S0-BOB-277

Collector's Library

THE BROTHERS KARAMAZOV

Fyodor Dostoevsky

Abridged edition

with an Afterword by
OLIVER FRANCIS

BARNES & NOBLE BOOKS
NEW YORK

© CRW 2004
Text and Afterword copyright ©
CRW Publishing Limited 2004

M 10 9 8 7 6 5 4 3 2 1

ISBN 0 7607 5772 0

All rights reserved. This publication may not be reproduced, stored in a retrieval system or transmitted in any form or by any means, electronic, mechanical, photocopying, recording or otherwise, without the prior permission in writing of the publishers.

Typeset in Great Britain by Antony Gray
Printed and bound in China by Imago

THE BROTHERS KARAMAZOV

Book One

I

Fyodor Pavlovitch Karamazov, a landowner well known in our district in his own day, and still remembered among us owing to his mysterious and tragic death, was a strange type, despicable and vicious and at the same time absurd. But he was one of those absurd persons who are very well capable of looking after their worldly affairs, and, apparently, after nothing else. Fyodor Pavlovitch, for instance, began with next to nothing; his estate was of the smallest; he ran to dine at other men's tables, and fastened on them as a toady, yet at his death it appeared that he had a hundred thousand roubles in hard cash.

He was married twice, and had three sons, the eldest Dmitri, by his first wife, and two, Ivan and Alexey, by his second. Fyodor Pavlovitch's first wife, Adelaïda Ivanovna, belonged to a fairly rich and distinguished noble family, also landowners in our district, the Miüsovs. How it came to pass that an heiress, who was also a beauty, and moreover one of those vigorous, intelligent girls, could have married such a worthless puny weakling, as we all called him, I won't attempt to explain. She wanted, perhaps, to prove her independence, to override class distinctions and the despotism of her family. What gave the marriage piquancy was that it was preceded by an elopement, and this greatly captivated Adelaïda Ivanovna's fancy. Fyodor Pavlovitch's position at the time made him specially eager for such a venture, for he was passionately anxious to make a career in one way or another. To marry into a good family and obtain a dowry was an alluring prospect. As for mutual love it did not exist apparently, either in the bride or in him, in spite of Adelaïda Ivanovna's beauty. This was, perhaps, a unique case of the kind in the life of Fyodor Pavlovitch, who was always of a voluptuous temper, and ready to run after any petticoat on the slightest encouragement. She seems to have been the only woman who made no particular appeal to his senses.

Immediately after the elopement Adelaïda Ivanovna discerned in a flash that she felt nothing for her husband but contempt. The marriage rapidly showed itself in its true colours. Although the family accepted the event pretty quickly and apportioned the runaway bride her dowry, the husband and wife began to lead a most disorderly life, and there were continual scenes between them.

It was said that the young wife showed incomparably more generosity and dignity than Fyodor Pavlovitch, who, as is now known, got hold of all her money up to twenty-five thousand roubles as soon as she received it, so that those thousands were lost to her for ever. The little village and the rather fine town house which formed part of her dowry he did his utmost for a long time to transfer to his name, by means of some deed of conveyance. He would probably have succeeded, if only because of her moral fatigue and desire to get rid of him. But, fortunately, Adelaïda Ivanovna's family intervened and circumvented his greediness. It is known for a fact that frequent fights took place between the husband and wife, but rumour had it that Fyodor

Pavlovitch did not beat his wife but was beaten by her, for she was a hot-tempered, bold, dark-browed, impatient woman, possessed of remarkable physical strength. Finally, she left the house and ran away from Fyodor Pavlovitch with a destitute divinity student, leaving Mitya, a child of three, in her husband's hands. Immediately Fyodor Pavlovitch introduced a regular harem into the house, and abandoned himself to orgies of drunkenness. In the intervals he used to drive all over the province, complaining tearfully to each and all of Adelaïda Ivanovna's desertion, going into details too disgraceful for a husband to mention in regard to his own married life. What seemed to gratify him and flatter his self-love most was to play the ridiculous part of the wronged husband, and to recite his woes with embellishments.

'One would think that you'd got a promotion, Fyodor Pavlovitch, you seem so pleased in spite of your sorrow,' scoffers said to him. Many even added that he was glad of a new comic part in which to play the buffoon, and that it was simply to make it funnier that he pretended to be unaware of his ludicrous position. But, who knows, it may have been just natural foolishness.

At last he succeeded in getting on the track of his runaway wife. The poor woman turned out to be in Petersburg, where she had gone with her divinity student, and where she had entered into a life of complete 'emancipation'. Fyodor Pavlovitch at once began bustling about, making preparations to go to Petersburg, with what object he could not himself have said. He would perhaps have really gone; but having determined to do so he felt at once entitled to fortify himself for the journey by another bout of reckless drinking. And just at that time his wife's family received the news of her death in Petersburg. She had died quite suddenly in a garret, according to one story, of typhus, or as another version had it, of starvation. Fyodor Pavlovitch was drunk when he heard of his wife's death, and the story is that he ran out into the street and began shouting with joy, raising his hands to heaven: 'Lord, now Thou hast released me,' but others say he wept without restraint like a little child, so much so that people were sorry for him, in spite of the repulsion he inspired. It is quite possible that both versions were true, that he rejoiced at his release, and at the same time wept for her who released him. As a general rule, people, even the wicked, are much more naïve and simple-hearted than we suppose. And we ourselves are too.

2

You can easily imagine what a father such a man could be and how he would bring up his children. His behaviour as a father was exactly what might be expected. He completely abandoned the child of his marriage with Adelaïda Ivanovna, not from malice, nor because of his matrimonial grievances, but simply because he forgot the boy's very existence. While he was wearying everyone with his tears and complaints, and turning his house into a sink of debauchery, a faithful servant of the family, Grigory, took the three-year-old Mitya into his care. If he hadn't looked after him, there would have been no one even to change the baby's little shirt.

It happened, moreover, that the child's relations on

his mother's side forgot him too at first. His grandfather was no longer living, his widow, Mitya's grandmother, had moved to Moscow, and was seriously ill, while her daughters were married, so that Mitya remained for almost a whole year in old Grigory's charge and lived with him in the servant's cottage. But if his father had remembered him (he could not, indeed, have been altogether unaware of his existence) he would have sent him back to the cottage, as the child would only have been in the way of his debaucheries. But a cousin of Mitya's mother, Peter Alexandrovitch Miüsov, happened to return from Paris. He was at that time quite a young man, and distinguished among the Miüsovs as a man of enlightened ideas and of European culture, who had been in the capitals and abroad. He personally 'owned', as we used to say, about a thousand serfs, which made him a wealthy man. His splendid estate lay on the outskirts of our little town. Hearing all about Adelaïda Ivanovna, whom he, of course, remembered, and in whom he had at one time been interested, and learning of the existence of Mitya, he intervened, in spite of all his youthful indignation and contempt for Fyodor Pavlovitch. He made the latter's acquaintance for the first time, and told him directly that he wished to undertake the child's education. He used long afterwards to tell as a characteristic touch, that when he began to speak of Mitya, Fyodor Pavlovitch looked for some time as though he did not understand what child he was talking about, and even as though he was surprised to hear that he had a little son in the house. The story may have been exaggerated, yet it must have had some truth in it.

Peter Alexandrovitch carried the business through

energetically, and was appointed, with Fyodor Pavlovitch, joint guardian of the child. Mitya did, in fact, pass into this cousin's keeping, but as the latter had no family of his own, and was in haste to return at once to Paris, he left the boy in charge of one of his cousins, a lady living in Moscow. Later when he settled permanently in Paris he too forgot the child. The Moscow lady died, and Mitya passed into the care of one of her married daughters. I believe he even changed his home a fourth time. I won't enlarge upon that now, as I shall have much to tell later of Fyodor Pavlovitch's first-born, and must confine myself now to the most essential facts about him, without which I could not begin my story.

In the first place, this Mitya, or rather Dmitri Karamazov, was the only one of Fyodor Pavlovitch's three sons who grew up in the belief that he had property, and that he would be independent on coming of age. He spent an irregular boyhood and youth. He did not finish his studies at the high school; he got into a military school, then went to the Caucasus, was promoted, fought a duel, and was degraded to the ranks, earned promotion again, led a wild life, and spent a good deal of money. He did not begin to receive any income from Fyodor Pavlovitch until he came of age, and until then got into debt. He saw and knew his father, Fyodor Pavlovitch, for the first time on coming of age, when he visited our neighbourhood in order to settle with him about his property. He seems not to have liked his father. He did not stay long with him, and made haste to get away, having succeeded only in obtaining a sum of money, and entered into an agreement for future payments from the estate, of the revenues and value of which he was unable (a fact worthy of note) upon this occasion, to get a statement from his father. Fyodor Pavlovitch remarked for the first time then (this, too, should be noted) that Mitya had a vague and exaggerated idea of his property. Fyodor Pavlovitch was very well satisfied with this, as it fell in with his own designs. He gathered only that the young man was frivolous, unruly, of violent passions, impatient, and dissipated and that if he could only obtain ready money, he would be satisfied, although only, of course, for a short time. So Fyodor Pavlovitch began to take advantage of this fact, sending him from time to time small doles, instalments. In the end, when four years later, Mitya, having lost patience, came a second time to our little town to settle up once for all with his father, it turned out to his amazement that he had nothing, that it was difficult to get even an accounting, that he had received the whole value of his property in sums of money from Fyodor Pavlovitch, and was perhaps even in debt to him, that by various agreements into which he had, of his own desire, entered at various previous dates, he had no right to expect anything more, and so on, and so on. The young man was overwhelmed, suspected deceit and cheating, and was almost beside himself. And, indeed, this circumstance led to the catastrophe, the account of which forms the subject of my first introductory story, or rather the external side of it. But before I pass to that story I must say a little of Fyodor Pavlovitch's other two sons, and of their origin.

3

Very shortly after getting his four-year-old Mitya off his hands, Fyodor Pavlovitch married a second time. His second marriage lasted eight years. He took this second wife, Sofya Ivanovna, also a very young girl, from another province, where he had gone upon some small piece of business. Sofya Ivanovna was the daughter of an obscure deacon, and was left from childhood an orphan without relations. She grew up in the house of a general's widow, a wealthy old lady of good social position, who was at once her benefactress and tormentor. I do not know the details, but I have only heard that the orphan girl, a meek and gentle creature, was once cut down from a noose in which she was hanging from a nail in the loft, so terrible were her sufferings from the caprice and everlasting nagging of this old woman, who was apparently not bad-hearted but had become an insufferable tyrant through idleness.

Fyodor Pavlovitch made her an offer; enquiries were made about him and he was refused. But again, as in his first marriage, he proposed an elopement to the orphan girl. There is very little doubt that she would not on any account have married him if she had known a little more about him at the time. But she lived in another province; besides, what could a young girl of sixteen know about life and marriage, except that she would be better at the bottom of the river rather than remain with her benefactress. So the poor child exchanged a benefactress for a benefactor. Fyodor Pavlovitch did not get a penny this time, for the general's widow was furious. She gave them nothing and cursed them both. But he had not reckoned on a dowry; what allured him was the remarkable beauty of the child-girl, above all her innocent appearance, which had a peculiar attraction for a vicious profligate, who had hitherto admired only the coarser types of feminine beauty.

'Those innocent eyes pierced my soul like a dagger,' he used to say afterwards, with his loathsome snicker. In a man so depraved this might, of course, mean no more than sensual attraction. As he had received no dowry with his wife, and had, so to speak, taken her 'out of the noose', he did not stand on ceremony with her. Making her feel that she was guilty, he took advantage of her phenomenal meekness and submissiveness to trample on the elementary decencies of marriage. He brought loose women into his house, and staged orgies of debauchery in his wife's presence. To show what a pass things had come to, I must add that Grigory, the gloomy, stupid, obstinate, argumentative servant, who had always hated his first mistress, Adelaïda Ivanovna, took the side of his new mistress. He championed her cause, abusing Fyodor Pavlovitch in a manner little befitting a servant, and on one occasion broke up the revels and drove all the bad women out of the house. In the end the unhappy young wife, terrorised from childhood, developed that kind of nervous disease suffered frequently by peasant women who are said to be 'possessed by devils'. At times, after terrible fits of hysterics, she even lost her reason. Yet she bore Fyodor Pavlovitch two sons, Ivan and Alexey, the older in the first year of marriage and the second three years later. When she died, little Alexey was in his fourth year, and, strange as it seems, I know that he remembered his mother all his life, like a dream, of course. At her death almost exactly the same thing happened to the two little boys as to their older brother, Mitya. Their father ignored and neglected them. They were looked after by the same Grigory and lived in his cottage, where they were found by the tyrannical old lady who had brought up their mother. She was still alive, and had not, in all those eight years, forgotten the insult done her. All that time she was obtaining exact information as to her Sofya's manner of life, and hearing of her illness and hideous surroundings, she declared aloud two or three times to her retainers: 'It serves her right. God has punished her for her ingratitude.'

Exactly three months after Sofya Ivanovna's death the general's widow suddenly appeared in town, and went straight to Fyodor Pavlovitch's house. She spent only half an hour in the town but she accomplished a great deal. It was evening, and Fyodor Pavlovitch, whom she had not seen for eight years, was quite drunk. The story is that instantly upon seeing him, without any sort of explanation, she gave him two good, resounding slaps on the face, grabbed him by the hair, and shook him three times up and down. Then, without a word, she went straight to the cottage to the two boys. Seeing, at first glance, that they were unwashed and clad in dirty linen, she promptly gave Grigory, too, a box on the ear, and announcing that she would carry off both the children she wrapped them just as they were in a blanket, put them in the carriage, and drove off to her own town. Grigory accepted the blow like a devoted slave, without a word, and when he escorted the old lady to her carriage he made her a low bow and said impressively, 'God will repay you for the orphans.'

'You are a blockhead all the same,' the old lady shouted to him as she drove away.

Fyodor Pavlovitch, thinking it over, decided that it was a good thing, and did not refuse the general's widow his formal consent to any proposition in regard to his children's education. As for the slaps she had given him, he drove all over town telling the story.

It happened that the old lady died soon after this, but in her will she left the boys a thousand roubles each 'for their instruction, and so that all be spent on them exclusively, with the condition that it be so portioned out as to last till they are twenty-one, for it is more than adequate provision for such children. If other people think fit to throw away their money, let them.' I have not read the will myself, but I heard there was something queer of the sort, very whimsically expressed.

The principal heir, Yefim Petrovitch Polenov, the Marshal of Nobility of the province, turned out, however, to be an honest man. He corresponded with Fyodor Pavlovitch, and having realised that he could extract nothing from him for the children's education (though Fyodor Pavlovitch never directly refused but only procrastinated as he always did in such cases, and was, indeed, at times effusively sentimental), assumed a personal interest in the orphans. He became especially fond of the younger, Alexey, who lived for a long while as one of his family. I beg the reader to note this from the beginning. And to Yefim Petrovitch, a man of generosity and humanity rarely to be met with, the young people were more indebted for their education and bringing up than to anyone. He kept the two thousand roubles left to them by the general's widow intact, so that by the time they came of age their portions had been doubled by the accumulation of interest. He educated them both at his own expense, and certainly spent far more than a thousand roubles upon each of them.

I won't enter into a detailed account of their boyhood and youth, but will only mention a few of the most important events. Of the elder, Ivan, I will say only that he grew into a somewhat morose and reserved, though far from timid boy. At ten years old he had realised that they were living not in their own home but on other people's charity, and that their father was a man of whom it was disgraceful to speak. This boy began very early, almost in his infancy (so they say at least), to show a brilliant and unusual aptitude for learning. I don't know precisely why, but he left the family of Yefim Petrovitch when he was hardly thirteen, entered a Moscow academy, and boarded with an experienced and celebrated teacher, an old friend of Yefim Petrovitch. Neither Yefim Petrovitch nor this teacher was living when the young man finished at the academy and entered the university. As Yefim Petrovitch had made no provision for the payment of the tyrannical old lady's legacy, it was delayed, owing to formalities inevitable in Russia, and the young man was in great straits for the first two years at the university. It must be noted that he did not even attempt to communicate with his father, perhaps from pride, from contempt for him, or perhaps from his cool common sense, which told him that from such a father he would get no real assistance. However that may have been, the young man was by no means despondent and succeeded in getting work, at first giving lessons for which he received a few pennies and afterwards getting paragraphs on street incidents into the newspapers under the signature of 'Eye-Witness'. In his latter years at the university he published brilliant reviews of books upon various special subjects, so that he became well known in literary circles. During his last year at college he succeeded in attracting the attention of a far wider circle of readers. One article was read in the famous monastery in our neighbourhood, and the inmates, on learning the author's name, were interested because he was a native of the town and the son of 'that Fyodor Pavlovitch'. It was just then that the author himself made his appearance among us.

Why Ivan Karamazov had come among us was, I remember, a question I put to myself at the time with a certain uneasiness. I never fully understood this fateful visit, which was the first step leading to so many consequences. It seemed strange on the face of it that a young man so learned, so proud, and apparently so cautious, should suddenly visit such an infamous house and a father who had ignored him all his life, hardly knew him, never thought of him, and would not under any circumstances have given him money, though he was always afraid that his sons Ivan and Alexey would come to ask him for it. And here the young man was staying in the house of such a father, had been living with him for two months; and they were on the best possible terms. This last fact was a special cause of wonder to many others as well as to me. Peter Alexandrovitch Miüsov, of whom we have spoken already, the cousin of Fyodor Pavlovitch's first wife, happened to be in the neighbourhood again on a visit to his estate. I remember that he was more surprised than anyone when he made the acquaintance of the young man, who interested him extremely, and with whom he sometimes argued and not without an inner pang compared himself in acquirements.

'He is proud,' he used to say; 'he will never be in want of cash; he has got money enough to go abroad now. What does he want here? Everyone can see that he hasn't come for money, for his father would never give him any. He has no taste for drink and dissipation, and yet his father can't do without him. They get on so well together!'

That was the truth; the young man had an unmistakable influence over his father, who appeared to be behaving more decently and even seemed at times ready to obey his son, though mostly he was extremely and even spitefully perverse.

It was only later that we learned that Ivan had come partly at the request of, and in the interests of, his elder brother, Dmitri, whom he saw for the first time on this very visit, though he had before leaving Moscow been in correspondence with him. I may add that Ivan appeared at the time in the light of a mediator between his father and his elder brother Dmitri, who was in open disagreement with his father and even planned to start legal action against him.

The family, I repeat, was now united for the first time, and some of its members met for the first time in their lives. The younger brother, Alexey, had been a year already among us, having been the first of the three to arrive. It is of that brother Alexey I find it most difficult to speak in this introduction. Yet I must give some preliminary account of him, if only to explain one queer fact, which is that I have to introduce my hero to the reader wearing the cassock of a novice. Yes, he had been for the last year in our monastery, and seemed willing to be cloistered there for the rest of his life.

4

He was only twenty; his brother Ivan was in his twenty-fourth year at the time, while their elder brother Dmitri was twenty-seven. First of all, I must explain that this young man, Alexey, whom we called Alyosha, was not a fanatic, and, in my opinion, at least, was not even a mystic. I may as well give my honest opinion from the beginning. He was simply a lover of humanity, and if he adopted the monastic life it was simply because at that time it seemed to him, so to say, the ideal escape for his soul in its struggle from the darkness of worldly wickedness to the light of love. And the reason this life attracted him was that he found in it at that time, as he thought, an extraordinary being, our celebrated elder, Zossima, to whom he became attached with all the warm first love of his ardent heart. But I do not dispute that he was very peculiar even at that time, and had been so indeed from his cradle. In his childhood and youth he was by no means expansive, and talked little indeed, but not from shyness or a sullen unsociability; quite the contrary. His habitual silence was due to something different, to a sort of inner preoccupation entirely personal and unconcerned with other people, but so important to him that he seemed, as it were, to forget others on account of it. But he was fond of people: he seemed throughout his life to put implicit trust in people: yet no one ever looked on him as a simpleton or naïve person. There was something about him which made one feel at once (and it was so all his life afterwards) that he did not care to be a judge of others – that he would never take it upon himself to criticise and would never condemn anyone for anything.

Coming at twenty to his father's house, which was a cesspool of filthy debauchery, he, chaste and pure as he was, simply withdrew in silence when to look on became unbearable, but withdrew without the slightest sign of contempt or condemnation. His father, who had once been in a dependent position, and so was sensitive and ready to take offence, met him at first with distrust and sullenness. 'He does not say much,' he used to say, 'and thinks the more.' Soon, within a fortnight indeed, he took to embracing him and kissing him often, with drunken tears, with sottish sentimentality, yet he evidently felt a real and deep affection for him, such as he had never been capable of feeling for anyone before.

Everyone, indeed, loved this young man wherever he went, and it was so from his earliest childhood. His talent for making himself loved was completely natural and unconscious, in his very nature so to speak. It was the same at school, though he should, it would seem, have been one of those children who are distrusted, sometimes ridiculed, and even disliked by their schoolfellows.

He was dreamy, for instance, and rather solitary. From his earliest childhood he liked to retire into a corner to read, and yet he was a general favourite all the while he was at school. He was rarely playful or merry, but anyone could see at the first glance that this was not from any sullenness. On the contrary, he was bright and good-tempered. He never tried to show off among his schoolfellows. Perhaps because of this, he was never afraid of anyone, yet the boys immediately understood that he was not proud of his fearlessness and seemed to be unaware that he was bold and courageous. He never resented an insult. It would happen that an hour after the offence he would address the offender or answer some question with as trustful and candid an expression as though nothing had happened between them. And it was not that he seemed to have forgotten or intentionally forgiven the affront, but simply that he did not regard it as an affront, and this completely conquered and captivated the boys.

He had one characteristic which made all his schoolfellows from the bottom class to the top want to mock at him, not from malice but because it amused them. This characteristic was a crazy fanatical modesty and chastity. He could not bear to hear certain words and certain conversations about women. There are 'certain' words and conversations unhappily impossible to eradicate in schools. Boys pure in mind and heart, almost children, are fond of talking in school among themselves, of things, pictures, and images of which even soldiers would sometimes hesitate to speak. More than that, much that soldiers have no knowledge or conception of is familiar to quite young children of our intellectual and higher classes. There is no moral depravity, no real corrupt inner cynicism in it, but there is the appearance of it, and it is often looked upon among them as something refined, subtle, daring, and worthy of imitation. Seeing that Alyosha Karamazov put his fingers in his ears when they talked of 'that', they used sometimes to crowd round him, pull his hands away, and shout nastiness into both ears, while he struggled, slipped to the floor, tried to hide himself without uttering one word of abuse, enduring their insults in silence. But at last they left him alone and gave up taunting him with being a 'regular girl', and what's more they looked upon his attitude with compassion as a weakness. He was always one of the best in the class but was never first.

At the slightest acquaintance with him anyone could see that Alyosha was one of those youths, almost of the type of religious enthusiast, who, if they were suddenly to come into possession of a large fortune, would not hesitate to give it away for the asking, either for good works or perhaps to a clever rogue. In general he seemed scarcely to know the value of money, not, of course, in a literal sense. When he was given pocket money, which he never asked for, he was either terribly careless of it so that it was gone in a moment, or he kept it for weeks, not knowing what to do with it.

In later years Peter Alexandrovitch Miüsov, a man very sensitive on the score of money and bourgeois honesty, pronounced the following judgment, after getting to know Alyosha: 'Here is perhaps the one man in the world whom you might leave alone without a penny, in the centre of an unknown town of a million inhabitants, and he would not come to harm, he would not die of cold and hunger, for he would be fed and sheltered at once; and if he were not, he would find a shelter for himself, and it would cost him no effort or humiliation. And to shelter him would be no burden, but, on the contrary, would probably be looked on as a pleasure.'

He did not finish his studies at the academy. A year before the end of the course he suddenly announced that he was going to see his father about a plan which had occurred to him. On his arrival in the town he made no answer to his father's first enquiry why he had come before completing his studies, and seemed, so they say, unusually thoughtful. It soon became apparent that he was looking for his mother's tomb. He practically admitted at the time that that was the sole object of his visit. But it can hardly have been the whole reason of it. It is more probable that he himself did not understand and could not explain what had suddenly arisen in his soul, and drawn him irresistibly into a new, unknown, but inevitable path. Fyodor Pavlovitch could not show him where his second wife was buried, for he had never visited her grave since he had thrown earth upon her coffin, and in the course of years had entirely forgotten where she was buried.

Fyodor Pavlovitch, by the way, had for some time previously not been living in our town. Three or four years after his wife's death he had gone to the south of Russia and then turned up in Odessa, where he spent several years. He finally returned to our town only three years before Alyosha's arrival. His former acquaintances found him terribly aged, although he was by no means an old man. He behaved not exactly with more dignity but with more effrontery. His depravity with women was not simply what it used to be, but even more revolting. Of late, too, he looked somehow bloated and seemed more irresponsible, more uneven, had sunk into a sort of incoherence, used to begin one thing and go on with another, as though he no longer had any self-control. He was more and more frequently drunk. If it had not been for the same servant Grigory, who by that time had aged considerably too, but who looked after him sometimes almost like a guardian, Fyodor Pavlovitch might have got into terrible scrapes. Alyosha's arrival seemed to affect even his mortal side, as though something had awakened in this prematurely old man which had long been dead in his soul.

'Do you know,' he used often to say, looking at Alyosha, 'that you are like her, "the crazy woman" ' – that was what he used to call his dead wife, Alyosha's mother. Grigory it was who pointed out the 'crazy woman's' grave to Alyosha. He took him to our town cemetery and showed him in a remote corner a cast-iron tombstone, cheap but decently kept, on which were inscribed the name and age of the deceased and the date of her death, and below a four-lined verse, such as is commonly used on old-fashioned middle-class tombs. To Alyosha's amazement this tomb turned out to be Grigory's doing. He had put it up on the poor 'crazy woman's' grave at his own expense, after Fyodor Pavlovitch, whom he had often pestered about the grave, had gone to Odessa, abandoning the grave and all his memories. Alyosha showed no particular emotion at the sight of his mother's grave. He only listened to Grigory's minute and solemn account of the erection of the tomb; he stood with bowed head and walked away without uttering a word. It was perhaps a year before he visited the cemetery again. But this little episode was not without an influence upon Fyodor Pavlovitch – and a very unexpected one. He suddenly took a thousand roubles to our monastery to pay for requiems for the soul of his wife; but not for the second, Alyosha's mother, the 'crazy woman', but for the first, Adelaïda Ivanovna, who used to thrash him. In the evening of the same day he got drunk and abused the monks to Alyosha. He himself was far from being religious; he had probably never put a penny candle before the image of a saint. Strange impulses of sudden feeling and sudden thought are common in such types.

I have mentioned already that he looked bloated.

His countenance at this time bore traces of something that testified unmistakably to the life he had led. Besides the long fleshy bags under his little, always insolent, suspicious, and ironical eyes; besides the multitude of deep wrinkles in his little fat face, the Adam's apple hung below his sharp chin like a great, fleshy goitre, which gave him a peculiar, repulsive, sensual appearance; add to that a long rapacious mouth with full lips, between which could be seen little stumps of black decayed teeth. He slobbered every time he began to speak. He was fond indeed of making fun of his own face, though, I believe, he was well satisfied with it. He used particularly to point to his nose, which was not very large, but very delicate and conspicuously aquiline. 'A regular Roman nose,' he used to say, 'with my goitre I've quite the countenance of an ancient Roman patrician of the decadent period.' He seemed proud of it.

Not long after visiting his mother's grave Alyosha suddenly announced that he wanted to enter the monastery, and that the monks were willing to receive him as a novice. He explained that this was his strong desire, and that he was solemnly asking the consent of his father. The old man knew that the elder Zossima, who was living in the monastery hermitage, had made a special impression upon his 'silent boy'.

'That is the most honest monk among them, of course,' he observed, after listening in thoughtful silence to Alyosha, and seeming scarcely surprised at his request. 'H'm! . . . So that's where you want to be, my silent boy?'

He was half drunk, and suddenly he grinned his slow half-drunken grin, which was not without a certain cunning and tipsy slyness. 'H'm! . . . I had a presentiment that you would end in something like this. Would you believe it? You were making straight for it. Well, to be sure you have your own two thousand. That's a dowry for you. And I'll never desert you, my angel. And I'll pay what's wanted for you there, if they ask for it. But, of course, if they don't ask, why should we worry them? What do you say? You know, you spend money like a canary, two little grains a week. H'm! . . . So you want to be a monk? And do you know I'm sorry to lose you, Alyosha; would you believe it, I've really grown fond of you? Well, it's a good opportunity. You'll pray for us sinners; we have sinned too much here. I've always wondered who would pray for me, and whether there's anyone in the world to do it. My dear boy, I'm awfully stupid about that. You wouldn't believe it. Awfully. You see, however stupid I am about it, I keep thinking, I keep thinking – from time to time, of course, not all the while. It's impossible, I think, for the devils to forget to drag me down to hell with their hooks when I die. Then I wonder – hooks? Where would they get them? What kind of hooks? Iron hooks? Where do they forge them? Have they a foundry there of some sort? If there are no hooks, there would be none to drag me down to hell, and if they don't drag me down what justice is there in the world? *Il faudrait les inventer*, those hooks, on purpose for me alone, for, if you only knew, Alyosha, what a blackguard I am.'

'But there are no hooks there,' said Alyosha, looking gently and seriously at his father.

'Yes, yes, only the shadows of hooks. I know, I know. That's how a Frenchman described hell. "*J'ai vu l'ombre d'un cocher qui avec l'ombre d'une brosse frottait l'ombre d'une carosse.*" How do you know there are no hooks, darling? But go and get at the truth there, and then come and tell me. Anyway it's easier going to the other world if one knows for sure what it will be like. Besides, it will be more seemly for you with the monks than here with me, with a drunken old man and young harlots . . . though you're like an angel, nothing touches you. And I dare say nothing will touch you there. That's why I let you go, because I hope for that. You've got all your wits about you. You will burn and you will burn out; you will be healed and come back again. And I will wait for you. I feel that you're the only creature in the world who has not condemned me. My dear boy, I feel it, you know. I can't help feeling it.'

And he even began snivelling. He was sentimental. He was wicked and sentimental.

5

Some of my readers may imagine that my young man was a sickly, ecstatic, poorly developed creature, a pale, wan dreamer. On the contrary, Alyosha was at this time a well-grown, red-cheeked, clear-eyed lad of nineteen, radiant with health. He was very handsome, too, graceful, moderately tall, with hair of a dark brown, with a regular, rather long, oval-shaped face, and wide-set dark grey, shining eyes; he was very thoughtful, and apparently very serene. I shall be told, perhaps, that red cheeks are not incompatible with fanaticism and mysticism; but I fancy that Alyosha was more of a realist than anyone. He entered upon this path only because, at that time, it alone struck his imagination and presented itself to him as offering an ideal means of escape for his soul from darkness to light. As soon as he reflected seriously he was convinced of the existence of God and immortality, and at once he instinctively said to himself: 'I want to live for immortality, and I will accept no compromise.' Alyosha would have found it strange and impossible to go on living as before.

It is written: 'Give all that thou hast to the poor and follow Me, if thou wouldst be perfect.'

Alyosha said to himself: 'I can't give two roubles instead of "all", and only go to Mass instead of "following Him".' Perhaps his memories of childhood brought back our monastery, to which his mother may have taken him to Mass. Perhaps the slanting sunlight and the holy image to which his poor 'crazy' mother had held him up still acted upon his imagination. Brooding on these things he may have come to us perhaps only to see whether here he could sacrifice all or only 'two roubles', and in the monastery he met this elder.

I must digress to explain what an 'elder' is in Russian monasteries, and I am sorry that I do not feel very competent to do so. I will try, however, to give a superficial account of it in a few words. Authorities on the subject assert that the institution of 'elders' is of recent date, not more than a hundred years old in our monasteries, though in the orthodox East, especially in Sinai and Athos, it has existed over a thousand years. It is maintained that it existed in ancient times in Russia also, but through the calamities which overtook Russia – the Tartars, civil war, the interruption of relations with the East after the destruction of Constantinople – this institution fell into oblivion. When and how it was introduced into our monastery I cannot say. There had already been three such elders and Zossima was the last of them. But he was almost dying of weakness and disease, and they had no one to take his place. The question for our monastery was an important one, for it had not been distinguished by anything in particular till then: they had neither relics of saints, nor wonder-working icons, nor glorious traditions, nor historical exploits. It had flourished and been glorious all over Russia through its elders, to see and hear whom pilgrims had flocked for thousands of miles from all parts.

What was such an elder? An elder was one who took your soul, your will, into his soul and his will. When you choose an elder, you renounce your own will and yield it to him in complete submission, complete self-abnegation. This institution of elders is not founded on theory, but was established in the East from the practice of a thousand years. The obligations due to an elder are not the ordinary 'obedience' which has always existed in our Russian monasteries.

The story is told, for instance, that in the early days of Christianity one novice, failing to fulfil some command laid upon him by his elder, left his monastery in Syria and went to Egypt. There, after great exploits he was found worthy at last to suffer torture and a martyr's death for the faith. When the Church, regarding him as a saint, was burying him, suddenly, at the deacon's exhortation, 'Depart all ye unbaptised', the coffin containing the martyr's body left its place and was cast forth from the church, and this took place three times. And only at last they learned that this holy man had broken his vow of obedience and left his elder, and, therefore, could not be forgiven without the elder's absolution in spite of his great deeds. Only after this could the funeral take place. This, of course, is only an old legend. But here is a recent instance.

A monk was suddenly commanded by his elder to quit Athos, which he loved as a sacred place and a haven of refuge, and to go, first to Jerusalem to do homage to the Holy Places and then to go to the north to Siberia: 'There is the place for thee and not here.' The monk, overwhelmed with sorrow, went to the Ecumenical Patriarch at Constantinople and besought him to release him from his obedience. But the Patriarch replied that not only was he unable to release him, but there was not and could not be on earth a power which could release him except the elder who had himself laid that duty upon him. In this way the elders are endowed in certain cases with unbounded and inexplicable authority.

The elder Zossima was sixty-five. He came of a family of landowners, had been in the army in early youth, and served in the Caucasus as an officer. He had, no doubt, impressed Alyosha by some peculiar quality of his soul. Alyosha lived in the cell of the elder, who was very fond of him and let him wait upon him. It must be noted that Alyosha was bound by no obligation and could go where he pleased and be absent for whole days. Though he wore the monastic dress it was voluntarily, not to be different from others in the monastery. No doubt he liked to do so. Possibly his youthful imagination was deeply stirred by the power and fame of his elder. Alyosha was particularly struck by the fact that Father Zossima was not at all stern. On the contrary, he was always almost gay. The monks used to say that he was more drawn to those who were more sinful, and the greater the sinner the more he loved him. There were, no doubt, up to the end of his life, among the monks some who hated and envied him, but the majority were on Father Zossima's side and very many of them loved him with all their hearts, warmly and sincerely. Some were almost fanatically devoted to him, and declared, though not quite aloud, that he was a saint. Alyosha had unquestioning faith in the miraculous power of the elder, just as he had unquestioning faith in the story of the coffin that flew out of the church.

The arrival of his two brothers, whom he had not known till then, seemed to make a great impression on Alyosha. He made friends more quickly with his half-brother Dmitri (though he arrived later) than with his own brother Ivan. He was extremely interested in his brother Ivan, but when the latter had been two months in the town, though they had met fairly often, they were still not intimate. Alyosha was naturally silent, and he seemed to be expecting something, ashamed about something, while his brother Ivan, though Alyosha noticed at first that he looked long and curiously at him, seemed soon to have left off thinking of him. Alyosha noticed it with some embarrassment. He ascribed his brother's indifference at first to the disparity of their age and education. Alyosha wondered, too, whether there was not some contempt on the part of the learned atheist for him – a foolish novice. He knew for certain that his brother was an atheist. He could not take offence at this contempt, if it existed; yet, with an uneasy embarrassment which he did not himself understand, he waited for his brother to come nearer to him. Dmitri used to speak of Ivan with the deepest respect and with a peculiar earnestness. Dmitri's enthusiastic references to Ivan were the more striking to Alyosha since Dmitri was, compared with Ivan, almost uneducated, and the two brothers were such a contrast in personality and character that it would be difficult to find two men more unlike.

It was at this time that the meeting, or rather gathering of the members of this inharmonious family took place in the cell of the elder who had such an extraordinary influence on Alyosha. The pretext for this gathering was a false one. It was at this time that the discord between Dmitri and his father seemed at its most acute stage and their relations had become insufferably strained. Fyodor Pavlovitch seems to have been the first to suggest, apparently as a joke, that they should all meet in Father Zossima's cell, and that, without appealing to his direct intervention, they might more decently come to an understanding under the conciliating influence of the elder's presence. Dmitri, who had never seen the elder, naturally supposed that his father was trying to intimidate him, but, as he secretly blamed himself for his outbursts of temper with his father on several recent occasions, he accepted the challenge. It must be noted that he was not, like Ivan, staying with his father, but living apart at the other end of the town. It happened that Peter Alexandrovitch Miüsov, who was staying in the district at the time, caught eagerly at the idea. A Liberal of the forties and fifties, a freethinker and atheist, he may have been led on by boredom or the hope of frivolous diversion. He was suddenly seized with the desire to see the monastery and the holy man. Influences from within the monastery were brought to bear on the elder, who of late had scarcely left his cell, and had been forced by illness to deny even his ordinary visitors. In the end he consented to see them, and the day was fixed.

'Who has made me a judge over them?' was all he said, smilingly, to Alyosha.

Alyosha was much perturbed when he heard of the proposed visit. Of all the wrangling, quarrelsome party, Dmitri was the only one who could regard the interview seriously. All the others would come from frivolous motives, perhaps insulting to the elder. Alyosha was well aware of that. Ivan and Miüsov would come from curiosity, perhaps of the coarsest kind, while his father might be contemplating some piece of buffoonery. Though he said nothing, Alyosha thoroughly understood his father. The boy, I repeat, was far from being so simple as everyone thought him. He awaited the day with a heavy heart. No doubt he was always pondering in his mind how the family discord could be ended. But his chief anxiety concerned the elder. He trembled for him, for his glory, and dreaded any affront to him, especially the refined, courteous irony of Miüsov and the supercilious half-utterances of the highly educated Ivan. He even thought of warning the elder, telling him something about them, but, on second thought, said nothing. He only sent word the day before, through a friend, to his brother Dmitri, that he loved him and expected him to keep his promise. Dmitri wondered, for he could not remember what he had promised, but he answered by letter that he would do his utmost not to let himself be provoked 'by vileness', but that, although he had a deep respect for the elder and for his brother Ivan, he was convinced that the meeting was either a trap for him or a cheap farce.

'Nevertheless I would rather bite out my tongue than be lacking in respect to the sainted man whom you reverence so highly,' he wrote in conclusion. Alyosha was not greatly cheered by the letter.

Book Two

I

It was a warm, bright day at the end of August. The interview with the elder had been fixed for half-past eleven, immediately after late Mass. Our visitors did not take part in the service, but arrived just as it was over. First an elegant open carriage, drawn by two high-priced horses, drove up with Miüsov and a distant relative of his, a young man of twenty, called Peter Fomitch Kalganov. He was a friend of Alyosha's.

In an ancient, jolting, but roomy, hired carriage, with a pair of old dappled-roan horses, a long way behind Miüsov's carriage, came Fyodor Pavlovitch, with his son Ivan. Dmitri was late, though he had been informed of the time the evening before. The visitors left their carriages at the hotel, outside the precincts, and went to the gates of the monastery on foot. Except Fyodor Pavlovitch, none of the party had ever seen the monastery, and Miüsov had probably not even been to church for thirty years. He looked about him with curiosity, and an air of assumed ease. But, except for the church and the domestic buildings, though these too were ordinary enough, he found nothing of interest in the interior of the monastery. The last of the worshippers were coming out of the church, bare-headed and crossing themselves. Among the humbler people were also a few of higher rank – two or three ladies and a very old general. They were all staying at the hotel. Our visitors were at once surrounded by beggars, but none of them gave anything, except young Kalganov, who took a ten-kopeck piece out of his purse, and, nervous and embarrassed – God knows why! – hurriedly gave it to an old woman, saying: 'Divide it equally.' None of his companions made any remark; so that he had no reason to be embarrassed; but, perceiving this, he grew even more uncomfortable.

A very pale, wan-looking monk of medium height, wearing a monk's cap, overtook them. Fyodor Pavlovitch and Miüsov stopped.

The monk, with an extremely courteous, profound bow, announced: 'The Father Superior invites all of you gentlemen to dine with him after your visit to the hermitage. At one o'clock, not later.'

'That I certainly will, without fail,' cried Fyodor Pavlovitch, hugely delighted at the invitation. 'And, believe me, we've all given our word to behave properly here . . . And you, Peter Alexandrovitch, will you go too?'

'Yes, of course. What have I come for but to study all the customs here? The only obstacle to me is your company . . .'

'Yes, Dmitri Fyodorovitch is nonexistent as yet.'

'It would be wonderful if he didn't turn up. Do you suppose I like all this business, and in your company too? So we will come to dinner. Thank the Father Superior,' he said to the monk.

'It is my duty first to conduct you to the elder,' answered the monk.

2

They entered the room almost at the same moment that the elder came in from his bedroom. There were already in the cell, awaiting the elder, two monks of the hermitage, one the Father Librarian, and the other Father Païssy, a very learned man, so they said, in delicate health, though not old. There was also a tall young man, who looked about twenty-two, standing in the corner throughout the interview. He had a broad, fresh face, and clever, observant, narrow brown eyes, and was wearing ordinary dress. He was a divinity student, living under the protection of the monastery. His expression was one of unquestioning, but self-respecting, reverence. Being in a subordinate and dependent position, and so not on an equality with the guests, he did not greet them with a bow.

Father Zossima was accompanied by a novice, and by Alyosha. The two monks rose and greeted him with very deep bows, touching the ground with their fingers; then kissed his hand. Blessing them, the elder replied with as deep a reverence to them, and asked their blessing. The whole ceremony was performed very seriously and with an appearance of emotion, not like an everyday rite. But Miüsov fancied that it was all done with intentional impressiveness. He stood in front of the other visitors. He ought – he had reflected upon it the evening before – from simple politeness, since it was the custom here, to have gone up to receive the elder's blessing, even if he did not kiss his hand. But when he saw all this bowing and kissing on the part of the monks he instantly changed his mind. With dignified gravity he made a rather deep, conventional bow, and moved away to a chair. Fyodor Pavlovitch did the same, mimicking Miüsov like an ape. Ivan bowed with great dignity and courtesy, but he too kept his hands at his sides, while Kalganov was so confused that he did not bow at all. The elder let fall the hand raised to bless them, and bowing to them again, asked them all to sit down. The blood rushed to Alyosha's cheeks. He was ashamed. His forebodings were coming true.

Father Zossima sat down on a very old-fashioned mahogany sofa, covered with leather, and made his visitors sit down in a row along the opposite wall on four mahogany chairs, covered with shabby black leather. The monks sat, one at the door and the other at the window. The divinity student, the novice and Alyosha remained standing. The cell was not very large and had a faded look. It contained nothing but the most necessary furniture, of coarse and poor quality. There were two pots of flowers in the window, and a number of holy pictures in the corner. Before one huge ancient icon of the Virgin a lamp was burning. Near it were two other holy pictures in shining metal settings, and, next them, carved cherubim, china eggs, a Catholic cross of ivory, with a Mater Dolorosa embracing it, and several foreign engravings from the great Italian artists of past centuries. Next to these costly and artistic engravings were several of the roughest Russian prints of saints and martyrs, such as are sold for a few pennies at all the fairs. On the other walls were portraits of Russian bishops.

Miüsov took a cursory glance at all these 'conventional' surroundings and bent an intent look upon the elder. At first he did not like Zossima. There was, indeed, something in the elder's face which many people besides Miüsov might not have liked. He was a short, bent, little man, with very weak legs, and though he was only sixty-five, he looked at least ten years older. His face was very thin and covered with a network of fine wrinkles, particularly numerous about his eyes, which were small, light-coloured, quick, and shining like two bright points. He had a sprinkling of grey hair about his temples. His pointed beard was small and scanty; and his lips, which smiled frequently, were as thin as two threads. His nose was not long, but sharp, like a bird's beak.

'To all appearances a malicious soul, full of petty pride,' thought Miüsov. He felt very dissatisfied with himself.

A cheap little clock on the wall struck twelve hurriedly, and helped start the conversation.

'We are exactly on time,' cried Fyodor Pavlovitch, 'but no sign of my son, Dmitri. I apologise for him, holy elder!' (Alyosha shuddered all over at 'holy elder'.) 'I am always punctual myself, to the minute, remembering that punctuality is the courtesy of kings . . .'

'But you are not a king, anyway,' Miüsov muttered, losing his self-restraint at once.

'Yes; that's true. I'm not a king, and, would you believe it, Peter Alexandrovitch, I was aware of that myself. But, there! I always say the wrong thing. Your reverence,' he cried, with sudden pathos, 'you behold before you a jester – a real jester! I introduce myself as such. It's an old habit, alas! And if I sometimes talk nonsense out of place, it's with an object, with the object of amusing people and making myself agreeable. Always injuring myself with my politeness. Once, many years ago, I said to an influential person: "Your wife is a ticklish lady," in an honourable sense, of the moral qualities, so to speak. But he asked me, "Why, have you tickled her?" I thought I'd be polite, so I couldn't help saying "Yes," and he gave me a fine tickling on the spot. Only that happened long ago, so

I'm not ashamed to tell the story. I'm always putting myself in the wrong like that.'

'You're doing it now,' muttered Miüsov, with disgust.

Father Zossima scrutinised them both in silence.

'Am I? Would you believe it, I was aware of that too, Peter Alexandrovitch, and let me tell you, indeed, I foresaw I should put my foot in it as soon as I began to speak. And do you know I foresaw, too, that you'd be the first to remark on it. The minute I see my joke isn't coming off, your reverence, both my cheeks feel as though they were drawn down to the lower jaw and there is almost a spasm in them. That's been so since I was young, when I had to make jokes for my living in noblemen's families. I am an inveterate buffoon, and have been from my birth up, your reverence, it's as though it were a craze in me. I dare say it's a devil within me. But only a little one. A more serious one would have chosen another lodging. But not in your soul, Peter Alexandrovitch; you're not a lodging worth having either. But I do believe – I believe in God, though I have had doubts of late. But now I sit and await words of wisdom. I'm like the philosopher, Diderot, your reverence. Did you ever hear, most holy father, how Diderot went to see the Metropolitan Platon, in the time of the Empress Catherine? He went in and said straight out, "There is no God." To which the great Bishop lifted up his finger and answered, "The fool has said in his heart there is no God." And Diderot fell down at the Bishop's feet on the spot. "I believe," he cried, "and will be christened." And so he was. Princess Dashkov was his godmother, and Potyomkin his godfather.'

'Fyodor Pavlovitch, this is unbearable! You know

you're telling lies and that that stupid anecdote isn't true. Why are you playing the fool?' cried Miüsov in a shaking voice.

'I suspected all my life that it wasn't true,' Fyodor Pavlovitch cried with conviction. 'But I'll tell you the whole truth, gentlemen. Great elder! Forgive me. The last thing about Diderot's christening I made up just now. I never thought of it before. I made it up to add zest. I play the fool, Peter Alexandrovitch, to make myself agreeable. Though I really don't know myself, sometimes, what I do it for. And as for Diderot, I heard as far as "the fool hath said in his heart" twenty times from the gentry about here when I was young. I heard your aunt, Peter Alexandrovitch, tell the story. They all believe to this day that the infidel Diderot came to dispute about God with the Metropolitan Platon . . . '

Miüsov got up, forgetting himself in his impatience. He was furious, and conscious of being ridiculous.

What was taking place in the cell was really incredible. For forty or fifty years past, from the times of former elders, no visitors had entered that cell without feelings of the profoundest veneration. Many remained kneeling during the whole visit. Of those visitors, many had been men of high rank and learning, some even freethinkers, attracted by curiosity, but all without exception had shown the profoundest reverence and delicacy, for here there was no question of money, but only, on the one side love and kindness, and on the other penitence and eager desire to decide some spiritual problem or crisis. So that such buffoonery amazed and bewildered the spectators, or at least some of them. Alyosha did not dare to look at Rakitin, the divinity student, whom he knew almost intimately. He alone in the monastery knew Rakitin's thoughts.

'Forgive me,' began Miüsov, addressing Father Zossima, 'for perhaps I seem to be taking part in this shameful foolery. I made a mistake in believing that *even* a man like Fyodor Pavlovitch would understand what was due on a visit to so honoured a personage. I did not suppose I should have to apologise simply for having come with him . . .'

Peter Alexandrovitch could say no more, and was about to leave the room, overwhelmed with confusion.

'Don't distress yourself, I beg.' The elder got on to his feeble legs, and taking Peter Alexandrovitch by both hands, made him sit down again. 'I beg you not to disturb yourself. I particularly beg you to be my guest.' And with a bow he went back and sat down again on his little sofa.

'Great elder, speak! Do I annoy you by my vivacity?' Fyodor Pavlovitch cried suddenly, clutching the arms of his chair in both hands, as though ready to leap up from it if the answer was unfavourable.

'I earnestly beg you, too, not to disturb yourself, and not to be uneasy,' the elder said impressively. 'Do not trouble. Make yourself quite at home. And, above all, do not be so ashamed of yourself, for that is at the root of it all.'

'Quite at home? To be my natural self? Oh, that is much too much . . . I will not go so far as that myself. I warn you for your own sake. But as for you, holy being, let me tell you, I am brimming over with ecstasy.'

He got up, and throwing up his hands, declaimed, 'When you said just now, "Don't be so ashamed of yourself for that is at the root of it all," you pierced right through me by that remark, and read me to the core. Indeed, I always feel when I meet people that I am lower than all, and that they all take me for a buffoon. So I say, "Let me really play the buffoon. I am not afraid of your opinion, for you are every one of you worse than I am." That is why I am a buffoon. It is from shame, great elder, from shame; it's simply over-sensitiveness that makes me rowdy. If I had only been sure that everyone would accept me as the kindest and wisest of men, oh, Lord, what a good man I should have been then! Teacher!' he fell suddenly on his knees, 'what must I do to gain eternal life?'

It was difficult even now to decide whether he was joking or really moved.

Father Zossima, raising his eyes, looked at him, and said with a smile: 'You have known for a long time what you must do. You have sense enough: don't give way to drunkenness and incontinence of speech; don't give way to sensual lust; and, above all, to the love of money.'

'Blessed man! Give me your hand to kiss.'

Fyodor Pavlovitch skipped up, and imprinted a rapid kiss on the elder's thin hand.

The elder suddenly rose from his seat. 'Excuse me, gentlemen, for leaving you a few minutes,' he said, addressing all his guests. 'I have visitors awaiting me who arrived before you. But don't you tell lies all the same,' he added, turning to Fyodor Pavlovitch with a good-humoured face. He went out of the cell. Alyosha and the novice flew to escort him down the steps. Alyosha was breathless: he was glad to get away, but he was glad, too, that the elder was good-humoured and not offended. Father Zossima was going towards the portico to bless the people waiting for him there.

3

Near the wooden veranda below, built on the outer wall of the precinct, there was a crowd of about twenty peasant women. They had been told that the elder was at last coming out, and they had gathered together in anticipation. Two ladies, Madame Hohlakov and her daughter, had also come out into the portico to wait for the elder, but in a separate part of it set aside for women of rank.

Madame Hohlakov was a wealthy lady, still young and attractive, and always dressed with taste. She was rather pale, and had lively black eyes. She was not more than thirty-three, and had been five years a widow. Her daughter, a girl of fourteen, was partially paralysed. The poor child had not been able to walk for the last six months, and was wheeled about in a long reclining chair. She had a charming little face, rather thin from illness, but full of gaiety. There was a gleam of mischief in her big dark eyes with their long lashes. Her mother had been intending to take her abroad ever since the spring, but they had been detained all summer by business connected with their estate. They had been staying a week in our town, where they had come more for purposes of business than devotion, but had visited Father Zossima once already, three days before. Though they knew that the elder scarcely saw anyone, they had now suddenly turned up again, and urgently entreated 'the happiness of looking once again on the great healer'.

But Father Zossima, when he came out, went first straight to the peasants who were crowded at the foot of the three steps that led up on to the veranda. Father Zossima stood on the top step, put on his stole, and began blessing the women who thronged about him. When the elder went up to Madame Hohlakov at last she met him enthusiastically.

'Ah, what I have been feeling, looking on at this touching scene! . . .' She could not go on for emotion. 'Oh, I understand the people's love for you. I love the people myself. I want to love them. And who could help loving them, our splendid Russian people, so simple in their greatness!'

'How is your daughter's health? You wanted to talk to me again?'

'Oh, I have been urgently begging for this meeting. I have prayed for it! I was ready to fall on my knees and kneel for three days at your windows until you let me in. We have come, great healer, to express our ardent gratitude. You have helped my Lise, healed her completely, merely by praying over her last Thursday and laying your hands upon her. We have hastened here to kiss those hands, to pour out our feelings and our homage.'

'What do you mean by healed? But she is still lying down in her chair.'

'But her night fevers have entirely ceased ever since Thursday,' said the lady with nervous haste. 'And that's not all. Her legs are stronger. This morning she got up well; she had slept all night. Look at her rosy cheeks, her bright eyes! She used to be always crying, but now she laughs and is gay and happy. This morning she insisted on my letting her stand up, and she stood up for a whole minute without any support. She wagers that in a fortnight she'll be dancing a quadrille. I've called in Dr Herzenstube. He shrugged his shoulders and said, "I am amazed; I can make nothing of it." And would you have us not come here to disturb you, not fly here to thank you? Lise, thank him – thank him!'

Lise's pretty little laughing face became suddenly serious. She rose in her chair as far as she could and, looking at the elder, clasped her hands before him, but could not restrain herself and broke into laughter.

'It's at him,' she said, pointing to Alyosha, with childish vexation at herself for not being able to repress her mirth.

If anyone had looked at Alyosha standing a step behind the elder, he could have caught a quick flush crimsoning his cheeks in an instant. His eyes shone and he looked down.

'She has a message for you, Alexey Fyodorovitch. How are you?' the mother went on, holding out her exquisitely gloved hand to Alyosha.

The elder turned round and all at once looked attentively at Alyosha. The latter went nearer to Lise and, smiling in a strangely awkward way, held out his hand to her. Lise assumed an important air.

'Katerina Ivanovna has sent you this through me.' She handed him a little note. 'She particularly begs you to go and see her as soon as possible; that you will not fail her, but will be sure to come.'

'She asks me to go and see her? Me? What for?' Alyosha mumbled in great astonishment. His face at once looked anxious.

'Oh, it's all to do with your brother Dmitri and – what has happened lately,' the mother explained hurriedly. 'Katerina Ivanovna has made up her mind, but she must see you about it . . . Why, of course, I can't say. But she wants to see you at once. And you will go to her, of course. It is a Christian duty.'

'I have seen her only once,' Alyosha protested.

'Oh, she is such a lofty, incomparable creature! If only for her suffering . . . Think what she has gone through, what she is enduring now! Think what awaits her! It's all terrible, terrible!'

'Very well, I will go,' Alyosha decided, after rapidly scanning the brief, enigmatic note, which consisted of an urgent entreaty that he would come, without any sort of explanation.

'Oh, how sweet and generous that would be of you!' cried Lise with sudden animation. 'I told mamma you wouldn't go. I said you were saving your soul. How splendid you are! I've always thought you were splendid. How glad I am to tell you so!'

'Lise!' said her mother impressively, though she smiled after she had said it. 'You have quite forgotten us, Alexey Fyodorovitch,' she said; 'you never come to see us. Yet Lise has told me twice that she is never happy except with you.'

Alyosha raised his downcast eyes and again flushed, and again smiled without knowing why.

'She does not deserve to be loved. I have seen her naughtiness all along,' the elder said jestingly. 'Why have you been laughing at Alexey?'

Lise had in fact been occupied in mocking at him all the time. She had noticed before that Alyosha was shy and tried not to look at her, and she found this extremely amusing. She waited intently to catch his eye. Alyosha, unable to endure her persistent stare, was irresistibly and suddenly drawn to glance at her, and at once she smiled triumphantly in his face. Alyosha was even more disconcerted and vexed. At last he turned away from her altogether and hid behind the elder's back. After a few minutes, drawn by the same irresistible force, he turned again to see whether he was being looked at or not, and found Lise almost hanging out of her chair to peep sideways at him, eagerly waiting for him to look. Catching his eye, she laughed so that the elder could not help saying, 'Why do you make fun of him like that, naughty girl?'

Lise suddenly and quite unexpectedly blushed. Her eyes flashed and her face became quite serious. She began speaking quickly and nervously in a warm and resentful voice: 'Why has he forgotten everything, then? He used to carry me about when I was little. We used to play together. He used to come to teach me to read, you know. Two years ago, when he went away, he said that he would never forget me, that we were friends for ever, for ever, for ever! And now he's afraid of me all at once. Am I going to eat him? Why doesn't he want to come near me? Why doesn't he talk? Why won't he come and see us? It's not that you won't let him. We know that he goes everywhere. It's not good manners for me to invite him. He ought to have thought of it first, if he hasn't forgotten me. No, now he's saving his soul! Why have you put that long gown on him? If he runs he'll fall.'

And suddenly she hid her face in her hand and went off into irresistible, prolonged, nervous, inaudible laughter. The elder listened to her with a smile, and blessed her tenderly. As she kissed his hand she suddenly pressed it to her eyes and began crying.

'Don't be angry with me. I'm silly and good for nothing . . . and perhaps Alyosha's right, quite right, in not wanting to come and see such a ridiculous girl.'

'I will certainly send him,' said the elder.

4

The elder's absence from his cell had lasted for about twenty-five minutes. It was more than half-past twelve, but Dmitri, on whose account they had all met there, had still not appeared. But he seemed almost to be forgotten, and when the elder entered the cell again, he found his guests engaged in eager conversation. Ivan and the two monks took the leading share in it. Miüsov, too, was trying to take a part, and apparently very eagerly, in the conversation. But he was unsuccessful in this also. He was evidently in the background, and his remarks were treated with neglect, which increased his irritability. He had had intellectual encounters with Ivan before and he could not endure the carelessness with which Ivan treated him.

'Hitherto at least I have stood in the front ranks of all that is progressive in Europe, and here the new generation positively ignores us,' he thought.

Fyodor Pavlovitch, who had given his word to sit still and be quiet, had actually been quiet for some time, but he watched his neighbour Miüsov with an ironical little smile, obviously enjoying his discomfiture. He had been waiting for some time to pay off old scores, and now he could not let the opportunity slip. Bending over his shoulder he began teasing him again in a whisper.

'Why didn't you go away just now? Why did you consent to remain in such unseemly company? Now you won't go till you've displayed your intellect to them.'

'You again? . . . On the contrary, I'm just going.'

'You'll be the last, the last of all to go!' Fyodor Pavlovitch delivered him another thrust, almost at the moment of Father Zossima's return.

The discussion died down for a moment, but the elder, seating himself in his former place, looked at them all as though cordially inviting them to go on. Alyosha, who knew every expression of his face, saw that he was fearfully exhausted and making a great effort. Of late he had been liable to fainting fits from exhaustion. His face had the pallor that was common before such attacks, and his lips were white. But he evidently did not want to break up the party. He seemed to have some special object of his own in keeping them. What object? Alyosha watched him intently.

The door opened, and the guest so long expected, Dmitri Fyodorovitch, came in. They had, in fact, given up expecting him, and his sudden appearance caused some surprise for a moment.

5

Dmitri Karamazov, a young man of twenty-eight, of medium height and agreeable countenance, looked older than his years. He was muscular, and showed signs of considerable physical strength. Yet there was something not healthy in his face. It was rather thin, his cheeks were hollow, and there was an unhealthy sallowness in their colour. His rather large, prominent, dark eyes had an expression of firm determination, and yet there was a vague look in them, too. Even when he was excited and talking irritably, his eyes somehow did not follow his mood, but betrayed something else, sometimes quite incongruous with what was passing. 'It's hard to tell what he's thinking,' those who talked to him sometimes declared. People who saw something pensive and sullen in his eyes were startled by his sudden laugh, which bore witness to mirthful and light-hearted thoughts at the very time when his eyes were so gloomy. The tense look in his face was easy to understand at this moment. Everyone knew or had heard of the extremely restless and dissipated life which he had been leading of late, as well as of the violent anger to which he had been roused in his quarrels with his father. There were several stories current in the town about it. It is true that he was irascible by nature, 'of an unstable and unbalanced mind', as our justice of the peace, Katchalnikov, aptly described him.

He was stylishly and irreproachably dressed in a carefully buttoned frock-coat. He wore black gloves and carried a top hat. Having only lately left the army, he still had moustaches and no beard. His dark brown hair was cropped short, and combed forward on his temples. He had the long determined stride of a military man. He stood still for a moment on the threshold, and glancing at the whole party went straight up to the elder, guessing him to be their host. He made him a low bow, and asked his blessing. Father Zossima, rising in his chair, blessed him. Dmitri kissed his hand respectfully, and with intense feeling, almost anger, he said: 'Be so generous as to forgive me for having kept you waiting so long, but Smerdyakov, the valet sent me by my father, in reply to my enquiries, told me twice over that the appointment was for one. Now I suddenly learn –'

'Don't disturb yourself,' interposed the elder. 'No

matter. You are a little late. It's of no consequence ...'

'I'm extremely obliged to you, and expected no less from your goodness.'

Saying this, Dmitri bowed once more. Then, turning suddenly towards his father, made him, too, a similarly low and respectful bow. He had evidently considered it beforehand, and made this bow in all seriousness, thinking it his duty to show his respect and good intentions.

Although Fyodor Pavlovitch was taken unawares, he was equal to the occasion. In response to Dmitri's bow he jumped up from his chair and made his son a bow as low in return. His face was suddenly solemn and impressive, which gave him a positively malignant look. Dmitri bowed generally to all present, and without a word walked to the window with his long, resolute stride, sat down on the only empty chair, near Father Païssy, and, bending forward, prepared to listen to the conversation he had interrupted.

Fyodor Pavlovitch jumped up from his seat.

'Most pious and holy elder,' he cried pointing to Ivan, 'that is my son, flesh of my flesh, the dearest of my flesh! While this son who has just come in, Dmitri, against whom I was seeking justice from you, is the undutiful one. Judge and save us! We need not only your prayers but your prophecies!'

'Speak without clowning, and don't begin by insulting the members of your family,' answered the elder, in a faint, exhausted voice. He was obviously getting more and more fatigued, and his strength was failing.

'An unseemly farce which I foresaw when I came here!' cried Dmitri indignantly. He too leaped up. 'Forgive it, reverend father,' he added, addressing the elder. 'I am not a cultivated man, and I don't even know how to address you properly, but you have been deceived and you have been too good-natured in letting us meet here. All my father wants is a scandal. Why he wants it only he can tell. He always has some motive. But I believe I know why – '

'They all blame me, all of them!' cried Fyodor Pavlovitch in his turn. 'Peter Alexandrovitch here blames me too. You have been blaming me, Peter Alexandrovitch, you have!' he turned suddenly to Miüsov, although the latter was not dreaming of interrupting him. 'They all accuse me of having hidden the children's money in my boots, and cheated them, but isn't there a court of law? There they will reckon out for you, Dmitri Fyodorovitch, from your notes, your letters, and your agreements, how much money you had, how much you have spent, and how much you have left. Why does Peter Alexandrovitch refuse to pass judgment? Dmitri is not a stranger to him. Because they are all against me, while Dmitri Fyodorovitch is in debt to me, and not a little, but some thousands of which I have documentary proof. The whole town is echoing with his debaucheries. And where he was stationed before, he several times spent a thousand or two for the seduction of some respectable girl; we know all about that, Dmitri Fyodorovitch, in its most secret details. I'll prove it . . . Would you believe it, holy father, he has captivated the heart of the most honourable of young ladies of good family and fortune, daughter of a gallant colonel, formerly his superior officer, who had received many honours and had the Anna Order on his breast. He compromised the girl by his promise of marriage, now she is an orphan and here; she is betrothed to him, yet before her very eyes he is dancing attendance on a certain enchantress. And although this enchantress has lived in, so to speak, civil marriage with a respectable man, yet she is of an independent character, an unapproachable fortress for everybody, just like a legal wife – for she is virtuous, yes holy father, she is virtuous. Dmitri Fyodorovitch wants to open this fortress with a golden key, and that's why he is insolent to me now, trying to get money from me, though he had wasted thousands on this enchantress already. He's continually borrowing money for the purpose. From whom do you think? Shall I say, Mitya?'

'Be silent!' cried Dmitri, 'wait till I'm gone. Don't dare in my presence to besmirch the good name of an honourable girl! That you should utter a word about her is an outrage, and I won't permit it!'

He was breathless.

'Dmitri! Dmitri darling!' cried Fyodor Pavlovitch hysterically, squeezing out a tear. 'And is your father's blessing nothing to you? If I curse you, what then?'

'Shameless hypocrite!' cried Dmitri furiously.

'He says that to his father! his father! What would he be with others? Gentlemen, only fancy; there's a poor but honourable man living here, burdened with a numerous family, a captain who got into trouble and was discharged from the army, but not publicly, not by court-martial, with no slur on his honour. And three weeks ago Dmitri seized him by the beard in a tavern, dragged him out into the street and beat him publicly, and all because he is an agent in a little business of mine.'

'It's all a lie! Outwardly it's the truth, but inwardly, a lie!' Dmitri was trembling with rage. 'Father, I don't justify my action. Yes, I confess it publicly, I behaved like a brute to that captain, and I regret it now, and I'm disgusted with myself for my brutal rage. But this captain, this agent of yours, went to that lady whom you call an enchantress, and suggested to her from you, that she should take IOUs of mine which were in your possession, and should sue me for the money so as to get me into prison by means of them, if I persisted in claiming an account from you of my property. Now you reproach me for having a weakness for that lady when you yourself incited her to captivate me! She told me so to my face . . . She told me the story and laughed at you . . . You wanted to put me in prison because you are jealous of her friendship with me, because you'd begun to force your attentions upon her; and I know all about that, too; she laughed at you for that as well – you hear – she laughed at you as she described it. So here you have this man, this father who reproaches his profligate son! Gentlemen, forgive my anger, but I foresaw that this crafty old man had only brought you together to create a scandal. I had come to forgive him if he held out his hand; to forgive him, and ask forgiveness! But as he has just this minute insulted not only me, but an honourable young lady for whom I feel such reverence that I dare not take her name in vain, I have made up my mind to show up his game, though he is my father . . .'

He could not go on. His eyes were glittering and he breathed with difficulty. But everyone in the cell was stirred. All except Father Zossima got up from their seats uneasily. The monks looked austere but waited for guidance from the elder. He sat still, pale, not from excitement but from the weakness of disease. An imploring smile lighted up his face; from time to time he raised his hand, as though to check the storm, and, of course, a gesture from him would have been enough to end the scene; but he seemed to be waiting for something and watched them intently as though trying to make out something which was not perfectly clear to him. At last Miüsov felt completely humiliated and disgraced.

'We are all to blame for this scandalous scene,' he said hotly. 'But I did not foresee it when I came, though I knew with whom I had to deal. This must be stopped at once! Believe me, your reverence, I had no precise knowledge of the details that have just come to light, I was unwilling to believe them, and I learn for the first time . . . A father is jealous of his son's relations with a woman of loose behaviour and intrigues with the creature to get his son into prison! This is the company in which I have been forced to be present! I was deceived. I declare to you all that I was as much deceived as anyone.'

'Dmitri Fyodorovitch,' yelled Fyodor Pavlovitch suddenly, in an unnatural voice, 'if you were not my son I would challenge you this instant to a duel . . . with pistols, at three paces . . . across a handkerchief,' he ended, stamping with both feet.

With old liars who have been acting all their lives there are moments when they enter so completely into their part that they tremble or shed tears of emotion in earnest, although at that very moment, or a second later, they are able to whisper to themselves, 'You know you are lying, you shameless old sinner! You're acting now, in spite of your "holy" wrath.'

Dmitri frowned painfully, and looked with unutterable contempt at his father.

'I thought . . . I thought,' he said, in a soft and, as it were, controlled voice, 'that I was coming to my native place with the angel of my heart, my betrothed, to cherish his old age, and I find nothing but a depraved profligate, a despicable clown!'

'A duel!' yelled the old wretch again, breathless and spluttering at each syllable. 'And you, Peter Alexandrovitch Miüsov, let me tell you that there has never been in all your family a loftier, and more honest – you hear – more honest woman than this "creature", as you have dared to call her! And you, Dmitri Fyodorovitch, have abandoned your betrothed for that "creature", so you must yourself have thought that your betrothed couldn't hold a candle to her. That's the woman called a "creature"!'

'Shameful!' broke from Father Iosif.

'Shameful and disgraceful!' Kalganov, flushing crimson, cried in a boyish voice, trembling with emotion. He had been silent till that moment.

'Why is such a man alive?' Dmitri, beside himself with rage, growled in a hollow voice, hunching up his shoulders till he looked almost deformed. 'Tell me, can he be allowed to go on defiling the earth?' He looked round at everyone and pointed at the old man. He spoke evenly and deliberately.

'Listen, listen, monks, to the parricide!' cried Fyodor Pavlovitch, rushing up to Father Iosif. 'That's the answer to your "Shameful!" What is shameful? That "creature", that "woman of loose behaviour" is perhaps holier than you are yourselves, you monks who are seeking salvation! She fell perhaps in her youth, ruined by her environment. But she loved much, and Christ himself forgave the woman "who loved much".'

'It was not for such love Christ forgave her,' broke impatiently from the gentle Father Iosif.

'Yes, it was for such, monks, it was! You save your souls here, eating cabbage, and think you are the righteous. You eat a fish a day, and you think you bribe God with fish.'

'This is unendurable!' was heard on all sides in the cell.

But this unseemly scene was cut short in a most unexpected way. Father Zossima rose suddenly from his seat. Almost distracted with anxiety for the elder and everyone else, Alyosha succeeded, however, in supporting him by the arm. Father Zossima moved towards Dmitri and reaching him sank on his knees before him. Alyosha thought that he had fallen from weakness, but this was not so. The elder distinctly and deliberately bowed down at Dmitri's feet till his forehead touched the floor. Alyosha was so astounded that he failed to assist him when he got up again. There was a faint smile on his lips.

'Goodbye! Forgive me, all of you!' he said, bowing on all sides to his guests.

Dmitri stood for a few moments in amazement. Bowing down to him – what did it mean? Suddenly he cried aloud, 'Oh, God!' hid his face in his hands, and rushed out of the room. All the guests flocked out after him, in their confusion not saying goodbye, or bowing to their host. Only the monks went up to him again for a blessing.

'What did it mean, falling at his feet like that? Was it symbolic or what?' said Fyodor Pavlovitch, suddenly quieted and trying to reopen conversation without venturing to address anybody in particular. They were all passing out of the precincts of the hermitage at the moment.

'I can't answer for a madhouse and for madmen,'

Miüsov answered at once ill-humouredly, 'but I will spare myself your company, Fyodor Pavlovitch, and, trust me, for ever. Where's that monk?'

'That monk', that is, the monk who had invited them to dine with the Superior, did not keep them waiting. He met them as soon as they came down the steps from the elder's cell, as though he had been waiting for them all the time.

'Reverend father, kindly do me a favour. Convey my deepest respect to the Father Superior, apologise for me, personally, Miüsov, to his reverence, telling him that I deeply regret that owing to unforeseen circumstances, I am unable to have the honour of being present at his table, greatly as I should desire to do so,' Miüsov said irritably to the monk.

'And that unforeseen circumstance, of course, is myself,' Fyodor Pavlovitch cut in immediately. 'Do you hear, father; this gentleman doesn't want to remain in my company or else he'd come at once. And you shall go, Peter Alexandrovitch, pray go to the Father Superior and good appetite to you. I will decline, and not you. Home, home, I'll eat at home, I don't feel equal to it here, Peter Alexandrovitch, my amiable relative.'

'I am not your relative and never have been, you contemptible man!'

'I said it on purpose to annoy you, because you always disclaim the relationship, though you really are a relation in spite of your evasions. I'll prove it by the church calendar. As for you, Ivan, stay if you like. I'll send the horses for you later. Propriety requires you to go to the Father Superior, Peter Alexandrovitch, to apologise for the disturbance we've been making . . . '

'Is it true that you are going home? Aren't you lying?'

'Peter Alexandrovitch! How could I dare after what's happened! Forgive me, gentlemen, I was carried away! And upset besides! And, indeed, I am ashamed. Gentlemen, one man has the heart of Alexander of Macedon and another the heart of the little dog Fido. Mine is that of the little dog Fido. I am abashed! After such an escapade how can I go to dinner, to gobble up the monastery's sauces? I am ashamed, I can't. You must excuse me!'

'The devil only knows, what if he deceives us,' thought Miüsov, still hesitating, and watching the retreating buffoon with distrustful eyes. The latter turned round, and noticing that Miüsov was watching him, waved him a kiss.

'Well, are you coming to the Superior?' Miüsov asked Ivan abruptly.

'Why not? I was especially invited yesterday.'

'Unfortunately I feel myself compelled to go to this confounded dinner,' said Miüsov with the same irritability, regardless of the fact that the monk was listening. 'We ought, at least, to apologise for the disturbance, and explain that it was not our doing. What do you think?'

'Yes, we must explain that it wasn't our doing. Besides, father won't be there,' observed Ivan.

'Well, I should hope not! Confound this dinner!'

6

Alyosha helped Father Zossima to his bedroom and seated him on his bed. It was a little room furnished with the bare necessities. There was a narrow iron bedstead, with a strip of felt for a mattress. In the corner, under the icons, was a reading-desk with a cross and the Gospel lying on it. The elder sank exhausted on the bed. His eyes glittered and he breathed hard. He looked intently at Alyosha, as though considering something.

'Go, my dear boy, go. Porfiry is enough for me. Make haste, you are needed there, go and wait at the Father Superior's table.'

'Let me stay here,' Alyosha entreated.

'You are more needed there. There is no peace there. You will wait, and be of service. If evil spirits rise up, repeat a prayer. And remember, my son' (the elder liked to call him that), 'this is not the place for you in the future. When it is God's will to call me, leave the monastery. Go away for good.'

Alyosha started.

'What is it? This is not your place for the time. I bless you for great service in the world. Yours will be a long pilgrimage. And you will have to take a wife, too. You will have to bear *all* before you come back. There will be much to do. But I have faith in you, and so I send you forth. Christ is with you. Do not abandon Him and He will not abandon you. You will see great sorrow, and in that sorrow you will be happy. This is my last message to you: in sorrow seek happiness. Work, work unceasingly. Remember my words, for although I shall talk with you again, not only my days but my hours are numbered.'

Alyosha's face again betrayed strong emotion. The corners of his mouth quivered.

'What is it again?' Father Zossima asked, smiling gently. 'The worldly may follow the dead with tears, but here we rejoice over the father who is departing. We rejoice and pray for him. Leave me, I must pray.

Go, and make haste. Be near your brothers. And not near one only, but near both.'

Father Zossima raised his hand to bless him. Alyosha could make no protest, though he had a great longing to remain. He longed, moreover, to ask the significance of his bowing to Dmitri, the question was on the tip of his tongue, but he dared not ask it. He knew that the elder would have explained it unasked if he had thought fit. But evidently it was not his will. That action had made a deep impression on Alyosha; he believed blindly in its mysterious significance. Mysterious, and perhaps awful.

As he hastened out of the hermitage precincts to reach the monastery in time to serve at the Father Superior's dinner, he felt a sudden pang at his heart, and stopped short. He seemed to hear again Father Zossima's words, foretelling his approaching end. What he had foretold so exactly must infallibly come to pass. Alyosha believed that implicitly. But how could he be left without him? How could he live without seeing and hearing him? Where should he go? Father Zossima had told him not to weep, and to leave the monastery. Good God! It was long since Alyosha had known such anguish. He hurried through the copse that divided the monastery from the hermitage, and unable to bear the burden of his thoughts, he gazed at the ancient pines beside the path. He had not far to go – about five hundred paces. He expected to meet no one at that hour, but at the first turn of the path he noticed Rakitin. He was waiting for someone.

'Are you waiting for me?' asked Alyosha, overtaking him.

'Yes,' grinned Rakitin. 'You are hurrying to the Father Superior, I know; he has a banquet. I shan't be there, but you go and hand the sauces. Tell me one thing, Alexey, what does that vision mean? That's what I want to ask you.'

'What vision?'

'That bowing to your brother, Dmitri. And didn't he tap the ground with his forehead, too!'

'You speak of Father Zossima?'

'Yes, of Father Zossima.'

'Tapped the ground?'

'Ah, an irreverent expression! Well, what of it? Anyway, what does this strange sight mean?'

'I don't know what it means, Misha.'

'I knew he wouldn't explain it to you! There's nothing wonderful about it, of course, only the usual sanctimonious mummery. But there was an object in the performance. All the pious people in the town will talk about it and spread the story through the province, wondering what it meant. To my thinking the old man really has a keen nose; he sniffed a crime. Your house stinks of it.'

'What crime?'

Rakitin evidently had something he was eager to speak of.

'It'll be in your family, this crime. Between your brothers and your rich old father. So Father Zossima flopped down to be ready for what may turn up. If something happens later on, it'll be: "Ah, the holy man foresaw it, prophesied it!" though it's a poor sort of prophecy, flopping like that. "Ah, but it was symbolic," they'll say, "an allegory," and the devil knows what all! It'll be remembered to his glory: "He predicted the crime and marked the criminal!" That's always the way with these crazy fanatics; they cross themselves at the tavern and throw stones at the temple. Like your elder, he takes a stick to a just man and falls at the feet of a murderer.'

'What crime? What murderer? What do you mean?'

Alyosha stopped dead. Rakitin stopped, too.

'What murderer? As though you didn't know! I'll bet you've thought of it before. That's interesting, too, by the way. Listen, Alyosha, you always speak the truth, though you're always between two stools. Have you thought of it or not? Answer.'

'I have,' answered Alyosha in a low voice. Even Rakitin was taken aback.

'What? Have you really?' he cried.

'I . . . I've not exactly thought it,' muttered Alyosha, 'but directly you began speaking so strangely, I fancied I had thought of it myself.'

'You see? (And how well you expressed it!) Looking at your father and your brother Mitya today you thought of a crime. Then I'm not mistaken?'

'But wait, wait a minute,' Alyosha broke in uneasily. 'What has led you to see all this? Why does it interest you? That's the first question.'

'Two questions, disconnected, but natural. I'll deal with them separately. What led me to see it? I wouldn't have seen it, if I hadn't suddenly understood your brother Dmitri, seen right into the very heart of him all at once. I caught the whole man from one trait. These very honest but passionate people have a line which mustn't be crossed. If it were, he'd run at your father with a knife. But your father's a drunken and abandoned old sinner, who can never draw the line – if they both let themselves go, they'll both come to grief.'

'No, Misha, no. If that's all, you've reassured me! It won't come to that.'

'But why are you trembling? Let me tell you; he may be honest, your Mitya (he is stupid, but honest) but he's – a sensualist. That's the very definition and inner essence of him. Your father has handed on his low sensuality to Dmitri. Do you know, I simply wonder at you, Alyosha, how you can have kept your purity. You're a Karamazov too, you know! In your family sensuality is actually a disease. But now, these three sensualists are watching one another, with their knives in their belts. The three of them are knocking their heads together, and you may be the fourth.'

'You are mistaken about that woman. Dmitri – despises her,' said Alyosha, with a sort of shudder.

'Grushenka? No, brother, he doesn't despise her. Since he has openly abandoned his betrothed for her, he doesn't despise her. There's something here, my dear boy, that you don't understand yet. A man will fall in love with some beauty (a sensualist can understand that) and he'll abandon his own children for her, sell his father and mother, and his country, even Russia. If he's honest, he'll steal; if he's humane, he'll murder; if he's faithful, he'll deceive. Pushkin, the poet of women's feet, sang of their feet in his verse. Others don't sing their praises, but they can't look at their feet without a thrill – and it's not only their feet. Contempt's no help here, brother, even if he did despise Grushenka. He does, but he can't tear himself away.'

'I understand that,' Alyosha jerked out suddenly.

'Really? Well, I dare say you do understand, since you blurt it out at the first word,' said Rakitin, malignantly. 'That escaped you unawares, and the confession's the more precious. So it's a familiar subject; you've thought about it already, about sensuality, I mean! Oh, you virgin soul! You're a quiet one, Alyosha, you're a saint, I know, but the devil only knows what you've thought about, and what you know already! You are pure, but you've been down into the depths . . . I've been watching you a long time. You're a Karamazov yourself; you're a thorough Karamazov – no doubt birth and selection have something to answer for. You're a sensualist from your father, a crazy saint from your mother. Why do you tremble? Is it true, then? Do you know, Grushenka has been begging me to bring you along. "I'll pull off his cassock," she says. You can't think how she keeps begging me to bring you. I wondered why she took such an interest in you. Do you know, she's an extraordinary woman, too!'

'Thank her and say I'm not coming,' said Alyosha, with a strained smile. 'Finish what you were saying, Misha. I'll tell you my idea after.'

'There's nothing to finish. It's all clear. It's the same old tune, brother. If even you are a sensualist at heart, what of your brother, Ivan? He's a Karamazov, too. He's trying to get Mitya's betrothed for himself, and I fancy he'll succeed too. And what's more, it's with Mitya's consent. For Mitya will surrender his betrothed to him to be rid of her, and escape to Grushenka. And he's ready to do that in spite of all his nobility and disinterestedness. Observe that. Those are the most fatal people! Who the devil can make you out? He recognises his vileness and goes on with it! Let me tell you, too, the old man, your father, is standing in Mitya's way now. He has suddenly gone crazy over Grushenka. His mouth waters at the sight of her. It's entirely on her account he made that scene in the cell just now, simply because Miüsov called her an "abandoned creature". He's worse than a tomcat in love. At first she was only employed by him in some shady business, but now he has suddenly realised all she is and has gone wild about her. He keeps pestering her with his offers, not honourable ones, of course. And they'll come into collision, the precious father and son, on that path! But Grushenka favours neither of them, she's still playing with them, and teasing them both, considering which she can get most out of. For though she could filch a lot of money from the papa he wouldn't marry her, and maybe he'll turn stingy in the end, and keep his purse shut. That's where Mitya's value comes in, he has no money, but he's ready to marry her. Yes, ready to marry her! to abandon his betrothed, a rare beauty, Katerina Ivanovna, who's rich, and the daughter of a colonel, and to marry Grushenka, who has been the mistress of a dissolute old merchant, Samsonov, a coarse, uneducated provincial mayor. Some murderous conflict may well come to pass from all this, and that's what your brother Ivan is waiting for. It would suit him down to the ground. He'll carry off Katerina Ivanovna, for whom he is languishing, and pocket her dowry of sixty thousand. That's very alluring to start with, for a man of no consequence and a beggar. And, take note, he won't be wronging Mitya, but doing him the greatest service. For I know as a fact that Mitya only last week, when he was with some gypsy girls drunk in a tavern, cried out aloud that he was unworthy of his betrothed, Katerina, but that his brother Ivan was the man who deserved her. And Katerina Ivanovna will not in the end refuse such a fascinating man as Ivan. She's hesitating between the two of them already. And how has that Ivan won you all, so that you all worship him?

He is laughing at you, and enjoying himself at your expense.'

'How do you know? How can you speak so confidently?' Alyosha asked sharply, frowning.

'Why do you ask, and are frightened at my answer? It shows that you know I'm speaking the truth.'

'You don't like Ivan. Ivan wouldn't be tempted by money.'

'Really? And the beauty of Katerina Ivanovna? It's not only the money, though a fortune of sixty thousand is an attraction.'

'Ivan is above that. He wouldn't make up to anyone for thousands. It is not money, it's not comfort Ivan is seeking. Perhaps it's suffering he is seeking?'

'What wild dream now? Oh, you – aristocrats!'

'I understand your getting hot about it, Misha. I guess from your warmth that you are not indifferent to Katerina Ivanovna yourself; I've suspected that for a long time, brother, that's why you don't like my brother Ivan. Are you jealous of him?'

'And jealous of her money too? Won't you add that?'

'I'll say nothing about money. I am not going to insult you.'

'I believe it, since you say so, but confound you, and your brother Ivan with you. Don't you understand that one might very well dislike him, apart from Katerina Ivanovna? And why the devil should I like him? He condescends to abuse me, you know. Why haven't I a right to abuse him?'

'I never heard of his saying anything about you, good or bad. He doesn't speak of you at all.'

'But I heard that the day before yesterday at Katerina Ivanovna's he was abusing me for all he was worth – you see what an interest he takes in your humble servant. And which is the jealous one after that, brother, I can't say.'

'Who can have told you all this? You can't have been at Katerina Ivanovna's yourself when he was talking about you?'

'I wasn't there, but Dmitri Fyodorovitch was; and I heard him tell it with my own ears; if you want to know, he didn't tell me, but I overheard him, unintentionally, of course, for I was sitting in Grushenka's bedroom and I couldn't go away because Dmitri Fyodorovitch was in the next room.'

'Oh, yes, I'd forgotten she was a relation of yours.'

'A relation! That Grushenka a relation of mine!' cried Rakitin, turning crimson. 'Are you mad? You're out of your mind!'

'Why, isn't she a relation of yours? I heard so.'

'Where can you have heard it? You Karamazovs brag of being an ancient, noble family, though your father used to run about playing the buffoon at other men's tables, and was only admitted to the kitchen as a favour. I may be only a priest's son, and dirt in the eyes of noblemen like you, but don't insult me so lightly and wantonly. I have a sense of honour, too, Alexey Fyodorovitch. I couldn't be a relation of Grushenka, a common harlot. I beg you to understand that!'

Rakitin was intensely irritated.

'Forgive me, for goodness' sake, I had no idea . . . besides . . . how can you call her a harlot? Is she . . . that sort of woman?' Alyosha flushed suddenly. 'I tell you again, I heard that she was a relation of yours. You often go to see her, and you told me yourself you're not her lover. I never dreamed that you of all people had such contempt for her! Does she really deserve it?'

'I may have reasons of my own for visiting her. That's not your business. But as for relationship, your brother, or even your father is more likely to make her yours, than mine. Well, here we are. You'd better go to the kitchen. Hullo! what's wrong, what is it? Are we late? They can't have finished dinner so soon! Have the Karamazovs been making trouble again? No doubt they have. Here's your father and your brother Ivan after him. They've broken out from the Father Superior's. And look, Father Isidor's shouting out something after them from the steps. And your father's shouting and waving his arms. I expect he's swearing. Bah, and there goes Miüsov driving away in his carriage. You see, he's going. There must have been a row. There can't have been any dinner. Surely they've not been beating the Father Superior! Or have they, perhaps, been beaten? It would serve them right!'

There was reason for Rakitin's exclamations. There had been a scandalous, an unprecedented scene. It had all come from the impulse of a moment.

7

Miüsov, as a man of breeding and delicacy, could not but feel some inward qualms, when he reached the Father Superior's with Ivan: he felt ashamed of having lost his temper. He felt that he ought to have disdained that despicable wretch, Fyodor Pavlovitch, too much to have been upset by him in Father Zossima's cell, and so to have forgotten himself. 'The monks were not to blame, in any case,' he reflected, on the steps. 'And if they're decent people here (and the Father Superior, I understand, is a nobleman) why not be friendly and courteous with them? I won't argue, I'll fall in with everything, I'll win them by politeness, and . . . and . . . show them that I've nothing to do with that Aesop, that buffoon, that Pierrot, and have merely been taken in over this affair, just as they have.'

These excellent intentions were strengthened when he entered the Father Superior's dining room, though, strictly speaking, it was not a dining room, for the Father Superior had only two rooms altogether; they were, however, much larger and more comfortable than Father Zossima's. But there was no great luxury about the furnishing of these rooms either. The furniture was of mahogany, covered with leather, in the old-fashioned style of 1820; the floor was not even stained, but everything was shining with cleanliness, and there were many choice flowers in the windows; the most sumptuous thing in the room at the moment was, of course, the beautifully decorated table. The cloth was clean, the service shone; there were three kinds of well-baked bread, two bottles of wine, two of excellent mead, and a large glass jug of kvass – both the latter made in the monastery, and famous in the neighbourhood. There was no vodka. Rakitin related afterwards that there were five courses: fish soup made of young sturgeon, served with little fish patties; then boiled fish served in a special way; then salmon cutlets, ice pudding and compote, and finally, blancmange. Rakitin found out about all these good things, for he could not resist peeping into the kitchen, where he already had a footing. He had a footing everywhere, and got information about everything.

Rakitin, of course, was a person of too little consequence to be invited to the dinner. Father Iosif, Father Païssy, and one other monk were the only inmates of the monastery who had received invitations. They were already waiting when Miüsov, Kalganov and Ivan arrived. The other guest, Maximov, stood a little aside, waiting also. The Father Superior stepped into the middle of the room to receive his guests. He was a tall, thin, but still vigorous old man, his black hair streaked with grey, and a long, grave, ascetic face. He bowed to his guests in silence. But this time they approached to receive his blessing. Miüsov even tried to kiss his hand, but the Father Superior drew it back in time to avoid the salute. Ivan and Kalganov went through the ceremony in the most simple-hearted and humble manner, kissing his hand as peasants do.

'We must apologise most humbly, your reverence,' began Miüsov, grinning amiably, and speaking in a dignified and respectful tone. 'Pardon us for having come alone without the gentleman you invited, Fyodor Pavlovitch. He felt obliged to decline the honour of your hospitality, and not without reason. In the reverend Father Zossima's cell he was carried away by the unhappy dissension with his son, and let fall words which were quite out of keeping . . . in fact, quite unseemly . . . as [he glanced at the monks] your reverence is, no doubt, already aware. And therefore, recognising that he had been to blame, he felt sincere regret and shame, and begged me, and his son Ivan Fyodorovitch, to convey to you his apologies and regrets. In brief, he hopes and desires to make amends later. He asks your blessing, and begs you to forget what has taken place.'

As he uttered the last word of his tirade, Miüsov completely recovered his self-complacency, and all traces of his former irritation disappeared. He fully and sincerely loved humanity again.

The Father Superior listened to him with dignity, and, with a slight bend of the head, replied: 'I sincerely deplore his absence. Perhaps at our table he might have learned to like us, and we him. Pray be seated, gentlemen.'

He stood before the holy image, and began to say grace, aloud. All bent their heads reverently, and Maximov clasped his hands before him with peculiar fervour.

It was at this moment that Fyodor Pavlovitch played his last prank. It must be noted that he really had meant to go home, and really had felt the impossibility of going to dine with the Father Superior as though nothing had happened, after his disgraceful behaviour in the elder's cell. Not that he was so very much ashamed of himself – quite the contrary perhaps. He did feel, however, that it would be unseemly to go to the dinner. Yet his creaking carriage had hardly been brought to the steps of the hotel, and he had hardly got into it, when he suddenly stopped short. He remembered his own words at the elder's: 'I always feel when I meet people that I am lower than all, and that they all take me for a buffoon; so I say let me play the buffoon, for you are, every one of you, stupider and lower than I.' He longed to revenge himself on everyone for his own unseemliness. He suddenly recalled how he had once in the past been asked, 'Why do you hate so and so, so much?' And he had answered them, with his shameless impudence, 'I'll tell you. He had done me no harm. But I played him a dirty trick, and ever since I have hated him.'

Remembering that now, he smiled quietly and malignantly, hesitating for a moment. His eyes gleamed, and his lips positively quivered. 'Well, since

I have begun, I may as well go on,' he decided. His predominant sensation at that moment might be expressed in the following words, 'Well, there is no rehabilitating myself now. So let me shame them for all I am worth. I will show them I don't care what they think – that's all!'

He told the coachman to wait, while with rapid steps he returned to the monastery and straight to the Father Superior's. He had no clear idea what he would do, but he knew that he could not control himself, and that a word might drive him to the utmost limits of obscenity, but only to obscenity, to nothing criminal, nothing for which he could be legally punished. In the last resort, he could always restrain himself, and had marvelled often at himself, on that score. He appeared in the Father Superior's dining room, at the moment when the prayer was over, and all were moving to the table. Standing in the doorway, he scanned the company, and laughing his prolonged, impudent, malicious chuckle, looked them all boldly in the face. 'They thought I had gone, and here I am again,' he cried to the whole room.

For one moment everyone stared at him without a word; and at once everyone felt that something revolting, grotesque, positively scandalous, was about to happen. Miüsov passed immediately from the most benevolent frame of mind to the most savage. All the feelings that had subsided and died down in his heart revived instantly.

'No! this I cannot endure!' he cried. 'I absolutely cannot! and . . . I certainly cannot!'

The blood rushed to his head. He positively stammered; but he was beyond thinking of style, and he seized his hat.

'What is it he cannot?' cried Fyodor Pavlovitch, 'that he absolutely cannot and certainly cannot? Your reverence, am I to come in or not? Will you receive me as your guest?'

'You are welcome with all my heart,' answered the Superior. 'Gentlemen!' he added, 'I venture to beg you most earnestly to lay aside your dissensions, and to be united in love and family harmony – with prayer to the Lord at our humble table.'

'No, no, it is impossible!' cried Miüsov, beside himself.

'Well, if it is impossible for Peter Alexandrovitch, it is impossible for me, and I won't stay. That is why I came here. I will go with Peter Alexandrovitch everywhere now. If you leave, Peter Alexandrovitch, I will leave too, if you remain, I will remain. You stung him by what you said about family harmony, Father Superior, he does not admit he is my relation.'

'What is happening? What's this?' voices were heard in the group of monks.

'Let us go,' cried Miüsov, addressing Kalganov.

'No, excuse me,' Fyodor Pavlovitch broke in shrilly, taking another step into the room. 'Allow me to finish. There in the cell you blamed me for behaving disrespectfully just because I spoke of eating fish, Peter Alexandrovitch. Miüsov, my relation, prefers to have *plus de noblesse que de sincerité* in his words, but I prefer in mine *plus de sincerité que de noblesse*, and – damn the noblesse! Allow me, Father Superior, though I am a buffoon and play the buffoon, yet I am the soul of honour, and I want to speak my mind. Yes, I am the soul of honour, while in Peter Alexandrovitch there is wounded vanity and nothing else. I came here perhaps to have a look and speak my mind. My son, Alexey, is here, being saved. I am his father; I care for his welfare, and it is my duty to care. While I've been playing the fool, I have been listening and having a look on the sly; and now I want to give you the last act of the performance. You know what people say? As a thing falls, so it lies. As a thing once has fallen, so it must lie for ever. That is nonsense. I want to get up again. Holy fathers, I am indignant with you. Confession is a great sacrament, before which even I am ready to bow down reverently; but there in the cell, they all suddenly kneel down and confess aloud. Can it be right to confess aloud? It was ordained by the holy fathers that confession shall be secret: then only your confession will be a mystery, and so it was of old. But how can I explain before everyone that I did this and that . . . well, you understand – sometimes it would not be proper to talk about certain acts. It would be quite scandalous! No, fathers, anyone who stays long enough with you might even become a Flagellant, I dare say . . . at the first opportunity I shall write to the Synod, and I shall take my son, Alexey, home.'

'How disgraceful!' cried Peter Alexandrovitch.

'Pardon me!' said the Father Superior. 'It was said of old "Many have begun to speak against me and have uttered evil sayings about me. And hearing it I have said to myself: it is the correction of the Lord and He has sent it to heal my vain soul." And so we humbly thank you, honoured guest!' and he made Fyodor Pavlovitch a low bow.

'Tut – tut – tut – sanctimoniousness and stock phrases! Old phrases and old gestures. The old lies and formal prostrations. We know all about them. I don't like falsehood, fathers, I want the truth. But the truth is not to be found in eating fish and that I proclaim aloud! Father monks, why do you fast? Why do you expect reward in heaven for that? Why, for reward like that I will come and fast too! No, saintly monk, you try being virtuous in the world, do good to society, without shutting yourself up in a monastery at other people's expense, and without expecting a reward from heaven for it – you'll find that a bit harder. I can talk sense, too, Father Superior. What have they got here?' He went up to the table. 'Old port wine, mead brewed by the Eliseyev Brothers. Fie, fie, fathers! That is something beyond fish. Look at the bottles the fathers have brought out, hoe! hoe! hoe! And who has provided it all? The Russian peasant, the labourer, brings here the pennies earned by his horny hand, wringing them from his family and the taxgatherer! You bleed the people, you know, holy fathers.'

'This is too disgraceful!' said Father Iosif.

Father Païssy kept obstinately silent. Miüsov rushed from the room, and Kalganov after him.

'Well, father, I will follow Peter Alexandrovitch! I am not coming to see you again. You may beg me on your knees, I shan't come. I sent you a thousand roubles, so now you are looking for more. I am taking my revenge for my youth, for all the humiliation I endured.' He thumped the table with his fist in a paroxysm of simulated feeling. 'This monastery has played a great part in my life! It has cost me many bitter tears. You used to set my wife, the crazy one, against me. You have slandered me all over the place, you spread stories about me among the neighbours. Enough, fathers! This is the age of liberalism, the age of steamers and railways. Neither a thousand, nor a hundred roubles, no, nor a hundred pennies will you get out of me!'

It must be noted again that our monastery never had played any great part in his life, and he never had shed a bitter tear owing to it. But he was so carried away by his simulated emotion, that for a moment he almost believed it himself. He was so touched he was almost weeping. But at that very instant, he felt that it was time to draw back.

The Father Superior bowed his head at the malicious lies, then spoke impressively: 'It is written again, "Bear circumspectly and gladly dishonour that cometh upon thee by no act of thine own, be not confounded and hate not him who hath dishonoured thee." And so will we.'

'Tut, tut, tut! Bethinking thyself and the rest of the rigmarole. Bethink yourselves, fathers, I will go. But I will take my son, Alexey, away from here for ever, on my parental authority. Ivan Fyodorovitch, my most dutiful son, permit me to order you to follow me.' He went out, shouting and gesticulating.

It was at that moment Rakitin saw him and pointed him out to Alyosha.

'Alexey!' his father shouted, from far off, catching sight of him. 'You come home to me today, for good, and bring your pillow and mattress, and leave no trace behind.'

Alyosha stood rooted to the spot, watching the scene in silence. Meanwhile, Fyodor Pavlovitch had stepped into the carriage, and Ivan followed him in grim silence without even turning to say goodbye to Alyosha.

After a pause, looking askance at his son, Fyodor Pavlovitch spoke, 'You got up all this monastery business. You urged it, you approved of it. Why are you angry now?'

'You've talked enough rubbish. You might rest a bit now,' Ivan snapped sullenly.

Fyodor Pavlovitch was silent again for a couple of minutes.

'A drop of brandy would be nice now,' he observed sententiously, but Ivan made no response.

'You shall have some, too, when we get home.'

Ivan remained silent.

Fyodor Pavlovitch waited a minute before speaking.

'But I shall take Alyosha away from the monastery, though you will dislike it so much.'

Ivan shrugged his shoulders contemptuously, and turning away stared at the road. They did not speak again all the way home.

Book Three

I

The Karamazovs' house was far from being in the centre of the town, but it was not quite outside it. It was a pleasant-looking old house of two storeys painted grey, with a red iron roof. It was roomy and snug, and might still last many years. There were all sorts of unexpected little alcoves and closets and staircases. There were rats in it, but Fyodor Pavlovitch did not altogether dislike them. 'One doesn't feel so solitary when one's left alone in the evening,' he used to say. It was his habit to send the servants away to the lodge for the night and to lock himself up alone. The lodge was a roomy and solid building in the yard. Fyodor Pavlovitch used to have the cooking done there, although there was a kitchen in the house; he did not like the smell of cooking, and, winter and summer alike, the dishes were carried in across the courtyard. The house was built for a large family; there was room for five times as many masters, with their servants. But at the time of our story there was no one living in the house but Fyodor Pavlovitch and his son Ivan. And in the lodge there were only three servants: old Grigory, and his old wife Marfa, and a young man called Smerdyakov.

Of these three we must say a few words. Of old Grigory we have said something already. He was firm and determined and went blindly and obstinately towards his goal, if once he had decided for any reasons (and they were often very illogical ones) to believe that his conclusion was immutably right. He was honest and incorruptible. His wife, Marfa Ignatyevna, had obeyed her husband's will implicitly all her life, yet she had pestered him terribly after the emancipation of the serfs. She was set on leaving Fyodor Pavlovitch and opening a little shop in Moscow with their small savings. But Grigory decided then, once for all, that 'the woman's talking nonsense, for every woman is dishonest', and that they ought not to leave their old master, whatever he might be, for 'that was now their duty'.

'Do you understand what duty is?' he asked Marfa Ignatyevna.

'I understand what duty means, Grigory Vassilyevitch, but why it's our duty to stay here I never shall understand,' Marfa answered.

'Well, don't understand then. But so it shall be. And you hold your tongue.'

And so it was. They did not go away, and Fyodor Pavlovitch promised them a small sum for wages, and paid it regularly. Grigory knew, too, that he had an indisputable influence over his master. It was true, and he was aware of it. Fyodor Pavlovitch was an obstinate and cunning buffoon; yet, though his will was strong enough 'in some of the affairs of life', as he expressed it, he found himself, to his surprise, extremely feeble in facing certain other emergencies. He knew his weaknesses and was afraid of them. There are positions in which one has to keep a sharp lookout. And that's not easy without a trustworthy man, and Grigory was a most trustworthy man. Many times in the course of his life Fyodor Pavlovitch only just escaped a sound thrashing through Grigory's intervention, and on each occasion the old servant gave him a regular lecture. But it wasn't only thrashings that Fyodor Pavlovitch was afraid of. There were graver occasions, very subtle and complicated ones, when Fyodor Pavlovitch could not have explained the extraordinary craving for someone faithful and devoted, which sometimes unaccountably came upon him all in a moment. It was almost a morbid condition. Corrupt and often cruel in his lust, like some poisonous insect, Fyodor Pavlovitch was sometimes, in moments of drunkenness, overcome by superstitious terror and a moral convulsion which took an almost physical form. 'My soul simply quakes in my throat at those times,' he used to say. At such moments he liked to feel that there was near at hand, in the lodge if not in the room, a strong, faithful man, virtuous and unlike himself, who had seen all his debauchery and knew all his secrets, but was ready in his devotion to overlook all that, not to oppose him, above all, not to reproach him or threaten him with anything, either in this world or in the next, and, in case of need, to defend him – from whom? From somebody unknown, but terrible and dangerous. What he needed was to feel that there was *another* man, an old and tried friend, whom he might call in his sick moments merely to look at his face, or, perhaps, exchange some quite irrelevant words with him. And if the old servant were not angry, he felt comforted, and if he were angry, he was more dejected. It happened even (very rarely however) that Fyodor Pavlovitch went at night to the lodge to wake Grigory and fetch him for a moment. When the old man came, Fyodor Pavlovitch would begin talking about the most trivial matters, and would soon let him go again, sometimes even with a jest. And after he had gone, Fyodor Pavlovitch would get into bed with a curse and sleep the sleep of the just. Something of the same sort had happened to Fyodor Pavlovitch on Alyosha's arrival. Alyosha 'pierced his heart' by 'living with him, seeing everything and blaming nothing'. Moreover, Alyosha brought with him something his father had never known before: a complete absence of contempt for him and an invariable kindness, a perfectly natural unaffected devotion to the old man who deserved it so little. All this was a complete surprise to the old profligate, who had dropped all family ties. It was a new and surprising experience for him, who had till then loved nothing but 'evil'. When Alyosha left him, he confessed to himself that he had learned something he had not till then been willing to learn.

I have mentioned already that Grigory had detested Adelaïda Ivanovna, the first wife of Fyodor Pavlovitch and the mother of Dmitri, and that he had, on the contrary, protected Sofya Ivanovna, the poor 'crazy woman', against his master and anyone who chanced to speak ill or lightly of her. His sympathy for the unhappy wife had become something sacred to him, so that even now, twenty years after, he could not bear a slighting allusion to her from anyone, and would at once check the offender. Externally, Grigory was cold, dignified and taciturn, and spoke, weighing his words, without frivolity. It was impossible to tell at first sight whether he loved his meek, obedient wife; but he really did love her, and she knew it.

God had not blessed them with children. One child was born but it died. Grigory was fond of children, and was not ashamed of showing it. When Adelaïda Ivanovna ran away, Grigory took Dmitri, then a child of three years old, combed his hair and washed him in a tub with his own hands, and looked after him for almost a year. Afterwards he had looked after Ivan and Alyosha, for which the general's widow had rewarded him with a slap in the face; but I have already related all that. The only happiness his own child had brought him had been in the anticipation of its birth. When it was born, he was overwhelmed with grief and horror. The baby had six fingers. Grigory was so crushed by this, that he was not only silent till the day of the christening, but kept away in the garden. It was spring, and he spent three days digging the kitchen garden. The third day was fixed for christening the boy: meantime Grigory had reached a conclusion. Going into the cottage where the clergy were assembled and the visitors had arrived, including Fyodor Pavlovitch, who was to stand godfather, he suddenly announced that the baby 'ought not to be christened at all'. He announced this quietly, briefly, forcing out his words and gazing with dull intentness at the priest.

'Why not?' asked the priest with good-humoured surprise.

'Because it's a dragon,' muttered Grigory.

'A dragon? What dragon?'

Grigory did not speak for some time. 'It's a confusion of nature,' he muttered vaguely, but firmly, and obviously unwilling to say more.

They laughed, and of course christened the poor baby. Grigory prayed earnestly at the font, but his opinion of the newborn child remained unchanged. Yet he did not interfere in any way. As long as the sickly infant lived he scarcely looked at it, tried indeed not to notice it, and for the most part kept out of the cottage. But when, at the end of a fortnight, the baby died of croup, he himself laid the child in its little coffin, looked at it in profound grief, and when they were filling up the shallow little grave he fell on his knees and bowed down to the earth. He did not for years afterwards mention his child, nor did Marfa speak of the baby before him, and, even if Grigory were not present, she never spoke of it except in a whisper. Marfa observed that, from the day of the burial, he devoted himself to 'religion', and took to reading the *Lives of the Saints*, for the most part sitting alone and in silence, and always putting on his big, round, silver-rimmed spectacles. He rarely read aloud, only sometimes during Lent. He was fond of the book of Job, and had somehow got hold of a copy of the sayings and sermons of 'the God-fearing Father Isaac the Syrian', which he read persistently for years together, understanding very little of it, but probably prizing and loving it the more for that. Of late he had begun to listen to the doctrines of the sect of Flagellants settled in the neighbourhood. He was evidently shaken by them, but judged it unfitting to go over to the new faith.

He was perhaps predisposed to mysticism. And the birth of his deformed child, and its death, had, as though by special design, been accompanied by another strange, unexpected and most peculiar event, which, as he said later, left a mark on his soul. It happened that, on the very night after the burial of his child, Marfa was awakened by the wail of a newborn baby. She was frightened and waked her husband. He listened and said he thought it was more like someone groaning, 'it might be a woman'. He got up and dressed. It was a rather warm night in May. As he went down the steps, he distinctly heard groans coming from the garden. But the gate from the yard into the garden was locked at night, and there was no other way of entering it, for it was enclosed all round by a strong, high fence. Going back into the house, Grigory lighted a lantern, took the garden key, and taking no notice of the hysterical fears of his wife, who was still persuaded that she heard a child crying, and that it was her own baby crying and calling for her, went into the garden in silence. There he heard at once that the groans came from the bathhouse that stood near the garden gate, and that they were groans of a woman. Opening the door of the bathhouse, he saw a sight which petrified him. An idiot girl, who wandered about the streets and was known to the whole town by the nickname of Lizaveta Smerdyastchaya (Stinking Lizaveta), had got into the bathhouse and had just given birth to a child. She lay dying with the baby beside her. She said nothing, for she had never been able to speak. But her story needs a chapter to itself.

2

There was one circumstance which struck Grigory particularly, and confirmed a very unpleasant and revolting suspicion. This Lizaveta was a dwarfish creature, 'not five foot within a wee bit', as many of the pious old women said pathetically about her, after her death. Her broad, healthy, red face had a look of blank idiocy and the fixed stare in her eyes was unpleasant, in spite of their meek expression. She wandered about, summer and winter alike, barefooted, wearing nothing but a rough cotton smock. Her coarse, almost black hair curled like lamb's wool, and formed a sort of huge cap on her head. It was always crusted with mud, and had leaves, bits of twigs, and wood shavings clinging to it, as she always slept on the ground and in the dirt. Her father, a homeless, sickly drunkard, called Ilya, had lost everything and lived many years as a workman with some well-to-do tradespeople. Her mother had long been dead. Spiteful and diseased, Ilya used to beat Lizaveta inhumanly whenever she returned to him. But she rarely did so, for everyone in the town was ready to look after her for, being an idiot, she was considered specially dear to God. Ilya's employers, and many others in the town, especially many of the tradespeople, tried to clothe her better, and always rigged her out with high boots and a sheepskin coat for the winter. But, although she allowed them to dress her up without resisting, she usually went away, preferably to the cathedral porch, and taking off all that had been given her – kerchief, sheepskin, skirt or boots – she left them there and walked away barefoot in her smock as before. It happened on one occasion that a new governor of the province, making a tour of inspection in our town, saw Lizaveta, and was wounded in his tenderest susceptibilities. And though he was told she was an idiot, he pronounced that for a young woman of twenty to wander about in nothing but a smock was a breach of the proprieties, and must not occur again. But the governor went his way, and Lizaveta was left as she was. At last her father died, leaving her an orphan, which made her even more acceptable in the eyes of the religious persons of the town. In fact, everyone seemed to like her; even the boys did not tease her, and the boys of our town, especially the schoolboys, are a mischievous set. She would walk into strange houses, and no one drove her away. Everyone was kind to her and gave her something. If she were given a copper, she would take it, and at once drop it in the alms jug of the church or prison. If she were given a roll or bun in the market, she would hand it to the first child she met. Sometimes she would stop one of the richest ladies in the town and give it to her, and the lady would be pleased to take it. She herself never tasted anything but black bread and water. If she went into an expensive shop, where there were costly goods or money lying about, no one kept watch on her, for they knew that if she saw thousands of roubles overlooked by them, she would not have touched a penny. She scarcely ever went to church. She slept either in the church porch or climbed over a hurdle (there are many hurdles instead of fences to this day in our town) into a kitchen garden. She used at least once a week to turn up 'at home', that is at the house of her father's former employers, and in the winter went there every night, and slept either in the hallway or in the cow house. People were amazed that she could stand such a life, but she was accustomed to it, and, although she was so tiny, she was of a robust constitution. Some of the townspeople declared that she did all this only from pride, but that is hardly credible. She could hardly speak, and only from time to time uttered an inarticulate grunt. How could she have been proud?

It happened one clear, warm, moonlight night in September (many years ago) that five or six drunken revellers were returning from the club at a very late hour, according to our provincial notions. They passed through the 'back-way', which led between the back gardens of the houses, with hurdles on either side. This way leads out on to the bridge over the long, stinking pool which we were accustomed to call a river. Among the nettles and burdocks under the hurdle our revellers saw Lizaveta asleep. They stopped to look at her, laughing, and began jesting with unbridled licentiousness. It occurred to one young gentleman to make the whimsical enquiry whether anyone could possibly look upon such an animal as a woman, and so forth . . . They all pronounced with lofty repugnance that it was impossible. But Fyodor Pavlovitch, who was among them, sprang forward and declared that it was by no means impossible, and that, indeed, there was a certain piquancy about it, and so on . . . It is true that at that time he was overdoing his part as a buffoon. He liked to put himself forward and entertain the company, ostensibly on equal terms, of course, though in reality he was on a servile footing with them. It was just at the time when he had received the news of his first wife's death in Petersburg, and, with a black crape band upon his hat, was drinking and behaving so shamelessly that even the most reckless among us were shocked at the sight of him. The revellers, of course, laughed at the unexpected opinion expressed by Fyodor Pavlovitch; one of them even began challenging him to act upon it. The others repelled the idea even more emphatically, although still with the utmost hilarity, and at last they went on their way. Later on, Fyodor Pavlovitch swore that he had gone with them, and perhaps it was so, no one knows for certain, and no one ever knew. But five or six months later, all the town was talking, with intense and sincere indignation, of Lizaveta's condition, and trying to find out who was the miscreant who had wronged her. Then suddenly a terrible rumour was all over the town that this miscreant was no other than

Fyodor Pavlovitch. Who set the rumour going? Of that drunken band five had left the town and the only one still among us was an elderly and much respected civil councillor, the father of grown-up daughters, who could hardly have spread the tale, even if there had been any foundation for it. But rumour pointed straight at Fyodor Pavlovitch, and persisted in pointing at him. Of course this was no great grievance to him: he would not have troubled to contradict a set of tradespeople. In those days he was proud, and did not condescend to talk except in his own circle of officials and nobles, whom he entertained so well.

At the time, Grigory stood up for his master vigorously. He provoked quarrels and altercations in defence of him and succeeded in bringing some people round to his side. 'It's the wench's own fault,' he asserted, and the culprit was Karp, a dangerous convict, who had escaped from prison and whose name was well known to us, as he had hidden in our town. This conjecture sounded plausible, for it was remembered that Karp had been in the neighbourhood just at that time in the autumn, and had robbed three people. But this affair and all the talk about it did not estrange popular sympathy from the poor idiot. She was better looked after than ever. A well-to-do merchant's widow named Kondratyev arranged to take her into her house at the end of April, intending to keep the girl in the house until after the confinement. The Kondratyev household kept a constant watch over her, but in spite of their vigilance she escaped on the very last day, and made her way into Fyodor Pavlovitch's garden. How, in her condition, she managed to climb over the high, strong fence remained a mystery. Some maintained that she must have been lifted over by somebody; others hinted at something more uncanny. The most likely explanation is that it happened naturally – that Lizaveta, accustomed to clambering over hurdles to sleep in gardens, had somehow managed to climb this fence, in spite of her condition, and had leaped down, injuring herself.

Grigory rushed to Marfa and sent her to Lizaveta, while he ran to fetch an old midwife who lived close by. They saved the baby, but Lizaveta died at dawn. Grigory took the baby, brought it home, and making his wife sit down, put it on her lap. 'A child of God – an orphan is akin to all,' he said, 'and to us above others. Our little lost one has sent us this gift, who is born of the devil's son and a holy innocent. Nurse him and weep no more.'

So Marfa brought up the child. He was christened Pavel, to which people were not slow in adding Fyodorovitch (son of Fyodor). Fyodor Pavlovitch did not object to any of this, and thought it amusing, though he persisted vigorously in denying his responsibility. The townspeople were pleased that Grigory and Marfa had adopted the foundling. Later on, Fyodor Pavlovitch invented a surname for the child, calling him Smerdyakov, after his mother's nickname.

So this Smerdyakov became Fyodor Pavlovitch's second servant, and was living in the lodge with Grigory and Marfa at the time our story begins. He was employed as cook. I ought to say something of this Smerdyakov, but I am ashamed of keeping my readers' attention so long occupied with these common menials, and I will go back to my story, hoping to say more of Smerdyakov later on.

3

Alyosha remained for some time irresolute after hearing the command his father shouted to him from the carriage. But in spite of his uneasiness he did not stand still. That was not his way. He went at once to the kitchen to find out what his father had been doing upstairs in the dining room. Then he set off, trusting that on the way he would find some answer to the doubt tormenting him. I hasten to add that his father's shouts, commanding him to return home 'with his mattress and pillow', did not frighten him in the least. He understood perfectly that those peremptory shouts were merely 'a flourish' to produce an effect. In the same way a tradesman in our town who was celebrating his saint's-day with a party of friends, getting angry at being refused more vodka, smashed up his own crockery and furniture and tore his own and his wife's clothes, and finally broke his windows, all for the sake of effect. Next day, of course, when he was sober, he regretted the broken cups and saucers. Alyosha knew that his father would let him go back to the monastery next day, possibly even that evening. Moreover, he was fully persuaded that his father might hurt anyone else, but would not hurt him. Alyosha was certain that no one in the whole world ever would want to hurt him, and, what is more, he knew that no one could hurt him. This was for him an axiom, assumed once for all without question, and he went his way without hesitation, relying on it.

But at that moment an anxiety of a different sort

disturbed him, and worried him the more because he could not formulate it. It was the fear of a woman, of Katerina Ivanovna, who had so urgently entreated him in the note handed to him by Madame Hohlakov to come and see her about something. This request and the necessity of going had at once aroused an uneasy feeling in his heart, and this feeling had grown more and more painful all the morning in spite of the scenes at the hermitage and at the Father Superior's. He was not uneasy because he did not know what she would speak of and what he must answer. And he was not afraid of her simply as a woman. Though he knew little of women, he had spent his life, from early childhood till he entered the monastery, entirely with women. He was afraid of that woman, Katerina Ivanovna. He had been afraid of her from the first time he saw her. He had only seen her two or three times, and had only chanced to say a few words to her. He thought of her as a beautiful, proud, imperious girl. It was not her beauty which troubled him, but something else. And the vagueness of his apprehension increased the apprehension itself. The girl's aims were of the noblest, he knew that. She was trying to save his brother Dmitri simply through generosity, though he had already behaved badly to her. Yet, although Alyosha recognised and did justice to all these fine and generous sentiments, a shiver began to run down his back as soon as he drew near her house.

He reflected that he would not find Ivan, who was so intimate a friend, with her, for Ivan was certainly now with his father. Dmitri he was even more certain not to find there, and he had a foreboding of the reason. And so his conversation would be with her alone. He had a great longing to run and see his brother Dmitri before that fateful interview. Without showing him the letter, he could talk to him about it. But Dmitri lived a long way off, and he was sure to be away from home too. Standing still for a minute, he reached a final decision. Crossing himself with a rapid and accustomed gesture, and at once smiling, he turned resolutely in the direction of his terrible lady.

He had to pass the garden adjoining his father's, which belonged to a little tumbledown house with four windows.

Over the hurdle in the garden, Dmitri, mounted on something, was leaning forward, gesticulating violently, beckoning to him, obviously afraid to utter a word for fear of being overheard. Alyosha ran up to the hurdle.

'It's a good thing you looked up. I was afraid I'd have to shout to you,' Mitya said in a joyful, hurried whisper. 'Climb in here quickly! How splendid that you've come! I was just thinking of you!'

Alyosha was delighted too, but he did not know how to get over the hurdle. Mitya put his powerful hand under his elbow to help him jump. Tucking up his cassock, Alyosha leaped over the hurdle with the agility of a bare-legged street urchin.

'Well done! Now come along,' said Mitya in an enthusiastic whisper.

'Where?' whispered Alyosha, looking about him and finding himself in a deserted garden with no one near but themselves. The garden was small, but the house was at least fifty paces away.

'There's no one here. Why do you whisper?' asked Alyosha.

'Why do I whisper? Deuce take it!' cried Dmitri at the top of his voice. 'You see what silly tricks nature plays one. I am here in secret, and on the watch. I'll explain later on, but, knowing it's a secret, I began whispering like a fool, when there's no need. Let us go. Over there. Till then be quiet. I want to embrace you.

> Glory to God in the world,
> Glory to God in me . . .

I was just repeating that, sitting here, before you came.'

The garden was about three acres in extent, and planted with trees only along the fence at the four sides. There were apple trees, maples, limes and birch trees. The middle of the garden was an open grass plot, from which several hundredweight of hay was carried in the summer. The garden was rented out for a few roubles for the summer. There were also rows of raspberries and currants and gooseberries laid out along the sides; a kitchen garden had been planted lately near the house.

Dmitri led his brother to the most secluded corner of the garden. There, in a thicket of lime trees and old bushes of black currant, elder, snowball tree, and lilac, there stood a tumbledown, green-painted summer-house, blackened with age. Its walls were of lattice-work, but there was a fairly sound roof which could give shelter. God knows when this summerhouse was built. It was all in decay, the floor was rotting, the planks were loose, the woodwork smelled musty. In the summerhouse there was a green wooden table fixed in the ground, and round it were some green benches upon which it was still possible to sit. Alyosha had at once observed his brother's exhilarated condition, and on entering the arbor he saw half a bottle of brandy and a wineglass on the table.

'That's brandy,' Mitya laughed. 'I see your look: "He's drinking again!" Distrust the apparition.

> Distrust the worthless, lying crowd,
> And lay aside thy doubts.

I'm not drinking, I'm only "indulging", as that pig, your Rakitin, says. He'll be a civil councillor one day, but he'll always talk about "indulging". Sit down. I could take you in my arms, Alyosha, and press you to my bosom till I crush you, for in the whole world – in reality – in re–al–i–ty – (can you take it in?) I love no one but you!'

He uttered the last words in a sort of exaltation.

'No one but you and one "jade" I have fallen in love with, to my ruin. But being in love doesn't mean loving. You may be in love with a woman and yet hate her. Remember that! I can talk about it gaily still. Sit down here by the table and I'll sit beside you and look at you, and go on talking. You shall keep quiet and I'll go on talking, for the time has come. But on reflection, you know, I'd better speak quietly, for here – here – you can never tell what ears are listening. I will explain everything, as they say, "the story will be continued." Why have I been longing for you? Why have I been thirsting for you all these days, and just now? (It's five days since I've cast anchor here.) Because it's only to you I can tell everything; because I must, because I need you, because tomorrow I shall fly from the clouds, because tomorrow life is ending and beginning. Have you ever felt, have you ever dreamed of falling down a precipice into a pit? That's just how I'm falling, but not in a dream. And I'm not afraid, and don't you be afraid. At least, I am afraid, but I enjoy it. It's not enjoyment though, but ecstasy. Damn it all, whatever it is! A strong spirit, a weak spirit, a womanish spirit – whatever it is! Let us praise nature: you see the beautiful sunshine, how clear the sky is, the leaves are all green, it's still summer; four o'clock in the afternoon and the stillness! Where were you going?'

'I was going to father's, but I meant to go to Katerina Ivanovna's first.'

'To her, and to father! O–o! What a coincidence! Why was I waiting for you? Hungering and thirsting for you in every cranny of my soul and even in my ribs? Why, to send you to father and to her, Katerina Ivanovna, so as to have done with her and with father. To send an angel. I might have sent anyone, but I wanted to send an angel. And here you are on your way to see father and her.'

'Did you really mean to send me?' cried Alyosha with a distressed expression.

'Stay! You knew it! And I see you understand it all at once. But be quiet, be quiet for a time. Don't be sorry, and don't cry.'

Dmitri stood up, thought a moment, and put his finger to his forehead.

'She's asked you, written you a letter or something, that's why you're going to her? You wouldn't be going except for that?'

'Here is her note.' Alyosha took it from his pocket. Mitya looked through it quickly.

'Listen, Alyosha, listen, brother! Now I mean to tell you everything, for I must tell someone. An angel in heaven I've told already; but I want to tell an angel on earth. You are an angel on earth. You will hear and judge and forgive. And that's what I need, that someone better than I should forgive. Listen! If two people break away from everything on earth and fly off into the unknown, or at least one of them, and before flying off or going to ruin he comes to someone else and says, "Do this for me" – some favour never asked before that could only be asked on one's deathbed – would that other refuse, if he were a friend or a brother?'

'I will do it, but tell me what it is, and make haste,' said Alyosha.

'Make haste! H'm! . . . Don't be in a hurry, Alyosha, you hurry and worry yourself. There's no need to hurry now. Now the world has taken a new turning. Ah, Alyosha, what a pity you can't understand ecstasy. But what am I saying to him? As though you didn't understand it. What an ass I am, what am I saying: "Be noble, oh, man!" who says that?'

Alyosha made up his mind to wait. He felt that, perhaps, indeed, his work lay here. Mitya sank into thought for a moment, with his elbow on the table and his head in his hand.

4

'I was leading a wild life then. Father said just now that I spent several thousand roubles in seducing young girls. That's a swinish invention. Nothing of the sort ever happened. And if it did, I don't need money simply for *that*. With me money is an accessory, the overflow of my heart, the framework. Today it might be my lady, tomorrow a wench out of the streets. I have entertained both kinds. I threw away money by the handful on music, rioting and gypsies. Sometimes I gave it to the ladies, too, for they'll take it greedily, that must be admitted, and be pleased and thankful for it. Ladies used to be fond of me: not all of them, but it happened, it happened. But I always liked sidepaths, little dark back-alleys behind the main road – there one finds adventures and surprises, and precious metal in the dirt. I am speaking figuratively, brother. In the town I was in, there were no such back-alleys in the literal sense, but morally there were. If you were like me, you'd know what that means. I loved vice, I loved the ignominy of vice. I loved cruelty; am I not a louse, am I not a noxious insect? In fact a Karamazov! Once we went, a whole lot of us, for a picnic, in seven sledges. It was dark, it was winter, and I began squeezing a girl's hand, and forced her to kiss me. She was the daughter of an official, a sweet, gentle, submissive creature. She allowed me, she allowed me much in the dark. She thought, poor thing, that I would come next day to make her an offer (I was looked upon as a good match too). But I didn't say a word to her for five months. I used to see her in a corner at dances (we were always having dances), her eyes watching me. I saw how they glowed with fire – a fire of gentle indignation. This game only tickled that vile lust I cherished in my soul. Five months later she married an official and left the town, still angry, and still, perhaps, in love with me. Now they live happily. Observe that I told no one. I didn't boast of it. Though I'm full of low desires, and love what's low, I'm not dishonourable. You're blushing; your eyes flashed. Enough of this filth with you. And all this was nothing much – wayside blossoms *à la* Paul de Kock – though the cruel insect had already grown strong in my soul. I've a perfect album of reminiscences, brother. God bless them, the darlings. I tried to break it off without quarrelling. And I never gave them away. I never bragged of one of them. But that's enough. You can't suppose I brought you here simply to talk of such nonsense. No, I'm going to tell you something more curious; and don't be surprised that I'm glad to tell you, instead of being ashamed.'

'You say that because I blushed,' Alyosha said suddenly. 'I wasn't blushing at what you were saying or at what you've done. I blushed because I am the same as you are.'

'You? Come, that's going a little too far!'

'No, it's not too far,' said Alyosha warmly (obviously the idea was not a new one). 'The ladder's the same. I'm at the bottom step, and you're above, somewhere about the thirteenth. That's how I see it. But it's all the same. Absolutely the same in kind. Anyone on the bottom step is bound to go up to the top one.'

'Then one ought not to step on it at all.'

'Anyone who can help it had better not.'

'But can you?'

'I think not.'

'Hush, Alyosha, hush, darling! I could kiss your hand, you touch me so. That rogue Grushenka has an eye for men. She told me once that she'd devour you one day. There, there, I won't! From this field of corruption fouled by flies, let's pass to my tragedy, also befouled by flies, that is by every sort of vileness. Although the old man told lies about my seducing innocence, there really was something of the sort in my tragedy, though it was only once, and then it did not come off. The old man who has reproached me with what never happened does not even know of this fact; I never told anyone about it. You're the first, except Ivan, of course – Ivan knows everything. He knew about it long before you. But Ivan's a tomb.'

'Ivan's a tomb?'

'Yes.'

Alyosha listened with great attention.

'I was lieutenant in a line regiment, but still I was under supervision, like a kind of convict. Yet I was awfully well received in the little town. I spent money right and left. I was thought to be rich; I thought so myself. But I must have pleased them in other ways as well. Although they shook their heads over me, they liked me. My colonel, who was an old man, took a sudden dislike to me. He was always down upon me, but I had powerful friends, and, moreover, all the town was on my side, so he couldn't do me much harm. I was at fault myself for refusing to treat him with proper respect. I was proud. This obstinate fellow, who was really a very good sort, kind-hearted and hospitable, had had two wives, both dead. His first wife, who was of a humble family, left a daughter as unpretentious as herself. She was a young woman of four and twenty when I was there, and was living with her father and an aunt, her mother's sister. The aunt was simple and illiterate; the niece was simple but lively. I like to say nice things about people. I never knew a woman of more charming character than Agafya – her name was Agafya Ivanovna! And she wasn't bad-looking either, in the Russian style: tall, stout, with a full figure, and beautiful eyes, though a rather coarse face. She had not married, although she had had two suitors. She refused them, but was as cheerful as ever. I was intimate with her, not in "that" way, it was pure friendship. I have often been friendly with women quite innocently. I used to talk to her with shocking frankness, and she only laughed. Many women like such freedom, and she was a girl too, which made it very amusing.

Another thing, one could never think of her as a young lady. She and her aunt lived in her father's house with a sort of voluntary humility, not putting themselves on an equality with other people. She was a general favourite, and of use to everyone, for she was a clever dressmaker. She had a talent for it. She gave her services freely without asking for payment, but if anyone offered her payment, she didn't refuse. The colonel, of course, was a very different matter. He was one of the chief personages in the district. He kept open house, entertained the whole town, gave suppers and dances. At the time I arrived and joined the battalion, all the town was talking of the expected return of the colonel's second daughter, a great beauty, who had just left a fashionable school in the capital. This second daughter is Katerina Ivanovna, and she was the child of the second wife, who belonged to a distinguished general's family; although, as I learned on good authority, she too brought the colonel no money. She had connections, and that was all. There may have been expectations, but they came to nothing.

'Yet, when the young lady arrived from boarding-school on a visit, the whole town woke up. Our most distinguished ladies – two "Excellencies" and a colonel's wife – and all the rest following their lead, at once took her up and gave entertainments in her honour. She was the belle of the balls and picnics, and they got up living pictures in aid of distressed governesses. I took no notice, I went on as wildly as before, and one of my exploits at the time set all the town talking. I saw her eyes taking my measure one evening at the battery commander's, but I didn't go up to her, as though I disdained her acquaintance. I did go up and speak to her at an evening party not long after. She scarcely looked at me, and compressed her lips scornfully. "Wait a bit. I'll have my revenge," thought I. I behaved like an awful fool on many occasions at that time, and I was conscious of it myself. What made it worse was that I felt that "Katenka" was not an innocent boarding-school miss, but a person of character, proud and really high-principled; above all, she had education and intellect, and I had neither. You think I meant to make her an offer? No, I simply wanted to revenge myself, because I was such a hero and she didn't seem to feel it.

'Meanwhile, I spent my time in drink and riot, till the lieutenant colonel put me under arrest for three days. Just at that time father sent me six thousand roubles in return for my sending him a deed giving up all claims upon him – settling our accounts, so to speak, and saying that I wouldn't expect anything more. I didn't understand a word of it at the time. Until I came here, Alyosha, till the last few days, indeed, perhaps even now, I haven't been able to make head or tail of my money affairs with father. But never mind that, we'll talk of it later.

'Just as I received the money, I got a letter from a friend telling me something that interested me immensely. The authorities, I learned, were dissatisfied with our lieutenant colonel. He was suspected of irregularities; in fact, his enemies were preparing a surprise for him. And then the commander of the division arrived, and kicked up the devil of a shindy. Shortly afterwards he was ordered to retire. I won't tell you how it all happened. He had enemies certainly. Suddenly there was a marked coolness in the town towards him and all his family. His friends all turned their backs on him. Then I took my first step. I met

Agafya Ivanovna, with whom I'd always kept up a friendship, and said, "Do you know there's a deficit of 4,500 roubles of government money in your father's accounts?"

' "What do you mean? What makes you say so? The general was here not long ago, and everything was all right."

' "Then it was, but now it isn't." '§§

'She was terribly scared.

' "Don't frighten me!" she said. "Who told you so?"

' "Don't be uneasy," I said, "I won't tell anyone. You know I'm as silent as the tomb. I only wanted, in view of 'possibilities', to add, that when they demand that 4,500 roubles from your father, and he can't produce it, he'll be tried, and made to serve as a common soldier in his old age, unless you like to send me your young sister secretly. I've just had money paid me. I'll give her four thousand, if you like, and keep the secret religiously."

' "Ah, you scoundrel!" that's what she said. "You wicked scoundrel! How dare you!"

'She went away furiously indignant, while I shouted after her once more that the secret should be kept sacred. Those two simple creatures, Agafya and her aunt, I may as well say at once, behaved like perfect angels all through this business. They genuinely adored their "Katya", thought her far above them, and waited on her hand and foot. But Agafya told her of our conversation. I found that out afterwards. She didn't keep it back, and of course that was all I wanted.

'Suddenly the new major arrived to take command of the battalion. The old lieutenant colonel was taken ill at once, couldn't leave his room for two days and didn't hand over the government money.

Dr Kravchenko declared that he really was ill. But I knew for a fact, and had known for a long time, that for the last four years the money had never been in his hands except when the commander made his visits of inspection. He used to lend it to a trustworthy person, a merchant of our town called Trifonov, an old widower, with a big beard and gold-rimmed spectacles. He used to go to the fair, do a profitable business with the money, and return the whole sum to the colonel, bringing with it a present from the fair, as well as interest on the loan. But this time (I heard all about it quite by chance from Trifonov's son and heir, a drivelling youth and one of the most vicious in the world) – this time, I say, Trifonov brought nothing back from the fair. The lieutenant colonel flew to him. "I've never received any money from you, and couldn't possibly have received any." That was all the answer he got. So now our lieutenant colonel is confined to the house, with a towel round his head, while they're all three busy putting ice on it. All at once an orderly arrives on the scene with the book and the order to "hand over the battalion money immediately, within two hours". He signed the book (I saw the signature in the book afterwards), stood up, saying he would put on his uniform, ran to his bedroom, loaded his double-barrelled gun with a service bullet, took the boot off his right foot, fixed the gun against his chest, and began feeling for the trigger with his foot. But Agafya, remembering what I had told her, had her suspicions. She stole up and peeped into the room just in time. She rushed in, flung herself upon him from behind, threw her arms round him, and the gun went off, hit the ceiling, but hurt no one. The others ran in, took away the gun, and held him by the arms. I heard all about this afterwards. I was at home, it was getting dusk, and I was just preparing to go out. I had dressed, brushed my hair, scented my handkerchief, and taken up my cap, when suddenly the door opened, and facing me in the room stood Katerina Ivanovna.

'It's strange how things happen sometimes. No one had seen her in the street, so that no one knew of it in the town. I lodged with two decrepit old ladies, who looked after me. They were most obliging old things, ready to do anything for me, and at my request were as silent afterwards as two cast-iron posts. Of course I grasped the position at once. She walked in and looked straight at me, her dark eyes determined, even defiant, but on her lips and round her mouth I saw uncertainty.

'"My sister told me," she began, "that you would give me 4,000 roubles if I came to you for it – myself. I have come . . . give me the money!"

'She couldn't keep it up. She was breathless, frightened, her voice failed her, and the corners of her mouth and the lines round it quivered. Alyosha, are you listening, or are you asleep?'

'Mitya, I know you will tell the whole truth,' said Alyosha in agitation.

'I am telling it. If I tell the whole truth just as it happened, I shan't spare myself. My first idea was a – Karamazov one. Once I was bitten by a centipede, brother, and laid up a fortnight with fever from it. Well, I felt a centipede biting at my heart then – a poisonous insect, you understand? I looked her up and down. You've seen her? She's a beauty. But she was beautiful in another way then. At that moment she was beautiful because she was noble, and I was a scoundrel; she in all the grandeur of her generosity and sacrifice for her father, and I – a louse! And, scoundrel as I was, she was altogether at my mercy, body and soul. She was hemmed in. I tell you frankly, that thought, that venomous thought, so possessed my heart that it almost swooned with suspense. It seemed as if there could be no resisting it; as though I should act like a louse, like a venomous spider, without a spark of pity. I could scarcely breathe. Understand, I should have gone next day to ask for her hand, so that it might end honourably, so to speak, and that nobody would or could know. For though I'm a man of base desires, I'm honest. And at that very second some voice seemed to whisper in my ear, "But when you come tomorrow to make your proposal, that girl won't even see you; she'll order her coachman to kick you out of the yard. 'Publish it through all the town,' she would say, 'I'm not afraid of you.' " I looked at the young lady, my instinct had not deceived me. That is how it would be, not a doubt of it. I could see from her face now that I should be turned out of the house. My spite was roused. I longed to play her the nastiest, most swinish cad's trick: to look at her with a sneer, and on the spot where she stood before me to stun her with a tone of voice that only a tradesman could use.

' "Four thousand! What do you mean? I was joking. You've been counting your chickens too easily, madam. Two hundred, if you like, with all my heart. But four thousand is not a sum to throw away on such frivolity. You've put yourself out to no purpose."

'I should have lost the game, of course. She'd have run away. But it would have been an infernal revenge. It would have been worth it all. I'd have howled with regret all the rest of my life, only to have played that trick. Would you believe it, it has never happened to me with any other woman, not one, to look at her at such a moment with hatred. But, on my oath, I looked at her for three seconds, or five perhaps, with fearful hatred – that hate which is only a hair's breadth from love, from the maddest love!

'I went to the window, put my forehead against the frozen pane, and I remember the cold burned my forehead like fire. I did not keep her long, don't be afraid. I turned round, went up to the table, opened the drawer and took out a banknote for five thousand roubles (it was lying in a French dictionary). Then I showed it to her in silence, folded it, handed it to her, opened the door into the passage, and, stepping back, made her a deep bow, a most respectful, a most impressive bow, believe me! She shuddered all over, gazed at me for a second, turned horribly pale – white as a sheet, in fact – and all at once, not impetuously but softly, gently, bowed down to my feet – not a boarding-school curtsy, but a Russian bow with her forehead to the floor. She jumped up and ran away. I was wearing my sword. I drew it and nearly stabbed myself with it on the spot; why, I don't know. It would have been frightfully stupid, of course. I suppose it was from delight. Can you understand that one might kill oneself from delight? But I didn't stab myself. I only kissed my sword and put it back in the scabbard – a detail which there is no need to have told you, by the way. And I fancy that in telling you about my inner conflict I have laid it on rather thick to glorify myself. But let it pass, and to hell with all who pry into the human heart! Well, so much for that "adventure" with Katerina Ivanovna. So now Ivan knows of it, and you – no one else.'

Dmitri got up, took a step or two in his excitement, pulled out his handkerchief and mopped his forehead, then sat down again, not in the same place as before, but on the opposite side, so that Alyosha had to turn around to face him.

5

'Now,' said Alyosha, 'I understand the first half.'

'You understand the first half. That half is a drama, and it was played out there. The second half is a tragedy, and it is being acted here.'

'And I understand nothing of that second half so far,' said Alyosha.

'And I? Do you suppose I understand it?'

'Stop, Dmitri. There's one important question. Tell me, you were betrothed, you are betrothed still?'

'We weren't betrothed at once, not for three months after that adventure. The next day I told myself that the incident was closed, concluded, that there would be no sequel. It seemed to me caddish to make her an offer. On her side she gave no sign of life for the six weeks that she remained in the town; except, indeed, for one action. The day after her visit the maidservant slipped round with an envelope addressed to me. I tore it open; it contained the change out of the banknote. Only 4,500 was needed, but there was a discount of about 200 on changing it. She only sent me about 260 roubles, I don't remember exactly, but not a note, not a word of explanation. I searched the packet for a pencil mark – nothing! I spent the rest of the money on such an orgy that the new major was obliged to reprimand me.

'Well, the lieutenant colonel produced the battalion money, to the astonishment of everyone, for nobody believed that he had the money intact. He'd no sooner paid it than he fell ill, took to his bed, and, three weeks later, softening of the brain set in, and he died five days afterwards. He was buried with military honours, for he had not had time to receive his discharge. Ten days after his funeral, Katerina Ivanovna, with her aunt and sister, went to Moscow. And, behold, on the very day they went away (I hadn't seen them, didn't see them off or take leave) I received a tiny note, a sheet of thin blue paper, and on it only one line in pencil: "I will write to you. Wait. K." And that was all.

'I'll explain the rest now, in two words. In Moscow their fortunes changed with the swiftness of lightning and the unexpectedness of an Arabian fairy tale. That general's widow, their nearest relation, suddenly lost the two nieces who were her heiresses and next-of-kin – both died in the same week of smallpox. The old lady, prostrated with grief, welcomed Katya as a daughter, as her one hope, clutched at her, altered her will in Katya's favour. But that concerned the future. Meanwhile she gave her, for present use, 80,000 roubles, as a marriage dowry, to do what she liked with. She was a hysterical woman. I saw something of her in Moscow, later.

'Well, suddenly I received by post four thousand five hundred roubles. I was speechless with surprise, as you may suppose. Three days later came the promised letter. I have it with me now. I always keep it, and shall keep it till I die. Shall I show you? You must read it. She offers to be my wife, offers herself to me. "I love you madly," she says, "even if you don't love me, never mind. Be my husband. Don't be afraid. I won't hamper you in any way. I will be your chattel. I will be the carpet under your feet. I want to love you for ever. I want to save you from yourself." Alyosha, I am not worthy to repeat those lines in my vulgar words and in my vulgar tone, my everlastingly vulgar tone, that I can never cure myself of. That letter stabs me even now. Do you think I don't mind – that I don't mind still? I wrote her an answer at once, as it was impossible for me to go to Moscow. I wrote to her with tears. One thing I shall be ashamed of for ever. I referred to her being rich and having a dowry while I was only a stuck-up beggar! I mentioned money! I ought to have borne it in silence, but it slipped from my pen. Then I wrote at once to Ivan, and told him all I could about it in a letter of six pages, and sent him to her. Why do you look like that? Why are you staring at me? Yes, Ivan fell in love with her; he's in love with her still. I know that. I did a stupid thing, in the world's opinion; but perhaps that one stupid thing may be the saving of us all now. Oh! Don't you see what a lot she thinks of Ivan, how she respects him? When she compares us, do you suppose she can love a man like me, especially after all that has happened here?'

'But I'm convinced that she does love a man like you, and not a man like him.'

'She loves her own *virtue*, not me.' The words broke involuntarily, and almost malignantly, from Dmitri. He laughed, but a minute later his eyes gleamed, he flushed crimson and struck the table violently with his fist.

'I swear, Alyosha,' he cried, with intense and genuine anger at himself; 'you may not believe me, but as God is holy, and as Christ is God, I swear that though I smiled at her lofty sentiments just now, I know that I am a million times baser in soul than she, and that these lofty sentiments of hers are as sincere as a heavenly angel's. That's the tragedy of it – that I know that for certain. What if anyone does show off a bit? Don't I do it myself? And yet I'm sincere, I'm sincere. As for Ivan, I can understand how he must be cursing nature now – with his intellect too! To see the preference given – to whom, to what? To a monster who, though he is betrothed and all eyes are fixed on him, can't restrain his debaucheries – and before the very eyes of his betrothed! And a man like me is preferred, while he is rejected. And why? Because a girl wants to sacrifice her life and destiny out of gratitude. It's ridiculous! I've never said a word of this to Ivan, and Ivan of course has never dropped a hint of the sort to me. But destiny will be accomplished, and the best man will hold his ground while the undeserving one will vanish into his back-alley for ever – his filthy back-alley, his beloved back-alley, where he is at home and where he will sink in filth and stench at his own free will and with enjoyment. I've been talking foolishly. I've no words left. I use them at random, but it will be as I have said. I shall drown in the back-alley, and she will marry Ivan.'

'Stop, Dmitri,' Alyosha interrupted again with great anxiety. 'There's one thing you haven't made clear yet: you are still betrothed all the same, aren't you? How can you break off the engagement if she, your betrothed, doesn't want to?'

'Yes, formally and solemnly betrothed. It was all done on my arrival in Moscow, with great ceremony, with icons, all in fine style. The general's wife blessed us, and – would you believe it? – congratulated Katya. "You've made a good choice," she said, "I see right through him." And, would you believe it, she didn't like Ivan, and hardly greeted him? I talked a lot with Katya in Moscow. I told her about myself – sincerely, honourably. She listened to everything.

There was sweet confusion,
There were tender words.

Though there were proud words too. She wrung out of me a solemn promise to reform. I gave my promise, and here – '

'What?'

'Why, I called to you and brought you out here today, this very day – remember it – to send you – this very day again – to Katerina Ivanovna, and – '

'What?'

'To tell her that I shall never come to see her again. Say "He sends you his compliments." '

'But is that possible?'

'That's just the reason I'm sending you, in my place, because it's impossible. How could I tell her myself?'

'And where are you going?'

'To the back-alley.'

'To Grushenka then!' Alyosha exclaimed mournfully, clasping his hands. 'Can Rakitin really have told the truth? I thought that you had just visited her, and that was all.'

'Can a betrothed man pay such visits? Is such a thing possible and with such a betrothed, and before the eyes of all the world? Confound it, I have some honour! As soon as I began visiting Grushenka, I ceased to be betrothed, and to be an honest man. I understand that. Why do you look at me? You see, I went in the first place to beat her. I had heard, and I know for a fact now, that that captain, father's agent, had given Grushenka an IOU of mine for her to sue me for payment, so as to put an end to me. They wanted to scare me. I went to beat her. I had had a glimpse of her before. She doesn't strike one at first sight. I knew about her old merchant, who's lying ill now, paralysed; but he's leaving her a decent little sum. I knew, too, that she was fond of money, that she hoarded it, and lent it at a wicked rate of interest, that she's a merciless cheat and swindler. I went to beat her, and I stayed. The storm broke – it struck me down like the plague. I'm plague-stricken still, and I know that everything is over, that there will never be anything more for me. The cycle of the ages is accomplished. That's my position. And though I'm a beggar, as fate would have it, I had three thousand just then in my pocket. I drove with Grushenka to Mokroe, a place fifteen miles from here. I got gypsies there and champagne and made all the peasants there drunk on it, and all the women and girls. I sent the thousands flying. In three days' time I was stripped bare, but a hero. Do you suppose the hero had gained his end? Not a sign of it from her. I tell you that rogue, Grushenka, has a supple curve all over her body. You can see it in her little foot, even in her little toe. I saw it, and kissed it, but that was all I swear! "I'll marry you if you like," she said, "you're a beggar you know. Say that you won't beat me, and will let me do anything I choose, and perhaps I will marry you." She laughed, and she's laughing still!'

Dmitri leaped up with a sort of fury. He seemed all at once as though he were drunk. His eyes became suddenly bloodshot.

'And do you really mean to marry her?'

'At once, if she will. And if she won't, I shall stay all the same. I'll be the porter at her gate. Alyosha!' he cried. He stopped short before him, and taking him by the shoulders began shaking him violently, 'Do you know, you innocent boy, that this is all delirium, senseless delirium, for there's a tragedy here. Let me tell you, that I may be a low man, with low and degraded passions, but a thief and a pickpocket Dmitri Karamazov never can be. Well, then; let me tell you that I am a thief and a pickpocket. That very morning, just before I went to beat Grushenka, Katerina Ivanovna sent for me, and in strict secrecy (why, I don't know, I suppose she had some reason) asked me to go to the chief town of the province and to post three thousand roubles to Agafya Ivanovna in Moscow, so that nothing should be known of it in the town here. So I had that three thousand roubles in my pocket when I went to see Grushenka, and it was that money we spent at Mokroe. Afterwards I pretended I had been to the town, but did not show her the post office receipt. I said I had sent the money and would bring the receipt, and so far I haven't brought it. I've forgotten it. Now what do you think you're going to her today to say? "He sends his compliments," and she'll ask you, "What about the money?" You might still have said to her, "He's a degraded sensualist, and a low creature, with uncontrolled passions. He didn't send your money then, but wasted it, because, like a low brute, he couldn't control himself." But still you might have added, "He isn't a thief though. Here is your three thousand; he sends it back. Send it yourself to Agafya Ivanovna. But he told me to say 'he sends his compliments'." But, as it is, she will ask, "But where is the money?" '

'Mitya, you are unhappy, yes! But not as unhappy as you think. Don't worry yourself to death with despair.'

'What, do you suppose I'd shoot myself because I can't get three thousand to pay back? That's just it. I shan't shoot myself. I haven't the strength now. Afterwards, perhaps. But now I'm going to Grushenka. I don't care what happens.'

'And what then?'

'I'll be her husband if she deigns to have me, and when lovers come, I'll go into the next room. I'll clean her friends' galoshes, heat up their samovar, run their errands.'

'Katerina Ivanovna will understand it all,' Alyosha said solemnly. 'She'll understand how great this trouble is and will forgive. She has a lofty mind, and no one could be more unhappy than you. She'll see that for herself.'

'She won't forgive everything,' said Dmitri, with a grin. 'There's something in it, brother, that no woman could forgive. Do you know what would be the best thing to do?'

'What?'

'Pay back the three thousand.'

'Where can we get it from? I say, I have two thousand. Ivan will give you another thousand – that makes three. Take it and pay it back.'

'And when would you get it, your three thousand? You're not of age, besides, and you must – you absolutely must – take my farewell to her today, with the money or without it, for I can't drag on any longer, things have come to such a pass. Tomorrow is too late. I shall send you to father.'

'To father?'

'Yes, to father first. Ask him for three thousand.'

'But, Mitya, he won't give it.'

'As though he would! I know he won't. Do you know the meaning of despair, Alexey?'

'Yes.'

'Listen. Legally he owes me nothing. I've had it all from him, I know that. But morally he owes me something, doesn't he? You know he started with twenty-eight thousand of my mother's money and made a hundred thousand with it. Let him give me back only three out of the twenty-eight thousand, and he'll pull my soul out of hell, and it will atone for many of his sins. For that three thousand – I give you my solemn word – I'll make an end of everything, and he shall hear nothing more of me. For the last time I give him the chance to be a father. Tell him God Himself sends him this chance.'

'Mitya, he won't give it for anything.'

'I know he won't. I know it perfectly well. Now, especially. That's not all. I know something more. Now, only a few days ago, perhaps only yesterday he found out for the first time *in earnest* (underline *in earnest*) that Grushenka is really perhaps not joking, and really means to marry me. He knows her nature; he knows the cat. And do you suppose he's going to give me money to help to bring that about when he's crazy about her himself? And that's not all, either. I can tell you more than that, I know that for the last five days he has had three thousand drawn out of the bank, changed into notes of a hundred roubles, packed into a large envelope, sealed with five seals, and tied across with red tape. You see how well I know all about it! On the envelope is written: "To my angel, Grushenka, when she will come to me." He scrawled it himself in silence and in secret, and no one knows that the money's there except the valet, Smerdyakov, whom he trusts like himself. So now he has been expecting Grushenka for the last three or four days; he hopes she'll come for the money. He has sent her word of it, and she has sent him word that perhaps she'll come. And if she does go to the old man, can I marry her after that? You understand now why I'm here in secret and what I'm on the watch for.'

'For her?'

'Yes, for her. Foma has a room in the house here. Foma comes from our parts; he was a soldier in our regiment. He does jobs for them. He's watchman at night and goes grouse shooting in the daytime; and that's how he lives. I've established myself in his room. Neither he nor the women of the house know the secret – that is, that I am on the watch here.'

'No one but Smerdyakov knows, then?'

'No one else. He will let me know if she goes to the old man.'

'It was he told you about the money, then?'

'Yes. It's a dead secret. Even Ivan doesn't know about the money, or anything. The old man is sending Ivan to Tchermashnya on a two- or three-days' trip. A purchaser has turned up for the wood there: he'll give eight thousand for the timber. So the old man keeps asking Ivan to help him by going to arrange it. It will take him two or three days. That's what the old man wants, so that Grushenka can come while Ivan is away.'

'Then he's expecting Grushenka today?'

'No, she won't come today; there are signs. She's certain not to come,' cried Mitya suddenly. 'Smerdyakov thinks so too. Father's drinking now. He's sitting at a table with Ivan. Go to him, Alyosha, and ask for the three thousand.'

'Mitya, dear, what's the matter with you?' cried Alyosha, jumping up from his place, and looking keenly at his brother's frenzied face. For one moment the thought struck him that Dmitri was mad.

'What is it? I'm not insane,' said Dmitri, looking

intently and earnestly at him. 'No fear. I am sending you to father, and I know what I'm saying. I believe in miracles.'

'In miracles?'

'In a miracle of Divine Providence. God knows my heart. He sees my despair. He sees the whole picture. Surely He won't let something awful happen. Alyosha, I believe in miracles. Go!'

'I am going. Tell me, will you wait for me here?'

'Yes. I know it will take some time. You can't go at him point blank. He's drunk now. I'll wait three hours – four, five, six, seven. Only remember you must go to Katerina Ivanovna today, if it has to be at midnight, *with the money or without the money*, and say, "He sends his compliments to you." I want you to say those words to her: "He sends his compliments to you." '

'Mitya! And what if Grushenka comes today – if not today, tomorrow, or the next day?'

'Grushenka? I shall see her. I shall rush out and prevent it.'

'And if – ?'

'If there's an if, it will be murder. I couldn't endure it.'

'Who will be murdered?'

'The old man. I shan't kill her.'

'Brother, what are you saying?'

'Oh, I don't know . . . I don't know. Perhaps I won't kill him, and perhaps I will. I'm afraid that he will suddenly become so loathsome to me with his face at that moment. I hate his ugly throat, his nose, his eyes, his shameless snicker. I feel a physical repulsion. That's what I'm afraid of. That's what may be too much for me.'

'I'll go, Mitya. I believe that God will order things for the best, that nothing awful may happen.'

'And I will sit and wait for the miracle. And if it doesn't come to pass – '

Alyosha went thoughtfully towards his father's house.

6

He did in fact find his father still at table. Though there was a dining room in the house, the table was laid as usual in the drawing-room, which was the largest room, and furnished with old-fashioned ostentation. The furniture was white and very old, upholstered in threadbare, red, silky material. In the spaces between the windows there were mirrors in elaborate white and gilt frames, of old-fashioned carving. On the walls, covered with white paper, which was torn in many places, there hung two large portraits – one of some prince who had been governor of the district thirty years before, and the other of some bishop, also long since dead. In the corner opposite the door there were several icons, before which a lamp was lighted at nightfall . . . not so much for devotional purposes as to light the room. Fyodor Pavlovitch used to go to bed very late, at three or four o'clock in the morning, and would wander about the room at night or sit in an armchair, thinking. This had become a habit with him. He often slept quite alone in the house, sending his servants to the lodge; but usually Smerdyakov remained, sleeping on a bench in the hall.

When Alyosha came in, dinner was over, but coffee and preserves had been served. Fyodor Pavlovitch liked sweet things with brandy after dinner. Ivan was also at table, sipping coffee. The servants, Grigory and

Smerdyakov, were standing by. Both the gentlemen and the servants seemed in singularly good spirits. Fyodor Pavlovitch was roaring with laughter. Before he entered the room, Alyosha heard the shrill laugh he knew so well, and could tell from the sound of it that his father had only reached the good-humoured stage, and was far from being completely drunk.

'Here he is! Here he is!' yelled Fyodor Pavlovitch, highly delighted at seeing Alyosha. 'Join us. Sit down. Coffee is a Lenten dish, but it's hot and good. I don't offer you brandy, you're keeping the fast. But would you like some? No; I'd better give you some of our famous liqueur. Smerdyakov, go to the cupboard, the second shelf on the right. Here are the keys. Look sharp!'

Alyosha refused the liqueur.

'Never mind. If you won't have it, we will,' said Fyodor Pavlovitch, beaming. 'But wait – have you dined?'

'Yes,' answered Alyosha, who had in truth only eaten a piece of bread and drunk a glass of kvass in the Father Superior's kitchen. 'Though I should be pleased to have some hot coffee.'

'Bravo, my darling! He'll have some coffee. Does it need warming? No, it's boiling. It's excellent coffee: Smerdyakov's making. My Smerdyakov's an artist at coffee and at fish patties, and at fish soup too. You must come one day and have some fish soup. Let me know beforehand . . . But, stay; didn't I tell you this morning to come home with your mattress and pillow and all? Have you brought your mattress? He, he, he!'

'No, I haven't,' said Alyosha, smiling too.

'Ah, but you were frightened, you were frightened this morning, weren't you? There, my darling, I couldn't do anything to vex you. Do you know, Ivan, I can't resist the way he looks one straight in the face and laughs? It makes me laugh all over. I'm so fond of him. Alyosha, let me give you my blessing – a father's blessing.'

Alyosha rose, but Fyodor Pavlovitch had already changed his mind.

'No, no,' he said, 'I'll just make the sign of the cross over you, for now. Sit still. Now we've a treat for you, in your own line too. It'll make you laugh. Balaam's ass has begun talking to us here – and how he talks! How he talks!'

Balaam's ass, it appeared, was the valet, Smerdyakov. He was a young man of about four and twenty, remarkably unsociable and taciturn. Not that he was shy or bashful. On the contrary, he was conceited and seemed to despise everybody.

But we must pause to say a few words about him now. He had been reared by Grigory and Marfa, but the boy grew up 'with no sense of gratitude', as Grigory expressed it; he was an unfriendly boy, and seemed to look at the world mistrustfully. In his childhood he was very fond of hanging cats and burying them with great ceremony. He used to dress up in a sheet as though it were a surplice, and sing and wave some object over the dead cat as though it were a censer. All this he did on the sly, with the greatest secrecy. Grigory caught him once at this diversion and gave him a sound beating. He shrank into a corner and sulked there for a week. 'He doesn't care for you or me, the monster,' Grigory used to say to Marfa, 'and he doesn't care for anyone. Are you a human being?' he said, addressing the boy directly. 'You're not a human being. You grew from the mildew in the bathhouse. [A proverbial expression in Russia.] That's what you are.' Smerdyakov, it appeared afterwards, could never forgive him those words. Grigory taught him to read and write, and when he was twelve years old began teaching him the Scriptures. But this teaching came to nothing. At the second or third lesson the boy suddenly grinned. 'What's that for?' asked Grigory, looking at him threateningly from under his spectacles.

'Oh, nothing. God created light on the first day, and the sun, moon, and stars on the fourth day. Where did the light come from on the first day?'

Grigory was thunderstruck. The boy looked sarcastically at his teacher. There was something positively condescending in his expression. Grigory could not restrain himself. 'I'll show you where!' he cried, and gave the boy a violent slap on the cheek. The boy took the slap without a word, but withdrew into his corner again for some days. A week later he had his first attack of the disease to which he was subject all the rest of his life – epilepsy. When Fyodor Pavlovitch heard of it, his attitude to the boy seemed to change at once. Till then he had taken no notice of him, though he never scolded him, and always gave him a copper coin when he met him. Sometimes, when he was in good humour, he would send the boy something sweet from his table. But as soon as he heard of his illness, he showed an active interest in him, sent for a doctor, and tried remedies, but the disease turned out to be incurable. The fits occurred, on an average, once a month, but at various intervals. The fits varied, too, in violence: some were light and some were very severe. Fyodor Pavlovitch strictly forbade Grigory to use corporal punishment on the boy, and began allowing him to come upstairs to him. He forbade him to be taught anything whatever for a time too. One day when the boy was about fifteen, Fyodor Pavlovitch noticed him lingering by the bookcase, and reading the titles through the glass. Fyodor Pavlovitch had a fair number of books – over a hundred – but no one ever saw him reading. He at once gave Smerdyakov the key of the bookcase. 'Come, read. You shall be my librarian. You'll be better sitting reading than hanging about the courtyard. Come, read this,' and Fyodor Pavlovitch gave him *Evenings in a Cottage Near Dikanka*.

He read a little, but didn't like it. He did not once smile, and ended by frowning.

'Why? Isn't it funny?' asked Fyodor Pavlovitch.

Smerdyakov did not speak.

'Answer, stupid!'

'It's all untrue,' mumbled the boy, with a grin.

'Then go to the devil! You have the soul of a lackey. Look, here's Smaragdov's *Universal History*. That's all true. Read that.'

But Smerdyakov thought it dull. So the bookcase was closed again.

Shortly afterwards Marfa and Grigory reported to Fyodor Pavlovitch that Smerdyakov was gradually beginning to show an extraordinary fastidiousness. He would sit before his soup, take up his spoon and look into the soup, bend over it, examine it, take a spoonful and hold it to the light.

'What is it? A beetle?' Grigory would ask.

'A fly, perhaps,' observed Marfa.

The squeamish youth never answered, but he did the same with his bread, his meat, and everything he ate. He would hold a piece on his fork to the light, scrutinise it microscopically, and only after long deliberation decide to put it in his mouth.

'Ah! What fine gentlemen's airs!' Grigory muttered, looking at him.

When Fyodor Pavlovitch heard of this development in Smerdyakov he determined to make him his cook, and sent him to Moscow to be trained. He spent some years there and came back remarkably changed in appearance. He looked extraordinarily old for his age. His face had grown wrinkled, yellow, and strangely emasculate. In character he seemed almost exactly the same as before he went away. He was just as unsociable, and showed not the slightest inclination for any companionship. In Moscow, too, as we heard afterwards, he had always been silent. Moscow itself had little interest for him; he saw very little there, and took scarcely any notice of anything. He went once to the theatre, but returned silent and displeased with it. On the other hand, he came back to us from Moscow well dressed, in a clean coat and clean linen. He brushed his clothes most scrupulously twice a day invariably, and was very fond of cleaning his smart calf boots with a special English polish, so that they shone like mirrors. He turned out to be a first-rate cook. Fyodor Pavlovitch paid him a salary, almost the whole of which Smerdyakov spent on clothes, pomade, perfumes, and such things. But he seemed to have as much contempt for the female sex as for men; he was discreet, almost unapproachable, with them. Fyodor Pavlovitch began to regard him rather differently. His fits were becoming more frequent, and on the days he was ill Marfa cooked, which did not suit Fyodor Pavlovitch at all.

'Why are your fits getting worse?' asked Fyodor Pavlovitch, looking askance at his new cook. 'Would you like to get married? Shall I find you a wife?'

But Smerdyakov turned pale with anger, and made

no reply. Fyodor Pavlovitch left him with an impatient gesture. The great thing was that he had absolute confidence in his honesty. It happened once, when Fyodor Pavlovitch was drunk, that he dropped in the muddy courtyard three hundred-rouble notes which he had only just received. He only missed them next day, and was just hastening to search his pockets when he saw the notes lying on the table. Where had they come from? Smerdyakov had picked them up and brought them in the day before.

'Well, my lad, I've never met anyone like you,' Fyodor Pavlovitch said shortly, and gave him ten roubles. We may add that he not only believed in his honesty, but had, for some reason, a liking for him, although the young man looked as morosely at him as at everyone and was always silent. He rarely spoke. If it had occurred to anyone to wonder at the time what the young man was interested in, and what was in his mind, it would have been impossible to tell by looking at him. Yet he used sometimes to stop suddenly in the house, or even in the yard or street, and would stand still for ten minutes, lost in thought. A physiognomist studying his face would have said that there was no thought in it, no reflection, but only a sort of contemplation.

7

But Balaam's ass had suddenly spoken. The subject was a strange one. Grigory had gone in the morning to make purchases, and had heard from the shopkeeper Lukyanov the story of a Russian soldier which had appeared in the newspaper of that day. This soldier had been taken prisoner in some remote part of Asia, and was threatened with an immediate agonising death if he did not renounce Christianity and follow Islam. He refused to deny his faith, and was tortured, flayed alive, and died, praising and glorifying Christ. Grigory had related the story at table. Fyodor Pavlovitch always liked, over the dessert after dinner, to laugh and talk, if only with Grigory. This afternoon he was in a particularly good-humoured and expansive mood. Sipping his brandy and listening to the story, he observed that they ought to make a saint of a soldier like that, and to take his skin to some monastery. 'That would make the people flock, and bring the money in.'

Grigory frowned, seeing that Fyodor Pavlovitch was by no means touched, but, as usual, was beginning to scoff. At that moment, Smerdyakov, who was standing by the door, smiled. Smerdyakov often waited at table towards the end of dinner, and since Ivan's arrival in our town he had done so every day.

'What are you grinning at?' asked Fyodor Pavlovitch, catching the smile instantly, and knowing that it referred to Grigory.

'Well, my opinion is,' Smerdyakov began suddenly and unexpectedly in a loud voice, 'that if that laudable soldier's exploit was so very great there would have been, to my thinking, no sin in it if he had on such an emergency renounced, so to speak, the name of Christ and his own christening, to save by that same his life, for good deeds, by which, in the course of years, to expiate his cowardice.'

'How could it not be a sin? You're talking nonsense. For that you'll go straight to hell and be roasted there like mutton,' put in Fyodor Pavlovitch.

It was at this point that Alyosha came in, and Fyodor

Pavlovitch, as we have seen, was highly delighted at his appearance.

'We're on your subject, your subject,' he chuckled gleefully, making Alyosha sit down to listen.

'As for mutton, that's not so, if it's according to justice,' Smerdyakov maintained stoutly.

'How do you mean "according to justice"?' Fyodor Pavlovitch cried still more gaily, nudging Alyosha with his knee.

'He's a rascal, that's what he is!' burst from Grigory. He looked Smerdyakov wrathfully in the face.

'As for being a rascal, wait a little, Grigory Vassilyevitch,' answered Smerdyakov with perfect composure. 'You'd better consider yourself that once I am taken prisoner by the enemies of the Christian race, and they demand from me to curse the name of God and to renounce my holy christening, I am fully entitled to act by my own reason, since there would be no sin in it.'

'But you've said that before. Don't waste words. Prove it,' cried Fyodor Pavlovitch.

'Soup maker!' muttered Grigory contemptuously.

'As for being a soup maker, wait a bit, too, and consider for yourself, Grigory Vassilyevitch, without abusing me. For as soon as I say to those enemies, "No, I'm not a Christian, and I curse my true God," then at once, by God's high judgment, I become immediately and specially anathema accursed, and I am cut off from the Holy Church, exactly as though I were a heathen, so that at that very instant, not only when I say it aloud, but when I think of saying it, before a quarter of a second has passed, I am cut off. Is that so or not, Grigory Vassilyevitch?'

He addressed Grigory with obvious satisfaction,

though he was really answering Fyodor Pavlovitch's questions, and was well aware of it, and intentionally pretending that Grigory had asked the questions.

'Ivan,' cried Fyodor Pavlovitch suddenly, 'stoop down for me to whisper. He's got this all up for your benefit. He wants you to praise him. Praise him.'

Ivan listened with perfect seriousness to his father's excited whisper.

'Listen, Smerdyakov, be quiet a minute,' cried Fyodor Pavlovitch once more. 'Ivan, your ear again.'

Ivan bent down again with a perfectly grave face.

'I love you as I do Alyosha. Don't think I don't love you. Some brandy?'

'Yes.' – 'But you're rather drunk yourself,' thought Ivan, looking steadily at his father.

He was watching Smerdyakov with great curiosity.

'You're anathema accursed, as it is,' Grigory suddenly burst out, 'and how dare you argue, you rascal, after that, if . . . '

'Don't scold him, Grigory, don't scold him,' Fyodor Pavlovitch cut him short.

'You should wait, Grigory Vassilyevitch, if only a short time, and listen, for I haven't finished all I had to say. For at the very moment I become accursed, at that same highest moment, I become exactly like a heathen, and my christening is taken off me and becomes of no avail. Isn't that so?'

'Make haste and finish, my boy,' Fyodor Pavlovitch urged him, sipping from his wineglass with relish.

'And if I've ceased to be a Christian, then I told no lie to the enemy when they asked whether I was a Christian or not a Christian, seeing I had already been relieved by God Himself of my Christianity by reason of the thought alone, before I had time to utter a word to the enemy. And if I have already been discharged, in what manner and with what sort of justice can I be held responsible as a Christian in the other world for having denied Christ, when, through the very thought alone, before denying Him I had been relieved from my christening? If I'm no longer a Christian, then I can't renounce Christ, for I've nothing then to renounce. Who will hold an unclean Tartar responsible, Grigory Vassilyevitch, even in heaven, for not having been born a Christian? And who would punish him for that, considering that you can't take two skins off one ox? For God Almighty Himself, even if He did make the Tartar responsible, when he dies would give him the smallest possible punishment, I imagine (since he must be punished), judging that he is not to blame if he has come into the world an unclean heathen, from heathen parents. The Lord God can't surely take a Tartar and say he was a Christian? That would mean that the Almighty would tell a real untruth. And can the Lord of Heaven and Earth tell a lie, even in one word?'

Grigory was thunderstruck and looked at the orator, his eyes nearly starting out of his head. Though he did not clearly understand what was said, he had caught something in this rigmarole, and stood looking like a man who has just hit his head against a wall.

The controversy was over. But, strange to say, Fyodor Pavlovitch, who had been so gay, suddenly began frowning. He frowned and gulped brandy, and it was already a glass too many.

'Get along with you, Jesuits!' he cried to the servants. 'Go away, Smerdyakov. I'll send you the gold piece I promised you today, but be off! Don't cry, Grigory. Go to Marfa. She'll comfort you and put you to bed. The rascals won't let us sit in peace after dinner,' he snapped peevishly, as the servants promptly withdrew at his word.

'Smerdyakov always pokes himself in now, after dinner. It's you he's so interested in. What have you done to fascinate him?' he added to Ivan.

'Nothing whatever,' answered Ivan. 'He's pleased to have a high opinion of me; he's a lackey and a mean soul. Raw material for revolution, however, when the time comes.'

'For revolution?'

'There will be others and better ones. But there will be some like him as well. His kind will come first, and better ones after.'

'And when will the time come?'

'The rocket will go off and fizzle out, perhaps. The peasants are not very fond of listening to these soup makers, so far.'

'Ah, brother, but a Balaam's ass like that thinks and thinks, and the devil knows where he gets to.'

'He's storing up ideas,' said Ivan, smiling.

'And you may be caught in the same way, though you are a philosopher. Shall I catch you? What do you bet that I'll catch you tomorrow. Speak, all the same, is there a God, or not? Only, be serious. I want you to be serious now.'

'No, there is no God.'

'Alyosha, is there a God?'

'There is.'

'Ivan, and is there immortality of some sort, just a little, just a tiny bit?'

'There is no immortality either.'

'None at all?'

'None at all.'

'There's absolute nothingness then. Perhaps there is just something? Anything is better than nothing!'

'Absolute nothingness.'

'Alyosha, is there immortality?'

'There is.'

'God and immortality?'

'God and immortality. In God is immortality.'

'H'm! It's more likely Ivan's right. Good Lord! to think what faith, what force of all kinds, man has lavished for nothing, on that dream, and for how many thousand years. Who is it laughing at man? Ivan! For the last time, once for all, is there a God or not? I ask for the last time!'

'And for the last time there is not.'

'Who is laughing at mankind, Ivan?'

'It must be the devil,' said Ivan, smiling.

'And the devil? Does he exist?'

'No, there's no devil either.'

'It's a pity. Damn it all, what wouldn't I do to the man who first invented God! Hanging on a bitter aspen tree would be too good for him.'

'There would have been no civilisation if they hadn't invented God.'

'Wouldn't there have been? Without God?'

'No. And there would have been no brandy either. But I must take your brandy away from you, anyway.'

'Stop, stop, stop, dear boy, one more little glass. I've hurt Alyosha's feelings. You're not angry with me, Alyosha? My dear little Alexey!'

'No, I am not angry. I know your thoughts. Your heart is better than your head.'

'My heart better than my head, is it? Oh, Lord! And that from you, Ivan, do you love Alyosha?'

'Yes.'

'You must love him.' (Fyodor Pavlovitch was by this time very drunk.) 'Come, another glass and that's enough. Take away the bottle, Ivan. I've been telling lies. Why didn't you stop me, Ivan, and tell me I was lying?'

'I knew you'd stop of yourself.'

'That's a lie. You did it from spite, from simple spite against me. You despise me. You have come to me and despised me in my own house.'

'Well, I'm going away. You've had too much brandy.'

'I've begged you for Christ's sake to go to Tchermashnya for a day or two and you don't go.'

'I'll go tomorrow if you're so set upon it.'

'You won't go. You want to keep an eye on me. That's what you want, spiteful fellow. That's why you won't go.'

The old man persisted. He had reached that state of drunkenness when the drunkard who has till then been inoffensive tries to pick a quarrel and to assert himself.

'Why are you looking at me? Why do you look like that? Your eyes look at me and say, "You ugly drunkard!" Your eyes are mistrustful. They're contemptuous . . . You've come here with some design. Alyosha, here, looks at me and his eyes shine. Alyosha doesn't despise me. Alexey, you mustn't love Ivan.'

'Don't be ill-tempered with my brother. Quit attacking him,' Alyosha said emphatically.

'Oh, all right. Ugh, my head aches. Take away the brandy, Ivan. It's the third time I've told you.'

He mused, and suddenly a slow, cunning grin spread over his face.

'Don't be angry with a feeble old man, Ivan. I know you don't love me, but don't be angry all the same.

You've nothing to love me for. You go to Tchermashnya. I'll come to you myself and bring you a present. I'll show you a little wench there. I've had my eye on her a long time. She's still running about barefoot. Don't be afraid of barefooted wenches – don't despise them – they're pearls!'

And he kissed his hand with a smack.

'To my thinking,' he revived at once, seeming to grow sober the instant he touched on his favourite topic. 'To my thinking . . . Ah, you boys! You children, little sucking pigs, to my thinking . . . I never thought a woman ugly in my life – that's been my rule! Can you understand that? How could you understand it? You've milk in your veins, not blood. You're not out of your shells yet. My rule has been that you can always find something devilishly interesting in every woman that you wouldn't find in any other. Only, one must know how to find it, that's the point! That's a talent! To my mind there are no ugly women. The very fact that she is a woman is half the battle . . . but how could you understand that? Even in *vieilles filles*, even in them you may discover something that makes you simply wonder that men have been such fools as to let them grow old without noticing them. Barefooted girls or unattractive ones, you must take by surprise. Didn't you know that? You must astound them till they're fascinated, upset, ashamed that a fine gentleman should fall in love with such a little slut. It's a damn good thing that there always are and will be masters and slaves in the world, so there always will be a little scrub-woman and her master, and you know, that's all that's needed for happiness. Wait . . . listen, Alyosha, I always used to surprise your mother, but in a different way. I paid no attention to her at all, but all at once, when the minute came, I'd be all devotion to her, crawl on my knees, kiss her feet, and I always, always – I remember it as though it were today – reduced her to that tinkling, quiet, nervous, queer little laugh. It was peculiar to her. I knew her attacks always used to begin like that, the next day she would begin shrieking hysterically, and that this little laugh was not a sign of delight, but it made a very good counterfeit. That's the great thing, to know how to take everyone. Once Belyavsky – he was a handsome fellow, and rich – used to like to come here and hang about her – suddenly gave me a slap in the face in her presence. And she – such a mild sheep – why, I thought she would have knocked me down for that blow. How she set on me! "You're beaten, beaten now," she said. "You've taken a blow from him. You have been trying to sell me to him," she said . . . "And how dared he strike you in my presence! Don't dare come near me again, never, never! Go at once, challenge him to a duel!" . . . I took her to the monastery then to bring her to her senses. The holy fathers prayed her back to reason. But I swear, by God, Alyosha, I never insulted the poor crazy girl! Only once, perhaps, in the first year; then she was very fond of praying. She used to keep the feasts of Our Lady particularly and used to turn me out of her room then. I'll knock that mysticism out of her, thought I! "Here," said I, "you see your holy image. Here it is. Here I take it down. You believe it's miraculous, but here, I'll spit on it directly and nothing will happen to me for it!" . . . When she saw it, good Lord! I thought she would kill me. But she only jumped up, wrung her hands, then suddenly hid her face in them, began trembling all over and fell on the floor . . . fell all of a heap. Alyosha, Alyosha, what's the matter?'

The old man jumped up in alarm. From the time he had begun speaking of the dead woman, a change had gradually come over Alyosha's face. He flushed crimson, his eyes glowed, his lips quivered. The old sot had gone spluttering on, noticing nothing, till the moment when something very strange happened to Alyosha. Precisely what he was describing in the crazy mother was suddenly repeated with Alyosha. He jumped up from his seat exactly as his mother was said to have done, wrung his hands, hid his face in them, and fell back in his chair, shaking all over in a hysterical paroxysm of sudden violent, silent weeping. His extraordinary resemblance to his mother particularly impressed the old man.

'Ivan, Ivan! Water, quickly! It's like her, exactly as she used to be then, his mother. Spurt some water on him from your mouth, that's what I used to do to her. He's upset about his mother, his mother,' he muttered to Ivan.

'But she was my mother, too, I believe, his mother. Was she not?' said Ivan, with uncontrolled anger and contempt. The old man shrank before his flashing eyes. But something very strange had happened, though only for a second; it seemed really to have escaped the old man's mind that Alyosha's mother actually was the mother of Ivan too.

'Your mother?' he muttered, not understanding. 'What do you mean? What mother are you talking about? Was she? . . . Why, damn it! of course she was yours too! Damn it! My mind has never been so dim before. Excuse me, why, I was thinking Ivan . . . He, he, he!' He stopped. A broad, drunken, half-senseless grin overspread his face.

At that moment a fearful noise and clamour was

heard in the hall, there were violent shouts, the door was flung open, and Dmitri burst into the room. The old man rushed to Ivan in terror.

'He'll kill me! He'll kill me! Don't let him get at me!' he screamed, clinging to the skirt of Ivan's coat.

8

Grigory and Smerdyakov ran into the room after Dmitri. They had been struggling with him in the passage, refusing to admit him, acting on instructions given them by Fyodor Pavlovitch some days before. Taking advantage of the fact that Dmitri stopped a moment on entering the room to look about him, Grigory ran round the table, closed the double doors on the opposite side of the room leading to the inner apartments, and stood before the closed doors, stretching wide his arms, prepared to defend the entrance, so to speak, with the last drop of his blood. Seeing this, Dmitri uttered a scream rather than a shout and rushed at Grigory.

'Then she's there! She's hidden there! Out of the way, scoundrel!'

He tried to pull Grigory away, but the old servant pushed him back. Beside himself with fury, Dmitri struck out, and hit Grigory with all his might. The old man fell like a log, and Dmitri, leaping over him, broke in the door. Smerdyakov remained pale and trembling at the other end of the room, huddling close to Fyodor Pavlovitch.

'She's here!' shouted Dmitri. 'I saw her turn towards the house just now, but I couldn't catch her. Where is she? Where is she?'

That shout, 'She's here!' produced an indescribable effect on Fyodor Pavlovitch. All his terror left him.

'Hold him! Hold him!' he cried, and dashed after Dmitri. Meanwhile Grigory had got up from the floor, but still seemed stunned. Ivan and Alyosha ran after their father. In the third room something was heard to fall on the floor with a ringing crash: it was a large glass vase – not an expensive one – on a marble pedestal which Dmitri had upset as he ran past it.

'At him!' shouted the old man. 'Help!'

Ivan and Alyosha caught the old man and were forcibly bringing him back.

'Why do you run after him? He'll murder you outright,' Ivan cried wrathfully at his father.

'Ivan! Alyosha! She must be here. Grushenka's here. He said he saw her himself, running.'

He was choking. He was not expecting Grushenka at the time, and the sudden news that she was here threw him into a frenzy. He was trembling all over. He seemed frantic.

'But you've seen for yourself that she hasn't come,' cried Ivan.

'But she may have come by that other entrance.'

'You know that entrance is locked, and you have the key.'

Dmitri suddenly reappeared in the drawing-room. He had, of course, found the other entrance locked, and the key actually was in Fyodor Pavlovitch's pocket. The windows of all the rooms were also closed, so Grushenka could not have come in anywhere nor have run out anywhere.

'Hold him!' shrieked Fyodor Pavlovitch, as soon as he saw Dmitri again. 'He's been stealing money from my bedroom.' And tearing himself from Ivan he rushed again at Dmitri. But Dmitri threw up both hands and suddenly clutched the old man by the two tufts of hair that remained on his temples, tugged at them, and flung him with a crash on the floor. He kicked him two or three times with his heel in the face. The old man moaned shrilly. Ivan, though not so strong as Dmitri, threw his arms round him, and with all his might pulled him away. Alyosha helped him with his slender strength, holding Dmitri in front.

'Madman! You've killed him!' cried Ivan.

'Serve him right!' shouted Dmitri breathlessly. 'If I haven't killed him, I'll come again and kill him. You can't protect him!'

'Dmitri! Go away at once!' cried Alyosha commandingly.

'Alexey! You tell me. It's only you I can believe; was she here just now, or not? I saw her myself creeping this way by the fence from the lane. I shouted, she ran away.'

'I swear she's not been here, and no one expected her.'

'But I saw her . . . So she must . . . I'll find out at once where she is . . . . Goodbye, Alexey! Not a word to Aesop about the money now. But go to Katerina Ivanovna at once and be sure to say, "He sends his compliments to you!" Compliments, his compliments! Just compliments and farewell! Describe the scene to her.'

Meanwhile Ivan and Grigory had raised the old man and seated him in an armchair. His face was covered with blood, but he was conscious and listened greedily to Dmitri's cries. He was still fancying that Grushenka really was somewhere in the house. Dmitri looked at him with hatred as he went out.

'I don't repent shedding your blood!' he cried. 'Beware, old man, beware of your dream, for I have my dream too. I curse you, and disown you altogether.'

He ran out of the room.

'She's here. She must be here. Smerdyakov! Smerdyakov!' the old man wheezed, scarcely audibly, beckoning to him with his finger.

'No, she's not here, you old lunatic!' Ivan shouted at him angrily. 'Here, he's fainting! Water! A towel! Make haste, Smerdyakov!'

Smerdyakov ran for water. At last they got the old man undressed, and put him to bed. They wrapped a wet towel round his head. Exhausted by the brandy, by his violent emotion, and the blows he had received, he shut his eyes and fell asleep as soon as his head touched the pillow. Ivan and Alyosha went back to the drawing-room. Smerdyakov removed the fragments of the broken vase, while Grigory stood by the table looking gloomily at the floor.

'Shouldn't you put a wet bandage on your head and go to bed too?' Alyosha said to him. 'We'll look after him. My brother gave you a terrible blow – on the head.'

'He's insulted me!' Grigory articulated gloomily and distinctly.

'He's "insulted" his father, not only you,' observed Ivan with a forced smile.

'I used to wash him in his tub. He's insulted me,' repeated Grigory.

'Damn it all, if I hadn't pulled him away perhaps he'd have murdered him. It wouldn't take much to do for Aesop, would it?' whispered Ivan to Alyosha.

'God forbid!' cried Alyosha.

'Why should He forbid?' Ivan went on in the same

whisper, with a malignant grimace. 'One reptile will devour the other. And serve them both right too.'

Alyosha shuddered.

'Of course I won't let him be murdered. I protected him just now, didn't I? Stay here, Alyosha, I'll go for a turn in the yard. My head's begun to ache.'

Alyosha went to his father's bedroom and sat by his bedside behind the screen for about an hour. The old man suddenly opened his eyes and gazed for a long while at Alyosha, evidently remembering and meditating. All at once his face betrayed extraordinary excitement.

'Alyosha,' he whispered apprehensively, 'where's Ivan?'

'In the yard. He's got a headache. He's on the watch.'

'Give me that looking glass. It stands over there. Give it to me.'

Alyosha gave him a little round folding looking glass which stood on the chest of drawers. The old man looked at himself in it; his nose was considerably swollen, and on the left side of his forehead there was a rather large crimson bruise.

'What does Ivan say? Alyosha, my dear, my only son, I'm afraid of Ivan. I'm more afraid of Ivan than the other. You're the only one I'm not afraid of . . . '

'Don't be afraid of Ivan either. He is angry, but he'll defend you.'

'Alyosha, and what of the other? He's run to Grushenka. My angel, tell me the truth, was she here just now or not?'

'No one has seen her. It was a mistake. She has not been here.'

'You know Mitya wants to marry her, to marry her.'

'She won't marry him.'

'She won't. She won't. She won't. She won't on any account!'

The old man fairly fluttered with joy, as though nothing more comforting could have been said to him. In his delight he seized Alyosha's hand and pressed it warmly to his heart. Tears positively glittered in his eyes.

'That image of the Mother of God of which I was telling you just now,' he said. 'Take it home and keep it for yourself. And I'll let you go back to the monastery . . . I was joking this morning, don't be angry with me. My head aches, Alyosha . . . Alyosha, comfort my heart. Be an angel and tell me the truth!'

'You're still asking whether she has been here or not?' Alyosha said sorrowfully.

'No, no, no. I believe you. I'll tell you what it is: you go to Grushenka yourself, or see her somehow; make haste and ask her; see for yourself, which she means to choose, him or me? Eh? What? Can you?'

'If I see her I'll ask her,' Alyosha muttered, embarrassed.

'No, she won't tell you,' the old man interrupted, 'she's a rogue. She'll begin kissing you and say that it's you she wants. She's a deceitful, shameless hussy. You mustn't go to her, you mustn't!'

'No, father, and it wouldn't be suitable, it wouldn't be right at all.'

'Where was he sending you just now? He shouted "Go" as he ran away.'

'To Katerina Ivanovna.'

'For money? To ask her for money?'

'No. Not for money.'

'He's no money; not a farthing. I'll settle down for the night, and think things over, and you can go. Perhaps you'll meet her . . . Only be sure to come to me tomorrow in the morning. Be sure to. I have a word to say to you tomorrow. Will you come?'

'Yes.'

'When you come, pretend you've come of your own accord to ask after me. Don't tell anyone I told you to. Don't say a word to Ivan.'

'Very well.'

'Goodbye, my angel. You stood up for me, just now. I shall never forget it. I've a word to say to you tomorrow – but I must think about it.'

'And how do you feel now?'

'I shall get up tomorrow and go out, perfectly well, perfectly well!'

Crossing the yard Alyosha found Ivan sitting on the bench at the gateway. He was sitting writing something in pencil in his notebook. Alyosha told Ivan that their father had waked up, was conscious, and had let him go back to sleep at the monastery.

'Alyosha, I should be very glad to meet you tomorrow morning,' said Ivan cordially, standing up. His cordiality was a complete surprise to Alyosha.

'I shall be at the Hohlakovs' tomorrow,' answered Alyosha, 'I may be at Katerina Ivanovna's, too, if I don't find her now.'

'But you're going to see her now, anyway? For that "compliments and farewell",' said Ivan smiling. Alyosha was disconcerted.

'I think I quite understand his exclamations just now, and part of what went before. Dmitri has asked you to go to her and say that he – well, in fact – takes his leave of her?'

'Brother, how will all this horror end between father and Dmitri?' exclaimed Alyosha.

'One can't tell for certain. Perhaps in nothing; it may all fizzle out. That woman is a beast. In any case we must keep the old man indoors and not let Dmitri in the house.'

'Brother, let me ask one thing more: has any man a right to look at other men and decide which is worthy to live?'

'Why bring in the question of worth? The matter is most often decided in men's hearts on other grounds much more natural. And as for rights – who has not the right to wish?'

'Not for another man's death?'

'What even if for another man's death? Why lie to oneself since all men live so and perhaps cannot help living so? Are you referring to what I said just now – that one reptile will devour the other? In that case let me ask you, do you think me, like Dmitri, capable of shedding Aesop's blood, murdering him, eh?'

'What are you saying, Ivan? Such an idea never crossed my mind. I don't think Dmitri is capable of it, either.'

'Thanks, if only for that,' smiled Ivan. 'Be sure, I should always defend him. But in my wishes I reserve myself full latitude in this case. Goodbye till tomorrow. Don't condemn me, and don't look on me as a villain,' he added with a smile.

They shook hands warmly as they had never done before. Alyosha felt that his brother had taken the first step towards him, and that he had certainly done this with some definite motive.

9

Alyosha left his father's house feeling even more exhausted and dejected in spirit than when he had entered it.

It was by now seven o'clock, and it was getting dark as Alyosha entered the very spacious and comfortable house in the High Street occupied by Katerina Ivanovna. Alyosha knew that she lived with two aunts. One of them, a woman of little education, was that aunt of her half-sister Agafya Ivanovna, who had looked after her in her father's house when she came from boarding-school. The other aunt was a Moscow lady of style and consequence, though in straitened circumstances. It was said that they both gave way in everything to Katerina Ivanovna, and that she only kept them with her as chaperones. Katerina Ivanovna herself gave way to no one but her benefactress, the general's widow, who had been kept by illness in Moscow, and to whom she was obliged to write twice a week a full account of all her doings.

When Alyosha entered the hall and asked the maid who opened the door to him to take his name up, it was evident that they were already aware of his arrival. Possibly he had been noticed from the window. At least Alyosha heard a noise, caught the sound of flying footsteps and rustling skirts. Two or three women perhaps had run out of the room.

Alyosha thought it strange that his arrival should cause such excitement. He was conducted, however, to the drawing-room at once. It was a large room, elegantly and amply furnished, not at all in provincial style. There were many sofas, lounges, settees, big and little tables. There were pictures on the walls, vases and lamps on the tables, masses of flowers, and even an aquarium in the window. It was twilight and rather dark. Alyosha made out a silk mantle thrown down on the sofa, where people had evidently just been sitting; and on a table in front of the sofa were two unfinished cups of chocolate, cakes, a glass dish with blue raisins, and another with sweetmeats. Alyosha saw that he had interrupted visitors, and frowned. But at that instant the portière was raised, and with rapid, hurrying footsteps Katerina Ivanovna came in, holding out both hands to Alyosha with a radiant smile of delight. At the same instant a servant brought in two lighted candles and set them on the table.

'Thank God! At last you have come too! I've been simply praying for you all day! Sit down.'

Alyosha had been struck by Katerina Ivanovna's beauty when, three weeks before, Dmitri had first brought him, at Katerina Ivanovna's special request, to be introduced to her. There had been no conversation between them at that interview, however. Supposing Alyosha to be very shy, Katerina Ivanovna had talked all the time to Dmitri to spare him. Alyosha had been silent, but he had seen a great deal very clearly. He was struck by the imperiousness, proud ease, and self-confidence, of the haughty girl. He thought her great glowing black eyes were very fine, especially with her pale, even rather sallow, longish face. But in those eyes and in the lines of her exquisite lips there was something with which his brother might well be passionately in love, but which perhaps could not be loved for long. He expressed this thought almost plainly to Dmitri when, after the visit, his brother besought and insisted that he should not conceal his impressions on seeing his betrothed.

'You'll be happy with her, but perhaps – not tranquilly happy.'

'Quite so, brother. Such people remain always the same. They don't yield to fate. So you think I shan't love her for ever.'

'No; perhaps you will love her for ever. But perhaps you won't always be happy with her.'

Alyosha had given his opinion at the time, blushing, and angry with himself for having yielded to his brother's entreaties and put such 'foolish' ideas into words. For his opinion had struck him as extremely foolish immediately after he had uttered it. He felt ashamed, too, of having given so confident an opinion about a woman. It was with the more amazement that he felt now, at the first glance at Katerina Ivanovna as she ran in to him, that he had perhaps been utterly mistaken. This time her face was beaming with spontaneous good-natured kindliness and direct warm-hearted sincerity. The 'pride and haughtiness', which had struck Alyosha so forcibly before, was only betrayed now in a frank, generous energy and a sort of bright strong faith in herself. Alyosha realised at the first glance, at the first word, that all the tragedy of her position in relation to the man she loved so dearly was no secret to her; that she perhaps already knew everything, positively everything. And yet, in spite of that, there was such brightness in her face, such faith in the future. Alyosha felt at once that he had gravely wronged her in his thoughts. He was conquered and captivated immediately. Besides all this, he noticed at her first words that she was greatly excited, an excitement perhaps quite exceptional and almost approaching ecstasy.

'I was so eager to see you, because I can learn from you the whole truth – from you and no one else.'

'I have come,' muttered Alyosha confusedly, 'I – he sent me.'

'Ah, he sent you! I foresaw that. Now I know everything – everything!' cried Katerina Ivanovna, her eyes flashing. 'Wait a moment, Alexey Fyodorovitch, I'll tell you why I have so longed to see you. You see, I know perhaps far more than you do yourself, and there's no need for you to tell me anything. I'll tell you what I want from you. I want to know your own last impression of him. I want you to tell me honestly, plainly, brutally even (oh, as crudely as you like!), what you thought of him just now and of his position after your meeting with him today. That will perhaps be better than if I had a personal explanation with him, as he does not want to come to me. Do you understand what I want from you? Now, tell me simply, tell me every word of the message he sent you with (I knew he would send you).'

'He told me to give you his compliments – and to say that he would never come again – but to give you his compliments.'

'His compliments? Was that what he said – his own expression?'

'Yes.'

'Accidentally perhaps he made a mistake in the word, perhaps he did not use the right word?'

'No; he told me precisely to repeat that word. He begged me two or three times not to forget to say so.'

Katerina Ivanovna flushed hotly.

'Help me now, Alexey Fyodorovitch. Now I really need your help. I'll tell you what I think, and you must simply say whether it's right or not. Listen! If he had sent me his compliments in passing, without insisting on your repeating the words, without emphasising them, that would be the end of everything! But if he particularly insisted on those words, if he particularly told you not to forget to repeat them to me, then perhaps he was excited, beside himself. He had made his decision and was frightened at it. He wasn't walking away from me with a resolute step, but running headlong. The emphasis on that phrase may have been simply bravado.'

'Yes, yes!' cried Alyosha warmly. 'I believe that is it.'

'And, if so, he's not altogether lost. I can still save him. Wait! Did he not tell you anything about money – about three thousand roubles?'

'He did speak about it, and it's that more than anything that's crushing him. He said he had lost his honour and that nothing matters now,' Alyosha answered warmly, feeling a rush of hope in his heart and believing that there really might be a way of escape and salvation for his brother. 'But do you know about the money?' he added, and suddenly broke off.

'I've known of it a long time; I telegraphed to Moscow to enquire, and heard long ago that the money had not arrived. He hadn't sent the money, but I said nothing. Last week I learned that he was still in need of money. My only object in all this was that he should know to whom to turn, and who was his true friend. But he won't admit that I am his truest friend; he won't see me, and looks on me merely as a woman. I've been tormented all the week, trying to think how to prevent him from being ashamed to face me because he spent that three thousand. Let him feel ashamed of himself, let him be ashamed of other people's knowing, but not of my knowing. He can tell God everything without shame. Why is it he still does not understand how much I am ready to bear for his sake? Why, why doesn't he understand me? How dare he not recognise me as I am after all that has happened? I want to save him for ever. Let him forget me as his betrothed. And here he fears that he is dishonoured in my eyes. Why, he wasn't afraid to be frank with you, Alexey Fyodorovitch. How is it that I don't deserve the same?'

As she spoke the last words, tears gushed from her eyes.

'I must tell you,' Alyosha began, his voice trembling too, 'what happened just now between him and my father.'

And he described the whole scene, how Dmitri had sent him to get the money, how later Dmitri had forced his way in, knocked his father down, and after that had again specially and emphatically begged Alyosha to give Katerina his compliments and convey his farewell. 'He went to that woman,' Alyosha added softly.

'And do you suppose that I can't put up with that woman? Does he think I can't? But he won't marry her,' she suddenly laughed nervously. 'Could such a passion last for ever in a Karamazov? It's passion, not love. He won't marry her because she won't marry him.' Again Katerina Ivanovna laughed strangely.

'He may marry her,' said Alyosha mournfully, looking down.

'He won't marry her, I tell you. That girl is an angel. Do you know that? Do you know that?' Katerina Ivanovna exclaimed suddenly with extraordinary warmth. 'She is one of the most fantastic of fantastic creatures. I know how bewitching she is, but I know, too, that she is kind, firm and noble. Why do you look at me like that, Alexey Fyodorovitch? Perhaps you are wondering at my words, perhaps you don't believe me? Agrafena Alexandrovna, my angel!' she cried suddenly to someone, peeping into the next room, 'come in to us. This is a friend. This is Alyosha. He knows all about our affairs. Show yourself to him.'

'I've only been waiting behind the curtain for you to call me,' said a soft, one might even say sugary, feminine voice.

The portière was raised and Grushenka herself, smiling and beaming, came up to the table. A violent revulsion passed over Alyosha. He fixed his eyes on her and could not take them away. Here she was, that awful woman, the 'beast', as Ivan had called her half an hour before. And yet one would have thought the creature standing before him most simple and ordinary, a good-natured, kind woman, handsome certainly, but so like other handsome ordinary women! It is true she was very, very good-looking with that Russian beauty so passionately loved by many men. She was a rather tall woman, though a little shorter than Katerina Ivanovna, who was exceptionally tall. She had a full figure, with soft, as it were, noiseless, movements, softened to a peculiar over-sweetness, like her voice. She moved, not like Katerina Ivanovna, with a vigorous, bold step, but noiselessly. Her feet made absolutely no sound on the floor. She sank softly into a low chair, softly rustling her sumptuous black silk dress, and delicately nestling her milk-white neck and broad shoulders in a costly black cashmere shawl. She was twenty-two years old, and her face looked exactly that age. She was very white in the face, with a pale pink tint on her cheeks. The modelling of her face might be said to be too broad, and the lower jaw was set a trifle forward. Her upper lip was thin, but the slightly prominent lower lip was at least twice as full, and looked pouting. But her magnificent, abundant dark brown hair, her sable-coloured eyebrows and charming grey-blue eyes with their long lashes would have made the most indifferent person, meeting her casually in a crowd in the street, stop at the sight of her face and remember it long after. What struck Alyosha most in that face was its expression of childlike good nature. There was a childlike look in her eyes, a look of childish delight. She came up to the table, beaming with delight, and seeming to expect something with childish, impatient, and confiding curiosity. The light in her eyes gladdened the soul – Alyosha felt that. There was something else in her which he could not understand, or would not have been able to define, and which yet perhaps unconsciously affected him. It was that softness, that voluptuousness of her bodily movements, that catlike noiselessness. Yet it was a vigorous, ample body. Under the shawl could be seen full broad shoulders, a high, still quite girlish bosom. Her figure suggested the lines of the Venus of Milo, though already in somewhat exaggerated proportions. That could be divined. Connoisseurs of Russian beauty could have foretold with certainty that this fresh, still youthful, beauty would lose its harmony by the age of thirty, would 'spread'; that the face would become puffy, and that wrinkles would very soon appear upon her forehead and round the eyes; the complexion would grow coarse and red perhaps – in fact, that it was the beauty of the moment, the fleeting beauty which is so often met with in Russian women. Alyosha, of course, did not think of this; but though he was fascinated, yet he wondered with an unpleasant sensation, and as it were regretfully, why she drawled in that way and could not speak naturally. She did so evidently feeling there was a charm in the exaggerated, honeyed modulation of the syllables. It was, of course, only a bad, underbred habit that showed bad education and a false idea of good manners. And yet this intonation and manner of speaking impressed Alyosha as almost incredibly incongruous with the childishly simple and happy expression of her face, the soft, babyish joy in her eyes. Katerina Ivanovna at once made her sit down in an armchair facing Alyosha, and ecstatically kissed her several times on her smiling lips. She seemed quite in love with her.

'This is the first time we've met, Alexey Fyodorovitch,' she said rapturously. 'I wanted to know her, to see her. I wanted to go to her, but I'd no sooner expressed the wish than she came to me. I knew we should settle everything together – everything. My heart told me so – I was begged not to take the step, but I foresaw it would be a way out of the difficulty, and I was not mistaken. Grushenka has explained everything to me, told me all she means to do. She flew here like an angel of goodness and brought us peace and joy.'

'You did not disdain me, sweet, excellent young lady,' drawled Grushenka in her singsong voice, still with the same charming smile of delight.

'Don't dare to speak to me like that, you sorceress, you witch! Disdain you! Here I must kiss your lower lip once more. It looks as though it were swollen, and now it will be more so, and more and more. Look how she laughs, Alexey Fyodorovitch! It does one's heart good to see the angel.'

Alyosha flushed, and faint, imperceptible shivers

kept running down him. 'You make so much of me, dear young lady, and perhaps I am not at all worthy of your kindness.'

'Not worthy! She's not worthy of it!' Katerina Ivanovna cried again with the same warmth. 'You know, Alexey Fyodorovitch, we're fanciful, we're self-willed, but proudest of the proud in our little heart. We're noble, we're generous, Alexey Fyodorovitch, let me tell you. We have only been unfortunate. We were too ready to make every sacrifice for an unworthy, perhaps, or fickle man. There was one man – one, an officer too, we loved him, we sacrificed everything to him. That was long ago, five years ago, and he has forgotten us, he has married. Now he is a widower, he has written, he is coming here, and, do you know, we've loved him, none but him, all this time, and we've loved him all our life! He will come, and Grushenka will be happy again. For the last five years she's been wretched. But who can reproach her, who can boast of her favour? Only that bedridden old merchant, but he is more like her father, her friend, her protector. He found her then in despair, in agony, deserted by the man she loved. She was ready to drown herself then, but the old merchant saved her – saved her!'

'You defend me very kindly, dear young lady. You are in a great hurry about everything,' Grushenka drawled again.

'Defend you! Is it for me to defend you? Should I dare to defend you? Grushenka, angel, give me your hand. Look at that charming soft little hand, Alexey Fyodorovitch! Look at it! It has brought me happiness and has lifted me up, and I'm going to kiss it, outside and inside, here, here, here!'

And three times she kissed the certainly charming,

though rather fat, hand of Grushenka in a sort of rapture. She held out her hand with a charming, musical, nervous little laugh, watched the 'sweet young lady', and obviously liked having her hand kissed.

'Perhaps there's rather too much rapture,' thought Alyosha. He blushed. He felt a peculiar uneasiness at heart the whole time.

'You won't make me blush, dear young lady, kissing my hand like this before Alexey Fyodorovitch.'

'Do you think I meant to make you blush?' said Katerina Ivanovna, somewhat surprised. 'Ah, my dear, how little you understand me!'

'Yes, and you too perhaps quite misunderstand me, dear young lady. Maybe I'm not so good as I seem to you. I've a bad heart; I will have my own way. I fascinated poor Dmitri that day simply for fun.'

'But now you'll save him. You've given me your word. You'll explain it all to him. You'll impress on him that you have long loved another man, who is now offering you his hand.'

'Oh, no! I didn't give you my word to do that. It was you kept talking about that. I didn't give you my word.'

'Then I didn't quite understand you,' said Katerina Ivanovna slowly, turning a little pale. 'You promised . . .'

'Oh, no, angel lady, I've promised nothing.' Grushenka interrupted softly and evenly, still with the same gay and simple expression. 'You see at once, dear young lady, what a wilful wretch I am compared with you. If I want to do a thing, I do it. I may have made you some promise just now. But now again I'm thinking: I may take to Mitya again. I liked him very much once – liked him for almost a whole hour. Now maybe I shall go and tell him to stay with me from this day forward. You see, I'm so changeable.'

'Just now you said – something quite different,' Katerina Ivanovna whispered faintly.

'Ah, just now! But, you know, I'm such a soft-hearted, silly creature. Only think what he's gone through on my account! What if when I go home I feel sorry for him? What then?'

'I never expected –'

'Ah, young lady, how good and generous you are compared with me! Now perhaps you won't care for a silly creature like me, now you know my character. Give me your sweet little hand, angelic lady,' she said tenderly, and with a sort of reverence took Katerina Ivanovna's hand.

'Here, dear young lady, I'll take your hand and kiss it as you did mine. You kissed mine three times, but I ought to kiss yours three hundred times to be even with you. Well, but let that pass. And then it shall be as God wills. Perhaps I shall be your slave entirely and want to do your bidding like a slave. Let it be as God wills, without any agreements and promises. What a sweet hand – what a sweet hand you have! You sweet young lady, you incredible beauty!'

She slowly raised the hand to her lips, with the strange object indeed of 'being even' with her in kisses.

Katerina Ivanovna did not take her hand away. She listened with timid hope to the last words, though Grushenka's promise to do her bidding like a slave was very strangely expressed. She looked intently into her eyes; she still saw in those eyes the same simple-hearted, confiding expression, the same bright gaiety.

'She's perhaps too naïve,' thought Katerina Ivanovna, with a gleam of hope.

Grushenka meanwhile seemed enthusiastic over the 'sweet hand'. She raised it deliberately to her lips. But she held it for two or three minutes near her lips, as though reconsidering something.

'Do you know, angel lady,' she suddenly drawled in an even more soft and sugary voice, 'do you know, after all, I think I won't kiss your hand?' And she laughed a little merry laugh.

'As you please. What's the matter with you?' said Katerina Ivanovna, starting suddenly.

'So that you may be left to remember that you kissed my hand, but I didn't kiss yours.'

There was a sudden gleam in her eyes. She looked with awful intentness at Katerina Ivanovna.

'Insolent creature!' cried Katerina Ivanovna, as though suddenly grasping something. She flushed deeply and jumped up from her seat. Grushenka too rose, but without haste.

'So I shall tell Mitya how you kissed my hand, but I didn't kiss yours at all. And how he will laugh!'

'Vile slut! Go away!'

'Ah, for shame, young lady! Ah, for shame! That's unbecoming for you, dear young lady, a word like that.'

'Go way! You're a creature for sale!' screamed Katerina Ivanovna. Every feature was working in her utterly distorted face.

'For sale indeed! You used to visit gentlemen in the dusk for money once; you brought your beauty for sale. You see, I know.'

Katerina Ivanovna shrieked, and would have rushed at her, but Alyosha held her with all his strength.

'Not a step, not a word! Don't speak, don't answer her. She'll go away – she'll go at once.'

At that instant Katerina Ivanovna's two aunts ran

in at her cry, and with them a maidservant. All hurried to her.

'I will go away,' said Grushenka, taking up her mantle from the sofa. 'Alyosha, darling, see me home!'

'Go away – go away, make haste!' cried Alyosha, clasping his hands imploringly.

'Dear little Alyosha, see me home! I've got a pretty little story to tell you on the way. I got up this scene for your benefit, Alyosha. See me home, dear, you'll be glad of it afterwards.'

Alyosha turned away, wringing his hands. Grushenka ran out of the house, laughing musically.

Katerina Ivanovna went into a fit of hysterics. She sobbed, and was shaken with convulsions. Everyone fussed round her.

'I warned you,' said the elder of her aunts. 'I tried to prevent your doing this. You're too impulsive. How could you do such a thing? You don't know these creatures, and they say she's worse than any of them. You are too self-willed.'

'She's a tigress!' yelled Katerina Ivanovna. 'Why did you hold me, Alexey Fyodorovitch! I'd have beaten her – beaten her!'

She could not control herself before Alyosha; perhaps she did not care to, indeed. 'She ought to be flogged in public on a scaffold!'

Alyosha withdrew towards the door.

'But, my God!' cried Katerina Ivanovna, clasping her hands. 'He! He! He could be so dishonourable, so inhuman! Why, he told that creature what happened on that fatal, accursed day! "You brought your beauty for sale, dear young lady." She knows it! Your brother's a scoundrel, Alexey Fyodorovitch.'

Alyosha wanted to say something, but he couldn't find a word. His heart ached.

'Go away, Alexey Fyodorovitch! It's shameful, it's awful for me! Tomorrow, I beg you on my knees, come tomorrow. Don't condemn me. Forgive me. I don't know what I shall do with myself now!'

Alyosha walked out into the street reeling. He could have wept as she did. Suddenly he was overtaken by the maid.

'The young lady forgot to give you this letter from Madame Hohlakov; it's been left with us since dinner time.'

Alyosha took the little pink envelope mechanically and put it, almost unconsciously, into his pocket.

10

It was little more than three-quarters of a mile from the town to the monastery. Alyosha walked quickly along the road, deserted at that hour. It was almost night, and too dark to see anything clearly at thirty paces ahead. There were crossroads halfway. A figure came into sight under a solitary willow at the crossroads. As soon as Alyosha reached the crossroads the figure moved out and rushed at him, shouting savagely: 'Your money or your life!'

'So it's you, Mitya,' cried Alyosha, in surprise, violently startled however.

'Ha, ha, ha! You didn't expect me? I wondered where to wait for you. By her house? There are three ways from it, and I might have missed you. At last I thought of waiting here, for you had to pass here, there's no other way to the monastery. Come, tell me the truth. Crush me like a beetle. But what's the matter?'

'Nothing, brother – it's the fright you gave me. Oh, Dmitri! Father's blood just now.' (Alyosha began to cry, he had been on the verge of tears for a long time, and now something seemed to snap in his soul.) 'You almost killed him – cursed him – and now – here – you're making jokes – Your money or your life!'

'Well, what of that? It's not seemly – is that it? Not suitable in my position?'

'No – I only – '

'Stop. Look at the night. You see what a dark night, what clouds, what a wind has risen. I hid here under the willow waiting for you. And as God's above, I suddenly thought, why go in misery any longer, what is there to wait for? Here I have a willow, a handkerchief, a shirt, I can twist them into a rope in a minute, and braces besides, and why go on burdening the earth, dishonouring it with my vile presence? And then I heard you coming – heavens, it was as though something flew down to me suddenly. So there is a man, then, whom I love. Here he is, that man, my dear little brother, whom I love more than anyone in the world, the only one I love in the world. And I loved you so much, so much at that moment that I thought, "I'll fall on his neck at once." Then a stupid idea struck me, to have a joke with you and scare you. I shouted, like a fool, "your money!" Forgive my foolery – it was only nonsense, and there's nothing unseemly in my soul . . . Damn it all, tell me what's happened. What did she say? Strike me, crush me, don't spare me! Was she furious?'

'No, not that . . . There was nothing like that, Mitya. There – I found them both there.'

'Both? Who?'

'Grushenka at Katerina Ivanovna's.'

Dmitri was struck dumb.

'Impossible!' he cried. 'You're raving! Grushenka with her?'

Alyosha described all that had happened from the moment he went to Katerina Ivanovna's. He was ten minutes telling his story. He can't be said to have told it fluently and consecutively, but he seemed to make it clear, not omitting any word or action of significance, and vividly describing, often in one word, his own sensations. Dmitri listened in silence, gazing at him with a terrible fixed stare, but it was clear to Alyosha that he understood it all, and had grasped every point. But as the story went on, his face became not merely gloomy, but menacing. He scowled, he gritted his teeth, and his fixed stare became still more rigid, more concentrated, more terrible, when suddenly, with incredible rapidity, his wrathful, savage face changed, his tightly compressed lips parted, and Dmitri Fyodorovitch broke into uncontrolled, spontaneous laughter. He literally shook with laughter. For a long time he could not speak.

'So she wouldn't kiss her hand! So she didn't kiss it; so she ran away!' he kept exclaiming with hysterical delight; insolent delight it might have been called, if it had not been so spontaneous. 'So the other one called her tigress! And a tigress she is! So she ought to be flogged on a scaffold! Yes, yes, so she ought. That's just what I think; she ought to have been whipped long ago. It's like this, brother, let her be punished, but I must get better first. I understand the queen of impudence. That's her all over! You saw her complete in that hand-kissing, the she-devil! She's the queen of all she-devils you can imagine in the world! She's magnificent in her own line! So she ran home? I'll go – ah – I'll run to her! Alyosha, don't blame me, I agree that hanging is too good for her.'

'But Katerina Ivanovna!' exclaimed Alyosha sorrowfully.

'I see her too! I see right through her, as I've never done before! It's a regular discovery of the four continents of the world, that is, of the five! What a thing to do! That's just like Katya, who was not afraid to face a coarse, unmannerly officer and risk a deadly insult on a generous impulse to save her father! But the pride, the recklessness, the defiance of fate, the unbounded defiance! You say that aunt tried to stop her? That aunt, you know, is overbearing, herself. She's the sister of the general's widow in Moscow, and even more stuck-up than she. But her husband was caught stealing government money. He lost everything, his estate and all, and the proud wife had to lower her colours, and hasn't raised them since. So she tried to prevent Katya, but she wouldn't listen to her! She thinks she can overcome everything, that everything will give way to her. She thought she could bewitch Grushenka if she liked, and she believed it herself; she plays a part to herself, and whose fault is it? Do you think she kissed Grushenka's hand first, on purpose, with a motive? No, she really was fascinated by Grushenka, that's to say, not by Grushenka, but by her own dream, her own delusion – because it was *her* dream, *her* delusion! Alyosha, darling, how did you escape from them, those women? Did you pick up your cassock and run? Ha, ha, ha!'

'Brother, you don't seem to have noticed how you've insulted Katerina Ivanovna by telling

Grushenka about that day. And she flung it in her face just now that she had gone to gentlemen in secret to sell her beauty! Brother, what could be worse than that insult?'

What worried Alyosha more than anything was that, incredible as it seemed, his brother appeared pleased at Katerina Ivanovna's humiliation.

'Bah!' Dmitri frowned fiercely, and struck his forehead with his hand. He only now realised it, though Alyosha had just told him of the insult, and Katerina Ivanovna's cry: 'Your brother is a scoundrel!'

'Yes, perhaps, I really did tell Grushenka about that "fatal day", as Katya calls it. Yes, I did tell her, I remember! It was that time at Mokroe. I was drunk, the gypsies were singing . . . But I was sobbing. I was sobbing then, kneeling and praying to Katya's image, and Grushenka understood it. She understood it all then. I remember, she cried herself . . . Damn it all! But it's bound to be so now . . . Then she cried, but now "the dagger in the heart"! That's how women are.' He looked down and sank into thought.

'Yes, I am a scoundrel, a thorough scoundrel!' he said suddenly, in a gloomy voice. 'It doesn't matter whether I cried or not, I'm a scoundrel! Tell her I accept the name, if that's any comfort. Come, that's enough. Goodbye. It's no use talking! It's not amusing. You go your way and I mine. And I don't want to see you again except as a last resource. Goodbye, Alexey!'

He warmly pressed Alyosha's hand, and still looking down, without raising his head, as though tearing himself away, turned rapidly towards the town.

Alyosha looked after him, unable to believe he would go away so abruptly.

'Wait, Alexey, one more confession to you alone!'

cried Dmitri, suddenly turning back. 'Look at me. Look at me well. You see here, here – there's terrible disgrace in store for me.' (As he said 'here', Dmitri struck his chest with his fist with a strange air, as though the dishonour lay precisely on his chest, in some spot, in a pocket, perhaps, or hanging round his neck.) 'You know me now, a scoundrel, an avowed scoundrel, but let me tell you that I've never done anything before and never shall again, anything that can compare in baseness with the dishonour which I bear now at this very minute on my breast, here, here, which will come to pass, though I'm perfectly free to stop it. I can stop it or carry it through, note that. Well, let me tell you, I shall carry it through. I shan't stop it. I told you everything just now, but I didn't tell you this, because even I had not brass enough for it. I can still pull up; if I do, I can give back the full half of my lost honour tomorrow. But I shan't pull up. I shall carry out my base plan, and you can bear witness that I told you so beforehand. Darkness and destruction! No need to explain. You'll find out in due time. The filthy back-alley and the she-devil. Goodbye. Don't pray for me, I'm not worth it. And there's no need, no need at all . . . I don't need it! Away!'

And he suddenly retreated, this time finally. Alyosha went towards the monastery.

'What? I shall never see him again! What is he saying?' he wondered wildly. 'Why, I shall certainly see him tomorrow. I shall look him up. I shall make a point of it. What does he mean?'

He went round the monastery, and crossed the pine wood to the hermitage. The door was opened to him, though no one was admitted at that hour. There was a tremor in his heart as he went into Father Zossima's cell.

'Why, why, had he gone forth? Why had the holy father sent him into the world? Here was peace. Here was holiness. But out there was confusion, there was darkness in which one lost one's way and went astray at once . . .'

In the cell he found the novice Porfiry and Father Païssy, who came every hour to enquire after Father Zossima. Alyosha learned with alarm that he was getting worse and worse.

Alyosha had no doubt that Father Zossima was dying, though he might live another day or two. Alyosha firmly and ardently resolved that in spite of his promises to his father, the Hohlakovs, and Katerina Ivanovna, he would not leave the monastery next day, but would remain with his elder to the end. His heart glowed with love, and he reproached himself bitterly for having been able for one instant to forget him whom he had left in the monastery on his deathbed, and whom he honoured above everyone in the world. He went into Father Zossima's bedroom, knelt down, and bowed to the ground before the elder, who slept quietly without stirring, with regular, hardly audible breathing and a peaceful face.

Alyosha returned to the other room, where Father Zossima had received his guests in the morning. Taking off his boots, he lay down on the hard, narrow, leather sofa, which he had long used as a bed, bringing nothing but a pillow. The mattress, about which his father had shouted to him that morning, he had long forgotten to lay on. He took off his cassock, which he used as a covering. But before going to bed, he fell on his knees and prayed a long time. In his fervent prayer he did not beseech God to lighten his darkness but only thirsted for the joyous emotion which always visited his soul after the praise and adoration, of which his evening prayer usually consisted. That joy always brought him light, untroubled sleep. As he was praying, he suddenly felt in his pocket the little pink note the servant had handed him as he left Katerina Ivanovna's. He was disturbed, but finished his prayer. Then, after some hesitation, he opened the envelope. In it was a letter to him, signed by Lise, the young daughter of Madame Hohlakov, who had laughed at him before the elder in the morning.

'Alexey Fyodorovitch,' she wrote, 'I am writing to you without anyone's knowledge, even mamma's, and I know how wrong it is. But I cannot live without telling you the feeling that has sprung up in my heart, and this no one but us two must know for a time. But how am I to say what I want so much to tell you? Paper, they say, does not blush, but I assure you it's not true and that it's blushing just as I am now, all over. Dear Alyosha, I love you, I've loved you from my childhood, since our Moscow days, when you were very different from what you are now, and I shall love you all my life. My heart has chosen you, to unite our lives, and pass them together till our old age. Of course, on condition that you will leave the monastery. As for our age, we will wait for the time fixed by the law. By that time I shall certainly be quite strong, I shall be walking and dancing. There can be no doubt of that.

'You see how I've thought of everything. There's only one thing I can't imagine: what you'll think of me when you read this? I'm always laughing and being naughty. I made you angry this morning, but I assure you before I took up my pen, I prayed before the image of the Mother of God, and now I'm praying, and almost crying.

'My secret is in your hands. When you come tomorrow, I don't know how I shall look at you. Ah, Alexey Fyodorovitch, what if I can't restrain myself like a silly and laugh when I look at you as I did today? You'll think I'm a naughty girl making fun of you, and you won't believe my letter. And so I beg you, dear one, if you've any pity for me, when you come tomorrow, don't look me straight in the face, for if I meet your eyes, it will be sure to make me laugh, especially, as you'll be in that long gown. I feel cold all over when I think of it, so when you come, don't look at me at all for a time, look at mamma or at the window . . .

'Here I've written you a love letter. Oh, dear, what have I done? Alyosha, don't despise me, and if I've done something very horrid and wounded you, forgive me. Now my reputation, ruined perhaps for ever, is in your hands.

'I shall certainly cry today. Goodbye till our meeting, our *awful* meeting. LISE

'P.S. – Alyosha! You must, must, must come!'

Alyosha read the note in amazement, read it through twice, thought a little, and suddenly laughed a soft, sweet laugh. Suddenly he was alarmed. That laugh seemed to him sinful. But a minute later he laughed again just as softly and happily. He slowly replaced the note in the envelope, crossed himself and lay down. The agitation in his heart passed quickly. 'God have mercy upon all of them, have all these unhappy and turbulent souls in Thy keeping, and set them in the right path. All ways are Thine. Save them according to Thy wisdom. Thou art love. Thou wilt send joy to all!' Alyosha murmured, crossing himself, and falling into peaceful sleep.

Book Four

I

Alyosha was roused early, before daybreak. Father Zossima woke up feeling very weak, though he wanted to get out of bed and sit up in a chair. His mind was quite clear; his face looked very tired, yet bright and almost joyful. It wore an expression of gaiety, kindness and cordiality. 'Maybe I shall not live through the coming day,' he said to Alyosha. Then he desired to confess and take the sacrament at once. He always confessed to Father Païssy. After taking the Communion, the service of extreme unction followed. The monks assembled and the cell was gradually filled by the inmates of the hermitage. Meantime it was daylight. People began coming from the monastery. After the service was over the elder desired to kiss and take leave of everyone. As the cell was so small the earlier visitors withdrew to make room for others. Alyosha stood beside the elder, who was seated again in his armchair. He talked as much as he could. Though his voice was weak, it was fairly steady.

'I've been teaching you so many years, and therefore I've been talking aloud so many years, that I've got into the habit of talking, and so much so that it's almost more difficult for me to hold my tongue than to talk, even now, in spite of my weakness, dear fathers and brothers,' he jested, looking with emotion at the group round him.

When Father Zossima, feeling tired again, had gone back to bed, he thought of Alyosha as he was closing his eyes, and sent for him. Alyosha came running. Only Father Païssy, Father Iosif, and the novice Porfiry were in the cell with Father Zossima. The elder, opening his weary eyes and looking intently at Alyosha, asked him suddenly: 'Are your people expecting you, my son?'

Alyosha hesitated.

'Haven't they need of you? Didn't you promise someone yesterday to see them today?'

'I did promise – to my father – my brothers – others too.'

'You see, you must go. Don't grieve. Be sure I shall not die without your being by to hear my last word. To you I will say that word, my son, it will be my last gift to you. To you, dear son, because you love me. But now go to keep your promise.'

Alyosha immediately obeyed, though it was hard to go. But the promise that he should hear Father Zossima's last word on earth, that it should be the last gift to him, Alyosha, sent a thrill of rapture through his soul. He made haste that he might finish what he had to do in the town and return quickly.

First of all, Alyosha went to his father. On the way he remembered that his father had insisted the day before that he should come without his brother Ivan's seeing him. 'Why so?' Alyosha wondered suddenly. 'Even if my father has something to say to me alone, why should I go in unseen? Most likely in his excitement yesterday he meant to say something different,' he decided. Yet he was very glad when Marfa Ignatyevna, who opened the garden gate to him (Grigory, it appeared, was ill in bed in the lodge), told him in answer to his question that Ivan had gone out two hours ago.

'And my father?'

'He is up, taking his coffee,' Marfa answered somewhat dryly.

Alyosha went in. The old man was sitting alone at the table, wearing slippers and a little old overcoat. He was amusing himself by looking through some accounts, rather inattentively, however. He was quite alone in the house, for Smerdyakov had gone out marketing. Though he had got up early and was trying to put a bold face on it, he looked tired and weak. His forehead, upon which huge purple bruises had come out during the night, was bandaged with a red handkerchief; his nose too had swollen terribly in the night, and some smaller bruises covered it in patches, giving his whole face a peculiarly spiteful and irritable look. The old man was aware of this, and turned a hostile glance on Alyosha as he came in.

'The coffee is cold,' he cried harshly; 'I won't offer you any. I've ordered nothing but a Lenten fish soup today, and I don't invite anyone to share it. Why have you come?'

'To find out how you are,' said Alyosha.

'That's right. Besides, I told you to come yesterday. It's all of no consequence. You need not have troubled. But I knew you'd come poking in directly.'

He said this with almost hostile feeling. At the same time he got up and looked anxiously in the mirror (perhaps for the fortieth time that morning) at his nose. He began to bind his red handkerchief more becomingly on his forehead.

'Red's better. A white one is too much like a hospital,' he observed sententiously. 'Well, how are things over there? How is your elder?'

'He is very sick; he may die today,' answered

Alyosha. But his father was not listening, and forgot his own question at once.

'Ivan's gone out,' he said suddenly. 'He is doing his utmost to carry off Mitya's betrothed. That's what he is staying here for,' he added maliciously, and, twisting his mouth, looked at Alyosha.

'Surely he did not tell you so?' asked Alyosha.

'Yes, he did, long ago. Would you believe it, he told me three weeks ago? You don't suppose he too came to murder me, do you? He must have had some object in coming.'

'What do you mean? Why do you say such things?' said Alyosha, troubled.

'He doesn't ask for money, it's true, and anyway he won't get a penny from me. I intend living as long as possible, you may as well know, my dear Alexey Fyodorovitch, and so I need every penny, and the longer I live, the more I shall need it,' he continued, pacing from one corner of the room to the other, keeping his hands in the pockets of his loose greasy overcoat made of yellow cotton material. 'I can still pass for a man at five and fifty, but I want to pass for one for another twenty years. As I get older, you know, I shan't be a pretty object. The wenches won't come to me of their own accord, so I shall need my money. So I am saving up more and more, simply for myself, my dear son Alexey Fyodorovitch. You may as well know. I mean to go on in my sinful ways to the end, let me tell you. For sin is sweet; all abuse it, but all men live in it, only others sin on the sly, and I openly. And so all the other sinners denounce me for being so simple. And your paradise, Alexey Fyodorovitch, is not to my taste, let me tell you that; and it's not the proper place for a gentleman, your paradise, even if it exists. I believe that I will fall asleep and won't wake up again, and that's all. You can pray for my soul if you like. And if you don't want to, don't, damn you! That's my philosophy. Ivan talked well here yesterday, though we were all drunk. Ivan is a conceited coxcomb, but he has no particular learning . . . nor education either. Mostly he sits silent and smiles without speaking – that's what pulls him through.'

Alyosha listened to him in silence.

'Why won't he talk to me? If he does speak, he gives himself airs. Your Ivan is a scoundrel! And I'll marry Grushenka in a minute if I want to. For if you've money, Alexey Fyodorovitch, you have only to want a thing and you can have it. That's what Ivan is afraid of, he is on the watch to prevent my getting married and that's why he is egging on Mitya to marry Grushenka himself. He hopes to keep me from Grushenka by that (as though I would leave him my money if I don't marry her!). Besides, if Mitya marries Grushenka, Ivan will carry off his rich betrothed, that's what he's reckoning on! He's a scoundrel, your Ivan!'

'How angry you are. It's because of yesterday; you had better lie down,' said Alyosha.

'There! you say that,' the old man observed suddenly, as though it had struck him for the first time, 'and I am not angry with you. But if Ivan said it, I should be angry with him. It is only with you I have good moments, with others, as you know, I am an ill-natured man.'

'You are not ill-natured, but distorted,' said Alyosha with a smile.

'Listen. I meant this morning to get that ruffian Mitya locked up and I don't know yet what I shall decide to do. Of course, in these fashionable days fathers and mothers are looked upon as a prejudice, but even now the law does not allow you to drag your old father about by the hair, to kick him in the face in his own house, and brag of murdering him outright – all in the presence of witnesses. If I liked, I could cook his goose, and have him locked up at once for what he did yesterday.'

'Then you don't mean to take proceedings?'

'Ivan has dissuaded me. I shouldn't care about Ivan, but there's another thing.'

And bending down to Alyosha, he went on in a confidential half-whisper.

'If I send the ruffian to prison, she'll hear of it and run to see him at once. But if she hears that he has beaten me, a weak old man, within an inch of my life, she may give him up and come to me . . . For that's her way, everything by contraries. I know her through and through! Won't you have a drop of brandy? Take some cold coffee and I'll pour a quarter of a glass of brandy into it, it's delicious, my boy.'

'No, thank you. I'll take that roll with me if I may,' said Alyosha, and taking a small French roll he put it in the pocket of his cassock. 'And you'd better not have brandy, either,' he suggested apprehensively, looking into the old man's face.

'You are quite right, it irritates my nerves instead of soothing them. Only one little glass. I'll get it out of the cupboard.' He unlocked the cupboard, poured out a glass, drank it, then locked the cupboard and put the key back in his pocket.

'That's enough. One glass won't kill me.'

'You see you are in a better humour now,' said Alyosha smiling.

'Um! I love you even without the brandy, but with scoundrels I am a scoundrel. Ivan is not going to Tchermashnya – why is that? He wants to spy how much I will give Grushenka if she comes. They are all scoundrels! But I don't recognise Ivan, I don't know him at all. Where does he come from? He is not one of us in soul. As though I'd leave him anything! I shan't leave a will at all, you may as well know. And I'll crush Mitya like a beetle. I squash black beetles at night with my slipper; they squelch when you tread on them. And your Mitya will squelch too. *Your* Mitya, for you love him. Yes, you love him and I am not afraid of your loving him. But if Ivan loved him I should be afraid for myself at his loving him. But Ivan loves nobody. Ivan is not one of us. People like Ivan are not our sort, my boy. They are like a cloud of dust. When the wind blows, the dust will be gone . . . I had a silly idea in my head when I told you to come today; I wanted to find out from you about Mitya. If I were to hand him over a thousand or maybe two now, would the beggarly wretch agree to take himself off altogether for five years or, better still, thirty-five, and without Grushenka, and give her up once for all, eh?'

'I – I'll ask him,' muttered Alyosha. 'If you would give him three thousand, perhaps he – '

'That's nonsense! You needn't ask him now, no need! I've changed my mind. It was a nonsensical idea of mine. I won't give him anything, not a penny, I want my money myself,' cried the old man, waving his hand. 'I'll crush him like a beetle without wasting money. Don't say anything to him or else he will begin hoping. There's nothing for you to do here, you needn't stay. Is that betrothed of his, Katerina Ivanovna, whom he has kept so carefully hidden from me all this time, going to marry him or not? You went to see her yesterday, I believe?'

'Nothing will induce her to abandon him.'

'There you see how dearly these fine young ladies love a rake and a scoundrel. They are poor creatures I tell you, those pale young ladies, very different from . . . Ah, if I had his youth and the looks I had then (for I was better-looking than he at twenty-eight), I'd have been a conquering hero just as he is. He is a low cad! But he shan't have Grushenka, anyway, he shan't! I'll crush him!'

His anger had returned with the last words.

'You can go. There's nothing for you to do here today,' he snapped harshly.

Alyosha went up to say goodbye to him, and kissed him on the shoulder.

'What's that for?' the old man was a little surprised. 'We shall see each other again, or do you think we shan't?'

'Not at all, I didn't mean anything.'

'Nor did I, I did not mean anything,' said the old man, looking at him. 'Listen, listen,' he shouted after him, 'make haste and come again and I'll have a fish soup for you, a fine one, not like today. Be sure to come! Come tomorrow, do you hear, tomorrow!'

And as soon as Alyosha had gone out of the door, he went to the cupboard again and poured out another half-glass.

'I won't have more!' he muttered, clearing his throat, and again he locked the cupboard and put the key in his pocket. Then he went into his bedroom, lay down on the bed, exhausted, and in one minute he was asleep.

2

'Thank goodness he did not ask me about Grushenka,' thought Alyosha, as he left his father's house and turned towards Madame Hohlakov's, 'or I might have had to tell him of my meeting with Grushenka yesterday.'

Alyosha felt painfully that since yesterday both combatants had renewed their energies, and that their hearts had grown hard again. 'Father is spiteful and angry, he's made some plan and will stick to it. And what of Dmitri? He too will be tougher than yesterday, he too must be spiteful and angry, and he too, no doubt, has made some plan. Oh, I must succeed in finding him today, whatever happens.'

But Alyosha had not long to meditate. An incident occurred on the road, which, though apparently of little consequence, made a great impression on him. Just after he had crossed the square and turned the corner into Mihailovsky Street, which is divided by a small ditch from the High Street (our whole town is intersected by ditches), he saw a group of schoolboys between the ages of nine and twelve, at the bridge. They were going home from school, some with their bags on their shoulders, others with leather satchels slung across them, some in short jackets, others in little overcoats. Some even had those high boots with creases round the ankles, such as little boys spoiled by rich fathers loved to wear. The whole group was talking eagerly about something, apparently holding a council. Alyosha had never from his Moscow days been able to pass children without taking notice of them, and although he was particularly fond of children of three or thereabouts, he liked schoolboys of ten and eleven too. And so, anxious as he was today, he wanted at once to turn aside to talk to them. He looked into their excited rosy faces, and noticed at once that all the boys had stones in their hands. Behind the ditch some thirty paces away, there was another schoolboy standing by a fence. He too had a satchel at his side. He was about ten years old, pale, delicate-looking and with sparkling black eyes. He kept an attentive and anxious watch on the other six, obviously his schoolfellows with whom he had just come out of school, but with whom he evidently had a feud.

Alyosha went up and addressing a fair, curly-headed, pink-cheeked boy in a black jacket observed: 'When I used to wear a satchel like yours, I always used to carry it on my left side, so as to have my right hand free, but you've got yours on your right side. So it will be awkward for you to get at it.'

Alyosha had no art or premeditation in beginning with this practical remark. But it is the only way for a grown-up person to get at once into confidential relations with a child, or still more with a group of children. One must begin in a serious businesslike way so as to be on a perfectly equal footing. Alyosha understood this by instinct.

'But he is left-handed,' another, a fine healthy-looking boy of eleven, answered promptly. All the others stared at Alyosha.

'He even throws stones with his left hand,' observed a third.

At that instant a stone flew into the group, but only just grazed the left-handed boy, though it was well and vigorously thrown by the boy standing the other side of the ditch.

'Give it to him, hit him back, Smurov,' they all shouted. But Smurov, the left-handed boy, needed no telling, and at once revenged himself; he threw a stone, but it missed the boy and hit the ground. The boy the other side of the ditch, the pocket of whose coat was visibly bulging with stones, flung another stone at the group; this time it flew straight at Alyosha and hit him painfully on the shoulder.

'He aimed it at you, he meant it for you. You are Karamazov, Karamazov!' the boys shouted, laughing. 'Come, all throw at him at once!' and six stones flew at the boy. One struck the boy on the head and he fell down, but at once leaped up and began ferociously returning their fire. Both sides threw stones incessantly. Many of the group had their pockets full too.

'What are you doing? Aren't you ashamed? Six against one! Why, you'll kill him,' cried Alyosha.

He ran forward and met the flying stones to screen the solitary boy. Three or four ceased throwing for a minute.

'He began first!' cried a boy in a red shirt in an angry childish voice. 'He is a beast, he stabbed Krassotkin in class the other day with a penknife. It bled. Krassotkin wouldn't tell tales, but he must be thrashed.'

'But what for? I suppose you tease him.'

'There, he sent a stone in your back again, he knows you,' cried the children. 'It's you he is throwing at now, not us. Come, all of you, at him again, don't miss, Smurov!' and again a fire of stones, and a very vicious one, began. The boy on the other side of the ditch was hit in the chest; he screamed, began to cry and ran away uphill towards Mihailovsky Street. They all shouted: 'Aha, he is scared, he is running away. Handful of hay!'

'You don't know what a beast he is, Karamazov, killing is too good for him,' said the boy in the jacket, with flashing eyes. He seemed to be the oldest.

'What's wrong with him?' asked Alyosha. 'Is he a tattletale or what?'

The boys looked at one another as though derisively.

'Are you going that way, to Mihailovsky?' the same boy went on. 'Catch him up . . . You see he's stopped again, he is waiting and looking at you.'

'He is looking at you,' the other boys chimed in.

'You ask him, does he like a handful of hay. Do you hear, ask him that!'

There was a general burst of laughter. Alyosha looked at them, and they at him.

'Don't go near him, he'll hurt you,' cried Smurov in a warning voice.

'I won't ask him about the handful of hay, for I suppose you tease him with that question somehow. But I'll find out from him why you hate him so.'

'Find out then, find out,' cried the boys, laughing.

Alyosha crossed the bridge and walked uphill by the fence, straight towards the boy.

'You'd better look out,' the boys called after him; 'he won't be afraid of you. He will stab you in a minute, on the sly, as he did Krassotkin.'

The boy waited for him without budging. Coming up to him, Alyosha saw facing him a child of about nine years old. He was an undersized, weakly boy with a thin long pale face, with large dark eyes that gazed at him vindictively. He was dressed in a rather shabby old overcoat, which he had monstrously outgrown. His bare arms stuck out beyond his sleeves. There was a large patch on the right knee of his trousers, and in his right boot just at the toe there was a big hole in the leather, carefully blackened with ink. Both the pockets of his great coat were weighed down with stones. Alyosha stopped two steps in front of him, looking enquiringly at him. The boy, seeing at once from Alyosha's eyes that he wouldn't beat him, became less defiant, and addressed him first.

'I am alone, and there are six of them. I'll beat them all, alone!' he said suddenly, with flashing eyes.

'I think one of the stones must have hurt you badly,' observed Alyosha.

'But I hit Smurov on the head!' cried the boy.

'They told me that you know me, and that you threw a stone at me on purpose,' said Alyosha. The boy scowled at him.

'I don't know you. Do you know me?' Alyosha continued.

'Let me alone!' the boy cried irritably, but he did not move, as though he were expecting something, and again there was a vindictive gleam in his eyes.

'Very well, I am going,' said Alyosha; 'only I don't know you and I don't tease you. They told me how they tease you, but I don't want to tease you. Good-bye!'

'Monk in fancy trousers!' cried the boy, following Alyosha with the same vindictive and defiant expression, and he threw himself into an attitude of defence, feeling sure that now Alyosha would fall upon him; but Alyosha turned, looked at him, and walked away. He had not gone three steps before the biggest stone the boy had in his pocket hit him a painful blow in the back.

'So you'll hit a man from behind! They tell the truth, then, when they say that you attack on the sly,' said

Alyosha, turning round again. This time the boy threw a stone savagely right into Alyosha's face; but Alyosha just had time to guard himself, and the stone struck him on the elbow.

'Aren't you ashamed? What have I done to you?' he cried.

The boy waited in silent defiance, certain that now Alyosha would attack him. Seeing that even now he would not, his rage was like a little wild beast's; he flew at Alyosha himself, and before Alyosha had time to move, the spiteful child had seized his left hand with both of his and bit his middle finger. He fixed his teeth in it and it was ten seconds before he let go. Alyosha cried out with pain and pulled his finger away with all his might. The child let go at last and retreated to his former distance. Alyosha's finger had been badly bitten to the bone, close to the nail; it began to bleed. Alyosha took out his handkerchief and bound it tightly round his injured hand. He was a full minute bandaging it.

The boy stood waiting all the time. At last Alyosha raised his gentle eyes and looked at him.

'Very well,' he said, 'you see how badly you've bitten me. That's enough, isn't it? Now tell me what have I done to you?'

The boy stared in amazement.

'Though I don't know you and it's the first time I've seen you,' Alyosha went on with the same serenity, 'yet I must have done something to you – you wouldn't have hurt me like this for nothing. So what have I done? How have I wronged you, tell me?'

Instead of answering, the boy broke into a loud tearful wail and ran away. Alyosha walked slowly after him towards Mihailovsky Street, and for a long time he saw the child running in the distance as fast as ever, not turning his head, and no doubt still keeping up his tearful wail. He made up his mind to look him up as soon as he had time, and to solve this mystery. Just now he had not the time.

3

Alyosha soon reached Madame Hohlakov's house, a handsome stone house of two storeys, one of the finest in our town. Though Madame Hohlakov spent most of her time in another province where she had an estate, or in Moscow, where she had a house of her own, yet she also kept her house in our town, inherited from her forefathers. The estate in our district was the largest of her three estates, though she had been very little in our province before this time. She ran out into the hall to Alyosha.

'He is dying today,' said Alyosha.

'I have heard, I know, oh, how I long to talk to you, to you, or someone about all this. No, to you, to you! And how sorry I am I can't see him! The whole town is excited, they are all in suspense. But now – do you know Katerina Ivanovna is here now?'

'Ah, that's lucky,' cried Alyosha. 'Then I shall see her here. She told me yesterday to be sure to come and see her today.'

'I know, I know all. I've heard exactly what happened yesterday – and the atrocious behaviour of that – creature. *C'est tragique*, and if I'd been in her place I don't know what I should have done. And your brother Dmitri Fyodorovitch, what do you think of him? – my goodness! Alexey Fyodorovitch, I am forgetting, only fancy; your brother is in there with her, not that dreadful brother who was so shocking yesterday, but the other, Ivan Fyodorovitch, he is sitting with her talking; they are having a serious conversation. If you could only imagine what's passing between them now – it's awful, I tell you it's heartbreaking, it's like some incredible tale of horror. They are ruining their lives for no reason anyone can see. They both recognise it and revel in it. I've been watching for you! I've been thirsting for you! It's too much for me, that's the worst of it. I'll tell you all about it presently, but now I must speak of something else, the most important thing – I had quite forgotten what's most important. Tell me, why has Lise been in hysterics? As soon as she heard you were here, she began to be hysterical!'

'Mamma, it's you who are hysterical now, not I.' Lise's voice carolled through a tiny crack of the door at the side. Her voice sounded as though she wanted to laugh, but was doing her utmost to control it. Alyosha at once noticed the crack, and no doubt Lise was peeping through it, but that he could not see.

'And no wonder, Lise, no wonder . . . your caprices will drive me to hysterics. But she is so ill, Alexey Fyodorovitch, she has been so ill all night, feverish and moaning! I could hardly wait for the morning and for Herzenstube to come. He says that he can make nothing of it, that we must wait. Herzenstube always comes and says that he can make nothing of it. As soon as you approached the house, she screamed, fell into hysterics, and insisted on being wheeled back into this room here.'

'Mamma, I didn't know he had come. It wasn't on his account I wanted to be wheeled into this room.'

'That's not true, Lise, Julia ran to tell you that

Alexey Fyodorovitch was coming. She was on the lookout for you.'

'My darling mamma, it's not at all clever of you. But if you want to make up for it and say something very clever, dear mamma, you'd better tell our honoured visitor, Alexey Fyodorovitch, that he has shown his lack of wit by coming to us after what happened yesterday and although everyone is laughing at him.'

'Lise, you go too far. I declare I shall have to be severe. Who laughs at him? I am so glad he has come, I need him, I can't do without him. Oh, Alexey Fyodorovitch, I am exceedingly unhappy!'

'But what's the matter with you, mamma darling?'

'Ah, your caprices, Lise, your moods, your illness, that awful night of fever, that awful everlasting Herzenstube, everlasting, everlasting, that's the worst of it! Everything, in fact, everything . . . And that tragedy in the drawing-room, it's more than I can bear, I warn you. I can't bear it. A comedy, perhaps, not a tragedy. Tell me, will Father Zossima live till tomorrow, will he? Oh, my God! What is happening to me? Every time I close my eyes I see that it's all nonsense, all nonsense.'

'I should be very grateful,' Alyosha interrupted suddenly, 'if you could give me a clean bandage to bind up my finger. I have hurt it, and it's very painful.'

Alyosha unbound his bitten finger. The handkerchief was soaked with blood. Madame Hohlakov screamed and shut her eyes.

'Good heavens, what a wound, how awful!'

But as soon as Lise saw Alyosha's finger through the crack, she flung the door wide open.

'Come, come here,' she cried, imperiously. 'No nonsense now! Good heaven, why did you stand there saying nothing about it all this time? He might have bled to death, mamma! How did you do it? Water, water! You must wash it first of all, simply hold it in cold water to stop the pain, and keep it there, keep it there . . . Make haste, mamma, some water in a bowl. But do make haste,' she finished nervously. She was quite frightened at the sight of Alyosha's wound.

'Shouldn't we send for Herzenstube?' cried Madame Hohlakov.

'Mamma, you'll be the death of me. Your Herzenstube will come and say that he can make nothing of it! Water, water! Mamma, for goodness' sake go yourself and hurry Julia, she is such a slow coach and never can come quickly! Make haste, mamma, or I shall die.'

'Why, it's nothing much,' cried Alyosha, frightened at all this fuss.

Julia ran in with water and Alyosha put his finger in it.

'A piece of clean linen, mamma, for mercy's sake, bring lint and that lotion for wounds, what's it called? We've got some. You know where the bottle is, mamma; it's in your bedroom in the right-hand closet, there's a big bottle of it there with the linen bandages.'

'I'll bring everything in a minute, Lise, only don't scream and don't fuss. You see how bravely Alexey Fyodorovitch bears it. Where did you get such a dreadful wound, Alexey Fyodorovitch?'

Madame Hohlakov hastened away. This was all Lise was waiting for.

'First of all, answer the question, where did you get hurt like this?' she asked Alyosha, quickly. 'And then I'll talk to you about something quite different. Well?'

Instinctively feeling that the time of her mother's absence was precious for her, Alyosha hastened to tell her in the fewest words possible of his strange meeting with the schoolboys. Lise clasped her hands at his story.

'How can you, and in that garb too, associate with schoolboys!' she cried angrily, as though she had a right to control him. 'You are nothing but a boy yourself if you can do that, a regular child! But you must find out for me about that horrid boy and tell me all about it, for there's some mystery in it. Now for the second thing, but first a question: does the pain prevent your talking about utterly unimportant things, but talking sensibly?'

'Of course not, and I don't feel much pain now.'

'That's because your finger is in the water. It must be changed directly, for it will get warm in a minute. Julia, bring some ice from the cellar and another bowl of water. Now she is gone, I can speak; will you give me the letter I sent you yesterday, dear Alexey Fyodorovitch – be quick, for mamma will be back in a minute and I don't want – '

'I haven't got the letter.'

'That's not true, you have. I knew you would say that. You've got it in that pocket. I've been regretting that joke all night. Give me back the letter at once, give it to me.'

'I've left it at home.'

'But you can't consider me as a child, a little girl, after that silly joke! I beg your pardon for that silliness, but you must bring me the letter, if you really haven't got it – bring it today, you must, you must.'

'Today, I can't possibly, for I am going back to the monastery and I shan't come and see you for the next two days – three or four perhaps – for Father Zossima – '

'Four days, what nonsense! Listen. Did you laugh at me very much?'

'I didn't laugh at all.'

'Why not?'

'Because I believed all you said.'

'You are insulting me!'

'Not at all. As soon as I read it, I thought that all that would come to pass, for as soon as Father Zossima dies, I am to leave the monastery. Then I shall go back and finish my studies, and when you reach the legal age we will be married. I shall love you. Though I haven't had time to think about it, I believe I couldn't find a better wife than you, and Father Zossima tells me I must marry.'

'But I am a cripple, wheeled about in a chair,' laughed Lise, flushing crimson.

'I'll wheel you about myself, but I'm sure you'll get well by then.'

'But you are mad,' said Lise, nervously, 'to make all this fuss out of a joke! Here's mamma, very apropos, perhaps. Mamma, how slow you always are, how can you be so long! And here's Julia with the ice.'

'Oh, Lise, don't scream, above all don't scream. That scream drives me . . . How can I help it when you put the bandages in another place. I've been hunting and hunting – I do believe you did it on purpose.'

'But I couldn't tell that he would come with a bad finger, or else perhaps I might have done it on purpose. My darling mamma, you begin to say really funny things.'

'Never mind my being funny, but I must say you show nice feeling for Alexey Fyodorovitch's sufferings. Oh, my dear Alexey Fyodorovitch, what's killing me is no one thing in particular, not Herzenstube, but everything together, that's what is too much for me.'

'That's enough, mamma, enough about Herzenstube,' Lise laughed gaily. 'Make haste with the bandages and the lotion, mamma. That's simply Goulard's water, Alexey Fyodorovitch, I remember the name now, but it's a splendid lotion. Would you believe it, mamma, on the way here he had a fight with the boys in the street, and a boy bit his finger, isn't he a child, a child himself? Is he fit to be married after that? For only fancy, he wants to be married, mamma. Just think of him married, wouldn't it be comical, wouldn't it be awful?'

And Lise kept laughing her high hysterical giggle, looking slyly at Alyosha.

'But why married, Lise? What makes you talk of such a thing? It's quite out of place – and perhaps the boy was rabid.'

'Why, mamma! As though there were rabid boys!'

'Why not, Lise, as though I had said something stupid! Your boy might have been bitten by a mad dog and he would become mad and bite anyone near him. How well she has bandaged it, Alexey Fyodorovitch. I couldn't have done it. Do you still feel the pain?'

'It's nothing much now.'

'You don't feel afraid of water?' asked Lise.

'Come, that's enough, Lise, perhaps I really was rather too quick talking of the boy being rabid, and you pounced upon it at once. Katerina Ivanovna has only just heard that you are here, Alexey Fyodorovitch, she simply rushed at me, she's dying to see you, dying!'

'Ah, mamma, go to them yourself. He can't go just now, he is in too much pain.'

'Not at all, I can go quite well,' said Alyosha.

'What! You are going away? Is that what you say?'

'Well, when I've seen them, I'll come back here and we can talk as much as you like. But I should like to see Katerina Ivanovna at once, for I am very anxious to be back at the monastery as soon as I can.'

'Mamma, take him away quickly. Alexey Fyodorovitch, don't trouble to come and see me afterwards, but go straight back to your monastery and a good riddance. I want to sleep, I didn't sleep all night.'

'Ah, Lise, you are only making fun, but how I wish you would sleep!' cried Madame Hohlakov.

'I don't know what I've done . . . I'll stay another three minutes, five if you like,' muttered Alyosha.

'Even five! Do take him away quickly, mamma, he is a monster.'

'Lise, you are crazy. Let us go, Alexey Fyodorovitch, she is too capricious today. I am afraid to cross her. Oh, the trouble one has with nervous girls! Perhaps she really will be able to sleep after seeing you. How quickly you have made her sleepy, and how fortunate it is!'

'Ah, mamma, how sweetly you talk. I must kiss you for it, mamma.'

'And I kiss you too, Lise. Listen, Alexey Fyodorovitch,' Madame Hohlakov began mysteriously and importantly, speaking in a rapid whisper. 'I don't want to suggest anything, I don't want to lift the veil, you will see for yourself what's going on. It's appalling. It's the most fantastic farce. Katerina Ivanovna loves your brother, Ivan, and she is doing her utmost to persuade herself she loves your other brother, Dmitri. It's appalling! I'll go in with you, and if they don't throw me out, I'll stay to the end.'

4

In the drawing-room the conversation was already over. Katerina Ivanovna was greatly excited, though she looked resolute. At the moment Alyosha and Madame Hohlakov entered, Ivan Fyodorovitch stood up to take leave. His face was rather pale, and Alyosha looked at him anxiously. For this moment was to solve a doubt, a harassing enigma which had for some time haunted Alyosha. During the preceding month it had been suggested to him several times that his brother Ivan was in love with Katerina Ivanovna, and, what was more, that he meant 'to take her away' from Dmitri. Until quite lately the idea seemed to Alyosha monstrous, though it worried him extremely. He loved both his brothers, and dreaded such rivalry between them. Meantime, Dmitri had said outright on the previous day that he was glad that Ivan was his rival, and that it was a great assistance to him, Dmitri. In what way did it assist him? To marry Grushenka? But that Alyosha considered the worst thing possible. Besides all this, Alyosha had till the evening before implicitly believed that Katerina Ivanovna had a steadfast and passionate love for Dmitri; but he had only believed it till the evening before. He had fancied, too, that she was incapable of loving a man like Ivan, and that she did love Dmitri, and loved him just as he was, in spite of all the strangeness of such a passion.

But during yesterday's scene with Grushenka another idea had struck him. The word 'heart-breaking', which Madame Hohlakov had just uttered, almost made him pause, because in his half-sleep towards daybreak that night he had cried out, 'Heartbreaking, heartbreaking', probably applying it to his dream. He had been dreaming all night of the previous day's scene at Katerina Ivanovna's. Now Alyosha was impressed by Madame Hohlakov's blunt and persistent assertion that Katerina Ivanovna was in love with Ivan, and was only deluding herself with some sort of pose of heartbreak, and was torturing herself by her pretended love for Dmitri from some fancied duty of gratitude. 'Yes,' he thought, 'perhaps the whole truth lies in those words.' But in that case what was Ivan's position? Alyosha felt instinctively that a character like Katerina Ivanovna's must dominate, and she could only dominate someone like Dmitri, and never a man like Ivan. For Dmitri might at last submit to her domination 'for his own happiness' (which was what Alyosha would have desired), but Ivan – no, Ivan could not submit to her, and such submission would not give him happiness. Alyosha could not help believing that of Ivan. And now all these doubts and reflections flitted through his mind as he entered the drawing-room. Another idea, too, forced itself upon him: 'What if she loved neither of them – neither Ivan nor Dmitri?'

It must be noted that Alyosha felt, as it were, ashamed of his own thoughts and blamed himself when they kept recurring to him during the last month. 'What do I know about love and women and how can I decide such questions?' he thought reproachfully, after such doubts and surmises. And yet it was impossible not to think about the situation. He felt instinctively that this rivalry was of immense importance in his brothers' lives and that a great deal depended upon it.

'One reptile will devour the other,' Ivan had said

the day before, speaking in anger of his father and Dmitri. So Ivan looked upon Dmitri as a reptile, and perhaps had long done so. Was it perhaps since he had known Katerina Ivanovna? The phrase had, of course, escaped Ivan unawares yesterday, but that only made it more important. If he felt like that, what chance was there of peace? Were there not, on the contrary, new grounds for hatred and hostility in their family? And with which side was Alyosha to sympathise? And what was he to wish for each of them? He loved them both, but what could he desire for each in the midst of these conflicting interests? He might go quite astray in this maze, and Alyosha's heart could not endure uncertainty, because his love was always of an active character. He was incapable of passive love. If he loved anyone, he set to work at once to help that person. And to do so he must know what he was aiming at; he must know for certain what was best for each, and having ascertained this it was natural for him to help them both. But instead of a definite aim, he found nothing but uncertainty and perplexity on all sides. 'It was heartbreaking,' as was said just now. What could he understand even in this 'heartbreak'? He did not understand the first thing in this perplexing tangle.

Seeing Alyosha, Katerina Ivanovna said quickly and joyfully to Ivan, who had already got up to go, 'Just a minute! Stay another minute! I want to hear the opinion of this person here whom I trust absolutely. Don't go away,' she added, addressing Madame Hohlakov. She made Alyosha sit down beside her, and Madame Hohlakov sat opposite, next to Ivan.

'You are all my friends here, all I have in the world, my dear friends,' she began warmly, in a voice which quivered with genuine tears of suffering, and Alyosha's heart warmed to her at once. 'You, Alexey Fyodorovitch, were witness yesterday of that abominable scene, and saw what I did. You did not see it, Ivan Fyodorovitch, Alyosha did. What he thought of me yesterday I don't know. I only know one thing, that if it were repeated today, this minute, I should express the same feelings again as yesterday – the same feelings, the same words, the same actions. You remember my actions, Alexey Fyodorovitch; you checked me in one of them . . . ' (as she said that, she flushed and her eyes shone). 'I must tell you that I can't get over it. Listen, Alexey Fyodorovitch. I don't even know whether I still love *him*. I feel *pity* for him, and that is a poor sign of love. If I loved him, if I still loved him, perhaps I wouldn't be sorry for him now, but would hate him.'

Her voice quivered, and tears glittered on her eyelashes. Alyosha shuddered inwardly. 'That girl is truthful and sincere,' he thought, 'and she does not love Dmitri any more.'

'That's true, that's true,' cried Madame Hohlakov.

'Wait, dear. I haven't told you the chief, the final decision I came to during the night. I feel that perhaps my decision is a terrible one – for me, but I foresee that nothing will induce me to change it – nothing. It will be so all my life. My dear, kind, ever-faithful and generous adviser, the one friend I have in the world, Ivan Fyodorovitch, with his deep insight into the heart, approves and commends my decision. He knows it.'

'Yes, I approve of it,' Ivan assented, in a subdued but firm voice.

'But I would like Alyosha, too (Ah! Alexey Fyodorovitch, forgive my calling you simply Alyosha), I would like Alexey Fyodorovitch, too, to tell me before my two friends whether I am right. I feel instinctively that you, Alyosha, my dear brother (for you are a dear brother to me),' she said again ecstatically, taking his cold hand in her hot one, 'I foresee that your decision, your approval, will bring me peace, in spite of all my sufferings, for, after your words, I shall be calm and submit – I feel that.'

'I don't know what you are asking me,' said Alyosha, flushing. 'I only know that I love you and at this moment wish for your happiness more than my own! . . . But I know nothing about such affairs,' something impelled him to add hurriedly.

'In such affairs, Alexey Fyodorovitch, in such affairs, the chief thing is honour and duty and something higher – I don't know what – but higher perhaps even than duty. I am conscious of this irresistible feeling in my heart, and it compels me irresistibly. But it may all be put in two words. I've already decided, even if he marries that – creature' (she began solemnly), 'whom I never, never can forgive, *even then I will not abandon him*. Henceforward I will never, never abandon him!' she cried, succumbing to a sort of pale, hysterical ecstasy. 'Not that I would run after him continually, get in his way and worry him. Oh, no! I will go away to another town – wherever you like – but I will watch over him all my life – I will watch over him all my life unceasingly. When he becomes unhappy with that woman, and that is bound to happen quite soon, let him come to me and he will find a friend, a sister . . . Only a sister, of course, and so for ever; but he will learn at least that that sister is really his sister, who loves him and has sacrificed all her life to him. I will gain my point. I will insist on his knowing me and confiding entirely in me, without reserve,' she cried, in a sort of frenzy. 'I will be a god to whom he can pray – and that, at least, he owes me for his treachery and for what I suffered yesterday through him. And let him know that all my life I will be true to him and the promise I gave him, in spite of his being untrue and betraying me. I will – I will become nothing but a means for his happiness, or – how shall I say? – an instrument, a machine for his happiness, and that for my whole life, my whole life, and this he may see all his life! That's my decision. Ivan Fyodorovitch fully approves me.'

She was breathless. She had perhaps intended to express her idea with more dignity, art and naturalness, but her speech was too hurried and crude. It was full of youthful impulsiveness, it betrayed that she was still smarting from yesterday's insult, and that her pride craved satisfaction. She felt this herself. Her face suddenly darkened, an unpleasant look came into her eyes. Alyosha at once saw it and felt a pang of sympathy. His brother Ivan made it worse by adding: 'I've only expressed my own view,' he said. 'From anyone else, this would have been affected and overstrained, but from you – no. Any other woman would have been wrong, but you are right. I don't know how to explain it, but I see that you are absolutely genuine and, therefore, you are right.'

'But that's only for the moment. And what does this moment stand for? Nothing but yesterday's insult.' Madame Hohlakov obviously had not intended to interfere, but she could not refrain from this very just comment.

'Quite so, quite so,' cried Ivan, with peculiar eagerness, obviously annoyed at being interrupted, 'in anyone else this moment would be only due to yesterday's impression and would be only a moment.

But with Katerina Ivanovna's character, that moment will last all her life. What for anyone else would be only a promise is for her an everlasting, burdensome, grim perhaps, but unflagging duty. And she will be sustained by the feeling of this duty being fulfilled. Your life, Katerina Ivanovna, will henceforth be spent in painful brooding over your own feelings, your own heroism, and your own suffering; but in the end that suffering will be softened and will pass into sweet contemplation of the fulfilment of a bold and proud design. Yes, proud it certainly is, and desperate in any case, but a triumph for you. And the consciousness of it will at last be a source of complete satisfaction and will make you resigned to everything else.'

This was unmistakably said with some malice and obviously with purpose; even perhaps with no desire to conceal that he spoke ironically and with purpose.

'Oh, dear, what a mistake it all is!' Madame Hohlakov cried again.

'Alexey Fyodorovitch, you speak. I want dreadfully to know what you will say!' cried Katerina Ivanovna, and burst into tears. Alyosha got up from the sofa.

'It's nothing, nothing!' she went on through her tears. 'I'm upset, I didn't sleep last night. But with two such friends as you and your brother I feel strong – for I know – you two will never desert me.'

'Unluckily I am obliged to return to Moscow – perhaps tomorrow – and to leave you for a long time – and, unluckily, it's unavoidable,' said Ivan suddenly.

'Tomorrow – to Moscow!' Her face was suddenly contorted. 'But – but, dear me, how fortunate,' she cried in a voice suddenly changed. In one instant there was no trace left of her tears. She underwent an instantaneous transformation, which amazed Alyosha.

Instead of a poor, insulted girl, weeping in a spasm of 'heartbreak', he saw a woman completely self-possessed and even exceedingly pleased, as though something agreeable had just happened.

'Oh, not fortunate that I am losing you, of course not,' she corrected herself suddenly, with a charming society smile. 'Such a friend as you are could not suppose that. I am only too unhappy at losing you.' She ran impulsively to Ivan, and seizing both his hands, pressed them warmly. 'But what is fortunate is that you will be able in Moscow to see auntie and Agafya and to tell them all the horror of my present position. You can speak with complete frankness to Agafya, but spare dear auntie. You will know how to do that. You can't think how wretched I was yesterday and this morning, wondering how I could write them that dreadful letter – for one can never tell such things in a letter . . . Now it will be easy for me to write, for you will see them and explain everything. Oh, how glad I am! But I am only glad of that, believe me. Of course, no one can take your place . . . I will run at once to write the letter,' she finished suddenly, and took a step as though to go out of the room.

'And what about Alyosha and his opinion, which you were so desperately anxious to hear?' cried Madame Hohlakov. There was a sarcastic, angry note in her voice.

'I had not forgotten that,' cried Katerina Ivanovna, coming to a sudden standstill, 'and why are you so antagonistic at such a moment?' she added, with warm and bitter reproachfulness. 'What I said, I repeat. I must have his opinion. More than that, I must have his decision! As he says, so it shall be. You see how anxious I am for your words, Alexey Fyodorovitch . . . But what's the matter?'

'I couldn't have believed it. I can't understand it!' Alyosha cried suddenly in distress.

'What? what?'

'He is going to Moscow, and you cry out that you are glad. You said that on purpose! And you begin explaining that you are not glad of that but sorry to be – losing a friend. But that was acting too – you were playing a part – as in a theatre!'

'In a theatre? What? What do you mean?' exclaimed Katerina Ivanovna, profoundly astonished, flushing crimson, and frowning.

'Though you assure him you are sorry to lose a friend in him, you persist in telling him to his face that it's fortunate he is going,' said Alyosha breathlessly. He was standing at the table and did not sit down.

'What are you talking about? I don't understand.'

'I don't understand myself . . . I seemed to see in a flash . . . I know I am not saying it properly, but I'll say it all the same,' Alyosha went on in the same shaking and broken voice. 'What I see is that perhaps you don't love Dmitri at all . . . and never have, from the beginning . . . And Dmitri, too, has never loved you . . . and only esteems you . . . I really don't know how I dare to say all this, but somebody must tell the truth . . . for nobody here will tell the truth.'

'What truth?' cried Katerina Ivanovna, and there was a hysterical edge to her voice.

'I'll tell you,' Alyosha went on with desperate haste, as though he were jumping from the top of a house. 'Call Dmitri; I will fetch him – and let him come here and take your hand and take Ivan's and join your hands. For you're torturing Ivan, simply because you love him – and torturing him, because you love Dmitri through "heartbreak" – with an unreal love – because you've persuaded yourself.'

Alyosha broke off and was silent.

'You . . . you . . . you are a little religious idiot – that's what you are!' Katerina Ivanovna snapped. Her face was white and her lips were writhing with anger.

Ivan suddenly laughed and got up. His hat was in his hand.

'You are mistaken, my good Alyosha,' he said, with an expression Alyosha had never seen in his face before – an expression of youthful sincerity and strong, irresistibly frank feeling. 'Katerina Ivanovna has never cared for me! She has known all the time that I cared for her – though I never said a word of my love to her – she knew, but she didn't care for me. I have never been her friend either, not for one moment; she is too proud to need my friendship. She kept me at her side as a means of revenge. She revenged through me and on me all the insults which she has been continually receiving from Dmitri ever since their first meeting. For even that first meeting has rankled in her heart as an insult – that's what her heart is like! She has talked to me of nothing but her love for him. I am going now; but, believe me, Katerina Ivanovna, you really love him. And the more he insults you, the more you love him – that's your "heartbreak". You love him just as he is; you love him for insulting you. If he reformed, you'd give him up at once and cease to love him. But you need him to contemplate continually your heroic fidelity and to reproach him for infidelity. And it all comes from your pride. Oh, there's a great deal of humiliation and self-abasement about it, but it all comes from pride . . . I am too young and I've loved you too much. I know that I ought not to say this, that it would be more dignified on my part simply to leave you, and it would be less offensive for you. But I am going far away, and shall never come back . . . It is for ever. I don't want to live beside a "heartbreak" . . . But I don't know how to speak now. I've said everything . . . Goodbye, Katerina Ivanovna; you can't be angry with me, for I am a hundred times more severely punished than you, if only by the fact that I shall never see you again. Goodbye! I don't want your hand. You have tortured me too deliberately for me to be able to forgive you at this moment. I shall forgive you later, but now I don't want your hand. "*Den Dank, Dame, begehr ich nicht,*" ' he added, with a forced smile, showing, however, that he could read Schiller, and read him till he knew him by heart – which Alyosha would never have believed. He went out of the room without saying goodbye even to his hostess, Madame Hohlakov. Alyosha clasped his hands.

'Ivan!' he cried desperately after him. 'Come back, Ivan! No, nothing will induce him to come back now!' he cried again, regretfully realising it; 'but it's my fault, my fault. I began it! Ivan spoke angrily, wrongly. Unjustly and angrily. He must come back here, come back,' Alyosha kept exclaiming frantically.

Katerina Ivanovna went suddenly into the next room.

'You have done no harm. You behaved beautifully, like an angel,' Madame Hohlakov whispered rapidly and ecstatically to Alyosha. 'I will do my utmost to prevent Ivan Fyodorovitch from going.'

Her face beamed with delight, to the great distress of Alyosha, but Katerina Ivanovna suddenly returned. She had two hundred-rouble notes in her hand.

'I have a great favour to ask of you, Alexey Fyodorovitch,' she began, addressing Alyosha with an apparently calm and even voice, as though nothing had happened. 'A week – yes, I think it was a week ago – Dmitri Fyodorovitch was guilty of a hasty and unjust action – a very ugly action. There is a low tavern here and in it he met that discharged officer, that captain, whom your father used to employ in some business. Dmitri Fyodorovitch somehow lost his temper with this captain, seized him by the beard and dragged him out into the street and for some distance along it, in that insulting fashion. And I am told that his son, a boy, quite a child, who is at the school here, saw it and ran beside them crying and begging for his father, appealing to everyone to defend him, while everyone laughed. You must forgive me, Alexey Fyodorovitch, I cannot think without indignation of that disgraceful action of *his* . . . one of those actions of which only Dmitri Fyodorovitch would be capable in his anger . . . and in his passions! I can't describe it even . . . I can't find the right words. I've made enquiries about his victim, and find he is quite a poor man. His name is Snegiryov. He did something wrong in the army and was discharged. I can't tell you what. And now he has sunk into terrible destitution, with his family – an unhappy family of sick children, and, I believe, an insane wife. He has been living here a long time; he used to work as a copying clerk, but now he is earning nothing. I thought if you . . . that is I thought . . . I don't know. I am so confused. You see, I wanted to ask you, my dear Alexey Fyodorovitch, to go to him, to find some excuse to go to them – I mean to that captain – oh, goodness, how badly I explain it! – and delicately, carefully, as only you know how to' (Alyosha blushed), 'manage to give him this assistance, these two hundred roubles. He will be sure to take it . . . I mean, persuade him to take it . . . Or, rather, what do I mean? You see it's not by way of compensation to prevent him from taking proceedings (for I believe he meant to), but simply as a token of sympathy, of a desire to assist him, a token from me, Dmitri Fyodorovitch's betrothed, not from Dmitri himself . . . But you understand . . . I would go myself, but you'll know how to do it so much better. He lives on Lake Street, in the house of a woman called Kalmikov . . . For God's sake, Alexey Fyodorovitch, do it for me, and now . . . now I am rather . . . tired. Goodbye!'

She turned so quickly and disappeared behind the portière that Alyosha had not time to utter a word, though he wanted to speak. He longed to beg her pardon, to blame himself, to say something, for his heart was full and he could not bear to go out of the room without expressing his feelings. But Madame Hohlakov took him by the hand and drew him along with her. In the hall she stopped him again as before.

'She is proud, she is struggling with herself; but kind, charming, generous,' she exclaimed, in a half-whisper. 'Oh, how I love her, especially sometimes, and how glad I am again of everything! Dear Alexey Fyodorovitch, you didn't know, but I must tell you, that we all, all – both her aunts, I and all of us, Lise, even – have been hoping and praying for nothing for the last month but that she may give up your favourite Dmitri, who takes no notice of her and does not care for her, and may marry Ivan Fyodorovitch – such an excellent and cultivated young man, who loves her more than anything in the world. We are in a regular plot to bring it about, and I am even staying on here chiefly on that account.'

'But she has been crying – she has been wounded again,' Alyosha exclaimed.

'Never trust a woman's tears, Alexey Fyodorovitch. I am never for the women in such cases. I am always on the side of the men.'

'Mamma, you are spoiling him,' Lise's little voice cried from behind the door.

'No, it was all my fault. I am horribly to blame,' Alyosha repeated unconsoled, hiding his face in his hands in an agony of remorse for his indiscretion.

'Quite the contrary; you behaved like an angel, like an angel. I am ready to say so a thousand times over.'

'Mamma, how has he behaved like an angel?' Lise's voice was heard again.

'I somehow fancied all at once,' Alyosha went on as though he had not heard Lise, 'that she loved Ivan, and so I said that stupid thing . . . What will happen now?'

'To whom, to whom?' cried Lise. 'Mamma, you really want to be the death of me. I ask you and you don't answer.'

At the moment the maid ran in.

'Katerina Ivanovna is ill . . . She is crying, struggling . . . hysterics.'

'What is the matter?' cried Lise, in a tone of real anxiety. 'Mamma, I should be having hysterics, and not she!'

'Lise, for mercy's sake, don't scream, don't persecute me. At your age one can't know everything that grown-up people know. I'll come and tell you everything you ought to know. Oh, mercy on us! I am coming, I am coming . . . Hysterics is a good sign, Alexey Fyodorovitch; it's an excellent thing that she is hysterical. That's just as it ought to be. In such cases I am always against the woman, against all these feminine tears and hysterics. Run and say, Julia, that I'll fly to her. As for Ivan Fyodorovitch's going away like that, it's her own fault. But he won't go away. Lise, for mercy's sake, don't scream! Oh, yes; you are not screaming. It's I am screaming. Forgive your mamma; but I am delighted, delighted, delighted! Did you notice, Alexey Fyodorovitch, how young, how young Ivan Fyodorovitch was just now when he went out, when he said all that and went out? I thought he was so learned, such a *savant*, and all of a sudden he behaved so warmly, openly, and youthfully, with such youthful inexperience, and it was all so fine, like you . . . And the way he repeated that German verse, it was just like you! But I must fly, I must fly! Alexey Fyodorovitch, make haste to carry out her commission, and then make haste back. Lise, do you want anything now? For mercy's sake, don't keep Alexey Fyodorovitch a minute. He will come back to you at once.'

Madame Hohlakov at last ran off. Before leaving, Alyosha would have opened the door to see Lise.

'On no account,' cried Lise. 'On no account now. Speak through the door. How have you come to be an angel? That's the only thing I want to know.'

'For an awful piece of stupidity, Lise! Goodbye!'

'Don't dare to go away like that!' Lise was beginning.

'Lise, I have a real sorrow! I'll be back directly, but I have a great, great sorrow!' And he ran out of the room.

5

He certainly was really grieved in a way he had seldom been before. He had rushed in like a fool, and meddled in what? In a love affair. 'But what do I know about it? What can I tell about such things?' he repeated to himself for the hundredth time, flushing crimson. 'Oh, being ashamed would be nothing; shame is only the punishment I deserve. The trouble is I shall certainly have caused more unhappiness . . . And Father Zossima sent me to reconcile and bring them together. Is this the way to bring them together?' Then he suddenly remembered how he had tried to join their hands, and he felt fearfully ashamed again. 'Though I acted quite sincerely, I must be more sensible in the future,' he concluded suddenly, and did not even smile at his conclusion.

Katerina Ivanovna's commission took him to Lake Street, and his brother Dmitri lived close by, in a turning out of Lake Street. Alyosha decided to go to him in any case before going to the captain, though he had a presentiment that he would not find his brother. He suspected that he would intentionally keep out of his way now, but he must find him anyhow. Time was passing: the thought of his dying elder had not left Alyosha for one minute from the time he set off from the monastery.

There was one point which interested him particularly about Katerina Ivanovna's commission; when she had mentioned the captain's son, the little schoolboy who had run beside his father crying, the idea had at once struck Alyosha that this must be the schoolboy who had bitten his finger when he, Alyosha, asked him what he had done to hurt him. Now Alyosha felt practically certain of this, though he could not have said why. Thinking of another subject was a relief, and he resolved to think no more about the 'mischief' he had done, and not to torture himself with remorse, but to do what he had to do, let come what would. At that thought he was completely comforted. Turning to the street where Dmitri lodged, he felt hungry, and taking out of his pocket the roll he had brought from his father's, he ate it. It made him feel stronger.

Dmitri was not at home. The people of the house, an old cabinetmaker, his son, and his old wife, looked with positive suspicion at Alyosha. 'He hasn't slept here for the last three nights. Maybe he has gone away,' the old man said in answer to Alyosha's persistent enquiries. Alyosha saw that he was answering in accordance with instructions. When he asked whether he were not at Grushenka's or in hiding at Foma's (Alyosha spoke so freely on purpose), all three looked at him in alarm. 'They are fond of him, they are doing their best for him,' thought Alyosha. 'That's good.'

At last he found the house in Lake Street. It was a decrepit little house, sunk on one side, with three windows looking into the street, and with a muddy yard, in the middle of which stood a solitary cow. He crossed the yard and found the door opening into the passage. On the left of the passage lived the old woman of the house with her old daughter. Both seemed to be deaf. In answer to his repeated enquiry for the captain, one of them at last understood that he was asking for their lodgers, and pointed to a door across the passage. The captain's lodging turned out to be a simple cottage room. Alyosha had his hand on the iron latch to open the door, when he was struck by the strange hush within. Yet he knew from Katerina Ivanovna's words that the man had a family. 'Either they are all asleep or perhaps they have heard me coming and are waiting for me to open the door. I'd better knock first,' and he knocked. An answer came, but not at once, after an interval of perhaps ten seconds.

'Who's there?' shouted someone in a loud and very angry voice.

Then Alyosha opened the door and crossed the threshold. He found himself in a regular peasant's room. Though it was large, it was crowded with domestic belongings of every kind, and there were several people in it. On the left was a large Russian stove. From the stove to the window near by a string was strung across the room, and on it hung a number of rags. There was a bedstead against the wall on each side, right and left, covered with knitted quilts. On the one on the left was a pyramid of four print-covered pillows, each smaller than the one beneath. On the other there was only one very small pillow. The opposite corner was screened off by a curtain or a sheet hung on a string. Behind this curtain could be seen a bed made up on a bench and a chair. The rough square table of plain wood had been moved to the middle window. The three windows, which consisted each of four tiny greenish murky panes, gave little light, and were close shut, so that the room was not very light and rather stuffy. On the table was a frying-pan with the remains of some fried eggs, a half-eaten piece of bread, and a small bottle with a few drops of vodka.

A woman of genteel appearance, wearing a cotton gown, was sitting on a chair by the bed on the left. Her face was thin and yellow, and her sunken cheeks betrayed at the first glance that she was ill. But what struck Alyosha most was the expression in the poor woman's eyes – a look of surprised enquiry and yet of haughty pride. And while he was talking to her husband, her big brown eyes moved from one speaker to the other with the same haughty and questioning expression. Beside her at the window stood a young girl, rather homely, with scanty reddish hair, poorly but very neatly dressed. She looked disdainfully at Alyosha as he came in. Beside the other bed sat another female figure. She was a very sad sight, a young girl of about twenty, but hunchbacked and crippled 'with withered legs', as Alyosha was told afterwards. Her crutches stood in the corner close by. The strikingly beautiful and gentle eyes of this poor girl looked with mild serenity at Alyosha. A man of about forty-five was sitting at the table, finishing the fried eggs. He was sparse, small and weakly built. He had reddish hair and a scanty light-coloured beard, like a handful of hay (this comparison and the phrase 'a handful of hay' flashed at once into Alyosha's mind for some reason, as he remembered afterwards). It was obviously this gentleman who had shouted to him, as there was no other man in the room. But when Alyosha went in, he jumped up from the bench on which he was sitting, and, hastily wiping his mouth with a ragged napkin, darted up to Alyosha.

'It's a monk come to beg for the monastery. A nice place to come to!' the girl standing in the left corner said aloud. The man spun round instantly towards her and answered her in an excited and breaking voice. 'No, Varvara, you are wrong. Allow me to ask,' he turned again to Alyosha, 'what has brought you to – our retreat?'

Alyosha looked attentively at him. It was the first time he had seen him. There was something angular, flurried and irritable about him. Though he had obviously just been drinking, he was not drunk. There was extraordinary impudence in his expression, and yet, strange to say, at the same time there was fear. He looked like a man who had long been kept in subjection and had submitted to it, and now had suddenly turned and was trying to assert himself. Or, perhaps even more, like a man who wants dreadfully to hit you but is horribly afraid you will hit him. In his words and in the intonation of his shrill voice there was a sort of crazy humour, at times spiteful and at times cringing, and continually shifting from one tone to another. The question about 'our retreat' he had asked as it were quivering all over, rolling his eyes, and skipping up so close to Alyosha that he instinctively drew back a step. He was dressed in a very shabby dark cotton coat, patched and spotted. He wore checked trousers of an extremely light colour, long out of fashion, and of very thin material. They were so crumpled and so short that he looked as though he had grown out of them like a boy.

'I am Alexey Karamazov,' Alyosha began in reply.

'I quite understand that, sir,' the gentleman snapped out at once to assure him that he knew who he was already. 'I am Captain Snegiryov, sir, but I am still desirous to know precisely what has led you – '

'Oh, I've come for nothing special. I wanted to have a word with you – if only you allow me.'

'In that case, here is a chair, sir; kindly be seated. That's what they used to say in the old comedies, "kindly be seated",' and with a rapid gesture he seized an empty chair (it was a rough wooden chair, not upholstered) and set it for him almost in the middle of the room; then, taking another similar chair for himself, he sat down facing Alyosha, so close to him that their knees almost touched.

'Nikolay Ilyitch Snegiryov, sir, formerly a captain in the Russian infantry, put to shame for his vices, but still a captain. Though I might not be one now for the way I talk; for the last half of my life I've learned to say "sir". It's a word you use when you've come down in the world.'

'That's very true,' smiled Alyosha. 'But is it used involuntarily or on purpose?'

'As God's above, it's involuntary, and I was never accustomed to use it! I didn't use the word "sir" all my life, but as soon as I sank into low water I began to say "sir". It's the will of a higher power. I see you are interested in our affairs, but how can I have excited your curiosity, living as I do in surroundings impossible for the exercise of hospitality?'

'I've come – about that business.'

'About what business?' the captain interrupted impatiently.

'About your meeting with my brother Dmitri Fyodorovitch,' Alyosha blurted out awkwardly.

'What meeting, sir? You don't mean that meeting? About my "handful of hay", then?' He moved closer so that his knees positively knocked against Alyosha. His lips were strangely compressed.

'What handful of hay?' muttered Alyosha.

'He has come to complain of me, Father!' cried a voice familiar to Alyosha – the voice of the schoolboy – from behind the curtain. 'I bit his finger a while back.' The curtain was drawn back, and Alyosha saw his assailant lying on a little bed made up on the bench and the chair in the corner under the icons. The boy lay covered with his coat and an old wadded quilt. He was evidently sick, and, judging by his glittering eyes, he was feverish. He looked at Alyosha without fear, as though he felt he was at home and could not be touched.

'What! Did he bite your finger?' The captain jumped up from his chair. 'Was it your finger he bit?'

'Yes. He was throwing stones at other schoolboys. There were six of them against him alone, I went up to him, and he threw a stone at me and then another at my head. I asked him what I had done to him. And then he rushed at me and bit my finger badly, I don't know why.'

'I'll thrash him, sir, at once – this minute!' The captain jumped up from his seat.

'But I am not complaining at all, I am simply telling you . . . I don't want him to be thrashed. Besides, he seems to be ill.'

'And do you suppose I'd thrash him? That I'd take my Iliusha and thrash him before you for your satisfaction? Would you like it done at once, sir?' said the captain, suddenly turning to Alyosha, as though he were going to attack him. 'I am sorry about your finger, sir; but instead of thrashing Iliusha, would you like me to chop off my four fingers with this knife here before your eyes to satisfy your just wrath? I should think four fingers would be enough to satisfy your thirst for vengeance. You won't ask for the fifth one too?' He stopped short with a catch in his throat. Every feature in his face was twitching and working; he looked extremely defiant. He was in a sort of frenzy.

'I think I understand it all now,' said Alyosha gently and sorrowfully, still keeping his seat. 'So your boy is a good boy, he loves his father, and he attacked me as the brother of your assailant . . . Now I understand it,' he repeated thoughtfully. 'But my brother Dmitri Fyodorovitch regrets his action, I know that, and if only it is possible for him to come to you, or better still, to meet you in that same place, he will ask your forgiveness before everyone – if you wish it.'

'After pulling out my beard, you mean, he will ask my forgiveness? And he thinks that will be a satisfactory finish, does he?'

'Oh, no! On the contrary, he will do anything you like and in any way you like.'

'So if I were to ask his highness to go down on his knees before me in that very tavern – the Metropolis it's called – or in the market place, he would do it?'

'Yes, he would even go down on his knees.'

'You've touched me to the heart, sir. Moved me to tears and touched me to the heart! I am only too sensible of your brother's generosity. Allow me to introduce my family, my two daughters and my son – my litter. If I die, who will care for them, and while I live who but they will care for a wretch like me? That's a great thing the Lord has ordained for every man of my sort, sir. For there must be someone who can love even a man like me.'

'Ah, that's perfectly true!' exclaimed Alyosha.

'Oh, do stop playing the fool! Some idiot comes in, and you put us to shame!' cried the girl by the window, suddenly turning to her father with a disdainful and contemptuous air.

'Wait a little, Varvara!' cried her father, speaking peremptorily but looking at her quite approvingly. 'That's her character,' he said, addressing Alyosha again.

'And in all nature there was nought
That could find favour in his eyes

or rather in the feminine: that could find favour in *her* eyes. But now let me present you to my wife, Arina Petrovna. She is crippled, she is forty-three; she can move, but very little. She is of humble origin. Arina Petrovna, compose your countenance. This is Alexey Fyodorovitch Karamazov. Get up, Alexey Fyodorovitch.' He took him by the hand and with unexpected force pulled him up. 'You must stand up to be introduced to a lady. It's not the Karamazov, mamma, who . . . h'm . . . etcetera, but his brother, radiant with modest virtues. Come, Arina Petrovna, come, mamma, first your hand to be kissed.'

And he kissed his wife's hand respectfully and even tenderly. The girl at the window turned her back indignantly on the scene; an expression of extraordinary gentleness lighted up the haughtily questioning face of the woman.

'How do you do! Sit down, Mr Tchernomazov,' she said.

'Karamazov, mamma, Karamazov (we are of humble origin),' he whispered again.

'Well, Karamazov, or whatever it is, but I always think of Tchernomazov . . . Sit down. Why did he make you get up? He calls me crippled but I am not, only my legs are swollen like tubs, and I am shrivelled up myself. Once I used to be so fat, but now it's as though I had swallowed a poker.'

'We are of humble origin,' the captain muttered again.

'Oh, Father, Father!' the hunchbacked girl, who had till then sat silent, said suddenly, and she hid her eyes with her handkerchief.

'Clown!' blurted out the girl at the window.

'Have you heard our news?' said the mother, pointing at her daughters. 'It's like clouds coming over; the clouds pass and we have music again. When we were with the army, we used to have many such guests. I don't mean to make any comparisons; everyone to his taste. The deacon's wife used to come then and say, "Alexander Alexandrovitch is a man of the noblest heart, but Nastasya Petrovna," he would say, "is of the brood of hell." "Well," I said, "that's a matter of taste; you may be a small lump, but you stink mighty strong." "And you want keeping in your place," says she. "You dirty thing," said I, "who asked you to teach me?" "But my breath," says she, "is clean, and yours is unclean." "You ask all the officers whether my breath is unclean." And ever since then I had it in my mind. Not long ago I was sitting here as I am now, when I saw that very general come in who came here for Easter, and I asked him: "Your Excellency," said I, "can a lady's breath be unpleasant?" "Yes," he answered; "you ought to open a windowpane or open the door, for the air is not fresh here." And they all go on like that! And what is my breath to them? The dead smell worse still! "I won't spoil the air," said I, "I'll get myself some shoes and go away." My darlings, don't blame your own mother! Nikolay Ilyitch, how is it I can't please you? There's only Iliusha who comes home from school and loves me. Yesterday he brought me an apple. Forgive your own mother – forgive a poor lonely creature! Why has my breath become unpleasant to you?'

And the poor mad woman broke into sobs, and tears streamed down her cheeks. The captain rushed up to her.

'Mamma, mamma, my dear, don't be so silly! You are not lonely. Everyone loves you, everyone adores you.' He began kissing both her hands again and tenderly stroking her face; taking up the dinner napkin, he began wiping away her tears. Alyosha fancied that he too had tears in his eyes. 'There, you see, you hear?' he turned with a sort of fury to Alyosha, pointing to the poor imbecile.

'I see and hear,' muttered Alyosha.

'Father, Father, how can you – with him! Don't talk to him!' cried the boy, sitting up in his bed and gazing at his father with burning eyes.

'Stop your fooling, stop your silly antics which never lead to anything!' shouted Varvara, stamping her foot with passion.

'Your anger is quite just this time, Varvara, and I'll make haste to satisfy you. Come, put on your cap, Alexey Fyodorovitch, and I'll put on mine. We will go out. I have a word to say to you in earnest, but not within these walls. This girl sitting here is my daughter Nina; I forgot to introduce her to you. She is an angel from heaven . . . who has flown down to us mortals . . . if you can understand.'

'There he is shaking all over, as though he is in convulsions!' Varvara went on indignantly.

'And the one over there stamping her foot at me and calling me a fool, she is another angel from heaven, and she has good reason to call me names. Come along, Alexey Fyodorovitch, we must finish this.'

And seizing Alyosha's hand, he drew him out of the room into the street.

6

'The air is fresh, but in my apartment it is not so in any sense of the word. Let us walk slowly, sir. I would be glad of your kind interest.'

'I too have something important to say to you,' observed Alyosha, 'only I don't know how to begin.'

'To be sure you must have business with me. You would never have dropped in to see me without some object. Unless you came simply to complain of the boy, and that's hardly likely. And, by the way, about the boy: I could not explain to you in there, but here I will describe that scene to you. My "hay" was thicker a week ago – I mean my beard. That's the nickname they give to my beard, the schoolboys most of all. Well, your brother Dmitri Fyodorovitch was pulling me by my beard, I'd done nothing, he was in a towering rage and happened to pick on me. He dragged me out of the tavern into the market place; at the very moment the boys were coming out of school, and with them Iliusha. As soon as he saw me in such a state he rushed up to me. "Father," he cried, "Father!" He caught hold of me, grabbed me, tried to pull me away, crying to my assailant, "Let go, let go, it's my father, forgive him!" – yes, he actually cried "forgive him". He clutched at that hand, that very hand, in his little hands and kissed it . . . I remember his little face at that moment. I haven't forgotten it and I never shall!'

'I swear,' cried Alyosha, 'that my brother will express his most deep and sincere regret, even if he has to go down on his knees in the market place . . . I'll make him or he is no brother of mine!'

'Aha, then it's only a suggestion! And it does not come from him but simply from the generosity of your own warm heart. You should have said so. No, in that case allow me to tell you of your brother's highly chivalrous soldierly generosity, for he did give expression to it at the time. He left off pulling at my beard and released me: "You are an officer," he said, "and I am an officer. If you can find a decent man to be your second send me your challenge. I will give you satisfaction, though you are a scoundrel." That's what he said. A chivalrous spirit indeed! I went off with Iliusha, and that scene is a family record imprinted for ever on Iliusha's soul. No, it's not for us to claim the privileges of noblemen. Judge for yourself. You've just been in our mansion, what did you see there? Three ladies, one a cripple and weak-minded, another a cripple and hunchback and the third not crippled but far too clever. She is a student, dying to get back to Petersburg, to work for the emancipation of the Russian woman on the banks of the Neva. I won't speak of Iliusha, he is only nine. I am alone in the world, and if I die, what will become of all of them, I ask you that. And if I challenge your brother and he kills me on the spot, what then? What will become of my family? And worse still, if he doesn't kill me but only cripples me: I couldn't work, but I should still be a mouth to feed. Who would feed it and who would feed them all? Must I take Iliusha from school and send him to beg in the streets? That's what it means for me to challenge your brother to a duel. It's a lot of silly talk and nothing else.'

'He will beg your forgiveness, he will bow down at your feet in the middle of the market place,' cried Alyosha, with shining eyes.

'I did think of prosecuting him,' the captain went on, 'but look in our code, could I get much compensation for a personal injury? And then Agrafena Alexandrovna (Grushenka) sent for me and shouted at me: "Don't dare to dream of it! If you take him to court, I'll tell the world that he beat you for your dishonesty, and then you will be prosecuted." I call God to witness whose was the dishonesty and by whose commands I acted, wasn't it by her own and Fyodor Pavlovitch's? "And what's more," she went on, "I'll dismiss you for good and you'll never earn another penny from me. I'll speak to my merchant too (that's what she calls her old man) and he will dismiss you!" And if he dismisses me, what can I earn then from anyone? Those two are all I have to look to, for your Fyodor Pavlovitch has not only dismissed me, for another reason, but he means to make use of papers I've signed to go to law against me. And so I kept quiet, and you have seen our retreat. But now let me ask you: did Iliusha hurt your finger much? I didn't like to go into it in our mansion before him.'

'Yes, very much, and he was in a great fury. He was avenging you on me as a Karamazov, I see that now. But if only you had seen how he was throwing stones at his schoolfellows! It's very dangerous. They might kill him. They are children and stupid. A stone may be thrown and break somebody's head.'

'That's just what has happened. He has been bruised by a stone today. Not on the head but on the chest, just above the heart. He came home crying and groaning and now he is ill.'

'But you know he attacks them first. He is bitter against them on your account. They say he stabbed a boy called Krassotkin with a penknife not long ago.'

'I've heard about that too, it's dangerous.

Krassotkin's father is an official here, we may hear more about it.'

'I would advise you,' Alyosha went on warmly, 'not to send him to school at all for a time till he is calmer . . . and his anger is passed.'

'Anger!' the captain repeated, 'that's just what it is. He is a little creature, but it's a mighty anger. You don't know all, sir. Let me tell you more. Since that incident all the boys have been teasing him about the "handful of hay". Schoolboys are a merciless race, individually they are angels, but together, especially in schools, they are often merciless. Their teasing has stirred up a gallant spirit in Iliusha. An ordinary boy, a weak son, would have submitted, have felt ashamed of his father, sir, but he stood up for his father against them all. For his father and for truth and justice. What he suffered when he kissed your brother's hand and cried to him "forgive father, forgive him" – that only God knows – and I, his father. For our children – not your children, but ours – the children of the poor gentlemen looked down upon by everyone – know what justice means, sir, even at nine years old. How should the rich know? They don't explore such depths once in their lives. But at that moment in the square when he kissed your brother's hand, at that moment my Iliusha grasped all that justice means. That truth entered into him and bruised him for ever, sir,' the captain said hotly again with a sort of frenzy, and he struck his right fist against his left palm as though he wanted to show how 'the truth' hit Iliusha. 'That very day, sir, he fell ill with fever and was delirious all night. All that day he hardly said a word to me, but I noticed he kept watching me from the corner, though he turned to the window and pretended to be learning his lessons. But I could see his mind was not on his lessons. Next day I got drunk to forget my troubles, sinful man that I am, and I don't remember much. Mamma began crying, too – I am very fond of mamma – well, I spent my last penny drowning my troubles. Don't despise me for that, sir, in Russia men who drink are the best. The best men among us are the greatest drunkards. I lay down and I don't remember about Iliusha, though all that day the boys had been jeering at him at school. "Handful of hay," they shouted, "your father was dragged out of the tavern by his handful of hay, you ran by and begged forgiveness."

'On the third day when he came back from school, I saw he looked pale and wretched. "What is it?" I asked. He wouldn't answer. Well, there's no talking in our mansion without mamma and the girls taking part in it. What's more, the girls had heard about it the very first day. Varvara had begun snarling. "You fools and clowns, can't you ever do anything rational?" "Quite so," I said, "can we ever do anything rational?" That time I got out of it with a joke. In the evening I took the boy out for a walk, for you must know we go for a walk every evening, always the same way, along which we are going now – from our gate to that big stone that lies in the road under the hurdle, and that marks the beginning of the town pasture. A beautiful and lonely spot, sir. Iliusha and I walked along hand in hand as usual. He has a little hand, his fingers are thin and cold – he suffers with his chest, you know. "Father," said he, "Father!" "Well?" said I. I saw his eyes flashing. "Father, how he treated you then!" "It can't be helped, Iliusha," I said. "Don't forgive him, Father, don't forgive him! At school they say that he has paid you ten roubles to forget." "No, Iliusha," said I, "I would not take money from him for anything." Then he began trembling all over, took my hand in both his and kissed it again. "Father," he said, "Father, challenge him to a duel. At school they say you are a coward and won't challenge him, and that you'll accept ten roubles from him." "I can't challenge him to a duel, Iliusha," I answered. And I told briefly what I've just told you. He listened. "Father," he said, "anyway don't forgive it. When I grow up I'll call him out myself and kill him." His eyes shone and glowed. And of course I am his father, and I had to put in a word: "It's a sin to kill," I said, "even in a duel." "Father," he said, "when I grow up, I'll knock him down, knock the sword out of his hand, I'll fall on him, wave my sword over him and say: 'I could kill you, but I forgive you, so there!' " You see what the workings of his little mind have been during these two days; he must have been planning that vengeance all day, and raving about it at night.

'Then he began to come home from school badly beaten. I found out about it the day before yesterday, and you are right, I won't send him to that school any more. I heard that he was standing up against all the class alone and defying them all, with his heart full of resentment, and bitterness – I was alarmed about him. We went for another walk. "Father," he asked, "are the rich people stronger than anyone else on earth?" "Yes, Iliusha," I said, "there are no people on earth stronger than the rich." "Father," he said, "I will get rich, I will become an officer and conquer everybody. The Czar will reward me, I will come back here and then no one will dare." . . . Then he was silent and his lips still kept trembling. "Father," he said, "what a horrid town this is." "Yes, Iliusha," I said, "it isn't a very nice town." "Father, let us move into another town, a nice one," he said, "where people don't know about us." "We will move, we will, Iliusha," said I, "only I must save up for it." I was glad to be able to turn his mind from painful thoughts, and we began to dream of how we would move to another town, how we would buy a horse and cart. "We will put mamma and your sisters inside, we will cover them up and we'll walk, you shall have a lift now and then, and I'll walk beside, for we must take care of our horse, we can't all ride. That's how we'll go." He was enchanted with the idea, most of all at the thought of having a horse and driving him. For of course, a Russian boy is born among horses. We chatted a long while. Thank God, I thought, I have diverted his mind and comforted him.

'That was the day before yesterday, in the evening, but last night everything was changed. He had gone to school in the morning, he came back depressed, terribly depressed. In the evening I took him by the hand and we went for a walk; he would not talk. There was a wind blowing and no sun, and a feeling of autumn; twilight was coming on. We walked along, both of us depressed. "Well, my boy," said I, "how about our setting off on our travels?" I thought I might bring him back to our talk of the day before. He didn't answer, but I felt his fingers trembling in my hand. Ah, I thought, it's a bad job; there's some new trouble. We had reached the stone where we are now. I sat down on the stone. And in the air there were lots of kites flapping and whirling. There were as many as thirty in sight. Of course, it's just the season for the kites. "Look, Iliusha," said I, "it's time we got out our last year's kite again. I'll mend it. Where have you hidden it?" My boy made no answer. He looked away and turned sideways to me. And then a gust of wind blew up the sand. He suddenly fell on me, threw both his little arms round my neck and held me tight. You know, when children are silent and proud, and try to keep back their tears when they are in great trouble and suddenly break down, their tears fall in streams. With those warm streams of tears, he suddenly wetted my face. He sobbed and shook as though he were in convulsions, and squeezed up against me as I sat on the stone. "Father," he kept crying, "dear Father, how he insulted you!" And I sobbed too. We sat shaking in each other's arms. "Iliusha," I said to him, "Iliusha darling." No one saw us then. God alone saw us, I hope he will record it to my credit. You must thank your brother, Alexey Fyodorovitch. No, sir, I won't thrash my boy for your satisfaction.'

He had gone back to his original tone of resentful clowning. Alyosha felt, though, that he trusted him, and that if there had been someone else in his, Alyosha's place, the man would not have spoken so openly and would not have told what he had just told. This encouraged Alyosha, whose heart was trembling on the verge of tears.

'Ah, how I would like to make friends with your boy!' he cried. 'If you could arrange it – '

'Certainly, sir,' muttered the captain.

'But now listen to something quite different!' Alyosha went on. 'I have a message for you. That same brother of mine, Dmitri, has insulted his betrothed, too, a noble-hearted girl of whom you have probably heard. I have a right to tell you of her trouble; I ought to do so, in fact, for when she heard of the insult done to you and learned all about your unfortunate position, she commissioned me at once – just now – to bring you this help from her – but only from her alone, not from

Dmitri, who has abandoned her. Nor from me, his brother, nor from anyone else, but from her, only from her! She entreats you to accept her help . . . You have both been insulted by the same man. She thought of you only when she had just received a similar insult from him – similar in its cruelty, I mean. She comes like a sister to help a brother in misfortune . . . She told me to persuade you to take these two hundred roubles from her, as from a sister, knowing that you are in such need. No one will know of it, it can give rise to no unjust slander. Here are the two hundred roubles, and I swear you must take them unless – unless all men are to be enemies on earth! But there are brothers even on earth . . . You have a generous heart . . . you must see that, you must,' and Alyosha held out two new rainbow-coloured hundred-rouble notes.

They were both standing at the time by the great stone close to the fence, and there was no one near. The notes seemed to produce a tremendous impression on the captain. He started, but at first only from astonishment. Such an outcome of their conversation was the last thing he expected. Nothing could have been farther from his dreams than help from anyone – and such a sum!

He took the notes, and for a minute he was almost unable to answer, quite a new expression came into his face.

'That for me? So much money – two hundred roubles! Good heavens! Why, I haven't seen so much money for the last four years! Mercy on us! And she says she is a sister . . . And is that the truth?'

'I swear that all I told you is the truth,' cried Alyosha.

The captain flushed red.

'Listen, my dear, listen. If I take it, I shan't be behaving like a scoundrel? In your eyes, Alexey Fyodorovitch, I shan't be a scoundrel? No, Alexey Fyodorovitch, listen, listen,' he hurried, touching Alyosha with both his hands. 'You are persuading me to take it, saying that it's a sister sends it, but inwardly, in your heart won't you feel contempt for me if I take it, eh?'

'No, no, on my salvation I swear I shan't! And no one will ever know but me – I, you and she, and one other lady, her great friend.'

'Never mind the lady! Listen, Alexey Fyodorovitch, at a moment like this you must listen, for you can't understand what these two hundred roubles mean to me now.' The poor fellow was talking himself gradually into a sort of incoherent, almost wild enthusiasm. He was thrown off his balance and talked extremely fast, as though afraid he would not be allowed to say all he had to say.

'Besides it's being honestly acquired from a "sister", so highly respected and revered, do you know that now I can look after mamma and Nina, my hunchback angel daughter? Dr Herzenstube came to me in the kindness of his heart and examined them both for a whole hour. "I can make nothing of it," said he, but he prescribed a mineral water which is sold at a chemist's here. He said it would be sure to do her good, and he ordered baths, too, with some medicine in them. The mineral water costs thirty kopecks, and she'd need to drink forty bottles perhaps; so I took the prescription and laid it on the shelf under the icons, and there it lies. And he ordered hot baths for Nina with something dissolved in them, morning and evening. But how can we carry out such a cure in our mansion, without servants, without help, without a bath, and without water? Nina is rheumatic all over, I don't think I told you that. All her right side aches at night, she is in agony, and, would you believe it, the angel bears it without groaning for fear of waking us. We eat what we can get, and she'll only take the leavings, what you'd scarcely give to a dog. "I am not worth it, I am taking it from you, I am a burden on you," that's what her angel eyes try to express. We wait on her, but she doesn't like it. "I am a useless cripple, no good to anyone." As though she were not worth it, when she is the saving of all of us with her angelic sweetness. Without her, without her gentle words, our life would be hell! She softens even Varvara. And don't judge Varvara harshly either, she is an angel too, she too has suffered wrong. She came to us for the summer, and she brought sixteen roubles she had earned by lessons and saved up, to go back with to Petersburg in September, that is now. But we took her money and lived on it, so now she has no money to go back. Though indeed she couldn't go back, for she has to work for us like a slave. She is like an overdriven horse with all of us on her back. She waits on us all, mends and washes, sweeps the floor, puts mamma to bed. And mamma is capricious and tearful and insane! And now I can get a servant with this money, you understand, Alexey Fyodorovitch, I can get medicines for the dear creatures, I can send my student to Petersburg, I can buy beef, I can feed them properly. Good Lord, but it's a dream!'

Alyosha was delighted that he had brought him such happiness and that the poor fellow had consented to be made happy.

'Wait, Alexey Fyodorovitch, wait,' the captain began

to talk with frenzied rapidity carried away by a new daydream. 'Do you know that Iliusha and I will perhaps really carry out our dream. We will buy a horse and cart, a black horse, he insists on its being black, and we will set off as we pretended the other day. I have an old friend, a lawyer in K. province, and I heard through a trustworthy man that if I were to go he'd give me a place as clerk in his office, and who knows, maybe he would. So I'd just put mamma and Nina in the cart, and Iliusha could drive, and I'd walk, I'd walk . . . Why, if I only succeed in getting one debt paid that's owing me, I should have perhaps enough for that too!'

'There would be enough!' cried Alyosha. 'Katerina Ivanovna will send you as much more as you need, and you know, I have money too, take what you want, as you would from a brother, from a friend, you can give it back later . . . (You'll get rich, you'll get rich!) And you know you couldn't have a better idea than to move to another province! It would be the saving of you, especially of your boy – and you ought to go quickly, before the winter, before the cold. You must write to us when you are there, and we will always be brothers . . . No, it's not a dream!'

Alyosha could have hugged him, he was so pleased. But glancing at him he stopped short. The man was standing with his neck outstretched and his lips protruding, with a pale and frenzied face. His lips were moving as though trying to articulate something; no sound came, but still his lips moved. It was uncanny.

'What is it?' asked Alyosha, startled.

'Alexey Fyodorovitch . . . I . . . you,' muttered the captain, faltering, looking at him with a strange, wild, fixed stare, and an air of desperate resolution. At the same time there was a sort of grin on his lips. 'I . . . you, sir . . . wouldn't you like me to show you a little trick I know?' he murmured, suddenly, in a firm rapid whisper, his voice no longer faltering.

'What trick?'

'A pretty trick,' whispered the captain. His mouth was twisted on the left side, his left eye was screwed up. He still stared at Alyosha.

'What is the matter, what trick?' Alyosha cried, now thoroughly alarmed.

'Why, look,' squealed the captain suddenly, and showing him the two notes which he had been holding by one corner between his thumb and forefinger during the conversation, he crumpled them up savagely and squeezed them tight in his right hand. 'Do you see, do you see?' he shrieked, pale and infuriated. And suddenly flinging up his hand, he threw the crumpled notes on the sand. 'Do you see?' he shrieked again, pointing to them. 'Look there!'

And with wild fury he began trampling them under his heel, gasping and exclaiming as he did so: 'So much for your money! So much for your money! So much for your money! So much for your money!'

Suddenly he darted back and drew himself up before Alyosha, and his whole figure expressed unutterable pride.

'Tell those who sent you that the handful of hay does not sell his honour,' he cried, raising his arm in the air. Then he turned quickly and began to run; but he had not run five steps before he turned completely round and kissed his hand to Alyosha. He ran another five paces and then turned round for the last time. This time his face was not contorted with laughter, but quivering all over with tears. In a tearful, faltering, sobbing voice he cried: 'What should I say to my boy if I took money from you for our shame?'

And then he ran on without turning. Alyosha looked after him, inexpressibly grieved. Oh, he saw that till the very last moment the man had not known he would crumple up and fling away the notes. He did not turn back. Alyosha knew he would not. He would not follow him and call him back, he knew why. When he was out of sight, Alyosha picked up the two notes. They were very much crushed and crumpled, and had been pressed into the sand, but were uninjured and even rustled like new ones when Alyosha unfolded them and smoothed them out. After smoothing them out, he folded them up, put them in his pocket and went to Katerina Ivanovna to report on the results of her commission.

Book Five

I

Madame Hohlakov was again the first to meet Alyosha. She was flustered; something important had happened. Katerina Ivanovna's hysterics had ended in a fainting fit, and then 'a terrible, awful weakness had followed, she lay with her eyes turned up and was delirious. Now she was running a temperature. They had sent for Herzenstube; they had sent for the aunts. The aunts were already here, but Herzenstube had not yet come. They were all sitting in her room, waiting. She was unconscious now, and what if it turned to brain fever!'

Madame Hohlakov looked gravely alarmed. 'This is serious, serious,' she added at every word, as though nothing that had happened to her before had been serious. Alyosha listened with distress, and was beginning to describe his adventures, but she interrupted him at the first words. She had not time to listen. She begged him to sit with Lise and wait for her there.

'Lise,' she whispered almost in his ear, 'Lise has greatly surprised me just now, dear Alexey Fyodorovitch. She touched me, too, and so my heart forgives her everything. Only fancy, as soon as you had gone, she began to be truly remorseful for having laughed at you today and yesterday, though she was not laughing at you, but only joking. But she was seriously sorry for it, almost ready to cry, so that I was quite surprised. She has never been really sorry for laughing at me, but has only made a joke of it. And you know she jeers at me every minute. But this time she was in earnest. She thinks a great deal of your opinion, Alexey Fyodorovitch, and don't take offence or be wounded by her if you can help it. I am never severe with her, for she's such a clever little thing – would you believe it? She said just now that you were a friend of her childhood, "the greatest friend of her childhood" – just think of that – "greatest friend" – and what about me? She has very strong feelings and memories, and, what's more, she uses these phrases, most unexpected words, which come out all of a sudden when you least expect them. She spoke the other day about a pine tree, for instance: there used to be a pine tree in our garden in her early childhood. Very likely it's standing there still; so there's no need to speak in the past tense. Pine trees are not like people, Alexey Fyodorovitch, they don't change quickly. "Mamma," she said, "I remember this pine tree as in a dream," only she said something so original about it that I can't repeat it. Besides, I've forgotten it. Well, goodbye! I am so worried I feel I shall go out of my mind. Ah! Alexey Fyodorovitch, I've been out of my mind twice in my life. Go to Lise, cheer her up, as you always can so charmingly. Lise,' she cried, going to her door, 'here I've brought you Alexey Fyodorovitch, whom you insulted so. He is not at all angry, I assure you; on the contrary, he is surprised that you could even think he was angry.'

'Thank you, mamma. Come in, Alexey Fyodorovitch.'

Alyosha went in. Lise looked rather embarrassed, and at once flushed crimson. She was evidently ashamed of something, and, as people do in such cases, she began immediately talking of other things, as though they were of absorbing interest to her at the moment.

'Mamma has just told me all about the two hundred roubles, Alexey Fyodorovitch, and your taking them to that poor officer . . . and she told me all the awful story of how he had been insulted . . . and you know, although Mamma muddles things – she always rushes from one thing to another – I cried when I heard. Well, did you give him the money; how is that poor man getting on?'

'The fact is I didn't give it to him, and it's a long story,' answered Alyosha, as though he too could think of nothing but his regret at having failed, yet Lise saw perfectly well that he too looked away, and that he too was trying to talk of other things.

Alyosha sat down by the table and began to tell his story, but at the first words he lost his embarrassment and gained the whole of Lise's attention as well. He spoke with deep feeling, under the influence of the strong emotion he had just experienced, and he succeeded in telling his story well and circumstantially. In the old days in Moscow he had been fond of coming to Lise and describing to her what had just happened to him, what he had read, or what he remembered of his childhood. Sometimes they had made daydreams and woven whole romances together – generally cheerful and amusing ones. Now they both felt suddenly transported to the past in Moscow, two years before. Lise was extremely touched by his story. Alyosha described Iliusha with warm feelings. When he finished describing how the luckless man trampled on the money, Lise could not help clasping her hands and crying out: 'So you didn't give him the money! So you let him run away! Oh, dear, you ought to have run after him!'

'No, Lise; it's better I didn't run after him,' said Alyosha, getting up from his chair and walking thoughtfully across the room.

'How so? How is it better? Now they are without food and their situation is hopeless.'

'Not hopeless, for the two hundred roubles will still come to them. He'll take the money tomorrow. Tomorrow he will be sure to take it,' said Alyosha, pacing up and down, pondering. 'You see, Lise,' he went on, stopping suddenly before her, 'I made one blunder, but that, even that, is all for the best.'

'What blunder, and why is it for the best?'

'I'll tell you. He is a man of weak and timorous character; he has suffered so much and yet is very good-natured. I keep wondering why he took offence so suddenly, for I assure you, up to the last minute, he did not know that he was going to trample on the notes. And I think now that there was a great deal to offend him . . . and it could not have been otherwise in his position . . . To begin with, he was sore at having been so glad of the money in my presence and not having concealed his joy from me. If he had been pleased, but not so much; if he had not shown it; if he had begun affecting scruples and difficulties, as other people do when they take money, he might still have taken it. But he was too genuinely delighted, and that was mortifying. Ah, Lise, he is a good and truthful man – that's the worst of the whole business. All the while he talked, his voice was so weak, so broken, he talked so fast, so fast, he kept laughing such a laugh, or perhaps he was crying – yes, I am sure he was crying, he was so delighted – and he talked about his daughters – and about the job he could get in another town . . . And when he had poured out his heart, he felt ashamed at having bared his inmost soul to me like that. So he began to hate me at once. He is one of those terribly sensitive poor people. What made him feel most ashamed was that he gave in too soon and accepted me as a friend, you see. At first he almost flew at me and tried to intimidate me, but as soon as he saw the money he began embracing me; he kept touching me with his hands. This must have been why he came to feel so humiliated and then I made a blunder, a very important one. I suddenly said to him that if he had not money enough to move to another town, we would give it to him, and, indeed, I myself would give him as much as he wanted out of my own money. That struck him all at once. Why, he thought, did I put myself forward to help him? You know, Lise, it's awfully hard for a man who has been injured, when other people suddenly behave as though they were his benefactors . . . I've heard that; Father Zossima told me so. I don't know how to put it, but I have often seen it myself. And I feel like that myself too. And the worst of it was that though he did not know, up to the very last minute, that he would trample on the notes, he had a kind of presentiment of it, I am sure of that. That's just what made him so ecstatic, that he had that presentiment . . . And though it's so dreadful, it's all for the best. In fact, I believe nothing better could have happened.'

'Why, why could nothing better have happened?' cried Lise, looking with great surprise at Alyosha.

'Because if he had taken the money, in an hour after getting home, he would be crying with mortification, that's just what would have happened. And most likely he would have come to me early tomorrow, and perhaps have flung the notes at me and trampled upon them as he did just now. But now he has gone home very proud and triumphant, though he knows he has "ruined himself". So now nothing could be easier than to make him accept the two hundred roubles by tomorrow, for he has already vindicated his honour, tossed away the money, and trampled it under foot . . . He couldn't know when he did it that I should bring it to him again tomorrow, and yet he is in terrible need of that money. Though he is proud of himself now, yet even today he'll be thinking what a help he has lost. He will think of it more than ever at night, will dream of it, and by tomorrow morning he may be ready to run to me to ask forgiveness. It's just then that I'll appear. "Here, you are a proud man," I shall say: "you have proved it; but now take the money and forgive us!" And then he will take it!' Alyosha was carried away with joy as he uttered the last words. Lise clapped her hands.

'Ah, that's true! I understand that perfectly now. Ah, Alyosha, how do you know all this? So young and yet you know what's in the heart . . . I should never have worked it out.'

'The great thing now is to persuade him that he is on an equal footing with us, in spite of his taking money from us,' Alyosha went on in his excitement, 'and not only on an equal, but even on a higher footing.'

'On a higher footing is charming, Alexey Fyodorovitch; but go on, go on!'

'You mean there isn't such an expression as "on a higher footing"; but that doesn't matter because – '

'Oh, no, of course it doesn't matter. Forgive me, Alyosha, dear . . . You know, I scarcely respected you till now – that is I respected you but on an equal footing; but now I shall begin to respect you on a higher footing. Don't be angry, dear, at my joking,' she put in at once, with strong feeling. 'I am absurd and small, but you, you! Listen, Alexey Fyodorovitch. Isn't there in all our analysis – I mean your analysis . . . no, better call it ours – aren't we showing contempt for him, for that poor man – in analysing his soul like this, as it were, from above, eh? In deciding so certainly that he will take the money?'

'No, Lise, it's not contempt,' Alyosha answered, as though he had prepared himself for the question. 'I was thinking of that on the way here. How can it be contempt when we are all like him, when we are all just the same as he is. For you know we are just the same, no better. If we are better, we should have been just the same in his place . . . I don't know about you, Lise, but I consider that I have a sordid soul in many ways, and his soul is not sordid; on the contrary, full of fine feeling . . . No, Lise, I have no contempt for him. Do you know, Lise, my elder told me once to care for most people exactly as one would for children, and for some of them as one would for the sick in hospitals.'

'Ah, Alexey Fyodorovitch, dear, let us care for people as we would for the sick!'

'Let us, Lise; I am ready. Though I am not altogether ready in myself. I am sometimes very impatient and at other times I don't see things. It's different with you.'

'Ah, I don't believe it! Alexey Fyodorovitch, how happy I am.'

'I am so glad to hear you say that, Lise.'

'Alexey Fyodorovitch, you are wonderfully good, but you are sometimes rather formal . . . And yet you are not a bit formal really. Go to the door, open it gently, and see whether mamma is listening,' said Lise, in a nervous, hurried whisper.

Alyosha went, opened the door, and reported that no one was listening.

'Come here, Alexey Fyodorovitch,' Lise went on, flushing redder and redder. 'Give me your hand – that's right. I have to make a great confession, I didn't write to you yesterday in joke, but in earnest,' and she hid her eyes with her hand. It was evident that she was greatly ashamed of the confession.

Suddenly she snatched his hand and impulsively kissed it three times.

'Ah, Lise, I am so happy!' cried Alyosha joyfully. 'You know, I was perfectly sure you were in earnest.'

'Sure? Upon my word!' She put aside his hand, but did not leave go of it, blushing hotly, and laughing a little happy laugh. 'I kiss his hand and he says, "I am so happy." '

But her reproach was undeserved; Alyosha, too, was greatly overcome.

'I should like to please you always, Lise, but I don't know how to do it,' he muttered, blushing too.

'Alyosha, dear, you are cold and rude. Do you see? He has chosen me as his wife and is quite settled about it. He is sure I was in earnest. What a thing to say! Why, that's impertinence – that's what it is.'

'Why, was it wrong of me to feel sure?' Alyosha asked, laughing suddenly.

'Ah, Alyosha, on the contrary, it was delightfully right,' cried Lise, looking tenderly and happily at him.

Alyosha stood still, holding her hand in his. Suddenly he stooped down and kissed her on her lips.

'Oh, what are you doing?' cried Lise. Alyosha was terribly abashed.

'Oh, forgive me if I shouldn't . . . Perhaps I'm awfully

stupid . . . You said I was cold, so I kissed you . . . But I see it was stupid.'

Lise laughed, and hid her face in her hands. 'And in that monk's garment!' she ejaculated in the midst of her mirth. But she suddenly ceased laughing and became serious, almost stern.

'Alyosha, we must put off kissing. We are not ready for that yet, and we shall have a long time to wait,' she ended suddenly. 'Tell me rather why you who are so clever, so intellectual, so observant, choose a little idiot, an invalid like me? Ah, Alyosha, I am awfully happy, for I don't deserve you a bit.'

'You do, Lise. I shall be leaving the monastery altogether in a few days. If I go into the world, I must marry. I know that. *He* told me to marry, too. Whom could I marry better than you – and who would have me except you? I have been thinking it over. In the first place, you've known me from a child and you've a great many qualities I haven't. You are more light-hearted than I am; above all, you are more innocent than I am. I have been brought into contact with many, many things already . . . Ah, you don't know, but I too am a Karamazov. What does it matter if you do laugh and make jokes, and at me too? Go on laughing. I am so glad you do. You laugh like a little child, but you think like a martyr.'

'Like a martyr? How?'

'Yes, Lise, your question just now: whether we weren't showing contempt for that poor man by dissecting his soul – that was the question of a sufferer . . . You see, I don't know how to express it, but anyone who thinks of such questions is capable of suffering. Sitting in your invalid chair you must have thought over many things already.'

'Alyosha, give me your hand. Don't take it away,' murmured Lise in a failing voice, weak with happiness. 'Listen, Alyosha. What will you wear when you come out of the monastery? What sort of suit? Don't laugh, don't be angry, it's very, very important to me.'

'I haven't thought about the suit, Lise; but I'll wear whatever you like.'

'I should like you to have a dark blue velvet coat, a white piqué waistcoat, and a soft grey felt hat . . . Tell me, did you believe that I didn't care for you when I said I didn't mean what I wrote?'

'No, I didn't believe it.'

'Oh, you odious creature, you are incorrigible.'

'You see, I knew that you – seemed to care for me, but I pretended to believe that you didn't care for me to make it – easier for you.'

'That makes it worse! Worse and better than all! Alyosha, I am awfully fond of you. Just before you came this morning, I made a wish. I decided I would ask you for my letter, and if you brought it out calmly and gave it to me (as might have been expected from you) it would mean that you did not love me at all, that you felt nothing, and were simply a stupid boy, good for nothing, and that I had ruined my reputation. But you left the letter at home and that cheered me. You left it behind on purpose, so as not to give it back, because you knew I would ask for it? That was it, wasn't it?'

'Ah, Lise, it was not so a bit. The letter is with me now, and it was this morning, in this pocket. Here it is.' Alyosha pulled the letter out laughing, and showed it to her at a distance.

'But I am not going to give it to you. Look at it from here.'

'Why, then you told a lie? You, a monk, told a lie!'

'I told a lie if you like,' Alyosha laughed, too. 'I told a lie so as not to give you back the letter. It's very precious to me,' he added suddenly, with strong feeling, and again he flushed. 'It always will be, and I won't give it up to anyone!'

Lise looked at him joyfully. 'Alyosha,' she murmured again, 'look at the door. Isn't mamma listening?'

'Very well, Lise, I'll look; but wouldn't it be better not to look? Why suspect your mother of such meanness?'

'What meanness? As for her spying on her daughter, it's her right, it's not meanness!' cried Lise, firing up. 'You may be sure, Alexey Fyodorovitch, that when I am a mother, if I have a daughter like myself I shall certainly spy on her!'

'Really, Lise? That's not right.'

'Oh, my goodness! What has meanness to do with it? If she were listening to some ordinary worldly conversation, it would be meanness, but when her own daughter is shut up with a young man . . . Listen, Alyosha, do you know I shall spy upon you as soon as we are married, and let me tell you I shall open all your letters and read them, so you may as well be prepared.'

'Yes, of course, if so –' muttered Alyosha, 'only it's not right.'

'Ah, how contemptuous! Alyosha, dear, don't let us quarrel the very first day. I'd better tell you the whole truth. Of course, it's very wrong to spy on people, and, of course, I am not right and you are, only I shall spy on you all the same.'

'Do, then; you won't find out anything,' laughed Alyosha.

'And Alyosha, will you give in to me? We must decide that too.'

'I shall be delighted to, Lise, and certain to, only not in the most important things. Even if you don't agree with me, I shall do my duty in the most important things.'

'That's right; but let me tell you I am ready to give in to you not only in the most important matters, but in everything. And I am ready to vow to do so now – in everything, and for all my life!' cried Lise fervently, 'and I'll do it gladly, gladly! What's more, I'll swear never to spy on you, never once, never to read one of your letters. For you are right and I am not. And though I shall be awfully tempted to spy, I know that I won't do it since you consider it dishonourable. You are my conscience now . . . Listen, Alexey Fyodorovitch, why have you been so sad lately – both yesterday and today? I know you have a lot of anxiety and trouble, but I see you have some special grief besides, some secret one, perhaps?'

'Yes, Lise, I have a secret one too,' answered Alyosha mournfully. 'I see you love me, since you guessed that.'

'What grief? What is troubling you? Can you tell me?' asked Lise with timid entreaty.

'I'll tell you later, Lise – afterwards,' said Alyosha, confused. 'Now you wouldn't understand it perhaps – and perhaps I couldn't explain it.'

'I know your brothers and your father are worrying you too?'

'Yes, my brothers too,' murmured Alyosha, pondering.

'I don't like your brother Ivan, Alyosha,' said Lise suddenly.

He noticed this remark with some surprise, but did not answer it.

'My brothers are destroying themselves,' he went on, 'my father, too. And they are destroying others with them. It's "the primitive force of the Karamazovs", as Father Païssy said the other day, a crude, unbridled, earthly force. Does the spirit of God move above that force? Even that I don't know. I only know that I too am a Karamazov . . . Me a monk, a monk! Am I a monk, Lise? You said just now that I was.'

'Yes, I did.'

'And perhaps I don't even believe in God.'

'You don't believe? What is the matter?' said Lise quietly and gently. But Alyosha did not answer. There was something too mysterious, too subjective in these last words of his, perhaps obscure to himself, but yet torturing him.

'And now on the top of it all, my friend, the best man in the world is going, is leaving the earth! If you knew, Lise, how bound up in soul I am with him! And then I shall be left alone . . . I shall come to you, Lise . . . For the future we will be together.'

'Yes, together, together! Henceforward we shall be always together, all our lives! Listen, kiss me, I allow you.' Alyosha kissed her.

'Come, now go. Christ be with you!' and she made the sign of the cross over him. 'Make haste back to *him* while he is alive. I see I've kept you selfishly. I'll pray today for him and you. Alyosha, we shall be happy! Will we be happy, will we?'

'I believe we will, Lise.'

Alyosha thought it better not to go in to Madame Hohlakov and was going out to leave without saying goodbye to her. But no sooner had he opened the door than he found Madame Hohlakov standing before him. From the first word Alyosha guessed that she had been waiting on purpose to see him.

'Alexey Fyodorovitch, this is awful. This is all childish nonsense and ridiculous. I trust you won't dream . . . It's foolishness, nothing but foolishness!' she said, attacking him at once.

'Only don't tell her that,' said Alyosha, 'or she will be upset, and that's bad for her now.'

'Sensible advice from a sensible young man. Am I to understand that you only agreed with her from compassion for her invalid state, because you didn't want to irritate her by contradiction?'

'Oh, no, not at all. I was quite serious in what I said,' Alyosha declared firmly.

'You can't be serious about this. It is impossible, unthinkable, and in the first place I shall never be at home to you again, and I will take her away, you may be sure of that.'

'But why?' asked Alyosha. 'It's all so far off. We may have to wait another year and a half.'

'Ah, Alexey Fyodorovitch, that's true, of course, and you'll have time to quarrel and separate a thousand times in a year and a half. But I am so unhappy! Though it's such nonsense, it's a great blow to me. I heard everything; I almost fainted. So this is the explanation of her dreadful night and her hysterics of late! It means love to the daughter but death to the mother. I might as well be in my grave at once. And a more serious matter still, what is this letter she has written? Show it me at once, at once!'

'No, there's no need. Tell me, how is Katerina Ivanovna now? I must know.'

'She still lies in delirium; she has not regained consciousness. Her aunts are here; but they do nothing but sigh and give themselves airs. Herzenstube came, and he was so alarmed that I didn't know what to do. I nearly sent for a doctor to look after him. He was driven home in my carriage. And on the top of it all, you and this letter! It's true nothing can happen for a year and a half. In the name of all that's holy, in the name of your dying elder, show me that letter, Alexey Fyodorovitch. I'm her mother. Hold it in your hand, if you like, and I will read it so.'

'No, I won't show it to you. Even if she sanctioned it, I wouldn't. I am coming tomorrow, and if you like, we can talk over many things, but now goodbye!'

And Alyosha ran downstairs and into the street.

2

He had no time to lose indeed. Even while he was saying goodbye to Lise, the thought had struck him that he must attempt some stratagem to find his brother Dmitri, who was evidently keeping out of his way. It was getting late, nearly three o'clock. Alyosha's whole soul turned to the monastery, to his dying saint, but the necessity of seeing Dmitri outweighed everything. The conviction that a great inevitable catastrophe was about to happen grew stronger in Alyosha's mind with every hour. What that catastrophe was, and what he would say at that moment to his brother, he could perhaps not have said definitely. 'Even if my benefactor must die without me, anyway I won't have to reproach myself all my life with the thought that I might have saved something and did not, but passed by and hastened home. If I do as I intend, I shall be following his great precept.'

His plan was to catch his brother Dmitri unawares, to climb over the fence, as he had the day before, get into the garden and sit in the summerhouse. If Dmitri were not there, thought Alyosha, he would not announce himself to Foma or the women of the house, but would remain hidden in the summerhouse, even if he had to wait there till evening. If, as before, Dmitri were lying in wait for Grushenka to come, he would be very likely to come to the summerhouse. Alyosha did not, however, give much thought to the details of his plan, but resolved to act upon it, even if it meant not getting back to the monastery that day.

Everything happened without hindrance, he climbed over the hurdle almost in the same spot as the day before, and stole into the summerhouse unseen. He did not want to be noticed. The women of the house and Foma too, if he were here, might be loyal to his brother and obey his instructions, and so refuse to let Alyosha come into the garden, or might warn Dmitri that he was being sought and enquired for.

There was no one in the summerhouse. Alyosha sat down and began to wait. He looked round the summerhouse, which somehow struck him as a great deal more ancient than before. Though the day was just as fine as yesterday, it seemed a wretched little place this time. There was a circle on the table, left no doubt from the glass of brandy that had been spilled the day before. Foolish and irrelevant ideas strayed through his mind, as they always do at a time of tedious waiting. He wondered, for instance, why he had sat down precisely in the same place as before, why not in the other seat. At last he felt very depressed – depressed by suspense and uncertainty. But he had not sat there more than a quarter of an hour, when he suddenly heard the thrum of a guitar somewhere quite close. People were sitting, or had only just sat down, somewhere in the bushes not more than twenty paces away. Alyosha suddenly recollected that on coming out of the summer-house the day before, he had caught a glimpse of an old green low garden seat among the bushes on the left, by the fence. The people must be sitting on it now. Who were they?

A man's voice suddenly began singing in a sugary falsetto, accompanying himself on the guitar:

> 'With invincible force
> I am bound to my dear.
> Oh, Lord, have mercy
> On her and on me!
> On her and on me!
> On her and on me!'

The voice ceased. It was a lackey's tenor and a lackey's song. Another voice, a woman's, suddenly asked insinuatingly and bashfully, though with mincing affectation: 'Why haven't you been to see us for so long, Pavel Fyodorovitch? Why do you always look down upon us?'

'Not at all,' answered a man's voice politely, but with emphatic dignity. It was clear that the man had the best of the position, and that the woman was making advances. 'I believe the man must be Smerdyakov,' thought Alyosha, 'from his voice. And the lady must be the daughter of the house here, who has come from Moscow, the one who wears the dress with a trailing skirt and goes to Marfa for soup.'

'I am awfully fond of verses of all kinds, if they rhyme,'

the woman's voice continued. 'Why don't you go on?'

The man sang again:

'What do I care for royal wealth
If but my dear one be in health?
Lord, have mercy
On her and on me!
On her and on me!
On her and on me!'

'It was even better last time,' observed the woman's voice. 'You sang "If my darling be in health"; it sounded more tender. I suppose you've forgotten today.'

'Poetry is rubbish!' said Smerdyakov curtly.

'Oh, no! I am very fond of poetry.'

'So far as it's poetry, it's essential rubbish. Consider yourself, who ever talks in rhyme? And if we were all to talk in rhyme, even though it were decreed by law, we shouldn't say much, should we? Poetry is no good, Marya Kondratyevna.'

'How clever you are! How is it you've gone so deep into everything?' The woman's voice was more and more insinuating.

'I could have done better than that. I could have known more than that, if it had not been for my destiny from my childhood up. I would have shot a man in a duel if he called me names because I am descended from a filthy beggar and have no father. They used to throw that in my teeth in Moscow. It had reached them from here, thanks to Grigory Vassilyevitch. Grigory Vassilyevitch blames me for rebelling against my birth, but I would have sanctioned their killing me before I was born that I might not have come into the world at all. They used to say in the market, and your mamma tried to tell me, with great lack of delicacy, that my mother's hair was always filthy and matted and that she was short of four foot by a wee bit. Why talk of a wee bit while she might have said "a little bit", like everyone else? She wanted to make it touching, a regular peasant's piece of sentimentality. Can a Russian peasant be said to feel, in comparison with an educated man? He can't be said to have feeling at all, in his ignorance. From my childhood up, when I hear "a wee bit", I am ready to burst with rage. I hate all Russia, Marya Kondratyevna.'

'If you'd been a cadet in the army, or a young hussar, you wouldn't have talked like that, but would have drawn your sabre to defend all Russia.'

'I don't want to be a hussar, Marya Kondratyevna, and, what's more, I should like to abolish all soldiers.'

'And when an enemy comes, who is going to defend us?'

'There's no need of defence. In 1812 there was a great invasion of Russia by Napoleon, first Emperor of the French, father of the present one, and it would have been a good thing if they had conquered us. A clever nation would have conquered a very stupid one and annexed it. We should have had quite different institutions.'

'Are they so much better in their own country than we are? I wouldn't change an elegant fellow I know of for three young Englishmen,' observed Marya Kondratyevna tenderly, doubtless accompanying her words with a most languishing glance.

'That's as one prefers.'

'But you are just like a foreigner – just like a most gentlemanly foreigner. I tell you that, though it makes me bashful.'

'If you care to know, the folks there and ours here are just alike in their vice. They are swindlers, only there the scoundrel wears polished boots and here he grovels in filth and sees no harm in it. The Russian people need thrashing, as Fyodor Pavlovitch said very truly yesterday, though he is mad, and so are all his children.'

'You said yourself you had so much respect for Ivan Fyodorovitch.'

'But he said I was a stinking lackey. He thinks that I might be disobedient. He is mistaken there. If I had a certain sum in my pocket, I would have left here long ago. Dmitri Fyodorovitch is lower than any lackey in his behaviour, in his mind, and in his poverty. He doesn't know how to do anything, and yet he is respected by everyone. I may be only a soup maker, but with luck I could open a café restaurant in Petrovka, in Moscow, for my cooking is something special, and there's no one in Moscow, except the foreigners, whose cooking is anything special. Dmitri Fyodorovitch is a beggar, but if he were to challenge the son of the highest nobleman in the country, he'd fight him. Though in what way is he better than I am? For he is ever so much stupider than I am. Look at the money he has wasted!'

'It must be lovely, a duel,' Marya Kondratyevna observed suddenly.

'How so?'

'It must be so dreadful and so brave, especially when young officers with pistols in their hands pop at one another for the sake of some lady. A perfect picture! Ah, if only girls were allowed to look on, I'd give anything to see one!'

'It's all very well when you are firing at someone, but

when he is firing straight in your mug, you must feel pretty silly. You'd be glad to run away, Marya Kondratyevna.'

'You don't mean you would run away?' But Smerdyakov did not deign to reply. After a moment's silence the guitar tinkled again, and he sang again in the same falsetto:

'Whatever you may say,
I shall go far away.
Life will be bright and gay
In the city far away.
I shall not grieve,
I shall not grieve at all,
I don't intend to grieve at all.'

Then something unexpected happened. Alyosha suddenly sneezed. They were silent. Alyosha got up and walked towards them. He found Smerdyakov dressed up and wearing polished boots, his hair pomaded, and perhaps curled. The guitar lay on the garden seat. His companion was the daughter of the house, wearing a light blue dress with a train a yard long. She was young and would not have been bad-looking, but that her face was so round and terribly freckled.

'Will my brother Dmitri soon be back?' asked Alyosha with as much composure as he could.

Smerdyakov got up slowly; Marya Kondratyevna rose too.

'How am I to know about Dmitri Fyodorovitch? It's not as if I were his keeper,' answered Smerdyakov quietly, distinctly, and superciliously.

'But I simply asked whether you do know?' Alyosha explained.

'I know nothing of his whereabouts and don't want to.'

'But my brother told me that you let him know all that goes on in the house, and promised to let him know when Agrafena Alexandrovna comes.'

Smerdyakov turned a deliberate, unmoved glance upon him.

'And how did you get in this time, since the gate was bolted an hour ago?' he asked, looking at Alyosha.

'I came in from the back-alley, over the fence, and went straight to the summerhouse. I hope you'll forgive me,' he added, addressing Marya Kondratyevna. 'I was in a hurry to find my brother.'

'Ah, as though we could take it amiss in you!' drawled Marya Kondratyevna, flattered by Alyosha's apology. 'For Dmitri Fyodorovitch often goes to the summerhouse in that way. We don't know he is here and he is sitting in the summerhouse.'

'I am very anxious to find him or to learn from you where he is now. Believe me, it's on business of great importance to him.'

'He never tells us,' lisped Marya Kondratyevna.

'Though I used to come here as a friend,' Smerdyakov began again, 'Dmitri Fyodorovitch has pestered me in a merciless way even here by his incessant questions about the master. "What news?" he'll ask. "What's going on in there now? Who's coming and going?" and can't I tell him something more. Twice already he's threatened me with death.'

'With death?' Alyosha exclaimed in surprise.

'Do you suppose he'd think much of that, with his temper, which you had a chance of observing yourself yesterday? He says if I let Agrafena Alexandrovna in and she passes the night there, I'll be the first to suffer for it. I am terribly afraid of him, and if I were not even more afraid of doing so, I ought to let the police know. God only knows what he might not do!'

'His honour said to him the other day, "I'll pound you in a mortar!" ' added Marya Kondratyevna.

'Oh, if it's pounding in a mortar, it may be only talk,' observed Alyosha. 'If I could meet him, I might speak to him about that.'

'Well, the only thing I can tell you is this,' said Smerdyakov, as though thinking better of it; 'I am here as an old friend and neighbour, and it would be odd if I didn't come. On the other hand, Ivan Fyodorovitch sent me first thing this morning to your brother's lodging in Lake Street, without a letter, but with a message to Dmitri Fyodorovitch to come to dine with him at the restaurant in the market place. I went, but didn't find Dmitri Fyodorovitch at home, though it was eight o'clock. "He's been here, but he is gone for good," those were the very words of his landlady. It's as though there was an understanding between them. Perhaps at this moment he is in the restaurant with Ivan Fyodorovitch, for Ivan Fyodorovitch has not been home to dinner and Fyodor Pavlovitch dined alone an hour ago, and is gone to lie down. But I beg you most particularly not to speak of me and of what I have told you, for he'd kill me for nothing at all.'

'Brother Ivan invited Dmitri to the restaurant today?' repeated Alyosha quickly.

'That's so.'

'The Metropolis tavern in the market place?'

'The very same.'

'That's quite likely,' cried Alyosha, much excited. 'Thank you, Smerdyakov; that's important. I'll go there at once.'

'Don't betray me,' Smerdyakov called after him.

'Oh, no, I'll go to the tavern as though by chance. Don't be anxious.'

'But wait a minute, I'll open the gate to you,' cried Marya Kondratyevna.

'No; it's a short cut, I'll get over the fence again.'

What he had heard threw Alyosha into great agitation. He ran to the tavern. It was impossible for him to go into the tavern in his monastic dress, but he could enquire at the entrance for his brothers and call them down. But just as he reached the tavern, a window was flung open, and his brother Ivan called down to him from it.

'Alyosha, can't you come up here to me? I shall be awfully grateful.'

'To be sure I can, only I don't quite know whether in this dress . . .'

'But I am in a room apart. Come up the steps; I'll run down to meet you.'

A minute later Alyosha was sitting beside his brother. Ivan was dining alone.

3

Ivan was not, however, in a separate room, but only in a place shut off by a screen, so that it was unseen by other people in the room. It was the first room from the entrance with a buffet along the wall. Waiters were continually darting to and fro in it. The only customer in the room was an old retired military man drinking tea in a corner. But there was the usual bustle going on in the other rooms of the tavern; there were shouts for the waiters, the sound of popping corks, the click of billiard balls, the drone of the organ. Alyosha knew that Ivan did not usually visit this tavern and disliked taverns in general. So he must have come here, he reflected, simply to meet Dmitri by arrangement. Yet Dmitri was not there.

'Shall I order you fish, soup, or anything? You don't live on tea alone, I suppose,' cried Ivan, apparently delighted at having got hold of Alyosha. He had finished dinner and was drinking tea.

'Let me have soup, and tea afterwards; I am hungry,' said Alyosha gaily.

'And cherry jam? They have it here. You remember how you used to love cherry jam when you were little?'

'You remember that? Let me have jam too; I like it still.'

Ivan rang for the waiter and ordered soup, jam and tea.

'I remember everything, Alyosha; I remember you till you were eleven, I was nearly fifteen. There's such a difference between fifteen and eleven that brothers are never companions at those ages. I don't know whether I was fond of you even. When I went away to Moscow for the first few years I never thought of you at all. Then, when you came to Moscow yourself, we only met once somewhere, I believe. And now I've been here more than three months, and so far we have scarcely said a word to each other. Tomorrow I am going away, and I was just thinking as I sat here how I could see you to say goodbye and just then you came by.'

'Were you very anxious to see me, then?'

'Very, I want to get to know you once for all, and I want you to know me. And then to say goodbye. I believe it's always best to get to know people just before leaving them. I've noticed how you've been looking at me these three months. There has been a continual look of expectation in your eyes, and I can't endure that. That's why I've kept away from you. But in the end I have learned to respect you. The little man stands firm, I thought. Though I am laughing, I am serious. You do stand firm, don't you? I like people who are firm like that whatever it is they stand by, even if they are such little fellows as you. Your expectant eyes ceased to annoy me, I grew fond of them in the end, those expectant eyes. You seem to love me for some reason, Alyosha?'

'I do love you, Ivan. Dmitri says of you – Ivan is a tomb! I say of you, Ivan is a riddle. You are a riddle to me even now. But I understand something in you, and I did not understand it till this morning.'

'What's that?' laughed Ivan.

'You won't be angry?' Alyosha laughed too.

'Well?'

'That you are just as young as other young men of twenty-three, that you are just a young and innocent and nice boy, green in fact! Now, have I insulted you dreadfully?'

'On the contrary, I am struck by a coincidence,' cried Ivan, warmly and good-humouredly. 'Would you believe it that ever since that scene with her, I have thought of nothing else but my youthful greenness, and just as though you guessed that, you talk about it. Do you know I've been sitting here thinking to myself: that if I didn't believe in life, if I lost faith in the woman I love, lost faith in the order of things, were convinced in fact that everything is a disorderly, damnable, and perhaps devil-ridden chaos, if I were struck by every horror of man's disillusionment – still I should want to live and, having once tasted of the cup, I would not turn away from it till I had drained it! At thirty, though, I shall be sure to leave the cup, even if I've not emptied it, and turn away – where I don't know. But till I am thirty, I know that my youth will triumph over everything – every disillusionment, every disgust with life. I've asked myself many times whether there is in the world any despair that would overcome this frantic and perhaps unseemly thirst for life in me, and I've come to the conclusion that there isn't, that is till I am thirty, and then I shall lose it of myself, I fancy. Some drivelling anaemic moralists – and poets especially – often call that thirst for life base. It's a feature of the Karamazovs it's true, that thirst for life regardless of everything; you have it no doubt too, but why is it base? The centripetal force on our planet is still fearfully strong, Alyosha. I have a longing for life, and I go on living in spite of logic. Though I may not believe in the order of the universe, yet I love the sticky little leaves as they open in spring. I love the blue sky, I love some people, whom one loves you know sometimes without knowing why. I love some great deeds done by men, though I've long ceased perhaps to have faith in them, yet from old habit one's heart treasures them. Here, they have brought the soup for you, eat it, it will do you good. It's first-rate soup, they know how to make it here. I want to travel in Europe, Alyosha, I shall set off from here. And yet I know that I am only going to a graveyard, but it's a most precious graveyard, that's what it is! Precious are the dead that lie there, every stone over them speaks of such burning life in the past, of such passionate faith in their work, their truth, their struggle and their science, that I know I shall fall on the ground and kiss those stones and weep over them; though I'm convinced in my heart that it's long been nothing but a graveyard. And I shall not weep from despair, but simply because I shall be happy in my tears, I shall steep my soul in my emotion. I love the sticky leaves in spring, the blue sky – that's all it is. It's not a matter of intellect or logic, it's loving with one's inside, with one's stomach. One loves the first strength of one's youth. Do you understand anything of my tirade, Alyosha?' Ivan laughed suddenly.

'I understand too well, Ivan. One longs to love with one's inside, with one's stomach. You said that so well and I am awfully glad that you have such a longing for life,' cried Alyosha. 'I think everyone should love life above everything in the world.'

'Love life more than the meaning of it?'

'Certainly, love it, regardless of logic as you say, it must be regardless of logic, and it's only then one will understand the meaning of it. I have thought so a long time. Half your work is done, Ivan, you love life, now you've only to try to do the second half and you are saved.'

'You are trying to save me, but perhaps I am not lost! And what does your second half mean?'

'Why, you must raise up your dead, who perhaps have not died after all. Come, let me have tea. I am so glad of our talk, Ivan.'

'I see you are feeling inspired. I am awfully fond of such "professions of faith" from such – novices. You are a steadfast person, Alexey. Is it true that you mean to leave the monastery?'

'Yes, my elder sends me out into the world.'

'We shall see each other then in the world. We shall meet before I am thirty, when I shall begin to turn aside from the cup. Father doesn't want to turn aside from his cup till he is seventy, he dreams of hanging on to eighty in fact, so he says. He means it only too seriously, though he is a buffoon. He stands on a firm rock, too, he stands on his sensuality – though after we are thirty, indeed, there may be nothing else to stand on . . . But to hang on to seventy is nasty, better only to thirty; one might retain "a shadow of nobility" by deceiving oneself. Have you seen Dmitri today?'

'No, but I saw Smerdyakov,' and Alyosha rapidly, though minutely, described his meeting with Smerdyakov. Ivan began listening anxiously and questioned him.

'But he begged me not to tell Dmitri that he had told me about him,' added Alyosha. Ivan frowned and pondered.

'Are you frowning on Smerdyakov's account?' asked Alyosha.

'Yes, on his account. Damn him, I certainly did want to see Dmitri, but now there's no need,' said Ivan reluctantly.

'But are you really going so soon, brother?'

'Yes.'

'What of Dmitri and father? How will it end?' asked Alyosha anxiously.

'You are always harping upon it! What have I to do with it? Am I my brother Dmitri's keeper?' Ivan snapped irritably, but then he suddenly smiled bitterly. 'Cain's answer to God about his murdered brother. Perhaps that's what you're thinking at this moment? Well, damn it all, I can't stay here to be their keeper, can I? I've finished what I had to do, and I am going. Do you imagine I am jealous of Dmitri, that I've been trying to steal his beautiful Katerina Ivanovna for the last three months? Nonsense, I had business of my own. I finished it. I am going. I finished it just now, you were witness.'

'At Katerina Ivanovna's?'

'Yes, and I've released myself once for all. And after all, what have I to do with Dmitri? Dmitri doesn't enter into it. I had my own business to settle with Katerina Ivanovna. You know, on the contrary, that Dmitri behaved as though there was an understanding between us. I didn't ask him to do it, but he solemnly handed her over to me and gave us his blessing. It's all too funny. Ah, Alyosha, if you only knew how light my heart is now! Would you believe it, I sat here eating my dinner and nearly ordered champagne to celebrate my first hour of freedom. Tfoo! It's been going on nearly six months, and all at once I've thrown it off. I could never have guessed, even yesterday, how easy it would be to put an end to it if I wanted.'

'You are speaking of your love, Ivan?'

'Of my love, if you like. I fell in love with the young lady, I worried myself over her and she worried me. I sat watching over her . . . and all at once it's collapsed! I spoke this morning with inspiration, but I went away and roared with laughter. Would you believe it? Yes, it's the literal truth.'

'You seem very merry about it now,' observed Alyosha, looking into his face, which had suddenly grown brighter.

'But how could I tell that I didn't care for her a bit! Ha-ha! It appears after all I didn't. And yet how she attracted me! How attractive she was just now when I made my speech! And do you know she attracts me awfully even now, yet how easy it is to leave her. Do you think I am boasting?'

'No, only perhaps it wasn't love.'

'Alyosha,' laughed Ivan, 'don't make reflections about love, it's unseemly for you. How you rushed into the discussion this morning! I've forgotten to kiss you for it . . . But how she tormented me! It certainly was nursing a "heartbreak". Ah, she knew how I loved her! She loved me and not Dmitri,' Ivan insisted gaily. 'Her feeling for Dmitri was simply self-torture. All I told her just now was perfectly true, but the worst of it is, it may take her fifteen or twenty years to find out that she doesn't care for Dmitri, and loves me whom she torments, and perhaps she may never find it out at all, in spite of her lesson today. Well, it's better so; I can simply go away for good. By the way, how is she now? What happened after I departed?'

Alyosha told him she had been hysterical, and that she was now, he heard, unconscious and delirious.

'Isn't Madame Hohlakov laying it on?'

'I think not.'

'I must find out. Nobody dies of hysterics though. They don't matter. God gave woman hysterics as a relief. I won't go to her at all. Why push myself forward again?'

'But you told her that she had never cared for you.'

'I did that on purpose. Alyosha, shall I call for some champagne? Let us drink to my freedom. Ah, if only you knew how glad I am!'

'No, brother, we had better not drink,' said Alyosha suddenly. 'Besides I feel somehow depressed.'

'Yes, you've been depressed a long time, I've noticed it.'

'Have you settled to go tomorrow morning then?'

'Morning? I didn't say I should go in the morning . . . But perhaps it may be in the morning. Would you believe it, I dined here today only to avoid dining with the old man, I loathe him so. I should have left long ago, so far as he is concerned. But why are you so worried about my going away? We've plenty of time before I go, an eternity!'

'If you are going away tomorrow, what do you mean by an eternity?'

'But what does it matter to us?' laughed Ivan. 'We've time enough for our talk, for what brought us here. Why do you look so surprised? Answer: why have we met here? To talk of my love for Katerina Ivanovna? of the old man and Dmitri? of foreign travel? of the fatal position of Russia? of the Emperor Napoleon? Is that it?'

'No.'

'Then you know what for. It's different for other people; but we in our green youth have to settle eternal questions first of all. That's what we care about. Young Russia is talking about nothing but the eternal questions now. Just when the old folks are all taken up with practical questions. Why have you been looking at me in expectation for the last three months? To ask me "what do you believe, or don't you believe at all?" That's what your eyes have been saying all these three months, haven't they?'

'Perhaps so,' smiled Alyosha. 'You are not laughing at me, now, Ivan?'

'Me laughing! I don't want to wound my little brother who has been watching me with such expectation for three months. Alyosha, look straight at me! Of course, I am just a little boy as you are, only not a novice. And what have Russian boys been doing up till now, some of them, I mean? In this stinking tavern, for instance, here, they meet and sit down in a corner. They've never met in their lives before and, when they go out of the tavern, they won't meet again for forty years. And what do they talk about in that momentary halt in the tavern? Of the eternal questions, of the existence of God and immortality. And those who do not believe in God talk of socialism or anarchism, of the remaking of all humanity on a new pattern, so that it all comes to the same, they're the same questions turned inside out. And masses, masses of the most original Russian boys do nothing but talk of the eternal questions. Isn't it so?'

'Yes, for real Russians the questions of God's existence and of immortality, or, as you say, the same question turned inside out, come first and foremost, of course, and so they should,' said Alyosha, still watching his brother with the same gentle and enquiring smile.

'Well, Alyosha, it's sometimes very unwise to be a Russian at all, but anything stupider than the way Russian boys spend their time one can hardly imagine. But there's one Russian boy called Alyosha I am awfully fond of.'

'How nicely you put that in!' Alyosha laughed suddenly.

'Well, tell me where to begin, give your orders. The existence of God, eh?'

'Begin where you like. You declared yesterday at father's that there was no God.' Alyosha looked searchingly at his brother.

'I said that yesterday at dinner on purpose to annoy you and I saw your eyes flash. But now I've no objection to discussing the subject with you, and I say so very seriously. I would like to be closer to you, Alyosha, for I have no friends and want to know what friendship is like. And, can you imagine, perhaps I too accept God,' laughed Ivan, 'that's a surprise for you, isn't it?'

'Yes, of course, if you are not joking now.'

'Joking? I was told at the elder's yesterday that I was joking. You know, dear boy, there was an old sinner in the eighteenth century who declared that, if there were no God, he would have to be invented: *S'il n'existait pas Dieu, il faudrait l'inventer*. And man has actually invented God. And what's strange, what would be marvellous, is not that God should really exist; the marvel is that such an idea, the idea of the necessity of God, could enter the head of such a savage, vicious beast as man. So holy it is, so touching, so wise and so great a credit it does to man. As for me, I've long resolved not to think whether man created God or God man. And I won't go through all the axioms laid down by Russian boys on that subject, all derived from European hypotheses; for what's a hypothesis there, is an axiom with the Russian schoolboy, and not only with the boys but with their teachers too, for our Russian professors are often just like boys themselves. And so I omit all the hypotheses. For what are we aiming at now? I am trying to explain as quickly as possible my essential nature, that is, what manner of man I am, what I believe in, and for what I hope, that's it, isn't it? And therefore I tell you that I accept God honestly and simply. But you must note this: if God exists and if He really did create the world, then, as we all know, He created it according to the geometry of Euclid and the human mind with the conception of only three dimensions in space. Yet there have been and still are geometricians and philosophers, and even some very distinguished ones, who doubt whether the whole universe, or to speak more generally the whole of being, was only created in Euclid's geometry; they even dare to dream that two parallel lines, which according to Euclid can never meet on earth, may meet somewhere in infinity. I have come to the conclusion that, since I can't understand even that, I can't expect to understand about God. I acknowledge humbly that I have no faculty for settling such questions, I have a Euclidian earthly mind, and how could I solve problems that are not of this world? And I advise you never to think about it either, my dear Alyosha, especially about God, whether He exists or not. All such questions are utterly inappropriate for a mind created with a conception of only three dimensions. And so I accept God and am glad to, and what's more I accept His wisdom, His purpose – which are utterly beyond our ken; I believe in the underlying order and the meaning of life; I believe in the eternal harmony in which they say we shall one day be blended. I believe in the Word to Which the universe is striving, and Which Itself was "with God", and Which Itself is God and so on, and so on, to infinity. There are all sorts of phrases for it. I seem to be on the right path, don't I? Yet would you believe it, in the final result I don't accept this world of God's, and, although I know it exists, I don't accept it at all. It's not that I don't accept God, you must understand, it's the world created by Him I don't and cannot accept. Let me make it plain. I believe like a child that suffering will be healed and made up for, that all the humiliating absurdity of human contradictions will vanish like a pitiful mirage, like the despicable fabrication of the impotent and infinitely small Euclidian mind of man, that in the world's finale, at the moment of eternal harmony, something so precious will come to pass that it will suffice for all hearts, for the comforting of all resentments, for the atonement of all the crimes of humanity, of all the blood they've shed; that it will make it not only possible to forgive but to justify all that has happened to men – but though all that may come to pass, I don't accept it. I won't accept it. Even if parallel lines do meet and I see it myself, I shall see it and say that they've met, but still I won't accept it. That's what's at the root of me, Alyosha; that's my creed. I am in earnest in what I say. I began our talk as stupidly as I could on purpose, but I've led up to my confession, for that's all you want. You didn't want to hear about God, but only to know what the brother you love lives by. And so I've told you.'

Ivan concluded his long tirade with marked and unexpected feeling.

4

'I must make you one confession,' Ivan said. 'I could never understand how one can love one's neighbours. It's just one's neighbours, to my mind, that one can't love, though one might love those at a distance. I once read somewhere of John the Merciful, a saint, that when a hungry, frozen beggar came to him, he took him into his bed, held him in his arms, and began breathing into his mouth, which was putrid and loathsome from some awful disease. I am convinced that he did that from "self-torture", from the self-torture of falsity, for the sake of the charity imposed by duty, as a penance laid on him. For anyone to love a man, he must be hidden, for as soon as he shows his face, love is gone.'

'Father Zossima has talked of that more than once,' observed Alyosha; 'he, too, said that the face of a man often hinders many people not practised in love, from loving him. But yet there's a great deal of love in mankind, and almost Christlike love. I know that myself, Ivan.'

'Well, I know nothing of it so far, and can't understand it, and the innumerable mass of mankind are with me there. The question is, whether that's due to men's bad qualities or whether it's inherent in their nature. To my thinking, Christlike love for men is a miracle impossible on earth. He was God. But we are not gods. Suppose I, for instance, suffer intensely. Another can never know how much I suffer, because he is another and not I. And what's more, a man is rarely ready to admit another's suffering (as though it were a distinction). Beggars, especially genteel beggars, ought never to show themselves, but to ask for charity through the newspapers. One can love one's neighbours in the abstract, or even at a distance, but at close quarters it's almost impossible.

'But enough of that. I simply wanted to show you my point of view. I meant to speak of the suffering of mankind generally, but we had better confine ourselves to the sufferings of the children. In the first place, children can be loved even at close quarters, even when they are dirty, even when they are ugly (I fancy, though, children never are ugly). Are you fond of children, Alyosha? I know you are, and will understand why I prefer to speak of them. If they, too, suffer horribly on earth, they must suffer for their fathers' sins, but that reasoning is of the other world and is incomprehensible for the heart of man here on earth. The innocent must not suffer for another's sins, and especially such innocents! You may be surprised at me, Alyosha, but I am awfully fond of children, too. And observe, cruel people, the violent, the rapacious, the Karamazovs, are sometimes very fond of children . . . You don't know why I am telling you all this, Alyosha? My head aches and I am sad.'

'You speak with a strange air,' observed Alyosha uneasily, 'as though you were not quite yourself.'

'By the way, a Bulgarian I met lately in Moscow,' Ivan went on, seeming not to hear his brother's words, 'told me about the crimes committed by Turks and Circassians in all parts of Bulgaria through fear of a general rising of the Slavs. They burn villages, murder, outrage women and children, they nail their prisoners by the ears to the fences, leave them so till morning, and in the morning they hang them – all sorts of things you can't imagine. People talk sometimes of bestial cruelty, but that's a great injustice and insult to the beasts; a beast can never be so cruel as a man, so artistically cruel. The tiger only tears and gnaws, that's all he can do. He would never think of nailing people by the ears, even if he were able to do it. These Turks took a pleasure in torturing children, too; cutting the unborn child from the mother's womb, and tossing babies up in the air and catching them on the points of their bayonets before their mothers' eyes. Doing it before the mothers' eyes was what gave zest to the amusement.'

'Brother, what are you driving at?' asked Alyosha.

'I think if the devil doesn't exist, but man has created him, he has created him in his own image and likeness.'

'Just as he did God, then?' observed Alyosha.

' "It's wonderful how you can turn words," as Polonius says in *Hamlet*,' laughed Ivan. 'You turn my words against me. Well, I am glad. Yours must be a fine God, if man created Him in His image and likeness. You asked just now what I was driving at.'

Ivan for a minute was silent, his face became all at once very sad.

'Listen! I took the case of children only to make my case clearer. Of the other tears of humanity with which the earth is soaked from its crust to its centre, I will say nothing. I have narrowed my subject on purpose. I am a bug, and I recognise in all humility that I cannot understand why the world is arranged as it is. Men are themselves to blame, I suppose; they were given paradise, they wanted freedom, and stole fire from heaven, though they knew they would become unhappy, so there is no need to pity them. And if the sufferings of children go to swell the sum of sufferings which was necessary to pay for truth, then I protest that the truth is not worth such a price; it's beyond our means to pay so much. And so I hasten to give back my entrance ticket, and if I am an honest man I am bound to give it back as soon as possible. And that I am doing. It's not God that I don't accept, Alyosha, only I most respectfully return Him the ticket.'

'That's rebellion,' murmured Alyosha, looking down.

'Rebellion? I am sorry you call it that,' said Ivan earnestly. 'One can hardly live in rebellion, and I want to live. Tell me yourself, I challenge you – answer. Imagine that you are creating a fabric of human destiny with the object of making men happy in the end, giving them peace and rest at last, but that it was essential and inevitable to torture to death only one tiny creature – that baby beating its breast with its fist, for instance – and to found that edifice on its unavenged tears, would you consent to be the architect on those conditions? Tell me, and tell the truth.'

'No, I wouldn't consent,' said Alyosha softly.

'And can you admit the idea that men for whom you are building it would agree to accept their happiness on the foundation of the unexpiated blood of a little victim? And accepting it would remain happy for ever?'

'No, I can't admit it. Brother,' said Alyosha suddenly, with flashing eyes, 'there is a Being and He can forgive everything, all and for all, because He gave His innocent blood for all and everything. You have forgotten Him, and on Him is built the edifice, and it is to Him they cry aloud, "Thou art just, O Lord, for Thy ways are revealed!" '

Ivan laughed. 'I told you, all I want is to live to thirty, and then . . . dash the cup to the ground!'

'But the little sticky leaves, and the precious tombs, and the blue sky, and the woman you love! How will you live, how will you love them?' Alyosha cried sorrowfully. 'With such hell in your heart and your head, how can you? No, that's just what you are going away for, to join them . . . if not, you will kill yourself, you can't endure it!'

'There is a strength to endure everything,' Ivan said with a cold smile.

'What strength?'

'The strength of the Karamazov – the strength of the Karamazov baseness.'

'You mean to sink into debauchery, to stifle your soul with corruption, yes?'

'Possibly even that . . . only perhaps till I am thirty I shall escape it, and then –'

'How will you escape it? By what will you escape it? That's impossible with your ideas.'

'In the Karamazov way, again.'

' "Everything is permitted," you mean? Everything is within the law, is that it?'

Ivan scowled, and all at once turned strangely pale. 'I thought that when I go away from here I would have you at least on my side,' Ivan said suddenly, with unexpected emotion; 'but now I see that there is no place for me even in your heart, my dear hermit. The formula, "all is within the law", I won't renounce – will you spurn me for that, yes?'

Alyosha got up, went to him and softly kissed him on the lips.

'Thank you,' cried Ivan, highly delighted. 'It's time we were going, both of us.' They went out, but stopped when they reached the entrance of the restaurant.

'Listen, Alyosha,' Ivan began in a determined voice, 'if I am really able to care for the sticky little leaves, I shall only love them, remembering you. It's enough for me that you are somewhere here, and I won't lose my desire for life yet. Is that enough for you? Take it as a declaration of affection if you like. And now you go to the right and I to the left. And it's enough, do you hear, enough. I mean even if I don't go away tomorrow (I think I certainly shall go) and we meet again, don't say a word more on these subjects. I beg that particularly. And about Dmitri too, I ask you specially never speak to me again,' he added, with sudden irritation; 'it's all exhausted, it has all been said over and over again, hasn't it? And I'll make you one promise in return for it. When at thirty, I want to "dash the cup to the ground", wherever I may be I'll come to have one more talk with you, even though it may be from America, you can be sure of that. I'll come specially for that talk.

It will be very interesting to have a look at you, to see what you'll be by that time. It's rather a solemn promise, you see. And we really may be parting for seven years or ten. Come, go now to your Pater Seraphicus, he is dying. If he dies without you, you will be angry with me for having kept you. Goodbye, kiss me once more; that's right, now go.'

Ivan turned suddenly and went his way without looking back. It was just as Dmitri had left Alyosha the day before, though the parting had been very different. The strange resemblance flashed like an arrow through Alyosha's mind in the distress and dejection of the moment. He waited a little, looking after his brother. He suddenly noticed that Ivan swayed as he walked and that his right shoulder looked lower than his left. He had never noticed it before. But all at once he turned too, and almost ran to the monastery. It was nearly dark, and he felt almost frightened; something new was growing up in him for which he could not account. The wind had risen again as on the previous evening, and the ancient pines murmured gloomily about him when he entered the hermitage copse. He almost ran. 'Pater Seraphicus – he got that name from somewhere – where from?' Alyosha wondered. 'Ivan, poor Ivan, and when shall I see you again? . . . Here is the hermitage. Yes, yes, that he is, Pater Seraphicus, he will save me – from him and for ever!'

Several times afterwards he wondered how he could on leaving Ivan so completely forget his brother Dmitri, though he had that morning, only a few hours before, so firmly resolved to find him and not to give up looking for him, even should he be unable to return to the monastery that night.

5

And Ivan, on parting from Alyosha, went home to Fyodor Pavlovitch's house. But, strange to say, he was overcome by insufferable depression, which grew greater at every step he took towards the house. There was nothing strange in his being depressed; what was strange was that Ivan could not have said what was the cause of it. He had often been depressed before, and there was nothing surprising at his feeling so at such a moment, when he had broken off with everything that had brought him here, and was preparing that day to make a new start and enter upon a new, unknown future. He would again be as solitary as ever, and though he had great hopes, and great – too great – expectations from life, he could not have given any definite account of his hopes, his expectations, or even his desires.

'I feel sick with depression and yet I can't tell what I want. Better not think, perhaps.'

Ivan tried 'not to think', but that too was no use. What made his depression so vexatious and irritating was that it had a kind of casual, external character – he felt that. Some person or thing seemed to be standing out somewhere, just as something will sometimes obtrude itself upon the eye, and though a man may be so busy with work or conversation that for a long time he does not notice it, yet it irritates and almost torments till at last he realises what the trouble is, and removes the offending object, often quite a trifling and ridiculous one – some article left about in the wrong place, a handkerchief on the floor, a book not replaced on the shelf, and so on.

At last, feeling very cross and ill-humoured, Ivan arrived home, and suddenly, about fifteen paces from the garden gate, he guessed what was fretting and worrying him.

On a bench in the gateway sat the valet Smerdyakov, enjoying the coolness of the evening, and at the first glance Ivan knew that the valet Smerdyakov had been on his mind, and that it was this man that his soul loathed. It all dawned upon him suddenly and became clear. Just before, when Alyosha had told of his meeting with Smerdyakov, Ivan had felt a sudden twinge of gloom and loathing, which had immediately stirred responsive anger in his heart. Afterwards, as he talked, Smerdyakov had been forgotten for the time; yet had been in his mind, and as soon as Ivan parted from Alyosha and was walking home, the forgotten sensation began to obtrude itself again. 'Is it possible that a miserable, contemptible creature like that can worry me so much?' he wondered, with acute irritation.

It was true that Ivan had come of late to feel an intense dislike for the man, especially during the last few days. He had even begun to notice in himself a growing feeling almost of hatred for the creature. Perhaps this hatred was accentuated by the fact that when Ivan first came to the neighbourhood he had felt quite differently. Then he had taken a marked interest in Smerdyakov, and had even thought him very unusual. He had encouraged him to talk, although he always wondered at Smerdyakov's incoherence, or rather the restlessness in his mind, and could not understand what it was that so continually and insistently worked upon the brain of 'the philosopher'. They discussed philosophical questions and even how there could have been light on the first day when the sun, moon, and stars were only created on the fourth day, and how that was to be understood. But Ivan soon saw that, though the sun, moon, and stars might be an interesting subject, yet it was quite secondary to Smerdyakov, and that he was looking for something altogether different. In one way and another, he began to betray a boundless vanity, and a wounded vanity too, and that Ivan disliked. It had first given rise to his aversion. Later on there had been trouble in the house. Grushenka had come on the scene, and there had been the scandals with his brother Dmitri – they discussed that, too. But though Smerdyakov always talked of the matter with great excitement, it was impossible to discover what he really hoped would come of it. There was, in fact, something surprising in the illogicality and incoherence of some of his desires, accidentally betrayed and always vaguely expressed. Smerdyakov was for ever enquiring, putting certain indirect but obviously premeditated questions, but what his object was he did not explain, and usually at the most important moment he would break off and relapse into silence or switch to another subject. But what finally irritated Ivan most and confirmed his dislike for Smerdyakov was the peculiar revolting familiarity which the fellow began to show more and more markedly. Not that he forgot himself and was rude; on the contrary, he always spoke very respectfully, yet he had obviously begun to consider – goodness knows why! – that there was some sort of understanding between him and Ivan Fyodorovitch. He always spoke in a tone that suggested that the two of them had some kind of compact, some secret between them, that had at some time been expressed on both sides and was only known to them beyond the comprehension of everyone around them. But for a long while Ivan did not recognise the real cause of his growing dislike and had only lately realised what was at the root of the whole business.

With a feeling of disgust and irritation he tried to pass through the gate without speaking or looking at Smerdyakov. But Smerdyakov rose from the bench, and from that action alone, Ivan knew instantly that Smerdyakov wanted particularly to talk to him. Ivan looked at him and stopped, and the fact that he did stop, instead of passing by, as he meant to the minute before, infuriated him. With anger and repulsion he looked at Smerdyakov's emasculate, sickly face, with the little curls combed forward on his forehead. His left eye winked and grinned as though to say, 'Where are you going? You won't pass by; you see that we two clever people have something to say to each other.'

Ivan shook. 'Get away, miserable idiot. What have I to do with you?' was on the tip of his tongue, but to his profound astonishment he heard himself say, 'Is my father still asleep, or has he waked?'

He asked the question softly and meekly, to his own surprise, and at once, again to his own surprise, sat down on the bench. For an instant he felt almost frightened; he remembered it afterwards. Smerdyakov stood facing him, his hands behind his back, looking at Ivan with assurance and almost severity.

'His honour is still asleep,' he articulated deliberately ('You were the first to speak, not I,' he seemed to say). 'I am surprised at you, sir,' he added, after a pause, dropping his eyes affectedly, setting his right foot forward, and pushing at the ground daintily with the tip of his polished boot.

'Why are you surprised at my visit?' Ivan asked abruptly and sullenly, doing his utmost to restrain himself, and realising suddenly with disgust, that he was feeling intense curiosity and would not, on any account, go away without satisfying it.

'Why don't you go to Tchermashnya, sir?' Smerdyakov suddenly raised his eyes and smiled familiarly. 'Why I smile you must understand of yourself, if you are a clever man,' his screwed-up left eye seemed to say.

'Why should I go to Tchermashnya?' Ivan asked in surprise.

Smerdyakov was silent again.

'Fyodor Pavlovitch himself has begged you to,' he said at last, slowly and apparently attaching no significance to his answer. 'I put you off with a secondary reason,' he seemed to suggest, 'simply to say something.'

'Damn you! Speak out what you have to say!' Ivan cried angrily at last, passing from meekness to violence.

Smerdyakov drew his right foot up to his left, pulled himself up, but still looked at Ivan with the same serenity and the same little smile.

'Substantially nothing – but just by way of conversation.'

Another silence followed. They did not speak for nearly a minute. Ivan knew that he ought to get up and show anger, and Smerdyakov stood before him and seemed to be waiting as though to see whether he would be angry or not. So at least it seemed to Ivan. Finally he made a move to get up. Smerdyakov seemed to seize the moment.

'I'm in an awful position, Ivan Fyodorovitch. I don't know how to help myself,' he said very distinctly, and at his last word he sighed. Ivan Fyodorovitch sat down again.

'They are both utterly crazy, they are no better than little children,' Smerdyakov went on. 'I am speaking of your parent and your brother Dmitri Fyodorovitch. Fyodor Pavlovitch will get up soon and begin worrying me every minute, "Has she come? Why hasn't she come?" and so on till midnight and even after midnight. And if Agrafena Alexandrovna doesn't come (for very likely she does not mean to come at all) then he will be at me again tomorrow morning, "Why hasn't she come? When will she come?" – as though I were to blame for it. On the other side it's no better. As soon as it gets dark, or even before, your brother will appear with his gun in his hands: "Look out, you rogue, you soup maker. If you miss her and don't let me know she's been here – I'll kill you first of all." When the night's over, in the morning, he too, like Fyodor Pavlovitch, begins worrying me to death. "Why hasn't she come? Will she come soon?" And he too thinks me to blame because his lady hasn't come. And every day and every hour they get angrier, so that I sometimes think I shall kill myself from sheer fright. I never know where I am with them, sir.'

'But why did you meddle in the whole business? Why did you begin to spy for Dmitri Fyodorovitch?' said Ivan irritably.

'How could I help meddling? Though, indeed, I haven't meddled at all, if you want to know the real truth. I kept quiet from the very beginning, not daring to answer; but he picked on me to be his servant. He has had only one thing to say since: "I'll kill you, you scoundrel, if you miss her." I feel certain, sir, that I shall have a bad fit tomorrow.'

'What do you mean by "a bad fit"?'

'A long fit, lasting a long time – several hours, or perhaps a day or two. Once it went on for three days. I fell from the attic that time. The struggling ceased and then began again, and for three days I couldn't come back to my senses. Fyodor Pavlovitch sent for Herzenstube, the doctor here, and he put ice on my head and tried another remedy too . . . I might have died.'

'But they say one can't tell with epilepsy when a fit is coming. What makes you say you will have one tomorrow?' Ivan enquired, with a peculiar, irritable curiosity.

'That's right. You can't tell beforehand.'

'Besides you fell from the attic then.'

'I climb up to the attic every day. I might fall from the attic again tomorrow. And, if not, I might fall down the cellar steps. I have to go into the cellar every day, too.'

Ivan took a long look at him.

'You are talking nonsense, I see, and I don't quite understand you,' he said softly, but with a sort of menace. 'Do you mean to pretend to be ill tomorrow for three days, eh?'

Smerdyakov, who was looking at the ground again, and making patterns with the toe of his right foot, set the foot down, moved the left one forward, and, grinning, articulated: 'If I were able to play such a trick, that is, pretend to have a fit – and it would not be difficult for a man accustomed to them – I should have a perfect right to use a means to save myself from death. For even if Agrafena Alexandrovna comes to see your father while I am ill, his honour can't blame a sick man for not telling. He'd be ashamed to.'

'Hang it all!' Ivan cried, his face working with anger. 'Why are you always in such a funk for your life? All my brother Dmitri's threats are only hasty words and mean nothing. He won't kill you; it's not you he'll kill!'

'He'd kill me first of all, like a fly. But even more than that, I am afraid I shall be taken for an accomplice of his when he does something crazy to his father.'

'Why should you be taken for an accomplice?'

'They'll think I am an accomplice, because I let him know the signals as a great secret.'

'What signals? Whom did you tell? Confound you, speak more plainly.'

'I'm bound to admit the fact,' Smerdyakov drawled with pedantic composure, 'that I have a secret with Fyodor Pavlovitch in this business. As you know yourself (if only you do know it) he has for several days past locked himself in as soon as night or evening comes. Of late you've been going upstairs to your room early every evening, and yesterday you did not come down at all, and so perhaps you don't know how carefully he has begun to lock himself in at night, and even if Grigory Vassilyevitch comes to the door he won't open to him till he hears his voice. But Grigory Vassilyevitch does not come, because I wait upon him alone in his room now. That's the arrangement he made himself ever since this to-do with Agrafena Alexandrovna began. But at night, by his orders, I go away to the lodge so that I don't get to sleep till midnight, but am on the watch, getting up and walking about the yard, waiting for Agrafena Alexandrovna to come. For the last few days he's been perfectly frantic expecting her. What he argues is, she is afraid of him, Dmitri Fyodorovitch (Mitya, as he calls him) "and so," says he, "she'll come the back way, late at night, to me. You look out for her," says he, "till midnight and later; and if she does come, you run up and knock at my door or at the window from the garden. Knock at first twice, rather gently, and then three times more quickly, then," says he, "I shall understand at once that she has come, and will open the door to you quietly." Another signal he gave me in case anything unexpected happens. At first, two knocks, and then, after an interval, another much louder. Then he will understand that something has happened suddenly and that I must see him, and he will open to me so that I can go in and speak to him. That's all in case Agrafena Alexandrovna can't come herself, but sends a message. Besides, Dmitri Fyodorovitch might come too, so I must let him know he is near. His honour is awfully afraid of Dmitri Fyodorovitch, so that even if Agrafena Alexandrovna had come and were locked in with him, and Dmitri Fyodorovitch were to turn up anywhere near at the time, I should be bound to let him know at once, knocking three times. So that the first signal of five knocks means Agrafena Alexandrovna has come, while the second signal of three knocks means "something important to tell you". His honour has shown me them several times and explained them. And as in the whole universe no one knows of these signals but myself and his honour, he'd open the door without the slightest hesitation and without calling out (he is awfully afraid of calling out aloud). Well, those signals are known to Dmitri Fyodorovitch too, now.'

'How are they known? Did you tell him? How dared you tell him?'

'I did it because I was terrified. How could I dare to

keep it back from him? Dmitri Fyodorovitch kept persisting every day, "You are deceiving me, you are hiding something from me! I'll break both your legs for you." So I told him about those secret signals to prove my absolute devotion, and to show that I was not deceiving him, but was telling him all I could.'

'If you think that he'll make use of those signals and try to get in, don't let him in.'

'But if I should be sick with a fit, how can I prevent him coming in then, even if I dared prevent him, knowing how desperate he is?'

'Damn it! How can you be so sure you are going to have a fit, confound you? Are you laughing at me?'

'How could I dare laugh at you, and I am in no laughing humour with this fear on me? I feel I am going to have a fit. I have a presentiment. Fright alone will bring it on.'

'Damn you! If you are laid up, Grigory will be on the watch. Let Grigory know beforehand; he will be sure not to let him in.'

'I would never dare tell Grigory Vassilyevitch about the signals without orders from my master. And as for Grigory Vassilyevitch hearing him and not admitting him, he has been ill since yesterday, and Marfa Ignatyevna intends to give him medicine tomorrow. They've just arranged it. It's a very strange remedy of hers. Marfa Ignatyevna knows of a preparation and always keeps it. It's a strong thing made from some herb. She has the secret of it, and she always gives it to Grigory Vassilyevitch three times a year when his lumbago's so bad he is almost paralysed by it. Then she takes a towel, wets it with the stuff, and rubs his whole back for half an hour till it's quite red and swollen, and what's left in the bottle she gives him to drink with a special prayer; but not quite all, for on such occasions she leaves some for herself, and drinks it herself. And as they never take strong drink, I assure you they both fall asleep at once and sleep sound a very long time. And when Grigory Vassilyevitch wakes up he is perfectly well after it, but Marfa Ignatyevna always has a headache from it. So, if Marfa Ignatyevna carries out her intention tomorrow, they won't hear anything and won't stop Dmitri Fyodorovitch. They'll be asleep.'

'What a rigmarole! And it all seems to happen at once, as though it were planned. You'll have a fit and they'll both be unconscious,' cried Ivan. 'But aren't you trying to arrange it so?' he said suddenly.

'How could I? . . . And why should I, when it all depends on Dmitri Fyodorovitch and his plans? . . . If he means to do anything, he'll do it; but if he doesn't, I won't be responsible for bringing him to his father.'

'And why should he go to father, especially on the sly, if, as you say yourself, Agrafena Alexandrovna won't come at all?' Ivan went on, turning white with anger. 'You say that yourself, and all the while I've been here, I've felt sure it was all the old man's fancy, and the creature won't come to him. Why should Dmitri break in on him if she doesn't come? Speak up, I want to know what you are thinking!'

'You know yourself why he'll come. What's the use of what I think? His honour will come simply because he is in a rage or suspicious on account of my illness perhaps, and he'll dash in, as he did yesterday through impatience to search the rooms, to see whether she hasn't escaped him on the sly. He is perfectly well aware, too, that Fyodor Pavlovitch has a big envelope with three thousand roubles in it, tied up with ribbon and sealed with three seals. On it is written in his own hand, "To my angel Grushenka, if she will come", to which he added three days later, "for my little chicken". There's no knowing what that might do.'

'Nonsense!' cried Ivan, almost beside himself. 'Dmitri won't come to steal money and kill my father to do it. He might have killed him yesterday on account of Grushenka, like the frantic, savage fool he is, but he won't steal.'

'He is in very great need of money now – the greatest need, Ivan Fyodorovitch. You don't know in what need he is,' Smerdyakov explained, with perfect composure and remarkable distinctness. 'He looks on that three thousand as his own, too. He told me so himself. "My father still owes me just three thousand," he said. And besides that, consider, Ivan Fyodorovitch, there is something else. It's as good as certain, so to say, that Agrafena Alexandrovna will force him, if only she cares to, to marry her – the master himself, I mean Fyodor Pavlovitch – if only she cares to, and of course she may care to. All I've said is that she won't come, but maybe she's looking for more than that – I mean to be mistress here. I know myself that Samsonov, her merchant, was laughing with her about it, telling her quite openly that it would not be at all a stupid thing to do. And she's got plenty of sense. She wouldn't marry a beggar like Dmitri Fyodorovitch. So, taking that into consideration, Ivan Fyodorovitch, reflect that then neither Dmitri Fyodorovitch nor yourself and your brother, Alexey Fyodorovitch, would have anything after the master's death, not a rouble, for Agrafena Alexandrovna would marry him simply to get hold of the whole, all the money there is. But if your father were to die now, there'd be some forty thousand for sure, even for

Dmitri Fyodorovitch whom he hates so, for he's made no will . . . Dmitri Fyodorovitch knows all that very well.'

A sort of shudder passed over Ivan's face. He suddenly flushed.

'Then why on earth,' he suddenly interrupted Smerdyakov, 'do you advise me to go to Tchermashnya? What did you mean by that? If I go away, you see what will happen here.' Ivan drew his breath with difficulty.

'Precisely so,' said Smerdyakov, softly and reasonably, watching Ivan intently, however.

'What do you mean by "precisely so"?' Ivan questioned him, with a menacing light in his eyes, restraining himself with difficulty.

'I spoke because I felt sorry for you. If I were in your place, I should simply throw it all up . . . rather than stay on in such a position,' answered Smerdyakov, with the most candid air looking at Ivan's flashing eyes. They were both silent.

'You seem to be a perfect idiot, and what's more . . . an awful scoundrel too.' Ivan rose suddenly from the bench. He was about to pass straight through the gate, but he stopped short and turned to Smerdyakov. Something strange followed. Ivan, in a sudden paroxysm, bit his lip, clenched his fists, and, in another minute, would have flung himself on Smerdyakov. The latter, anyway, noticed it at the same moment, shuddered, and shrank back. But the moment passed without danger to Smerdyakov, and Ivan turned in silence, as it seemed in perplexity, to the gate.

'I am going away to Moscow tomorrow, if you care to know – early tomorrow morning. That's all!' he suddenly said aloud angrily, and wondered himself afterwards what need there was to say this then to Smerdyakov.

'That's the best thing you can do,' he responded, as though he had expected to hear it; 'except that you can always be telegraphed for from Moscow, if anything should happen here.'

Ivan stopped again, and again turned quickly to Smerdyakov. But a change had passed over him too. All his familiarity and carelessness had completely disappeared. His face expressed attention and expectation, intent but timid and cringing.

'Haven't you something more to say – something to add?' could be read in the intent gaze he fixed on Ivan.

'And couldn't I be sent for from Tchermashnya, too – in case anything happened?' Ivan shouted suddenly, for some unknown reason raising his voice.

'From Tchermashnya, too . . . you could be sent for,' Smerdyakov muttered, almost in a whisper, looking disconcerted, but gazing intently into Ivan's eyes.

'Only Moscow is farther and Tchermashnya is nearer. Is it to save my spending money on the fare, or to save my going so far out of my way, that you insist on Tchermashnya?'

'Precisely so . . . ' muttered Smerdyakov, with a breaking voice. He looked at Ivan with a revolting smile, and again made ready to draw back. But to his astonishment Ivan broke into a laugh, and went through the gate still laughing. Anyone who had seen his face at that moment would have known that he was not laughing from lightness of heart, and he could not have explained himself what he was feeling at that instant. He moved and walked as though in a nervous frenzy.

6

And in the same nervous frenzy, too, he spoke. Meeting Fyodor Pavlovitch in the drawing-room directly he went in, he shouted to him, waving his hands, 'I am going upstairs to my room, I don't want to see you. Goodbye!' and passed by, trying not even to look at his father. Very possibly the old man was too hateful to him at that moment; but such an unceremonious display of hostility was a surprise even to Fyodor Pavlovitch. The old man evidently wanted to tell him something at once and had come to meet him in the drawing-room on purpose. On receiving this unexpected greeting, he stood still in silence and with an ironical air watched his son going upstairs, till he passed out of sight.

'What's the matter with him?' he promptly asked Smerdyakov, who had followed Ivan.

'Angry about something. Who can tell?' the valet muttered evasively.

'To hell with him! Let him be angry. Bring in the samovar, and get along with you. Look sharp! No news?'

Then followed a series of questions such as Smerdyakov had just complained of to Ivan, all relating to his expected visitor, and these questions we will omit. Half an hour later the house was locked, and the crazy old man was wandering alone through the rooms in excited expectation of hearing every minute the five knocks agreed upon. Now and then he peered out into the darkness, seeing nothing.

It was very late, but Ivan was still awake and thinking things over. He sat up late that night, till two o'clock. But we will not give an account of his thoughts, and this is not the place to look into that soul – its turn will come. And even if we tried, it would be very hard to give an account of them, for there were no thoughts in his brain, but some very vague, intense excitement. He felt himself that he had lost his bearings. He was fretted, too, by all sorts of strange and almost surprising desires; for instance, after midnight he suddenly had an intense irresistible inclination to go down, open the door, go to the lodge and beat up Smerdyakov. But if he had been asked why, he could not have given any exact reason, except perhaps that he loathed the valet as one who had insulted him more gravely than anyone in the world. On the other hand, he was overcome more than once that night by a sort of inexplicable humiliating terror, which he felt positively paralysed his physical powers. His head ached and he was dizzy. A feeling of hatred was rankling in his heart, as though he meant to avenge himself on someone. He even hated Alyosha, recalling the conversation he had just had with him. At moments he hated himself intensely. Of Katerina Ivanovna he almost forgot to think, and wondered greatly at this afterwards, especially as he remembered perfectly that when he had protested so valiantly to Katerina Ivanovna that he would go away next day to Moscow, something had whispered in his heart, 'That's nonsense, you are not going, and it won't be so easy to tear yourself away as you are boasting of doing now.'

Remembering that night long afterwards, Ivan recalled with peculiar repulsion how he had suddenly got up from the couch and stealthily, as though he were afraid of being watched, had opened the door, gone out on the staircase and listened to Fyodor Pavlovitch stirring down below, had listened a long while – some five minutes – with a sort of strange curiosity, holding his breath while his heart throbbed. And why he had done all this, why he was listening, he could not have said. That 'action' all his life afterwards he called 'infamous', and at the bottom of his heart, he thought of it as the basest action of his life. For Fyodor Pavlovitch himself he felt no hatred at that moment, but was simply intensely curious to know how he was walking down there below and what he must be doing now. He wondered and imagined how he must be peeping out of the dark windows and stopping in the middle of the room, listening, listening – for someone to knock. Ivan went out on to the stairs twice to listen like this.

About two o'clock when everything was quiet, and even Fyodor Pavlovitch had gone to bed, Ivan got into bed, firmly resolved to fall asleep at once, as he felt terribly exhausted. And he did fall asleep at once, and slept soundly without dreams, but waked early, at seven o'clock, when it was broad daylight. Opening his eyes, he was surprised to feel himself extraordinarily vigorous. He jumped up at once and dressed quickly; then dragged out his trunk and began packing immediately. His linen had come back from the laundress the previous morning. Ivan positively smiled at the thought that everything was helping his sudden departure. And his departure certainly was sudden. Though Ivan had said the day before (to Katerina Ivanovna, Alyosha, and Smerdyakov) that he was leaving next day, yet he remembered that he had no thought of departure when he went to bed, or, at least, had not dreamed that his first act in the morning would be to pack his trunk. At last his trunk and bag were ready. It was about nine o'clock when Marfa Ignatyevna came in with her usual enquiry, 'Where will your honour take your tea, in your own room or downstairs?' He looked almost cheerful, but there was about him, about his words and gestures, something hurried and absent-minded. Greeting his father affably, and even enquiring specially after his health, though he did not wait to hear the answer to the end, he announced that he was starting off in an hour to return to Moscow for good, and begged his father to send for the horses. His father heard this announcement with no sign of surprise, and forgot in an unmannerly way to show regret at losing him. Instead of doing so, he flew into a great flutter at the recollection of some important business of his own.

'What a fellow you are! Not to tell me yesterday! Never mind; we'll manage it all the same. Do me a great service, my dear boy. Go to Tchermashnya on the way. It's only a turn to the left from the station at Volovya, only another eight miles and you come to Tchermashnya.'

'I'm sorry, I can't. It's fifty miles to the railway and the train starts for Moscow at seven o'clock tonight. I can only just catch it.'

'You'll catch it tomorrow or the day after, but today turn off to Tchermashnya. It won't put you out much to humour your father! If I hadn't had something to keep me here, I would have run over myself long ago, for I've some business there in a hurry. But here I . . . it's not the time for me to go now . . . You see, I've two pieces of young timber land there. The Maslovs, an old merchant and his son, will give eight thousand for the timber. But last year I just missed a purchaser who would have given twelve. There's no getting anyone about here to buy it. The Maslovs have it all their own way. One has to take what they'll give, for no one here dare bid against them. The priest at Ilyinskoe wrote to me last Thursday that a merchant called Gorstkin, a man I know, had turned up. What makes him valuable is that he is not from these parts, so he's not afraid of the Maslovs. He says he will give me eleven thousand for the copse. Do you hear? But he'll only be here, the priest writes, for a week altogether, so you must go at once and make a bargain with him.'

'Well, you write to the priest; he'll make the bargain.'

'He can't do it. He has no eye for business. He is a perfect saint, I'd give him twenty thousand to take care of for me without a receipt; but he has no eye for business, he is a child, a chicken could fool him. And yet he is a learned man, would you believe it? This Gorstkin looks like a peasant, he wears a long blue coat, but he is a regular rogue. That's the common complaint. He is a liar. Sometimes he tells such lies that you wonder why he is doing it. He told me the year before last that his wife was dead and that he had married another, and would you believe it, there was not a word of truth in it? His wife has never died at all, she is alive to this day and gives him a beating twice a week. So what you have to find out is whether he is lying or speaking the truth, when he says he wants to buy it and would give eleven thousand.'

'I won't be of any use in such a business. I have no eye for the telltale signs.'

'Now, wait a bit! You will be of use, for I will tell you the signs by which you can judge about Gorstkin. I've done business with him a long time. You see, you must watch his beard; he has a nasty, thin, red beard. If his beard shakes when he talks and he gets cross, it's all right, he is saying what he means, he wants to do business. But if he strokes his beard with his left hand and grins – he is trying to cheat you. Don't watch his eyes, you won't find out anything from his eyes, he is a deep one, a rogue – but watch his beard! I'll give you a note and you show it to him. He's called Gorstkin, though his real name is Lyagavy, like the setter dog; but don't call him so, he will be offended. If you come to an understanding with him, and see it's all right, write to me at once. You need only say: "He's not lying." Stand out for eleven thousand; one thousand you can knock off, but not more. Just think! there's a difference between eight thousand and eleven thousand. It's as good as picking up three thousand; it's not so easy to find a buyer, and I'm in desperate need of money. Just let me know it's serious, and I'll run over and fix it up. I'll find the time somehow. But what's the good of my chasing over there, if it's all a wild idea of the priest's? Now, will you go?'

'But, I can't spare the time. You must excuse me.'

'Come, you might oblige your father. I shan't forget it. You've no heart, any of you – that's what it is! What's a day or two to you? Where are you going now – to Venice? Your Venice will keep another two days. I would have sent Alyosha, but what use is Alyosha in an affair like this? I send you just because you are a clever fellow. Do you suppose I don't know that? You understand nothing about timber, but you've got an eye. All that is wanted is to see whether the man is in earnest. I tell you, watch his beard – if his beard shakes, you know he means business.'

'You force me to go to that damned Tchermashnya yourself, then?' cried Ivan, with a malignant smile.

Fyodor Pavlovitch did not catch, or would not catch, the malignancy, but he caught the smile.

'Then you'll go, you'll go? I'll scribble the note for you at once.'

'I don't know whether I shall go. I don't know. I'll decide on the way.'

'Nonsense! Decide at once. My dear fellow, decide! If you settle the matter, write me a line; give it to the priest and he'll send it on to me at once. And I won't delay you more than that. You can go to Venice. The priest will give you horses back to Volovya station.'

The old man was quite delighted. He wrote the note, and sent for the horses. A light lunch was brought in, with brandy. When Fyodor Pavlovitch was pleased, he usually became expansive, but today he seemed to restrain himself. Of Dmitri, for instance, he did not say a word. He was quite unmoved by the parting, and seemed, in fact, at a loss for something to say. Ivan noticed this particularly. 'He must be bored with me,' he thought. Only when accompanying his son out on to the steps, the old man began to fuss. He would have kissed him, but Ivan made haste to hold out his hand, obviously avoiding the kiss. His father noticed the gesture at once, and instantly pulled himself up.

'Well, good luck to you, good luck to you!' he repeated from the steps. 'You'll come again some time or other? Mind you do come. I shall always be glad to see you. Well, Christ be with you!'

Ivan got into the carriage.

'Goodbye, Ivan! Don't be too hard on me!' his father called for the last time.

The whole household came out to take leave – Smerdyakov, Marfa and Grigory. Ivan gave them ten roubles each. When he had seated himself in the carriage, Smerdyakov jumped up to arrange the rug.

'You see . . . I am going to Tchermashnya,' broke suddenly from Ivan. Again, as the day before, the words seemed to drop of themselves, and he laughed, too, a peculiar, nervous laugh. He remembered it long after.

'It's a true saying then, that "a word to the wise is sufficient",' answered Smerdyakov firmly, looking significantly at Ivan.

The carriage rolled away. Nothing was clear in Ivan's soul, but he looked eagerly around him at the fields, at the hills, at the trees, at a flock of geese flying high overhead in the bright sky. And all of a sudden he felt very happy. He tried to talk to the driver, and he felt intensely interested in an answer the peasant made him; but a minute later he realised that he was not really listening, and that he had not even taken in the peasant's answer. He was silent, and it was pleasant even so. The air was fresh, pure and cool, the sky bright. The images of Alyosha and Katerina Ivanovna floated into his mind. But he smiled gently, blew softly on the friendly phantoms, and they flew away. 'There's plenty of time for them,' he thought. They reached the station quickly, changed horses, and galloped to Volovya. 'In what way is "a word to the wise sufficient"? What did he mean by that?' The thought seemed suddenly to stop his breathing. 'And why did I tell him I was going to Tchermashnya?' They reached Volovya Station. Ivan got out of the carriage, and the drivers stood round him bargaining over the journey of eight miles to Tchermashnya. He told them to harness the horses. He went into the station house, looked around, glanced at the overseer's wife, and suddenly went back to the entrance.

'I won't go to Tchermashnya. Am I too late to reach the railway by seven, brothers?'

'We can just make it. Shall we get the carriage out?'

'At once. Will any one of you be going to the town tomorrow?'

'To be sure. Mitri here will.'

'Can you do me a service, Mitri? Go to my father's, to Fyodor Pavlovitch Karamazov, and tell him I didn't go to Tchermashyna. Can you?'

'Of course I can. I've known Fyodor Pavlovitch a long time.'

'And here's something for you, for I dare say he won't give you anything,' said Ivan, laughing gaily.

'You may depend on it he won't.' Mitri laughed too. 'Thank you, sir. I'll be sure to deliver your message.'

At seven o'clock Ivan got into the train and set off for Moscow. 'Away with the past. I've done with the old world for ever, and may I have no news, no echo, from it. To a new life, new places, and no looking back!' But instead of delight, his soul was filled with such gloom, and his heart ached with such anguish as he had never known in his life before. He lay awake thinking all night. The train raced on, and only at daybreak, when he was approaching Moscow, did he suddenly rouse himself from his meditation.

'I am a scoundrel,' he whispered to himself.

Fyodor Pavlovitch remained well satisfied with having seen his son off. For two hours afterwards he felt almost happy, and sat drinking brandy. But suddenly something happened which was very annoying and unpleasant for everyone in the house, and completely upset Fyodor Pavlovitch's equanimity at once. Smerdyakov went to the cellar and fell down from the top of the steps. Fortunately, Marfa Ignatyevna was in the yard and heard him in time. She did not see the fall, but heard his scream – the strange, peculiar scream, long familiar to her – the scream of the epileptic falling in a fit. They could not tell whether the fit had come on him at the moment he was descending the steps, so that he must have fallen unconscious, or whether it was the fall and the shock that had caused the fit in Smerdyakov, who was known to be liable to them. They found him at the bottom of the cellar steps, writhing in convulsions and foaming at the mouth. It was thought at first that he must have broken some bone – an arm or a leg – and hurt himself, but 'God had preserved him', as Marfa Ignatyevna expressed it – nothing of the kind had happened. But it was difficult to get him out of the cellar. They asked the neighbours to help and managed it somehow. Fyodor Pavlovitch himself was present at the whole ceremony. He helped, evidently alarmed and upset. The sick man did not regain consciousness; the convulsions ceased for a time, but then began again, and everyone concluded the same thing would happen, as had happened a year before, when he accidentally fell from the attic. They remembered that ice had been put on his head then. There was still ice in the cellar, and Marfa Ignatyevna had some brought up. In the evening, Fyodor Pavlovitch sent for Dr Herzenstube, who arrived at once. He was a most estimable old man, and the most careful and conscientious doctor in the province. After a meticulous examination, he concluded that the fit was a very violent one and might have serious consequences; that meanwhile he, Herzenstube, did not fully understand it, but that by tomorrow morning, if the present remedies were unavailing, he would venture to try something else. The invalid was taken to the lodge, to a room next to Grigory's and Marfa Ignatyeyna's.

Then Fyodor Pavlovitch had one misfortune after another to put up with that day. Marfa Ignatyevna cooked the dinner, and the soup, compared with Smerdyakov's, was no 'better than dish water', and the fowl was so dried up that it was impossible to masticate it. To her master's bitter, though deserved, reproaches, Marfa Ignatyevna replied that the fowl was a very old one to begin with, and that she had never been trained as a cook. In the evening there was more trouble in store for Fyodor Pavlovitch; he was informed that Grigory, who had not been well for the last three days, was completely laid up by his lumbago. Fyodor Pavlovitch finished his tea as early as possible and locked himself up alone in the house. He was terribly excited and filled with anticipation. That evening he reckoned on Grushenka's coming almost as a certainty. He had received from Smerdyakov that morning an assurance 'that she had promised to come without fail'. The incorrigible old man's heart throbbed with excitement; he paced up and down his empty rooms listening. He had to be on the alert. Dmitri might be on the watch for her somewhere, and when she knocked on the window (Smerdyakov had informed him two days before that he had told her where and how to knock) the door must be opened at once. She must not be a second in the passage, for fear – which God forbid! – that she should be frightened and run away. Fyodor Pavlovitch had much to think of, but never had his heart been steeped in such voluptuous hopes. This time he was almost certain that she would come!

Book Six

I

When with an anxious and aching heart Alyosha went into his elder's cell, he stood still almost astonished. Instead of a sick man at his last gasp, perhaps unconscious, as he had feared to find him, he saw the elder sitting up in his chair and, though weak and exhausted, his face was bright and cheerful; he was surrounded by visitors and engaged in a quiet and happy conversation. But he had only got up from his bed a quarter of an hour before Alyosha's arrival; his visitors had gathered together in his cell earlier, waiting for him to wake, having received a most confident assurance from Father Païssy that 'the teacher would get up, and as he had himself promised in the morning, converse once more with those dear to his heart'. Father Païssy put implicit trust in this promise and indeed in every word of the dying elder. If he had seen him unconscious, if he had seen him breathe his last, and yet had his promise that he would rise up and say goodbye to him, he would not have believed perhaps even in death, but would still have expected the dead man to recover and fulfil his promise. In the morning as he lay down to sleep, Father Zossima had told him positively: 'I shall not die without the pleasure of another conversation with you, beloved of my heart. I shall look once more on your dear face and pour out my heart to you once again.' The monks, who had gathered for what would probably be the last conversation with Father Zossima, had all been his devoted friends for many years. There were four of them: Father Iosif and Father Païssy. Father Mihail, the warden of the hermitage, a man not very old and far from being learned. He was of humble origin, of strong will and steadfast faith, of austere appearance, but of deep tenderness, though he obviously concealed it as though he were almost ashamed of it. The fourth, Father Anfim, was a very old and humble little monk of the poorest peasant class. He was almost illiterate, and very quiet, scarcely speaking to anyone. He was the humblest of the humble, and looked as though he had been frightened by something great and awful beyond the scope of his intelligence. Father Zossima had a great affection for this timorous man, and always treated him with marked respect, though perhaps there was no one he had known to whom he had said less, in spite of the fact that he had spent years wandering about holy Russia with him. That was very long ago, forty years before, when Father Zossima first began his life as a monk in a poor small monastery at Kostroma, and when, shortly after, he had accompanied Father Anfim on his pilgrimage to collect alms for their poor monastery.

The whole party was in the bedroom, which, as we mentioned before, was very small, so that there was scarcely room for the four of them (in addition to Porfiry, the novice, who stood) to sit round Father Zossima on chairs brought from the sitting-room. It was already beginning to grow dark; the room was illuminated by the lamps and the candles before the icons.

Seeing Alyosha standing embarrassed in the

doorway, Father Zossima smiled at him joyfully and held out his hand.

'Welcome, my quiet one, welcome, my dear, here you are too. I knew you would come.'

Alyosha went up to him, bowed down before him to the ground and wept. Something surged up from his heart, he wanted to sob.

'Come, don't weep over me yet,' Father Zossima smiled, laying his right hand on Alyosha's head. 'You see I am sitting up talking; maybe I shall live another twenty years yet, as that dear good woman from Vishegorye, with her little Lizaveta in her arms, wished me yesterday. God bless the mother and the little girl Lizaveta,' he crossed himself. 'Porfiry, did you take her offering where I told you?'

He meant the sixty kopecks brought him the day before by the good-humoured woman to be given 'to someone poorer than me'. Such offerings, always of money gained by personal toil, are made by way of penance voluntarily undertaken. The elder had sent Porfiry the evening before to a widow, whose house had been burned down lately, and who after the fire had gone with her children begging alms. Porfiry hastened to reply that he had given the money, as he had been instructed, from 'an unknown benefactress'.

'Get up, my dear boy,' the elder went on to Alyosha. 'Let me look at you. Have you been home and seen your brother?' It seemed strange to Alyosha that he asked so confidently and precisely, about one of his brothers only – but which one? Then perhaps he had sent him out both yesterday and today for the sake of that brother.

'I have seen one of my brothers,' answered Alyosha.

'I mean the older one, to whom I bowed down.'

'I only saw him yesterday and could not find him today,' said Alyosha.

'Make haste to find him, go again tomorrow and make haste, leave everything and make haste. Perhaps you may still have time to prevent something terrible. I bowed down yesterday to the great suffering in store for him.'

He was suddenly silent and seemed to be pondering. The words were strange. Father Iosif, who had witnessed the scene yesterday, exchanged glances with Father Païssy. Alyosha could not resist asking: 'Father and teacher,' he began with extreme emotion, 'your words are too obscure . . . What is this suffering in store for him?'

'Don't enquire. I seemed to see something terrible yesterday . . . as though his whole future were expressed in his eyes. A look came into his eyes – so that I was instantly horror-stricken at what that man is preparing for himself. Once or twice in my life I've seen such a look in a man's face . . . reflecting as it were his future fate, and that fate, alas, came to pass. I sent you to him, Alexey, for I thought your brotherly face would help him. But everything and all our destiny is from the Lord. "Except a corn of wheat fall into the ground and die, it abideth alone; but if it die, it bringeth forth much fruit." Remember that. You, Alexey, I've many times silently thanked the Lord for your face, know that,' added the elder with a gentle smile. 'This is what I think of you, you will go forth from these walls, but will live like a monk in the world. You will have many enemies, but even your foes will love you. Life will bring you many misfortunes, but you will find your happiness in them, and will bless life and will make others bless it – which is what matters most. Well, that is your character.

Fathers and teachers,' he addressed his friends with a tender smile, 'I have never till today told even him why the face of his youth is so dear to me. Now I will tell you. His face has been as it were a remembrance and a prophecy for me. At the dawn of my life when I was a child I had an older brother who died before my eyes at seventeen. And later on in the course of my life I gradually became convinced that that brother had been a guidance and a sign from on high for me. For had he not come into my life, I should never perhaps, so I fancy at least, have become a monk and entered on this sacred path. He appeared first to me in my childhood and here at the end of my pilgrimage he seems to have come to me over again. It is miraculous, fathers and teachers, that Alexey, who has some, though not a great, resemblance in face, seems to me so like him spiritually, that many times I have taken him for that young man, my brother, mysteriously come back to me at the end of my pilgrimage, as a reminder and an inspiration. So that I positively wondered at so strange a dream in myself. Do you hear this, Porfiry?' he turned to the novice who waited on him. 'Many times I've seen in your face as it were a look of mortification that I love Alexey more than you. Now you know why that was so, but I love you too, know that, and many times I grieved at your mortification.'

The elder's death came in the end quite unexpectedly. For although those who were gathered about him that last evening realised that his death was approaching, yet it was difficult to imagine that it would come so suddenly. On the contrary, his friends, as I observed already, seeing him that night apparently so cheerful and talkative, were convinced that there was at least a temporary change for the better in his condition. Even five minutes before his death, they said afterwards wonderingly, it was impossible to foresee it. He seemed suddenly to feel an acute pain in his chest, he turned pale and pressed his hands to his heart. All rose from their seats and hastened to him. But though suffering, he still looked at them with a smile, sank slowly from his chair on his knees, then bowed his face to the ground, stretched out his arms and as though in joyful ecstasy, praying and kissing the ground, quietly and joyfully gave up his soul to God.

The news of his death spread at once through the hermitage and reached the monastery. The nearest friends of the deceased and those whose duty it was from their position began to lay out the corpse according to the ancient ritual, and all the monks gathered together in the church. And before dawn the news of the death reached the town. By the morning all the town was talking of the event, and crowds flocked from the town to the monastery. I will only add here that before a day had passed something happened so unexpected, so strange, upsetting, and bewildering in its effect on the monks and the townspeople, that after all these years, that day of general suspense is still vividly remembered in the town.

2

It had begun to get dusk when Rakitin, crossing the pine wood from the hermitage to the monastery, suddenly noticed Alyosha, lying face down on the ground under a tree, not moving and apparently asleep. He went up and called him by his name.

'You here, Alexey? Can you have . . .' he began wondering but broke off. He had meant to say, 'Can you have come to this?'

Alyosha did not look at him, but from a slight movement Rakitin at once saw that he heard and understood him.

'What's the matter?' continued Rakitin; but the surprise in his face gradually merged into a smile that became more and more ironical.

'I say, I've been looking for you for the last two hours. You suddenly disappeared. What are you doing? What nonsense is this? You might just look at me . . .'

Alyosha raised his head, sat up and leaned his back against the tree. He was not crying, but there was a look of suffering and irritability in his face. He did not look at Rakitin, however, but looked away to one side of him.

'Do you know your face is quite changed? There's none of your famous mildness to be seen in it. Are you angry with someone? Have they been ill-treating you?'

'Let me alone,' said Alyosha suddenly, with a weary gesture of his hand, still looking away.

'Oho! So that's how we are feeling! So you can shout at people like other mortals. That is a comedown from the angels. I say, Alyosha, you have surprised me, do you hear? I mean it. It's long since I've been surprised at anything. I always took you for an educated man . . .'

Alyosha at last looked at him, but vaguely, as though scarcely understanding what he said.

'Can you really be so upset simply because your old man has begun to stink? You don't mean to say you seriously believed that he was going to work miracles?' exclaimed Rakitin, genuinely surprised again.

'I believed, I believe, I want to believe, and I will believe, what more do you want?' cried Alyosha irritably.

'Nothing at all, my boy. Damn it all, why no schoolboy of thirteen believes in that now. But there . . . So now you are angry with your God, you rebel against Him; He hasn't given promotion. He hasn't bestowed the order of merit! Ah, you!'

Alyosha gazed a long while with his eyes half closed at Rakitin, and there was a sudden gleam in his eyes . . . but not of anger at Rakitin.

'I am not rebelling against my God; I simply "don't accept His world".' Alyosha suddenly smiled a forced smile.

'How do you mean, you don't accept the world?' Rakitin thought a moment over his answer. 'What idiocy is this?'

Alyosha did not answer.

'Come, that's enough nonsense, now to business. Have you had anything to eat today?'

'I don't remember . . . I think I have.'

'You need nourishment, to judge by your face. It makes one sorry to look at you. You didn't sleep all night either, I hear, you had a meeting in there. And then all this fuss and flurry afterwards. Most likely you've had nothing to eat but a mouthful of holy bread. I've got some sausage in my pocket; I've brought it from the town in case of need, only you won't eat sausage . . .'

'Give me some.'

'Well, I must say. So that's how it is. Why, it's a regular mutiny, with barricades! Well, my boy, we must make the most of it. Come to my place . . . I wouldn't mind a drop of vodka myself, I am tired to death. Vodka is going too far for you, I suppose . . . or would you like some?'

'Give me some vodka too.'

'Well, well! You surprise me, brother!' Rakitin looked at him in amazement. 'Anyway, one way or another, vodka or sausage, this is a fine chance and mustn't be missed. Come along.'

Alyosha got up in silence and followed Rakitin.

'If your little brother Ivan could see this – wouldn't he be surprised! By the way, your brother Ivan set off to Moscow this morning, did you know?'

'Yes,' answered Alyosha listlessly, and suddenly the image of his brother Dmitri rose before his mind. But only for a moment, and though it reminded him of something that must not be put off for an instant, some duty, some terrible obligation, even that reminder made no impression on him, did not reach his heart, and faded immediately out of his mind and was forgotten. But, a long while afterwards, Alyosha remembered this.

'Your brother Ivan declared once that I was a "liberal fool with no talents whatever". Once you too could not resist letting me know I was "dishonourable". Well! I should like to see what your talents and sense of honour will do for you now.' This phrase Rakitin finished to himself in a whisper.

'Listen!' he said aloud, 'let's go by the path beyond the monastery straight to the town.' He suddenly stopped and taking Alyosha by the shoulder made him stop too.

'Do you know, Alyosha – ' He looked inquisitively into Alyosha's eyes, absorbed in a sudden new thought which had dawned on him, and though he was laughing outwardly he was evidently afraid to utter that new idea aloud, so difficult he still found it to believe in the strange and unexpected mood in which he now saw Alyosha. 'Alyosha, do you know where we had better go?' he brought out at last timidly, and insinuatingly.

'I don't care . . . where you like.'

'Let's go to Grushenka, eh? Will you come?' pronounced Rakitin at last, trembling with timid suspense.

'Let's go to Grushenka,' Alyosha answered calmly, at once, and this prompt and calm agreement was such a surprise to Rakitin that he almost stepped back.

'Well! I must say!' he cried in amazement, but seizing Alyosha firmly by the arm he led him along the path still dreading that Alyosha would change his mind.

They walked on in silence; Rakitin was positively afraid to talk.

'And how glad she will be, how delighted,' he muttered, but lapsed into silence again. And indeed it was not to please Grushenka that he was taking Alyosha to her. He was a practical creature and never undertook anything without a prospect of gain for himself.

3

Grushenka lived in the busiest part of the town, near the cathedral square, in a small wooden house in the courtyard belonging to the big house of the widow Morozov. The big house was a large stone building of two storeys, old and very ugly. The widow led a secluded life with her two unmarried nieces, who were also elderly women. She had no need to rent her small house, but everyone knew that she had taken in Grushenka as a lodger, four years before, solely to please her kinsman, the merchant Samsonov, who was known to be the girl's protector. It was said that the jealous old man's object in placing his 'favourite' with the widow Morozov was that the old woman could keep a sharp eye on her new lodger's conduct. But this sharp eye soon proved to be unnecessary, and in the end the widow Morozov seldom met Grushenka and did not worry her by looking after her in any way. It is true that four years had passed since the old man had brought the slim, delicate, shy, timid, dreamy, and sad girl of eighteen from the chief town of the province, and much had happened since then. Little was known of the girl's history in the town and that little was vague. Nothing more had been learned during the last four years, even after many persons had become interested in the beautiful young woman into whom Agrafena Alexandrovna had meanwhile developed. There were rumours that she had been at seventeen betrayed by someone, some officer, and immediately afterwards abandoned by him. The officer had gone away and afterwards married, while Grushenka had been left in poverty and disgrace. It was said, however, that though Grushenka had been raised from destitution by the old man, Samsonov, she came of a respectable family belonging to the clerical class, that she was the daughter of a deacon or something of the sort.

And now after four years the sensitive, injured and pathetic little orphan had become a plump, rosy beauty of the Russian type, a woman of bold and determined character, proud and insolent. She had a good head for business, was acquisitive, thrifty and careful, and by fair means or foul had succeeded, it was said, in amassing a little fortune. There was only one point on which all were agreed. Grushenka was not easy to approach and except for her aged protector there had not been one man who could boast of her favours during those four years. It was a positive fact, for there had been a good many, especially during the last two years, who had attempted to obtain those favours. But all their efforts had been in vain and some of these suitors had been forced to beat an undignified and even comic retreat, owing to the firm and ironical resistance they met from the strong-willed young person. It was known, too, that the young person had, especially of late, been given to what is called 'speculation', and that she had shown marked abilities in that direction. It was known, for instance, that she had for some time past, in partnership with old Karamazov, actually invested in the purchase of bad debts for a trifle, a tenth of their nominal value, and afterwards had made out of them ten times their value.

The old widower Samsonov, a man of large fortune, was stingy and merciless. He tyrannised over his grown-up sons, but, for the last year, during which he had been ill and lost the use of his swollen legs, he had fallen greatly under the influence of his protégée, whom he had at first kept strictly and in humble surroundings 'on Lenten fare' as the wits said at the time. But Grushenka had succeeded in emancipating herself, while she established in him a boundless belief in her fidelity. The old man, now long since dead, had had a large business in his day and was also a noteworthy character, miserly and hard as flint. Though Grushenka's hold upon him was so strong that he could not live without her (it had been so especially for the last two years), he did not settle any considerable fortune on her and would not have been moved to do so, if she had threatened to leave him. But he had presented her with a small sum, and even that was a surprise to everyone when it became known.

'You are a wench with brains,' he said to her, when he gave her eight thousand roubles, 'and you must look after yourself, but let me tell you that except your yearly allowance as before, you'll get nothing more from me to the day of my death, and I'll leave you nothing in my will either.'

And he kept his word; he died and left everything to his sons, whom, with their wives and children, he had treated all his life as servants. Grushenka was not even mentioned in his will. All this became known afterwards. He helped Grushenka with his advice to increase her capital and put business in her way.

When Fyodor Pavlovitch, who first came into contact with Grushenka over a piece of speculation, ended to his own surprise by falling madly in love with her, old Samsonov, gravely ill as he was, was immensely amused. It is remarkable that throughout their whole acquaintance Grushenka was absolutely and spontaneously open with the old man, and he seems to have been the only person in the world with whom she was so. Of late, when Dmitri, too, had come on the scene with his love, the old man left off laughing. On the contrary, he once gave Grushenka a stern and earnest piece of advice.

'If you have to choose between the two, father or son, you'd better choose the old man, if only you make sure the old scoundrel will marry you and settle some fortune on you beforehand. But don't keep on with the captain, you'll get no good out of that.'

These were the very words of the old profligate, who felt already that his death was not far off and who actually died five months later.

I will note, too, in passing, that, although many in our town knew of the grotesque and monstrous rivalry of the Karamazovs, father and son, the object of which was Grushenka, scarcely anyone understood what really underlay her attitude to both of them. Even Grushenka's two servants later testified in court that she received Dmitri Fyodorovitch simply from fear because 'he threatened to murder her'. These servants were an old cook, sickly and almost deaf, who came from Grushenka's old home, and her granddaughter, a smart young girl of twenty, who performed the duties of a maid. Grushenka lived very economically and her surroundings were anything but luxurious. Her home consisted of three rooms furnished with mahogany furniture in the fashion of 1820, belonging to her landlady.

It was quite dark when Rakitin and Alyosha entered her rooms, yet they were not lighted up. Grushenka was lying down in her drawing-room on the big, hard, clumsy sofa, with a mahogany back. The sofa was covered with shabby and ragged leather. Under her head she had two white down pillows taken from her bed. She was lying stretched out motionless on her back with her hands behind her head. She was dressed as though expecting someone, in a black silk dress, with a dainty lace fichu on her head, which was very becoming. A lace shawl pinned with a massive gold brooch was draped over her shoulders. She certainly was expecting someone. She lay as though impatient and weary, her face rather pale and her lips and eyes hot, restlessly tapping the arm of the sofa with the tip of her right foot. The appearance of Rakitin and Alyosha caused a slight excitement. From the hall they could hear Grushenka leap up from the sofa and cry out in a frightened voice, 'Who's there?' But the maid met the visitors and at once called back to her mistress.

'It's not he, it's nothing, only other visitors.'

'What can be the matter?' muttered Rakitin, leading Alyosha into the drawing-room.

Grushenka was standing by the sofa as though still alarmed. A thick coil of her dark brown hair escaped from its lace covering and fell on her right shoulder, but she did not notice it and did not put it back till she had gazed at her visitors and recognised them.

'Ah, it's you, Rakitin? You quite frightened me. Whom have you brought? Who is this with you? Good heavens, you have brought him!' she exclaimed, recognising Alyosha.

'Do send for candles!' said Rakitin, with the free-and-easy air of a most intimate friend, who is privileged to give orders in the house.

'Candles . . . of course, candles . . . Fenya, go get a candle for him . . . Well, you have chosen a moment to bring him!' she exclaimed again, nodding towards Alyosha and turning to the looking-glass she began quickly fastening up her hair with both hands. She seemed displeased.

'Haven't I managed to please you?' asked Rakitin, instantly almost offended.

'You frightened me, Rakitin, that's what.' Grushenka turned with a smile to Alyosha. 'Don't be afraid of me, my dear Alyosha, you can't think how glad I am to see you, my unexpected visitor. But you frightened me, Rakitin, I thought it was Mitya breaking in. You see, I deceived him just now, I made him promise to believe me and I told him a lie. I told him that I was going to spend the evening with my old man, Kuzma Kuzmitch, and would be there till late counting up his money. I always spend one whole evening a week with him making up his accounts. We lock ourselves in and he counts on the abacus while I sit and put things down in the book. I am the only person he trusts. Mitya believes that I am there, but I came back and have been sitting locked in here, expecting some news. How was it Fenya let you in? Fenya, Fenya, run out to the gate, open it and see whether the captain is anywhere near! Perhaps he is hiding and spying, I am dreadfully frightened.'

'There's no one there, Agrafena Alexandrovna, I've just looked out, I keep running to peep through the crack, I am in fear and trembling myself.'

'Are the shutters fastened, Fenya? And we must draw the curtains – that's better!' She drew the heavy curtains herself. 'He'd rush in at once if he saw a light. I am afraid of your brother Mitya today, Alyosha.'

Grushenka spoke aloud, and, though she was alarmed, she seemed very happy about something.

'Why are you so afraid of Mitya today?' enquired Rakitin. 'I should have thought you were not timid with him, you can twist him round your little finger.'

'I tell you, I am expecting news, priceless news, so I don't want Mitya at all. And he didn't believe, I feel he didn't, that I would stay at Kuzma Kuzmitch's. He must be in his ambush now, behind Fyodor Pavlovitch's, in the garden, watching for me. And if he's there, he won't come here, so much the better! But I really have been to Kuzma Kuzmitch's, Mitya escorted me there. I told him I should stay there till midnight, and I asked him to be sure to come at midnight to fetch me home. He went away and I sat ten minutes with Kuzma Kuzmitch and came back here again. Oh, I was afraid, I ran for fear of meeting him.'

'And why are you so dressed up? What a curious headdress you've got on!'

'How inquisitive you are, Rakitin! I tell you, I am expecting a message. If the message comes, I shall fly, I shall gallop away and you will see no more of me. That's why I am dressed up, so as to be ready.'

'And where are you flying to?'

'If you know too much, you'll get old too soon.'

'Upon my word! You are highly delighted . . . I've never seen you like this before. You are dressed up as if you were going to a ball.' Rakitin looked her up and down.

'Much you know about balls.'

'And do you know much about them?'

'I have seen a ball. The year before last, Kuzma Kuzmitch's son was married and I looked on from the gallery. Do you suppose I want to be talking to you, Rakitin, while a prince like this is standing here. Such a visitor! Alyosha, my dear boy, I gaze at you and can't believe my eyes. Good heavens, can you have come here to see me! To tell you the truth, I never had a thought of seeing you and I didn't think that you would ever come and see me. Though this is not the moment now, I am awfully glad to see you. Sit down on the sofa, here, that's right, my bright young moon. I really can't take it in even now . . . Oh, Rakitin, if only you had brought him yesterday or the day before! But I am glad as it is! Perhaps it's better he has come now, at such a moment, and not the day before yesterday.'

She gaily sat down beside Alyosha on the sofa, looking at him with positive delight. And she really was glad, she was not lying when she said so. Her eyes glowed, her lips laughed, but it was a good-natured merry laugh. Alyosha had not expected to see such a kind expression in her face . . . He had barely met her till the day before, he had formed an alarming idea of her, and had been horribly distressed the day before by the spiteful and treacherous trick she had played on Katerina Ivanovna. He was greatly surprised to find her now altogether different from what he had expected. And, crushed as he was by his own sorrow, his eyes involuntarily rested on her with attention. Her whole manner seemed changed for the better since yesterday, there was scarcely any trace of that mawkish sweetness in her speech, of that voluptuous softness in her movements. Everything was simple and good-natured, her gestures were rapid, direct, confiding, but she was greatly excited.

'Dear me, how everything comes together today,' she chattered on again. 'And why I am so glad to see you, Alyosha, I couldn't say myself! If you ask me, I couldn't tell you.'

'Come, don't you know why you're glad?' said Rakitin, grinning. 'You used to be always pestering me to bring him, you'd some object, I suppose.'

'I had a different object once, but now that's over, this is not the moment. I say, I want you to have something nice. I am so good-natured now. Let me sit on your knees, Alyosha, like this.' She suddenly skipped forward and jumped, laughing, on his knee, like a nestling kitten, with her right arm about his neck. 'I'll cheer you up, my pious boy. Yes, really, will you let me sit on your knee, you won't be angry? If you tell me, I'll get off.'

Alyosha did not speak. He sat afraid to move, he

heard her words, 'If you tell me, I'll get off,' but he did not answer. But there was nothing in his heart such as Rakitin, for instance, watching him malignantly from his corner, might have expected or fancied. The great grief in his heart swallowed up every sensation that might have been aroused, and, if only he could have thought clearly at that moment, he would have realised that he had now the strongest armour to protect him from every lust and temptation. Yet in spite of the dim uncertainty of his spirit and the sorrow that overwhelmed him, he could not help wondering at a new and strange sensation in his heart. This woman, this 'dreadful' woman, had no terror for him now, none of that terror that had stirred in his soul at any passing thought of woman. On the contrary, this woman, dreaded above all women, sitting now on his knee, holding him in her arms, aroused in him now a quite different, unexpected, peculiar feeling, a feeling of intense and pure interest without a trace of fear, of his former terror. That was what instinctively surprised him.

'You've talked enough nonsense,' cried Rakitin. 'You'd much better give us some champagne. You owe it to me, you know you do!'

'Yes, I really do. Do you know, Alyosha, I promised him champagne as a reward, if he'd bring you? I'll have some too! Fenya, Fenya, bring us the bottle Mitya left! Be quick! Though I am so stingy, I'll stand a bottle, not for you, Rakitin, you're a nasty little fellow, but he is a prince! And though my heart is full of something very different, so be it, I'll drink with you. I long for some dissipation.'

'But what is the matter with you? And what is this message may I ask, or is it a secret?' Rakitin put in inquisitively, doing his best to pretend not to notice the snubs that were being continually aimed at him.

'Oh, it's not a secret, and you know it too,' Grushenka said, in a voice suddenly anxious, turning her head towards Rakitin, and drawing a little away from Alyosha, though she still sat on his knee with her arm round his neck. 'My officer is coming, Rakitin, my officer is coming.'

'I heard he was coming, but is he so near?'

'He is at Mokroe now. He'll send a messenger from there, so he wrote. I got a letter from him today. I am expecting the messenger every minute.'

'You don't say so! Why at Mokroe?'

'That's a long story, I've told you enough.'

'Mitya'll be up to something now! Does he know or doesn't he?'

'He know! Of course he doesn't. If he knew, there would be murder. But I am not afraid of that now, I am not afraid of his knife. Be quiet, Rakitin, don't remind me of Dmitri Fyodorovitch, he has bruised my heart. And I don't want to think of that at this moment. I can think of Alyosha here, I can look at Alyosha . . . smile at me, dear, cheer up, smile at my foolishness, at my pleasure . . . Ah, he's smiling, he's smiling! How kindly he looks at me! And you know, Alyosha, I've been thinking all this time you were angry with me, because of the day before yesterday, because of that young lady. I was a bitch, that's the truth . . . But it's a good thing it happened so. It was a horrid thing, but a good thing too.' Grushenka smiled dreamily and a little cruel line showed in her smile. 'Mitya told me that she screamed out that I "ought to be flogged". I did insult her dreadfully. She sent for me, she wanted to make a conquest of me, to win me over with her chocolate . . . No, it's a good thing it ended like that.' She smiled again. 'But I am still afraid you may be angry.'

'Yes, that's really true,' Rakitin put in suddenly with genuine surprise. 'Alyosha, she is really afraid of a chicken like you.'

'He is a chicken to you, Rakitin . . . because you've no conscience, that's why! You see, I love him with all my soul, that's how it is! Alyosha, do you believe I love you with all my soul?'

'Ah, you shameless woman! She is making you a declaration, Alexey!'

'Well, what of it, I love him!'

'And what about your officer? And the priceless message from Mokroe?'

'That is quite different.'

'That's a woman's way of looking at it!'

'Don't you make me angry, Rakitin.' Grushenka caught him up hotly. 'This is quite different. I love Alyosha in a different way. It's true, Alyosha, I had sly designs on you before. For I am a horrid, violent creature. But at other times I've looked upon you, Alyosha, as my conscience. I've kept thinking "how anyone like that must despise a nasty thing like me". I thought that the day before yesterday, as I ran home from the young lady's. I have thought of you a long time in that way, Alyosha, and Mitya knows; I've talked to him about it. Mitya understands. Would you believe it, I sometimes look at you and feel ashamed, utterly ashamed of myself . . . And how, and since when, I began to think about you like that, I can't say, I don't remember . . .'

Fenya came in and put a tray with an uncorked bottle and three glasses of champagne on the table.

'Here's the champagne!' cried Rakitin. 'You're excited, Grushenka, and not yourself. When you've had a glass of champagne, you'll be ready to dance. Oh, the fools, they can't even do that properly,' he added, looking at the bottle. 'The old woman's poured it out in the kitchen and the bottle's been brought in warm and without a cork. Well, let me have some, anyway.'

He went up to the table, took a glass, emptied it at one gulp and poured himself out another.

'One doesn't often stumble upon champagne,' he said, licking his lips. 'Now, Alyosha, take a glass, show what you can do! What shall we drink to? The gates of paradise? Take a glass, Grushenka, you drink to the gates of paradise, too.'

'What gates of paradise?'

She took a glass, Alyosha took his, tasted it and put it back.

'No, I'd better not,' he smiled gently.

'And you bragged!' cried Rakitin.

'Well, if so, I won't either,' chimed in Grushenka, 'I really don't want any. You can drink the whole bottle alone, Rakitin. If Alyosha has some, I will.'

'What touching sentimentality!' said Rakitin tauntingly, 'and she's sitting on his knee, too! He's got something to grieve over, but what's the matter with you? He is rebelling against his God and ready to eat sausage . . . '

'How so?'

'His elder died today, Father Zossima, the saint.'

'So Father Zossima is dead,' cried Grushenka. 'Good God, I did not know!' She crossed herself devoutly. 'Goodness, what have I been doing, sitting on his knee like this at such a moment!' She started up as though in dismay, instantly slipped off his knee and sat down on the sofa.

Alyosha bent a long wondering look upon her and a light seemed to dawn in his face.

'Rakitin,' he said suddenly, in a firm and loud voice; 'don't taunt me with having rebelled against God. I don't want to feel angry with you, so you must be kinder, too. I've lost a treasure such as you have never had, and you cannot judge me now. You had much better look at her – do you see how she has pity on me? I came here to find a wicked soul – I felt drawn to evil because I was base and evil myself, and I've found a true sister, I have found a treasure – a loving heart. She had pity on me just now . . . Agrafena Alexandrovna, I am speaking of you. You've raised my soul from the depths.'

Alyosha's lips were quivering and he caught his breath.

'She has saved you, it seems,' laughed Rakitin spitefully. 'And she meant to get you in her clutches, do you realise that?'

'Be quiet, Rakitin.' Grushenka jumped up. 'Hush, both of you. Now I'll tell you all about it. Hush, Alyosha, your words make me ashamed, for I am bad and not good – that's what I am. And you hush, Rakitin, because you are telling lies. I had the low idea of trying to get him in my clutches, but now you are lying, now it's all different. And don't let me hear anything more from you, Rakitin.'

All this Grushenka said with extreme emotion.

'They are both crazy,' said Rakitin, looking at them with amazement. 'I feel as though I were in a madhouse. They're both getting so feeble they'll begin crying in a minute.'

'I shall begin to cry, I shall,' repeated Grushenka. 'He called me his sister and I shall never forget that. Only let me tell you, Rakitin, though I am bad, I did give away an onion.'

'An onion? Hang it all, you really are crazy.'

Rakitin wondered at their enthusiasm. He was aggrieved and annoyed, though he might have reflected that each of them was just passing through a spiritual crisis such as does not come often in a lifetime. But though Rakitin was very sensitive about everything that concerned himself, he was very obtuse as regards the feelings and sensations of others – partly from his youth and inexperience, partly from his intense egoism.

'You see, Alyosha,' Grushenka turned to him with a nervous laugh. 'I was boasting when I told Rakitin I had given away an onion, but it's not to boast I tell you about it. It's only a story, but it's a nice story. I used to hear it when I was a child from Matryona, my cook, who is still with me. It's like this. Once upon a time there was a peasant woman and a very wicked woman she was. And she died and did not leave a single good deed behind. The devils caught her and plunged her into the lake of fire. So her guardian angel stood and wondered what good deed of hers he could remember to tell to God; "She once pulled up an onion in her garden," said he, "and gave it to a beggar woman." And God answered: "You take that onion then, hold it out to her in the lake, and let her take hold and be pulled out. And if you can pull her out of the lake, let her come to Paradise, but if the onion breaks, then the woman must stay where she is." The angel ran to the woman and held out the onion to her; "Come," said he, "catch hold and I'll pull you out." And he began cautiously pulling her out. He had just pulled her right out, when the other sinners in the lake, seeing how she was being drawn out, began catching hold of her so as to be pulled out with her. But she was a very wicked woman and she began kicking them. "I'm to be pulled out, not you. It's my onion, not yours." As soon as she said that, the onion broke. And the woman fell into the lake and she is burning there to this day. So the angel wept and went away. So that's the story, Alyosha; I know it, by heart, for I am that wicked woman myself. I boasted to Rakitin that I had given away an onion, but to you I'll say: "I've done nothing but give away one onion all my life, that's the only good deed I've done." So don't praise me, Alyosha, don't think me good, I am bad, I am a wicked woman and you make me ashamed if you praise me. Oh, I must confess everything. Listen, Alyosha. I was so anxious to get hold of you that I promised Rakitin twenty-five roubles if he would bring you to me.'

She went with rapid steps to the table, opened a drawer, pulled out a purse and took from it a twenty-five-rouble note.

'What nonsense! What nonsense!' cried Rakitin, disconcerted.

'Take it, Rakitin, I owe it you, there's no fear of your refusing it, you asked for it yourself.' And she threw the note to him.

'Likely I should refuse it,' boomed Rakitin, obviously abashed, but carrying off his confusion with a swagger. 'That will come in very handy; fools are made for wise men's profit.'

'And now hold your tongue, Rakitin, what I am going to say now is not for your ears. Sit down in that corner and keep quiet. You don't like us, so hold your tongue.'

'What should I like you for?' Rakitin snarled, not concealing his ill-humour. He put the twenty-five-rouble note in his pocket, and he felt ashamed at Alyosha's seeing it. He had reckoned on receiving his payment later, without Alyosha's knowing of it, and now, feeling ashamed, he lost his temper. Till that moment he had thought it discreet not to contradict Grushenka too flatly in spite of her snubbing, since he had something to get out of her. But now he too was angry: 'One loves people for some reason, but what have either of you done for me?'

'You should love people without a reason, as Alyosha does.'

'How does he love you? How has he shown it, that you make such a fuss about it?'

Grushenka was standing in the middle of the room; she spoke with heat and there were hysterical overtones in her voice.

'Hush, Rakitin, you know nothing about us! And don't dare to speak to me like that again. How dare you be so familiar? Sit in that corner and be quiet, as though you were my footman! And now, Alyosha, I'll tell you the whole truth, that you may see what a wretch I am! I am not talking to Rakitin, but to you. I wanted to ruin you, Alyosha, that's the holy truth; I quite meant to. I wanted to so much, that I bribed Rakitin to bring you. And why did I want to do such a thing? You knew nothing about it, Alyosha, you turned away from me, if you passed me you dropped your eyes. And I've looked at you a hundred times before today, I began asking everyone about you. Your face haunted my heart. "He despises me," I thought, "he won't even look at me." And I felt it so much at last that I wondered at myself for being so frightened of a boy. I'll get him in my clutches and laugh at him. I was full of spite and anger. Would you believe it, nobody here dares talk or think of coming to Agrafena Alexandrovna with any evil purpose. Old Kuzma is the only man I have anything to do with here, I was bound and sold to him, Satan brought us together, but there has been no one else. But looking at you I thought, I'll get him in my clutches and laugh at him. You see what a spiteful creature I am, and you called me your sister! And now that man who wronged me has come; I sit here waiting for a message from him. And do you know what that man has been to me? Five years ago, when Kuzma brought me here, I used to shut myself up, that no one might have sight or sound of me. I was a silly slip of a girl; I used to sit here sobbing, I used to lie awake all night, thinking: "Where is he now, the man who wronged me? He is laughing at me with another woman, most likely. If only I could see him, if I could meet him again, I'd pay him out, I'd pay him out!" At night I used to lie sobbing into my pillow in the dark, and I used to brood over it, I used to tear my heart on purpose and gloat over my anger. "I'll pay him out, I'll pay him out!" That's what I used to cry out in the dark. And when I suddenly thought that I should really do nothing to him, and that he was laughing at me then, or perhaps had utterly forgotten me, I would fling myself on the floor, melt into helpless tears, and lie there shaking till dawn. In the morning I would get up more spiteful than a dog, ready to tear the whole world to pieces. And then what do you think? I began saving money, I became hard-hearted, grew stout –

grew wiser, would you say? No, no one in the whole world sees it, no one knows it, but when night comes on, I sometimes lie as I did five years ago, when I was a silly girl, clenching my teeth and crying all night, thinking: "I'll pay him out, I'll pay him out!" Do you hear? Well then, now you understand me. A month ago a letter came to me – he was coming, he was a widower, he wanted to see me. It took my breath away, then I suddenly thought: "If he comes and whistles to call me, I shall creep back to him like a beaten dog." I couldn't believe myself. Am I so abject? Shall I run to him or not? And I've been in such a rage with myself all this month that I am worse than I was five years ago. Do you see now, Alyosha, what a violent, vindictive creature I am? I have shown you the whole truth! I played with Mitya to keep me from running to that other. Hush, Rakitin, it's not for you to judge me, I am not speaking to you. Before you came in, I was lying here waiting, brooding, deciding my whole future life and you can never know what was in my heart. Yes, Alyosha, tell your young lady not to be angry with me for what happened the day before yesterday . . . Nobody in the whole world knows what I am going through now, and no one ever can know . . . For perhaps I shall take a knife with me today. I can't make up my mind . . .'

And at this 'tragic' phrase Grushenka broke down, hid her face in her hands, flung herself on the sofa pillows, and sobbed like a child.

Alyosha got up and went to Rakitin.

'Misha,' he said, 'don't be angry. She wounded you, but don't be angry. You heard what she said just now? You mustn't ask too much of human endurance, one must be merciful.'

Alyosha said this at the instinctive prompting of his heart. He felt obliged to speak and he turned to Rakitin. If Rakitin had not been there, he would have spoken to the air. But Rakitin looked at him ironically and Alyosha stopped short.

'You were so primed up with your elder's teaching last night that now you have to work it off on me, Alexey, man of God!' said Rakitin, with a vicious grin.

'Don't laugh, Rakitin, don't smile, don't talk of the dead – he was better than anyone in the world!' cried Alyosha, with tears in his voice. 'I didn't speak to you as a judge but as the lowest of the judged. What am I beside her? I came here seeking my ruin, and said to myself, "what does it matter?" in my cowardliness, but she after five years in torment, as soon as anyone says a word from the heart to her – it makes her forget everything, forgive everything, in her tears! The man who has wronged her has come back, he sends for her and she forgives him everything, and hastens joyfully to meet him and she won't take a knife with her. She won't! . . . She is more loving than we . . . Have you heard her speak before of what she has just told us? No, you haven't; if you had, you'd have understood her long ago . . . and the person insulted the day before yesterday must forgive her, too! She will, when she knows . . . and she shall know . . . This soul is not yet at peace with itself, one must be tender with it . . . there may be a treasure in that soul . . .'

Alyosha stopped, because he caught his breath. In spite of his ill-humour, Rakitin looked at him with astonishment. He had never expected such a tirade from the gentle Alyosha.

'She's found someone to plead her cause! Why, are you in love with her? Agrafena Alexandrovna, our monk's really in love with you, you've made a conquest!' he cried, with a coarse laugh.

Grushenka lifted her head from the pillow and looked at Alyosha with a tender smile shining on her tear-stained face.

'Let him alone, Alyosha, my angel, you see what he is, he is not a person for you to speak to.' She turned to Rakitin, 'I meant to beg your pardon for being rude to you, but now I don't want to. Alyosha, come to me, sit down here.' She beckoned to him with a happy smile. 'That's right, sit here. Tell me,' she took him by the hand and peeped into his face, smiling, 'tell me, do I love that man or not? the man who wronged me, do I love him or not? Before you came, I lay here in the dark, asking my heart whether I loved him. Decide for me, Alyosha, the time has come, it shall be as you say. Am I to forgive him or not?'

'But you have forgiven him already,' said Alyosha, smiling.

'Yes, I really have forgiven him,' Grushenka murmured thoughtfully. 'What an abject heart! To my abject heart!' She snatched up a glass from the table, emptied it at a gulp, lifted it in the air and flung it on the floor. The glass broke with a crash. A little cruel line came into her smile.

'Perhaps I haven't forgiven him, though,' she said, with a sort of menace in her voice, and she dropped her eyes to the ground as though she were talking to herself. 'Perhaps my heart is only getting ready to forgive, I shall struggle with my heart. You see, Alyosha, I've grown to love my tears in these five years . . . Perhaps I only love my resentment, not him . . .'

'Well, I shouldn't care to be in his shoes,' hissed Rakitin.

'Well, you won't be, Rakitin, you'll never be in his shoes. You shall black my shoes, Rakitin, that's the place you are fit for. You'll never get a woman like me . . . and he won't either, perhaps . . . '

'Won't he? Then why are you dressed up like that?' said Rakitin, with a venomous sneer.

'Don't taunt me with dressing up, Rakitin, you don't know all that is in my heart! If I choose to tear off my finery, I'll tear it off at once, this minute,' she cried in a resonant voice. 'You don't know what that finery is for, Rakitin! Perhaps I shall see him and say: "Have you ever seen me look like this before?" He left me a thin, sick crybaby of seventeen. I'll sit by him, fascinate him and get him excited. "Do you see what I am like now?" I'll say to him; "well, and that's enough for you, my dear sir, there's many a slip twixt the cup and the lip!" That may be what the finery is for, Rakitin.' Grushenka finished with a malicious laugh. 'I'm violent and resentful, Alyosha, I'll tear off my finery, I'll destroy my beauty, I'll burn my face, slash it with a knife, and turn beggar. If I choose, I won't go anywhere now to see anyone. If I choose, I'll send Kuzma back all he has ever given me, tomorrow, and all his money, and I'll go out as a scrub-woman for the rest of my life. You think I wouldn't do it, Rakitin, that I would not dare to do it? I would, I would, I could do it directly, only don't exasperate me . . . and I'll send him about his business, I'll snap my fingers in his face, he shall never see me again!'

She uttered the last words in a hysterical scream, but broke down again, hid her face in her hands, buried it in the pillow and shook with sobs.

Rakitin got up.

'It's time we were off,' he said, 'it's late, we shall be shut out of the monastery.'

Grushenka leaped up from her place.

'Surely you don't want to go, Alyosha!' she cried, in mournful surprise. 'What are you doing to me? You've stirred up my heart, tortured me, and now you'll leave me to face this night alone!'

'He can hardly spend the night with you! Though if he wants to, let him! I'll go alone,' Rakitin scoffed jeeringly.

'Hush, evil tongue!' Grushenka cried angrily at him; 'you never said such words to me as he has said.'

'What has he said to you so special?' asked Rakitin irritably.

'I can't say, I don't know. I don't know what he said to me, it went straight to my heart; he has wrung my heart . . . He is the first, the only one who has pitied me, that's what it is. Why did you not come before, you angel?' She fell on her knees before him as though in a sudden frenzy. 'I've been waiting all my life for someone like you, I knew that someone like you would come and forgive me. I believed that, nasty as I am, someone would really love me, not only with a shameful love!'

'What have I done to you?' answered Alyosha bending over her with a tender smile, and gently taking her by the hands; 'I only gave you an onion, nothing but a tiny little onion, that was all!'

He was moved to tears himself as he said it. At that moment there was a sudden noise in the passage, someone came into the hall. Grushenka jumped up, seeming greatly alarmed. Fenya ran noisily into the room, crying out: 'Mistress, mistress darling, a messenger has galloped up,' she cried, breathless and joyful. 'A carriage from Mokroe for you, Timofey the driver, with three horses, they are just putting in fresh horses . . . A letter, here's the letter, mistress.'

A letter was in her hand and she waved it in the air all the while she talked. Grushenka snatched the letter from her and carried it to the candle. It was only a note, a few lines. She read it in one instant.

'He has sent for me,' she cried, her face white and distorted, with a wan smile; 'he whistles! Crawl back, little dog!'

But only for one instant she stood as though hesitating; suddenly the blood rushed to her head and sent a glow to her cheeks.

'I will go,' she cried; 'five years of my life! Goodbye! Goodbye, Alyosha, my fate is sealed. Go, go, leave me all of you, don't let me see you again! Grushenka is flying to a new life . . . Don't you remember evil against me either, Rakitin. I may be going to my death! Oh, oh! I feel as though I were drunk!'

She suddenly left them and ran into her bedroom.

'Well, she has no thoughts for us now!' grumbled Rakitin. 'Let's go, or we may hear that feminine shriek again. I am sick of all these tears and cries.'

Alyosha mechanically let himself be led out. In the yard stood a carriage. Horses were being taken out of the shafts, men were running to and fro with a lantern. Three fresh horses were being led in at the open gate. But when Alyosha and Rakitin reached the bottom of the steps, Grushenka's bedroom window was suddenly opened and she called in a ringing voice after Alyosha: 'Alyosha, give my greetings to your brother Mitya and tell him not to remember evil against me, though I have brought him misery. And tell him, too, in my words: "Grushenka has fallen to a scoundrel, and not to you, noble heart." And add, too, that Grushenka loved him only one hour, only one short hour she loved him – so let him remember that hour all his life – say, "Grushenka tells you to!" '

She ended in a voice full of sobs. The window was shut with a slam.

'H'm, h'm!' growled Rakitin, laughing, 'she murders your brother Mitya and then tells him to remember it all his life! What ferocity!'

Alyosha made no reply; he seemed not to have heard. He walked fast beside Rakitin as though in a terrible hurry. He was lost in thought and moved mechanically. Rakitin felt a sudden twinge as though he had been touched on an open wound. He had expected something quite different by bringing Grushenka and Alyosha together. Something very different from what he had hoped for had happened.

'He is a Pole, that officer of hers,' he began again, restraining himself; 'and indeed he is not an officer at all now. He served in the customs in Siberia, somewhere on the Chinese frontier, some puny little beggar of a Pole, I expect. Lost his job, they say. He's heard now that Grushenka's saved a little money, so he's turned up again – that's the explanation of the mystery.'

Again Alyosha seemed not to hear. Rakitin could not control himself.

'Well, so you've saved the sinner?' he laughed spitefully. 'Have you turned the Magdalene to the true path? Driven out the seven devils, eh? So you see the miracles you were looking out for just now have come to pass!'

'Hush, Rakitin,' Alyosha answered, with an aching heart.

'So you despise me now for those twenty-five

roubles? I've sold my friend, you think. But you are not Christ, you know, and I am not Judas.'

'Oh, Rakitin, I assure you I'd forgotten about it,' cried Alyosha, 'you remind me of it yourself . . . '

But this was the last straw for Rakitin.

'Damn you all and each of you!' he cried suddenly, 'why the devil did I take you up? I don't want to know you from this time forward. Go alone, there's your road!'

And he turned abruptly into another street, leaving Alyosha alone in the dark. Alyosha came out of the town and walked across the fields to the monastery.

Book Seven

I

But Dmitri, to whom Grushenka had left her last greeting, knew nothing of what had happened to her, and was at that moment in a condition of feverish agitation and activity. For the last two days he had been in such an inconceivable state of mind that he might have fallen ill with brain fever, as he said later.

He had spent those two days literally rushing in all directions, 'struggling with his destiny and trying to save himself', as he expressed it himself afterwards.

He felt that whatever might follow, whatever turn things might take, his final conflict with Fyodor Pavlovitch was very close, and must be decided before anything else. With a sinking heart he was expecting momentarily Grushenka's decision, always believing that it would come suddenly, on the impulse of the moment. All of a sudden she would say to him: 'Take me, I'm yours for ever,' and it would all be over. He would seize her and bear her away at once to the ends of the earth. Oh, then he would bear her away at once, as far, far away as possible; to the farthest end of Russia, if not of the earth, then he would marry her, and settle down with her incognito, so that no one would know anything about them, there, here, or anywhere. Then, oh, then, a new life would begin at once!

Of this different, reformed and 'virtuous' life ('it must, it must be virtuous') he dreamed feverishly at every moment. He thirsted for that reformation and renewal. The filthy morass, in which he had sunk of his own free will, was too revolting to him, and, like very many men in such cases, he put his faith above all in change of place. If only it were not for these people, if only it were not for these circumstances, if only he could fly away from this accursed place – he would be altogether regenerated, would enter on a new path. That was what he believed in, and for what he yearned.

But all this could only be on condition of the first, the *happy* solution of the question. There was another possibility, a different and awful ending. Suddenly she might say to him: 'Go away. I have just come to terms with Fyodor Pavlovitch. I am going to marry him and don't want you' – and then . . . but then . . . But Mitya did not know what would happen then. Up to the last hour he didn't know. That must be said to his credit. He had no definite intentions, had planned no crime. He was simply watching and spying in agony, while he prepared himself for the first, happy solution of his destiny. He drove away any other idea, in fact. But for that ending a quite different anxiety arose, a new, incidental, but yet fatal and insoluble difficulty presented itself.

If she were to say to him: 'I'm yours; take me away,' how could he take her away? Where had he the means, the money to do it? It was just at this time that all sources of revenue from Fyodor Pavlovitch, doles which had gone on without interruption for so many years, ceased. Grushenka had money, of course, but with regard to this Mitya suddenly evinced extraordinary pride; he wanted to carry her away and begin the new life with her himself, at his own expense, not at hers. He could not conceive taking her money, and the very idea caused him a pang of intense repulsion. I won't enlarge on this fact or analyse it here, but confine myself to remarking that this was his attitude at the moment. All this may have arisen indirectly and unconsciously from the secret stings of his conscience for the money of Katerina Ivanovna that he had dishonestly appropriated. 'I've been a scoundrel to one of them, and I shall be a scoundrel to the other very soon,' was his feeling then, as he explained after: 'and when Grushenka knows, she won't care for such a scoundrel.'

Where, then, was he to get the means, where was he to get the fateful money? Without it, all would be lost and nothing could be done, 'and only because I hadn't the money. Oh, the shame of it!'

To anticipate things: he did, perhaps, know where to get the money, knew, perhaps, where it lay at that moment. I will say no more of this here, as it will all be clear later. But his chief trouble, I must explain however obscurely, lay in the fact that to have the sum he knew of, to *have the right* to take it, he must first restore Katerina Ivanovna's three thousand – if not, 'I'm a common pickpocket, I'm a scoundrel, and I don't want to begin a new life as a scoundrel,' Mitya decided. And so he made up his mind to move heaven and earth to return Katerina Ivanovna that three thousand, and that *first of all*.

Strange to say, though one would have supposed there was nothing left for him but despair – for what chance had he, with nothing in the world, to raise such a sum? – yet to the very end he persisted in hoping that he would get that three thousand, that the money would somehow come to him, of itself, as though it might drop from heaven. That is just how it is with people who, like Dmitri, have never had anything to do with money, except to squander what had come to them by inheritance without any effort of their own, and have no notion how money is obtained. A vortex of the most fantastic notions took possession of his brain immediately after he had parted with Alyosha two days before, and threw his thoughts into a tangle of confusion. This is why he picked first on a perfectly wild enterprise. And perhaps to men of that kind in such circumstances the most impossible, fantastic schemes occur first, and seem most practical.

He suddenly determined to go to Samsonov, the merchant who was Grushenka's protector, and to propose a 'scheme' to him, and by means of it to obtain at once the whole sum required. Of the commercial value of his scheme he had no doubt, not the slightest, and was only uncertain how Samsonov would look upon his crazy idea, supposing he were to consider it from any but the commercial point of view. Though Mitya knew the merchant by sight, he was not acquainted with him and had never spoken a word to him. But for some unknown reason he had long entertained the conviction that the old reprobate, who was lying at death's door, would perhaps not object now to Grushenka's securing a respectable position, and marrying a man 'to be depended upon'. And he believed not only that he would not object, but that this was what he desired, and, if opportunity arose, that he would be ready to help. From some rumour, or perhaps from some stray words of Grushenka's, he had gathered further that the old man would perhaps prefer him to Fyodor Pavlovitch for Grushenka.

After his conversation with Alyosha, at the cross-roads, he hardly slept all night, and, at ten o'clock next morning, he was at the house of Samsonov and telling the servant to announce him. It was a very large and gloomy old house, of two storeys, with a lodge and outhouses. In the lower storey lived Samsonov's two married sons with their families, his old sister, and his unmarried daughter. In the lodge lived two of his clerks, one of whom also had a large family. Both the lodge and the lower storey were overcrowded, but the old man kept the upper floor to himself, and would not even let the daughter live there with him, though she waited upon him, and in spite of her asthma was obliged at certain fixed hours, and at any time he might call her, to run upstairs to him from below.

This upper floor contained a number of large rooms kept purely for show, furnished in the old-fashioned merchant style, with long, monotonous rows of clumsy mahogany chairs along the walls, with glass chandeliers enclosed in muslin bags, and dim mirrors on the walls. All these rooms were entirely empty and unused, for the old man kept to one room, a small, remote bedroom, where he was waited upon by an old servant with a kerchief on her head, and by a lad who used to sit on the locker in the passage. Owing to his swollen legs, the old man could hardly walk at all, and was only rarely lifted from his leather armchair, when the old woman supporting him led him up and down the room once or twice. He was morose and taciturn even with this old woman.

When he was informed of the arrival of the 'captain', he at once refused to see him. But Mitya persisted and sent his name up again. Samsonov questioned the lad minutely: What he looked like? Whether he was drunk?

Was he going to make a row? The answer he received was: that he was sober, but wouldn't go away. The old man again refused to see him. Then Mitya, who had foreseen this, and purposely brought pencil and paper with him, wrote clearly on the piece of paper the words: 'On most important business closely concerning Agrafena Alexandrovna', and sent it up to the old man.

After thinking a little, Samsonov told the lad to take the visitor to the drawing-room, and sent the old woman downstairs with a summons to his younger son to come upstairs to him at once. The younger son, a man over six feet and of exceptional physical strength, who was closely shaven and dressed in the European style, though his father still wore a caftan and a beard, came at once without a comment. All the family trembled before the father. The old man had sent for this giant, not because he was afraid of the 'captain' (he was by no means of a timorous temper), but in order to have a witness in case of an emergency. Supported by his son and the servant lad, he waddled at last into the drawing-room. It may be assumed that he felt considerable curiosity. The drawing-room in which Mitya was awaiting him was a vast, dreary room that laid a weight of depression on the heart. It had a double row of windows, a gallery, marbled walls, and three immense chandeliers with glass lustres all concealed in the muslin bags.

Mitya was sitting on a little chair at the entrance, awaiting his fate with nervous impatience. When the old man appeared at the opposite door, seventy feet away, Mitya jumped up at once, and with his long, military stride walked to meet him. Mitya was well dressed, in a frock-coat, buttoned up, with a round hat and black gloves in his hands, just as he had been three days before at the elder's, at the family meeting with his father and brothers. The old man waited for him, standing dignified and unbending, and Mitya felt at once that he had looked him through and through as he advanced. Mitya was greatly impressed, too, with Samsonov's immensely swollen face. His lower lip, which had always been thick, hung down now, looking like a large biscuit. He bowed to his guest in dignified silence, motioned him to a low chair by the sofa, and, leaning on his son's arm he began lowering himself on to the sofa opposite, groaning painfully, so that Mitya, seeing his painful exertion, immediately felt remorseful and sensitively conscious of his insignificance in the presence of the dignified person he had ventured to disturb.

'What is it you want of me, sir?' said the old man, deliberately, distinctly, severely, but courteously, when he was at last seated.

Mitya jumped up, but sat down again quickly. Then he began at once to speak with loud, nervous haste, gesticulating, and in a positive frenzy. He was unmistakably a man driven into a corner, on the brink of ruin, catching at the last straw, ready to sink if he failed. Old Samsonov probably grasped all this in an instant, though his face remained cold and immovable as a statue's.

'Most honoured sir, Kuzma Kuzmitch, you have no doubt heard, more than once, of my disputes with my father, Fyodor Pavlovitch Karamazov, who robbed me of my inheritance from my mother . . . seeing the whole town is gossiping about it . . . for here everyone's gossiping of what they shouldn't . . . and besides, it might have reached you through Grushenka . . . I beg your pardon, through Agrafena Alexandrovna . . .

Agrafena Alexandrovna, the lady for whom I have the highest respect and esteem . . . '

So Mitya began, and broke down at the first sentence. We will not reproduce his speech word for word, but will only summarise the gist of it. Three months ago, he said, he had of express intention (Mitya purposely used these words instead of 'intentionally') consulted a lawyer in the chief town of the province, 'a distinguished lawyer, Kuzma Kuzmitch, Pavel Pavlovitch Korneplodov. You have perhaps heard of him? A man of vast intellect, the mind of a statesman . . . he knows you too . . . spoke of you in the highest terms . . .' Mitya broke down again. But these breaks did not deter him. He strode instantly over the gaps, and struggled on and on.

This Korneplodov, after questioning him minutely, and inspecting the documents he was able to bring (Mitya alluded somewhat vaguely to these documents, and slurred over the subject with special haste), reported that they certainly might take proceedings concerning the village of Tchermashnya, which ought, he said, to have come to him, Mitya, from his mother, and so checkmate the old villain, his father . . . 'because every door was not closed and justice might still find a loophole'. In fact, he might reckon on an additional sum of six or even seven thousand roubles from Fyodor Pavlovitch, as Tchermashnya was worth, at least, twenty-five thousand, he might say twenty-eight thousand, in fact, 'thirty, thirty, Kuzma Kuzmitch, and, would you believe it, I didn't get seventeen from that heartless man!' So he, Mitya, had thrown the business up, for the time, knowing nothing about the law, but on coming here was struck dumb by a cross-claim made upon him (here Mitya went adrift again, and again took a flying leap forward), 'so will not you, excellent and honoured Kuzma Kuzmitch, be willing to take up all my claims against that unnatural monster, and pay me a sum down of only three thousand? . . . You see, you cannot, in any case, lose over it. On my honour I swear that. Quite the contrary, you may make six or seven thousand instead of three' . . . Above all, he wanted this concluded that very day.

'I'll do the business with you at a notary's, or whatever it is . . . in fact, I'm ready to do anything . . . I'll hand over all the deeds . . . whatever you want, sign anything . . . and we could draw up the agreement at once . . . and if it were possible, if it were only possible, this very morning . . . You could pay me that three thousand, for there isn't a capitalist in this town to compare with you, and so would save me from . . . would save me, in fact . . . for a good, I might say an honourable, action . . . For I cherish the most honourable feelings for a certain person, whom you know well, and care for as a father. I would not have come, indeed, if those were not your sentiments. And, indeed, it's a struggle of three in this business, for it's fate – that's a fearful thing, Kuzma Kuzmitch! A tragedy, Kuzma Kuzmitch, a tragedy! And as you've dropped out long ago, it's a tug-of-war between two. I'm expressing it awkwardly, perhaps, but I'm not a literary man. You see, I'm on the one side, and that monster on the other. So you must choose. It's either I or the monster. It all lies in your hands – the fate of three lives, and the happiness of two . . . Excuse me, I'm making a mess of it, but you understand . . . I see from your venerable eyes that you understand . . . and if you don't understand, I'm done for . . . so you see!'

Mitya broke off his clumsy speech with that 'so you see!' and, jumping up from his seat, awaited the answer to his foolish proposal. At the last phrase he had suddenly become hopelessly aware that it had all fallen flat, above all, that he had been talking utter nonsense.

'How strange it is! On the way here it seemed all right, and now it's nothing but nonsense.' The idea suddenly dawned on his despairing mind. All the while he had been talking, the old man sat motionless, watching him with an icy expression in his eyes. After keeping him for a moment in suspense, Kuzma Kuzmitch pronounced at last, in the most positive and chilling tone: 'Excuse me, we don't undertake such business.'

Mitya suddenly felt his legs growing weak under him.

'What am I to do now, Kuzma Kuzmitch?' he muttered, with a pale smile. 'I suppose it's all up with me – what do you think?'

'Excuse me . . .'

Mitya remained standing, motionless, staring. He suddenly noticed a movement in the old man's face. He made an agitated gesture.

'You see, sir, business of that sort's not in our line,' said the old man slowly. 'There's the court, and the lawyers – it's a perfect misery. But if you like, there is a man here you might apply to.'

'Good heavens! Who is it? You're my salvation, Kuzma Kuzmitch,' faltered Mitya.

'He doesn't live here, and he's not here just now. He is a peasant, he does business in timber. His name is Lyagavy. He's been haggling with Fyodor Pavlovitch for the last year, over your woodland at Tchermashnya. They can't agree on the price, maybe you've heard? Now he's come back again and is staying with the priest at Ilyinskoe, about eight miles from Volovya Station. He wrote to me, too, about the business of the woodland asking my advice. Fyodor Pavlovitch means to go and see him, himself. So if you were to be beforehand with Fyodor Pavlovitch and to make Lyagavy the offer you've made me, he might possibly . . .'

'A brilliant idea!' Mitya interrupted ecstatically. 'He's the very man, it would just suit him. He's haggling with my father for it, being asked too much, and here he would have all the documents entitling him to the property itself. Ha–ha–ha!'

And Mitya suddenly went off into his short, stiff laugh, startling Samsonov.

'How can I thank you, Kuzma Kuzmitch?' cried Mitya effusively.

'Don't mention it,' said Samsonov, inclining his head.

'But you don't know, you've saved me. Oh, it was a true presentiment brought me to you . . . So now to this priest!'

'No need of thanks.'

'I'll make haste and fly there. I'm afraid I've overtaxed your strength. I shall never forget it. It's a Russian says that, Kuzma Kuzmitch, a R–r–russian!'

'To be sure!'

Mitya seized his hand to press it, but there was a malignant gleam in the old man's eye. Mitya drew back his hand, but at once blamed himself for his mistrustfulness.

'It's because he's tired,' he thought.

'For her sake! For her sake, Kuzma Kuzmitch! You understand that it's for her,' he cried, his voice ringing through the room. He bowed, turned sharply round, and with the same long stride walked to the door without looking back. He was trembling with delight. 'Everything was on the verge of ruin and my guardian angel saved me,' was the thought in his mind. And if such a businessman as Samsonov (a most worthy old man, and what dignity!) had suggested this course, then . . . then success was assured. He would start immediately. 'I will be back before night, I shall be back at night and the business is done. Could the old man have been laughing at me?' exclaimed Mitya, as he strode towards his lodging. He could, of course, imagine nothing, but that the advice was practical 'from such a businessman' with an understanding of the business, with an understanding of this Lyagavy (curious name!). Or – the old man was laughing at him.

Alas! the second alternative was the correct one. Long afterwards, when the catastrophe had happened, old Samsonov himself confessed, laughing, that he had made a fool of the 'captain'. He was a cold, spiteful and sarcastic man, subject to violent antipathies. Whether it was the 'captain's' excited face, or the foolish conviction of the 'rake and spendthrift', that he, Samsonov, could be taken in by such a cock-and-bull story as his scheme, or jealousy over Grushenka, in whose name this 'scapegrace' had rushed in on him with such a tale to get money – which worked on the old man I can't tell. But, at the instant when Mitya stood before him, feeling his legs grow weak under him, and frantically exclaiming that he was ruined, at that moment the old man looked at him with intense spite, and resolved to make a laughing-stock of him. When Mitya had gone, Kuzma Kuzmitch, white with rage, turned to his son and bade him see to it that that beggar be never seen again, and never admitted even into the yard, or else he'd . . .

He did not utter his threat. But even his son, who often saw him enraged, trembled with fear. For a whole hour afterwards, the old man was shaking with anger, and by evening he was really sick, and sent for the doctor.

2

So he must drive at full speed, and he had not the money for horses. He had forty kopecks, and that was all, all that was left after so many years of prosperity! But he had at home an old silver watch which had long ceased to go. He snatched it up and carried it to a Jewish watchmaker, who gave him six roubles for it.

'And I didn't expect that,' cried Mitya, ecstatically. (He was still in a state of ecstasy.) He seized his six roubles and ran home. At home he borrowed three roubles from the people of the house, who loved him so much that they were pleased to give it to him, though it was all they had. Mitya in his excitement told them on the spot that his fate would be decided that day, and he described, in desperate haste, the whole scheme he had put before Samsonov, the latter's decision, his own hopes for the future, and so on. These people had been told many of their lodger's secrets before, and so looked upon him as a gentleman who was not at all proud, and almost one of themselves. Having thus collected nine roubles Mitya sent for posting-horses to take him to the Volovya Station. This was how the fact came to be remembered and established that 'at midday, on the day before the event, Mitya had not a farthing, and that he had sold his watch to get money and had borrowed three roubles from his landlord, all in the presence of witnesses'.

I note this fact; later on it will be apparent why I do so.

Though he was radiant with the joyful anticipation that he would at last solve all his difficulties, yet, as he drew near Volovya Station, he trembled at the thought of what Grushenka might be doing in his absence. What if she made up her mind today to go to Fyodor Pavlovitch? This was why he had gone off without telling her and why he left orders with his landlady not to tell where he had gone, if anyone came to enquire for him.

'I must, I must get back tonight,' he repeated, as he was jolted along in the carriage, 'and I dare say I shall have to bring this Lyagavy back here . . . to draw up the deed.' So mused Mitya, with a throbbing heart, but alas! his dreams were not fated to be carried out.

To begin with, he was late, taking a short cut from Volovya Station which turned out to be twelve miles instead of eight. Secondly, he did not find the priest at home at Ilyinskoe; he had gone off to a neighbouring village. While Mitya, setting off there with the same exhausted horses, was looking for him, it was almost dark.

The priest, a shy and amiable-looking little man, informed him at once that, though Lyagavy had been staying with him at first, he was now at Suhoy Possyolok, that he was staying the night in the forester's cottage, as he was buying timber there too. At Mitya's urgent request that he would take him to Lyagavy at once, and by so doing 'save him, so to speak', the priest agreed, after some demur, to conduct him to Suhoy Possyolok; his curiosity was obviously aroused. But, unluckily, he advised their going on foot, as it would not be 'much over' a mile. Mitya, of course, agreed, and marched off with his yard-long strides, so that the poor priest almost ran after him. He was a very cautious man, though not old.

Mitya at once began talking to him, too, of his plans, nervously and excitedly asking advice in regard to Lyagavy, and talking all the way. He turned off Mitya's questions with: 'I don't know. Ah, I can't say. How can I tell?' and so on. When Mitya began to speak of his quarrel with his father over his inheritance, the priest was positively alarmed, as he was in some way dependent on Fyodor Pavlovitch. He enquired, however, with surprise, why he called the peasant-trader Gorstkin, Lyagavy, and obligingly explained to Mitya, that, though the man's name really was Lyagavy, he was never called so, as he would be grievously offended at the name, and that he must be sure to call him Gorstkin, 'or you'll do nothing with him; he won't even listen to you', said the priest in conclusion.

Mitya was taken aback for a moment, and explained that that was what Samsonov had called him. On hearing this fact, the priest dropped the subject, though he would have done well to put into words his doubt whether, if Samsonov had sent him to the peasant, calling him Lyagavy, there might not be something wrong about it, and that perhaps Mitya was the butt of a bad joke. But Mitya had no time to pause over such trifles. He hurried, striding along, and only when he reached Suhoy Possyolok did he realise that they had come not one mile, nor one and one half, but at least two. This annoyed him, but he controlled himself.

They went into the log cabin. The forester lived in one half, and Gorstkin lodged in the other. They went into that room and lighted a tallow candle. The cabin was extremely overheated. On the table there was a samovar that had gone out, a tray with cups, an empty rum bottle, a bottle of vodka partly full, and some half-eaten crusts of bread. The visitor himself lay stretched at full length on the bench, with his coat rolled up under his head for a pillow, snoring heavily. Mitya stood in perplexity.

'Of course I must wake him. My business is too important. I've come in such haste. I'm in a hurry to get back today,' he said in great agitation. But the priest and the forester stood in silence, not giving their opinion. Mitya went up and tried to wake Gorstkin; he shook him, but the sleeper did not wake.

'He's drunk,' Mitya decided. 'Good Lord! What am I to do? What am I to do?' And terribly impatient, he began pulling the arms, the legs, shaking his head, lifting him up and making him sit on the bench. Yet, after prolonged exertions, he could only succeed in getting the drunken man to utter absurd grunts, and violent, inarticulate oaths.

'No, you'd better wait a little,' the priest said at last, 'for he's obviously not in a fit state.'

'He's been drinking the whole day,' the forester chimed in.

'Good heavens!' cried Mitya. 'If only you knew how important it is to me and how desperate I am!'

'Well, you'd better wait till morning,' the priest insisted.

'Till morning? My God! that's impossible!'

And in his despair he was on the point of attacking the sleeping man again, but stopped short at once, realising the uselessness of his efforts. The priest said nothing, the sleepy forester looked gloomy.

'What terrible tragedies real life contrives for people,' said Mitya, in complete despair. The perspiration was streaming down his face. The priest seized the moment to suggest, very reasonably, that even if he succeeded in wakening the man, he would still be drunk and incapable of conversation. 'And your business is important,' he said, 'so you'd certainly better put it off till morning.' With a gesture of despair Mitya agreed.

'Father, I will stay here with a candle, and seize the favourable moment. As soon as he wakes I'll begin. I'll pay you for the light,' he said to the forester, 'for the night's lodging, too; you'll remember Dmitri Karamazov. Only, father, I don't know what we're to do with you. Where will you sleep?'

'I'm going home. I'll take his horse and get home,' said the priest, indicating the forester. 'And now I'll say goodbye. I wish you all success.'

So it was settled. The priest rode off on the forester's horse, delighted to escape, though he shook his head uneasily, wondering whether he ought not next day to inform his benefactor Fyodor Pavlovitch of this curious incident, 'or he may in an unlucky hour hear of it, be angry, and withdraw his favour'.

The forester, scratching himself, went back to his room without a word, and Mitya sat on the bench to 'seize the favourable moment', as he expressed it. Profound dejection clung about his soul like a heavy mist. A profound, intense dejection! He sat thinking, but could reach no conclusion. The candle burned dimly, a cricket chirped; it became insufferably close in the overheated room. He suddenly pictured the garden, the path behind the garden, the door of his father's house mysteriously opening and Grushenka running in. He sprang up from the bench.

'It's a tragedy!' he said, grinding his teeth. Mechanically he approached the sleeping man and looked in his face. He was a lean, middle-aged peasant, with a very long face, flaxen curls, and a long, thin, reddish beard, wearing a blue cotton shirt and a black waistcoat, from the pocket of which hung the chain of a silver watch. Mitya looked at his face with intense hatred, and for some unknown reason the curly hair irritated him particularly.

It was insufferably humiliating that, after leaving things of such importance and making such sacrifices, he, Mitya, utterly worn out, should with business of such urgency be standing over this dolt on whom his whole fate depended, while the fool snored as though there were nothing the matter, as though he'd dropped from another planet.

'Oh, the irony of fate!' cried Mitya, and, quite losing his head, he began again to rouse the tipsy peasant. He worked with a sort of ferocity, pulled the man, pushed him, even beat him; but after five minutes of vain exertions, he returned to his bench in helpless despair, and sat down.

'Stupid! Stupid!' cried Mitya. 'And how dishonourable it all is!' something made him add. His head began to ache horribly. 'Should he give up and go away altogether?' he wondered. 'No, wait till tomorrow now. What else did I come for? Besides, I've no means of going. How am I to get away from here now? Oh, the idiocy of it!'

His head ached more and more. He sat without moving, and unconsciously dozed off and fell asleep as he sat. He seemed to have slept two hours or more. He was waked up by his head aching so unbearably that he could have screamed. There was a hammering in his temples, and the top of his head ached. It was a long time before he could wake up fully and understand what had happened to him.

At last he realised that the room was full of charcoal fumes from the stove, and that he might die of suffocation. And the drunken peasant still lay snoring. The candle guttered and was about to go out. Mitya cried out, and ran staggering across the passage into the forester's room. The forester woke up at once, but hearing that the other room was full of fumes, to Mitya's surprise and annoyance accepted the fact with strange unconcern, though he did go to see to it.

'But he's dead, he's dead! and . . . what am I to do then?' cried Mitya frantically.

They threw open the doors, opened a window and the chimney. Mitya brought a pail of water from the passage. First he wetted his own head, then, finding a rag of some sort, dipped it into the water, and put it on Lyagavy's head. The forester still treated the matter contemptuously, and when he opened the window said grumpily: 'It'll be all right, now.'

He went back to sleep, leaving Mitya a lighted lantern. Mitya fussed about the drunken peasant for half an hour, wetting his head, and gravely resolved not to sleep all night. But he was so worn out that when he sat down for a moment to take breath, he closed his eyes, unconsciously stretched himself full length on the bench and slept like the dead.

It was dreadfully late when he waked. It was somewhere about nine o'clock. The sun was shining brightly in the two little windows of the cabin. The curly-headed peasant was sitting on the bench and had his coat on. He had another samovar and another bottle in front of him. Yesterday's bottle had already been finished, and the new one was more than half empty. Mitya jumped up and saw at once that the cursed peasant was drunk again, hopelessly and completely. He stared at him for a moment with wide eyes. The peasant was silently and slyly watching him, with insulting composure, and even a sort of contemptuous condescension, so Mitya fancied. He rushed up to him.

'Excuse me, you see . . . I . . . you've most likely heard from the forester here in the hut. I'm Lieutenant Dmitri Karamazov, the son of the old Karamazov whose woodland you are buying.'

'That's a lie!' said the peasant, calmly and confidently.

'A lie? You know Fyodor Pavlovitch?'

'I don't know any of your Fyodor Pavlovitches,' said the peasant, speaking thickly.

'You're bargaining with him for the wood, for the wood. Do wake up, and collect yourself. Father Pavel of Ilyinskoe brought me here. You wrote to Samsonov, and he has sent me to you,' Mitya gasped breathlessly.

'You're l–lying!' Lyagavy blurted out again. Mitya's legs grew cold.

'For mercy's sake! It isn't a joke! You're drunk, perhaps. Yet you can speak and understand . . . or else . . . I understand nothing!'

'You're a painter!'

'For mercy's sake! I'm Karamazov, Dmitri Karamazov. I have an offer to make you, an advantageous offer . . . very advantageous offer, concerning the woodland!'

The peasant stroked his beard importantly.

'No, you've contracted for the job and turned out a scamp. You're a scoundrel!'

'I assure you you're mistaken,' cried Mitya, wringing his hands in despair. The peasant still stroked his beard, and suddenly screwed up his eyes cunningly.

'You show me this: you tell me the law that allows roguery. D'you hear? You're a scoundrel! Do you understand that?'

Mitya stepped back gloomily, and suddenly 'something seemed to hit him on the head', as he said afterwards. In an instant a light seemed to dawn in his mind, 'a light was kindled and I grasped it all'. He stood, stupefied, wondering how he, after all a man of intelligence, could have yielded to such folly, have been led into such an adventure, and have kept it up for almost twenty-four hours, fussing round this Lyagavy, wetting his head.

'Why, the man's drunk, dead drunk, and he'll go on drinking now for a week; what's the use of waiting here? And what if Samsonov sent me here on purpose? What if she? . . . Oh, God, what have I done?'

The peasant sat watching him and grinning. Another time Mitya might have killed the fool in a fury, but now he felt as weak as a child. He went quietly to the bench, took up his overcoat, put it on without a word, and went out of the hut. He did not find the forester in the next room; there was no one there. He took fifty kopecks in small change out of his pocket and put them on the table for his night's lodging, the candle, and the trouble he had given. Coming out of the hut he saw nothing but forest all round. He walked at hazard, not knowing which way to turn out of the hut, to the right or to the left. Hurrying there the evening before with the priest, he had not noticed the road. He had no revengeful feeling for anybody, even for Samsonov, in his heart. He strode along a narrow forest path, aimless, dazed, without heeding where he was going. A child could have knocked him down, so weak was he in body and soul. He got out of the forest somehow, however, and a vista of fields, bare after the harvest, stretched as far as the eye could see.

'What despair! What death all round!' he repeated striding on and on.

He was saved by meeting an old merchant who was being driven across country in a hired trap. When he overtook him, Mitya asked the way, and it turned out that the old merchant, too, was going to Volovya. After some discussion Mitya got into the trap. Three hours later they arrived. At Volovya, Mitya at once ordered posting-horses to drive to the town, and suddenly realised that he was appallingly hungry. While the horses were being harnessed, an omelette was prepared for him. He ate it all in an instant, ate a huge hunk of bread, ate a sausage, and swallowed three glasses of vodka. After eating, his spirits and his heart grew lighter. He flew towards the town, urged on the driver, and suddenly made a new and 'unalterable' plan to procure that 'accursed money' before evening. 'And to think, only to think that a man's life should be ruined for the sake of that paltry three thousand!' he cried, contemptuously. 'I'll settle it today.' And if it had not been for the thought of Grushenka and of what might have happened to her, which never left him, he would perhaps have become quite cheerful again . . . But the thought of her was stabbing him to the heart every moment, like a sharp knife.

At last they arrived, and Mitya at once ran to Grushenka.

3

This was the visit of Mitya of which Grushenka had spoken to Rakitin with such horror. She was just then expecting the 'message', and was much relieved that Mitya had not been to see her that day or the day before. She hoped that 'please God he won't come till I'm gone away', and he suddenly burst in on her. The rest we know already. To get him off her hands she suggested at once that he should walk with her to Samsonov's, where she said she absolutely must go 'to settle his accounts', and when Mitya accompanied her at once, she said goodbye to him at the gate, making him promise to come at twelve o'clock to take her home again. Mitya, too, was delighted at this arrangement. If she was sitting at Samsonov's, she could not be going to Fyodor Pavlovitch's, 'if only she's not lying', he added at once. But he thought she was not lying from what he saw.

After leaving Grushenka at the gate he rushed home. Oh, he had so much still to do that day! But a load had been lifted from his heart, anyway.

'Now I must only make haste and find out from Smerdyakov whether anything happened there last night, whether, by any chance, she went to Fyodor Pavlovitch; ouch!' floated through his mind.

Before he had time to reach his lodging, jealousy had surged up again in his restless heart.

At the sight of Grushenka, Mitya's jealousy vanished, and for an instant he became trustful and generous, and positively despised himself for his evil feelings. But that only proved that, in his love for this woman, there was an element of something far higher than he himself imagined, that it was not only a sensual passion, not only the 'curve of her body', of which he had talked to Alyosha. But, as soon as Grushenka had gone, Mitya began to suspect her of all the low cunning of faithlessness, and he felt no sting of conscience at his thoughts.

And so jealousy rose up in him again. He had, in any case, to make haste. The first thing to be done was to get hold of at least a small, temporary loan of money. The nine roubles had almost all gone on his expedition. And, as we all know, one can't take a step without money. But he had thought over in the carriage where he could get a loan. He had a brace of fine duelling pistols in a case, which he had not pawned till then because he prized them above all his possessions.

In the Metropolis tavern he had some time since made acquaintance with a young official and had learned that this very opulent bachelor was passionately fond of weapons. He bought pistols, revolvers, daggers, hung them on his wall and showed them to acquaintances. He prided himself on them, and was quite a specialist on the mechanism of the revolver. Mitya, without stopping to think, went straight to him, and offered to pawn his pistols to him for ten roubles. The official, delighted, began trying to persuade him to sell them outright. But Mitya would not consent, so the young man gave him ten roubles, protesting that nothing would induce him to take interest. They parted friends.

Mitya was in haste; he rushed towards Fyodor Pavlovitch's by the back way, to his arbour, to get hold of Smerdyakov as soon as possible. In this way the fact was established that three or four hours before a certain event, of which I shall speak later on, Mitya had not a penny, and pawned for ten roubles a possession he valued, though, three hours later, he was in possession of thousands . . . But I am anticipating. From Marya Kondratyevna (the woman living near Fyodor Pavlovitch's) he learned the very disturbing fact of Smerdyakov's illness. He heard the story of his fall in the cellar, his fit, the doctor's visit, Fyodor Pavlovitch's anxiety; he heard with interest, too, that his brother Ivan had set off that morning for Moscow.

He was terribly distressed about Smerdyakov. 'What will happen now? Who'll keep watch for me? Who'll bring me word?' he thought. He began greedily questioning the women whether they had seen anything the evening before. They quite understood what he was trying to find out, and completely reassured him. No one had been there. Ivan Fyodorovitch had been there all night; everything had been perfectly as usual. Mitya grew thoughtful. He would certainly have to keep watch today, but where? Here or at Samsonov's gate? He decided that he must be on the lookout both here and there, and meanwhile . . . meanwhile . . . The difficulty was that he had to carry out the new plan that he had made on the journey back. He was sure of its success, but he must not delay acting upon it. Mitya resolved to sacrifice an hour to it: 'In an hour I shall know everything, I shall settle everything, and then, then, first of all to Samsonov's. I'll enquire whether Grushenka's there and instantly be back here again, stay till eleven, and then to Samsonov's again to bring her home.' This was what he decided.

He rushed home, washed, combed his hair, brushed

his clothes, dressed, and went to Madame Hohlakov's. Alas! he had built his hopes on her. He had resolved to borrow three thousand from that lady. And what was more, he felt suddenly convinced that she would not refuse to lend it to him.

Yet the fact was that he had never known Madame Hohlakov well, and had seen nothing of her for the last month, and that he knew she could not endure him. She had detested him from the first because he was engaged to Katerina Ivanovna, while she had, for some reason, suddenly conceived the desire that Katerina Ivanovna should throw him over, and marry the 'charming, chivalrously refined Ivan, who had such excellent manners'. Mitya's manners she detested. Mitya positively laughed at her, and had once said about her that she was just as lively and at her ease as she was uncultivated. But that morning in the carriage a brilliant idea had struck him: 'If she is so anxious I should not marry Katerina Ivanovna' (and he knew she was positively hysterical upon the subject), 'why should she refuse me now that three thousand, just to enable me to leave Katya and get away from her for ever? These spoiled fine ladies, if they set their hearts on anything, will spare no expense to satisfy their caprice. Besides, she's so rich,' Mitya argued.

At first fortune seemed to smile upon him. As soon as he was announced he was received with extraordinary rapidity. 'As though she were waiting for me,' thought Mitya, and as soon as he had been led to the drawing-room, the lady of the house herself ran in, and declared at once that she was expecting him.

'I was expecting you! I was expecting you! Though I'd no reason to suppose you would come to see me, as you will admit yourself. Yet, I did expect you. You may marvel at my instinct, Dmitri Fyodorovitch, but I was convinced all the morning that you would come.'

'That is certainly wonderful, Madame,' observed Mitya, sitting down limply, 'but I have come to you on a matter of great importance . . . On a matter of supreme importance for me that is, Madame . . . for me alone . . . and I hasten . . .'

'I know you've come on most important business, Dmitri Fyodorovitch; it's not a case of presentiment, this is a case of mathematics: you couldn't help coming, after all that has passed with Katerina Ivanovna; you couldn't, you couldn't; that's a mathematical certainty.'

'The realism of actual life, Madame, that's what it is. But allow me to explain . . .'

'Realism indeed, Dmitri Fyodorovitch. I'm all for realism now. I've seen too much of miracles. You've heard that Father Zossima is dead?'

'No, Madame, it's the first time I've heard of it.' Mitya was a little surprised. The image of Alyosha rose to his mind.

'Last night, and only imagine . . .'

'Madame,' said Mitya, 'I can imagine nothing except that I'm in a desperate position, and that if you don't help me, everything will go to pieces, and I first of all. Excuse me, for the triviality of the expression, but I'm in a fever . . .'

'I know, I know that you're in a fever. You could hardly fail to be, and whatever you may say to me, I know beforehand. I have long been thinking over your destiny, Dmitri Fyodorovitch, I am watching over it and studying it . . . Oh, believe me, I'm an experienced doctor of the soul, Dmitri Fyodorovitch.'

'Madame, if you are an experienced doctor, I'm certainly an experienced patient,' said Mitya, with an effort to be polite, 'and I feel that if you are watching over my destiny in this way, you will come to my help in my despair, and so allow me, at least to explain to you the plan with which I have ventured to come to you . . . and what I am hoping of you . . . I have come, Madame . . . '

'Don't explain it. It's of secondary importance. But as for help, you're not the first I have helped, Dmitri Fyodorovitch. You have most likely heard of my cousin, Madame Belmesov. Her husband was ruined, "had gone to pieces", as you characteristically express it, Dmitri Fyodorovitch. I advised him to take up horse-breeding, and now he's doing well. Have you any idea of horse-breeding, Dmitri Fyodorovitch?'

'Not the faintest, Madame; ah, Madame, not the faintest!' cried Mitya, in nervous impatience, positively starting from his seat. 'I simply implore you, Madame, to listen to me. Only give me two minutes of free speech that I may just explain to you everything, the whole plan with which I have come. Besides I am short of time. I'm in a fearful hurry,' Mitya cried hysterically, feeling that she was just going to begin talking again, and hoping to cut her short. 'I have come in despair . . . in the last gasp of despair, to beg you to lend me the sum of three thousand, a loan, but on safe, most safe security, Madame, with the most trustworthy guarantees! Only let me explain . . . '

'You must tell me all that afterwards, afterwards!' Madame Hohlakov with a gesture demanded silence in her turn, 'and whatever you may tell me, I know it all beforehand; I've told you so already. You ask for a certain sum, for three thousand, but I can give you more, immeasurably more, I will save you, Dmitri Fyodorovitch, but you must listen to me.'

Mitya started from his seat again.

'Madame, will you really be so good!' he cried, with a strong feeling. 'Good God, you've saved me! You have saved a man from violent death, from a bullet . . . My eternal gratitude . . .'

'I will give you more, infinitely more than three thousand!' cried Madame Hohlakov, looking with a radiant smile at Mitya's ecstasy.

'Infinitely? But I don't need so much. I only need that fatal three thousand, and on my part I can give security for that sum with infinite gratitude, and I propose a plan which . . . '

'Enough, Dmitri Fyodorovitch, it's said and done.' Madame Hohlakov cut him short, with the modest triumph of beneficence: 'I have promised to save you, and I will save you. I will save you as I did Belmesov. What do you think of the gold mines, Dmitri Fyodorovitch?'

'Of gold mines, Madame? I have never thought anything about them.'

'But I have thought of them for you. Thought of them over and over again. I have been watching you for the last month. I've watched you a hundred times as you've walked past, saying to myself: that's a man of energy who ought to be at the gold mines. I've studied your gait and come to the conclusion: that's a man who would find gold.'

'From my gait, Madame?' said Mitya, smiling.

'Yes, from your gait. You surely don't deny that character can be told from the way people walk, Dmitri Fyodorovitch? Science supports the idea. I'm all for science and realism now. After all this business with Father Zossima, which has so upset me, from this very day I'm a realist and I want to devote myself to practical causes. I'm cured. "Enough!" as Turgenev says.'

'But, Madame, the three thousand you so generously promised to lend me . . .'

'It is yours, Dmitri Fyodorovitch,' Madame Hohlakov cut in at once. 'The money is as good as in your pocket, not three thousand, but three million, Dmitri Fyodorovitch, in less than no time. I'll make you a present of the idea: you shall find gold mines, make millions, return and become a leading man, and wake us up and lead us to better things.'

'Madame, Madame!' Dmitri interrupted with an uneasy presentiment. 'I shall indeed, perhaps, follow your advice, your wise advice, Madame . . . I shall perhaps set off . . . to the gold mines . . . I'll come and see you again about it . . . many times, indeed . . . but now, that three thousand you so generously . . . oh, that would set me free, and if you could today . . . you see, I haven't a minute to lose today . . . '

'Enough, Dmitri Fyodorovitch, enough!' Madame Hohlakov interrupted emphatically. 'The question is, will you go to the gold mines or not; have you quite made up your mind? Answer yes or no.'

'I will go, Madame, afterwards . . . I'll go where you like . . . but now . . .'

'Wait!' cried Madame Hohlakov. And jumping up and running to a handsome bureau with numerous little drawers, she began pulling out one drawer after another, looking for something with desperate haste.

'The three thousand,' thought Mitya, his heart almost stopping, 'and at the instant . . . without any papers or formalities . . . that's doing things in gentlemanly style! She's a splendid woman, if only she didn't talk so much!'

'Here!' cried Madame Hohlakov, running back joyfully to Mitya, 'here is what I was looking for!'

It was a tiny silver icon on a cord, such as is sometimes worn next to the skin with a cross.

'This is from Kiev, Dmitri Fyodorovitch,' she went on reverently, 'from the relics of the Holy Martyr, Varvara. Let me put it on your neck myself, and with it dedicate you to a new life, to a new career.'

And she actually put the cord round his neck, and began arranging it. In extreme embarrassment, Mitya bent down and helped her, and at last he got it under his necktie and collar through his shirt to his chest.

'Now you can set off,' Madame Hohlakov pronounced, sitting down triumphantly in her place again.

'Madame, I am so touched. I don't know how to thank you, indeed . . . for such kindness, but . . . If only you knew how precious time is to me . . . That sum of money, for which I shall be indebted to your generosity . . . Oh, Madame, since you are so kind, so touchingly generous to me,' Mitya exclaimed impulsively, 'then let me reveal to you . . . though, of course, you've known it a long time . . . that I love somebody here . . . I have been false to Katya . . . Katerina Ivanovna I should say . . . Oh, I've behaved inhumanly, dishonourably to her, but I fell in love here with another woman . . . a woman whom you, Madame, perhaps, despise, for you know everything already, but whom I cannot leave on any account; therefore that three thousand now . . .'

'Leave everything, Dmitri Fyodorovitch,' Madame Hohlakov interrupted in the most decisive tone. 'Leave everything, especially women. Gold mines are your goal, and there's no place for women there. Afterwards, when you come back rich and famous, you will find the girl of your heart in the highest society. That will be a modern girl, a girl of education and advanced ideas. By that time the question of women's rights will have gained ground, and the new woman will have appeared.'

'Madame!' cried Mitya, jumping up at last, clasping his hands before her in helpless entreaty. 'You will make me weep if you delay what you have so generously . . . '

'Oh, do weep, Dmitri Fyodorovitch, do weep! That's a noble feeling . . . such a path lies open before you! Tears will ease your heart, and later on you will return rejoicing. You will hasten to me from Siberia on purpose to share your joy with me . . . '

'But allow me, too!' Mitya cried suddenly. 'For the last time I entreat you, tell me, can I have the sum you promised me today, if not, when may I come for it?'

'What sum, Dmitri Fyodorovitch?'

'The three thousand you promised me . . . that you so generously . . . '

'There thousand? Roubles? Oh, no, I haven't got three thousand,' Madame Hohlakov announced with serene amazement. Mitya was stupefied.

'Why, you just now . . . you said . . . you said it was as good as in my hands . . . '

'Oh, no, you misunderstood me, Dmitri Fyodorovitch. In that case you misunderstood me. I was talking of the gold mines. It's true I promised you more, infinitely more than three thousand, I remember it all now, but I was referring to the gold mines.'

'But the money? The three thousand?' Mitya exclaimed, awkwardly.

'Oh, if you meant money, I haven't any. I haven't a penny, Dmitri Fyodorovitch. I'm quarrelling with my agent about it, and I've just borrowed five hundred roubles from Miüsov, myself. No, no, I've no money.

And, do you know, Dmitri Fyodorovitch, if I had, I wouldn't give it to you. In the first place, I never lend money. Lending money means losing friends. And I wouldn't give it to you particularly. I wouldn't give it you, because I like you and want to save you, for all you need is the gold mines, the gold mines, the gold mines!'

'Oh, the devil!' roared Mitya, and with all his might brought his fist down on the table.

'Aie! Aie!' cried Madame Hohlakov, alarmed, and she ran to the other end of the drawing-room.

Mitya spat on the floor, and strode rapidly out of the room, out of the house, into the street, into the darkness! He walked like one possessed, and beating himself on the breast, on the spot where he had struck himself two days previously, before Alyosha, the last time he saw him in the dark, on the road. What those blows upon his breast signified, *on that spot*, and what he meant by it – that was, for the time, a secret which was known to no one in the world, and had not been told even to Alyosha. But that secret meant for him more than disgrace; it meant ruin, suicide. So he had determined, if he did not get hold of the three thousand that would pay his debt to Katerina Ivanovna, and so remove from his breast, from *that spot on his breast*, the shame he carried upon it, that weighed on his conscience. All this will be fully explained to the reader later on, but now that his last hope had vanished, this man, so strong in appearance, began to sob like a little child a few steps from the Hohlakovs' house. He walked on, and not knowing what he was doing, wiped away his tears with his fist. In this way he reached the square, and suddenly became aware that he had stumbled against something. He heard a piercing wail from an old woman whom he had almost knocked down.

'Good Lord, you've nearly killed me! Why don't you look where you're going, scapegrace?'

'Why, it's you!' cried Mitya, recognising the old woman in the dark. It was the old servant who waited on Samsonov, whom Mitya had particularly noticed the day before.

'And who are you, my good sir?' said the old woman in quite a different voice. 'I don't know you in the dark.'

'You live at Kuzma Kuzmitch's. You're the servant there?'

'Just so, sir, I was only running out to Prohoritch's . . . But I don't know you.'

'Tell me, my good woman, is Agrafena Alexandrovna there now?' said Mitya, beside himself with suspense. 'I saw her to the house some time ago.'

'She has been there, sir. She stayed a little while, and went off again.'

'What? Went away?' cried Mitya. 'When did she go?'

'Why, as soon as she came. She only stayed a minute. She only told Kuzma Kuzmitch a tale that made him laugh; then she ran away.'

'You're lying, damn you!' roared Mitya.

'Aie! Aie!' shrieked the old woman, but Mitya had vanished.

He ran with all his might to the house where Grushenka lived. At the moment he reached it, Grushenka was on her way to Mokroe. It was not more than a quarter of an hour after her departure.

Fenya was sitting with her grandmother, the old cook, Matryona, in the kitchen when 'the captain' ran in. Fenya uttered a piercing shriek on seeing him.

'You scream?' roared Mitya; 'where is she?'

But without giving the terror-stricken Fenya time to utter a word, he fell at her feet.

'Fenya, for Christ's sake, tell me, where is she?'

'I don't know. Dmitri Fyodorovitch, my dear, I don't know. You may kill me but I can't tell you.' Fenya swore and protested. 'You went out with her yourself not long ago . . .'

'She came back!'

'Indeed she didn't. By God I swear she didn't come back.'

'You're lying!' shouted Mitya. 'From your terror I know where she is.'

He rushed away. Fenya in her fright was glad she had got off so easily. But she knew very well that it was only that he was in such haste, or she might not have fared so well. But as he ran, he surprised both Fenya and old Matryona by an unexpected action. On the table stood a brass mortar, with a pestle in it, a small brass pestle, not much more than six inches long. Mitya already had opened the door with one hand when, with the other, he snatched up the pestle, and thrust it in his side pocket.

'Oh Lord! He's going to murder someone!' cried Fenya, flinging up her hands.

4

Where was he running? Where could she be except at Fyodor Pavlovitch's? She must have run straight to him from Samsonov's, that was clear now. The whole intrigue, the whole deceit was evident . . . It all rushed whirling through his mind. He did not run to Marya Kondratyevna's. There was no need to go there . . . not the slightest need . . . he must raise no alarm . . . they would run and tell directly . . . Marya Kondratyevna was clearly in the plot, Smerdyakov too, he too, all had been bought over!

He formed another plan of action: he ran a long way round Fyodor Pavlovitch's house, crossing the lane, running down Dmitrovsky Street, then over the little bridge, and so came straight to the deserted alley at the back, which was empty and uninhabited, with on one side the hurdle fence of a neighbour's kitchen-garden, on the other, the strong high fence, that ran all round Fyodor Pavlovitch's garden. Here he chose a spot, apparently the very place where, according to the tradition, he knew Lizaveta had once climbed over it: 'If she could climb over it,' the thought, God knows why, occurred to him, 'surely I can.' He did in fact jump up, and instantly contrived to catch hold of the top of the fence. Then he vigorously pulled himself up and sat astride on it. Close by, in the garden stood the bathhouse, but from the fence he could see the lighted window of the house too.

'Yes, the old man's bedroom is lighted up. She's there!' and he jumped from the fence into the garden. Though he knew Grigory was ill and very likely Smerdyakov, too, and that there was no one to hear him, he instinctively hid himself, stood still, and began to listen. But there was dead silence on all sides and, as though of design, complete stillness, not the slightest breath of wind.

'And nought but the whispering silence,' the line for some reason rose to his mind. 'If only no one heard me jump over the fence! I think not.' Standing still for a minute, he walked softly over the grass in the garden, avoiding the trees and shrubs. He walked slowly, creeping stealthily at every step, listening to his own footsteps. It took him five minutes to reach the lighted window. He remembered that just under the window there were several thick high bushes of elder and snowball tree. The door from the house into the garden, on the left-hand side, was shut; he had carefully looked to see, in passing. At last he reached the bushes and hid behind them. He held his breath. 'I must wait now,' he thought, 'to reassure them, in case they heard my footsteps and are listening . . . If only I don't cough or sneeze.'

He waited two minutes. His heart was beating violently, and, at moments, he could scarcely breathe. 'No, this throbbing at my heart won't stop,' he thought. 'I can't wait any longer.' He was standing behind a bush in the shadow. The light of the window fell on the front part of the bush.

'How red the berries are!' he murmured, not knowing why. Softly and noiselessly, step by step, he approached the window, and raised himself on tiptoe. All Fyodor Pavlovitch's bedroom lay open before him. It was not a large room, and was divided in two parts by a red screen, 'Chinese', as Fyodor Pavlovitch used to call it. The word 'Chinese' flashed into Mitya's mind, 'and behind the screen, is Grushenka', thought Mitya. He began watching Fyodor Pavlovitch, who was wearing his new striped-silk dressing gown, which Mitya had never seen, a tasselled silk cord round the waist. A clean, dandified shirt of fine linen with gold studs showed under the collar of the dressing gown. On his head Fyodor Pavlovitch had the same red bandage which Alyosha had seen.

'He has fixed himself up,' thought Mitya.

His father was standing near the window, apparently

lost in thought. Suddenly he jerked up his head, listened a moment, and, hearing nothing, went up to the table, poured out half a glass of brandy from a decanter, and drank it off. Then he uttered a deep sigh, again stood still a moment, walked carelessly up to the looking-glass on the wall, with his right hand raised the red bandage on his forehead a little, and began examining his bruises and scars, which had not yet disappeared.

'He's alone,' thought Mitya, 'in all probability he's alone.'

Fyodor Pavlovitch moved away from the looking-glass, turned suddenly to the window and looked out. Mitya instantly slipped away into the shadow.

'She may be there behind the screen. Perhaps she's asleep by now,' he thought, with a pang at his heart. Fyodor Pavlovitch moved away from the window. 'He's looking for her out of the window, so she's not there. Why should he stare out into the dark? He's wild with impatience.' . . . Mitya slipped back at once, and fell to gazing in at the window again. The old man was sitting down at the table, apparently disappointed. At last he put his elbow on the table, and laid his right cheek against his hand. Mitya watched him eagerly.

'He's alone, he's alone!' he repeated again. 'If she were here, his face would be different.'

Strange to say, a queer, irrational vexation rose up in his heart that she was not here. 'It's not that she's not here,' he explained to himself, immediately, 'but that I can't tell for sure whether she is or not.' Mitya remembered afterwards that his mind was, at that moment, exceptionally clear, that he took in everything to the slightest detail, and missed no point. But a feeling of misery, the misery of uncertainty and indecision was growing in his heart with every instant. 'Is she here or not?' The angry doubt filled his heart, and suddenly, making up his mind, he put out his hand and softly knocked on the window frame. He knocked the signal the old man had agreed upon with Smerdyakov, twice slowly and then three times more quickly, the signal that meant 'Grushenka is here!'

The old man started, jerked up his head, and jumping up quickly, ran to the window. Mitya slipped away into the shadow. Fyodor Pavlovitch opened the window and thrust his whole head out.

'Grushenka, is it you? Is it you?' he said, in a sort of trembling half-whisper. 'Where are you, my angel, where are you?' He was fearfully agitated and breathless.

'He's alone,' Mitya decided.

'Where are you?' cried the old man again; and he thrust his head out farther, thrust it out to the shoulders, gazing in all directions, right and left. 'Come here, I've a little present for you. Come, I'll show you . . .'

'He means the three thousand,' thought Mitya.

'But where are you? Are you at the door? I'll open it at once.'

And the old man almost climbed out of the window, peering out to the right, where there was a door into the garden, trying to see into the darkness. In another second he would certainly have run out to open the door without waiting for Grushenka's answer.

Mitya looked at him from the side without stirring. The old man's profile that he loathed so, his pendant Adam's apple, his hooked nose, his lips that smiled in greedy expectation, were all brightly lighted up by the slanting lamplight falling on the left from the room. A horrible fury of hatred suddenly surged up in Mitya's heart. 'There he was, his rival, the man who had tormented him, had ruined his life!' It was a rush of that sudden, furious, revengeful anger of which he had spoken, as though foreseeing it, to Alyosha, four days ago in the arbour, when, in answer to Alyosha's question, 'How can you say you'll kill our father?' 'I don't know, I don't know,' he had said then. 'Perhaps I shall not kill him, perhaps I shall. I'm afraid he'll suddenly be so loathsome to me at that moment. I hate his double chin, his nose, his eyes, his shameless grin. I feel a personal repulsion. That's what I'm afraid of, that's what may be too much for me . . . ' This personal repulsion was growing unendurable. Mitya was beside himself. He suddenly pulled the brass pestle out of his pocket.

'God was watching over me then,' Mitya himself said afterwards. At that very moment Grigory waked up on his bed of sickness. Earlier in the evening he had undergone the treatment which Smerdyakov had described to Ivan. He had rubbed himself all over with vodka mixed with a secret very strong decoction, had drunk what was left of the mixture while his wife repeated a 'certain prayer' over him, after which he had gone to bed. Marfa Ignatyevna had tasted the stuff, too, and, being unused to strong drink, slept like the dead beside her husband.

But Grigory waked up in the night, quite suddenly, and, after a moment's reflection, though he immediately felt a sharp pain in his back, he sat up in bed. Then he deliberated again, got up and dressed hurriedly. Perhaps his conscience was uneasy at the thought of sleeping while the house was unguarded 'in such perilous times'. Smerdyakov, exhausted by his fit, lay motionless in the next room. Marfa

Ignatyevna did not stir. 'The stuff's been too much for the woman,' Grigory thought, glancing at her, and groaning, he went out on the steps. No doubt he only intended to look out from the steps, for he was hardly able to walk, the pain in his back and his right leg was intolerable. But he suddenly remembered that he had not locked the little gate into the garden that evening. He was the most punctual and precise of men, a man who adhered to an unchangeable routine, and habits that lasted for years. Limping and writhing with pain he went down the steps and towards the garden. Yes, the gate stood wide open. Mechanically he stepped into the garden. Perhaps he fancied something, perhaps caught some sound, and, glancing to the left he saw his master's window open. No one was looking out of it then.

'What's it open for? It's not summer now,' thought Grigory, and suddenly, at that very instant he caught a glimpse of something extraordinary before him in the garden. Forty paces in front of him a man seemed to be running in the dark, a sort of shadow was moving very fast.

'Good Lord!' cried Grigory beside himself, and forgetting the pain in his back, he hurried to intercept the running figure. He took a short cut, evidently he knew the garden better; the flying figure went towards the bathhouse, ran behind it and rushed to the garden fence. Grigory followed, not losing sight of him, and ran, forgetting everything. He reached the fence at the very moment the man was climbing over it. Grigory cried out, beside himself, pounced on him, and clutched his leg in his two hands.

Yes, his foreboding had not deceived him. He recognised him, it was he, the 'monster', the 'parricide'.

'Parricide!' the old man shouted so that the whole neighbourhood could hear, but he had not time to shout more, he fell at once, as though struck by lightning.

Mitya jumped back into the garden and bent over the fallen man. In Mitya's hands was a brass pestle, and he flung it mechanically in the grass. The pestle fell two paces from Grigory, not in the grass but on the path, in a most conspicuous place. For some seconds he examined the prostrate figure before him. The old man's head was covered with blood. Mitya put out his hand and began feeling it. He remembered afterwards clearly, that he had been terribly anxious to make sure whether he had broken the old man's skull, or simply stunned him with the pestle. But the blood was flowing horribly; and in a moment Mitya's fingers were drenched with the hot stream. He remembered taking out of his pocket the clean white handkerchief with which he had provided himself for his visit to Madame Hohlakov, and putting it to the old man's head, senselessly trying to wipe the blood from his face and temples. But the handkerchief was instantly soaked with blood.

'Good heavens! what am I doing it for?' thought Mitya, suddenly pulling himself together. 'If I have broken his skull, how can I find out now? And what difference does it make now?' he added, hopelessly. 'If I've killed him, I've killed him . . . you've come to grief, old man, so there you must lie!' he said aloud. And suddenly, turning to the fence, he vaulted over it into the lane and fell to running – the handkerchief soaked with blood he held, crushed up, in his right fist, and, as he ran, he thrust it into the back pocket of his coat. He ran headlong, and the few passers-by who met him in the dark, in the streets, remembered afterwards that they had met a man running that night. He flew back again to the widow Morozov's house.

Immediately after he had left it, that evening, Fenya had rushed to the chief porter, Nazar Ivanovitch, and besought him, for Christ's sake, 'not to let the captain in again today or tomorrow'. Nazar Ivanovitch promised, but went upstairs to his mistress who had suddenly sent for him, and meeting his nephew, a boy of twenty, who had recently come from the country, on the way up told him to take his place, but forgot to mention 'the captain'. Mitya, running up to the gate, knocked. The lad instantly recognised him, for Mitya had more than once tipped him. Opening the gate at once he let him in, and hastened to inform him with a good-humoured smile that 'Agrafena Alexandrovna is not at home now, you know'.

'Where is she then, Prohor?' asked Mitya, stopping short.

'She set off this evening, some two hours ago, with Timofey, to Mokroe.'

'What for?' cried Mitya.

'That I can't say. To see some officer. Someone invited her and horses were sent to fetch her.'

Mitya left him, and ran like a madman to Fenya.

5

She was sitting in the kitchen with her grandmother; they were both just going to bed. Relying on Nazar Ivanovitch, they had not locked themselves in. Mitya ran in, pounced on Fenya and seized her by the throat.

'Speak at once! Where is she? With whom is she now, at Mokroe?' he roared furiously.

Both the women squealed.

'Aie! I'll tell you. Aie, Dmitri Fyodorovitch, darling, I'll tell you everything directly, I won't hide anything,' gabbled Fenya, frightened to death; 'she's gone to Mokroe, to her officer.'

'What officer?' roared Mitya.

'To her officer, the same one she used to know, the one who threw her over five years ago,' cackled Fenya, as fast as she could speak.

Mitya withdrew the hands with which he was squeezing her throat. He stood facing her, pale as death, unable to utter a word, but his eyes showed that he realised it all, all, from the first word, and guessed the whole position. Poor Fenya was not in a condition at that moment to observe whether he understood or not. She remained sitting as she had been when he ran into the room, trembling all over, holding her hands out before her as though trying to defend herself. She seemed to have grown rigid in that position. Her wide-opened, scared eyes were fixed immovably upon him. And to make matters worse, both his hands were smeared with blood. On the way, as he ran, he must have touched his forehead with them, wiping off perspiration, so that on his forehead and his right cheek were bloodstained patches. Fenya was on the verge of hysterics. The old cook had jumped up and was staring at him like a mad woman, almost unconscious with terror.

Mitya stood for a moment, then mechanically sank on to a chair next to Fenya. He sat, not reflecting but, as it were, terror-stricken, benumbed. Yet everything was clear as day: that officer, he knew about him, he knew everything perfectly, he had known it from Grushenka herself, and known that a letter had come from him a month before. So that for a month, for a whole month this had been going on in secret from him, till the very arrival of this new man, and he had never thought of him! But how could he, how could he not have thought of him? Why was it he had forgotten this officer, like that, forgotten him as soon as he heard of him? That was the question that faced him like some monstrous thing. And he looked at this monstrous thing with horror, growing cold with horror.

But suddenly, as gently and mildly as a gentle and affectionate child, he began speaking to Fenya as though he had utterly forgotten how he had scared and hurt her just now. He fell to questioning Fenya with an extreme preciseness, astonishing in his position, and though the girl looked wildly at his bloodstained hands, she too, with wonderful readiness and rapidity, answered every question as though eager to put the whole truth and nothing but the truth before him. Little by little, even with a sort of enjoyment, she began explaining every detail, not wanting to torment him, but, as it were, eager to be of the utmost service to him. She described the whole of that day, in great detail, the visit of Rakitin and Alyosha, how she, Fenya, had stood on the watch, how the mistress had set off, and how she had called out of the window to Alyosha to give him, Mitya, her greetings, and to tell him 'to remember for ever how she had loved him for an hour'.

Hearing of the message, Mitya suddenly smiled, and there was a flush of colour on his pale cheeks. At the same moment Fenya said to him, not a bit afraid now to be inquisitive: 'Look at your hands, Dmitri Fyodorovitch. They're all over blood!'

'Yes,' answered Mitya mechanically. He looked carelessly at his hands and at once forgot them and Fenya's question.

He sank into silence again. Twenty minutes had passed since he had run in. His first horror was over, but evidently some new fixed determination had taken possession of him. He suddenly stood up, smiling dreamily.

'What has happened to you, sir?' said Fenya, pointing to his hands again. She spoke compassionately, as though she felt very near to him now in his grief. Mitya looked at his hands again.

'That's blood, Fenya,' he said, looking at her with a strange expression. 'That's human blood, and, my God! why was it shed? But . . . Fenya . . . there's a fence here' (he looked at her as though setting her a riddle), 'a high fence, and terrible to look at. But, at dawn tomorrow, when the sun rises, Mitya will leap over that fence . . . You don't understand what fence, Fenya, and, never mind . . . You'll hear tomorrow and understand . . . and now, goodbye. I won't stand in her way. I'll step aside, I know how to step aside. Live, my joy . . . You loved me for an hour, remember "little" Mitya Karamazov so for ever . . . She always used to call me little Mitya, do you remember?'

And with those words he went suddenly out of the

kitchen. Fenya was almost more frightened at this sudden departure than she had been when he ran in and attacked her.

Just ten minutes later Dmitri went to Peter Ilyitch Perhotin, the young official with whom he had pawned his pistols. It was by now half-past eight, and Peter Ilyitch had finished his evening tea, and had just put his coat on again to go to the Metropolis to play billiards. Mitya caught him coming out.

Seeing him with his face all smeared with blood, the young man uttered a cry of surprise.

'Good Heavens! What is the matter?'

'I've come for my pistols,' said Mitya, 'and brought you the money. And thanks very much. I'm in a hurry, Peter Ilyitch, please make haste.'

Peter Ilyitch grew more and more surprised; he suddenly caught sight of a bundle of bank notes in Mitya's hand, and what was more, he had walked in holding the notes as no one walks in and no one carries money: he had them in his right hand, and held them outstretched as if to show them. Perhotin's servant boy, who met Mitya in the passage, said afterwards that he walked into the passage in the same way, with the money outstretched in his hand, so he must have been carrying them like that even in the street. They were all rainbow-coloured hundred-rouble notes, and the fingers holding them were covered with blood.

When Peter Ilyitch was questioned later on as to the sum of money, he said that it was difficult to judge at a glance, but that it might have been two thousand, or perhaps three, but it was a big, 'fat' bundle. 'Dmitri Fyodorovitch,' so he testified afterwards, 'seemed unlike himself, too; not drunk, but, as it were, exalted, lost to everything, but at the same time, as it were, absorbed, as though pondering and searching for something and unable to come to a decision. He was in great haste, answered abruptly and very strangely, and at moments seemed not at all dejected but quite cheerful.'

'But what *is* the matter with you? What's wrong?' cried Peter Ilyitch, looking wildly at his guest. 'How is it that you're all covered with blood? Have you had a fall? Look at yourself!'

He took him by the elbow and led him to the glass.

Seeing his bloodstained face, Mitya recoiled and scowled wrathfully.

'Damnation! That's the last straw,' he muttered angrily, hurriedly changing the notes from his right to the left, and impulsively jerked the handkerchief out of his pocket. But the handkerchief turned out to be soaked with blood, too (it was the handkerchief he had used to wipe Grigory's face). There was scarcely a white spot on it, and it had not merely begun to dry, but had stiffened into a crumpled ball and could not be pulled apart. Mitya threw it angrily on the floor.

'Oh, damn it!' he said. 'Haven't you a rag of some sort . . . to wipe my face?'

'So you're only stained, not wounded? You'd better wash,' said Peter Ilyitch. 'Here's a washstand. I'll pour you out some water.'

'A washstand? That's all right . . . but where am I to put this?'

With the strangest perplexity he indicated his bundle of hundred-rouble notes, looking enquiringly at Peter Ilyitch as though it were for him to decide what he, Mitya, was to do with his own money.

'In your pocket, or on the table here. They won't be lost.'

'In my pocket? Yes, in my pocket. All right . . . But, I say, that's all nonsense,' he cried, as though suddenly coming out of his absorption. 'Look here, let's settle that business of the pistols. Give them back to me. Here's your money . . . because I am in great need of them . . . and I haven't a minute, a minute to spare.'

And taking the topmost note from the bundle he held it out to Peter Ilyitch.

'But I shan't have change enough. Haven't you less?'

'No,' said Mitya, looking again at the bundle, and as though not trusting his own words he turned over two or three of the topmost ones.

'No, they're all alike,' he added, and again he looked inquiringly at Peter Ilyitch.

'How have you grown so rich?' the latter asked. 'Wait, I'll send my boy to Plotnikov's, they close late – to see if they won't change it. Here, Misha!' he called into the passage.

'To Plotnikov's shop – first rate!' cried Mitya, as though struck by an idea. 'Misha,' he turned to the boy as he came in, 'look here, run to Plotnikov's and tell them that Dmitri Fyodorovitch sends his greetings, and will be there directly . . . But listen, listen, tell them to have champagne, three dozen bottles ready before I come, and packed as it was to take to Mokroe. I took four dozen with me then,' he added (suddenly addressing Peter Ilyitch); 'they know all about it, don't you trouble, Misha,' he turned again to the boy. 'Listen; tell them to put cheese, Strasbourg pies, smoked fish, ham, caviar, and everything, everything they've got, up to a hundred roubles, or a hundred and twenty as before . . . But wait: don't let them forget dessert, sweets, pears, watermelons, two or three or four – no, one melon's enough, and chocolate, candy, toffee, fondants; in fact, everything I took to Mokroe before, three hundred roubles' worth with the champagne . . . let it be just the same again. And remember, Misha, if you are called Misha . . . His name is Misha, isn't it?' He turned to Peter Ilyitch again.

'Wait a minute,' Peter Ilyitch intervened, listening and watching him uneasily, 'you'd better go yourself and tell them. He'll muddle it.'

'He will, I see he will! Eh, Misha! Why, I was going to kiss you for the commission . . . If you don't make a mistake, there's ten roubles for you, run along, make haste . . . Champagne's the chief thing, let them bring up champagne. And brandy, too, and red and white wine, and all I had then . . . They know what I had then.'

'But listen!' Peter Ilyitch interrupted with some impatience. 'I say, let him simply run and change the money and tell them not to close, and you go and tell them . . . Give him your note. Be off, Misha! Hurry!'

Peter Ilyitch seemed to hurry Misha off on purpose, because the boy remained standing with his mouth and eyes wide open, apparently understanding little of Mitya's orders, gazing up with amazement and terror at his bloodstained face and the trembling bloodstained fingers that held the notes.

'Well, now come and wash,' said Peter Ilyitch, sternly. 'Put the money on the table or else in your pocket . . . That's right, come along. But take off your coat.'

And beginning to help him off with his coat, he cried out again: 'Look, your coat's covered with blood, too!'

'That . . . it's not the coat. It's only a little here on the sleeve . . . And that's only here where the handkerchief lay. It must have soaked through. I must have sat on the handkerchief at Fenya's, and the blood's come through,' Mitya explained at once with a childlike unconsciousness that was astounding. Peter Ilyitch listened, frowning.

'Well, you must have been up to something; you must have been fighting with someone,' he muttered.

They began to wash. Peter Ilyitch held the jug and poured out the water. Mitya, in desperate haste, scarcely soaped his hands (they were trembling, and Peter Ilyitch remembered it afterwards). But the young official insisted on his soaping them thoroughly and rubbing them more. He seemed to exercise more and more sway over Mitya, as time went on. It may be noted in passing that he was a young man of sturdy character.

'Look, you haven't got your nails clean. Now rub your face; here, on your temples, by your ear . . . Will you go in that shirt? Where are you going? Look, the cuff of your right sleeve is covered with blood.'

'Yes, it's all bloody,' observed Mitya, looking at the cuff of his shirt.

'Then change your shirt.'

'I haven't time. You see I'll . . . ' Mitya went on with the same confiding ingenuousness, drying his face and hands on the towel, and putting on his coat. 'I'll turn it up at the wrist. It won't be seen under the coat . . . You see!'

'Tell me now, what have you done? Have you been fighting with someone? In the tavern again, as before? Have you been beating that captain again?' Peter Ilyitch asked him reproachfully. 'Whom have you been beating now . . . or killing, perhaps?'

'Nonsense!' said Mitya.

'Why "nonsense"?'

'Don't worry,' said Mitya, and he suddenly laughed. 'I knocked down an old woman in the market place just now.'

'Knocked down? An old woman?'

'An old man!' cried Mitya, looking Peter Ilyitch straight in the face, laughing, and shouting at him as though he were deaf.

'Confound it! An old woman, an old man . . . Have you killed someone?'

'We made it up. We had a row – and made it up. In a place I know of. We parted friends. A fool . . . He's forgiven me . . . He's sure to have forgiven me by now . . . if he had got up, he wouldn't have forgiven me' – Mitya suddenly winked – 'only, damn him, you know, I say, Peter Ilyitch, damn him! Don't worry about him! I don't want to just now!' Mitya snapped out, resolutely.

'Whatever do you want to go picking quarrels with everyone for? . . . Just as you did with that captain over some nonsense . . . You've been fighting and now you're rushing off on the spree – that's you all over! Three dozen champagne – what do you want all that for?'

'Bravo! Now give me the pistols. Upon my honour I've no time now. I should like to have a chat with you, my dear boy, but I haven't the time. And there's no need, it's too late for talking. Where's my money? Where have I put it?' he cried, thrusting his hands into his pockets.

'You put it on the table . . . yourself . . . Here it is. Had you forgotten? Money's like dirt or water to you, it seems. Here are your pistols. It's an odd thing, at six o'clock you pledged them for ten roubles, and now you've got thousands. Two or three I should say.'

'Three, you bet,' laughed Mitya, stuffing the notes into the side pocket of his trousers.

'You'll lose it like that. Have you found a gold mine?'

'The mines? The gold mines?' Mitya shouted at the top of his voice and went off in a roar of laughter. 'Would you like to go to the mines, Perhotin? There's a lady here who'll stump up three thousand for you, if only you'll go. She did it for me, she's so awfully fond of gold mines. Do you know Madame Hohlakov?'

'I don't know her, but I've heard of her and seen her. Did she really give you three thousand? Did she really?' said Peter Ilyitch.

'As soon as the sun rises tomorrow, as soon as Phoebus, ever young, flies upward, praising and glorifying God, you go to her, this Madame Hohlakov, and ask her whether she did stump up that three thousand or not. Try and find out.'

'I don't know on what terms you are . . . since you say it so positively, I suppose she did give it to you. You've got the money in your hand, but instead of going to Siberia you're spending it all . . . Where are you really off to now, eh?'

'To Mokroe.'

'To Mokroe? But it's night!'

'Once the lad had all, now the lad has nought,' cried Mitya.

'How "nought"? You say that with all those thousands!'

'I'm not talking about thousands. Damn thousands! I'm talking of the female character.

'Fickle is the heart of woman
Treacherous and full of vice;

I agree with Ulysses. That's what he says.'

'I don't understand you!'

'Am I drunk?'

'Not drunk, but worse.'

'I'm drunk in spirit, Peter Ilyitch, drunk in spirit! But that's enough!'

'What are you doing, loading the pistol?'

'I'm loading the pistol.'

Unfastening the pistol case, Mitya actually opened the powder horn, and carefully sprinkled and rammed in the charge. Then he took the bullet and before inserting it, held it in two fingers in front of the candle.

'Why are you looking at the bullet?' asked Peter Ilyitch, watching him with uneasy curiosity.

'Oh, a fancy. Why, if you meant to put that bullet in your brain, would you look at it or not?'

'Why look at it?'

'It's going into my brain, so it's interesting to look and see what it's like. But that's foolishness, a moment's foolishness. Now that's done,' he added, putting in the bullet and driving it home with the ramrod. 'Peter Ilyitch, my dear fellow, that's nonsense, all nonsense, and if only you knew what nonsense! Give me a little piece of paper now.'

'Here's some paper.'

'No, a clean new piece, writing paper. That's right.'

And taking a pen from the table, Mitya rapidly wrote two lines, folded the paper in four, and thrust it in his waistcoat pocket. He put the pistols in the case, locked it up, and kept it in his hand. Then he looked at Peter Ilyitch with a slow, thoughtful smile.

'Now, let's go,' he said.

'Where are we going? No, wait a minute . . . Are you thinking of putting that bullet in your brain, perhaps?' Pyotr Ilyitch asked uneasily.

'I was fooling about the bullet! I want to live. I love life! You may be sure of that. I love golden-haired Phoebus and his warm light . . . Dear Peter Ilyitch, do you know how to step aside?'

'What do you mean by "stepping aside"?'

'Making way. Making way for a dear creature, and for one I hate. And to let the one I hate become dear – that's what making way means! And to say to them: God bless you, go your way, pass on, while I . . . '

'While you?'

'That's enough, let's go.'

'Upon my word. I'll tell someone to prevent your going there,' said Peter Ilyitch, looking at him. 'What are you going to Mokroe for, now?'

'There's a woman there, a woman. That's enough for you. You shut up.'

'Listen, though you're such a savage I've always liked you . . . I feel anxious.'

'Thanks, old fellow. I'm a savage you say. Savages, savages! That's what I am always saying. Savages! Why, here's Misha! I was forgetting him.'

Misha ran in, posthaste, with a handful of notes in change, and reported that everyone was in a bustle at the Plotnikovs'. 'They're carrying down the bottles, and the fish, and the tea; it will all be ready directly.' Mitya seized ten roubles and handed it to Peter Ilyitch, then tossed another ten-rouble note to Misha.

'Don't dare to do such a thing!' cried Peter Ilyitch. 'I won't have it in my house, it's a bad, demoralising habit. Put your money away. Here, put it here, why waste it? It would come in handy tomorrow, and I dare say you'll be coming to me to borrow ten roubles again. Why do you keep putting the notes in your side pocket? Ah, you'll lose them!'

'I say, my dear fellow, let's go to Mokroe together.'

'What should I go for?'

'I say, let's open a bottle at once, and drink to life! I want to drink, and especially to drink with you. I've never drunk with you, have I?'

'Very well, we can go to the Metropolis. I was just going there.'

'I haven't time for that. Let's drink at the Plotnikovs', in the back room. Shall I ask you a riddle?'

'Ask away.'

Mitya took the piece of paper out of his waistcoat pocket, unfolded it and showed it. In a large, distinct hand was written: 'I punish myself for my whole life, my whole life I punish!'

'I certainly will speak to someone. I'll go at once,' said Peter Ilyitch, after reading the paper.

'You won't have time, dear boy, come and have a drink. March!'

Plotnikov's shop was at the corner of the street, next door but one to Peter Ilyitch's house. It was the largest grocery shop in our town, and by no means a bad one, belonging to some rich merchants. They kept everything that could be got in a Petersburg shop, grocery of every kind, wines 'bottled by the brothers Eliseyev', fruits, cigars, tea, coffee, sugar, and so on. There were three sales clerks and two delivery boys always employed. Though our part of the country had grown poorer, the landowners had gone away, and trade had got worse, yet the grocery stores flourished as before.

They were awaiting Mitya with impatience in the shop. They had vivid recollections of how he had bought, three or four weeks ago, wine and delicacies of every sort to the value of several hundred roubles, paid for in cash (they would never have let him have anything on credit, of course). They remembered that then, as now, he had had a bundle of hundred-rouble notes in his hand, and had scattered them at random, without bargaining, without reflecting, or caring to reflect what use so much wine and provisions would be to him. The story was told all over the town that, driving off then with Grushenka to Mokroe he had 'spent three thousand in one night and the following day, and had come back from the spree without a penny'. He had picked up a whole troop of gypsies (encamped in our neighbourhood at the time), who for two days got money without stint out of him while he was drunk, and drank expensive wine without stint. People used to tell, laughing at Mitya, how he had given champagne to grimy-handed peasants, and feasted the village women and girls on candy and Strasbourg pies. Though to laugh at Mitya to his face was rather a risky proceeding, there was much laughter behind his back, especially in the tavern, at his own ingenuous public avowal that all he had got out of Grushenka by this 'escapade' was 'permission to kiss her foot, and that was the utmost she had allowed him'.

By the time Mitya and Peter Ilyitch reached the shop, they found a carriage with three horses harnessed abreast with bells, and with Andrey, the driver, ready waiting for Mitya at the entrance. In the shop they had almost entirely finished packing one box of provisions, and were only waiting for Mitya's arrival to nail it down and put it in the carriage. Peter Ilyitch was astounded.

'Where did this carriage come from in such a hurry?' he asked Mitya.

'I met Andrey as I ran to you, and told him to drive straight here to the shop. There's no time to lose. Last time I drove with Timofey, but Timofey now has gone on before me with the witch. Shall we be very late, Andrey?'

'They'll only get there an hour at most before us, not even that maybe. I got Timofey ready to start. I know how he'll go. Their pace won't be ours, Dmitri Fyodorovitch. How could it be? They won't get there an hour earlier!' Andrey, a lanky, red-haired, middle-aged driver, wearing a full-skirted coat, and with a caftan on his arm, replied warmly.

'Fifty roubles for vodka if we're only an hour behind them.'

'I guarantee the time, Dmitri Fyodorovitch. Eh, they won't be half an hour before us, let alone an hour.'

Though Mitya bustled about seeing after things, he gave his orders strangely, as it were disconnectedly, and inconsecutively. He began a sentence and forgot the end of it. Peter Ilyitch found himself obliged to come to the rescue.

'Four hundred roubles' worth, not less than four hundred roubles' worth, just as it was then,' commanded Mitya. 'Four dozen champagne, not a bottle less.'

'What do you want with so much? What's it for? Stay!' cried Peter Ilyitch. 'What's this box? What's in it? Surely there isn't four hundred roubles' worth here?'

The officious shopmen began explaining with oily politeness that the first box contained only half a dozen bottles of champagne, and only 'the most indispensable articles' such as savoury snacks, candies, fruit drops. But the main part of the food ordered would be packed and sent off, as on the previous occasion, in a special cart, also with three horses, travelling at full speed, so that it would arrive not more than an hour later than Dmitri Fyodorovitch himself.

6

All was confusion, confusion, in Mitya's soul, but although many things were tormenting his heart, at that moment he yearned most for her, his queen, to whom he was hastening for a last meeting. One thing I can say for certain; his heart did not waver for one instant. I shall perhaps not be believed when I say that this jealous lover felt not the slightest jealousy of his new rival, who seemed to have sprung out of the earth. If any other had appeared on the scene, he would have been jealous at once, and would perhaps have stained his fierce hands with blood again. But as he sped through the night, he felt no envy, no hostility even, for the man who had been her first lover . . . It is true he had not yet seen him.

'Here there was no room for dispute; it was her right and his; this was her first love whom, after five years, she had not forgotten; so she loved only him for those five years, and I, how do I come in? What right have I? Step aside, Mitya, and make way! What am I now? Now everything is over apart from the officer – even if he had not appeared, everything would be over . . . '

These words would roughly have expressed his feelings, if he had been capable of reasoning. But he could not reason at that moment. His present plan of action had arisen without reasoning. He had written his own sentence of death with pen and paper: 'I punish myself,' and the paper was there in his pocket, ready; the pistol was loaded; he had already resolved how, next morning, he would meet the first warm ray of 'golden-haired Phoebus'.

'She's now with *him*,' he thought, 'now I shall see what she looks like with him, her first love, and that's all I want.' Never had this woman, who was such a fateful influence in his life, aroused such love in his breast, such new and unknown feeling, surprising even to himself, a feeling of tender devoutness, of self-effacement before her! 'I will efface myself!' he said, in a rush of almost hysterical ecstasy.

They had been galloping nearly an hour. Mitya was silent, and though Andrey was, as a rule, a talkative peasant, he did not utter a word, either. He seemed afraid to talk, he only whipped up briskly his three lean, but mettlesome, bay horses. Suddenly Mitya cried out in horrible anxiety: 'Andrey! What if they're asleep?'

This thought fell upon him like a blow. It had not occurred to him before.

'It may well be that they're gone to bed, by now, Dmitri Fyodorovitch.'

Mitya frowned as though in pain. Yes, indeed . . . he was rushing there . . . with such feelings . . . while they were asleep . . . she was asleep, perhaps, there too . . . An angry feeling surged up in his heart.

'Drive on, Andrey! Whip them up! Look alive!' he cried, beside himself.

'But maybe they're not in bed!' Andrey went on after a pause. 'Timofey said there were a lot of them there . . .'

'At the station?'

'Not at the posting-station, but at Plastunov's, at the inn, where they hire out horses, too.'

'I know. So you say there are a lot of them? How's that? Who are they?' cried Mitya, greatly dismayed at this unexpected news.

'Well, Timofey was saying they're all gentlefolk. Two from our town – who they are I can't say – and there are two others, strangers, maybe more besides. I didn't ask particularly. They sat down to play cards, so Timofey said.'

'Cards?'

'So, maybe they're not in bed if they're at cards. It's most likely not more than eleven.'

But Mitya did not hear. He was frantically praying and muttering to himself.

'Lord, have mercy on me, with all my lawlessness, and do not condemn me. Let me pass by Thy judgment . . . do not condemn me, for I have condemned myself, do not condemn me, for I love Thee, O Lord. I am a wretch, but I love Thee. If Thou sendest me to hell, I shall love Thee there, and from there I shall cry out that I love Thee for ever and ever . . . But let me love to the end . . . Here and now for just five hours . . . till the first light of Thy day . . . for I love the queen of my soul . . . I love her and I cannot help loving her. Thou seest my whole heart . . . I shall gallop up, I shall fall on my knees before her and say, "You are right to pass on and leave me. Farewell and forget your victim . . . never fret yourself about me!" '

'Mokroe!' cried Andrey, pointing ahead with his whip.

Through the pale darkness of the night loomed a solid black mass of buildings, flung down, as it were, in the vast plain. The village of Mokroe numbered two thousand inhabitants, but at that hour all were asleep, and only here and there a few lights still twinkled.

'Drive on, Andrey, I come!' Mitya exclaimed, feverishly.

'They're not asleep,' said Andrey again, pointing with his whip to the Plastunovs' inn, which was at the entrance to the village. The six windows, looking on the street, were all brightly lighted up.

'They're not asleep,' Mitya repeated joyously. 'Faster, Andrey! Gallop! Drive up with a dash! Set the bells ringing! Let all know that I have come. I'm coming! I'm coming, I myself!'

Andrey lashed his exhausted team into a gallop, drove with a dash and pulled up his steaming, panting horses at the steps.

Mitya jumped out of the carriage just as the innkeeper, on his way to bed, glanced out from the door curious to see who had arrived.

'Trifon Borissovitch, is that you?'

The innkeeper bent down, looking intently, ran down the steps, and rushed up to the guest with obsequious delight.

'Dmitri Fyodorovitch, your honour! Do I see you again?'

Trifon Borissovitch was a thickset, healthy peasant, of middle height, with a rather fat face. His expression was severe and uncompromising, particularly in his dealings with the peasants of Mokroe, but he had the power of assuming the most obsequious countenance when he had an inkling that it was to his advantage. He dressed in Russian style, with a shirt buttoning down on one side, and a full-skirted coat. He had saved a good sum of money, but was for ever dreaming of improving his position.

In spite of the thousands of roubles he had saved, Trifon Borissovitch was very fond of emptying the pockets of a drunken guest, and, remembering that not a month ago he had, in twenty-four hours, made two if not three hundred roubles out of Dmitri, when he had come on his escapade with Grushenka, he met him now with eager welcome, scenting his prey the moment Mitya drove up to the steps.

'Dmitri Fyodorovitch, dear sir, we see you once more!'

'Look, Trifon Borissovitch,' began Mitya, 'first and foremost, where is she?'

'Agrafena Alexandrovna?' The innkeeper understood at once, looking sharply into Mitya's face. 'She's here too . . . '

'With whom? With whom?'

'Some strangers. One is an official gentleman, a Pole, to judge from his speech. He sent the horses for her from here; and there's another with him, a friend of his, or a fellow traveller, there's no telling. They're dressed like civilians.'

'Well, are they feasting? Have they money?'

'Poor sort of a feast! Nothing to boast of, Dmitri Fyodorovitch.'

'Nothing to boast of? And who are the others?'

'They're two gentlemen from the town . . . They've come back from Tcherny, and are putting up here. One's quite a young gentleman, a relative of Mr Miüsov, he must be, but I've forgotten his name . . . and I expect you know the other, too, a gentleman called Maximov. He's been on a pilgrimage, so he says, to the monastery in the town. He's travelling with this young relation of Mr Miüsov.'

'Is that all?'

'Yes.'

'Now listen, Trifon Borissovitch. Tell me the chief thing. What of her? How is she?'

'Oh, she's only just arrived. She's sitting with them.'

'Is she cheerful? Is she laughing?'

'No. I think she's not laughing much. She's sitting quite dull. She's combing the young gentleman's hair.'

'The Pole – the officer?'

'He's not young, and he's not an officer, either. Not him, sir. It's the young gentleman that's Mr Miüsov's relation . . . I've forgotten his name.'

'Kalganov?'

'That's it, Kalganov!'

'All right. I'll see for myself. Are they playing cards?'

'They have been playing, but they've stopped. They've been drinking tea, the official gentleman asked for liqueurs.'

'Wait, Trifon Borissovitch, wait, my good soul, I'll see for myself. Now answer one more question: are the gypsies here?'

'You can't have the gypsies now, Dmitri Fyodorovitch. The authorities have sent them away. But we've Jews that play the cymbals and the fiddle in the village, so one might send for them. They'd come.'

'Send for them. Certainly send for them!' cried Mitya. 'And you can get the girls together as you did then. Marya especially, Stepanida, too, and Arina. Two hundred roubles for a chorus!'

'Oh, for a sum like that I can get all the village together, though by now they're asleep. Are the peasants here worth such kindness, Dmitri Fyodorovitch, or the girls either? To spend a sum like that on such coarseness and vulgarity! What's the good of giving a peasant a cigar to smoke, the stinking swine!

And the girls are all lousy. Besides, I'll get my daughters up for nothing, let alone a sum like that. They've only just gone to bed, I'll give them a kick and set them singing for you. You gave the peasants champagne to drink the other day, e–ech!'

For all his pretended compassion for Mitya, Trifon Borissovitch had hidden half a dozen bottles of champagne on the last occasion, and had picked up a hundred-rouble note under the table, and it had remained in his clutches.

'Trifon Borissovitch, I sent more than one thousand flying last time I was here. Do you remember?'

'You did send it flying. I well remember. You must have left three thousand behind you.'

'Well, I've come to do the same thing again, do you see?'

And he pulled out his roll of notes, and held them up before the innkeeper's nose.

'Now, listen and remember. In an hour's time the wine will arrive, snacks, pies, and candies – bring them all up at once. That box Andrey has got is to be brought up at once, too. Open it, and hand champagne immediately. And the girls, we must have the girls, Marya especially.'

He turned to the cart and pulled out the box of pistols.

'Here, Andrey, let's settle. Here's fifteen roubles for the drive, and fifty for vodka . . . for your willingness, for your love . . . Remember Karamazov!'

'I'm afraid, sir,' faltered Andrey. 'Give me five roubles extra, but more I won't take. Trifon Borissovitch, bear witness. Forgive my foolish words . . . '

'What are you afraid of?' asked Mitya, scanning him. 'Well, go to the devil, if that's it!' he cried, flinging him five roubles. 'Now, Trifon Borissovitch, take me up quietly and let me first get a look at them, so that they don't see me. Where are they? In the blue room?'

Trifon Borissovitch looked apprehensively at Mitya, but at once obediently did his bidding. Leading him into the passage, he went himself into the first large room, adjoining that in which the visitors were sitting, and took the light away. Then he stealthily led Mitya in, and put him in a corner in the dark, whence he could freely watch the company without being seen. But Mitya did not look long, and, indeed, he could not see them, he saw her, his heart throbbed violently, and all was dark before his eyes.

She was sitting sideways to the table in a low chair, and beside her, on the sofa, was the pretty youth, Kalganov. She was holding his hand and seemed to be laughing, while he, seeming vexed and not looking at her, was saying something in a loud voice to Maximov, who sat the other side of the table, facing Grushenka. Maximov was laughing violently at something. On the sofa sat *he*, and on a chair by the sofa there was another stranger. The one on the sofa was lolling backward, smoking a pipe, and Mitya had an impression of a stoutish broad-faced short little man, who was apparently angry about something. His friend, the other stranger, struck Mitya as extraordinarily tall, but he could make out nothing more. He caught his breath. He could not bear it for a minute, he put the pistol case on a chest, and with a throbbing heart he walked, feeling cold all over, straight into the blue room to face the company.

'Aie!' shrieked Grushenka, the first to notice him.

7

With his long, rapid strides, Mitya walked straight up to the table. 'Gentlemen,' he said in a loud voice, almost shouting, yet stammering at every word, 'I . . . I'm all right! Don't be afraid!' he exclaimed, 'I – there's nothing the matter,' he turned suddenly to Grushenka, who had shrunk back in her chair towards Kalganov, and clasped his hand tightly. 'I . . . I'm coming along too. I'm here till morning. Gentlemen, may I stay with you till morning? Only till morning, for the last time, in this same room?'

So he finished, turning to the fat little man, with the pipe, sitting on the sofa. The latter removed his pipe from his lips with dignity and observed severely: 'Sir, we're here in private. There are other rooms.'

'Why, it's you, Dmitri Fyodorovitch! What do you mean?' answered Kalganov suddenly. 'Sit down with us. How are you?'

'Delighted to see you, my dear man . . . and my dear boys, I always thought a lot of you,' Mitya responded, joyfully and eagerly, at once holding out his hand across the table.

'Aie! What a strong handshake you have! You've quite broken my fingers,' laughed Kalganov.

'He always squeezes like that, always,' Grushenka put in gaily, with a timid smile, suddenly convinced from Mitya's expression that he was not going to make a scene. She was watching him with intense curiosity and still some uneasiness. She was impressed by something about him, and indeed the last thing she expected of him was that he would come in and speak like this at such a moment.

'Good-evening,' Maximov ventured blandly, on the left. Mitya rushed up to him too.

'Good-evening. You're here too! How glad I am to find you here too! Gentlemen, gentlemen, I . . . ' (He addressed the Polish gentleman with the pipe again, evidently taking him for the most important person present.) 'I rushed here . . . I wanted to spend my last day, my last hour in this room, in this very room . . . where I too adored . . . my queen . . . Forgive me, sir,' he cried wildly, 'I rushed here and vowed . . . Oh, don't be afraid, it's my last night! Let's drink to our good understanding. They'll bring the wine at once . . . I brought this with me.' (Something made him pull out his bundle of notes.) 'Allow me, sir! I want to have music, singing, a revel, as we had before. But the worm, the unnecessary worm, will crawl away, and there'll be no more of him. I will commemorate my day of joy and my last night.'

He was almost choking. There was so much, so much he wanted to say, but strange exclamations were all that came from his lips. The Pole gazed fixedly at him, at the bundle of notes in his hand; looked at Grushenka, and was evidently perplexed.

'If my suverin lady is permitting . . . ' he began.

'What does "suverin" mean? "Sovereign", I suppose?' interrupted Grushenka. 'I can't help laughing at you, the way you pronounce your words. Sit down, Mitya, what are you talking about? Don't frighten us, please. You won't frighten us, will you? If you won't, I am glad to see you . . . '

'Me, me frighten you?' cried Mitya, flinging up his hands. 'Oh, forget about me, go your way, I won't hinder you!' . . .

And suddenly he surprised them all, and no doubt

himself as well, by flinging himself on a chair, and bursting into tears, turning his head away to the opposite wall, while his arms clasped the back of the chair tight, as though embracing it.

'Come, come, what a fellow you are!' cried Grushenka reproachfully. 'That's just how he comes to see me – he begins talking, and I can't make out what he means. He cried like that once before, and now he's crying again! It's shameful! Why are you crying? *As though you had anything to cry for!*' she added enigmatically, emphasising each word with some irritability.

' . . . I'm not crying . . . Well, good-evening!' he instantly turned round in his chair, and suddenly laughed, not his abrupt, wooden laugh but a long, quivering, inaudible nervous laugh.

'There you go again . . . Come, cheer up, cheer up,' Grushenka said to him persuasively. 'I'm very glad you've come, very glad, Mitya, do you hear, I'm very glad! I want him to stay here with us,' she said peremptorily, addressing the whole company, though her words were obviously meant for the man sitting on the sofa. 'I wish it, I wish it! And if he leaves I shall go too!' she added.

'What my queen commands is law!' pronounced the Pole, gallantly kissing Grushenka's hand. 'I beg you, sir, to join our company,' he added politely, addressing Mitya.

Mitya jumped up with the obvious intention of delivering another tirade, but the words did not come.

'Let's drink, sirs,' he blurted out, instead of making a speech. Everyone laughed.

'Good heavens! I thought he was going to begin again!' Grushenka exclaimed nervously. 'Do you hear, Mitya,' she went on insistently, 'don't prance about, but it's nice you've brought the champagne. I want some myself, and I can't bear liqueurs. And best of all, you've come yourself. We were fearfully dull here . . . You've come for a spree again, I suppose? But put your money in your pocket. Where did you get such a lot?'

Mitya all this time had been holding in his hand the crumpled bundle of notes on which the eyes of all, especially the Pole's, were fixed. In confusion he thrust them hurriedly into his pocket. He flushed. At that moment the innkeeper brought in an uncorked bottle of champagne, and glasses on a tray. Mitya snatched up the bottle, but he was so bewildered that he did not know what to do with it. Kalganov took it from him and poured out the champagne.

'Another! Another bottle!' Mitya cried to the innkeeper, and, forgetting to clink glasses with the Pole whom he had so solemnly invited to drink to their good understanding, he downed his glass without waiting for anyone. His whole countenance suddenly changed. The solemn and tragic expression with which he had entered vanished completely, and a childlike expression irradiated his face. He seemed to become suddenly gentle and subdued. He looked shyly and happily at everyone, with a continual nervous little laugh, and the blissful expression of a dog who has done wrong, been punished, and forgiven. He seemed to have forgotten everything, and looked round at everyone with a childlike smile of delight. He gazed at Grushenka, laughing continually, and brought his chair close up to her. By degrees he had gained some idea of the two Poles, though he had formed no definite conception of them yet.

The Pole on the sofa struck him by his dignified demeanour and his Polish accent; and, above all, by his pipe. 'Well, what of it? It's a good thing he's smoking a pipe,' he reflected. The Pole's puffy, middle-aged face, with its tiny nose and two very thin, pointed, dyed and impudent-looking moustaches, had not so far roused the faintest doubts in Mitya. He was not even particularly struck by the Pole's absurd wig made in Siberia, with love-locks foolishly combed forward over the temples. 'I suppose it's all right for him to wear a wig,' he mused blissfully. The other, younger Pole, who was staring insolently and defiantly at the company and listening to the conversation with silent contempt, still only impressed Mitya by his great height, which was in striking contrast to the Pole on the sofa. 'If he stood up, he'd be six foot three.' The thought flitted through Mitya's mind. It occurred to him, too, that this Pole must be the friend of the other, as it were, a 'bodyguard', and no doubt the big Pole got his orders from the little Pole with the pipe. But this all seemed to Mitya perfectly natural and not to be questioned. In his state of doglike submissiveness all feeling of rivalry had died away.

Grushenka's mood and the enigmatic tone of some of her words he completely failed to grasp. All he understood, with a fast-beating heart, was that she was being kind to him, that she had forgiven him, and made him sit by her. He was beside himself with delight, watching her sip her glass of champagne. The silence of the company seemed somehow to strike him, however, and he looked round at everyone with expectant eyes.

'Why are we sitting here though, gentlemen? Why

don't you begin doing something?' his smiling eyes seemed to ask.

'He keeps talking nonsense, and we were all laughing,' Kalganov began suddenly, as though divining his thoughts, and pointing to Maximov.

Mitya immediately stared at Kalganov and then at Maximov.

'Oh, it's certainly anything but amusing!' Kalganov mumbled.

'Let's play faro again, as we did just now,' Maximov tittered suddenly.

'Begin, gentlemen,' Mitya assented, pulling his notes out of his pocket, and laying two hundred-rouble notes on the table. 'I want to lose a lot to you. Take your cards. Make the bank.'

'We'll have cards from the landlord, gentlemen,' said the little Pole, gravely and emphatically.

'That's much the best way,' chimed in Pan Vrublevsky.

'From the landlord? Very good, I understand, let's get them from him. Cards!' Mitya shouted to the landlord.

The landlord brought in a new, unopened pack, and informed Mitya that the girls were getting ready, and that the Jews with the cymbals would most likely be here soon; but the cart with the provisions had not yet arrived.

'Take your places, gentlemen,' cried Pan Vrublevsky.

'No, I'm not going to play any more,' observed Kalganov, 'I've lost fifty roubles to them just now.'

'The Polish gentleman had no luck, perhaps he'll be lucky this time,' the Pole on the sofa observed in his direction.

'How much in the bank? To correspond?' asked Mitya.

'That's according, sirs, maybe a hundred, maybe two hundred, as much as you will stake.'

'A million!' laughed Mitya.

'The Sir Captain has heard of Pan Podvysotsky, perhaps?'

'What Podvysotsky?'

'In Warsaw there was a bank and anyone comes and stakes against it. Podvysotsky comes, sees a thousand gold pieces, stakes against the bank. The banker says, "Podvysotsky, are you laying down the gold, or must we trust to your honour?" "To my honour, *pan*," says Podvysotsky. "So much the better." The banker throws the dice. Podvysotsky wins. "Take it, *pan*," says the banker, and pulling out the drawer gives him a million. "Take it, *pan*, this is your gain." There was a million in the bank. "I didn't know that," says Podvysotsky. "*Pan* Podvysotsky," said the banker, "you pledged your honour and we pledged ours." Podvysotsky took the million.'

'That's not true,' said Kalganov.

'Pan Kalganov, in gentlemanly society one doesn't say such things.'

'As if a Polish gambler would give away a million!' cried Mitya, but checked himself at once. 'Forgive me, gentlemen, it's my fault again, he would, he would give away a million, for honour, for Polish honour. You see how I talk Polish, ha-ha! Here, I stake ten roubles, the knave leads.'

'And I put a rouble on the queen, the queen of hearts, the pretty little *panienotchka*, he-he!' laughed Maximov, pulling out his queen, and, as though trying to conceal it from everyone, he moved right up and crossed himself hurriedly under the table. Mitya won. The rouble won too.

'A corner!' cried Mitya.

'I'll bet another rouble, a "single" stake,' Maximov muttered gleefully, hugely delighted at having won a rouble.

'Lost!' shouted Mitya. 'A "double" on the seven!'

The seven too was trumped.

'Stop!' cried Kalganov suddenly.

'Double! Double!' Mitya doubled his stakes, and each time he doubled the stake, the card he doubled was trumped by the Poles. The rouble stakes kept winning.

'On the double!' shouted Mitya, furiously.

'You've lost two hundred, sir. Will you stake another hundred?' the Pole on the sofa enquired.

'What? Lost two hundred already? Then another two hundred! All doubles!'

And pulling his money out of his pocket, Mitya was about to fling two hundred roubles on the queen, but Kalganov covered it with his hand.

'That's enough!' he shouted in his ringing voice.

'What's the matter?' Mitya stared at him.

'That's enough! I don't want you to play any more. Don't!'

'Why?'

'Because I don't. Hang it, come away. That's why. I won't let you go on playing.'

Mitya gazed at him in astonishment.

'Give it up, Mitya. He may be right. You've lost a lot as it is,' said Grushenka, with a curious note in her voice. Both the Poles rose from their seats with a deeply offended air.

'Are you joking?' said the short man, looking severely at Kalganov.

'How dare you!' Pan Vrublevsky, too, growled at Kalganov.

'Don't dare to shout like that,' cried Grushenka. 'Ah, you turkey-cocks!'

Mitya looked at each of them in turn. But something in Grushenka's face suddenly struck him, and at the same instant something new flashed into his mind – a strange new thought!

'Madame Agrippina,' the little Pole began, crimson with anger, when Mitya suddenly went up to him and slapped him on the shoulder.

'Sir, two words with you.'

'What do you want?'

'In the next room, I've two words to say to you, something pleasant, very pleasant. You'll be glad to hear it.'

The little Pole was taken aback and looked apprehensively at Mitya. He agreed at once, however, on condition that Pan Vrublevsky went with them.

'The bodyguard? Let him come, and I want him too. I must have him!' cried Mitya. 'March, gentlemen!'

'Where are you going?' asked Grushenka, anxiously.

'We'll be back in one moment,' answered Mitya.

There was a sort of boldness, a sudden confidence shining in his eyes. His face had looked very different when he entered the room an hour before.

He led the Poles, not into the large room where the chorus of girls was assembling and the table was being laid, but into the bedroom on the right. The Poles looked severe but were evidently inquisitive.

'What can I do for you, sir?' lisped the little Pole.

'Look, gentlemen, I won't keep you long. There's money for you,' he pulled out his notes. 'Would you like three thousand? Take it and go your way.'

The Pole gazed, wide-eyed, at Mitya, with a searching look.

'Three thousand?' He exchanged glances with Vrublevsky.

'Three, three! Listen, sir, I see you're a sensible man. Take three thousand and go to the devil, and Vrublevsky with you – d'you hear? But, at once, this very minute, and for ever. You understand that, for ever. Here's the door, you go out of it. What have you got there, a top coat, a fur coat? I'll bring it out to you. They'll get the horses out directly, and then – good-bye, good sirs!'

Mitya awaited an answer with assurance. He had no doubts. An expression of extraordinary resolution passed over the Pole's face.

'And the money, sir?'

'The money, gentlemen? Five hundred roubles I'll give you this moment for the journey, and as a first instalment, and two thousand five hundred tomorrow, in the town – I swear on my honour, I'll get it, I'll get it at any cost!' cried Mitya.

The Poles exchanged glances again. The short man's face looked more forbidding.

'Seven hundred, seven hundred, not five hundred, at once, this minute, cash down!' Mitya added, feeling something wrong. 'What's the matter, gentlemen? Don't you trust me? I can't give you the whole three thousand straight off. If I give it, you may come back to her tomorrow . . . besides, I haven't the three thousand with me. I've got it at home in the town,' faltered Mitya, his spirit sinking at every word he uttered. 'Upon my word, the money's there, hidden.'

In an instant an extraordinary sense of personal dignity showed itself in the little man's face.

'What next?' he asked ironically. 'For shame!' and he spat on the floor. Pan Vrublevsky spat too.

'You do that, gentlemen,' said Mitya, recognising with despair that all was over – 'because you hope to make more out of Grushenka? You're a couple of pimps, that's what you are?'

'This is a mortal insult!' The little Pole turned as red as a lobster, and he went out of the room, briskly, as though unwilling to hear another word. Vrublevsky swung out after him, and Mitya followed, confused and crestfallen. He was afraid of Grushenka, afraid that the Polish gentleman would at once raise an outcry. And so indeed he did. The Pole walked into the room and threw himself in a theatrical attitude before Grushenka.

'Lady Agrippina, I have received a mortal insult!' he exclaimed. But Grushenka suddenly lost all patience, as though they had wounded her in the tenderest spot.

'Speak Russian! Speak Russian!' she cried, 'not another word of Polish! You used to talk Russian. You can't have forgotten it in five years.' She was red with passion.

'Lady Agrippina . . . '

'My name's Agrafena, Grushenka, speak Russian or I won't listen!'

The Pole gasped with offended dignity, and quickly and pompously delivered himself in broken Russian: 'Lady Agrafena, I came here to forget the past and forgive it, to forget all that has happened till today . . . '

'Forgive? Come here to forgive me?' Grushenka cut him short, jumping up from her seat.

'Just so, Lady, I'm not a coward, I'm magnanimous. But I was astounded when I saw your lovers. Sir Mitya offered me three thousand, in the other room, to depart. I spat in the Sir's face.'

'What? He offered you money for me?' cried Grushenka, hysterically. 'Is it true, Mitya? How dare you? Am I for sale?'

'Sweet lady, my lady,' yelled Mitya, 'she's pure and shining, and I have never been her lover! That's a lie . . . '

'How dare you defend me to him?' shrieked Grushenka. 'It wasn't virtue kept me pure, and it wasn't that I was afraid of Kuzma, but that I might hold up my head when I met him, and tell him he's a scoundrel. And did he actually refuse the money?'

'He took it! He took it!' cried Mitya; 'only he wanted to get the whole three thousand at once, and I could only give him seven hundred straight off.'

'I see: he heard I had money, and came here to marry me!'

'Lady Agrippina!' cried the little Pole. 'I'm – a knight, I'm – a nobleman, and not a peon. I came here to make you my wife and I find you a different woman, perverse and shameless.'

'Oh, go back where you came from! I'll tell them to turn you out and you'll be turned out,' cried Grushenka, furious. 'I've been a fool, a fool, to have been miserable these five years! And it wasn't for his sake, it was my anger made me miserable. And this isn't he at all! Was he like this? It might be his father! Where did you get your wig from? He was an eagle, but this is a gander. He used to laugh and sing to me . . . And I've been crying for five years, damned fool, abject, shameless creature that I was!'

She sank back in her low chair and hid her face in her hands. At that instant the chorus of Mokroe girls began singing in the room on the left – a rollicking dance song.

'A regular Sodom!' Vrublevsky roared suddenly. 'Landlord, send the shameless hussies away!'

The landlord, who had been for some time past inquisitively peeping in at the door, hearing shouts and guessing that his guests were quarrelling, at once entered the room.

'What are you shouting for? D'you want to split your throat?' he said, addressing Vrublevsky, with surprising rudeness.

'Swine!' bellowed Pan Vrublevsky.

'Swine? And what sort of cards were you playing with just now? I gave you a pack and you hid it. You played with marked cards! I could send you to Siberia for playing with false cards, d'you know that, for it's just the same as false bank notes . . .'

And going up to the sofa he thrust his fingers between the sofa back and the cushion, and pulled out an unopened pack of cards.

'Here's my pack unopened!'

He held it up and showed it to all in the room. 'From where I stood I saw him slip my pack away, and put his in place of it – you're a cheat and not a gentleman!'

'And I twice saw the Pole change a card!' cried Kalganov.

'How shameful! How shameful!' exclaimed Grushenka, clasping her hands, and blushing for genúine shame. 'Good Lord, he's come to that!'

'I thought so too!' said Mitya. But before he had uttered the words, Vrublevsky, with a contorted and infuriated face, shook his fist at Grushenka, shouting: 'You low harlot!'

Mitya flew at him at once, clutched him in both hands, lifted him in the air, and in one instant had carried him into the room on the right, from which they had just come.

'I've thrown him on the floor, there,' he announced, returning at once, gasping with excitement. 'He's struggling, the scoundrel! But he won't come back, no fear of that . . . '

He closed one half of the folding doors, and holding the other ajar called out to the little Pole: 'Most illustrious, will you be pleased to retire at once?'

'My dear Dmitri Fyodorovitch,' said Trifon Borissovitch, 'make them give you back the money you lost. It's as good as stolen from you.'

'I don't want my fifty roubles back,' Kalganov declared suddenly.

'I don't want my two hundred, either,' cried Mitya, 'I wouldn't take it for anything! Let him keep it as a consolation.'

'Bravo, Mitya! You're tops, Mitya!' cried Grushenka, and there was a note of fierce anger in the exclamation.

The little Pole, crimson with fury, but still mindful of his dignity, was making for the door, but he stopped short and said suddenly, addressing Grushenka: 'Lady, if you want to come with me, come. If not, goodbye.'

And swelling with indignation and importance he went to the door. This was a man of character: he had so good an opinion of himself that after all that had happened, he still expected that she would marry him. Mitya slammed the door after him.

'Lock it,' said Kalganov. But the key clicked on the other side, they had locked it from within.

'That's wonderful!' exclaimed Grushenka relentlessly. 'Serves them right!'

8

What followed was almost an orgy, a feast to which all were welcome. Grushenka was the first to call for wine.

'I want to drink. I want to be quite drunk, as I was when we were here before. Do you remember, Mitya, do you remember how we made friends here last time!'

Mitya himself was almost delirious, feeling that his happiness was at hand.

But Grushenka kept sending him away from her: 'Go and enjoy yourself. Tell them to dance, to make merry, "let the stove and cottage dance"; as we had it last time,' she kept exclaiming. She was tremendously excited. And Mitya hastened to obey her. Grushenka settled herself near the door. Mitya set an easy-chair for her. She had sat in the same place to watch the dancing and singing 'the time before', when they had made merry there. All the girls who had come had been there then; the Jewish band with fiddles and zithers had come, too, and at last the long-expected cart arrived with the wines and provisions.

Mitya bustled about. All sorts of people began coming into the room to look on, peasants and their women, who had been roused from sleep and attracted by the hope of another marvellous entertainment such as they had enjoyed a month before.

An absurd chaotic confusion followed, but Mitya was in his natural element, and the more foolish it became, the more his spirits rose. If the peasants had asked him for money at that moment, he would have pulled out his notes and given them away right and left. This was probably why the landlord, Trifon Borissovitch, kept hovering about Mitya to protect him.

Mitya remembered Andrey again, and ordered punch to be sent out to him. 'I was rude to him just now,' he repeated with a sinking, softened voice. Kalganov did not want to drink, and at first did not care for the girls' singing but after he had drunk a couple of glasses of champagne he became extraordinarily lively, strolling about the room, laughing and praising the music and the songs, admiring everyone and everything. Maximov, blissfully drunk, never left his side. Grushenka, too, was beginning to get drunk. Pointing to Kalganov, she said to Mitya: 'What a dear, charming boy he is!'

And Mitya, delighted, ran to kiss Kalganov and Maximov. Oh, great were his hopes! She had said nothing yet, and seemed, indeed, purposely to refrain from speaking. But she looked at him from time to time with caressing and passionate eyes. At last she suddenly gripped his hand and drew him vigorously to her. She was sitting at that moment in the low chair by the door.

'How was it you came just now, eh? How you walked in! . . . I *was* frightened. So you wanted to give me up to him, did you? Did you really want to?'

'I didn't want to spoil your happiness!' Mitya faltered blissfully. But she did not need his answer.

'Well, go and enjoy yourself . . .' she sent him away once more. 'Don't cry, I'll call you back again.'

He walked away, and though she listened to the singing and looked at the dancing, her eyes followed him wherever he went. But in another quarter of an hour she summoned him once more and again he ran back to her.

'Come, sit beside me, tell me, how did you hear about me, and my coming here yesterday? From whom did you first hear it?'

And Mitya began telling her all about it, disconnectedly, incoherently, feverishly. He spoke strangely, often frowning, and stopping abruptly.

'What are you frowning at?' she asked.

'Nothing . . . I left a man ill there. I'd give ten years of my life for him to get well, to know he was all right!'

'Well, never mind him, if he's ill. So you meant to shoot yourself tomorrow! What a silly boy! What for? I like such reckless fellows as you,' she lisped, with a rather halting tongue. 'So you would go any length for me, eh? Did you really mean to shoot yourself tomorrow, you stupid? No, wait a little. Tomorrow I may have something to say to you . . . I won't say it today, but tomorrow. You'd like it to be today? No, I don't want to today. Go along now, go and amuse yourself.'

Once, however, she called him, as it were, puzzled and uneasy.

'Why are you sad? I see you're sad . . . Yes, I see it,' she added, looking intently into his eyes. 'Though you keep kissing the peasants and shouting, I see something. No, be merry. I'm merry; you be merry too . . . I love somebody here. Guess who it is. Ah, look, my boy has fallen asleep, poor dear, he's drunk.'

She meant Kalganov. He was, in fact, drunk, and had dropped asleep for a moment, sitting on the sofa. But he was not merely drowsy from drink; he felt suddenly dejected, or, as he said, 'bored'. He was intensely depressed by the girls' songs, which, as the drinking went on, gradually became coarse and more reckless.

'Well, let them! Let them!' said Grushenka sententiously, with an ecstatic expression on her face. 'When they do get a day to enjoy themselves, why shouldn't simple country folk be happy?'

Kalganov looked as though he had been besmirched with dirt.

'It's swinish, all this peasant foolery,' he murmured, moving away; 'it's the games they play when it's light all night in summer.'

Mitya's head was burning. He went outside to the wooden balcony which ran around the whole building on the inner side, overlooking the courtyard. The fresh air revived him. He stood alone in a dark corner, and suddenly clutched his head in both hands. His scattered thoughts came together; his sensations blended into a whole and threw a sudden light into his mind. A fearful and terrible light! 'If I'm to shoot myself, why not now?' passed through his mind. 'Why not go for the pistols, bring them here, and here, in this dark, dirty corner, make an end?' Almost a minute he stood, undecided. A few hours earlier, when he had been rushing here, he was pursued by disgrace, by the theft he had committed, and that blood, that blood! . . . But yet it was easier for him then. Then everything was over: he had lost her, given her up. She was lost to him – oh, then his death sentence had been easier for him; at least it had seemed necessary, inevitable, for what had he to stay on earth for?

But now? Was it the same as then? Now one phantom, one terror at least was at an end: that first, rightful lover, that fateful figure had vanished, leaving no trace. The terrible phantom had turned into something so small, so comic; it had been carried into the bedroom and locked in. It would never return. She was ashamed, and from her eyes he could see now whom she loved. Now he had everything to make life happy . . . but he could not go on living, he could not; oh, damnation! 'Oh, God! restore to life the man I knocked down at the fence! Let this fearful cup pass from me! Lord, Thou hast wrought miracles for such sinners as me! But what, what if the old man's alive? Oh, then the shame of the other disgrace I would wipe away. I would restore the stolen money. I'd give it back; I'd get it somehow . . . No trace of that shame will remain except in my heart for ever! But no, no; oh, impossible cowardly dreams! Oh, damnation!'

Yet there was a ray of light and hope in his darkness. He jumped up and ran back to the room – to her, to her, his queen for ever! Was not one moment of her love worth all the rest of life, even in the agonies of disgrace? This wild question clutched at his heart. 'To her, to her alone, to see her, to hear her, to think of nothing, to forget everything, if only for that night, for an hour, for a moment!' But she was not there. She was not in the blue room either; there was no one but Kalganov asleep on the sofa. Mitya looked behind the curtain – she was there. She was sitting in the corner, on a trunk. Bent forward, with her head and arms on the bed close by, she was crying bitterly, doing her utmost to stifle her sobs that she might not be heard. Seeing Mitya, she beckoned him to her, and when he went to her, she grasped his hand tightly.

'Mitya, Mitya, I loved him, you know. How I have loved him these five years, all that time! Did I love him or only my own anger? No, him, him! It's a lie that it was my anger I loved and not him. Mitya, I was only seventeen then; he was so kind to me, so merry; he used to sing to me . . . Or so it seemed to a silly girl like me . . . And now, O Lord, it's not the same man. Even his face is not the same; he's different altogether. I wouldn't have known him. I drove here with Timofey, and all the way I was thinking how I should meet him, what I should say to him, how we should look at one another. My soul was faint, and all of a sudden it was just as though he had emptied a pail of dirty water over me. He talked to me like a schoolmaster, so grave and learned; he met me so solemnly that I was struck dumb. I couldn't get a word in. At first I thought he was ashamed to talk before his great big Pole. I sat staring at him and wondering why I couldn't say a word to him now. It must have been his wife that ruined him; you know he threw me over to get married. She must have changed him like that. Mitya, how shameful it is! Oh, Mitya, I'm ashamed, I'm ashamed for all my life. Curse it, curse it, curse those five years!'

And again she burst into tears, but clung tight to Mitya's hand and did not let it go.

'Mitya darling, stay, don't go away. I want to say one word to you,' she whispered, and suddenly raised her face to him. 'Listen, tell me who it is I love? I love one man here. Who is that man? That's what you must tell me.'

A smile lighted up her face that was swollen with weeping, and her eyes shone in the half darkness.

'An eagle flew in, and my heart sank. "Fool! that's the man you love!" That was what my heart whispered to me at once. You came in and all grew bright. What's he afraid of? I wondered. For you were frightened; you couldn't speak. It's not them he's afraid of – could you be frightened of anyone? It's me he's afraid of, I thought, only me. So Fenya told you, you little stupid, how I called to Alyosha out of the window that I'd loved Mitya for one hour, and that I was going now to love . . . another. Mitya, Mitya, how could I be such a fool as to think I could love anyone after you? Do you forgive me, Mitya? Do you forgive me or not? Do you love me? Do you love me?' She jumped up and held him with both hands on his shoulders. Mitya, dumb with rapture, gazed into her eyes, at her face, at her smile, and suddenly clasped her tightly in his arms and kissed her passionately.

'You will forgive me for having tormented you? It was through spite I tormented you all. It was for spite I drove the old man out of his mind . . . Do you remember how you drank at my house one day and broke the wineglass? I remembered that and I broke a glass today and drank "to my vile heart". Mitya, my darling, why don't you kiss me? He kissed me once, and now he draws back and looks and listens. Why listen to me? Kiss me, kiss me hard, that's right. If you love, well then love! I'll be your slave now, your slave for the rest of my life. It's sweet to be a slave. Kiss me! Beat me, ill-treat me, do what you will with me . . . And I do deserve to suffer. Stay, wait, afterwards, I won't have that . . . ' she suddenly thrust him away. 'Go along, Mitya, I'll come and have some wine, I want to be drunk, I'm going to get drunk and dance; I must, I must!' She tore herself away from him and disappeared behind the curtain. Mitya followed like a drunken man.

'Yes, come what may – whatever may happen now, for one minute I'd give the whole world,' he thought.

Grushenka did, in fact, toss off a whole glass of champagne at one gulp, and became at once very tipsy. She sat down in the same chair as before, with a blissful smile on her face. Her cheeks were glowing, her lips were burning, her flashing eyes were moist; there was passionate appeal in her eyes. Even Kalganov felt his heart stir and went up to her.

'Did you feel how I kissed you when you were asleep just now?' she said thickly. 'I'm drunk now, that's what . . . And aren't you drunk? And why isn't Mitya drinking? Why don't you drink, Mitya? I'm drunk, and you don't drink . . . '

'I am drunk! I'm drunk as it is . . . drunk with you . . . and now I'll be drunk with wine too.'

He drank off another glass, and – he thought it strange himself – that glass made him completely drunk. He was suddenly drunk, although till that moment he had been quite sober, he remembered that. From that moment everything whirled about him, as though he were delirious. He walked, laughed, talked to everybody, without knowing what he was doing. Only one persistent burning sensation made itself felt continually, 'like a red-hot coal in his heart', he said afterwards. He went up to her, sat beside her, gazed at her, listened to her . . . She became very talkative, kept calling everyone to her, and beckoned to different girls out of the chorus. When the girl came up, she either kissed her, or made the sign of the cross over her.

She bowed to the chorus, and then began bowing in all directions.

'I'm sorry . . . Forgive me . . . '

'The lady's been drinking. The pretty lady has been drinking,' voices were heard saying.

'The lady's drunk too much,' Maximov explained to the girls, giggling.

'Mitya, lead me away . . . take me,' said Grushenka helplessly. Mitya pounced on her, snatched her up in his arms, and carried the precious burden through the curtains.

'Well, now I'll go,' thought Kalganov, and walking out of the blue room, he closed the two halves of the door after him. But the orgy in the larger room went on and grew louder and louder. Mitya laid Grushenka on the bed and kissed her on the lips.

'Don't touch me . . . ' she faltered, in an imploring voice. 'Don't touch me, till I'm yours . . . I've told you I'm yours, but don't touch me . . . spare me . . . With them here, with them close, you mustn't. He's here. It's nasty here . . . '

'I'll obey you! I won't think of it . . . I worship you!' muttered Mitya. 'Yes, it's nasty here, it's abominable.'

And still holding her in his arms, he sank on his knees by the bedside.

'I know, though you're a brute, you're generous,' Grushenka articulated with difficulty. 'It must be honourable . . . it shall be honourable for the future . . . and let us be honest, let us be good, not animals, but good . . . take me away, take me far away, do you hear? I don't want it to be here, but far, far away . . . '

'Oh, yes, yes, it must be!' said Mitya, pressing her in his arms. 'I'll take you and we'll fly away . . . Oh, I'd give my whole life for one year only to know about that blood!'

'What blood?' asked Grushenka, bewildered.

'Nothing,' muttered Mitya, through his teeth. 'Grushenka, you wanted to be honest, but I'm a thief. I've stolen money from Katya . . . Disgrace, a disgrace!'

'From Katya, from that young lady? No, you didn't steal it. Give it her back, take it from me . . . Why make a fuss? Now everything of mine is yours. What does money matter? We shall waste it anyway . . . Folks like us are bound to waste money. But we'd better go and work the land. I want to dig the earth with my own hands. We must work, do you hear? Alyosha said so. I won't be your mistress, I'll be faithful to you, I'll be your slave, I'll work for you. We'll go to the young lady and bow down to her together, so that she may forgive us, and then we'll go away. And if she won't forgive us, we'll go, anyway. Take her her money and love me . . . Don't love her . . . Don't love her any more. If you love her, I shall strangle her . . . I'll put out both her eyes with a needle . . .'

'I love you. I love only you. I'll love you in Siberia . . .'

'Why Siberia? Never mind, Siberia if you like. I don't care . . . we'll work . . . there's snow in Siberia . . . I love driving in the snow . . . and must have bells . . . Do you hear, there's a bell ringing? Where is that bell ringing? There are people coming . . . Now it's stopped.'

She closed her eyes, exhausted, and suddenly fell asleep for an instant. There had certainly been the sound of a bell in the distance, but the ringing had ceased. Mitya let his head sink on her breast. He did not notice that the bell had ceased ringing, nor did he notice that the songs had ceased, and that instead of singing and drunken clamour there was absolute stillness in the house. Grushenka opened her eyes.

'What's the matter? Was I asleep? Yes . . . a bell . . . I've been asleep and dreamed I was driving over the snow with bells, and I dozed. I was with someone I loved, with you. And far, far away. I was holding you and kissing you, nestling close to you. I was cold, and the snow glistened . . . You know how the snow glistens at night when the moon shines. It was as though I was not on earth. I woke up, and my dear one is close to me. How sweet that is . . .'

'Close to you,' murmured Mitya, kissing her dress, her bosom, her hands. And suddenly he had a strange fancy: it seemed to him that she was looking straight before her, not at him, not into his face, but over his head, with an intent, almost uncanny fixity. An expression of wonder, almost of alarm, came suddenly into her face.

'Mitya, who is that looking at us?' she whispered.

Mitya turned, and saw that someone had, in fact, parted the curtains and seemed to be watching them. And not one person alone, it seemed.

He jumped up and walked quickly to the intruder.

'Here, come to us, come here,' said a voice, speaking not loudly, but firmly and peremptorily.

Mitya passed to the other side of the curtain and stood rooted to the ground. The room was filled with people, but not those who had been there before. A sudden shiver ran down his back, and he shuddered. He recognised all those people instantly. That tall, stout old man in the overcoat and forage cap with a cockade – was the police captain, Mihail Makarovitch. And that 'consumptive-looking' trim dandy, 'who always has such polished boots' – that was the deputy prosecutor. 'He has a chronometer worth four hundred roubles; he showed it to me.' And that small young man in spectacles . . . Mitya forgot his surname though he knew him, had seen him: he was the 'investigating lawyer', from the 'school of jurisprudence', who had only lately come to the town.

And this man – the inspector of police, Mavriky Mavrikyevitch, a man he knew well. And those fellows with the brass shields, why are they here? And those other two . . . peasants . . . And there at the door Kalganov with Trifon Borissovitch . . .

'Gentlemen! What's this for, gentlemen?' began Mitya, but suddenly, as though beside himself, not knowing what he was doing, he cried aloud, at the top of his voice: 'I un–der–stand!'

The young man in spectacles moved forward suddenly, and stepping up to Mitya, began with dignity, though hurriedly: 'We have to make . . . in brief, I beg you to come this way, this way to the couch . . . It is absolutely imperative that you should give an explanation.'

'The old man!' cried Mitya frantically. 'The old man and his blood! . . . I understand.'

And he sank, almost fell, on a chair close by, as though he had been mown down by a scythe.

'You understand? He understands it! Monster and parricide! Your father's blood cries out against you!' the old captain of police roared suddenly, stepping up to Mitya.

He was beside himself, crimson in the face and quivering all over.

'This is impossible!' cried the small young man. 'Mihail Makarovitch, Mihail Makarovitch, this won't do! . . . I beg you'll allow me to speak. I should never have expected such behaviour from you . . .'

'This is delirium, gentlemen, raving delirium,' cried the captain of police; 'look at him: drunk, at this time of night, in the company of a disreputable woman, with the blood of his father on his hands . . . It's delirium! . . .'

'I beg you most earnestly, dear Mihail Makarovitch, to restrain your feelings,' the prosecutor said in a rapid whisper to the old police captain, 'or I shall be forced to resort to . . . '

But the little lawyer did not allow him to finish. He turned to Mitya, and delivered himself in a loud, firm, dignified voice: 'Ex-Lieutenant Karamazov, it is my duty to inform you that you are charged with the murder of your father, Fyodor Pavlovitch Karamazov, perpetrated this night . . . '

He said something more, and the prosecutor, too, put in something, but though Mitya heard them he did not understand them. He stared at them all with wild eyes.

Book Eight

I

Our police captain, Mihail Makarovitch Makarov, a retired lieutenant colonel, was a widower and an excellent man. He had only come to us three years previously, but had won general esteem, chiefly because he 'knew how to keep society together'. He was never without visitors, and could not have got on without them. As it happened, on that occasion the prosecutor, and Varvinsky, our district doctor, a young man, who had only just come to us from Petersburg after taking a brilliant degree at the Academy of Medicine, were playing whist at the police captain's.

Ippolit Kirillovitch, the prosecutor (he was really the deputy prosecutor, but we always called him the prosecutor), was rather a peculiar man, of about five and thirty, inclined to be tubercular, and married to a fat and childless woman. He was vain and irritable, though he had a good intellect, and even a kind heart. It seemed that all that was wrong with him was that he had a better opinion of himself than his ability warranted. In gloomy moments he even threatened to give up his post, and practice as a barrister in criminal cases.

Nikolay Parfenovitch Nelyudov, the young investigating lawyer, who had only come from Petersburg two months before, was sitting in the next room with the young ladies. People talked about it afterwards and wondered that all the gentlemen should, as though intentionally, on the evening of 'the crime' have been gathered together at the house of the executive authority. Yet it was perfectly simple and happened quite naturally.

Ippolit Kirillovitch's wife had had a toothache for the last two days, and he was obliged to go out to escape from her groans. The doctor, from the very nature of his being, could not spend an evening except at cards. Nikolay Parfenovitch Nelyudov had been intending for three days past to drop in that evening at Mihail Makarovitch's, so to speak casually, so as slyly to startle the oldest granddaughter, Olga Mihailovna, by showing that he knew her secret, that he knew it was her birthday, and that she was trying to conceal it on purpose, so as not to be obliged to give a party. He anticipated a great deal of merriment, many playful jests about her age, and her being afraid to reveal it, about his knowing her secret and telling everybody, and so on. The charming young man was a great adept at such teasing; the ladies had christened him 'the naughty man', and he seemed to be delighted at the name. He was extremely well bred, however, of good family, education and feelings, and, though leading a life of pleasure, his sallies were always innocent and in good taste. He was short and delicate looking. On his white, slender, little fingers he always wore a number of big, glittering rings. When he was engaged in his official duties, he always became extraordinarily grave, as though realising his position and the sanctity of the obligations laid upon him. He had a special gift for mystifying murderers and other criminals of the peasant class during interrogation, and if he did not win their respect, he certainly succeeded in arousing their wonder.

The news reached them in the following manner.

Marfa Ignatyevna, the wife of old Grigory, who had been knocked senseless near the fence, was sleeping soundly in her bed and might well have slept till morning after the draught she had taken. But, all of a sudden she waked up, no doubt roused by a fearful epileptic scream from Smerdyakov, who was lying in the next room unconscious. That scream always preceded his fits, and always terrified and upset Marfa Ignatyevna. She could never get accustomed to it. She jumped up and ran half-awake to Smerdyakov's room. But it was dark there, and she could only hear the invalid beginning to gasp and struggle. Then Marfa Ignatyevna herself screamed out and was going to call her husband, but suddenly realised that when she had got up, he was not beside her in bed. She ran back to the bedstead and began groping with her hands, but the bed was really empty. Then he must have gone out – where? She ran to the steps and timidly called him. She got no answer, of course, but she caught the sound of groans far away in the garden in the darkness. She listened. The groans were repeated, and it was evident they came from the garden.

'Good Lord! Just as it was with Lizaveta Smerdyastchaya!' she thought distractedly. She went timidly down the steps and saw that the gate into the garden was open.

'He must be out there, poor dear,' she thought. She went up to the gate and all at once she distinctly heard Grigory calling her by name, 'Marfa! Marfa!' in a weak, moaning, dreadful voice.

'Lord, preserve us from harm!' Marfa Ignatyevna murmured, and ran towards the voice, and that was how she found Grigory. But she found him not by the fence where he had been knocked down, but about twenty paces off. It appeared later that he had crawled away on regaining consciousness, and probably had been a long time getting so far, losing consciousness again several times. She noticed at once that he was covered with blood, and screamed at the top of her voice. Grigory was muttering incoherently: 'He has murdered . . . his father murdered . . . Why scream, silly . . . run . . . fetch someone . . .'

But Marfa continued screaming, and seeing that her master's window was open and that there was a candle alight in the window, she ran there and began calling Fyodor Pavlovitch. But when she looked in at the window, she saw a fearful sight. Her master was lying on his back, motionless, on the floor. His light-coloured dressing-gown and white shirt were soaked with blood. The candle on the table brightly illuminated the blood and the motionless dead face of Fyodor Pavlovitch. Terror-stricken, Marfa rushed away from the window, ran out of the garden, drew the bolt of the big gate, and ran headlong by the back way to the neighbour, Marya Kondratyevna. Both mother and daughter were asleep, but they woke up at Marfa's desperate and persistent screaming and knocking at the shutter. Marfa, shrieking and screaming incoherently, managed to tell them the main facts, and to beg for assistance. It happened that Foma had come back from his wanderings and was staying the night with them. They roused him up immediately and all three ran to the scene of the crime. On the way, Marya Kondratyevna remembered that at about eight o'clock she heard a dreadful scream from their garden, and this was no doubt Grigory's scream, 'Parricide!' uttered when he caught hold of Mitya's leg.

'Someone screamed out and then was silent,' Marya Kondratyevna explained as she ran. Running to the place where Grigory lay, the two women with the help of Foma carried him to the lodge. They lighted a candle and saw that Smerdyakov was no better, that he was writhing in convulsions, his eyes fixed in a squint, and that foam was flowing from his lips. They moistened Grigory's forehead with water mixed with vinegar, and the water revived him at once. He asked immediately: 'Is the master murdered?'

Then Foma and both women ran to the house and saw this time that not only the window, but also the door into the garden was wide open, though Fyodor Pavlovitch had for the last week locked himself in every night and did not allow even Grigory to come in on any pretext. Seeing that door open, they were afraid to go in to Fyodor Pavlovitch 'for fear anything should happen afterwards'. And when they returned to Grigory, the old man told them to go straight to the police captain. Marya Kondratyevna ran there and gave the alarm to the whole party at the police captain's.

It was resolved to act with energy. The deputy police inspector of the town was commissioned to take four witnesses, to enter Fyodor Pavlovitch's house and there to open an enquiry on the spot, according to the regular forms, which I will not go into here.

The district doctor, a zealous man, new to his work, almost insisted on accompanying the police captain, the prosecutor, and the investigating lawyer.

I will note briefly that Fyodor Pavlovitch was found to be quite dead, with his skull battered in. But with what? Most likely with the same weapon with which Grigory had been attacked later. And immediately that weapon was found, Grigory, to whom all possible medical assistance was at once given, described in a weak and faltering voice how he had been knocked down. With a lantern they began looking by the fence and found the brass pestle dropped in a most conspicuous place on the garden path. There were no signs of disturbance in the room where Fyodor Pavlovitch was lying. But by the bed, behind the screen, they picked up from the floor a big and thick envelope with the inscription: 'A present of three thousand roubles for my angel Grushenka, if she is willing to come.' And below had been added by Fyodor Pavlovitch, 'For my little chicken.' There were three seals of red sealing-wax on the envelope, but it had been torn open and was empty; the money had been removed. They found also on the floor a piece of narrow pink ribbon, with which the envelope had been tied up.

The doctor was particularly interested in the condition of the servant, Smerdyakov.

'Such violent and protracted epileptic fits, recurring continually for twenty-four hours, are rarely to be met with, and are of interest to science,' he declared enthusiastically to his companions, and, as they left, they laughingly congratulated him on his find. The prosecutor and the investigating lawyer distinctly remembered the doctor's saying that Smerdyakov could not outlive the night.

After these long, but, I think, necessary explanations, we will return to that moment of our story at which we broke off.

2

And so Mitya sat looking wildly at the people round him, not understanding what was said to him. Suddenly he got up, flung up his hands and shouted aloud: 'I'm not guilty! I'm not guilty of that blood! I'm not guilty of my father's blood . . . I meant to kill him. But I'm not guilty. Not I.'

But he had hardly said this, before Grushenka rushed from behind the curtain and flung herself at the police captain's feet.

'It was my fault! Mine! My wickedness!' she cried, in a heartrending voice, bathed in tears, stretching out her clasped hands towards them. 'He did it because of me. I tortured him and drove him to it. I tortured that poor old man that's dead, too, in my wickedness, and brought him to this! It's my fault, mine first, mine most, my fault!'

'Yes, it's your fault! You're the chief criminal! You fury! You harlot! You're the most to blame!' shouted the police captain, threatening her with his hand. But he was quickly and resolutely suppressed. The prosecutor firmly seized hold of him.

'This is absolutely irregular, Mihail Makarovitch!' he cried. 'You are positively hindering the enquiry . . . You're ruining the case . . . ' he almost gasped.

'Follow the regular course! Follow the regular course!' cried Nikolay Parfenovitch, fearfully excited too, 'otherwise it's absolutely impossible! . . . '

'Judge us together!' Grushenka cried frantically, still kneeling. 'Punish us together. I will go with him now, if it's to death!'

'Grushenka, my life, my blood, my holy one!' Mitya

fell on his knees beside her and held her tight in his arms. 'Don't believe her,' he cried, 'she's not guilty of anything, of any blood, of anything!'

He remembered afterwards that he was forcibly dragged away from her by several men, and that she was led out, and that when he recovered himself he was sitting at the table. Beside him and behind him stood the men with metal shields. Facing him on the other side of the table sat Nikolay Parfenovitch, the investigating lawyer. He kept persuading him to drink a little water out of a glass that stood on the table.

'That will refresh you, that will calm you. Be calm, don't be frightened,' he added, most politely. Mitya (he remembered it afterwards) became suddenly intensely interested in his big rings, one with an amethyst, and another with a transparent bright yellow stone, of great brilliance. And long afterwards he remembered with wonder how those rings had riveted his attention through all those terrible hours of interrogation, so that he was utterly unable to tear himself away from them and dismiss them, as things that had nothing to do with his position. On Mitya's left side, in the place where Maximov had been sitting at the beginning of the evening, the prosecutor was now seated, and on Mitya's right hand, where Grushenka had been, was a rosy-cheeked young man in a sort of shabby hunting jacket, with ink and paper before him. This was the secretary of the investigating lawyer, who had brought him along. The police captain was now standing by the window at the other end of the room, beside Kalganov, who was sitting there.

'Drink some water,' said the investigating lawyer softly, for the tenth time.

'I have drunk it, gentlemen, I have . . . but . . . come,

gentlemen, strangle me, behead me, decide my fate!' cried Mitya, staring with protruding eyes at the investigating lawyer.

'So you positively declare that you are not guilty of the death of your father, Fyodor Pavlovitch?' asked the investigating lawyer, softly but insistently.

'I am not guilty. I am guilty of the blood of another old man, but not of my father's. And I weep for it! I killed, I killed the old man and knocked him down . . . But it's hard to have to answer for that murder with another, a terrible murder of which I am not guilty . . . It's a terrible accusation, gentlemen, a knockout blow. But who killed my father, who killed him? Who can have killed him if I didn't? It's extraordinary, absurd, impossible.'

'Yes, who can have killed him?' the investigating lawyer began, but Ippolit Kirillovitch, the prosecutor, glancing at him, addressed Mitya.

'There is no need to have the old servant, Grigory Vassilyevitch on your conscience. He is alive, he has recovered, and in spite of the terrible blows inflicted, according to his own and your evidence, by you, there seems no doubt that he will live, so the doctor says, at least.'

'Alive? He's alive?' cried Mitya, flinging up his hands. His face beamed. 'Lord, I thank Thee for the great miracle Thou hast wrought for me, a sinner and evildoer. That's an answer to my prayer. I've been praying all night.' And he crossed himself three times. He was almost breathless.

'So from this Grigory we have received such important evidence concerning you, that . . . ' the prosecutor would have continued, but Mitya suddenly jumped up from his chair.

'One minute, gentlemen, for God's sake, one minute; I will run to her –'

'Excuse me, at this moment it's quite impossible,' Nikolay Parfenovitch almost shrieked. He too sprang to his feet. Mitya was seized by the men with the metal shields, but he sat down of his own accord.

'Gentlemen, what a pity! I wanted to see her for one minute only; I wanted to tell her that it has been washed away, it has gone, that crime that was weighing on my heart all night, and that I am not a murderer now! Gentlemen, she is my betrothed!' he said ecstatically and reverently, looking round at them all. 'Oh, thank you, gentlemen! Oh, in one minute you have given me new life, new courage! . . . That old man used to carry me in his arms, gentlemen. He used to wash me in the tub when I was a baby three years old, abandoned by everyone, he was like a father to me! . . .'

'And so you . . . ' the investigating lawyer began.

'Allow me, gentlemen, allow me one minute more,' interposed Mitya, putting his elbows on the table and covering his face with his hands. 'Let me have a moment to think, let me breathe, gentlemen. All this has shattered me, shattered me completely. A man can bear only so much, gentlemen!'

'Drink a little more water,' murmured Nikolay Parfenovitch. Mitya took his hands from his face and laughed. His eyes were confident. He seemed completely transformed in a moment. His whole bearing was changed; he was once more the equal of these men, with all of whom he was acquainted, as though they had all met the day before, when nothing had happened, at some social gathering. We may note in passing that, on his first arrival, Mitya had been made very welcome at the police captain's, but later, during the last month especially, Mitya had hardly called at all, and when the police captain met him, in the street, for instance, Mitya noticed that he frowned and only bowed out of politeness. His acquaintance with the prosecutor was less intimate, though he sometimes paid his wife, a nervous and fanciful lady, visits of courtesy, without quite knowing why, and she always received him graciously and had, for some reason, taken an interest in him up to the last. He had not had time to get to know the investigating lawyer, though he had met him and talked to him twice, each time about the fair sex.

'You're a most skilful lawyer, I see, Nikolay Parfenovitch,' cried Mitya, laughing gaily, 'but I can help you now. Oh, gentlemen, I feel like a new man, and don't be offended at my addressing you so simply and directly. I'm rather drunk, too, I'll tell you that frankly. I believe I've had the honour and pleasure of meeting you, Nikolay Parfenovitch, at my kinsman Miüsov's. Gentlemen, gentlemen, I don't pretend to be on equal terms with you. I understand, of course, what my position is as I sit here before you. Oh, of course, there's a horrible suspicion . . . hanging over me . . . if Grigory has given evidence . . . A horrible suspicion! It's awful, awful, I understand that! But to business, gentlemen, I am ready, and we will make an end of it in one moment; for, listen, listen, gentlemen! Since I know I'm innocent, we can put an end to it in a minute. Can't we? Can't we?'

Mitya spoke freely and rapidly, nervously and effusively, as though he positively took his listeners to be his best friends.

'So, for the present, we will put down that you absolutely deny the charge brought against you,' said

Nikolay Parfenovitch, impressively, and bending down to the secretary he dictated to him in an undertone what to write.

'Write it down? You want to write that down? Well, write it; I consent, I give my full consent, gentlemen, only . . . do you see . . . Wait, wait, write this. Of disorderly conduct I am guilty, of violence on a poor old man, I am guilty. And there is something else at the bottom of my heart, of which I am guilty, too – but that you need not write down (he turned suddenly to the secretary); that's my personal life, gentlemen, that doesn't concern you, the bottom of my heart, that's to say . . . But of the murder of my old father I'm not guilty. That's a wild idea. It's a crazy idea! . . . I will prove you that and you'll be convinced directly . . . You will laugh, gentlemen. You'll laugh yourself at your suspicion! . . .'

'Be calm, Dmitri Fyodorovitch,' said the investigating lawyer, evidently trying to allay Mitya's excitement by his own composure. 'Before we go on with our enquiry, I should like, if you will consent to answer, to hear you confirm the statement that you disliked your father, Fyodor Pavlovitch, that you were involved in continual disputes with him. Here at least, a quarter of an hour ago, you exclaimed that you wanted to kill him: "I didn't kill him," you said, "but I wanted to kill him." '

'Did I say that? Ah, that may be so, gentlemen! Yes, unhappily, I would have liked to kill him . . . many times I wanted to . . . unhappily, unhappily!'

'You wanted to. Would you consent to explain what motives precisely led you to such a sentiment of hatred for your parent?'

'What is there to explain, gentlemen?' Mitya

shrugged his shoulders sullenly, looking down. 'I have never concealed my feelings. All the town knows about it – everyone knows in the tavern. Only lately I declared them in Father Zossima's cell . . . And the very same day, in the evening I beat my father. I nearly killed him, and I swore I'd come again and kill him, before witnesses . . . Oh, a thousand witnesses! I've been shouting it aloud for the last month, anyone can tell you that! . . . The fact stares you in the face, it speaks for itself, it cries aloud, but, feelings, gentlemen, feelings are another matter. You see, gentlemen' (Mitya frowned), 'it seems to me that about feelings you've no right to question me. I know that you are bound by your office, I quite understand that, but that's my affair, my private, intimate affair, yet . . . since I haven't concealed my feelings in the past . . . in the tavern, for instance, I've talked to everyone, so . . . so I won't make a secret of it now. You see, I understand, gentlemen, that there are terrible facts against me in this business. I told everyone that I'd kill him, and now, all of a sudden, he's been killed. So it must have been me! Ha, ha! I can make allowances for you, gentlemen, I can certainly make allowances. I'm thunderstruck myself, for who can have murdered him, if not I? That's what it comes to, doesn't it? If not I, who can it be, who? Gentlemen, I want to know, I insist on knowing!' he exclaimed suddenly. 'Where was he murdered? How was he murdered? How, and with what? Tell me,' he asked quickly, looking at the two lawyers.

'We found him in his study, lying on his back on the floor, with his head battered in,' said the prosecutor.

'That's horrible!' Mitya shuddered and, leaning on the table, hid his face in his right hand.

'We will continue,' interposed Nikolay Parfenovitch. 'So what was it that impelled you to this sentiment of hatred? You have asserted in public, I believe, that it was based upon jealousy?'

'Well, yes, jealousy. And not only jealousy.'

'Disputes about money?'

'Yes, about money too.'

'There was a dispute about three thousand roubles, I think, which you claimed as part of your inheritance?'

'Three thousand! More, more,' cried Mitya hotly; 'more than six thousand, more than ten, perhaps. I told everyone so, shouted it at them. But I made up my mind to let it go at three thousand. I was desperately in need of that three thousand . . . so the bundle of notes for three thousand that I knew he kept under his pillow, ready for Grushenka, I considered as simply stolen from me. Yes, gentlemen, I looked upon it as mine, as my own property . . . '

The prosecutor looked significantly at the investigating lawyer, and had time to wink at him on the sly.

'We will return to that subject later,' said the lawyer promptly. 'You will allow us to note that point and write it down; that you looked upon that money as your own property?'

'Write it down, by all means. I know that's another fact that tells against me, but I'm not afraid of facts and I tell them against myself. Do you hear? Do you know, gentlemen, you take me for a different sort of man than I really am,' he added, suddenly, gloomy and dejected. 'You have to deal with a man of honour, a man of the highest honour; above all – don't lose sight of it – a man who's done a lot of nasty things, but has always been, and still is, honourable at bottom, in his inner being. I don't know how to express it. That's just what's made me wretched all my life, that I yearned to be honourable, that I was, so to say, a martyr to a sense of honour, seeking for it with a lantern, with the lantern of Diogenes and yet, all my life I've been doing filthy things like all of us, gentlemen . . . that is like me alone. That was a mistake, like me alone, me alone! . . . Gentlemen, my head aches . . . ' His brows contracted with pain. 'You see, gentlemen, I couldn't bear the look of him, there was something in him ignoble, impudent, trampling on everything sacred, something sneering and irreverent, loathsome, loathsome. But now that he's dead, I feel differently.'

'How do you mean?'

'I don't feel differently, but I wish I hadn't hated him so.'

'You feel penitent?'

'No, not penitent, don't write that. I'm not much good myself, I'm not very beautiful, so I had no right to consider him repulsive. That's what I mean. Write that down, if you like.'

Saying this Mitya became very mournful. He had grown more and more gloomy as the enquiry continued.

At that moment an unexpected scene occurred. Though Grushenka had been removed, she had not been taken far away, only into the room next but one from the blue room, in which the examination was proceeding. It was a little room with one window, next beyond the large room in which they had danced and feasted so lavishly. She was sitting there with no one by her but Maximov, who was terribly depressed, terribly scared, and clung to her side, as though for security. At their door stood one of the peasants with a metal shield dangling on his breast. Grushenka was crying, and suddenly her grief was too much for her, she jumped up, flung up her arms, and with a loud wail of sorrow, rushed out of the room to him, to her Mitya, and so unexpectedly that no one had time to stop her. Mitya, hearing her cry, trembled, jumped up, and with a shriek rushed impetuously to meet her, not knowing what he was doing. But they were not allowed to come together, though they saw one another. He was seized by the arms; he struggled, and tried to tear himself away. It took three or four men to hold him. She was seized too, and he saw her stretching out her arms to him, crying aloud as they carried her away. When the scene was over, he came to himself again, sat down in the same place as before, opposite the investigating lawyer, and cried out to them: 'What do you want with her? Why do you torment her? She's done nothing, nothing! . . . '

The lawyers tried to soothe him. About ten minutes passed like this. At last Mihail Makarovitch, who had been absent, came hurriedly into the room, and said in a loud and excited voice to the prosecutor: 'She's been removed, she's downstairs. Will you allow me to say one word to this unhappy man, gentlemen? In your presence, gentlemen, in your presence.'

'By all means, Mihail Makarovitch,' answered the investigating lawyer. 'At the moment we have nothing against it.'

'Listen, Dmitri Fyodorovitch, my dear fellow,' began the police captain, and there was a look of warm, almost fatherly, feeling for the luckless prisoner on his excited face, 'I took your Agrafena Alexandrovna downstairs myself, and confided her to the care of the landlord's daughters, and that old fellow Maximov is with her all the time. And I soothed her, do you hear? I soothed and calmed her. I impressed on her that you have to clear yourself, so she mustn't hinder you, must not depress you, or you may lose your head and say the wrong thing in your evidence. In fact, I talked to her and she understood. She's a sensible girl, my boy, a good-hearted girl, she would have kissed my old hands, begging help for you. She sent me herself, to tell you not to worry about her. And I must go, my dear fellow, I must go and tell her that you are calm and comforted about her. And so you must be calm, do you understand? I was unfair to her; she is a Christian soul, gentlemen, yes, I tell you, she's a gentle soul, and not to blame for anything. So what am I to tell her, Dmitri Fyodorovitch, will you sit quiet or not?'

The good-natured police captain said a great deal that was irregular, but Grushenka's suffering, a fellow creature's suffering, touched his good-natured heart, and tears stood in his eyes. Mitya jumped up and rushed towards him.

'Forgive me, gentlemen, oh, allow me, allow me!' he cried. 'You've the heart of an angel, an angel, Mihail Makarovitch, I thank you for her. I will, I will be calm, cheerful, in fact. Tell her, in the kindness of your heart, that I am cheerful, quite cheerful, that I shall be laughing in a minute, knowing that she has a guardian angel like you. I shall have done with all this directly, and as soon as I'm free, I'll be with her, she'll see, let her wait. Gentlemen,' he said, turning to the two lawyers, 'now I'll open my whole soul to you; I'll pour out everything. We'll finish this off directly, finish it off happily. We shall laugh at it in the end, won't we? But, gentlemen, that woman is the queen of my heart. Oh, let me tell you that. That one thing I'll tell you now . . . I see I'm with honourable men. She is my light, she is my holy one, and if only you knew! Did you hear her cry, "I'll go to death with you"? And what have I, a penniless beggar, done for her? Why such love for me? How can a clumsy, ugly brute like me, with my ugly face, deserve such love, that she is ready to go to exile with me? And how she fell down at your feet for my sake, just now? . . . and yet she's proud and has done nothing! How can I help adoring her, how can I help crying out and rushing to her as I did just now? Gentlemen, forgive me! But now, now I am comforted.'

And he sank back in his chair and covering his face with his hands, burst into tears. But they were happy tears. He recovered himself instantly. The old police captain seemed much pleased, and the lawyers also. They felt that the examination was passing into a new phase. When the police captain went out, Mitya was positively gay.

'Now, gentlemen, I am at your disposal, entirely at your disposal. And if it were not for all these trivial details, we should understand one another in a minute. I'll take up those details again. I'm at your disposal, gentlemen, but I declare that we must have mutual confidence, you in me and I in you, or there'll be no end to it. I speak in your interests. To business, gentlemen, to business, and don't rummage in my soul; don't tease me with trifles, but only ask me about facts and what matters, and I will satisfy you at once. And damn the details!'

So spoke Mitya. The interrogation began again.

3

'You don't know how you encourage us, Dmitri Fyodorovitch, by your readiness to answer,' said Nikolay Parfenovitch, with an animated air, and obvious satisfaction beaming in his bulging, short-sighted, light grey eyes, from which he had removed his spectacles a moment before. 'And you have made a very just remark about mutual confidence, without which it is sometimes positively impossible to get on in cases of such importance, if the suspected party really hopes and desires to defend himself and is in a position to do so. We, on our side, will do everything in our power, and you can see for yourself how we are conducting the case. You approve, Ippolit Kirillovitch?' He turned to the prosecutor.

'Oh, undoubtedly,' replied the prosecutor. His tone was somewhat cold, compared with Nikolay Parfenovitch's impulsiveness.

I will note once for all that Nikolay Parfenovitch, who had but lately arrived among us, had from the first felt marked respect for Ippolit Kirillovitch, our prosecutor, and had become almost his bosom friend. He was practically the only person who put implicit faith in Ippolit Kirillovitch's extraordinary talents as a psychologist and orator and in his unappreciated talent. He had heard of him in Petersburg. On the other hand, young Nikolay Parfenovitch was the only person in the whole world whom our 'unappreciated' prosecutor genuinely liked. On their way to Mokroe they had time to come to an understanding about the present case. And now as they sat at the table, the sharp-witted junior caught and interpreted every indication on his senior colleague's face, at half a word, at a glance, or at a wink.

'Gentlemen, only let me tell my own story and don't interrupt me with trival questions and I'll tell you everything in a moment,' said Mitya excitedly.

'Excellent! Thank you. But before we proceed to listen to your statement, will you allow me to enquire as to another little fact of great interest to us. I mean the ten roubles you borrowed yesterday at about five o'clock on the security of your pistols, from your friend, Pyotr Ilyitch Perhotin.'

'I pledged them, gentlemen. I pledged them for ten roubles. What more? That's all about it. As soon as I got back to town I pledged them.'

'You got back to town? Then had you been out of town?'

'Yes, I went on a journey of twenty-five miles into the country. Didn't you know?'

The prosecutor and Nikolay Parfenovitch exchanged glances.

'Well, how would it be if you began your story with a systematic description of all you did yesterday, from the morning onwards? Allow us, for instance, to enquire why you were absent from the town, and just when you left and when you came back – all those facts.'

'You should have asked me that from the beginning,' cried Mitya, laughing aloud, 'and, if you like, we won't begin from yesterday, but from the morning of the day before; then you'll understand how, why, and where I went. I went the day before yesterday, gentlemen, to a merchant of the town, called Samsonov, to borrow three thousand roubles from him on safe security. It was a pressing matter, gentlemen, it was a sudden necessity.'

'Allow me to interrupt you,' the prosecutor put in politely. 'Why were you in such pressing need for just that sum, three thousand?'

'Oh, gentlemen, you needn't go into details, how, when and why, and why just so much money, and not more or less, and all that rigmarole. Why, it'll run to three volumes, and then you'll want an epilogue!'

Mitya said all this with the good-natured but impatient familiarity of a man who is anxious to tell the whole truth and is full of the best intentions.

'We have treated you reasonably from the beginning,' said Nikolay Parfenovitch, laughing. 'We haven't tried to put you out by asking how you got up in the morning and what you had for breakfast. We began, indeed, with questions of the greatest importance.'

'I understand. I noted that and appreciated your attitude, and I appreciate still more your present kindness to me, an unprecedented kindness, worthy of your noble hearts. We three here are gentlemen, and let everything be on the footing of mutual confidence between educated, well-bred people, who have the common bond of noble birth and honour. In any case, allow me to look upon you as my best friends at this moment of my life, at this moment when my honour is assailed. That's no offence to you, gentlemen, is it?'

'On the contrary. You've expressed it all so well, Dmitri Fyodorovitch,' Nikolay Parfenovitch answered with dignified approbation.

'And enough of those trivial questions, gentlemen, all those tricky questions!' cried Mitya enthusiastically. 'Or there's simply no knowing where we shall get to! Is there?'

'I will follow your sensible advice entirely,' the prosecutor interposed, addressing Mitya. 'But I don't withdraw my question, however. It is now vitally important for us to know exactly why you needed that sum, I mean precisely three thousand.'

'Why I needed it? . . . Oh, for one thing and another . . . Well, it was to pay a debt.'

'A debt to whom?'

'That I absolutely refuse to answer, gentlemen. Not because I couldn't, or because I wouldn't dare, or because it would be damaging, for it's all a paltry matter and absolutely trifling, but – I won't, because it's a matter of principle: that's my private life, and I won't allow any intrusion into my private life. That's my principle. Your question has no bearing on the case, and whatever has nothing to do with the case is my private affair. I wanted to pay a debt. I wanted to pay a debt of honour, but to whom I won't say.'

'Allow me to make a note of that,' said the prosecutor.

'By all means. Write down that I won't say, that I won't. Write that I would think it dishonourable to say. Yes! You can write it down; you've nothing else to do with your time.'

'Allow me to caution you, sir, and to remind you once more, if you are unaware of it,' the prosecutor began, with an unusual and stern impressiveness, 'that you have a perfect right not to answer the questions put to you now, and we on our side have no right to extort an answer from you, if you decline to give it for one reason or another. That is entirely a matter for your personal decision. But it is our duty, on the other hand, in such cases as the present, to explain and set before you the degree of injury you will be doing yourself by refusing to give this or that piece of evidence. After which I will beg you to continue.'

'Gentlemen, I'm not angry . . . I . . . ' Mitya muttered

in a rather disconcerted tone. 'Well, gentlemen, you see, that Samsonov to whom I went then . . .'

We will, of course, not reproduce his account of what is known to the reader already. Mitya was impatiently anxious not to omit the slightest detail. At the same time he was in a hurry to get it over. But as he gave his evidence it was written down, and therefore they had continually to pull him up. Mitya disliked this, but submitted; got impatient, though still good-humouredly. He did, it is true, exclaim, from time to time, 'Gentlemen, that's enough to make an angel angry!' Or, 'Gentlemen, it's no good your irritating me.'

But even though he exclaimed he still preserved for a time his genially expansive mood. So he told them how Samsonov had made a fool of him two days before. (He had completely realised by now that he had been fooled.) The sale of his watch for six roubles to obtain money for the journey was something new to the lawyers. They were at once greatly interested, and even, to Mitya's intense indignation, thought it necessary to write the fact down as a secondary confirmation of the circumstance that he had hardly a penny in his pocket at the time. Little by little Mitya began to grow surly. When he came to telling of his visit to Madame Hohlakov, he regained his spirits and even wished to tell a little anecdote of that lady which had nothing to do with the case. But the investigating lawyer stopped him, and civilly suggested that he should pass on to 'more essential matters'. At last, when he described his despair and told them how, when he left Madame Hohlakov's, he thought that he'd 'get three thousand if he had to murder someone to do it,' they stopped him again and noted down that he had 'meant to murder someone'. Mitya let them write it without protest. At last he reached the point in his story when he learned that Grushenka had deceived him and had returned from Samsonov's as soon as he left her there, though she had said that she would stay there till midnight.

'If I didn't kill Fenya then, gentlemen, it was only because I hadn't time,' broke from him suddenly at that point in his story. That, too, was carefully written down. Mitya waited gloomily, and was beginning to tell how he ran into his father's garden when the investigating lawyer suddenly stopped him, and opening the big portfolio that lay on the sofa beside him he brought out the brass pestle.

'Do you recognise this object?' he asked, showing it to Mitya.

'Oh, yes,' he laughed gloomily. 'Of course I recognise it. Let me have a look at it . . . Damn it, never mind!'

'You have forgotten to mention it,' observed the investigating lawyer.

'Hang it all, I shouldn't have concealed it from you. Do you suppose I could have managed without it? It simply escaped my memory.'

'Be so good as to tell us precisely how you came to arm yourself with it.'

'Certainly I will be so good, gentlemen.'

And Mitya described how he took the pestle and ran.

'But what object had you in view in arming yourself with such a weapon?'

'What object? No object. I just picked it up and ran off.'

'What for, if you had no object?'

Mitya's wrath flared up. He looked intently at 'the boy' and smiled gloomily and malignantly. He was feeling more and more ashamed at having told 'such people' the story of his jealousy so sincerely and spontaneously.

'Bother the pestle!' broke from him suddenly.

'But still . . . '

'Oh, to keep off dogs . . . Oh, because it was dark . . . In case anything turned up.'

'But have you ever on previous occasions taken a weapon with you when you went out, since you're afraid of the dark?'

'Damn it all, gentlemen! There's positively no talking to you!' cried Mitya, exasperated beyond endurance, and turning to the secretary, crimson with anger, he said quickly, with a note of fury in his voice: 'Write down at once . . . at once . . . "that I snatched up the pestle to go and kill my father . . . Fyodor Pavlovitch . . . by hitting him on the head with it!" Well, now are you satisfied, gentlemen? Are your minds relieved?' he said, glaring defiantly at the lawyers.

'We quite understand that you made that statement just now through exasperation with us and the questions we put to you, which you consider trivial, though they are, in fact, essential,' the prosecutor remarked dryly in reply.

'Well, upon my word, gentlemen! Yes, I took the pestle . . . What does one pick things up for at such moments? I don't know what for. I snatched it up and ran – that's all. Now let's get on with this business, gentlemen, or I declare I won't tell you any more.'

He sat with his elbows on the table and his head in his hand. He sat sideways to them and gazed at the wall, struggling against a feeling of nausea. He had, in fact, an awful inclination to get up and declare that he wouldn't say another word, 'not if you hang me for it'.

'You see, gentlemen,' he said at last, with difficulty controlling himself, 'you see. I listen to you and am haunted by a dream . . . It's a dream I have sometimes, you know . . . I often dream it – it's always the same . . . that someone is hunting me, someone I'm awfully afraid of . . . that he's hunting me in the dark, in the night . . . tracking me, and I hide somewhere from him, behind a door or in a closet, hide in a degrading way, and the worst of it is, he always knows where I am, but he pretends not to know where I am on purpose, to prolong my agony, to enjoy my terror . . . That's just what you're doing now. It's just like that!'

'Is that the sort of thing you dream about?' enquired the prosecutor.

'Yes, it is. Don't you want to write it down?' said Mitya, with a distorted smile.

'No; no need to write it down. But still you do have curious dreams.'

'It's not a question of dreams now, gentlemen – this is reality, this is real life! I'm a wolf and you're the hunters. Well, hunt him down!'

'You are wrong to make such comparisons . . .' began Nikolay Parfenovitch, with extraordinary softness.

'No, I'm not wrong, not at all!' Mitya flared up again, though his outburst of wrath had obviously relieved his heart. He grew more good-humoured at every word. 'You may not trust a criminal or a man on trial tortured by your questions, but an honourable man, the honourable impulses of the heart (I say that boldly!) – no! That you must believe you have no right indeed . . . but –

' "Be silent, heart,
Be patient, humble, hold thy peace."

Well, shall I go on?' he broke off gloomily.

'If you'll be so kind,' answered Nikolay Parfenovitch.

4

Though Mitya spoke sullenly, it was evident that he was trying more than ever not to forget or miss a single detail of his story. He told them how he had jumped over the fence into his father's garden; how he had gone up to the window; told them all that had happened under the window. Clearly, precisely, distinctly, he described the feelings that troubled him during those moments in the garden when he longed so terribly to know whether Grushenka was with his father or not. But, strange to say, both the lawyers listened now with a sort of awful reserve, looked coldly at him, asked few questions. Mitya could gather nothing from their faces.

'They're angry and offended,' he thought. 'Well, to hell with them!'

When he described how he made up his mind at last to make the 'signal' to his father that Grushenka had come, so that he would open the window, the lawyers paid no attention to the word 'signal', as though they entirely failed to grasp the meaning of the word in this connection: so much so that Mitya noticed it. Coming at last to the moment when, seeing his father peering out of the window, his hatred flared up and he pulled the pestle out of his pocket, he suddenly, as though of design, stopped short. He sat gazing at the wall and was aware that their eyes were fixed upon him.

'Well?' said the investigating lawyer. 'You pulled out the weapon and . . . and what happened then?'

'Then? Why, then I murdered him . . . hit him on the

head and cracked his skull . . . I suppose that's your story. That's it!'

His eyes suddenly flashed. All his smothered wrath suddenly flamed up with extraordinary violence in his soul.

'Our story?' repeated Nikolay Parfenovitch. 'Well – and yours?'

Mitya dropped his eyes and was a long time silent.

'My story, gentlemen? Well, it was like this,' he began softly. 'Whether it was someone's tears, or my mother prayed to God, or a good angel held me back at that instant, I don't know. But the devil was conquered. I rushed from the window and ran to the fence. My father was alarmed and, for the first time, he saw me then, cried out, and sprang back from the window. I remember that very well. I ran across the garden to the fence . . . and there Grigory caught me, when I was sitting on the fence.'

At that point he raised his eyes at last and looked at his listeners. They seemed to be staring at him with perfectly unruffled attention. A sort of paroxysm of indignation seized on Mitya's soul.

'Why, you're laughing at me at this moment, gentlemen!' he broke off suddenly.

'What makes you think that?' observed Nikolay Parfenovitch.

'You don't believe one word – that's why! I understand, of course, that I have come to the vital point. The old man's lying there now with his skull broken, while I – after dramatically describing how I wanted to kill him, and how I snatched up the pestle – I suddenly run away from the window. A nice story! Romance! As though one could believe a fellow on his word. Ha, ha! You are scoffers, gentlemen!'

And he swung round on his chair so that it creaked.

'And did you notice,' asked the prosecutor suddenly, as though not observing Mitya's excitement, 'did you notice when you ran away from the window, whether the door into the garden was open?'

'No, it was not open.'

'It was not?'

'It was shut. And who could open it? Bah! the door. Wait a bit!' he seemed suddenly to bethink himself, and almost with a start: 'Why, did you find the door open?'

'Yes, it was open.'

'Why, who could have opened it if you did not open it yourselves?' cried Mitya, greatly astonished.

'The door stood open, and your father's murderer undoubtedly went in at that door, and, having accomplished the crime, went out again by the same door,' the prosecutor pronounced deliberately, as though chiselling out each word separately. 'That is perfectly clear. The murder was committed in the room and *not through the window*; that is absolutely certain from the examination that has been made, from the position of the body, and everything. There can be no doubt of that circumstance.'

Mitya was absolutely dumfounded.

'But that's utterly impossible!' he cried, completely at a loss. 'I . . . I didn't go in . . . I tell you positively, definitely, the door was shut the whole time I was in the garden, and when I ran out of the garden. I only stood at the window and saw him through the window. That's all, that's all . . . I remember to the last minute. And if I didn't remember, it would be just the same. I know it, for no one knew the signals except Smerdyakov, and me, and the dead man. And he wouldn't have opened the door to anyone in the world without the signals.'

'Signals? What signals?' asked the prosecutor, with greedy, almost hysterical, curiosity. He instantly lost all trace of his reserve and dignity. He asked the question with a sort of cringing timidity. He scented an important fact of which he had known nothing, and was already filled with dread that Mitya might be unwilling to disclose it.

'So you didn't know!' Mitya winked at him with a malicious and mocking smile. 'What if I won't tell you? From whom could you find out? No one knew about the signals except my father, Smerdyakov, and me: that was all. Heaven knew, too, but it won't tell you. But it's an interesting fact. There's no knowing what you might build on it. Ha, ha! Take comfort, gentlemen, I'll reveal it. You've some foolish idea in your hearts. You don't know the man you have to deal with! You have to do with a prisoner who gives evidence against himself, to his own damage! Yes, for I'm a man of honour and you – are not.'

The prosecutor swallowed this without a murmur. He was trembling with impatience to hear the new fact. Minutely and diffusely Mitya told them everything about the signals invented by Fyodor Pavlovitch for Smerdyakov. He told them exactly what every tap on the window meant, tapped the signals on the table, and when Nikolay Parfenovitch said that he supposed he, Mitya, had tapped the signal 'Grushenka has come', when he tapped to his father, he answered precisely that he had tapped that signal, that 'Grushenka had come'.

'So now you can build up your tower,' Mitya broke off, and again turned away from them contemptuously.

'So no one knew of the signals but your dead father, you, and the valet Smerdyakov? And no one else?' Nikolay Parfenovitch enquired once more.

'Yes. The valet Smerdyakov, and heaven. Write down about heaven. That may be of use. Besides, you will need God yourselves.'

And they had already, of course, begun writing it down. But while they wrote, the prosecutor said suddenly, as though catching at a new idea: 'But if Smerdyakov also knew of these signals and you absolutely deny all responsibility for the death of your father, was it not he, perhaps, who knocked the signal agreed upon, induced your father to open to him, and then . . . committed the crime?'

Mitya turned upon him a look of profound irony and intense hatred. His silent stare lasted so long that it made the prosecutor blink.

'You've caught the fox again,' commented Mitya at last; 'you've got the beast by the tail. Ha, ha! I see through you, Mr Prosecutor. You thought, of course, that I should jump at that, catch at your prompting, and shout with all my might, "Aie, it's Smerdyakov; he's the murderer." Confess that's what you thought. Confess, and I'll go on.'

But the prosecutor did not confess. He held his tongue and waited.

'You're mistaken. I'm not going to shout "it's Smerdyakov",' said Mitya.

'And you don't even suspect him?'

'Why, do you suspect him?'

'He is under suspicion too.'

Mitya fixed his eyes on the floor.

'Joking apart,' he said gloomily. 'Listen. From the very beginning, almost from the moment when I ran out to you from behind the curtain, I've had the thought of Smerdyakov in my mind. I've been sitting here, shouting that I'm innocent and thinking all the time "Smerdyakov!" I can't get Smerdyakov out of my head. In fact, I too thought of Smerdyakov just now; but only for a second. Almost at once I thought, "No, it's not Smerdyakov." It's not his doing, gentlemen.'

'In that case is there anybody else you suspect?' Nikolay Parfenovitch enquired cautiously.

'I don't know anyone it could be, whether it's the hand of heaven or of Satan, but . . . not Smerdyakov,' Mitya jerked out with decision.

'But what makes you affirm so confidently and emphatically that it's not he?'

'From my conviction – my impression. Because Smerdyakov is a man of the most abject character and a coward. He's not a coward, he's the epitome of all the cowardice in the world walking on two legs. He has the heart of a chicken. When he talked to me, he was always trembling for fear I would kill him, though I never raised my hand against him. He fell at my feet and snivelled; he has kissed these very boots, literally, beseeching me "not to frighten him". Do you hear? "Not to frighten him". What a thing to say! Why, I offered him money. He's a puling chicken – sickly, epileptic, weak-minded – a child of eight could thrash him. He has no character worth talking about. It's not Smerdyakov, gentlemen. He doesn't care for money; he wouldn't take my presents. Besides, what motive had he for murdering the old man? Why, he's very likely his son, you know – his natural son. Do you know that?'

'We have heard that legend. But you are your father's son, too, you know; yet you yourself told everyone you meant to murder him.'

'That's a thrust! And a nasty, mean one too! I'm not afraid! Oh, gentlemen, isn't it too base of you to say that to my face? It's base, because I told you that myself. I not only wanted to murder him, but I might have done it. And, what's more, I went out of my way to tell you of my own accord that I nearly murdered him. But, you see, I didn't murder him; you see, my guardian angel saved me – that's what you've not taken into account. And that's why it's so base of you. For I didn't kill him, I didn't kill him! Do you hear, I did not kill him.'

He was almost choking. He had not been so moved before during the whole interrogation.

'And what has he told you, gentlemen – Smerdyakov, I mean?' he added suddenly, after a pause. 'May I ask that question?'

'You may ask any question,' the prosecutor replied with frigid severity, 'any question relating to the facts of the case, and we are, I repeat, bound to answer every enquiry you make. We found the servant Smerdyakov, concerning whom you enquire, lying unconscious in his bed, in an epileptic fit of extreme severity, that had recurred, possibly, ten times. The doctor who was with us told us, after seeing him, that he may not outlive the night.'

'Well, if that's so, the devil must have killed him,' broke suddenly from Mitya, as though until that moment he had been asking himself: 'Was it Smerdyakov or not?'

'We will come back to this later,' Nikolay Parfenovitch decided. 'Now, wouldn't you like to continue your statement?'

Mitya asked for a rest. His request was courteously granted. After resting, he went on with his story. But he was evidently depressed. He was exhausted, mortified and morally shaken. To make things worse the prosecutor exasperated him, as though intentionally, by vexatious interruptions about 'trifling points'. Scarcely had Mitya described how, while straddling the wall, he had struck Grigory on the head with the pestle, while the old man had hold of his left leg, and how he had then jumped down to look at him, when the prosecutor stopped him to ask him to describe exactly how he was sitting on the wall. Mitya was surprised.

'Oh, I was sitting like this, astride, one leg on one side of the wall and one on the other.'

'And the pestle?'

'The pestle was in my hand.'

'Not in your pocket? Do you remember that precisely? Was it a violent blow you gave him?'

'It must have been a violent one. But why do you ask?'

'Would you mind sitting on the chair just as you sat on the wall then and showing us just how you moved your arm, and in what direction?'

'You're making fun of me, aren't you?' asked Mitya, looking haughtily at the speaker; but the latter did not flinch.

Mitya turned abruptly, sat astride on his chair, and swung his arm.

'This was how I struck him! That's how I knocked him down! What more do you want?'

'Thank you. May I trouble you now to explain why you jumped down, with what object, and what you had in view?'

'Oh, hang it! . . . I jumped down to look at the man I'd hurt . . . I don't know what for!'

'Though you were so excited and were running away?'

'Yes, though I was excited and running away.'

'You wanted to help him?'

'Help! . . . Yes, perhaps I did want to help him . . . I don't remember.'

'You don't remember? Then you didn't quite know what you were doing?'

'Not at all. I remember everything – every detail. I jumped down to look at him, and wiped his face with my handkerchief.'

'We have seen your handkerchief. Did you hope to restore him to consciousness?'

'I don't know whether I hoped it. I simply wanted to make sure whether he was alive or not.'

'Ah! You wanted to be sure? Well, what then?'

'I'm not a doctor. I couldn't decide. I ran away thinking I'd killed him. And now he's recovered.'

'Excellent,' commented the prosecutor. 'Thank you. That's all I wanted. Kindly proceed.'

Alas! it never entered Mitya's head to tell them, though he remembered it, that he had jumped back from pity, and standing over the prostrate figure had even uttered words of regret: 'You've come to grief, old man – there's no help for it. Well, there you must lie.'

The prosecutor could only draw one conclusion: that the man had jumped back 'at such a moment and in such excitement simply with the object of ascertaining whether the *only* witness of his crime were dead; that he must therefore have been a man of great strength, coolness, decision and foresight even at such a moment', . . . and so on. The prosecutor was satisfied: 'I've provoked the nervous fellow by "trifles" and he has said more than he meant to.'

With painful effort Mitya went on. But this time he was pulled up immediately by Nikolay Parfenovitch.

'How came you to run to the servant, Fenya, with your hands so covered with blood, and, as it appears, your face too?'

'Why, I didn't notice the blood at all at the time,' answered Mitya.

'That's quite likely. It does happen sometimes.' The prosecutor exchanged glances with Nikolay Parfenovitch.

'I simply didn't notice. You're quite right there, prosecutor,' Mitya assented suddenly.

Next came the account of Mitya's sudden determination to 'step aside' and make way for Grushenka's happiness. But he could not make up his mind to open his heart to them as before, and tell them about 'the queen of his soul'. He disliked speaking of her before these chilly persons 'who were fastening on him like bedbugs'. And so in response to their reiterated questions he answered briefly and abruptly: 'Well, I made up my mind to kill myself. What had I left to live for? That question stared me in the face. Her first rightful lover had come back, the man who wronged her but who'd hurried back to offer his love, after five years, and atone for the wrong with marriage . . . So I knew it was all over for me . . . And behind me disgrace, and that blood – Grigory's . . . What had I to live for? So I went to redeem the pistols I had pledged, to load them and put a bullet in my brain tomorrow.'

'And a grand feast the night before?'

'Yes, a grand feast the night before. Damn it all, gentlemen! Do make haste and finish it. I meant to shoot myself not far from here, beyond the village, and I'd planned to do it at five o'clock in the morning. And

I had a note in my pocket already. I wrote it at Perhotin's when I loaded my pistols. Here's the letter. Read it! It's not for you I tell it,' he added contemptuously. He took it from his waistcoat pocket and flung it on the table. The lawyers read it with curiosity, and added it to the papers connected with the case.

'And you didn't even think of washing your hands at Perhotin's? You were not afraid then of arousing suspicion?'

'What suspicion? Suspicion or not, I would have galloped here just the same, and shot myself at five o'clock, and you wouldn't have been in time to do anything. If it hadn't been for what's happened to my father, you would have known nothing about it, and wouldn't have come here. Oh, it's the devil's doing. It was the devil murdered father, it was through the devil that you found it out so soon. How did you manage to get here so quick? It's unbelievable, a nightmare!'

'Mr Perhotin informed us that when you came to him, you held in your hands . . . your bloodstained hands . . . your money . . . a lot of money . . . a bundle of hundred-rouble notes, and that his servant boy saw it too.'

'That's true, gentlemen. I remember it was so.'

'Now, there's one little point presents itself. Can you inform us,' Nikolay Parfenovitch began, with extreme gentleness, 'where did you get so much money all of a sudden, when it appears from the facts, from the reckoning of time, that you had not been home?'

The prosecutor's brows contracted at the question's being asked so plainly, but he did not interrupt Nikolay Parfenovitch.

'No, I didn't go home,' answered Mitya, apparently perfectly composed, but looking at the floor.

'Allow me, then, to repeat my question,' Nikolay Parfenovitch went on as though creeping up to the subject. 'Where were you able to procure such a sum all at once, when, by your confession, at five o'clock the same day you . . . '

'I was in want of ten roubles and pledged my pistols with Perhotin, and then went to Madame Hohlakov to borrow three thousand which she wouldn't give me, and so on, and all the rest of it,' Mitya interrupted sharply. 'Yes, gentlemen, I was in want of it, and suddenly thousands turned up, eh? Do you know, gentlemen, you're both afraid now "what if he won't tell us where he got it?" That's just how it is. I'm not going to tell you, gentlemen. You've guessed right. You'll never know,' said Mitya, chipping out each word with extraordinary determination. The lawyers were silent for a moment.

'You must understand, Mr Karamazov, that it is of vital importance for us to know,' said Nikolay Parfenovitch, softly and suavely.

'I understand; but still I won't tell you.'

The prosecutor, too, intervened, and again reminded him that the prisoner was at liberty to refuse to answer questions, if he thought it to his interest, and so on. But in view of the damage he might do himself by his silence, especially in a case of such importance as . . .

'And so on, gentlemen, and so on. Enough! I've heard that rigmarole before,' Mitya interrupted again. 'I can see for myself, how important it is, and that this is the vital point, and still I won't say.'

'What is it to us? It's not our business, but yours. You are doing yourself harm,' observed Nikolay Parfenovitch nervously.

'You see, gentlemen, joking apart' – Mitya lifted his

eyes and looked firmly at them both – 'I had an inkling from the first that we would come to loggerheads at this point. But at first when I began to give my evidence, it was all still far away and misty; it was all nebulous, and I was so simple that I began with the supposition of mutual confidence existing between us. Now I can see for myself that such confidence is out of the question, for in my case we were bound to come to this cursed stumbling-block. And now we've come to it! It's impossible and there's an end of it! But I don't blame you. You can't believe it all just on my word. I understand that, of course.'

He relapsed into gloomy silence.

'Couldn't you, without abandoning your resolution to be silent about the chief point, could you not, at the same time, give us some slight hint as to the nature of the motives which are strong enough to induce you to refuse to answer, at a crisis so full of danger to you?'

Mitya smiled mournfully, almost dreamily.

'I'm much more good-natured than you think, gentlemen. I'll tell you the reason why and give you that hint, though you don't deserve it. I won't speak of that, gentlemen, because it would be a stain on my honour. The answer to the question where I got the money would expose me to far greater disgrace than the murder and robbing of my father, if I had murdered and robbed him. That's why I can't tell you. I can't for fear of disgrace. What, gentlemen, are you going to write that down too?'

'Yes, we'll write it down,' lisped Nikolay Parfenovitch.

'You ought not to write that down about "disgrace". I only told you that in the goodness of my heart. I needn't have told you. I made you a present of it, so to speak, and you pounce upon it at once. Oh, well, write – write what you like,' he concluded, with scornful disgust. 'I'm not afraid of you and I can still hold up my head before you.'

'And can't you tell us the nature of that disgrace?' Nikolay Parfenovitch hazarded.

The prosecutor frowned darkly.

'No, no, *c'est fini,* don't trouble yourself. It's not worth while soiling one's hands. I have soiled myself enough through you as it is. You're not worth it – no one is . . . Enough, gentlemen. I'm not going on.'

This was said too peremptorily. Nikolay Parfenovitch did not insist further, but from Ippolit Kirillovitch's eyes he saw that he had not given up hope.

'Can you not, at least, tell us what sum you had in your hands when you went into Mr Perhotin's – how many roubles exactly?'

'I can't tell you that.'

'You spoke to Mr Perhotin, I believe, of having received three thousand from Madame Hohlakov.'

'Perhaps I did. Enough, gentlemen. I won't say how much I had.'

'Will you be so good, then, as to tell us how you came here and what you have done since you arrived?'

'Oh! you might ask the people here about that. But I'll tell you if you like.'

He proceeded to do so, but we won't repeat his story. He told it dryly and curtly. Of the raptures of his love he said nothing, but told them that he abandoned his determination to shoot himself, owing to 'new factors in the case'. He told the story without going into motives or details. And this time the lawyers did not worry him much. It was obvious that there was no essential point of interest to them here.

'We shall verify all that. We will come back to it during the examination of the witnesses, which will, of course, take place in your presence,' said Nikolay Parfenovitch in conclusion. 'And now allow me to request you to lay on the table everything in your possession, especially all the money you still have about you.'

'My money, gentlemen? Certainly. I understand that that is necessary. I'm surprised, indeed, that you haven't enquired about it before. It's true I couldn't get away anywhere. I'm sitting here where I can be seen. But here's my money – count it – take it. That's all, I think.'

He turned it all out of his pockets; even the small change – two small silver coins – he pulled out of his waistcoat pocket. They counted the money, which amounted to eight hundred and thirty-six roubles, and forty kopecks.

'And is that all?' asked the investigating lawyer.

'Yes.'

'You stated just now in your evidence that you spent three hundred roubles at Plotnikov's. You gave Perhotin ten, your driver twenty, here you lost two hundred, then . . . '

Nikolay Parfenovitch reckoned it all up. Mitya helped him readily. They recollected every penny and included it in the reckoning. Nikolay Parfenovitch hurriedly added up the total.

'With this eight hundred you must have had about fifteen hundred at first?'

'I suppose so,' snapped Mitya.

'How is it they all assert there was much more?'

'Let them assert it.'

'But you asserted it yourself.'

'Yes, I did too.'

'We will compare all this with the evidence of other persons not yet examined. Don't be anxious about your money. It will be properly taken care of and be at your disposal at the conclusion of . . . what is beginning . . . if it appears, or, so to speak, is proved that you have undisputed right to it. Well, and now . . . '

Nikolay Parfenovitch suddenly got up, and informed Mitya firmly that it was his duty and obligation to conduct a minute and thorough search 'of your clothes and everything else . . .'

'By all means, gentlemen. I'll turn out all my pockets, if you like.'

And he did, in fact, begin turning out his pockets.

'It will be necessary to take off your clothes, too.'

'What! Undress! Well! Damn it. Won't you search me as I am? Can't you?'

'It's utterly impossible, Dmitri Fyodorovitch. You must take off your clothes.'

'As you like,' Mitya submitted gloomily; 'only, please, not here, but behind the curtains. Who will search them?'

'Behind the curtains, of course.'

Nikolay Parfenovitch bent his head in assent. His small face wore an expression of peculiar solemnity.

5

Something utterly unexpected and amazing to Mitya followed. He could never, even a minute before, have conceived that anyone could behave like that to him, Mitya Karamazov. What was worst of all, there was something humiliating in it, and on their side something 'supercilious and scornful'. It was nothing to take off his coat, but he was asked to undress further, or rather not asked but 'commanded', he quite understood that. From pride and contempt he submitted without a word. Several peasants accompanied the lawyers and remained on the same side of the curtain. 'To be ready if force is required,' thought Mitya, 'and perhaps for some other reason, too.'

'Well, must I take off my shirt too?' he asked sharply, but Nikolay Parfenovitch did not answer. He was busily engaged with the prosecutor in examining the coat, the trousers, the waistcoat and the cap; and it was evident that they were both much interested in the scrutiny. 'They make no bones about it,' thought Mitya, 'they don't keep up the most elementary politeness.'

'I ask you for the second time – need I take off my shirt or not?' he said, still more sharply and irritably.

'Don't trouble yourself. We will tell you what to do,' Nikolay Parfenovitch said, and his voice was positively peremptory, or so it seemed to Mitya.

Meantime a consultation was going on in undertones between the lawyers. There turned out to be on the coat, especially on the left side at the back, a huge patch of blood, dry, and still stiff. There were bloodstains on the trousers too. Nikolay Parfenovitch, moreover, in the presence of the peasant witnesses, passed his fingers along the collar, the cuffs, and all the seams of the coat and trousers, obviously looking for something – money, of course. He didn't even hide from Mitya his suspicion that he was capable of sewing money up in his clothes.

'He treats me not as an officer but as a thief,' Mitya muttered to himself. They communicated their ideas to one another with amazing frankness. The secretary, for instance, who was also behind the curtain, fussing about and listening, called Nikolay Parfenovitch's attention to the cap, which they were also fingering.

'You remember Gridyenko, the copying-clerk,' observed the secretary. 'Last summer he received the wages of the whole office, and pretended to have lost the money when he was drunk. And where was it found? Why, in just such pipings in his cap. The hundred-rouble notes were screwed up in little rolls and sewed in the piping.'

Both the lawyers remembered Gridyenko's case perfectly, and so laid aside Mitya's cap, and decided that all his clothes must be more thoroughly examined later.

'Excuse me,' cried Nikolay Parfenovitch, suddenly, noticing that the right cuff of Mitya's shirt was turned in, and covered with blood, 'excuse me, what's that, blood?'

'Yes,' Mitya jerked out.

'That is, what blood . . . and why is the cuff turned in?'

Mitya told him how he had got the sleeve stained with blood looking after Grigory, and had turned it inside when he was washing his hands at Perhotin's.

'You must take off your shirt too. That's very important as material evidence.'

Mitya flushed red and flew into a rage.

'What, am I to stay naked?' he shouted.

'Don't disturb yourself. We will arrange something. And meanwhile take off your socks.'

'You're not joking? Is that really necessary?' Mitya's eyes flashed.

'We are in no mood for joking,' answered Nikolay Parfenovitch sternly.

'Well, if I must . . .' muttered Mitya, and sitting

down on the bed, he took off his socks. He felt unbearably awkward. All were clothed, while he was naked, and strange to say, when he was undressed he felt somehow guilty in their presence, and was almost ready to believe himself that he was inferior to them, and that now they had a perfect right to despise him.

'When all are undressed, one is somehow not ashamed, but when one's the only one undressed and everybody is looking, it's degrading,' he kept repeating to himself, again and again. 'It's like a dream, I've sometimes dreamed of being in such degrading positions.' It was a misery to him to take off his socks. They were very dirty, and so were his underclothes, and now everyone could see it. And what was worse, he disliked his feet. All his life he had thought both his big toes hideous. He particularly loathed the coarse, flat, crooked nail on the right one, and now they would all see it. Feeling intolerably ashamed made him, at once and intentionally, rougher. He pulled off his shirt himself.

'Would you like to look anywhere else if you're not ashamed to?'

'No, there's no need to, at present.'

'Well, am I to stay naked like this?' he added savagely.

'Yes, that can't be helped for the time . . . Kindly sit down here for a while. You can wrap yourself in a quilt from the bed, and I . . . I'll see to all this.'

All the things were shown to the witnesses. The report of the search was drawn up, and at last Nikolay Parfenovitch went out, and the clothes were carried out after him. Ippolit Kirillovitch went out too. Mitya was left alone with the peasants, who stood in silence, never taking their eyes off him. Mitya wrapped himself up in the quilt. He felt cold. His bare feet stuck out, and he couldn't pull the quilt over so as to cover them. Nikolay Parfenovitch seemed to be gone a long time, 'an insufferable time'. 'He thinks of me as a puppy,' thought Mitya, gnashing his teeth. 'That rotten prosecutor has gone, too, contemptuous no doubt, it disgusts him to see me naked!'

Mitya imagined, however, that his clothes would be examined and returned to him. But what was his indignation when Nikolay Parfenovitch came back with quite different clothes, carried in by a peasant who followed behind.

'Here are clothes for you,' he observed airily, seeming well satisfied with the success of his mission. 'Mr Kalganov has kindly provided these for this unusual emergency, as well as a clean shirt. Luckily he had them all in his trunk. You can keep your own socks and underclothes.'

Mitya flew into a passion.

'I won't have other people's clothes!' he shouted menacingly, 'give me my own!'

'It's impossible!'

'Give me my own. Damn Kalganov and his clothes too!'

It was a long time before they could persuade him. But they succeeded somehow in quieting him down. They impressed upon him that, his clothes being stained with blood, must be 'included with the other material evidence', and that they 'had not even the right to let him have them now . . . taking into consideration the possible outcome of the case'. Mitya at last understood this. He subsided into gloomy silence and hurriedly dressed himself. He merely observed, as he put them on, that the clothes were much better than his old ones, and that he disliked 'gaining by the change'. They were, besides, 'ridiculously tight. Am I to be dressed up like a fool . . . for your amusement?'

They urged upon him again that he was exaggerating, that Kalganov was only a little taller, so that only the trousers might be a little too long. But the coat turned out to be really tight in the shoulders.

'Damn it all! I can hardly button it,' Mitya grumbled. 'Be so good as to tell Mr Kalganov from me that I didn't ask for his clothes, and it's not my doing that they've dressed me up like a clown.'

'He quite understands that, and is sorry . . . I mean, not sorry to lend you his clothes, but sorry about all this business,' mumbled Parfenovitch.

'Confound his sorrow! Well, where now, or am I to go on sitting here?'

He was asked to go back to the 'other room'. Mitya went in, scowling with anger, and trying to avoid looking at anyone. Dressed in another man's clothes he felt himself disgraced, even in the eyes of the peasants, and of Trifon Borissovitch, whose face appeared, for some reason, in the doorway, and vanished immediately. 'He's come to see me looking like a scarecrow,' thought Mitya. He sat down on the same chair as before. He had an absurd nightmarish feeling, as though he were out of his mind.

'Well, what now? Are you going to flog me? That's all that's left for you,' he said, clenching his teeth and addressing the prosecutor. He would not turn to Nikolay Parfenovitch, as though he disdained to speak to him. ('He looked too closely at my socks, and turned them inside out on purpose to show everyone how dirty they were – the scoundrel!')

'Well, now we must proceed to the examination of witnesses,' observed Nikolay Parfenovitch, as though in reply to Mitya's question.

'Yes,' said the prosecutor thoughtfully, as though reflecting on something.

'We've done what we could in your interest, Dmitri Fyodorovitch,' Nikolay Parfenovitch went on, 'but having received from you such an uncompromising refusal to explain to us the source from which you obtained the money found upon you, we are, at the present moment . . .'

'What is the stone in your ring?' Mitya interrupted suddenly, as though awakening from a reverie. He pointed to one of the three large rings adorning Nikolay Parfenovitch's right hand.

'Ring?' repeated Nikolay Parfenovitch with surprise.

'Yes, that one . . . on your middle finger, with the little veins in it, what stone is that?' Mitya persisted, like a peevish child.

'That's a smoky topaz,' said Nikolay Parfenovitch, smiling. 'Would you like to look at it? I'll take it off . . .'

'No, don't take it off,' cried Mitya furiously, suddenly waking up, and angry with himself. 'Don't take it off . . . there's no need . . . Damn it . . . Gentlemen, you've defiled my heart! Can you suppose that I would conceal it from you, if I really had killed my father, that I would shuffle, lie, and hide myself? No, that's not like Dmitri Karamazov, that he couldn't do, and if I were guilty, I swear I wouldn't have waited for your coming, or for the sunrise as I meant at first, but should have killed myself before this, without waiting for the dawn! I know that about myself now. I couldn't have learned so much in twenty years as I've found out in this accursed night! . . . And should I have been like this on this night, and at this moment, sitting with you, could I have talked like this, could I have moved like this, could I have looked at you and at the world like this, if I had really been the murderer of my father, when the very thought of having accidentally killed Grigory gave me no peace all night – not from fear – oh, not simply from fear of your punishment! The disgrace of it! And you expect me to be frank with such scoffers as you, who see nothing and believe in nothing, blind moles and scoffers, and to tell you another nasty thing I've done, another disgrace, even if that would save me from your accusation! No, better Siberia! The man who opened the door to my father and went in at that door, he killed him, he robbed him. Who was he – I'm racking my brains and can't think who. But I can tell you it was not Dmitri Karamazov, and that's all I can tell you, and that's enough, enough, leave me alone . . . Exile me, punish me, but don't persecute me any more. I'll say no more. Call your witnesses!'

Mitya uttered his sudden monologue as though he were determined to be absolutely silent for the future. The prosecutor watched him the whole time and only when he had ceased speaking, observed, as though it were the most ordinary thing, with the most frigid and composed air: 'Oh, about the open door of which you spoke just now, we may as well inform you, by the way, now, of a very interesting piece of evidence of the greatest importance both to you and to us, that has been given us by Grigory, the old man you wounded. On his recovery, he clearly and emphatically stated, in reply to our questions, that when, on coming out to the steps, and hearing a noise in the garden, he made up his mind to go into it through the little gate which stood open, before he noticed you running, as you have told us already, in the dark from the open window where you saw your father, he, Grigory, glanced to the left, and, while noticing the open window, observed at the same time, much nearer to him, the door, standing wide open – that door which you have stated to have been shut the whole time you were in the garden. I will not conceal from you that Grigory himself confidently affirms and bears witness that you must have run from that door, though, of course, he did not see you do so with his own eyes, since he only noticed you first some distance away in the garden, running towards the fence.'

Mitya had leaped up from his chair halfway through this speech.

'Nonsense!' he yelled, in a sudden frenzy, 'it's a barefaced lie. He couldn't have seen the door open because it was shut. He's lying!'

'I consider it my duty to repeat that he is firm in his statement. He does not waver. He adheres to it. We've cross-examined him several times.'

'Precisely. I have cross-examined him several times,' Nikolay Parfenovitch confirmed warmly.

'It's false, false! It's either an attempt to slander me, or the hallucination of a madman,' Mitya still shouted. 'He's simply raving, from loss of blood, from the wound. He must have fancied it when he came to . . . He's raving.'

'Yes, but he noticed the open door, not when he came to after his injuries, but before that, as soon as he went into the garden from the lodge.'

'But it's false, it's false! It can't be so! He's slandering me from spite . . . He couldn't have seen it . . . I didn't come from the door,' gasped Mitya.

The prosecutor turned to Nikolay Parfenovitch and said to him impressively: 'Confront him with it.'

'Do you recognise this object?'

Nikolay Parfenovitch laid upon the table a large and thick official envelope, on which three seals still remained intact. The envelope was empty, and slit open at one end. Mitya stared at it with open eyes.

'It . . . it must be that envelope of my father's, the envelope that contained the three thousand roubles . . . and if there's inscribed on it, allow me, "For my little chicken" . . . yes – three thousand!' he shouted, 'do you see, three thousand, do you see?'

'Of course, we see. But we didn't find the money in it. It was empty, and lying on the floor by the bed, behind the screen.'

For some seconds Mitya stood as though thunderstruck.

'Gentlemen, it's Smerdyakov!' he shouted suddenly, at the top of his voice. 'It's he who's murdered him! He's robbed him! No one else knew where the old man hid the envelope. It's Smerdyakov, that's clear, now!'

'But you, too, knew of the envelope and that it was under the pillow.'

'I never knew it. I've never seen it. This is the first time I've looked at it. I'd only heard of it from Smerdyakov . . . He was the only one who knew where the old man kept it hidden, I didn't know . . . ' Mitya was completely breathless.

'But you told us yourself that the envelope was under your deceased father's pillow. You especially stated that it was under the pillow, so you must have known it.'

'We've got it written down,' confirmed Nikolay Parfenovitch.

'Nonsense! It's absurd! I'd no idea it was under the pillow. And perhaps it wasn't under the pillow at all . . . It was just a chance guess that it was under the pillow. What does Smerdyakov say? Have you asked him where it was? What does Smerdyakov say? that's the chief point . . . And I went out of my way to tell lies against myself . . . I told you without thinking that it was under the pillow, and now you . . . Oh, you know how one says the wrong thing, without meaning it. No one knew but Smerdyakov, only Smerdyakov, and no one else . . . He didn't even tell me where it was! But it's his doing, his doing; there's no doubt about it, he murdered him, that's as clear as daylight now,' Mitya exclaimed more and more frantically, repeating himself incoherently, and growing more and more exasperated and excited. 'You must understand that, and arrest him at once . . . He must have killed him while I was running away and while Grigory was unconscious, that's clear now . . . He gave the signal and father opened to him . . . for no one but he knew the signal, and without the signal father would never have opened the door . . . '

'But you're again forgetting the circumstance,' the prosecutor observed, still speaking with the same restraint, though with a note of triumph, 'that there was no need to give the signal if the door already stood open when you were there, while you were in the garden . . . '

'The door, the door,' muttered Mitya, and he stared speechless at the prosecutor. He sank back helpless in his chair. All were silent.

'Yes, the door! . . . It's a nightmare! God is against me!' he exclaimed, staring before him in complete stupefaction.

'Come, you see,' the prosecutor went on with dignity, 'and you can judge for yourself, Dmitri Fyodorovitch. On the one hand we have the evidence of the open door from which you ran out, a fact which overwhelms you and us. On the other side your incomprehensible, persistent, and, so to speak, obdurate silence with regard to the source from which you obtained the money which was so suddenly seen in your hands, when only three hours earlier, on your own showing, you pledged your pistols for ten roubles! In view of all these facts, judge for yourself. What are we to believe, and what can we depend upon? And don't accuse us of being "frigid, cynical, scoffing people", who are incapable of believing in the generous impulses of your heart . . . . Try to enter into our position . . .'

Mitya was indescribably agitated. He turned pale.

'Very well!' he exclaimed suddenly, 'I will tell you my secret. I'll tell you where I got the money! . . . I'll reveal my shame, that I may not have to blame myself or you hereafter.'

'And believe me, Dmitri Fyodorovitch,' put in Nikolay Parfenovitch, in a voice of almost pathetic delight, 'that a sincere and complete confession on your part at this moment may, later on, have an immense influence in your favour, and may, indeed, moreover . . .'

But the prosecutor gave him a slight kick under the table, and he checked himself in time. Mitya, it is true, had not heard him.

6

'Gentlemen,' he began, still in the same agitation, 'I want to make a full confession: that money was *my own.*'

The lawyers' faces lengthened. That was not at all what they expected.

'How do you mean?' faltered Nikolay Parfenovitch, 'when at five o'clock on the same day, from your own confession . . .'

'Damn five o'clock on the same day and my own confession. That's nothing to do with it now! That money was my own, my own, that is, stolen by me . . . not mine, I mean, but stolen by me, and it was fifteen hundred roubles, and I had it on me all the time, all the time . . .'

'But where did you get it?'

'I took it off my neck, gentlemen, off this very neck . . . it was here, round my neck, sewn up in a rag, and I'd had it round my neck a long time, it's a month since I put it round my neck . . . to my shame and disgrace!'

'And from whom did you . . . appropriate it?'

'You mean, "steal it"? Speak out plainly now. Yes, I consider that I practically stole it, but, if you prefer, I "appropriated it". I consider I stole it. And last night I stole it finally.'

'Last night? But you said that it's a month since you . . . obtained it? . . .'

'Yes. But not from my father. Not from my father, don't be uneasy. I didn't steal it from my father, but from her. Let me tell you without interrupting. It's hard to do, you know. You see, a month ago, I was sent for by Katerina Ivanovna, formerly my betrothed. Do you know her?'

'Yes, of course.'

'I know you know her. She's a noble creature, noblest of the noble. But she has hated me ever so long, oh, ever so long . . . and hated me with good reason, good reason!'

'Katerina Ivanovna!' Nikolay Parfenovitch exclaimed with wonder. The prosecutor, too, stared.

'Oh, don't take her name in vain! I'm a scoundrel to bring her into it. Yes, I've seen that she hated me . . . a long while . . . From the very first, even that evening at my lodging . . . but enough, enough. You're unworthy even to know of that. No need of that at all . . . I need only tell you that she sent for me a month ago, gave me three thousand roubles to send to her sister and another relative in Moscow (as though she couldn't have sent it off herself!), and I . . . it was just at that fatal moment in my life when I . . . Well, in fact, when I'd just come to love another, *her*, she's sitting down below now, Grushenka. I carried her off here to Mokroe then, and wasted here in two days half that damned three thousand, but the other half I kept on me. Well, I've kept that other half, that fifteen hundred like a locket round my neck, but yesterday I undid it, and spent it. What's left of it, eight hundred roubles, is in your hands now, Nikolay Parfenovitch. That's the change out of the fifteen hundred I had yesterday.'

'Excuse me. How's that? Why, when you were here a month ago you spent three thousand, not fifteen hundred, everybody knows that.'

'Who knows it? Who counted the money? Did I let anyone count it?'

'Why you told everyone yourself that you'd spent exactly three thousand.'

'It's true, I did. I told the whole town so, and the whole town said so. And here, at Mokroe, too, everyone reckoned it was three thousand. Yet I didn't spend three thousand, but fifteen hundred. And the other fifteen hundred I sewed into a little bag. That's how it was, gentlemen. That's where I got that money yesterday . . .'

'This is almost miraculous,' murmured Nikolay Parfenovitch.

'Allow me to enquire,' observed the prosecutor at last, 'have you informed anyone whatever of this circumstance before, I mean that you had fifteen hundred left about you a month ago?'

'I told no one.'

'That's strange. Do you mean absolutely no one?'

'Absolutely no one. No one and nobody.'

'What was your reason for this reticence? What was your motive for making such a secret of it? To be more precise: You have told us at last your secret, in your words, so "disgraceful", though in reality – that is, of course, comparatively speaking – this action, that is, the appropriation of three thousand roubles belonging to someone else, and, of course, only for a time is, in my view at least, only an act of the greatest recklessness and not so disgraceful, when one takes into consideration your character . . . Even admitting that it was an action in the highest degree discreditable, still, discreditable is not "disgraceful". . . . Many people have already guessed, during this last month, about the three thousand of Katerina Ivanovna's, that you have spent, and I had heard the legend myself, apart from your confession . . . Mihail Makarovitch, for instance, had heard it, too, so that indeed, it was scarcely a legend, but the gossip of the whole town. There are indications, too, if I am not mistaken, that you confessed this yourself to someone, I mean that the money was Katerina Ivanovna's, and so, it's extremely surprising to me that hitherto, that is, up to the present moment, you have made such an extraordinary secret of the fifteen hundred you say you put by, apparently connecting a feeling of positive horror with that secret . . . It's not easy to believe that it could cause you such distress to confess such a secret . . . You cried out, just now, that Siberia would be better than confessing it . . . '

The prosecutor ceased speaking. He was provoked. He did not conceal his vexation, which was almost anger, and gave vent to all his accumulated spleen, without choosing words, disconnectedly and incoherently.

'It's not the fifteen hundred that's the disgrace, but that I put it apart from the rest of the three thousand,' said Mitya firmly.

'Why,' smiled the prosecutor irritably, 'what is there disgraceful, to your thinking, in your having set aside half of the three thousand you had discreditably, if you prefer, "disgracefully", appropriated? Your taking the three thousand is more important than what you did with it. And by the way, why did you do that – why did you set apart that half, for what purpose, for what object did you do it? Can you explain that to us?'

'Oh, gentlemen, the purpose is the whole point!' cried Mitya. 'I put it aside because I was vile, that is, because I was calculating, and to be calculating in such a case is vile . . . and that vileness has been going on a whole month.'

'It's incomprehensible.'

'I wonder at you. But I'll make it clearer. Perhaps it really is incomprehensible. You see, attend to what I say. I appropriate three thousand entrusted to my honour, I spend it on a spree, say I spend it all, and next morning I go to her and say, "Katya, I've done wrong, I've squandered your three thousand," well, is that right? No, it's not right – it's dishonest and cowardly, I'm a beast, with no more self-control than a beast, that's so, isn't it? But still I'm not a thief? Not a downright thief, you'll admit! I squandered it, but I didn't steal it. Now a second, rather more favourable alternative: follow me carefully, or I may get confused again – my head's going round – and so for the second alternative: I spend here only fifteen hundred out of the three thousand, that is, only half. Next day I go and take that half to her: "Katya, take this fifteen hundred from me, I'm a low beast, and an untrustworthy scoundrel, for I've wasted half the money, and I shall waste this, too, so keep me from temptation!" Well, what of that alternative? I should be a beast and a scoundrel, and whatever you like; but not a thief, not altogether a thief, or I should not have brought back what was left, but have kept that too. She would see at once that since I brought back half, I should pay back what I'd spent, that I should never give up trying to, that I should work to get it and pay it back. So in that case I should be a scoundrel, but not a thief, you may say what you like, not a thief!'

'I admit that there is a certain distinction,' said the prosecutor, with a cold smile. 'But it's strange that you see such a vital difference.'

'Yes, I see a vital difference! Every man may be a scoundrel, and perhaps every man is a scoundrel, but not everyone can be a thief, it takes an arch-scoundrel to be that. Oh, of course, I don't know how to make these fine distinctions . . . but a thief is lower than a scoundrel, that's my conviction. Listen, I carry the money about me a whole month, I may make up my mind to give it back tomorrow, and I'm a scoundrel no longer, but I cannot make up my mind, you see, though I'm making up my mind every day, and every day spurring myself on to do it, and yet for a whole month I can't bring myself to it, you see. Is that right to your thinking, is that right?'

'Certainly, that's not right, that I can quite understand, and that I don't dispute,' answered the prosecutor with reserve. 'And let us give up all discussions of these subtleties and distinctions, and, if you will be so kind, get back to the point. And the point is, that you have still not told us, although we've asked you, why, in the first place, you halved the money, squandering one half and hiding the other? For what purpose exactly did you hide it, what did you mean to do with that fifteen hundred? I insist upon that question, Dmitri Fyodorovitch.'

'Yes, of course!' cried Mitya, striking himself on the forehead; 'forgive me, I'm worrying you, and am not explaining the chief point, or you'd understand in a minute, for it's just the motive of it that's the disgrace! You see, it was all to do with the old man, my dead father. He was always pestering Agrafena Alexandrovna, and I was jealous; I thought then that she was hesitating between me and him. So I kept thinking every day, suppose she were to make up her mind all of a sudden, suppose she were to leave off tormenting me, and were suddenly to say to me, "I love you, not him; take me to the other end of the world." And I'd only a few pennies; how could I take her away, what could I do? Why, I'd be lost. You see, I didn't know her then, I didn't understand her, I thought she wanted money, and that she wouldn't forgive my poverty. And so I fiendishly counted out the half of that three thousand, sewed it up, calculating on it, sewed it up before I was drunk, and after I had sewn it up; I went off to get drunk on the rest. Yes, that was base. Do you understand now?'

Both the lawyers laughed aloud.

'I should have called it sensible and moral on your part not to have squandered it all,' chuckled Nikolay Parfenovitch, 'for after all what does it amount to?'

'Why, that I stole it, that's what it amounts to! Oh, God, you horrify me by not understanding! Every day that I had that fifteen hundred sewn up in the little bag and hanging round my neck, every day and every hour I said to myself, "you're a thief! you're a thief!" Yes, that's why I've been so savage all this month, that's why I fought in the tavern, that's why I attacked my father, it was because I felt I was a thief. I couldn't make up my mind, I didn't dare even to tell Alyosha, my brother, about that fifteen hundred: I felt I was such a scoundrel and such a pickpocket. But, do you know, while I carried it I said to myself at the same time every hour: "No, Dmitri Fyodorovitch, you may yet not be a thief." Why? Because I might go next day and pay back that fifteen hundred to Katya. And only yesterday I made up my mind to tear my amulet off my neck, on my way from Fenya's to Perhotin. I hadn't been able till that moment to bring myself to it. And it was only when I tore it off that I became a downright thief, a thief and a dishonest man for the rest of my life. Why? Because, with that I destroyed, too, my dream of going to Katya and saying, "I'm a scoundrel, but not a thief!" Do you understand now? Do you understand?'

'What was it made you decide to do it yesterday?' Nikolay Parfenovitch interrupted.

'Why? It's absurd to ask. Because I had condemned myself to die at five o'clock this morning, here, at dawn. I thought it made no difference whether I died a thief or a man of honour. But I see it's not so, it turns out that it does make a difference. Believe me, gentlemen, what has tortured me most during this night has not been the thought that I'd killed the old servant, and that I was in danger of Siberia just when my love was being rewarded, and heaven was open to me again. Oh, that did torture me, but not in the same way; not so much as the damned consciousness that I had torn that damned money off my breast at last and spent it, and had become a downright thief! Oh, gentlemen, I tell you again, with a bleeding heart, I have learned a great deal this night. I have learned that it's not only impossible to live a scoundrel, but impossible to die a scoundrel . . . No, gentlemen, one must die honest . . . '

Mitya was pale. His face had a haggard and exhausted look, in spite of his being intensely excited.

'I am beginning to understand you, Dmitri Fyodorovitch,' the prosecutor said slowly, in a soft and almost compassionate tone. 'But all this, if you'll excuse my saying so, is a matter of nerves, in my opinion . . . your overwrought nerves, that's what it is. And why, for instance, should you not have saved yourself such misery for almost a month, by going and returning that fifteen hundred to the lady who had entrusted it to you? And why could you not have explained things to her, and in view of your position, which you describe as being so awful, why could you not have had recourse to the plan which would so naturally have occurred to one's mind, that is, after honourably confessing your errors to her, why could you not have asked her to lend you the sum needed for your expenses, which, with her generous heart, she would certainly not have refused you in your distress, especially if it had been with some guarantee, or even on the security you offered to the merchant Samsonov, and to Madame Hohlakov. I suppose you still regard that security as of value?'

Mitya suddenly crimsoned.

'Surely you don't think me such an out-and-out scoundrel as that? You can't be speaking in earnest?' he said, with indignation, looking the prosecutor straight in the face, and seeming unable to believe his ears.

'I assure you I'm in earnest . . . Why do you imagine I'm not serious?' It was the prosecutor's turn to be surprised.

'Oh, how base that would have been! Gentlemen, do you know, you are torturing me! Let me tell you everything, so be it. I'll confess all my infernal wickedness, but to put you to shame, and you'll be surprised yourself at the depths of ignominy to which a medley of human passions can sink. You must know that I already had that plan myself, that plan you spoke of, just now, prosecutor! Yes, gentlemen, I too have had that thought in my mind all this current month, so that I was on the point of deciding to go to Katya – I was mean enough for that. But to go to her, to tell her of my treachery, and for that very treachery, to carry it out, for the expenses of that treachery, to beg for money from her, Katya (to beg, do you hear, to beg), and to go straight from her to run away with the other, the rival, who hated and insulted her – to think of it! You must be mad, prosecutor!'

'Mad I am not, but I did speak in haste, without thinking . . . of that feminine jealousy . . . if there could be jealousy in this case, as you assert . . . yes, perhaps there is something of the kind,' said the prosecutor, smiling.

'But that would have been so infamous!' Mitya brought his fist down on the table fiercely. 'That would have been filthy beyond everything! Yes, do you know that she might have given me that money, yes, and she would have given it too; she'd have given it to satisfy her vengeance, to show her contempt for me, for hers is an infernal nature, too, and she's a woman of great wrath. I'd have taken the money, too, oh, I should have taken it; I should have taken it, and then, for the rest of my life . . . oh, God! Forgive me, gentlemen, I'm making such an outcry because I've had that thought in my mind so lately, only the day before yesterday, that night when I was having all that trouble with Lyagavy, and afterwards yesterday, all day yesterday, I remember, till that happened . . . '

'Till what happened?' put in Nikolay Parfenovitch inquisitively, but Mitya did not hear it.

'I have made you an awful confession,' Mitya said gloomily in conclusion. 'You must appreciate it, and what's more, you must respect it, for if not, if that leaves your souls untouched, then you've simply no respect for me, gentlemen, I tell you that, and I shall die of shame at having confessed it to men like you! Oh, I shall shoot myself! Yes, I see, I see already that you don't believe me. What, you want to write that down too?' he cried in dismay.

'Yes, what you said just now,' said Nikolay Parfenovitch, looking at him in surprise, 'that is, that up to the last hour you were still contemplating going to Katerina Ivanovna to beg that sum from her . . . I assure you, that's a very important piece of evidence for us, Dmitri Fyodorovitch, I mean for the whole case . . . and particularly for you, particularly important for you.'

'Have mercy, gentlemen!' Mitya flung up his hands. 'Don't write that, anyway; have some shame. Here I've torn my heart asunder before you, and you seize the opportunity and are fingering the wounds in both halves . . . Oh, my God!'

In despair he hid his face in his hands.

'Don't torture yourself so, Dmitri Fyodorovitch,' observed the prosecutor, 'everything that is written down will be read over to you afterwards, and what you don't agree to we'll alter as you like. But now I'll ask you one little question for the second time. Has no one, absolutely no one, heard from you of that money you sewed up? That, I must tell you, is almost impossible to believe.'

'No one, no one, I told you so before, or you've not understood anything! Let me alone!'

'Very well, this matter is bound to be explained, and there's plenty of time for it, but meantime, consider; we have perhaps a dozen witnesses that you yourself spread it abroad, and even shouted almost everywhere about the three thousand you'd spent here; three thousand, not fifteen hundred. And now, too, when you got hold of the money you had yesterday, you gave many people to understand that you had brought three thousand with you.'

'You've got not dozens, but hundreds of witnesses, two hundred witnesses, two hundred have heard it, thousands have heard it!' cried Mitya.

'Well, you see, all bear witness to it. And the word *all* means something.'

'It means nothing. I talked nonsense, and everyone began repeating it.'

'But what need had you to "talk nonsense", as you call it?'

'The devil knows. From bravado perhaps . . . at having wasted so much money . . . To try and forget that money I had sewn up, perhaps . . . yes, that was why . . . damn it . . . how often will you ask me that question? Well, I told a lie, and that was the end of it, once I'd said it, I didn't care to correct it. Why does a man tell lies sometimes?'

'That's very difficult to decide, Dmitri Fyodorovitch, what makes a man tell lies,' observed the prosecutor impressively. 'Tell me, though, was that "amulet", as you call it, on your neck, a big thing?'

'No, not big.'

'How big, for instance?'

'If you fold a hundred-rouble note in half, that would be the size.'

'You'd better show us the remains of it. You must have them somewhere.'

'Damnation, what nonsense! I don't know where they are.'

'But excuse me: where and when did you take it off your neck? According to your own evidence you didn't go home.'

'When I was going from Fenya's to Perhotin's, on the way I tore it off my neck and took out the money.'

'In the dark?'

'Why would I need a light? I did it with my fingers in one minute.'

'Without scissors, in the street?'

'In the market place I think it was. Why scissors? It was an old rag. It was torn in a minute.'

'Where did you put it afterwards?'

'I dropped it there.'

'Where was that, exactly?'

'In the market place, in the market place! The devil knows whereabouts. What do you want to know for?'

'That's extremely important, Dmitri Fyodorovitch. It would be material evidence in your favour. How is it you don't understand that? Who helped you to sew it up a month ago?'

'No one helped me. I did it myself.'

'Can you sew?'

'A soldier has to know how to sew. No knowledge was needed to do that.'

'Where did you get the material, that is, the rag in which you sewed the money?'

'Are you laughing at me?'

'Not at all. And we are in no mood for laughter, Dmitri Fyodorovitch.'

'I don't know where I got the rag from – somewhere, I suppose.'

'I should have thought you couldn't have forgotten it?'

'Upon my word, I don't remember. I might have torn a bit off my linen.'

'That's very interesting. We might find in your lodgings tomorrow the shirt or whatever it is from which you tore the rag. What sort of rag was it, cloth or linen?'

'Goodness only knows what it was. Wait a bit . . . I believe I didn't tear it off anything. It was a bit of calico . . . I believe I sewed it up in a cap of my landlady's.'

'In your landlady's cap?'

'Yes. I took it from her.'

'How did you get it?'

'You see, I remember once taking a cap for a rag, perhaps to wipe my pen on. I took it without asking, because it was a worthless rag. I tore it up, and I took the notes and sewed them up in it. I believe it was in that very rag I sewed it. An old piece of calico, washed a thousand times.'

'And you remember that for certain now?'

'I don't know whether for certain. I think it was in the cap. But, hang it, what does it matter?'

'In that case your landlady will remember that the thing was lost?'

'No, she won't, she didn't miss it. It was an old rag, I tell you, an old rag not worth a penny.'

'And where did you get the needle and thread?'

'I'll stop now. I won't say any more. Enough of it!' said Mitya, losing his temper at last.

'It's strange that you should have so completely forgotten where you threw the pieces in the market place.'

'Give orders for the market place to be swept tomorrow, and perhaps you'll find it,' said Mitya sneering. 'Enough, gentlemen, enough!' he decided, in an exhausted voice. 'I see you don't believe me! Not for a moment! It's my fault, not yours. I ought not to have been so ready. Why, why did I degrade myself by confessing my secret to you? It's a joke to you. I see that from your eyes. You led me on to it, prosecutor! Sing a hymn of triumph if you can . . . Damn you, you torturers!'

He bent his head, and hid his face in his hands. The lawyers were silent. A minute later he raised his head and looked at them almost vacantly. His face expressed now complete, hopeless despair, and he sat mute and passive as though hardly conscious of what was happening. In the meantime they had to finish what they were about. They had immediately to begin examining the witnesses. It was by now eight o'clock in the morning. The lights had been extinguished long ago. Mihail Makarovitch and Kalganov, who had been continually in and out of the room all the while the interrogation had been going on, had now both gone out again. The lawyers, too, looked very tired. It was a wretched morning, the whole sky was overcast, and the rain streamed down in bucketfuls.

Mitya gazed blankly out of the window.

'May I look out of the window?' he asked Nikolay Parfenovitch, suddenly.

'Oh, as much as you like,' the latter replied.

Mitya got up and went to the window. The rain lashed against the little greenish panes of the window. He could see the muddy road just below the window, and farther away, in the rainy mist, a row of poor, black, dismal cabins, looking even blacker and poorer in the rain. Mitya thought of 'Phoebus the golden-haired', and how he had meant to shoot himself when the first ray illumined the sky. 'Perhaps it would be even better on a morning like this,' he thought with a smile, and suddenly, flinging his hand downward, he turned to his 'torturers'.

'Gentlemen,' he cried, 'I see that I am lost! But she? Tell me about her, I beseech you. Surely she need not be ruined with me? She's innocent, you know, she was out of her mind when she cried last night "it's all my fault!" She's done nothing, nothing! I've been grieving over her all night as I sat with you . . . Can't you, won't you tell me what you are going to do with her now?'

'You can set your mind quite at rest on that score, Dmitri Fyodorovitch,' the prosecutor answered at once, with evident alacrity. 'We have, so far, no grounds for interfering with the lady in whom you are so interested. I trust that it may be the same in the later development of the case . . . On the contrary, we'll do everything that lies in our power in that matter. Set your mind completely at rest.'

'Gentlemen, I thank you. I knew that you were honest, straightforward people in spite of everything. You've taken a load off my heart . . . Well, what are we to do now? I'm ready.'

'Well, we ought to make haste. We must pass to examining the witnesses without delay. That must be done in your presence and therefore . . . '

'Shouldn't we have some tea first?' interposed Nikolay Parfenovitch, 'I think we've deserved it!'

They decided that if tea were ready downstairs (Mihail Makarovitch had, no doubt, gone down to get some) they would have a glass and then 'go on and on', putting off their proper breakfast until a more favourable opportunity. Tea really was ready below, and was soon brought up. Mitya at first refused the glass that Nikolay Parfenovitch politely offered him, but afterwards he asked for it himself and drank it greedily. He looked surprisingly exhausted. It might have been supposed from his herculean strength that one night of carousing, even accompanied by the most violent emotions, could have had little effect on him. But he felt that he could hardly hold his head up, and from time to time all the objects about him seemed heaving and dancing before his eyes. 'A little more and I shall begin raving,' he said to himself.

7

The examination of the witnesses began. But we will not continue our story in such detail as before. And so we will not dwell on how Nikolay Parfenovitch impressed on every witness called that he must give evidence in accordance with truth and conscience, and that the witness would later have to repeat that evidence on oath, how every witness was called upon to sign the protocol of the evidence given, and so on. We will only note that the point principally insisted upon in the examination was the question of the three thousand roubles, that is, was the sum spent here, at Mokroe, by Mitya on the first occasion, a month before, three thousand or fifteen hundred? And again had he spent three thousand or fifteen hundred yesterday? Alas, all the evidence given by everyone turned out to be against Mitya. There was none in his favour, and some witnesses introduced new, overwhelming facts, in contradiction of his, Mitya's, story.

The first witness examined was Trifon Borissovitch. He was not in the least abashed as he stood before the lawyers. He had, on the contrary, an air of stern and severe indignation with the accused, which gave him an appearance of truthfulness and personal dignity. He spoke little, and with reserve, waited to be questioned, answered precisely and deliberately. Firmly and unhesitatingly he bore witness that the sum spent a month before could not have been less than three thousand, that all the peasants about here would testify that they had heard the sum of three thousand mentioned by Dmitri Fyodorovitch himself.

'The money he flung away on the gypsy girls alone. He wasted a thousand, I dare say, on them alone.'

'I don't believe I gave them five hundred,' was Mitya's gloomy comment on this. 'It's a pity I didn't count the money at the time, but I was drunk . . .'

Mitya was sitting sideways with his back to the curtains. He listened sullenly, with a melancholy and exhausted air, as though he would say: 'Oh, say what you like. It makes no difference now.'

'More than a thousand went on them, Dmitri Fyodorovitch,' retorted Trifon Borissovitch firmly. 'You flung it about at random and they picked it up. They were a rascally, thievish lot, horse-stealers, they've been driven away from here, or maybe they'd bear witness themselves how much they got from you. I saw the sum in your hands, myself – count it I didn't, you didn't let me, that's true enough – but by the look of it I should say it was far more than fifteen hundred . . . fifteen hundred, indeed! We've seen money too. We can judge of amount . . .'

As for the sum spent yesterday he asserted that Dmitri Fyodorovitch had told him, as soon as he arrived, that he had brought three thousand with him.

'Come now, is that so, Trifon Borissovitch?' replied Mitya. 'Surely I didn't declare so positively that I'd brought three thousand?'

'You did say so, Dmitri Fyodorovitch. You said it before Andrey. Andrey himself is still here. Send for him. And in the hall, when you were treating the chorus, you shouted straight out that you would leave your sixth thousand here – that is with what you spent before, we must say. Stepan and Semyon heard it, and Peter Fomitch Kalganov, too, was standing beside you at the time. Maybe he'd remember it . . .'

The evidence as to the 'sixth' thousand made an extraordinary impression on the two lawyers. They were delighted with this new mode of reckoning, three and three made six, three thousand then and three now made six, that was clear.

The Poles, too, were examined. Though they had gone to bed in their room, they had not slept all night, and on the arrival of the police officers they hastily dressed and got ready, realising that they would certainly be sent for. They gave their evidence with dignity, though not without some uneasiness. The little Pole turned out to be a retired official of the twelfth class, who had served in Siberia as a veterinary surgeon. His name was Mussyalovitch. Pan Vrublevsky turned out to be an uncertificated dentist. One piece of evidence given by the Poles roused special interest in the lawyers: that was how, in that very room, Mitya had tried to buy off Pan Mussyalovitch, and had offered him three thousand roubles to resign his claims, seven hundred roubles down, and the remaining two thousand three hundred 'to be paid next day in the town'. He had sworn at the time that he had not the whole sum with him at Mokroe, but that his money was in the town. Mitya observed hotly that he had not said that he would be sure to pay him the remainder next day in the town. But Pan Vrublevsky confirmed the statement, and Mitya, after thinking for a moment admitted, frowning, that it must have been as the Poles stated, that he had been excited at the time, and might indeed have said so.

The prosecutor really pounced on this piece of evidence. It seemed to establish for the prosecution (and they did, in fact, base this deduction on it) that half, or a part of, the three thousand that had come into

Mitya's hands might actually have been left somewhere hidden in the town, or even, perhaps, somewhere here, in Mokroe. This would explain the circumstance, so baffling for the prosecution, that only eight hundred roubles were to be found in Mitya's hands. This circumstance had been the one piece of evidence which, insignificant as it was, had hitherto told, to some extent, in Mitya's favour. Now this only bit of evidence in his favour had broken down. In answer to the prosecutor's enquiry, where he would have got the remaining two thousand three hundred roubles, since he himself had denied having more than fifteen hundred, Mitya confidently replied that he had meant to offer the 'little chap', not money, but a formal deed of conveyance of his rights to the village of Tchermashnya, those rights which he had already offered to Samsonov and Madame Hohlakov. The prosecutor smiled ironically at the 'innocence of this subterfuge'.

'And you imagine he would have accepted such a deed as a substitute for two thousand three hundred roubles in cash?'

'He certainly would have accepted it,' Mitya declared warmly. 'Why, look here, he might have grabbed not two thousand, but four or six, for it. He would have put his lawyers on to the job, and might have got, not three thousand, but the whole property out of the old man.'

The evidence of Pan Mussyalovitch was, of course, entered into the protocol in the fullest detail.

At last it was Grushenka's turn. Nikolay Parfenovitch was obviously apprehensive of the effect her appearance might have on Mitya, and he muttered a few words of admonition to him, but Mitya bowed his head in silence, giving him to understand 'that he would not make a scene'. Mihail Makarovitch, himself, led Grushenka in. She entered with a stern and gloomy face, that looked almost composed, and sat down quietly on the chair offered her by Nikolay Parfenovitch. She was very pale, she seemed to be cold, and wrapped herself closely in her magnificent black shawl. She was suffering from a slight feverish chill – the first symptom of the long illness which followed that night. Her grave air, her direct earnest look and quiet manner made a very favourable impression on everyone. Nikolay Parfenovitch was even a little bit 'fascinated'. He admitted himself, when talking about it afterwards, that only then had he seen 'how handsome the woman was', for, though he had seen her several times before, he had always looked upon her as something of a 'provincial hetaera'. 'She has the manners of the best society,' he said enthusiastically, gossiping about her in a circle of ladies. But this was received with definite indignation by the ladies, who immediately called him a 'naughty man', to his great satisfaction.

As she entered the room, Grushenka glanced for only an instant at Mitya, who looked at her uneasily. But her face reassured him at once. After the first inevitable enquiries and warnings, Nikolay Parfenovitch asked her, hesitating a little, maintaining the most courteous manner, on what terms she was with the retired lieutenant, Dmitri Fyodorovitch Karamazov. To this Grushenka firmly and quietly replied: 'He was an acquaintance. He came to see me as an acquaintance during the last month.' To further inquisitive questions she answered clearly and with complete frankness, that, though 'at times' she had thought him attractive, she had not loved him, but had won his heart as well as his old father's 'in my nasty spite', that she had seen that Mitya was very jealous of Fyodor Pavlovitch and everyone else; but that had only amused her. She had never meant to go to Fyodor Pavlovitch, she had simply been laughing at him. 'I had no thoughts for either of them all this last month. I was expecting another man who had wronged me. But I think,' she said in conclusion, 'that there's no need for you to enquire about that, nor for me to answer you, for that's my own affair.'

Nikolay Parfenovitch immediately dismissed the 'romantic' aspect of the case and passed to the serious one, concerning the three thousand roubles. Grushenka confirmed the statement that three thousand roubles had certainly been spent on the first carousal at Mokroe, and, though she had not counted the money herself, she had heard that it was three thousand from Dmitri Fyodorovitch's own lips.

'Did he tell you that alone, or before someone else, or did you only hear him speak of it to others in your presence?' the prosecutor enquired immediately.

To which Grushenka replied that she had heard him say so before other people, and had heard him say so when they were alone.

'Did he say it to you alone once, or several times?' enquired the prosecutor, and learned that he had told Grushenka so several times.

Ippolit Kirillovitch was very well satisfied with this piece of evidence. Further examination elicited that Grushenka knew, too, where that money had come from, and that Dmitri Fyodorovitch had got it from Katerina Ivanovna.

'And did you never, once, hear that the money spent a month ago was not three thousand, but less, and that

Dmitri Fyodorovitch had saved half that sum for his own use?'

'No, I never heard that,' answered Grushenka.

It was explained further that Mitya had, on the contrary, often told her that he hadn't a penny.

'He was always expecting to get some from his father,' said Grushenka in conclusion.

'Did he never say before you . . . casually, or in a moment of irritation,' Nikolay Parfenovitch put in suddenly, 'that he intended to make an attempt on his father's life?'

'Yes, he did say so,' sighed Grushenka.

'Once or several times?'

'He mentioned it several times, always in anger.'

'And did you believe he would do it?'

'No, I never believed it,' she answered firmly. 'I had faith in his noble heart.'

'Gentlemen, allow me,' cried Mitya suddenly, 'allow me to say one word to Agrafena Alexandrovna, in your presence.'

'You can speak,' Nikolay Parfenovitch assented.

'Agrafena Alexandrovna!' Mitya got up from his chair, 'have faith in God and in me. I am not guilty of my father's murder!'

Having uttered these words Mitya sat down again on his chair. Grushenka stood up and crossed herself devoutly before the icon.

'Thanks be to Thee, O Lord,' she said, in a voice vibrant with emotion, and still standing, she turned to Nikolay Parfenovitch and added: 'As he has spoken now, believe it! I know him. He'll say anything as a joke or from obstinacy, but he'll never deceive you against his conscience. He's telling the whole truth, you may believe it.'

'Thanks, Agrafena Alexandrovna, you've given me fresh courage,' Mitya responded in a trembling voice.

As to the money spent the previous day, she declared that she did not know what sum it was, but had heard him tell several people that he had three thousand with him. And to the question where he got the money, she said that he had told her that he had 'stolen' it from Katerina Ivanovna, and that she had replied to that that he hadn't stolen it, and that he must pay the money back next day. When the prosecutor asked her solemnly whether the money he said he had stolen from Katerina Ivanovna was what he had spent yesterday, or what he had squandered there a month ago, she declared that he meant the money spent a month ago, and that that was how she understood him.

Grushenka was at last released, and Nikolay Parfenovitch informed her impulsively that she might at once return to the town and that if he could be of any assistance to her, with horses for example, or if she would care for an escort he . . . would be . . .

'I thank you sincerely,' said Grushenka, bowing to him, 'I'm going with this old gentleman, I am driving him back to town with me, and meanwhile, if you'll allow me, I'll wait below to hear what you decide about Dmitri Fyodorovitch.'

She went out. Mitya was calm, and even looked more cheerful, but only for a moment. He felt more and more oppressed by a strange physical weakness. His eyes were closing with fatigue. The examination of the witnesses was, at last, over. They proceeded to a final revision of the protocol. Mitya got up, moved from his chair to the corner by the curtain, lay down on a large chest covered with a rug, and instantly fell asleep.

8

When the protocol had been signed, Nikolay Parfenovitch turned solemnly to the prisoner and read him the 'Committal', setting forth, that in such a year, on such a day, in such a place, the investigating lawyer of such-and-such a district court, having examined so-and-so (to wit, Mitya) accused of this and of that (all the charges were carefully written out) and having considered that the accused, not pleading guilty to the charges made against him, had brought forward nothing in his defence, while the witnesses, so-and-so, and so-and-so, and the circumstances such-and-such testify against him, acting in accordance with such-and-such articles of the Statute Book, and so on, has ruled, that, in order to preclude such-and-such (Mitya) from all means of evading pursuit and judgment he be detained in such-and-such a prison, which he hereby notifies to the accused and communicates a copy of this same 'Committal' to the deputy prosecutor, and so on, and so on.

In brief, Mitya was informed that he was, from that moment, a prisoner, and that he would be driven at once to the town, and there shut up in a very unpleasant place. Mitya listened attentively, and only shrugged his shoulders.

'Well, gentlemen, I don't blame you. I'm ready . . . I understand that there's nothing else for you to do.'

Nikolay Parfenovitch informed him gently that he would be escorted at once by the rural police officer, Mavriky Mavrikyevitch, who happened to be on the spot . . .

'Listen,' Mitya interrupted, suddenly, and impelled by uncontrollable emotion he pronounced, addressing all in the room: 'Gentlemen, we're all cruel, we're all monsters, we all make men weep, and mothers, and babes at the breast, but of all, let it be settled here, now, of all I am the lowest reptile! I've sworn to reform, and every day I've done the same filthy things. I understand now that such men as I need a jolt, a jolt from destiny to jerk them as with a noose, and bind them by a force from without. Never, never would I have risen of myself! But the thunderbolt has fallen. I accept the torture of accusation, and my public shame, I want to suffer and by suffering I shall be purified. Perhaps I shall be purified, gentlemen? But listen, for the last time, I am not guilty of my father's blood. I accept my punishment, not because I killed him, but because I meant to kill him, and perhaps I really might have killed him. Still I mean to fight it out with you, I warn you of that. I'll fight it out with you to the end, and then God will decide. Goodbye, gentlemen, don't be angry with me for having shouted at you during the examination. Oh, I was still such a fool then . . . In another minute I shall be a prisoner, but now, for the last time, as a free man, Dmitri Karamazov offers you his hand. Saying goodbye to you, I say it to all men.'

His voice trembled and he stretched out his hand, but Nikolay Parfenovitch, who happened to stand nearest to him, with a sudden, almost nervous movement, hid his hands behind his back. Mitya instantly noticed this, and started. He let his outstretched hand fall at once.

'The preliminary enquiry is not yet over,' Nikolay Parfenovitch faltered, somewhat embarrassed. 'We will continue it in the town, and I, for my part, of course, am ready to wish you all success . . . in your defence . . . As a matter of fact, Dmitri Fyodorovitch, I've always been disposed to regard you as, so to speak, more unfortunate than guilty. All of us here, if I may make bold to speak for all, we are all ready to recognise that you are, at bottom, a young man of honour, but, alas, one who has been carried away by certain passions to a somewhat excessive degree . . .'

'Gentlemen, you are good, you are humane, may I see *her* to say "goodbye" for the last time?' asked Mitya.

'Certainly, but considering . . . in fact, now it's impossible except in the presence of . . .'

'Oh, well, if it must be so, it must!'

Grushenka was brought in, but the farewell was brief, and of few words, and did not at all satisfy Nikolay Parfenovitch. Grushenka made a deep bow to Mitya.

'I have told you I am yours, and I will be yours. I will follow you for ever, wherever they may send you. Farewell; you are guiltless, though you've been your own undoing.'

Her lips quivered, tears flowed from her eyes.

'Forgive me, Grushenka, for my love, for ruining you, too, with my love.'

Mitya would have said something more, but he broke off and went out. He was at once surrounded by men who kept a constant watch on him. At the bottom of the steps to which he had driven up with such a show the day before with Andrey's three horses, two carts stood in readiness. Mavriky Mavrikyevitch, a sturdy, thickset man with a wrinkled face, was annoyed about something, some sudden irregularity. He was shouting angrily. He asked Mitya to get into the cart with somewhat excessive surliness.

'When I stood him drinks in the tavern, the man had quite a different face,' thought Mitya, as he got in. At the gates stood a crowd of people, peasants, women and drivers. Trifon Borissovitch came down the steps too. All stared at Mitya.

'Forgive me at parting, good people!' Mitya shouted suddenly from the cart.

'Forgive us too!' he heard two or three voices.

'Goodbye to you, too, Trifon Borissovitch!'

But Trifon Borissovitch did not even turn round. He was, perhaps, too busy. He too was shouting and fussing about something. It appeared that everything was not yet ready in the second cart, in which two constables were to accompany Mavriky Mavrikyevitch. The peasant who had been ordered to drive the second cart was pulling on his smock, stoutly maintaining that it was not his turn to go, but Akim's. But Akim was not to be seen. They ran to look for him. The peasant persisted and besought them to wait.

'But what do we want a second cart for?' Mitya put in. 'Let's start with the one, Mavriky Mavrikyevitch. I won't be unruly, I won't run away from you, old man. What do we want an escort for?'

'I'll trouble you, sir, to learn how to speak to me if you've never been taught. I'm not "old man" to you, and you can keep your advice for another time!' Mavriky Mavrikyevitch snapped out savagely, as though glad to vent his wrath.

Mitya was reduced to silence. He flushed all over. A moment later he felt suddenly very cold. The rain had ceased, but the dull sky was still overcast with clouds, and a keen wind was blowing straight in his face.

'I've taken a chill,' thought Mitya, twitching his shoulders.

At last Mavriky Mavrikyevitch, too, got into the cart, sat down heavily, and, as though without noticing it, squeezed Mitya into the corner. It is true that he was out of humour and greatly disliked the task that had been laid upon him.

'Goodbye, Trifon Borissovitch!' Mitya shouted again, and felt himself, that he had not called out this time from good nature, but involuntarily, from resentment.

But Trifon Borissovitch stood proudly, with both hands behind his back, and, staring straight at Mitya with a stern and angry face, he made no reply.

'Goodbye, Dmitri Fyodorovitch, goodbye!' he heard all at once the voice of Kalganov, who had suddenly darted out. Running up to the cart he held out his hand to Mitya. He had no cap on.

Mitya had time to seize and press his hand.

'Goodbye, dear fellow! I shan't forget your generosity,' he cried warmly.

But the cart moved and their hands parted. The bell on the harness began to tinkle and Mitya was driven off.

Book Nine

I

Alyosha went towards the cathedral square to the widow Morozov's house to see Grushenka, who had sent Fenya to him early in the morning with an urgent message begging him to come. Questioning Fenya, Alyosha learned that her mistress had been particularly distressed since the previous day. During the two months that had passed since Mitya's arrest, Alyosha had called frequently, both from his own inclination and to take messages for Mitya. Three days after Mitya's arrest, Grushenka was taken very ill and was ill for nearly five weeks. For one whole week she was unconscious. She was very much changed – thinner and a little sallow, though she had for the past fortnight been well enough to go out. But to Alyosha her face was even more attractive than before, and he liked to meet her eyes when he went in to her. A look of resolution and intelligent purpose had developed in her face. There were signs of spiritual transformation in her, and a steadfast, fine and humble determination that nothing could shake showed in her face. There was a small vertical line between her brows which gave her charming face a look of concentrated thought, almost austere at the first glance. There was scarcely a trace of her former frivolity.

It seemed strange to Alyosha, too, that in spite of the calamity that had overtaken the poor girl, betrothed to a man who had been arrested for a terrible crime, almost at the instant of their betrothal, in spite of her illness and the almost inevitable sentence hanging over Mitya, Grushenka had yet not lost her youthful cheerfulness. There was a soft light in the once proud eyes, though at times they gleamed with the old vindictive fire when she was visited by one disturbing thought stronger than ever in her heart. The object of that uneasiness was the same as ever – Katerina Ivanovna, of whom Grushenka had even raved when she lay in delirium. Alyosha knew that she was fearfully jealous of her. Yet Katerina Ivanovna had not once visited Mitya in his prison, though she might have done it whenever she liked. All this made a difficult problem for Alyosha, for he was the only person to whom Grushenka opened her heart.

Full of anxiety, he entered her lodging. She was at home. She had returned from visiting Mitya half an hour before, and from the rapid movement with which she rose from her chair to meet him he saw that she had been awaiting him with great impatience. A pack of cards dealt for a game of 'fools' lay on the table.

Grushenka saw scarcely anyone besides Alyosha, who did not come every day and never stayed long. Her old merchant lay seriously ill at this time, 'at his last gasp' as they said in the town, and he did, in fact, die a week after Mitya's trial. Three weeks before his death, feeling the end approaching, he made his sons, their wives and children, come upstairs to him at last and bade them not leave him again. From that moment he gave strict orders to his servants not to admit Grushenka and to tell her if she came, 'The master wishes you long life and happiness and tells you to forget him.' But Grushenka sent almost every day to enquire after him.

'You've come at last!' she cried, flinging down the

cards and joyfully greeting Alyosha. 'Ah, how I need you! Sit down to the table. What will you have – coffee?'

'Yes, please,' said Alyosha, sitting down at the table. 'I am very hungry.'

'That's right. Fenya, Fenya, coffee,' cried Grushenka. 'It's been made a long time all ready for you. And bring some little pies, and mind they are hot. Do you know, we had a row over a batch of pies today. I took them to the prison for him, and would you believe it, he threw them back at me: he would not eat them. He flung one of them on the floor and stamped on it. So I said to him: "I shall leave them with the warder; if you don't eat them before evening, it will be that your venomous spite is enough for you!" With that I went away. We quarrelled again, would you believe it? Whenever I go we quarrel.'

Grushenka said all this in one breath in her agitation.

'What did you quarrel about this time?' asked Alyosha.

'I didn't expect it in the least. Only fancy, he is jealous of the Pole. "Why are you keeping him?" he said. "So you've begun keeping him." He is jealous, jealous of me all the time, jealous eating and sleeping! He even took it into his head to be jealous of Kuzma last week.'

'But he knew about the Pole before?'

'Of course, but there it is. He has known about him from the very beginning, but today he suddenly stood up and began scolding about him. If only that Pole didn't exist, Alyosha. He's taken it into his head to fall ill, too, today. I went to see him. And now I shall send him some pies, too, on purpose. I hadn't sent him any, but Mitya accused me of sending some, so now I will send them. Ah, here's Fenya with a letter! Yes, it's from the Poles – begging again!'

Pan Mussyalovitch had indeed sent an extremely long and characteristically eloquent letter in which he begged her to lend him three roubles. In the letter was enclosed a receipt for the sum, with a promise to repay it within three months, signed by Pan Vrublevsky as well. Grushenka had received many such letters, accompanied by such receipts, from her former lover during the fortnight of her convalescence. But she knew that the two Poles had been to ask after her health during her illness. The first letter Grushenka got from them was a long one, written on large note paper and with a big family crest on the seal. It was so obscure and rhetorical that Grushenka put it down before she had read half, unable to make head or tail of it. She could not attend to letters then. The first letter was followed next day by another in which Pan Mussyalovitch begged her for a loan of two thousand roubles for a very short period. Grushenka left that letter, too, unanswered. A whole series of letters had followed – one every day – all as pompous and rhetorical, but the loan asked for, gradually diminishing, dropped to a hundred roubles, then to twenty-five, to ten, and finally Grushenka received a letter in which both the Poles begged her for only one rouble and included a receipt signed by both.

Then Grushenka suddenly felt sorry for them, and at dusk she went round herself to their lodgings. She found the two Poles in great poverty, almost destitute, without food or fuel, without cigarettes, in debt to their landlady. The two hundred roubles they had carried off from Mitya at Mokroe had soon disappeared. But Grushenka was surprised at their meeting her with arrogant dignity and self-assertion, with the greatest punctilio and pompous speeches. Grushenka simply laughed, and gave her former admirer ten roubles. Then, laughing, she told Mitya of it and he was not in the least jealous. But ever since, the Poles had attached themselves to Grushenka and bombarded her daily with requests for money and she had always sent them small sums. And now suddenly Mitya had taken it into his head to be fearfully jealous.

'Like a fool, I went round to him just for a minute, on the way to see Mitya, for he is ill, too, my Pole,' Grushenka began again with nervous haste. 'I laughed, telling Mitya about it. "Fancy," I said "my Pole had the happy thought to play the guitar and sing his old songs. He thought I would be touched and marry him!" Mitya jumped up swearing . . . So, there, I'll send them the pies! Fenya, is it that little girl they've sent? Here, give her three roubles and pack a dozen pies up in some paper and tell her to take them. And you, Alyosha, be sure to tell Mitya that I did send them the pies.'

'I wouldn't tell him for anything,' said Alyosha, smiling.

'O-oh! You think he is unhappy about it? Why, he's shamming to annoy me. He doesn't care,' said Grushenka bitterly.

'Shamming?' queried Alyosha.

'I tell you you are silly, Alyosha. You know nothing about such matters, for all your cleverness. I am not offended that he is jealous of a girl like me. I would be offended if he were not jealous. I am like that. I am not offended at jealousy. I have a fierce heart, too. I can be jealous myself. Only what offends me is that he doesn't love me at all. I tell you he is jealous now on *purpose*. Am I blind? Don't I see? He began talking to me just now of that woman, of Katerina, saying she was this and that, how she had ordered a doctor from Moscow for him, to try and save him; how she had ordered the best counsel, the most learned one too. So he loves her, if he'll praise her to my face, more shame to him! He's treated me badly himself, so he attacked me, to make out I am at fault first and to throw it all on me. "You were with your Pole before me, so I can't be blamed for Katerina," that's what it amounts to. He wants to throw the whole blame on me. He attacked me on purpose, on purpose, I tell you, but I'll . . .'

Grushenka could not finish saying what she had begun. She hid her eyes in her handkerchief and sobbed violently.

'He doesn't love Katerina Ivanovna,' said Alyosha firmly.

'Well, whether he loves her or not, I'll soon find out for myself,' said Grushenka, with a menacing note in her voice, taking the handkerchief from her eyes. Her face was distorted. Alyosha saw sorrowfully that from being mild and serene, it had become sullen and spiteful.

'Enough of this foolishness,' she said suddenly; 'it's not for that I sent for you. Alyosha, darling, tomorrow – what will happen tomorrow? That's what worries me! And it's only me it worries! I look at everyone and no one is thinking of it. No one cares about it. Are you thinking about it even? Tomorrow he'll be tried, you know. Tell me, how will he be tried? You know it's the valet, the valet killed him! Good heavens! Can they condemn him in place of the valet and will no one stand up for him? They haven't gone after the valet at all, have they?'

'He's been severely cross-examined,' observed

Alyosha thoughtfully; 'but everyone came to the conclusion it was not he. Now he is lying very ill. He has been ill ever since that attack. Really ill,' added Alyosha.

'Oh, dear! couldn't you go to that counsel yourself and tell him the whole thing yourself? He's been brought from Petersburg for three thousand roubles, they say.'

'We gave these three thousand together – Ivan, Katerina Ivanovna and I – but she paid two thousand for the doctor from Moscow herself. The counsel Fetyukovitch would have charged more, but the case has become known all over Russia; it's talked of in all the papers and journals. Fetyukovitch agreed to come more for the glory of the thing, because the case has become so notorious. I saw him yesterday.'

'Well? Did you talk to him?' Grushenka put in eagerly.

'He listened and said nothing. He told me that he had already formed his opinion. But he promised to give my words consideration.'

'Consideration! Ah, they are swindlers! They'll ruin him. And why did she send for the doctor?'

'As an expert. They want to prove that Mitya's mad and committed the murder when he didn't know what he was doing,' Alyosha smiled gently; 'but Mitya won't agree to that.'

'Yes; but that would be the truth if he had killed him!' cried Grushenka. 'He was mad then, perfectly mad, and that was my fault, wretch that I am! But, of course, he didn't do it, he didn't do it! And they are all against him, the whole town. Even Fenya's evidence went to prove he had done it. And the people at the shop, and that official, and at the tavern, too, before, people had heard him say so! They are all, all against him, all crying out against him.'

'Yes, there's a fearful accumulation of evidence,' Alyosha observed grimly.

'And Grigory – Grigory Vassilyevitch – sticks to his story that the door was open, persists that he saw it – there's no shaking him. I went and talked to him myself. He's rude about it too.'

'Yes, that's perhaps the strongest evidence against Mitya,' said Alyosha.

'And as for Mitya's being mad, he certainly seems to be crazy now,' Grushenka began with a peculiarly anxious and mysterious air. 'Do you know, Alyosha, I've been wanting to talk to you about it for a long time. It's his brother Ivan Fyodorovitch upsetting him. It's his going to see him, that's what it is,' Grushenka began, and suddenly broke off. Alyosha gazed at her in amazement.

'Ivan's going? Has he been to see him? Mitya told me himself that Ivan hasn't been once.'

'There . . . there! What a girl I am! Blurting things out!' exclaimed Grushenka, confused and suddenly blushing. 'Wait, Alyosha, hush! Since I've said so much I'll tell the whole truth – he's been to see him twice, the first time directly he arrived. He galloped here from Moscow at once, before I was taken ill; and the second time was a week ago. He told Mitya not to tell you about it, under any circumstances; and not to tell anyone, in fact. He came secretly.'

Alyosha sat plunged in thought, considering something. The news evidently impressed him.

'Ivan doesn't talk to me of Mitya's case,' he said slowly. 'He's said very little to me these last two months. And whenever I go to see him, he seems vexed at my coming, so I've not been to him for the last three weeks. Hm! . . . if he was there a week ago . . . there certainly has been a change in Mitya this week.'

'There has been a change,' Grushenka assented quickly.

'They have a secret, they have a secret! Mitya told me himself there was a secret, and such a secret that Mitya can't rest. Before then, he was cheerful – and, indeed, he is cheerful now – but when he shakes his head like that, you know, and strides about the room and keeps pulling at the hair on his right temple with his right hand, I know there is something on his mind worrying him . . . I know! He was cheerful before, though, indeed, he is cheerful today.'

'But you said he was worried.'

'Yes, he is worried and yet cheerful. He is irritable for a minute and then cheerful and then irritable again. And you know, Alyosha, he amazes me – with this awful thing hanging over him, he sometimes laughs at trifles as though he were a baby himself.'

'And did he really tell you not to tell me about Ivan? Did he say "don't tell him"?'

'Yes, he told me "don't tell him". It's you that Mitya's most afraid of. Because it's a secret: he said himself it was a secret. Alyosha, darling, go to him and find out what their secret is and come and tell me,' Grushenka besought him with sudden eagerness. 'Set my mind at rest that I may know the worst that's in store for me. That's why I sent for you.'

'You think it's something to do with you? If it were, he wouldn't have told you there was a secret.'

'I don't know. Perhaps he wants to tell me, but doesn't dare to. He warns me. There is a secret, he tells me, but he won't tell me what it is.'

'What do you think yourself?'

'What do I think? It's the end for me, that's what I think. They all three have been plotting my end, for Katerina's in it. It's all Katerina, it all comes from her. He is planning to throw me over, that's the whole secret. They've planned it together, the three of them – Mitya, Katerina, and Ivan Fyodorovitch. Alyosha, I've been wanting to ask you a long time. A week ago he suddenly told me that Ivan was in love with Katerina, because he often goes to see her. Did he tell me the truth or not? Tell me, on your conscience, tell me the worst.'

'I won't tell you a lie. Ivan is not in love with Katerina Ivanovna, I think.'

'Oh, that's what I thought! He is lying to me, shameless deceiver, that's what it is! And he was jealous of me just now, so as to put the blame on me afterwards. He is stupid, he can't disguise what he is doing; he is so guileless, you know . . . But I'll pay him back, I'll pay him back! "You believe I did it," he said. He said that to me, to me. He reproached me with that! God forgive him! You wait, I'll make it hot for Katerina at the trial! I'll just say a word then . . . I'll tell everything then!'

And again she wept bitterly.

'This I can tell you for certain, Grushenka,' Alyosha said, getting up. 'First, that he loves you, loves you more than anyone in the world, and you only, believe me. I know. I do know. The second thing is that I don't want to worm his secret out of him, but if he'll tell me of himself today, I shall tell him straight out that I have promised to tell you. Then I'll come to you today and tell you. Only . . . I fancy . . . Katerina Ivanovna has nothing to do with it, and that the secret is about something else. That's certain. It isn't likely it's about Katerina Ivanovna, it seems to me. Goodbye for now.'

Alyosha shook hands with her. Grushenka was still crying. He saw that she put little faith in his consolation, but she was better for having revealed her sorrow, for having spoken of it. He was sorry to leave her in such a state of mind, but he was in haste. He had still a great many things to do.

2

The first of these was a visit to the house of Madame Hohlakov, and he hurried there to get it over as quickly as possible and not to be too late for Mitya. Madame Hohlakov had been slightly ailing for the last three weeks: her foot had for some reason swollen up and though she was not in bed, she lay all day half-reclining on the couch in her boudoir. Lise had sent a maid to him the previous day, specially asking him to come to her 'about something very important', a request which, for certain reasons, interested Alyosha. But while the maid went to take his name in to Lise, Madame Hohlakov heard of his arrival from someone, and immediately sent to beg him to come to her 'just for one minute'. Alyosha reflected that it was better to accede to the mamma's request, or else she would send down to Lise's room every minute that he was there. Madame Hohlakov was lying on a couch. She was unusually well dressed and was evidently in a state of extreme nervous excitement. She greeted Alyosha with cries of rapture.

'It's ages, ages, perfect ages since I've seen you! It's

a whole week – only think of it! Ah, but you were here only four days ago, on Wednesday. You have come to see Lise. I'm sure you meant to slip into her room on tiptoe, without my hearing you. My dear, dear Alexey Fyodorovitch, if you only knew how worried I am about her! But of that later, though that's the most important thing, of that later. Dear Alexey Fyodorovitch, I trust you implicitly with my Lise. Since the death of Father Zossima – God rest his soul!' (she crossed herself) ' – I look upon you as a monk, though you look charming in your new suit. Where did you find such a tailor in these parts? No, no, that's not the chief thing – of that later. Forgive me for sometimes calling you Alyosha; an old woman like me may take liberties,' she smiled coquettishly; 'but that will do later too. The important thing is that I shouldn't forget what is important. Please remind me of it yourself. As soon as my tongue runs away with me, you just say "the important thing?" Oh dear! how do I know now what is of most importance? Ever since Lise took back her promise – her childish promise, Alexey Fyodorovitch – to marry you, you've realised, of course, that it was only the playful fancy of a sick child who had been so long confined to her chair – thank God, she can walk now! . . . that new doctor Katya sent for from Moscow for your unhappy brother, who will tomorrow . . . But why speak of tomorrow? I am ready to die at the very thought of tomorrow. Ready to die of curiosity . . . That doctor was with us yesterday and saw Lise . . . I paid him fifty roubles for the visit. But that's not the point, that's not the point again. You see, I'm mixing everything up. I am in such a hurry. Why am I in a hurry? I don't understand. It's awful how I seem unable to understand anything these days.

Everything seems mixed up in a sort of tangle. I am afraid you are so bored you will jump up and run away, and that will be all I shall see of you. Goodness! Why are we sitting here and no coffee? Julia, Glafira, coffee!'

Alyosha made haste to thank her, and said that he had only just had coffee.

'Where?'

'At Agrafena Alexandrovna's.'

'At . . . that woman's? Ah, it's she has brought ruin on everyone. I know nothing about it though. They say she has become a saint, though it's rather late in the day. She had better have done it before. What use is it now? Now be quiet, Alexey Fyodorovitch, for I have so much to say to you that I am afraid I shall tell you nothing. This awful trial . . . I shall certainly go, I am making arrangements. I shall be carried there in my chair; besides I can sit up. I shall have people with me. And, you know, I am a witness. How shall I speak, how shall I speak? I don't know what I shall say. One has to take an oath, hasn't one?'

'Yes; but I don't think you will be able to go.'

'I can sit up. Ah, you put me out; Ah! this trial, this savage act, and then they are all going to Siberia, some are getting married, and all this so quickly, so quickly, everything's changing, and at last – nothing. All grow old and have death to look forward to. Well, so be it! I am weary. This Katya, *cette charmante personne*, has disappointed all my hopes. Now she is going to follow one of your brothers to Siberia, and your other brother is going to follow her, and will live in the nearest town, and they will all torment one another. It drives me out of my mind. Worst of all – the publicity. The story has been told a million times over in all the papers in Moscow and Petersburg. Ah! yes, would you believe it, there's a paragraph that I was a "dear friend" of your brother's – I can't repeat the horrid word. Just fancy, just fancy!'

'Impossible! Where was the paragraph? What did it say?'

'I'll show you directly. I got the paper and read it yesterday. Here, in the Petersburg paper *Gossip*. The paper began coming out this year. I am awfully fond of gossip, and I take it in, and now it drags me in – this is what gossip comes to! Here it is, here, this passage. Read it.'

And she handed Alyosha a sheet of newspaper which had been under her pillow.

Alyosha was well aware that the story of the terrible case had spread all over Russia. And, good heavens! what wild rumours about his brother, about the Karamazovs, and about himself he had read in the course of the past two months, among other equally credible items. One paper had even stated that he had gone into a monastery and become a monk, in horror at his brother's crime. Another contradicted this, and stated that he and his elder, Father Zossima, had broken into the monastery chest and 'made tracks from the monastery'. The present paragraph in the paper *Gossip* was brief, and Madame Hohlakov was not directly mentioned in it. No names appeared, in fact. It was merely stated that the criminal, whose approaching trial was making such a sensation – retired army captain, an idle swaggerer, and reactionary bully – was continually involved in amorous intrigues, and particularly popular with certain ladies 'who were pining in solitude'. One such lady, a pining widow, who tried to seem young though she had a grown-up daughter, was so fascinated by him that only two hours before the crime she offered him three thousand roubles, on condition that he would elope with her to the gold mines. But the criminal, counting on escaping punishment, had preferred to murder his father to get the three thousand, rather than go off to Siberia with the middle-aged charms of his pining lady. This playful paragraph finished, of course, with an outburst of generous indignation at the wickedness of parricide and at the lately abolished institution of serfdom. Reading it with curiosity, Alyosha folded up the paper and handed it back to Madame Hohlakov.

'Well, that must be me,' she hurried on again. 'Of course I am meant. Scarcely more than an hour before, I suggested gold mines to him, and here they talk of "middle-aged charms" as though that were my motive!'

'It's very important for me to be in time to see my brother today,' Alyosha faltered.

'To be sure, to be sure! You bring it all back to me. Listen, what is an aberration?'

'What aberration?' asked Alyosha, wondering.

'In the legal sense. An aberration in which everything is pardonable. Whatever you do, you will be acquitted at once.'

'What do you mean?'

'I'll tell you. This Katya . . . Ah! she is a charming, charming creature, only I never can make out who it is she is in love with. She was with me some time ago and I couldn't get anything out of her. Especially as she won't talk to me except on the surface now. She is always talking about my health and nothing else, and she takes such a tone with me too. I simply said to myself, "Well, so be it. I don't care" . . . Oh, yes. I was talking of aberration. This doctor has come. You know a doctor has come? Of course you know it – the one who discovers madmen. You wrote for him. No, it wasn't you, but Katya. It's all Katya's doing. Well, you see, a man may be perfectly sane and suddenly have an aberration. He may be conscious and know what he is doing and yet be in a state of aberration. And there's no doubt that Dmitri Fyodorovitch was suffering from aberration. They found out about aberration as soon as the law courts were reformed. It's all the good effect of the reformed law courts. The doctor has been here and questioned me about that evening, about the gold mines. "How did he seem then?" he asked me. He must have been in a state of aberration. He came in shouting, "Money, money, three thousand! Give me three thousand!" and then went away and immediately did the murder. "I don't want to murder him," he said, and he suddenly went and murdered him. That's why they'll acquit him, because he struggled against it and yet he murdered him.'

'But he didn't murder him,' Alyosha interrupted rather sharply. He felt more and more sick with anxiety and impatience.

'Yes, I know it was that old man Grigory murdered him.'

'Grigory?' cried Alyosha.

'Yes, yes; it was Grigory. He fell as Dmitri Fyodorvitch struck him down, and then got up, saw the door open, went in and killed Fyodor Pavlovitch.'

'But why, why?'

'Suffering from aberration. When he recovered from the blow Dmitri Fyodorovitch gave him on the head, he was suffering from aberration: he went and committed the murder. As for his saying he didn't, he very likely doesn't remember. Only, you know, it'll be better, ever so much better, if Dmitri Fyodorovitch murdered him. And that's how it must have been, though I say it was Grigory. It certainly was Dmitri Fyodorovitch, and that's better, ever so much better! Oh! not better that a son should have killed his father, I don't defend that. Children ought to honour their parents, and yet it would be better if it were he, as you'd have nothing to cry over then, for he did it when he was unconscious or rather when he was conscious, but did not know what he was doing. Let them acquit him – that's so humane, and would show what a blessing reformed law courts are. I knew nothing about it, but they say they have been so a long time. And when I heard it yesterday, I was so struck by it that I wanted to send for you at once. And if he is acquitted, make him come straight from the law courts to dinner with me, and I'll have a party of friends, and we'll drink to the reformed law courts. I don't believe he'd be dangerous; besides, I'll invite a great many friends, so that he can always be led out if he does anything. And then he might be made a justice of the peace or something in another town, for those who have been in trouble themselves make the best judges. And, besides, who isn't suffering from aberration, nowadays? – you, I, all of us are in a state of aberration, and there are ever so many examples of it: a man sits singing a song, suddenly something annoys him, he takes a pistol and shoots the first person he comes across, and no one blames him for it. I read that lately, and all the doctors confirm it. The doctors are always confirming; they confirm anything. Why, my Lise is in a state of aberration. She made me cry again yesterday, and the day before, too, and today I suddenly realised that it's all due to aberration. Oh, Lise grieves me so! I believe she's quite mad. Why did she send for you? Did she send for you or did you come of yourself?'

'Yes, she sent for me, and I am just going to her.' Alyosha got up resolutely.

'Oh, my dear, Alexey Fyodorovitch, perhaps that's what's most important,' Madame Hohlakov cried, suddenly bursting into tears. 'God knows I trust Lise to you with all my heart, and it's no matter her sending for you on the sly, without telling her mother. But forgive me, I can't trust my daughter so easily to your brother Ivan Fyodorovitch, though I still consider him the most chivalrous young man. But only fancy, he's been to see Lise and I knew nothing about it!'

'How? What? When?' Alyosha was exceedingly surprised. He had not sat down again and listened standing.

'I will tell you, that's perhaps why I asked you to come, for I don't know now why I did ask you to come. Well, Ivan Fyodorovitch has been to see me twice, since he came back from Moscow. First time he came as a friend to call on me, and the second time Katya was here and he came because he heard she was here. I didn't, of course, expect him to come often, knowing what a lot he has to do as it is, you understand, this affair and the terrible death of your father. But I suddenly heard he'd been here again, not to see me but to see Lise. That's six days ago now. He came, stayed five minutes, and went away. And I didn't hear of it till three days afterwards, from Glafira, so it was a great shock to me. I sent for Lise directly. She laughed. "He thought you were asleep," she said, "and came in to me to ask after your health." Of course, that's how it happened. But Lise, Lise, mercy on us, how she distresses me! Would you believe it, one night, four days ago, just after you saw her last time, and had gone away, she suddenly had a fit, screaming, shrieking, hysterics! Why is it I never have hysterics? Then, next day another fit and the same thing on the third, and yesterday too, and then yesterday that aberration. She suddenly screamed out, "I hate Ivan Fyodorovitch. I insist on your never letting him come to the house again." I was struck dumb at these amazing words, and answered, "On what grounds could I refuse to see such an excellent young man, a young man of such learning too, and so unfortunate," for all this business is a misfortune, isn't it? She suddenly burst out laughing at my words, and so rudely, you know. Well, I was pleased, I thought I had amused her and the fit would pass off, especially as I wanted to refuse to see Ivan Fyodorovitch anyway on account of his strange visits without my knowledge, and meant to ask him for an explanation. But early this morning Lise waked and flew into a passion with Julia and, would you believe it, slapped her in the face. That's monstrous, I am always polite to my servants. And an hour later she was hugging Julia's feet and kissing them. She sent a message to me, that she wasn't coming to me at all, and would never come and see me again, and when I dragged myself down to her, she rushed to kiss me, crying, and as she kissed me, she pushed me out of the room without saying a word, so I couldn't find out what was the matter. Now, dear Alexey Fyodorovitch, I rest all my hopes on you, and, of course, my whole life is in your hands. I simply beg you to go to Lise and find out everything from her, as you alone can, and come back and tell me – me, her mother, for you understand it will be the death of me, simply the death of me, if this goes on, or else I shall run away. I can stand no more. I have patience; but I may lose patience, and then . . . Where are you off to, Alexey Fyodorovitch?'

'To Lise.'

'Oh, yes. You won't forget, you won't forget what I asked you? It's a question of life and death!'

'Of course, I won't forget, if I can . . . but I am so late', muttered Alyosha, beating a hasty retreat.

'No, be sure, be sure to come in; don't say "if you can." I shall die if you don't,' Madame Hohlakov called after him, but Alyosha had already left the room.

3

Going in to Lise, he found her half reclining in the invalid chair, in which she had been wheeled when she was unable to walk. She did not move to meet him, but her sharp keen eyes were riveted on his face. There was a feverish look in her eyes, her face was pale and sallow. Alyosha was amazed at the change that had taken place in her in three days. She was much thinner. She did not hold out her hand to him. He touched the slim long fingers which lay motionless on her dress, then he sat down facing her, without a word.

'I know you are in a hurry to get to the prison,' Lise said curtly, 'and mamma's kept you there for hours. She's just been telling you about me and Julia.'

'How do you know?' asked Alyosha.

'I've been listening. Why do you stare at me? I want to listen and I do listen, there's no harm in that. I don't apologise.'

'You are upset about something?'

'On the contrary, I am very happy. I've only just been reflecting for the thirtieth time what a good thing it is I refused you and shall not be your wife. You are not fit to be a husband. If I were to marry you and give you a note to take to the man I loved after you, you'd take it and be sure to give it to him and bring an answer back too. If you were forty, you would still go on taking my love letters for me.'

She suddenly laughed.

'There is something spiteful and yet open-hearted about you,' Alyosha smiled to her.

'The open-heartedness consists in my not being ashamed of myself with you. What's more, I don't want to feel ashamed with you, just with you. Alyosha, why is it I don't respect you? I am very fond of you, but I don't respect you. If I respected you, I shouldn't talk to you without shame, should I?'

'No.'

'But do you believe that I am not ashamed with you?'

'No, I don't believe it.'

Lise laughed nervously again; she spoke rapidly.

'I sent your brother, Dmitri Fyodorovitch, some candy to the prison. Alyosha, you know, you are quite handsome! I shall love you always for having so quickly allowed me not to love you.'

'Why did you send for me today, Lise?'

'I wanted to tell you of a longing I have. I should like someone to torture me, marry me and then torture me, deceive me and go away. I don't want to be happy.'

'You are in love with disorder?'

'Yes, I want disorder. I keep wanting to set fire to the house. I keep imagining how I'll creep up and set fire to the house on the sly, it must be on the sly. They'll try to put it out, but it'll go on burning. And I shall know and say nothing. Ah, what silliness! And how bored I am!' She waved her hand with a look of repulsion.

'It's your luxurious life,' said Alyosha, softly.

'Is it better then to be poor?'

'Yes, it is better.'

'That's what your monk taught you. That's not true. Let me be rich and all the rest be poor, I'll eat candies and drink cream and not give any to anyone else. Oh, don't speak, don't say anything,' she shook her hand at him, though Alyosha had not opened his mouth. 'You've told me all that before, I know it all by heart. It bores me. If I am ever poor, I shall murder somebody, and even if I am rich, I may murder someone, perhaps – one must do something! But do you know, I should like to reap, cut the rye? I'll marry you, and you shall become a peasant, a real peasant; we'll keep a colt, shall we? Do you know Kalganov?'

'Yes.'

'He is always wandering about, dreaming. He says, why live in real life, it's better to dream. One can dream the most delightful things, but real life is a bore. But he'll be married soon for all that, he's been making love to me already. Can you spin tops?'

'Yes.'

'Well, he's just like a top: he wants to be wound up and set spinning and then to be lashed, lashed, lashed with a whip. If I marry him, I'll keep him spinning all his life. You are not ashamed to be with me?'

'No.'

'You are annoyed, because I don't talk about holy things. I don't want to be holy. What will they do to me in the next world for the greatest sin? You must know all about that.'

'God will censure you.' Alyosha was watching her steadily.

'That's just what I should like. I would go up and they would censure me and I would burst out laughing in their faces. I should dreadfully like to set fire to the house, Alyosha, to our house; you still don't believe me?'

'Why not? There are children of twelve years who have a longing to set fire to something and they do set things on fire too. It's a sort of disease.'

'That's not true, that's not true, there may be children, but that's not what I mean.'

'You take evil for good; it's a passing crisis, it's the result of your illness, perhaps.'

'You do despise me though! It's simply that I don't want to do good, I want to do evil, and it has nothing to do with illness.'

'Why do evil?'

'So that everything may be destroyed. Ah, how wonderful it would be if everything were destroyed! You know, Alyosha, I sometimes think of doing a fearful lot of harm and everything bad, and doing it for a long while on the sly and then suddenly everyone would find it out. Everyone would stand round and point their fingers at me and I would look back at them all. That would be wonderful. Why would it be so wonderful, Alyosha?'

'I don't know. It's a craving to destroy something good or, as you say, to set fire to something. It happens sometimes.'

'I not only talk about it, I shall do it.'

'I believe you.'

'Ah, how I love you for saying you believe me. And you are not lying one little bit. But perhaps you think that I am saying all this on purpose to annoy you?'

'No, I don't think that . . . though perhaps there is some desire to do that, too, in what you say.'

'There is a little. I never can tell lies to you,' she declared, with a strange light in her eyes.

What struck Alyosha above everything was her earnestness. There was not a trace of humour or jesting in her face now, though, in old days, fun and gaiety never deserted her even at her most 'earnest' moments.

'There are moments when people love crime,' said Alyosha thoughtfully.

'Yes, yes! You have uttered my thought, they love crime, everyone loves crime, they love it always, not just "sometimes". You know, it's as though people have made an agreement to lie about this love of crime and have lied about it ever since. They all declare that they hate evil, but secretly they all love it.'

'And are you still reading nasty books?'

'Yes, I am. Mamma reads them and hides them under her pillow and I steal them.'

'Aren't you ashamed to destroy yourself?'

'I want to destroy myself. Listen, your brother is being tried now for murdering his father and everyone loves his having killed his father.'

'Loves his having killed his father?'

'Yes, loves it, everyone loves it! Everybody says it's so awful, but secretly they simply love it. I for one love it.'

'There is some truth in what you say about everyone,' said Alyosha softly.

'Oh, what ideas you have!' Lise shrieked in delight. 'And you a monk too! You wouldn't believe how I respect you, Alyosha, for never telling lies. Oh, I must tell you a funny dream of mine. I sometimes dream of devils. It's night, I am in my room with a candle and suddenly there are devils all over the place, in all the corners, under the table, and they open the doors, there's a crowd of them behind the doors and they want to come and seize me. And they are just coming, just seizing me. But I suddenly cross myself and they all draw back, though they don't go away altogether, they stand at the doors and in the corners, waiting. And suddenly I have a frightful longing to revile God aloud, and so I begin, and then they come crowding back to me, delighted, and seize me again and I cross myself again and they all draw back. It's awful fun, it takes one's breath away.'

'I've had the same dream too,' said Alyosha suddenly.

'Really?' cried Lise, surprised. 'Listen, Alyosha, don't laugh, that's awfully important. Could two different people have the same dream?'

'It seems they can.'

'Alyosha, I tell you, it's awfully important,' Lise went on, with intense amazement. 'It's not the dream that's important, but your having the same dream that I have. You never lie to me, don't lie now: is it true? You are not joking?'

'It's true.'

Lise seemed extraordinarily impressed and for half a minute she was silent.

'Alyosha, come and see me, come and see me more often,' she said suddenly, in a pleading voice.

'I'll always come to see you, all my life,' answered Alyosha firmly.

'Do you know, Alyosha, do you know, I should like . . . Alyosha, save me!' she suddenly jumped from the couch, rushed to him and seized him with both hands. 'Save me!' she almost groaned. 'Is there anyone in the world I could tell what I've told you? I've told you the truth, the truth. I shall kill myself, because I loathe everything! I don't want to live, because I loathe everything! I loathe everything, everything. Alyosha, why don't you love me in the least?' she finished in a frenzy.

'But I do love you!' answered Alyosha warmly.

'And will you weep over me, will you?'

'Yes.'

'Not because I won't be your wife, but simply weep for me?'

'Yes.'

'Thank you! It's only your tears I want. Everyone else may crucify me and trample me underfoot, everyone, everyone, not excepting *anyone*. For I don't love anyone. Do you hear, not anyone! On the contrary, I hate everyone! Go, Alyosha, it's time you went to your brother,' she tore herself away from him suddenly.

'How can I leave you like this?' said Alyosha, alarmed.

'Go to your brother, the prison will be closed, go, here's your hat. Give my love to Mitya, go, go!'

And she almost forcibly pushed Alyosha out of the door. He looked at her with pained surprise, when he was suddenly aware of a letter in his right hand, a tiny letter folded up tight and sealed. He glanced at it and instantly read the address 'to Ivan Fyodorovitch Karamazov'. He looked quickly at Lise. Her face had become almost menacing.

'Give it to him, you must give it to him!' she ordered him, trembling and beside herself. 'Today, at once, or I'll poison myself! That's why I sent for you.'

And she slammed the door quickly. The bolt clicked. Alyosha put the note in his pocket and went straight downstairs, without going back to Madame Hohlakov, forgetting her, in fact. As soon as Alyosha had gone, Lise unbolted the door, opened it a little, put her finger in the crack and slammed the door with all her might, pinching her finger. Ten seconds after, releasing her finger, she walked softly, slowly to her chair, sat up straight in it and looked intently at her blackened finger and at the blood that oozed from under the nail. Her lips were quivering and she kept whispering rapidly to herself: 'I am wicked, wicked, wicked, wicked!'

4

It was quite late (days are short in November) when Alyosha rang the bell at the prison gate. It was beginning to grow dark. But Alyosha knew that he would be admitted to see Mitya without difficulty. Such matters were arranged in our little town, as everywhere else. At first, of course, when the preliminary enquiry was finished, relatives and a few other persons could only obtain interviews with Mitya by going through certain inevitable formalities. But later, though the formalities were not relaxed, exceptions were made for some, at least, of Mitya's visitors. So much so, that sometimes the interviews with the prisoner in the room set aside for the purpose were practically tête-à-tête.

These exceptions, however, were few in number; only Grushenka, Alyosha and Rakitin had this privilege.

When Mitya was summoned from his cell, he always went downstairs, to the place set aside for interviews. As Alyosha entered the room he came upon Rakitin, who was just taking leave of Mitya.

They were both talking loudly. Mitya was laughing heartily as he saw him out, while Rakitin seemed grumbling. Rakitin did not like meeting Alyosha, especially of late. He scarcely spoke to him, and bowed to him stiffly. Seeing Alyosha enter now, he frowned and looked away, as though he was entirely absorbed in buttoning his big, warm, fur-trimmed overcoat. Then he began looking at once for his umbrella.

'I must remember not to forget my belongings,' he muttered, simply to say something.

'Mind you, don't forget other people's belongings,' said Mitya, as a joke, and laughed at once at his own wit. Rakitin fired up instantly.

'You'd better give that advice to your own family, who've always been a slave-driving lot, and not to Rakitin,' he cried, suddenly trembling with anger.

'What's the matter? I was joking,' cried Mitya. 'Damn it all! They are all like that,' he turned to Alyosha, nodding towards Rakitin's hurriedly retreating figure. 'He was sitting here, laughing and cheerful, and all at once he boils up like that. He didn't even nod to you. Have you broken with him completely? Why are you so late? I've not only been waiting, but thirsting for you the whole morning. But never mind. We'll make up for it now. Well, Alexey, it's all over for me now.'

He sat down on the bench and made Alyosha sit down beside him.

'Yes, the trial's tomorrow. Are you so hopeless, brother?' Alyosha said, with an apprehensive feeling.

'What are you talking about?' said Mitya, looking at him rather uncertainly. 'Oh, you mean the trial! Damn it all! Till now we've been talking of things that don't matter, about this trial, but I haven't said a word to you about the chief thing. Yes, the trial is tomorrow;

but it wasn't the trial I meant, when I said it was all over with me. Why do you look at me so critically?'

'What do you mean, Mitya?'

'Ideas, ideas, that's all! Ethics! What is ethics?'

'Ethics?' asked Alyosha, wondering.

'Yes; is it a science?'

'Yes, there is such a science . . . but . . . I confess I can't explain to you what sort of science it is.'

'Rakitin knows. Rakitin knows a lot, damn him! He's not going to be a monk. He means to go to Petersburg. There he'll go in for criticism on a high level. Who knows, he may even do some good and make himself a career in the bargain. Well! they are experts, these people, at making a career! Damn ethics. I am done for, Alexey, I am, you man of God!'

He walked across the room with a harassed air.

'Brother, I cannot stay long,' Alyosha said, after a pause. 'Tomorrow will be a great and awful day for you, the judgment of God will be accomplished . . . I am amazed at you, you walk about here, talking of I don't know what . . . '

'No, don't be amazed at me,' Mitya broke in warmly. 'Am I to talk of that stinking dog? Of the murderer? We've talked enough of him. I don't want to say more of the stinking son of Stinking Lizaveta! God will kill him, you will see. Hush!'

He went up to Alyosha excitedly and kissed him. His eyes glowed.

'Rakitin wouldn't understand it,' he began in a sort of exaltation; 'but you, you'll understand it all. That's why I longed for you. You see, there's so much I've been wanting to tell you for ever so long, here, within these peeling walls, but I haven't said a word about what matters most; the moment never seems to have come. Now I can wait no longer. I must pour out my heart to you. Brother, these last two months I've found in myself a new man. A new man has risen up in me. He was hidden in me, but would never have come to the surface, if it hadn't been for this blow from heaven. I am afraid! And what do I care if I spend twenty years in the mines, breaking out ore with a hammer? I am not a bit afraid of that – it's something else I am afraid of now: that that new man may leave me. Even there, in the mines, underground, I may find a human heart in another convict and murderer by my side, and I may make friends with him, for even there one may live and love and suffer. One may thaw and revive a frozen heart in that convict, one may wait upon him for years, and at last bring up from the dark depths a lofty soul, a sentient, suffering creature; one may bring forth an angel, create a hero! There are so many of them, hundreds of them, and we are all to blame for them. I will suffer for all, because someone must suffer for all. I didn't kill father, but I have to suffer. I accept that. It's all come to me here, here, within these peeling walls. There are numbers of them there, hundreds of them underground, with hammers in their hands. Oh, yes, we shall be in chains and there will be no freedom, but then, in our great sorrow, we shall rise again to joy, without which man cannot live nor God exist, for God gives joy: it's His privilege – a magnificent one. Ah, man should be purified in prayer! What would I be underground there without God? Rakitin's laughing! If they drive God from the earth, we shall shelter Him underground. One cannot exist in prison without God; it's even more impossible than out of prison. And then we men underground will sing from the bowels of the earth a glorious hymn to God, with Whom is joy. Hail to God and His joy! I love Him!'

Mitya was almost gasping for breath as he uttered his wild speech. He turned pale, his lips quivered, and tears rolled down his cheeks.

'Yes, life is full, there is life even underground,' he began again. 'You wouldn't believe, Alexey, how I want to live now, what a thirst for existence and consciousness has sprung up in me within these peeling walls. Rakitin doesn't understand that; all he cares about is building a house and renting apartments. But I've been waiting, so that I could talk with you. And what is suffering? I am not afraid of it, even if it were beyond reckoning. I am not afraid of it now. I was afraid of it before. Do you know, perhaps I won't answer at the trial at all . . . And I seem to have such strength in me now, that I think I could stand anything, any suffering, only to be able to say and to repeat to myself every moment, "I exist." In thousands of agonies – I exist. I'm tormented on the rack – but I exist! Though I stand alone on the scaffold – I exist! I see the sun, and if I don't see the sun, I know it's there. And there's a whole life in that, in knowing that the sun is there. Alyosha, my angel, all these philosophies are the death of me. Damn them! Brother Ivan . . .'

'What did he say?' Alyosha took it up quickly.

'I said to him, "Then everything is lawful, if it is so?" He frowned. "Fyodor Pavlovitch, our papa," he said, "was a pig, but his ideas were right enough." That was what he dropped. That was all he said. That was going one better than Rakitin.'

'Yes,' Alyosha assented bitterly. 'When was he with you?'

'Of that later, now I must speak of something else. I

have said nothing about Ivan to you before. I put it off to the last. When my business here is over and the verdict has been given, then I'll tell you something. I'll tell you everything. We've something tremendous on hand . . . And you shall be my judge in it. But don't begin about that now; be silent. You talk of tomorrow, of the trial; but, would you believe it, I know nothing about it.'

'Have you talked to the counsel?'

'What's the use of the counsel? I told him all about it. He's a smooth, city-bred rogue! But he doesn't believe me – not a bit of it. Only imagine, he believes I did it. I see it. "In that case," I asked him, "why have you come to defend me?" To hell with them all! They've brought a doctor down, too; they want to prove I'm mad. I won't have that! Katerina Ivanovna wants to do her "duty" to the end, whatever the cost!' Mitya smiled bitterly. 'The hellcat! Hard-hearted creature! She knows that I said of her at Mokroe that she was a woman of "great wrath". They repeated it. Yes, the facts against me have been numerous as the sands of the sea. Grigory sticks to his point. Grigory's honest, but a fool. Many people are honest because they are fools: that's Rakitin's idea. Grigory's my enemy. And there are some people who are better as foes than friends. I mean Katerina Ivanovna. I am afraid, oh, I am afraid she will tell how she bowed to the ground after that four thousand. She'll pay it back to the last farthing. I don't want her sacrifice; they'll put me to shame at the trial. I wonder how I can stand it. Go to her, Alyosha, ask her not to speak of that in the court, can't you? But damn it all, it doesn't matter! I shall get through somehow. I don't pity her. It's her own doing. She deserves what she gets. I shall have my own story to tell, Alexey.'

He smiled bitterly again. 'Only . . . only Grushenka, Grushenka! Good Lord! Why should she have such suffering to bear?' he exclaimed suddenly, with tears. 'Grushenka's killing me; the thought of her's killing me, killing me. She was with me just now . . . '

'She told me she was very much grieved by you today.'

'I know. Confound my temper! It was jealousy. I was sorry, I kissed her when she was leaving. I didn't ask her forgiveness.'

'Why didn't you?' exclaimed Alyosha.

Suddenly Mitya laughed almost gaily.

'God preserve you, my dear boy, from ever asking forgiveness for a fault from a woman you love. From one you love especially, however greatly you may have been in fault. For women are hell to understand, yet I really do know something about them. Just try admitting to a woman that you are at fault. Say "I'm sorry, forgive me," and a torrent of reproaches will follow. Nothing will make her forgive you in a simple, straightforward way. Oh, no, she will make you crawl, she will reproach you with things that never happened, recall everything, forget nothing, add something of her own, and only then forgive you. And even the best, the best of them do it. She'll scrape up all the scrapings and load them on your head. They are ready to flay you alive, I tell you, every one of them, all these angels without whom we cannot live! I tell you frankly, dear boy, every decent man ought to be under some woman's thumb. That's my conviction – not conviction, but feeling. A man ought to be magnanimous, and it's no disgrace to a man! No disgrace to a hero, not even a Caesar! But don't ever beg her pardon, never. Remember that rule given you by your brother Mitya, who's come to ruin through women. No, I'd better make it up to Grushenka somehow, without asking her forgiveness. I worship her, Alyosha, worship her. Only she doesn't see it. No, she still thinks I don't love her enough. And she tortures me, tortures me with her love. The past was nothing! In the past it was only those damned curves of hers that tortured me, but now I've taken all her soul into my soul and through her I've become a man myself. Will they consent to marry us? If they don't, I shall die of jealousy. I imagine something every day . . . What did she say to you about me?'

Alyosha related everything Grushenka had said to him that day. Mitya listened, made him repeat things, and seemed pleased.

'Then she is not angry at my being jealous?' he exclaimed. 'She is a fine woman! "I've a fierce heart myself!" Ah, I love such fierce hearts, though I can't bear anyone's being jealous of me. I can't endure it. We shall fight. But I shall love her, I shall love her infinitely. Will they marry us? Do they let convicts marry? That's the question. And without her I can't exist . . .'

Mitya walked frowning across the room. It was almost dark. He suddenly seemed terribly worried.

'So there's a secret, she says, a secret? We have got up a plot against her, and Katya is mixed up in it, she thinks. No, my good Grushenka, that's not it. You are very wide of the mark, in your foolish feminine way. Alyosha, darling, well, here goes! I'll tell you our secret!'

He looked round, went up quickly to Alyosha, who was standing before him, and whispered to him with an air of mystery, though no one could hear them: the old warder was dozing in the corner, and not a word could reach the ears of the soldiers on guard.

'I will tell you of our secret,' Mitya whispered hurriedly. 'I meant to tell you later, for how could I decide on anything without you? You are everything to me. Though I say that Ivan is superior to us, you are my good angel. It's your decision that will decide everything. Perhaps it's you that is superior and not Ivan. You see, it's a question of conscience, a question of the higher conscience – the secret is so important that I can't settle it myself, and I've put it off till I could speak to you. But anyway it's too early to decide now, for we must wait for the verdict. As soon as the verdict is given, you shall decide my fate. Don't decide it now. I'll tell you now. You listen, but don't decide. Just keep quiet. I won't tell you everything. I'll only tell you the idea, without details, and you keep quiet. Not a question, not a gesture. You agree? But, goodness, what shall I do with your eyes? I'm afraid your eyes will tell me your decision, even if you don't speak. Oh! I'm afraid! Alyosha, listen! Ivan suggests my *escaping*. I won't tell you the details; it's all been thought out; it can all be arranged. Hush, don't decide. I could go to America with Grushenka. You know I can't live without Grushenka! But what if they won't let her follow me to Siberia? Do they let convicts get married? Ivan thinks not. And without Grushenka, what would I do there underground with a pick? I should only smash my skull with the pick! On the other hand, my conscience? I should have run away from suffering. A sign has come, I reject the sign. I have a way of salvation and I turn my back on it. Ivan says that in America, "with good will", I can be of more use than underground. But what becomes of our hymn from underground? What's America? America is vanity again! And there's a lot of swindling in America, too, I expect. I would have run away from crucifixion! I tell you, you know, Alexey, because you are the only person who can understand this. There's no one else. It's folly, madness to others. They'll say I'm out of my mind or a fool. I am not out of my mind and I am not a fool. Ivan understands, only he doesn't believe. Don't speak, don't speak. I see how you look! You have already decided. Don't decide, spare me! I can't live without Grushenka. Wait till after the trial!'

Mitya ended his tirade tense and exalted. He held Alyosha with both hands on his shoulders, and his yearning, feverish eyes were fixed on his brother's.

'They don't permit convicts to marry, do they?' he repeated for the third time in a supplicating voice.

Alyosha listened with extreme surprise and was deeply moved.

'Tell me one thing,' he said, 'is Ivan very keen on it, and whose idea was it?'

'His, his, and he is very keen on it. He didn't come to see me at first, then he suddenly came a week ago and he began about it straight away. He is quite set on it. He doesn't ask me, but orders me to escape. He doesn't doubt that I will obey him, though I showed him all my heart as I have to you. He told me he'd arrange it; he's found out about everything. But of that later. He's simply set on it. It's all a matter of money: he'll pay ten thousand for escape and give me twenty thousand for America. And he says we can arrange a magnificent escape for ten thousand.'

'And he told you on no account to tell me?' Alyosha asked again.

'To tell no one, and especially not you; on no account to tell you. He is afraid, no doubt, that you'll stand before me as my conscience. Don't tell him I told you. Don't tell him, for heaven's sake.'

'You are right,' Alyosha pronounced; 'it's impossible to decide anything before the trial is over. After the trial you'll decide of yourself. Then you'll find that new man in yourself and he will decide. But, brother, have you no hope then of being acquitted?'

Mitya shrugged his shoulders nervously and shook his head.

'Alyosha, darling, it's time you were going,' he said, with sudden urgency. 'There's the superintendent shouting in the yard. He'll be here directly. We are late; it's irregular. Embrace me quickly. Kiss me! Make the sign of the cross over me, dear brother, for the cross I have to bear tomorrow.'

They embraced and kissed.

'Ivan,' said Mitya suddenly, 'suggests my escaping; but, of course, he believes I did it.'

A mournful smile came on to his lips.

'Have you asked him whether he believes it?' asked Alyosha.

'No, I haven't. I wanted to, but I couldn't. I hadn't the courage. But I saw it in his eyes. Well, goodbye!'

Once more they kissed hurriedly, and Alyosha was just going out, when Mitya suddenly called him back.

'Stand facing me! That's right!' And again he seized Alyosha, putting both hands on his shoulders. His face became suddenly quite pale, so that it was quite noticeable, even in the gathering darkness. His lips twitched, his eyes fastened upon Alyosha.

'Alyosha, tell me the whole truth, as you would before God. Do you believe I did it? Do you, do you in yourself, believe it? The whole truth, don't lie!' he cried desperately.

The whole room seemed to swim before Alyosha, and he felt something like a stab at his heart.

'What do you mean?' he faltered helplessly.

'The whole truth, the whole, don't lie!' repeated Mitya.

'I've never for one instant believed that you were the murderer!' broke in a shaking voice from Alyosha's lips, and he raised his right hand in the air, as though calling God to witness his words.

Mitya's whole face lighted up with happiness.

'Thank you!' he articulated slowly, as though letting a sigh escape him. 'Now you have given me new life. Would you believe it, till this moment I've been afraid to ask you, you, even you. Well go! You've given me strength for tomorrow. God bless you! Come, go along! Love Ivan!' was Mitya's last word.

Alyosha went out with tears in his eyes. Mitya's lack of confidence even in him, in Alyosha, suddenly opened before Alyosha an unsuspected depth of hopeless grief and despair in the soul of his unhappy brother. Intense, infinite compassion overwhelmed him instantly. There was a poignant ache in his torn heart. 'Love Ivan' – he suddenly recalled Mitya's words. And he was going to Ivan. He had badly wanted to see Ivan all day. He was as much worried about Ivan as about Mitya, and more than ever now.

5

On the way to Ivan he had to pass the house where Katerina Ivanovna lived. The windows were lighted up. He stopped suddenly and decided to go in. He had not seen Katerina Ivanovna for more than a week. But now it struck him that Ivan might be with her, especially on the eve of the terrible day. Ringing, and mounting the staircase, dimly lighted by a Chinese lantern, he saw a man coming down, and as they met, he recognised him as his brother. So he was just coming from Katerina Ivanovna.

'Ah, it's only you,' said Ivan dryly. 'Well, goodbye! You are going to her?'

'Yes.'

'I don't advise you to; she's upset and you'll upset her more.'

A door was instantly flung open above, and a voice cried suddenly: 'No, no! Alexey Fyodorovitch, have you come from him?'

'Yes, I have been with him.'

'Has he sent me any message? Come up, Alyosha, and you, Ivan Fyodorovitch, you must come back, you must. Do you hear?'

There was such a peremptory note in Katya's voice that Ivan, after a moment's hesitation, made up his mind to go back with Alyosha.

'She was listening,' he murmured angrily to himself, but Alyosha heard it.

'Excuse my keeping my topcoat on,' said Ivan, entering the drawing-room. 'I won't sit down. I won't stay more than a minute.'

'Sit down, Alexey Fyodorovitch,' said Katerina Ivanovna, though she remained standing. She had changed very little during this time, but there was an ominous gleam in her dark eyes. Alyosha remembered afterwards that she looked particularly handsome at that moment.

'What did he ask you to tell me?'

'Only one thing,' said Alyosha, looking her straight in the eyes, 'that you would spare yourself and say nothing at the trial of what (he was a little confused) . . . passed between you . . . at the time of your first acquaintance . . . in that town.'

'Ah! that I bowed down to the ground for that money!' She broke into a bitter laugh. 'Why? Is he afraid for me or for himself? He asks me to spare – whom? Him or myself? Tell me, Alexey Fyodorovitch!'

Alyosha watched her intently, trying to understand her.

'Both yourself and him,' he answered softly.

'I am glad to hear it,' she snapped out maliciously, and she suddenly blushed.

'You don't know me yet, Alexey Fyodorovitch,' she said menacingly. 'And I don't know myself yet. Perhaps you'll want to trample me underfoot after my examination tomorrow.'

'You will give your evidence honourably,' said Alyosha; 'that's all that's needed.'

'Women are often dishonourable,' she muttered. 'Only an hour ago I was thinking I felt afraid to touch that monster . . . as though he were a reptile . . . but no, he is still a human being to me! But did he do it? Is he the murderer?' she cried, all of a sudden, hysterically, turning quickly to Ivan. Alyosha saw at once that she had asked Ivan that question before, perhaps only a moment before he came in, and not for the first time, but for the hundredth, and that they had ended by quarrelling.

'I've been to see Smerdyakov . . . It was you, you who persuaded me that he murdered his father. It's only you I believed!' she continued, still addressing Ivan. He gave her a sort of strained smile. Alyosha was shocked at her tone. He had not suspected such intimacy between them.

'Well, that's enough, anyway,' Ivan cut short the conversation. 'I am going. I'll come tomorrow.' And turning at once, he walked out of the room and went straight downstairs.

With an imperious gesture Katerina Ivanovna seized Alyosha by both hands.

'Follow him! Overtake him! Don't leave him alone for a minute!' she said, in a hurried whisper. 'He's mad! Don't you know that he's mad? He is in a fever, nervous fever. The doctor told me so. Go, run after him . . . '

Alyosha jumped up and ran after Ivan, who was not fifty paces ahead of him.

'What do you want?' He turned quickly on his brother, when he saw Alyosha. 'She told you to follow me, because I'm mad. I know it all by heart,' he added irritably.

'She is mistaken, of course; but she is right that you are sick,' said Alyosha. 'I was looking at your face just now. You look very ill, Ivan.'

Ivan walked on without stopping. Alyosha followed him.

'And do you know, Alyosha, how people do go crazy?' Ivan asked in a voice suddenly quiet, without a trace of irritation, with a note of simple curiosity.

'No, I don't. I suppose there are all kinds of insanity.'

'And can one observe that one's going mad oneself?'

'I imagine one can't see oneself clearly in such circumstances,' Alyosha answered with surprise.

Ivan paused for half a minute.

'If you want to talk to me, please change the subject,' he said suddenly.

'Oh, while I think of it, I have a letter for you,' said Alyosha timidly, and he took Lise's note from his pocket and held it out to Ivan. They were right under a street light. Ivan recognised the handwriting at once.

'Ah, from that little devil!' he laughed maliciously, and, without opening the envelope, he tore it into bits and threw it in the air. The bits were scattered by the wind.

'She's not sixteen yet, I believe, and already offering herself,' he said contemptuously, striding along the street again.

'How do you mean, offering herself?' exclaimed Alyosha.

'As wanton women offer themselves, to be sure.'

'How can you, Ivan, how can you?' Alyosha cried warmly in a grieved voice. 'She is a child; you are insulting a child! She is ill; she is very ill, too. She is on the verge of insanity, too, perhaps . . . I had hoped to hear something from you . . . that would save her.'

'You'll hear nothing from me. If she is a child, I am not her nurse. Be quiet, Alexey. Don't talk about her. I am not even thinking about it.'

They were silent again for a moment.

'She will be praying all night now to the Mother of God to show her how to act tomorrow at the trial,' he said sharply and angrily again.

'You . . . you mean Katerina Ivanovna?'

'Yes. Whether she's to save Mitya or ruin him. She'll pray for light from above. She can't make up her mind for herself, you see. She has not had time to decide yet. She takes me for her nurse too. She wants me to sing lullabies to her.'

'Katerina Ivanovna loves you, brother,' said Alyosha sadly.

'Perhaps; but I am not interested in her.'

'She is suffering. Why do you . . . sometimes say things to her that give her hope?' Alyosha went on, with timid reproach. 'I know that you've given her hope. Forgive me for speaking to you like this,' he added.

'I can't behave with her as I should – break off altogether and tell her so straight out,' said Ivan, irritably. 'I must wait till sentence is passed on the murderer. If I break off with her now, she will avenge herself on me by ruining that scoundrel tomorrow at the trial, for she hates him and knows she hates him. It's all a lie – lie upon lie! As long as I don't break off with her, she goes on hoping, and she won't ruin that monster, knowing how I want to get him out of trouble. If only that damned verdict would come!'

The words 'murderer' and 'monster' echoed painfully in Alyosha's heart.

'But how can she ruin Mitya?' he asked, pondering on Ivan's words. 'What evidence can she give that would ruin Mitya?'

'You don't know that yet. She's got a document in her hands, in Mitya's own writing, that proves conclusively that he did murder Fyodor Pavlovitch.'

'That's impossible!' cried Alyosha.

'Why is it impossible? I've read it myself.'

'There can't be such a document!' Alyosha repeated warmly. 'There can't be, because he's not the murderer. It's not he murdered father, not he!'

Ivan suddenly stopped.

'Who is the murderer then, according to you?' he asked, with apparent coldness. There was even a supercilious note in his voice.

'You know who,' Alyosha pronounced in a low, penetrating voice.

'Who? You mean the myth about that crazy idiot, the epileptic, Smerdyakov?'

Alyosha suddenly felt himself trembling all over.

'You know who,' broke helplessly from him. He could scarcely breathe.

'Who? Who?' Ivan cried almost fiercely. All his restraint suddenly vanished.

'I only know one thing,' Alyosha went on, still almost in a whisper, '*it wasn't you* killed father.'

'Not you! What do you mean by "not you"?' Ivan was thunderstruck.

'It was not you killed father, not you!' Alyosha repeated firmly.

The silence lasted for half a minute.

'I know I didn't. Are you raving?' said Ivan, with a pale, distorted smile. His eyes were riveted on Alyosha. They were standing again under a street lamp.

'No, Ivan. You've told yourself several times that you are the murderer.'

'When did I say so? I was in Moscow . . . When have I said so?' Ivan faltered helplessly.

'You've said so to yourself many times, when you've been alone during these two dreadful months,' Alyosha went on softly and distinctly as before. Yet he was speaking now, as it were, not of his own will, but as though obeying some irresistible command. 'You have accused yourself and have confessed to yourself that you are the murderer and no one else. But you didn't do it: you are mistaken: you are not the murderer. Do you hear? It was not you! God has sent me to tell you so.'

They were both silent. The silence lasted a long minute. They were both standing quite still, gazing into each other's eyes. They were both pale. Suddenly Ivan began trembling all over, and clutched Alyosha's shoulder.

'You've been in my room!' he whispered hoarsely. 'You've been there at night, when he came . . . Confess . . . have you seen him?'

'Whom do you mean – Mitya?' Alyosha asked, bewildered.

'Not him, damn the monster!' Ivan shouted, in a frenzy. 'Do you know that he visits me? How did you find out? Speak!'

'Who is *he*? I don't know whom you are talking about,' Alyosha faltered, beginning to be alarmed.

'Yes, you do know . . . or how could you . . . ? It's impossible that you don't know.'

Suddenly he seemed to check himself. He stood still and seemed to reflect. A strange grin contorted his lips.

'Brother,' Alyosha began again, in a shaking voice, 'I have said this to you, because you'll believe my word, I know that. I tell you once and for all, it's not you. You hear, once for all! God has put it into my heart to say this to you, even though it may make you hate me from this hour.'

But by now Ivan had apparently regained his self-control.

'Alyosha,' he said, with a cold smile, 'I can't endure

prophets and epileptics – messengers from God especially – and you know that only too well. I sever all relations with you from this moment and probably for ever. I beg you to leave me at this corner. It's the way to your lodgings too. You'd better be particularly careful not to come to me today! Do you hear?'

He turned and walked on with a firm step, not looking back.

'Brother,' Alyosha called after him, 'if anything happens to you today, turn to me first of all!'

But Ivan made no reply. Alyosha stood under the street lamp at the crossroads till Ivan had vanished into the darkness. Then he turned and walked slowly homewards. Both Alyosha and Ivan were living in lodgings; neither of them was willing to live in Fyodor Pavlovitch's empty house. Alyosha had a furnished room in the house of some working people. Ivan lived some distance from him. He had taken a roomy and fairly comfortable cottage attached to a fine house that belonged to a well-to-do lady, the widow of an official. But his only attendant was a deaf and rheumatic old crone who went to bed at six o'clock every evening and got up at six in the morning. Ivan had grown remarkably indifferent to his comforts of late, and very fond of being alone. He did everything for himself in the one room he lived in, and rarely entered any of the other rooms in his abode.

He reached the gate of the house and had his hand on the bell, when he suddenly stopped. He felt that he was trembling all over with anger. Suddenly he let go of the bell, turned back with a curse, and walked with rapid steps in the opposite direction. He walked a mile and a half to a tiny, crooked, wooden house, almost a hut, where Marya Kondratyevna, the neighbour who used to come to Fyodor Pavlovitch's kitchen for soup and to whom Smerdyakov had once sung his songs and played on the guitar, was now living. She had sold her little house, and now lived here with her mother. Smerdyakov, who was ill – almost dying – had been with them ever since Fyodor Pavlovitch's death. It was to him Ivan was going now, drawn by a sudden and irresistible impulse.

6

This would be the third time that Ivan had been to see Smerdyakov since his return from Moscow. The first time he had seen him and talked to him was on the first day of his arrival, then he had visited him once more, a fortnight later. But his visits had ended with that second one, so that it was now over a month since he had seen Smerdyakov. And he had scarcely heard anything of him.

Ivan had returned five days after his father's death, so that he was not present at the funeral, which took place the day before he came back. The cause of his delay was that Alyosha, not knowing his Moscow address, had to apply to Katerina Ivanovna to telegraph to him, and she, not knowing his address either, telegraphed to her sister and aunt, reckoning on Ivan's going to see them as soon as he arrived in Moscow. But he did not go to them till four days after his arrival. When he got the telegram, he had, of course, set off posthaste to our town. The first to meet him was Alyosha, and Ivan was greatly surprised to find that in opposition to the general opinion of the town, he refused to entertain a suspicion against Mitya, and spoke openly of Smerdyakov as the murderer. Later on, after seeing the police captain and the prosecutor, and hearing the details of the charge and the arrest, he was still more surprised at Alyosha, and ascribed his opinion only to his exaggerated brotherly affection and sympathy with Mitya, of whom Alyosha, as Ivan knew, was very fond.

By the way, let us say a word or two of Ivan's sentiment for his brother Dmitri. He positively disliked him; at most, felt sometimes a compassion for him, and even that was mixed with great contempt, almost repugnance. Mitya's whole personality, even his appearance, was extremely unattractive to him. Ivan looked with indignation on Katerina Ivanovna's love for his brother. Yet he went to see Mitya on the first day of his arrival, and that interview, far from shaking Ivan's belief in his guilt, positively strengthened it. He found his brother agitated, nervously excited. Mitya had been talkative, but very absent-minded and incoherent. He used violent language, accused Smerdyakov, and was fearfully muddled. He talked principally about the three thousand roubles, which he said had been 'stolen' from him by his father.

'The money was mine, it was my money,' Mitya kept repeating. 'Even if I had stolen it, I would have had the right.'

He hardly contested the evidence against him, and if he tried to turn a fact to his advantage, it was in an absurd and incoherent way. He hardly seemed to wish to defend himself to Ivan or anyone else. Quite the contrary, he was angry and proudly scornful of the charges against him; he was continually flaring up and abusing everyone. He only laughed contemptuously at

Grigory's evidence about the open door, and declared that it was 'the devil who opened it'. But he could not bring forward any coherent explanation of the fact. He even succeeded in insulting Ivan during their first interview, telling him sharply that it was not for people who declared that 'everything was lawful' to suspect and question him. Altogether he was anything but friendly with Ivan on that occasion. Immediately after that interview with Mitya, Ivan went for the first time to see Smerdyakov.

In the railway train on his way from Moscow, he kept thinking of Smerdyakov and of his last conversation with him on the evening before he went away. Many things seemed to him puzzling and suspicious. But when he gave his evidence to the investigating lawyer Ivan said nothing, for the time, of that conversation. He put that off till he had seen Smerdyakov, who was in the hospital at the time.

Dr Herzenstube and Varvinsky, the doctor he met in the hospital, confidently asserted in reply to Ivan's persistent questions, that Smerdyakov's epileptic attack was unmistakably genuine, and were quite surprised at Ivan's asking whether he might not have been shamming on the day of the catastrophe. They gave him to understand that the attack was an exceptional one, the fits persisting and recurring several times, so that the patient's life was actually in danger, and it was only now, after they had applied remedies, that they could assert with confidence that the patient would survive. 'Though it might well be,' added Dr Herzenstube, 'that his reason may be impaired for a considerable period, if not permanently.' On Ivan's asking impatiently whether that meant that he was now mad, they told him that this was not yet the case, in the full sense of the word, but that certain abnormalities were perceptible. Ivan decided to find out for himself what those abnormalities were.

At the hospital he was at once allowed to see the patient. Smerdyakov was lying on a cot in a separate ward. There was only one other bed in the room, and in it lay a tradesman of the town, swollen with dropsy, who was obviously near death; he could be no hindrance to their conversation. Smerdyakov grinned uncertainly on seeing Ivan, and for the first instant seemed nervous. So at least Ivan fancied. But that was only momentary. For the rest of the time he was struck, on the contrary, by Smerdyakov's composure. From the first glance Ivan had no doubt that he was very ill. He was very weak; he spoke slowly, seeming to move his tongue with difficulty; he was much thinner and more sallow. Throughout the interview, which lasted twenty minutes, he kept complaining of headache and of pain in all his limbs. His thin emasculate face seemed to have become so tiny; his hair was ruffled, and his crest of curls in front stood up in a thin tuft. But in the left eye, which was screwed up and seemed to be insinuating something, Smerdyakov showed himself unchanged. 'A word to the wise is always sufficient.' Ivan was reminded of that at once. He sat down on the stool at his feet. Smerdyakov, with painful effort, shifted his position in bed, but he was not the first to speak. He remained silent, and did not even look much interested.

'Can you talk to me?' asked Ivan. 'I won't tire you.'

'Certainly I can,' mumbled Smerdyakov, in a faint voice.

'Has your honour been back long?' he added patronisingly, as though encouraging a nervous visitor.

'I only arrived today . . . To see the mess you are in here.'

Smerdyakov sighed.

'Why do you sigh, you knew of it all along?' Ivan blurted out. Smerdyakov was stolidly silent for a while.

'How could I help knowing? It was clear beforehand. But how could I tell it would turn out like that?'

'What would turn out? Don't prevaricate! You'd foretold you'd have a fit; on the way down to the cellar, you know. You mentioned the very spot.'

'Have you said so at the enquiry yet?' Smerdyakov queried with composure.

Ivan felt suddenly angry.

'No. I haven't yet, but I certainly shall. You must explain a great deal to me, my man, and let me tell you, I am not going to let you play with me!'

'Why should I play with you, when I put my whole trust in you, as in God Almighty?' said Smerdyakov, with the same composure, only for a moment closing his eyes.

'In the first place,' began Ivan. 'I know that epileptic fits can't be foretold beforehand. I've enquired; don't try and take me in. You can't foretell the day and the hour. How was it you told me the day and the hour beforehand, and about the cellar too? How could you tell that you would fall down the cellar stairs in a fit, if you didn't sham a fit on purpose?'

'I had to go to the cellar anyway, several times a day, indeed,' Smerdaykov drawled deliberately. 'I fell from the garret just in the same way a year ago. It's quite true you can't foretell the day and hour of a fit beforehand, but you can always have a presentiment of it.'

'But you did foretell the day and the hour!'

'In regard to my epilepsy, sir, you had much better enquire of the doctors here. You can ask them whether it was a real fit or a sham; it's no use my saying any more about it.'

'And the cellar? How could you know beforehand of the cellar?'

'You don't seem able to get over that cellar! As I was going down to the cellar, I was in terrible dread and doubt. What frightened me most was losing you and being left without defence in all the world. So I went down into the cellar thinking, "Here it'll come on directly, it'll strike me down directly, shall I fall?" And it was through this fear that I suddenly felt the spasm that always comes . . . and so I fell headlong. All that and all my previous conversation with you at the gate the evening before when I told you how frightened I was and spoke of the cellar, I told all that to Dr Herzenstube and Nikolay Parfenovitch, the investigating lawyer, and it's all been written down in the protocol. And the doctor here, Mr Varvinsky, maintained to all of them that it was just the thought of it brought it on, the apprehension that I might fall. It was just then that the fit seized me. And so they've written it down, that it's just how it must have happened, simply from fear.'

As he finished, Smerdyakov drew a deep breath, as though exhausted.

'Then you have said all that in your evidence?' said Ivan, somewhat taken aback. He had meant to frighten him with the threat of repeating their conversation, and it appeared that Smerdyakov had already reported it all himself.

'What have I to be afraid of? Let them write down the whole truth,' Smerdyakov pronounced firmly.

'And have you told them every word of our conversation at the gate?'

'No, not to say every word.'

'And did you tell them that you can sham fits, as you boasted then?'

'No, I didn't tell them that either.'

'Tell me now, why did you send me then to Tchermashnya?'

'I was afraid you'd go away to Moscow, Tchermashnya is nearer, anyway.'

'You are lying, you suggested my going away yourself; you told me to get out of the way of trouble.'

'That was simply out of affection and my sincere devotion to you, foreseeing trouble in the house, to spare you. Only I wanted to spare myself even more. That's why I told you to get out of harm's way, that you might understand that there would be trouble in the house, and would remain at home to protect your father.'

'You might have said it more directly, you blockhead!' Ivan suddenly flared up.

'How could I have said it more directly then? It was simply my fear that made me speak, and you might have been angry, too. I might well have been apprehensive that Dmitri Fyodorovitch would make a scene and carry away that money, for he considered it as good as his own, but who could tell that it would end in a murder like this? I thought that he would only carry off the three thousand that lay under the master's mattress in the envelope, and you see, he's murdered him. How could you guess it either, sir?'

'But if you say yourself that it couldn't be guessed, how could I have guessed and stayed at home? You contradict yourself!' said Ivan, pondering.

'You might have guessed from my sending you to Tchermashnya and not to Moscow.'

'How could I guess it from that?'

Smerdyakov seemed much exhausted, and again he was silent for a minute.

'You might have guessed from the fact of my asking you not to go to Moscow, but to Tchermashnya, that I wanted to have you nearer, for Moscow's a long way off, and Dmitri Fyodorovitch, knowing you not far off, would not be so bold. And if anything had happened, you might have come to protect me, too, for I warned you of Grigory Vassilyevitch's illness, and that I was afraid of having a fit. And when I explained those knocks to you, by means of which one could go in to the deceased, and that Dmitri Fyodorovitch knew them all through me, I thought that you would guess yourself that he would be sure to do something, and so wouldn't go to Tchermashnya even, but would stay.'

'He talks very coherently,' thought Ivan, 'though he does mumble; what's the derangement of his faculties that Herzenstube talked of?'

'You are being tricky with me, damn you,' he exclaimed, getting angry.

'But I thought at the time that you quite guessed,' Smerdyakov parried with the most innocent expression.

'If I'd guessed, I would have stayed,' cried Ivan.

'Why, I thought that it was because you guessed that you went away in such a hurry, just to get out of trouble, just to run away and save yourself in your fright.'

'You think that everyone is as great a coward as yourself?'

'Forgive me, I thought you were like me.'

'Of course, I ought to have guessed,' Ivan said with

agitation, 'and I did guess there you were planning some mischief . . . only you are lying, you are lying again,' he cried, suddenly recollecting. 'Do you remember how you went up to the carriage and said to me, "A word to the wise is sufficient"? So you were glad I went away, since you praised me?'

Smerdyakov sighed again and again. A trace of colour came into his face.

'If I was pleased,' he articulated rather breathlessly, 'it was simply because you agreed not to go to Moscow, but to Tchermashnya. For it was nearer, anyway. Only when I said those words to you, it was not by way of praise, but of reproach. You didn't understand it.'

'What reproach?'

'Why, that foreseeing such a calamity you deserted your own father, and would not protect us, for I might have been arrested any time for stealing that three thousand.'

'Damn you!' Ivan swore again. 'Did you tell the prosecutor and the investigating lawyer about those knocks?'

'I told them everything just as it was.'

Ivan wondered inwardly again.

'If I thought of anything then,' he began again, 'it was solely of some wickedness on your part. Mitya might kill him, but that he would steal – I did not believe that then . . . But I was prepared for any wickedness from you. You told me yourself you could sham a fit. What did you say that for?'

'That was my foolishness. I never have shammed a fit on purpose in my life. And I only said so then to boast to you. It was just foolishness. I liked you so much then, and was open-hearted with you.'

'My brother accuses you of the murder and theft.'

'What else is left for him to do?' said Smerdyakov, with a bitter smile. 'And who will believe him with all the proofs against him? Grigory Vassilyevitch saw the door open. What can he say after that? But never mind him! He is frantic to save himself.'

He slowly ceased speaking, and suddenly, as though on reflection, added: 'And look here again. He wants to throw the blame on me and make out that it is the work of my hands – I've heard that already. But as to my being clever at shamming a fit: would I have told you beforehand that I could sham one, if I really had had such a design against your father? If I had been planning such a murder, would I have been such a fool as to give such evidence against myself beforehand? And to his son too! Upon my word! Is that likely? As if that could be, such a thing has never happened. No one hears this talk of ours now, except Providence itself, and if you were to tell of it to the prosecutor and Nikolay Parfenovitch you might defend me completely by doing so, for who would be likely to be such a criminal, if he is open-hearted beforehand? Anyone can see that.'

'Well,' and Ivan rose to cut short the conversation, struck by Smerdyakov's last argument. 'I don't suspect you at all, and I think it's absurd indeed to suspect you. On the contrary, I am grateful to you for setting my mind at rest. Now I am going, but I'll come again. Meanwhile, goodbye. Get well. Is there anything you want?'

'I am very thankful for everything. Marfa Ignatyevna does not forget me, and provides me anything I want, out of the kindness of her heart. Good people visit me every day.'

'Goodbye. But I won't say anything of your being able to sham a fit, and I don't advise you to, either,' something prompted Ivan to say suddenly.

'I quite understand. And if you don't speak of that, I shall say nothing of that conversation of ours at the gate.'

Then Ivan went out, and only when he had gone a dozen steps along the corridor, he suddenly felt that there was an insulting significance in Smerdyakov's last words. He was almost on the point of turning back, but it was only a passing impulse, and muttering, 'nonsense!' he left the hospital.

His chief feeling was one of relief at the fact that it was not Smerdyakov, but Mitya, who had committed the murder, though he might have been expected to feel the opposite. He did not want to analyse the reason for this feeling, and even felt a positive repugnance at prying into his sensations. He felt as though he wanted to make haste to forget something.

In the following days he became convinced of Mitya's guilt, as he learned all the weight of evidence against him. There was evidence of people of no importance, Fenya and her mother, for instance, but the effect of it was almost overwhelming. As to Perhotin, the people at the tavern, and at Plotnikov's shop, as well as the witnesses at Mokroe, their evidence seemed conclusive. It was the details that were so damning. The secret of the knocks impressed the lawyers almost as much as Grigory's evidence as to the open door. Grigory's wife, Marfa, in answer to Ivan's questions, declared that Smerdyakov had lain all night the other side of the partition wall. 'He was not three paces from our bed,' and that although she was a sound sleeper she waked several times and heard him moaning. 'He was moaning the whole time, moaning continually.'

Talking to Herzenstube, and expressing his opinion that Smerdyakov was not mad, but only rather weak, Ivan only evoked a subtle smile from the old man.

'Do you know how he spends his time now?' he asked, 'learning lists of French words by heart. He has an exercise book under his pillow with the French words written out in Russian letters for him by someone, he, he, he!'

Ivan ended by dismissing all doubts. He could not think of Dmitri without revulsion. Only one thing was strange, however. Alyosha persisted that Dmitri was not the murderer, and that 'in all probability' Smerdyakov was. Ivan always felt that Alyosha's opinion meant a great deal to him, and so he was astonished at it now. Another thing that was strange was that Alyosha did not make any attempt to talk about Mitya with Ivan, that he never brought up the matter and only answered questions. This, too, struck Ivan particularly.

But he was very much preoccupied at that time with something quite apart from Mitya's fate. On his return from Moscow, he abandoned himself hopelessly to his mad and consuming passion for Katerina Ivanovna. When Ivan, on leaving Katerina Ivanovna with Alyosha, as I've related already, told him, 'I am not interested in her,' it was an absolute lie: he loved her madly, though at times he hated her so that he felt like killing her. Many causes helped to bring about this feeling. Shattered by what had happened to Mitya, she rushed on Ivan's return to meet him as her one salvation. She was hurt, insulted and humiliated in her feelings. And here the man had come back to her, who had loved her so ardently before (oh, she knew that very well), and whose heart and intellect she considered so superior to her own. But the sternly virtuous girl did not abandon herself altogether to the man she loved, in spite of the Karamazov violence of passion and the great fascination he had for her. She was continually tormented at the same time by remorse for having deserted Mitya, and in moments of discord and violent anger (and they were numerous) she told Ivan so plainly. This was what he had called to Alyosha 'lies upon lies'. There was, of course, much that was false in it, and that angered Ivan intensely . . . But of all this later.

He did, in fact, for a time almost forget Smerdyakov's existence, and yet, a fortnight after his first visit to him, he began to be haunted by the same strange thoughts as before. It's enough to say that he was continually asking himself, why was it that on that last night in Fyodor Pavlovitch's house he had crept out on to the stairs like a thief and listened to hear what his father was doing below? Why had he recalled that afterwards with disgust; why, next morning, had he been suddenly so depressed on the journey; why, as he reached Moscow, had he said to himself 'I am a scoundrel'? And now he almost fancied that these tormenting thoughts would make him forget even Katerina Ivanovna, so completely did they take possession of him again. It was just after fancying this, that he met Alyosha in the street. He stopped him at once, and put a question to him: 'Do you remember when Dmitri burst in after dinner and beat father, and afterwards I told you in the yard that I reserved "the right to desire" . . . tell me, did you think then that I desired father's death or not?'

'I did think so,' answered Alyosha, softly.

'It was so, too; it was not a matter of guessing. But didn't you fancy then that what I wished was just that "one reptile should devour another"; that is, just that Dmitri should kill father, and as soon as possible . . . and that I myself was even prepared to help to bring that about?'

Alyosha turned rather pale, and looked silently into his brother's face.

'Speak!' cried Ivan, 'I want above everything to know what you thought then. I want the truth, the truth!'

He drew a deep breath, looking angrily at Alyosha before his answer came.

'Forgive me, I did think that, too, at the time,' whispered Alyosha, and he did not add one softening phrase.

'Thanks,' snapped Ivan, and, leaving Alyosha, he went quickly on his way. From that time Alyosha noticed that Ivan began obviously to avoid him and seemed to have taken a dislike to him, so much so that Alyosha gave up going to see him. Immediately after that meeting with him, Ivan had not gone home, but went straight to Smerdyakov again.

7

By that time Smerdyakov had been discharged from the hospital. Ivan knew his new lodging, the dilapidated little wooden house, divided in two by a passage on one side of which lived Marya Kondratyevna and her mother, and on the other, Smerdyakov. No one knew on what terms he lived with them, whether as a friend or as a lodger. It was supposed afterwards that he had come to stay with them as Marya Kondratyevna's betrothed, and was living there for a time without paying for board or lodging. Both mother and daughter had the greatest respect for him and looked upon him as greatly superior to themselves.

Ivan knocked, and, when the door opened, went into the passage. Following Marya Kondratyevna's directions, he went straight to the better room on the left, occupied by Smerdyakov. There was a tiled stove in the room, and it was extremely hot. The walls were gay with blue paper, which was badly worn however, and in the torn places cockroaches swarmed in amazing numbers, so that there was a continual rustling from them. The furniture was very scanty: two benches against each wall and two chairs by the table. The table of plain wood was covered with a cloth with pink patterns. There was a pot of geraniums on the sill of each of the two little windows. In the corner there was a frame filled with icons. On the table stood a small copper samovar with many dents in it, and a tray with two cups. But Smerdyakov had finished tea and the samovar was cold. He was sitting at the table on a bench. He was looking at an exercise book and slowly writing with a pen. There was a bottle of ink by him and a low iron candlestick, with a candle in it. Ivan saw at once from Smerdyakov's face that he had completely recovered from his illness. His face was fresher, fuller, his hair stood up jauntily in front and was plastered down at the sides. He was sitting in a flowered quilted robe, rather dirty and frayed, however. He had spectacles on his nose, which Ivan had never seen him wear before. This trifling circumstance suddenly redoubled Ivan's anger: 'A creature like that with spectacles!'

Smerdyakov slowly raised his head and looked intently at his visitor through his glasses; then he slowly took them off and rose from the bench, but by no means respectfully, almost lazily, doing the least possible required by common civility. All this struck Ivan instantly, he took it all in and noted it at once – most of all the look in Smerdyakov's eyes, definitely malicious, churlish and haughty. 'What brings you here?' it seemed to say; 'we settled everything then, why have you come again?' Ivan could scarcely control himself.

'It's hot here,' he said, still standing, and unbuttoned his overcoat.

'Take off your coat,' Smerdyakov conceded.

Ivan took off his coat and threw it on a bench with trembling hands. He took a chair, moved it quickly to the table and sat down. Smerdyakov managed to sit down on his bench before him.

'To begin with, are we alone?' Ivan asked sternly and impulsively. 'Can they overhear us in there?'

'No one can hear anything. You've seen for yourself: there's a passage.'

'Listen, my good fellow, what was that you babbled, as I was leaving the hospital, that if I said nothing about your ability to sham fits, you wouldn't tell the investigating lawyer all our conversation at the gate. What do you mean by *all*? What could you mean by it? Were you threatening me? Have I entered into some sort of pact with you? Do you suppose I am afraid of you?'

Ivan said this in a perfect fury, giving Smerdyakov to understand with obvious intention that he scorned any subterfuge or indirectness and meant to show his cards. Smerdyakov's eyes gleamed resentfully, his left eye winked and he at once gave his answer, with his habitual composure and deliberation: 'You want to have everything above-board, very well, you shall have it,' he seemed to say.

'This is what I meant then, and this is why I said that, that you, knowing beforehand of this murder of your own parent, left him to his fate, and that people might not after that conclude any evil about your feelings and perhaps of something else, too – that's what I promised not to tell the authorities.'

Though Smerdyakov spoke without haste and with obvious control, yet there was something in his voice, determined and emphatic, resentful and insolently defiant. He stared impudently at Ivan. For a moment Ivan could not focus his eyes.

'How? What? Are you out of your mind?'

'I'm in perfect possession of all my faculties.'

'Do you suppose I *knew* of the murder?' Ivan cried at last, and he crashed his fist violently on the table. 'What do you mean by "something else too"? Speak, scoundrel!'

Smerdyakov was silent and still scanned Ivan with the same insolent stare.

'Speak, you filthy swine, what is that "something else, too"?'

'The "something else" I meant was that you probably too were very desirous of your parent's death.'

Ivan jumped up and struck him with all his might on the shoulder, so that Smerdyakov fell back against the wall. In an instant his face was bathed in tears. Saying, 'It's a shame, sir, to strike a sick man,' he dried his eyes with a very dirty chequered blue handkerchief and sank into quiet weeping. A minute passed.

'That's enough! Stop it,' Ivan said peremptorily, sitting down again. 'Don't exasperate me so.'

Smerdyakov took the rag from his eyes. Every line of his puckered face reflected the insult he had just received.

'So you thought then, you scoundrel, that together with Dmitri I meant to kill my father?'

'I didn't know what thoughts were in your mind then,' said Smerdyakov resentfully; 'and so I stopped you then at the gate to sound you on that very point.'

'To sound what, what?'

'Why, that very matter, whether you wanted your father to be murdered or not.'

What infuriated Ivan more than anything was the aggressive, insolent tone to which Smerdyakov persistently adhered.

'It was you who murdered him?' he cried suddenly.

Smerdyakov smiled contemptuously.

'You know yourself, for a fact, that it wasn't I who murdered him. And I should have thought that there was no need for a sensible man to speak of it again.'

'But why, why had you such a suspicion about me at the time?'

'As you know already, it was simply from fear. For I was in such a position, shaking with fear, that I suspected everyone. I resolved to sound you out, too, for I thought if you wanted the same as your brother, then the business was as good as settled and I should be caught like a fly in a web.'

'Look here, you didn't say that a fortnight ago.'

'I meant the same when I talked to you in the hospital, only I thought you'd understand without wasting words, and that being such a sensible man you wouldn't care to talk of it openly.'

'What next! Come, answer, answer, I insist: what was it . . . what could I have done to put such a degrading suspicion into your mean soul?'

'As for the murder, you couldn't have done that and didn't want to, but as for wanting someone else to do it, that was just what you did want.'

'And how coolly, how coolly he speaks! But why should I have wanted it, what grounds had I for wanting it?'

'What grounds had you? What about the inheritance?' said Smerdyakov sarcastically, and as it were vindictively. 'Why, after your parent's death there was at least forty thousand to come to each of you, and very likely more, but if Fyodor Pavlovitch got married then to that lady, Agrafena Alexandrovna, she would have had all his capital made over to her directly after the wedding, for she has plenty of sense, so that your parent would not have left you two roubles between the three of you. And were they far from a wedding, either? Not a hair's breadth: that lady had only to lift her little finger and he would have run after her to church, with his tongue out.'

Ivan restrained himself with painful effort.

'Very good,' he commented at last, 'you see, I haven't jumped up, I haven't knocked you down, I haven't killed you. Speak on. So, according to you, I had fixed on Dmitri to do it, I was reckoning on him?'

'How could you help reckoning on him? If he killed him, then he would lose all the rights of a nobleman, his rank and property, and would go off to exile, so his share of the inheritance would come to you and your brother Alexey Fyodorovitch, in equal parts, so you'd each have not forty, but sixty thousand each. There's not a doubt you did reckon on Dmitri Fyodorovitch.'

'What I put up with from you! Listen, scoundrel, if I had reckoned on anyone then, it would have been on you, not on Dmitri, and I swear I did expect some wickedness from you . . . at the time . . . I remember my impression!'

'I thought, too, for a minute, at the time, that you were reckoning on me as well,' said Smerdyakov, with a sarcastic grin. 'So it was just by that more than by anything else you showed me what was in your mind. For if you had a foreboding about me and yet went away, you as good as said to me, "You can murder my parent, I won't hinder you!" '

'You scoundrel! So that's how you understood it!'

'It was all that going to Tchermashnya. Why! You meant to go to Moscow and refused all your father's entreaties to go to Tchermashnya – and simply at a foolish word from me you consented at once! What reason had you to consent to Tchermashnya? Since you went to Tchermashnya with no reason, simply at my word, it shows that you must have expected something from me.'

'No, I swear I didn't!' shouted Ivan, grinding his teeth.

'You didn't? Then you ought, as your father's son, to have had me taken to the prison, and thrashed at once for my words then . . . or at least, to have given me a punch in the face on the spot, but you were not a bit angry, if you please, and at once in a friendly way acted on my foolish word and went away, which was utterly absurd, for you ought to have stayed to save your parent's life. How could I help drawing my conclusions?'

Ivan sat scowling, both his fists convulsively pressed on his knees.

'Yes, I am sorry I didn't punch you in the face,' he

said with a bitter smile. 'I couldn't have taken you to the hoosegow just then. Who would have believed me and what charge could I bring against you? But the punch in the face . . . oh, I'm sorry I didn't think of it. Though blows are forbidden, I should have pounded your ugly face to a jelly.'

Smerdyakov looked at him almost with relish.

'In the ordinary circumstances of life,' he said in the same complacent and sententious tone in which he had taunted Grigory and argued with him about religion at Fyodor Pavlovitch's table, 'in the ordinary circumstances of life, blows on the face are forbidden nowadays by law and people have given up the habit, but in exceptional circumstances of life people still resort to blows, not only among us but all over the world, be it even the most complete Republic of France, just as in the time of Adam and Eve, and they never will leave off, but you, even in an exceptional case, did not dare.'

'What are you learning French words for?' Ivan nodded towards the exercise book lying on the table.

'Why shouldn't I learn them so as to improve my education, supposing that I may myself chance to go some day to those happy parts of Europe.'

'Listen, you unnatural monster,' Ivan's eyes flashed and he trembled all over. 'I am not afraid of your accusations, you can say what you like about me, and if I don't beat you to death, it's simply because I suspect you of that crime and I'll drag you to justice. I'll unmask you.'

'To my thinking, you'd better keep quiet, for what can you accuse me of, considering my absolute innocence; and who would believe you? Only if you begin, I shall tell everything, too.'

'Do you think I am afraid of you now?'

'If the court doesn't believe all I've said to you just now, the public will, and you will be ashamed.'

'That's as much as to say "A word to the wise is sufficient," ' snarled Ivan.

'You hit the mark, indeed. And you'd better be wise.'

Ivan got up, shaking all over with indignation, put on his coat, and without replying further to Smerdyakov, without even looking at him, walked quickly out of the cottage. The cool evening air refreshed him. There was a bright moon in the sky. A nightmare of ideas and sensations filled his soul. 'Shall I go at once and give information against Smerdyakov? But what information can I give? He is not guilty, anyway. On the contrary, he'll accuse me. And in fact why did I set off for Tchermashnya then? What for? What for?' Ivan asked himself. 'Yes, of course, I was expecting something and he is right . . .' And he remembered for the hundredth time how, on that last night in his father's house, he had listened on the stairs. But he remembered it now with such anguish that he stopped suddenly as though he had been stabbed. 'Yes, I expected it then, that's true! I wanted the murder, I did want the murder! Did I want the murder? Did I want it? I must kill Smerdyakov! If I don't dare kill Smerdyakov now, life is not worth living!'

Ivan did not go home, but went straight to Katerina Ivanovna and alarmed her by his appearance. He was like a madman. He repeated all his conversation with Smerdyakov, every syllable of it. He couldn't be calmed, however much she tried to soothe him: he kept walking about the room, speaking strangely, disconnectedly. At last he sat down, put his elbows on the table, leaned his head on his hands and pronounced this strange sentence: 'If it's not Dmitri, but Smerdyakov who's the murderer, I share his guilt, for I put him up to it. Whether I did, I don't know yet. But if he is the murderer, and not Dmitri, then, of course, I am the murderer too.'

When Katerina Ivanovna heard that, she got up from her seat without a word, went to her writing table, opened a box standing on it, took out a sheet of paper and laid it before Ivan. This was the document of which Ivan spoke to Alyosha later on as a 'conclusive proof' that Mitya had killed his father. This was the letter written by Mitya to Katerina Ivanovna when he was drunk, on the very evening he met Alyosha at the crossroads on the way to the monastery, after the scene at Katerina Ivanovna's, when Grushenka had insulted her. Then, parting from Alyosha, Mitya had rushed to Grushenka. I don't know whether he saw her, but in the evening he was at the Metropolis, where he got thoroughly drunk. Then he asked for pen and paper and wrote a document of weighty consequence to himself. It was a wordy, disconnected, frantic letter, a drunken letter in fact. It was like the talk of a drunken man, who, on his return home, begins with extraordinary heat telling his wife or one of his household how he has just been insulted, what a rascal has just insulted him, what a fine fellow he is on the other hand, and how he will pay that scoundrel out; and all that at great length, with great excitement and incoherence, with drunken tears and thumpings on the table. The letter was written on a dirty piece of ordinary paper of the cheapest kind. It had been provided by the tavern and there were figures scrawled on the back of it. There was evidently not space enough for his drunken verbosity and Mitya not only filled the margins but had written the last line right across the rest. The letter ran as follows:

FATAL KATYA! – Tomorrow I will get the money and repay your three thousand and farewell, woman of great wrath, but farewell too my love! Let us make an end! Tomorrow I shall try and get it from everyone, and if I can't borrow it, I give you my word of honour I shall go to my father and break his skull and take the money from under the pillow, if only Ivan has gone. If I had to go to Siberia for it, I'll give you back your three thousand. And farewell. I bow down to the ground before you, for I've been a scoundrel to you. Forgive me! No, better not forgive me, you'll be happier and so shall I! Better Siberia than your love, for I love another woman and you got to know her too well today, so how can you forgive? I will murder the man who's robbed me! I'll leave you all and go to the East so as to see no one again. Not her either, for you are not my only tormentress, she is too. Farewell!

P.S. I write my curse, but I adore you! I hear it in my heart. One string is left, and it vibrates. Better tear my heart in two! I shall kill myself, but first of all that cur. I shall tear three thousand from him and fling it to you. Though I've been a scoundrel to you, I am not a thief! You can expect three thousand. The cur keeps it under his mattress, with pink ribbon. I am not a thief, but I'll murder my thief. Katya, don't look disdainful. Mitya is not a thief; but a murderer! He has murdered his father and ruined himself to hold his ground, rather than endure your pride. And he doesn't love you.

P.P.S. I kiss your feet, farewell!

P.P.P.S. Katya, pray to God that some one'll give me the money. Then I shall not be steeped in gore, and if no one does – I shall! Kill me!

Your slave and enemy,

D. KARAMAZOV

When Ivan read this 'document', he was convinced. So then it was his brother, not Smerdyakov. And if not Smerdyakov, then not he, Ivan. This letter at once assumed in his eyes the aspect of a logical proof. There could be no longer the slightest doubt of Mitya's guilt. The suspicion never occurred to Ivan, by the way, that Mitya might have committed the murder in conjunction with Smerdyakov, and indeed such a theory did not fit in with the facts. Ivan was completely reassured. The next morning he only thought of Smerdyakov and his gibes with contempt. A few days later he even wondered how he could have been so horribly distressed at his suspicions. He resolved to dismiss him with contempt and forget him. So passed a month. He made no further enquiry about Smerdyakov, but twice he happened to hear that he was very ill and out of his mind.

'He'll end in the madhouse,' the young doctor, Varvinsky, observed about him and Ivan remembered this. During the last week of that month Ivan himself began to feel very ill. He went to consult the Moscow doctor who had been sent for by Katerina Ivanovna just before the trial. And just at that time his relations with Katerina Ivanovna became acutely strained. They were like two enemies in love with one another. Katerina Ivanovna's 'returns' to Mitya, that is, her brief but violent revulsions of feeling in his favour, drove Ivan to complete frenzy. Strange to say, until the time when Alyosha came from Mitya to Katerina Ivanovna, Ivan had never once, during that month, heard her express a doubt of Mitya's guilt, in spite of those 'returns' that were so hateful to him. It is remarkable, too, that while he felt that he hated Mitya more and more every day, he realised that it was not on account of Katya's 'returns' that he hated him, but just *because he was the murderer of his father.* He was conscious of this and fully recognised it to himself.

Nevertheless, he went to see Mitya ten days before the trial and proposed to him a plan of escape – a plan he had obviously thought over a long time. He was partly impelled to do this by a sore place still left in his heart from a phrase of Smerdyakov, that it was to his, Ivan's, advantage that his brother should be convicted, as that would increase his inheritance and Alyosha's from forty to sixty thousand roubles. He determined to sacrifice thirty thousand to Mitya's escape. On returning from a visit to the prison, he was very mournful and dispirited, he suddenly began to feel that he was anxious for Mitya's escape, not only to heal that sore place by sacrificing thirty thousand, but for another reason. 'Is it because I am as much a murderer at heart?' he asked himself. Something very deep down seemed to burn and rankle in his soul. His pride above all suffered cruelly all that month. But of that later . . .

When, after his conversation with Alyosha, Ivan suddenly decided with his hand on the bell of his lodging to go to Smerdyakov, he obeyed a sudden and peculiar impulse of indignation. He suddenly remembered how Katerina Ivanovna had only just cried out to him in Alyosha's presence: 'It was you,

you, persuaded me of his (that is, Mitya's) guilt!' Ivan was thunderstruck when he recalled it. He had never once tried to persuade her that Mitya was the murderer; on the contrary, he had suspected himself in her presence, that time when he came back from Smerdyakov. It was she, *she*, who had produced that 'document' and proved his brother's guilt. And now she suddenly exclaimed: 'I've been at Smerdyakov's myself!' When had she been there? Ivan had known nothing of it. So she was not at all so sure of Mitya's guilt! And what could Smerdyakov have told her? What, what, had he said to her? His heart burned with violent anger. He could not understand how he could, half an hour before, have let those words pass and not have cried out at the moment. He let go of the bell and rushed off to Smerdyakov. 'I shall kill him perhaps this time,' he thought on the way.

8

When he was halfway there, the keen dry wind that had been blowing early that morning rose again, and a fine dry snow began falling thickly. It did not lie on the ground, but was whirled about by the wind and soon there was a real snowstorm. There were scarcely any street lamps in the part of the town where Smerdyakov lived. Ivan walked alone in the darkness, unconscious of the storm, instinctively picking his way. His head ached and there was a painful throbbing in his temples. He felt his hands twitching convulsively. Not far from Marya Kondratyevna's cottage, Ivan suddenly came upon a solitary drunken little peasant. He wore a coarse and patched coat, and was walking in zigzags, grumbling and swearing to himself. Then suddenly he began to sing in a husky drunken voice:

'Oh, Vanka's gone to Petersburg,
I won't wait till he comes back.'

But he broke off every time at the second line and started to swear again; then he would begin the same song again. Ivan felt an intense hatred for him before he had thought about him at all. Suddenly he realised his presence and felt an irresistible impulse to knock him down. At that moment they met, and the peasant with a violent lurch fell full tilt against Ivan, who pushed him back furiously. The peasant went flying backwards and toppled like a log on the frozen ground. He uttered one plaintive 'O-oh!' and then was silent. Ivan stepped up to him. He was lying on his back, without movement or consciousness. 'He will be frozen,' thought Ivan, and he went on his way.

In the corridor, Marya Kondratyevna, who ran out to open the door with a candle in her hand, whispered that Smerdyakov was very ill; 'It's not that he's laid up, but he seems not himself, and he even told us to take the tea away; he wouldn't have any.'

'Why, is he making a row?' asked Ivan coarsely.

'Oh, dear, no, quite the contrary, he's very quiet. Only please don't talk to him too long,' Marya Kondratyevna begged him. Ivan opened the door and stepped into the room.

It was overheated as before, but there were changes in the room. One of the benches at the side had been removed, and in its place stood a large old mahogany and leather sofa, on which a bed had been made up, with fairly clean white pillows. Smerdyakov was sitting on the sofa, wearing the same quilted robe. The table had been placed in front of the sofa, so that there was hardly room to move. On the table lay a thick book in a yellow cover, but Smerdyakov was not reading it. He seemed to be sitting doing nothing. He turned a slow silent look on Ivan, and was apparently not at all surprised at his coming. There was a great change in his face; he was much thinner and more sallow. His eyes were sunken and there were blue rings under them.

'Why, you really are ill?' Ivan stopped short. 'I won't keep you long, I won't even take off my coat. Where can one sit down?'

He went to the other end of the table, moved up a chair and sat down on it.

'Why do you look at me without speaking? I've only come with one question, and I swear I won't go without an answer. Has the young lady, Katerina Ivanovna, been with you?'

Smerdyakov still remained silent, looking quietly at Ivan as before. Suddenly, making a gesture with his hand, he turned his face away.

'What's the matter with you?' cried Ivan.

'Nothing.'

'What do you mean by "nothing"?'

'Yes, she has. It's no business of yours. Let me alone.'

'No, I won't let you alone. Tell me, when was she here?'

'Why, I'd quite forgotten about her,' said Smerdyakov, with a scornful smile, and turning his face to Ivan again, he stared at him with a look of frenzied hatred, the same look that he had fixed on him at their last interview, a month before.

'You seem very ill yourself, your face is sunken; you don't look like yourself,' he said to Ivan.

'Never mind my health, tell me what I ask you.'

'But why are your eyes so yellow? The whites are quite yellow. Are you so worried?' He smiled contemptuously and suddenly laughed outright.

'Listen, I've told you I won't go away without an answer!' Ivan cried, intensely irritated.

'Why do you keep pestering me? Why do you torment me?' said Smerdyakov, with a look of suffering.

'Damn it! I've nothing to do with you. Just answer my question and I'll go away.'

'I've no answer to give you,' said Smerdyakov, looking down again.

'You may be sure I'll make you answer!'

'Why are you so uneasy?' Smerdyakov stared at him, not simply with contempt, but almost with disgust. 'Is this because the trial begins tomorrow? Nothing will happen to you, can't you believe that at last? Go home, go to bed and sleep in peace, don't be afraid of anything.'

'I don't understand you . . . What have I to be afraid of tomorrow?' Ivan articulated in astonishment, and suddenly a chill breath of fear did in fact pass over his soul. Smerdyakov measured him with his eyes.

'You don't understand?' he drawled reproachfully. 'It's a strange thing a sensible man should care to play such a farce!'

Ivan looked at him speechless. The startling, incredibly supercilious tone of this man who had once been his valet was extraordinary in itself. He had not spoken in such a tone even at their last interview.

'I tell you, you've nothing to be afraid of. I won't say anything about you, there's no proof against you. Look how your hands are trembling! Why are your fingers jerking like that? Go home, *you* did not murder him.'

Ivan shivered. He thought of Alyosha.

'I know it was not I,' he faltered.

'Do you?' Smerdyakov caught him up again.

Ivan jumped up and seized him by the shoulder.

'Tell me everything, you foul creature! Tell me everything!'

Smerdyakov was not in the least scared. He only fixed his eyes on Ivan with insane hatred.

'Well, it was you who murdered him, if that's it,' he whispered furiously.

Ivan sank back on his chair, as though pondering something. He laughed malignantly.

'You mean my going away. What you talked about last time?'

'You stood before me last time and understood it all, and you understand it now.'

'All I understand is that you are crazy.'

'Aren't you tired of it? Here we are face to face; what's the use of playing games with each other? Are you still trying to throw it all on me, to my face? *You* murdered him; you are the real murderer, I was only your instrument, your faithful servant, and it was in obedience to your words I did it.'

'*Did* it? Why, did you murder him?' Ivan turned cold.

Something seemed to give way in his brain, and he shuddered all over with a cold shiver. Then Smerdyakov himself looked at him wonderingly; probably the genuineness of Ivan's horror struck him.

'You don't mean to say you really did not know?' he faltered mistrustfully, looking with a crooked smile into his eyes. Ivan still gazed at him, and seemed unable to speak.

Oh, Vanka's gone to Petersburg,
I won't wait till he comes back,

suddenly echoed in his head.

'Do you know, I am afraid that you are a dream, a phantom sitting before me,' he muttered.

'There's no phantom here, but only us two and one other. No doubt he is here, that third, between us.'

'Who is he? Who is here? What third person?' Ivan cried in alarm, looking about him, his eyes hastily searching in every corner.

'That third is God Himself, Providence. He is the third beside us now. Only don't look for Him, you won't find Him.'

'It's a lie that you killed him!' Ivan cried madly. 'You are mad, or mocking me again!'

Smerdyakov, as before, watched him curiously, with no sign of fear. He could still scarcely get over his incredulity; he still fancied that Ivan knew everything and was trying to 'blame it all on him to his face'.

'Wait a minute,' he said at last in a weak voice, and suddenly bringing up his left leg from under the table, he turned up his trouser leg. He was wearing long white stockings and slippers. Slowly he took off his garter and fumbled to the bottom of his stocking. Ivan gazed at him, and suddenly shuddered in a paroxysm of terror.

'He's mad!' he cried, and rapidly jumping up, he drew back, so that he knocked his back against the wall and stood up against it, stiff and straight. He looked with insane terror at Smerdyakov, who, entirely unaffected by the outcry, continued to fumble in his stocking, as though he were making an effort to get hold of something with his fingers and pull it out. At last he got hold of it and began pulling it out. Ivan saw that it was a piece of paper, or perhaps a roll of papers. Smerdyakov pulled it out and laid it on the table.

'Here,' he said quietly.

'What is it?' responded Ivan, trembling.

'Kindly look at it,' Smerdyakov answered, in the same low tone.

Ivan stepped up to the table, took up the roll of paper and began unfolding it, but suddenly he drew back his fingers, as though from contact with a loathsome reptile.

'Your hands keep twitching,' observed Smerdyakov, and he deliberately unfolded the bundle himself. Under the wrapper were three packets of hundred-rouble notes.

'They are all here, all the three thousand roubles. You need not count them. Take them,' Smerdyakov suggested to Ivan, nodding at the notes. Ivan sank back in his chair. He was as white as a handkerchief.

'You frightened me . . . with your stocking,' he said, with a strange grin.

'Did you really not know till now?' Smerdyakov asked once more.

'No, I did not know. I kept thinking of Mitya. Brother, brother! Oh!' He suddenly clutched his head in both hands.

'Listen. Did you kill him alone? With my brother's help or without?'

'It is only with you, with your help, I killed him, and Dmitri Fyodorovitch is quite innocent.'

'All right, all right. Talk about me later. Why do I keep on trembling? I can't speak properly.'

'You were bold enough then. You said "everything was lawful", and how frightened you are now,'

Smerdyakov muttered in surprise. 'Won't you have some lemonade? I'll ask for some at once. It's very refreshing. Only I must hide this first.'

And again he motioned at the notes. He was just going to get up and call at the door to Marya Kondratyevna to make some lemonade and bring it to them, but, looking for something to cover up the notes that she might not see them, he first took out his handkerchief, and as it turned out to be very dirty, took up the big yellow book that Ivan had noticed at first lying on the table, and put it over the notes. The book was *The Sayings of the Holy Father Isaac the Syrian*. Ivan read it mechanically.

'I won't have any lemonade,' he said. 'Talk of me later. Sit down and tell me how you did it. Tell me all about it.'

'You'd better take off your overcoat, or you'll be too hot.' Ivan, as though he'd only just thought of it, took off his coat, and, without getting up from his chair, threw it on the bench.

'Speak, please, speak.'

He seemed calmer. He waited, feeling sure that Smerdyakov would tell him *all* about it.

'How it was done?' sighed Smerdyakov. 'It was done in a most natural way, following your very words.'

'Of my words later,' Ivan broke in again, apparently with complete self-possession, firmly uttering his words, and not shouting as before. 'Only tell me in detail how you did it. Everything, as it happened. Don't forget anything. The details, above everything, the details, I beg you.'

'You'd gone away, then I fell into the cellar.'

'In a fit or in a sham one?'

'A sham one, naturally. I shammed it all. I went quietly down the steps to the very bottom and lay down quietly, and as I lay down I gave a scream, and struggled, till they carried me out.'

'Wait! And were you shamming all along, afterwards, and in the hospital?'

'No, not at all. Next day, in the morning, before they took me to the hospital, I had a real attack and a more violent one than I've had for years. For two days I was quite unconscious.'

'All right, all right. Go on.'

'They laid me on the bed. I knew I'd be the other side of the partition, for whenever I was ill, Marfa Ignatyevna used to put me there, near them. She's always been very kind to me from my birth up. At night I moaned, but quietly. I kept expecting Dmitri Fyodorovitch to come.'

'Expecting him? To come to you?'

'Not to me. I expected him to come into the house, for I'd no doubt that he'd come that night, for since I was not there and he had no news, he'd be sure to come and climb over the fence, as he used to and do something.'

'And if he hadn't come?'

'Then nothing would have happened. I should never have brought myself to it without him.'

'All right, all right . . . speak more intelligibly, don't hurry; above all, don't leave anything out!'

'I expected him to kill Fyodor Pavlovitch. I thought that was certain, for I had prepared him for it . . . during the last few days . . . He knew how to tap on the window, as agreed, that was the chief thing. With his suspiciousness and the fury which had been growing in him all those days, he was bound to get into the house by means of those taps. That was inevitable, so I was expecting him.'

'But,' Ivan interrupted, 'if he had killed him, he would have taken the money and carried it away; you must have considered that. What would you have from that afterwards? I don't see.'

'But he would never have found the money. That was only what I told him, that the money was under the mattress. But that wasn't true. It was hidden, at first, in a box. Afterwards I suggested to Fyodor Pavlovitch, as I was the only person he trusted, to hide the envelope with the notes in the corner behind the icons, for no one would guess that place, especially if they came in a hurry. So that's where the envelope was, in the corner behind the icons. It would have been absurd to keep it under the mattress; the box, anyway, could be locked. But all believe it was under the mattress. A stupid thing to believe. So if Dmitri Fyodorovitch had committed the murder, finding nothing, he would either have run away in a hurry, afraid of every sound, as always happens with murderers, or he would have been arrested. So I could always have climbed up to the icons and taken away the money next morning or even that night, and it would have all been put down to Dmitri Fyodorovitch. I could reckon upon that.'

'But what if he did not kill him, but only knocked him down?'

'If he did not kill him, of course, I would not have ventured to take the money, and nothing would have happened. But I calculated that he would beat him senseless, and I should have time to take it, and then I'd make out to Fyodor Pavlovitch that it was no one but Dmitri Fyodorovitch who had taken the money after beating him.'

'Wait . . . I am getting mixed. Then it was Dmitri after all who killed him, you only took the money?'

'No, he didn't kill him. Well, I might as well have told you now that he was the murderer . . . But I don't want to lie to you now, because . . . because if you really haven't understood till now, as I see for myself, and are not pretending, so as to throw your guilt on me to my very face, you are still responsible for it all, since you knew of the murder and charged me to do it, and went away knowing all about it. And so I want to prove to your face this evening that you are the only real murderer in the whole affair, and I am not the real murderer, though I did kill him. You are the rightful murderer.'

'Why, why, am I a murderer? Oh, God!' Ivan cried, unable to restrain himself at last, and forgetting that he had put off discussing himself till the end of the conversation. 'You still mean that trip to Tchermashnya? Tell, tell me, why did you want my consent, if you really took Tchermashnya for consent? How will you explain that now?'

'Assured of your consent, I knew that you wouldn't make an outcry over the disappearance of those three thousand, even if I'd been suspected, instead of Dmitri Fyodorovitch, or as his accomplice; on the contrary, you would have protected me from others . . . And when you got your inheritance you would have rewarded me when you were able, all the rest of your life. For you'd have received your inheritance through me, seeing that if he had married Agrafena Alexandrovna, you wouldn't have had a penny.'

'Ah! Then you intended to persecute me all my life afterwards,' snarled Ivan. 'And what if I hadn't gone away then, but had informed against you?'

'What could you have informed? That I persuaded you to go to Tchermashnya? That's all nonsense. Besides, after our conversation you would either have gone away or have stayed. If you had stayed, nothing would have happened. I should have known that you didn't want it done, and I wouldn't have attempted anything. As soon as you went away, it meant you assured me that you wouldn't dare to inform against me at the trial, and that you'd overlook my having the three thousand. And, indeed, you couldn't have prosecuted me afterwards, because then I should have told it all in the court; that is, not that I had stolen the money or killed him – but that you'd put me up to the theft and the murder, though I didn't consent to it. That's why I needed your consent, so that you couldn't corner me later, for what proof could you have had? I could always have cornered you, by revealing your eagerness for your father's death, and I tell you the public would have believed it all, and you would have been ashamed for the rest of your life.'

'Was I so eager then, was I?' Ivan snarled again.

'To be sure you were and by your consent you silently sanctioned my doing it.' Smerdyakov looked boldly at Ivan. He was very weak and spoke slowly and wearily, but some hidden inner force urged him on. He obviously had some plan. Ivan felt that.

'Go on,' he said. 'Tell me what happened that night.'

'What more is there to tell! I lay there and I thought I heard the master shout. And before that Grigory Vassilyevitch suddenly got up and came out and he suddenly gave a scream and then all was silence and darkness. I lay there waiting, my heart beating; I couldn't bear it. I got up at last, went out. I saw the window open on the left into the garden, and I stepped to the left to listen whether he was sitting there alive, and I heard the master moving about, sighing, so I knew he was alive. Oh-ho! I thought. I went to the window and called to the master, "It's I." And he shouted to me, "He came, he came; he's run away." He meant Dmitri Fyodorovitch had come. "He's killed Grigory!" "Where?" I whispered. "There in the corner," he pointed. He was whispering too. "Wait a bit," I said. I went to the corner of the garden to look, and there I came upon Grigory Vassilyevitch lying by the wall, covered with blood, senseless. So it's true that Dmitri Fyodorovitch has been here, was the thought that came into my head, and I determined on the spot to make an end of it, as Grigory Vassilyevitch, even if he were alive, would see nothing of it, as he lay there senseless. The only risk was that Marfa Ignatyevna might wake up. I felt that at the moment, but the longing to get it over with came over me, till I could scarcely breathe. I went back to the window to the master and said, "She's here, she's come; Agrafena Alexandrovna has come. She wants to be let in." And he quivered like a baby. "Where is she?" he fairly gasped, but couldn't believe it. "She's standing there," said I, "open." He looked out of the window at me, half believing and half distrustful, but afraid to open. "Why, he is afraid of me now," I thought. And it was funny. I remembered to knock out on the window frame those taps we'd agreed upon as a signal that Grushenka had come, in his presence, before his eyes. He didn't seem to believe my words, but as soon as he heard the taps, he ran at once to open the door. He opened it. I would have gone in, but he stood in the way to prevent me from entering. "Where is she?

Where is she?" He looked at me, all of a tremble. Well, thought I, if he's as frightened of me as all that, it's a bad lookout! And my legs went weak with fright that he wouldn't let me in or would call out, or Marfa Ignatyevna would run up, or something else might happen. I don't remember now, but I must have stood pale, facing him. I whispered to him, "Why, she's there, there, under the window, how is it you don't see her?" I said. "Bring her then, bring her." "She's afraid," said I, "she was frightened at the noise, she's hidden in the bushes; go and call to her yourself from the study." He ran to the window, put the candle in the window. "Grushenka," he cried, "Grushenka, are you here?" Though he cried that, he didn't want to lean out of the window, he didn't want to move away from me, for he was panic-stricken; he was so frightened he didn't dare to turn his back on me. "Why, here she is," said I. I went up to the window and leaned right out of it. "Here she is, she's in the bush, laughing at you, don't you see her?" He suddenly believed it; he was trembling – he was completely crazy about her – and he leaned right out of the window. I snatched up that iron paper weight from his table; do you remember, weighing about three pounds? I swung it and hit him on the top of the skull with the corner of it. He didn't even cry out. He only sank down suddenly, and I hit him again and a third time. And the third time I knew I'd broken his skull. He suddenly rolled on his back, face upward, covered with blood. I looked around. There was no blood on me, not a spot. I wiped the paper weight, put it back, went up to the icons, took the money out of the envelope, and flung the envelope on the floor and the pink ribbon beside it. I went out into the garden shaking, straight to the apple tree with a hollow in it – you know that hollow. I'd picked it long before and had a rag and a piece of paper ready in it. I wrapped all the notes in the rag and stuffed the package deep down in the hole. And there it stayed for over a fortnight. I took it out later, when I came out of the hospital. I went back to my bed, lay down and thought, "If Grigory Vassilyevitch has been killed outright, it may be a bad job for me, but if he is not killed and recovers, it will be fine, for then he'll bear witness that Dmitri Fyodorovitch was here, and so he must have killed his father and taken the money." Then I began groaning with suspense and impatience, so as to wake Marfa Ignatyevna as soon as possible. At last she got up, and she rushed to me, but when she saw Grigory Vassilyevitch was not there, she ran out, and I heard her scream in the garden. And that started the whole business and set my mind at rest.'

He stopped. Ivan had listened all the time in dead silence without stirring or taking his eyes off him. As he told his story Smerdyakov glanced at Ivan from time to time, but for the most part kept his eyes averted. When he had finished he was evidently agitated and was breathing hard. The perspiration stood out on his face. But it was impossible to tell whether it was remorse he was feeling, or what.

'Well,' cried Ivan, pondering. 'What about the door? If he only opened the door to you, how could Grigory have seen it open before? For Grigory saw it before you got there.'

It was remarkable that Ivan spoke quite amicably, in a different tone, not angry as before, so that if anyone had opened the door at that moment and peeped in at them, he would certainly have concluded that they were talking peaceably about some ordinary, though interesting, subject.

'As for that door and Grigory Vassilyevitch's having seen it open, that's only his fancy,' said Smerdyakov, with a wry smile. 'He is not a man, I assure you, but an obstinate mule. He didn't see it, but fancied he had seen it, and there's no shaking him. It's just our luck he took that notion into his head, for they can't fail to convict Dmitri Fyodorovitch after that.'

'Listen . . .' said Ivan, apparently bewildered again and making an effort to grasp something. 'Listen. There are a lot of questions I want to ask you, but I forget them . . . I keep forgetting and getting mixed up. Yes. Tell me this at least, why did you open the envelope and leave it there on the floor? Why didn't you simply carry off the envelope? . . . When you were telling me, I thought you spoke about it as though it were the right thing to do . . . but why, I can't understand . . .'

'I did that for a good reason. For if a man had known all about it, as I did for instance, if he'd seen those notes before, and perhaps had put them in that envelope himself, and had seen the envelope sealed and addressed, with his own eyes, if such a man had done the murder, what could make him tear open the envelope afterwards, especially in such desperate haste, since he'd known for certain the notes must be in the envelope? No, if the robber had been someone like me, he'd simply have put the envelope straight in his pocket and got away with it as fast as he could. But it'd be quite different with Dmitri Fyodorovitch. He only knew about the envelope by hearsay; he had never seen it, and if he'd found it, for instance, under the mattress, he'd have torn it open as quickly as possible to make sure the notes were in it. And he'd have thrown the envelope down, without having time to think that it would be evidence against him. Because he was not a habitual thief and had never stolen anything before, for he is a gentleman born, and if he did bring himself to steal, it would not be regular stealing, but simply taking what was his own, for he'd told the whole town he meant to get his *own* money back, and had even bragged aloud before everyone that he'd go and take his property from Fyodor Pavlovitch. I didn't say that openly to the prosecutor when I was being examined, but quite the contrary, I brought him to it by a hint, as though I didn't see it myself, and as though he'd thought of it himself and I hadn't prompted him so that Mr Prosecutor's mouth positively watered at my suggestion.'

'But can you possibly have thought of all that on the spot?' cried Ivan, overcome with astonishment. He looked at Smerdyakov again with alarm.

'Mercy on us! Could anyone think of it all in such a desperate hurry? It was all thought out beforehand.'

'Well . . . well, it was the devil helped you!' Ivan cried again. 'No, you are not a fool, you are far cleverer than I thought . . .'

He got up, obviously intending to walk across the room. He was terribly agitated. But as the table blocked his way, and there was hardly room to pass between the table and the wall, he only turned round where he stood and sat down again. Perhaps the impossibility of moving irritated him, as he suddenly cried out almost as furiously as before.

'Listen, you miserable, contemptible creature! Don't you understand that if I haven't killed you, it's simply because I am keeping you to answer tomorrow at the trial. God sees,' Ivan raised his hand, 'perhaps I too was guilty; perhaps I really had a secret desire for my father's . . . death, but I swear I was not as guilty as you think, and perhaps I didn't urge you on at all. No, no, I didn't urge you on! But no matter, I will give evidence against myself tomorrow, at the trial. I'm determined to! I shall tell everything, everything. But we'll make our appearance together. And whatever you may say against me at the trial, whatever evidence you give, I'll face it, I am not afraid of you. I'll corroborate it all myself! But you must confess too! You must, you must, we'll go together. That's how it shall be!'

Ivan said this solemnly and resolutely, and from his flashing eyes alone it could be seen that it would be so.

'You are sick, I see, you are quite sick. Your eyes are yellow,' Smerdyakov commented, without the least irony, with apparent sympathy in fact.

'We'll go together,' Ivan repeated. 'And if you won't go, no matter, I'll go alone.'

Smerdyakov paused as though pondering.

'Nothing of the sort will happen, and you won't go,' he concluded at last positively.

'You don't understand me,' Ivan exclaimed reproachfully.

'You'll be too much ashamed, if you confess it all. And, what's more, it will be no use at all, for I shall say at once that I never said anything of the sort to you, and that you are either sick (and you look it, too), or that you're so sorry for your brother that you are sacrificing yourself to save him and have invented the whole story all against me, for you've always thought no more of me than if I'd been a fly. And who will believe you, and what single proof have you got?'

'Listen, you showed me those notes just now to convince me.'

Smerdyakov lifted the book off the notes and laid it on one side.

'Take that money away with you,' Smerdyakov sighed.

'Of course I shall take it. But why do you give it to me, if you committed the murder for the sake of it?' Ivan looked at him with great surprise.

'I don't want it,' Smerdyakov articulated in a shaking voice, with a gesture of refusal. 'I did have an idea of beginning a new life with that money in Moscow or, better still, abroad. I did dream of it, chiefly because "all things are lawful". That was quite right what you taught me, for you talked a lot to me about that. But if there's no eternal God, there's no such thing as virtue, and there's no need of it. You were right there. So that's how I look at it.'

'Did you arrive at that conclusion yourself?' asked Ivan, with a wry smile.

'With your guidance.'

'And now, I suppose, you believe in God, since you are giving back the money?'

'No, I don't believe,' whispered Smerdyakov.

'Then why are you giving it back?'

'Be quiet . . . that's enough!' Smerdyakov waved his hand again. 'You used to say yourself that everything was lawful, so now why are you so upset? You even want to go and give evidence against yourself . . . Only there'll be nothing of the sort! You won't go to give evidence,' Smerdyakov decided with conviction.

'You'll see,' said Ivan.

'It isn't possible. You are very clever. You are fond of money, I know that. You like to be respected, too, for you're very proud; you are far too fond of female charms, too, and you love most of all to live in undisturbed comfort, without having to depend on anyone – that's what you care most about. You won't want to spoil your life for ever by taking such a disgrace on yourself. You are like Fyodor Pavlovitch, you are more like him than any of his children; you've the same soul as he had.'

'You are not a fool,' said Ivan, evidently astonished. The blood rushed to his face. 'You are serious now!' he observed, looking suddenly at Smerdyakov with a different expression.

'It was your pride made you think I was a fool. Take the money.'

Ivan took the three rolls of notes and put them in his pocket without wrapping them in anything.

'I shall show them at the court tomorrow,' he said.

'Nobody will believe you, as you've plenty of money of your own; you could simply have taken it out of your cash box and brought it to the court.'

Ivan rose from his seat.

'I repeat,' he said, 'the only reason I haven't killed you is that I need you for tomorrow, remember that, don't forget it!'

'Well, kill me. Kill me now,' Smerdyakov said, all at once looking strangely at Ivan. 'You don't dare do that even!' he added, with a bitter smile. 'You don't dare to do anything, you, who used to be so bold!'

'Till tomorrow,' cried Ivan, and moved to go out.

'Wait a moment . . . Show me those notes again.'

Ivan took out the notes and showed them to him. Smerdyakov looked at them for ten seconds.

'Well, you can go,' he said, with a wave of his hand. 'Ivan Fyodorovitch!' he called after him again.

'What do you want?' Ivan turned without stopping.

'Goodbye!'

'Till tomorrow!' Ivan cried again, and he walked out of the cottage.

The snowstorm was still raging. He walked the first few steps boldly, but suddenly began staggering. 'It's something physical,' he thought with a grin. Something like joy was springing up in his heart. He was conscious of unbounded resolution; he would make an end of the wavering that had so tortured him of late. His decision was taken, 'and now it will not be changed', he thought with relief. At that moment he stumbled against something and almost fell down; stopping short, he made out at his feet the peasant he had knocked down, still lying senseless and motionless. The snow had almost covered his face. Ivan seized him and lifted him in his arms. Seeing a light in the little house to the right he went up, knocked at the shutters, and asked the man to whom the house belonged to help him carry the peasant to the police station, promising him three roubles. The man got ready and came out. I won't describe in detail how Ivan succeeded in his enterprise, how he brought the peasant to the police station and arranged for a doctor to see him at once, providing with a liberal hand for the expenses. I will only say that this business took a whole hour, but Ivan was well content with it. His mind wandered and worked incessantly.

'If I had not taken my decision so firmly for tomorrow,' he reflected with satisfaction, 'I would not have stayed a whole hour to look after the peasant, but would have passed by, without caring about his being frozen. I am quite capable of taking care of myself, by the way,' he thought at the same instant, with still greater satisfaction, 'although they have decided that I am going out of my mind!'

Just as he reached his own house he stopped short, asking himself suddenly hadn't he better go at once now to the prosecutor and tell him everything. He decided the question by turning back to the house. 'Everything together tomorrow!' he whispered to himself, and, strange to say, almost all his gladness and self-satisfaction passed in one instant.

As he entered his own room he felt something like a touch of ice on his heart, like a recollection or, more exactly, a reminder, of something agonising and revolting that was in that room now, at that moment, and had been there before. He sank wearily on his sofa. The old woman brought him a samovar; he made tea, but did not touch it. He sat on the sofa and felt dizzy. He felt that he was sick and helpless. He began to fall asleep, but got up uneasily and walked across the room to shake off his drowsiness. At moments he fancied he was delirious, but it was not sickness that he thought of most. Sitting down again, he began looking round, as though searching for something. This happened several times. At last his eyes fastened intently on one point. Ivan smiled, but an angry flush suffused his face. He sat a long time in his place, his head propped on both arms, though he looked sideways at the same point, at the sofa that stood against the opposite wall. There was evidently something, some object, that irritated him there, worried him and tormented him.

A loud, persistent knocking was suddenly heard at the window. Ivan jumped up from the sofa. He rushed to the window and opened the movable pane.

'Alyosha, I told you not to come,' he cried fiercely to

his brother. 'What do you want? Tell me. In two words, do you hear?'

'An hour ago Smerdyakov hanged himself,' Alyosha answered from the yard.

'Come around to the steps, I'll open at once,' said Ivan, going to open the door to Alyosha.

9

Alyosha told Ivan that a little over an hour ago Marya Kondratyevna had run to his rooms and informed him Smerdyakov had taken his own life. 'I went in to clear away the samovar and he was hanging from a nail in the wall.' When Alyosha enquired whether she had informed the police, she answered that she had told no one, 'but I ran straight to you, I've run all the way'. She seemed almost out of her mind, Alyosha reported, and was trembling like a leaf. When Alyosha ran with her to the cottage, he found Smerdyakov still hanging. On the table lay a note: 'I destroy my life of my own will and desire, so as to throw no blame on anyone.' Alyosha left the note on the table and went straight to the police captain and told him about it. 'And from him I've come straight to you,' said Alyosha, in conclusion, looking intently into Ivan's face. He had not taken his eyes off him while he told his story, as though struck by something in his expression.

'Brother,' he cried suddenly, 'you must be terribly ill. You stare and don't seem to understand what I tell you.'

'It's a good thing you came,' said Ivan, as though brooding, and not hearing Alyosha's exclamation. 'I knew he had hanged himself.'

'From whom?'

'I don't know. But I knew. Did I know? Yes, he told me. He told me so just now.'

Ivan stood in the middle of the room, and still spoke in the same brooding tone, looking at the ground.

'Who is *he*?' asked Alyosha, involuntarily looking round.

'He's slipped away.'

Ivan raised his head and smiled softly.

'He was afraid of you, of a gentle dove like you. You are a "pure angel". Mitya calls you an angel. Angel! . . . the seraphim's loud hymn of ecstasy. What are seraphim? Perhaps a whole constellation. But perhaps that constellation is only a chemical molecule. There's a constellation of the Lion and the Sun. Do you know that?'

'Brother, sit down,' said Alyosha in alarm. 'For goodness' sake, sit down on the sofa! You are delirious; put your head on the pillow, that's right. Would you like a wet towel on your head? Perhaps it will do you good.'

'Give me the towel: it's here on the chair. I just threw it down there.'

'It's not here. Don't worry yourself. I know where it is – here,' said Alyosha, finding a clean towel folded up and unused, by Ivan's dressing table in the other corner of the room. Ivan looked strangely at the towel.

'Listen' – he got up from the sofa – 'an hour ago I took that fresh towel from there and soaked it in water. I wrapped it round my head and threw it down here . . . How is it it's dry? There was no other.'

'You put that towel on your head?' asked Alyosha.

'Yes, and walked up and down the room an hour ago . . . Why have the candles burnt down so? What's the time?'

'Nearly twelve.'

'No, no, no!' Ivan cried suddenly. 'It was not a dream. He was here; he was sitting here, on that sofa. When you knocked at the window, I threw a glass at him . . . this one. Wait a minute. I was asleep last time, but this dream was not a dream. It has happened before. I have dreams now, Alyosha . . . yet they are not dreams, but reality. I walk about, talk and see . . . though I am asleep. But he was sitting here, on that sofa there . . . He is frightfully stupid, Alyosha, frightfully stupid.' Ivan laughed suddenly and began pacing about the room.

'Who is stupid? Of whom are you talking, brother?' Alyosha asked anxiously again.

'The devil! He's taken to visiting me. He's been here twice, almost three times. He pretended that I was angry with him for being a simple devil and not Satan, with scorched wings, in thunder and lightning. But he is not Satan: that's a lie. He is an impostor. He is simply a devil – a paltry, trivial devil. He goes to the baths. If you undressed him, you'd be sure to find he had a tail, long and smooth like a Danish dog's, a yard long, dun colour . . . Alyosha, you are cold. You've been in the snow. Would you like some tea? What? Is it cold? Shall I tell her to bring some? You wouldn't put a dog outdoors . . . '

Alyosha ran to the washbowl, soaked the towel, persuaded Ivan to sit down again, and put the wet towel round his head. He sat down beside him.

'What were you telling me just now about Lise?' Ivan began again. (He was growing very talkative.) 'I like Lise. I said something nasty about her. It was a lie. I like her . . . I am afraid for Katya tomorrow. I am more afraid of her than of anything. On account of the future.

She will cast me off tomorrow and trample me underfoot. She thinks that I am ruining Mitya from jealousy on her account! Yes, she thinks that! But it's not so. Tomorrow the cross, but not the gallows. No, I shan't hang myself. Do you know, I can never commit suicide, Alyosha. Is it because I am base? I am not a coward. Is it from love of life? How did I know that Smerdyakov had hanged himself? Yes, it was *he* told me so.'

'And you are quite convinced that there has been someone here?' asked Alyosha.

'Yes, on that sofa in the corner. You would have driven him away. You did drive him away: he disappeared when you arrived. I love your face, Alyosha. Did you know that I loved your face? And *he* is myself, Alyosha. All that's base in me, all that's mean and contemptible. Yes, I am a romantic. He guessed it . . . though it's a libel. He is frightfully stupid; but it's to his advantage. He has cunning, animal cunning – he knew how to infuriate me. He kept taunting me for believing in him, and that was how he made me listen to him. He fooled me as you fool a little boy. He told me a great deal that was true about myself, though. I would never have acknowledged such things to myself. Do you know, Alyosha,' Ivan added in an intensely earnest and confidential tone, 'I would be awfully glad to think it was *he* and not I.'

'He has exhausted you,' said Alyosha, looking compassionately at his brother.

'He's been taunting me. And you know he does it so cleverly, so cleverly. "Conscience! What is conscience? I invent conscience for myself. Why am I tormented by it? From habit. From the universal habit of mankind for seven thousand years. So let us give it up, and we shall be gods." It was he said that, it was he said that!'

'And not you, not you?' Alyosha could not help crying, looking frankly at his brother. 'Never mind him, anyway; have done with him and forget him. And let him take with him all that you curse now, and never come back!'

'Yes, but he is spiteful. He laughed at me. He was impudent, Alyosha,' Ivan said, with a shudder of distaste. 'But he was unfair to me, unfair to me about lots of things. He told lies about me to my face. "Oh, you are going to perform an act of heroic virtue: to confess you murdered your father, that the valet murdered him at your instigation." '

'Brother,' Alyosha interposed, 'restrain yourself. It was not you murdered him. It's not true!'

'That's what he says, he, and he knows it. "You are going to perform an act of heroic virtue, and you don't believe in virtue; that's what tortures you and makes you angry, that's why you are so vindictive." He said that to me about me and he knows what he says.'

'It's you say that, not he,' exclaimed Alyosha mournfully, 'and you say it because you are ill and delirious, tormenting yourself.'

'No, he knows what he says. "Pride is driving you to the trial," he says. "You'll stand up and say it was I killed him, and why do you writhe with horror? You are lying! I despise your opinion, I despise your horror!" He said that about me. "And do you know you long for their praise – 'He is a criminal, a murderer, but what a generous soul; he wanted to save his brother and he confessed.' " That's a lie, Alyosha!' Ivan cried suddenly, with flashing eyes. 'I don't want the low rabble to praise me, I swear I don't! That's a lie! That's why I threw the glass at him and it broke against his ugly face.'

'Brother, calm yourself, stop!' Alyosha entreated him.

'Yes, he knows how to torment one. He's cruel,' Ivan went on, unheeding. 'I had an inkling from the first what he came for. "Granted that you go there through pride, still you had a hope that Smerdyakov might be convicted and sent to Siberia, and Mitya would be acquitted, while you would only be punished with *moral* condemnation" ("Do you hear?" he laughed then) – "and some people will praise you. But now Smerdyakov's dead, he has hanged himself, and who'll believe you alone? But yet you are going, you are going, you'll go all the same, you've decided to go. What are you going for now?" That's awful, Alyosha. I can't endure such questions. Who has the right to ask me such questions?'

'Brother,' interposed Alyosha. His heart sank with terror, but he still hoped to bring Ivan to reason. 'How could he have told you of Smerdyakov's death before I came when no one knew of it and there was no time for anyone to know of it?'

'He told me,' said Ivan firmly, refusing to admit a doubt. 'It was all he did talk about, if you come to that. "And it would be all right if you believed in virtue," he said. "No matter if they disbelieve you, you are going for the sake of principle. But you are a little pig like Fyodor Pavlovitch and what do you want with virtue? Why do you want to go meddling if your sacrifice is of no use to anyone? Because you don't know yourself why you go! Oh, you'd give a great deal to know yourself why you go! And can you have made up your mind? You've not made up your mind. You'll sit all night deliberating whether to go or not. But you will go; you know you'll go. You know that whichever way you decide, the decision does not depend on you. You'll go because you won't dare not to go. Why won't you dare to stay away? You must guess that for yourself. That's a riddle for you!" He got up and went away. You came and he went. He called me a coward, Alyosha! The truth is that I am a coward. "It is not for such eagles to soar above the earth." It was he added that – he! And Smerdyakov said the same. He must be killed! Katya despises me. I've seen that for a month past. Even Lise will begin to despise me! "You are going in order to be praised." That's a brutal lie! And you despise me too, Alyosha. Now I am going to hate you again! And I hate the monster too! I hate the monster! I don't want to save the monster. Let him rot in Siberia! Oh, tomorrow I'll go, stand before them, and spit in their faces!'

He jumped up in a frenzy, flung off the towel, and began to pace up and down the room again. Alyosha recalled what he had just said. 'I seem to be sleeping awake . . . I walk, I speak, I see, but I am asleep.' He seemed in just this state now. Alyosha did not leave him. The thought passed through his mind to run for a doctor, but he was afraid to leave his brother alone; there was no one to whom he could leave him. By degrees Ivan completely lost consciousness. He still went on talking, talking incessantly, but quite incoherently, and even articulated his words with difficulty. Suddenly he staggered violently; but Alyosha was in time to support him. Ivan let him lead him to the bed. Alyosha undressed him somehow and put him to bed. He sat watching over him for another two hours. The sick man slept soundly, without stirring, breathing softly and evenly. Alyosha took a pillow and lay down on the sofa, without undressing.

As he fell asleep he prayed for Mitya and Ivan. He began to understand Ivan's illness. 'The anguish of a proud determination. An earnest conscience!' God, in whom Ivan did not believe, and His truth were gaining mastery over his heart, which still refused to submit. 'Yes,' the thought floated through Alyosha's head as it lay on the pillow, 'yes, if Smerdyakov is dead, no one will believe Ivan's evidence; but he will go and give it.' Alyosha smiled softly. 'God will conquer!' he thought. 'He will either rise up in the light of truth, or . . . he'll perish in hate, revenging on himself and on everyone his service to a cause he does not believe in,' Alyosha added bitterly, and again he prayed for Ivan.

Book Ten

I

At ten o'clock on the morning of the day following the events I have described, the trial of Dmitri Karamazov began in our district court.

Visitors had arrived not only from the chief town of our province, but from several other Russian towns, as well as from Moscow and Petersburg. Among them were lawyers, ladies, and even several distinguished personages. Every ticket of admission had been snatched up. A special place behind the table at which the three judges sat was set apart for the most distinguished and important of the men visitors; a row of armchairs had been placed there – something exceptional, which had never been allowed before. A large proportion – not less than half of the public – were ladies.

Some of the ladies, especially those who came from a distance, made their appearance in the gallery very smartly dressed, but the majority of the ladies were oblivious even of dress. Their faces betrayed hysterical, intense, almost morbid, curiosity. A peculiar fact – established afterwards from many observations – was that almost all the ladies, or, at least the vast majority of them, were on Mitya's side and in favour of his being acquitted. This was perhaps chiefly owing to his reputation as a conqueror of female hearts. It was known that two women rivals were to appear in the case. One of them – Katerina Ivanovna – was an object of general interest. All sorts of extraordinary tales were told about her, amazing anecdotes of her passion for Mitya, in spite of his crime. Her pride and 'aristocratic connections' were particularly stressed (she had called upon scarcely anyone in the town). People said she intended to petition the Government for leave to accompany the criminal to Siberia and to be married to him somewhere in the mines. The appearance of Grushenka in court was awaited with no less impatience. The public was looking forward with anxious curiosity to the meeting of the two rivals – the proud aristocratic girl and the paramour, but Grushenka was a more familiar figure to the local ladies than Katerina Ivanovna. They had already seen 'the woman who had ruined Fyodor Pavlovitch and his unhappy son', and all, almost without exception, wondered how father and son could be so in love with 'such a very common, ordinary Russian girl, who was not even pretty'.

In brief, there was a great deal of talk. I know for a fact that there were several serious family quarrels on Mitya's account in our town. Many ladies quarrelled violently with their husbands over differences of opinion about the dreadful case, and it was only natural that the husbands of these ladies, far from being favourably disposed to the prisoner, should enter the court bitterly prejudiced against him. In fact, one may say with fair certainty that the masculine, as distinguished from the feminine part of the audience, were biased against the prisoner. There were numbers of severe, frowning, even vindictive, faces. Mitya, indeed, had managed to offend many people during his stay in the town.

The court was packed and overflowing long before

the judges made their appearance. Our court is the best hall in the town – spacious, lofty, and good for sound. On the right of the judges, who were on a raised platform, a table and two rows of chairs had been prepared for the jury. On the left was the place for the prisoner and the counsel for the defence. In the middle of the court, near the judges, was a table with the 'material evidence'. On it lay Fyodor Pavlovitch's white silk dressing gown, stained with blood; the fatal brass pestle with which the murder had supposedly been committed; Mitya's shirt, with a bloodstained sleeve; his coat, stained with blood in patches over the pocket in which he had put his handkerchief; the handkerchief itself, stiff with blood and by now quite yellow; the pistol loaded by Mitya at Perhotin's with a view to suicide, and taken from him on the sly at Mokroe by Trifon Borissovitch; the envelope in which the three thousand roubles had been put ready for Grushenka, the narrow pink ribbon with which it had been tied, and many other articles.

At ten o'clock the three judges arrived – the President, one honorary justice of the peace, and one other. The prosecutor, of course, entered immediately after. The President was a short, stout, thickset man of fifty, with a dyspeptic complexion, dark hair turning grey and cut short, and a red ribbon, of what Order I don't recollect. The prosecutor struck me and the others, too, as looking particularly pale, almost green. His face seemed to have grown suddenly thinner, for I had seen him looking as usual only two days before. The President began by asking the court whether all the jury were present.

Neither side objected to very many of the jurymen. I remember the twelve jurymen – four were petty officials of the town, two were merchants, and six peasants and artisans of the town. I remember, long before the trial, questions were continually asked with some surprise, especially by ladies, 'Can such a delicate, complex and psychological case be submitted for decision to petty officials and even peasants?' Yet their faces made a strangely imposing, almost menacing, impression; they were stern and frowning.

At last the President opened the case of the murder of Fyodor Pavlovitch Karamazov. I don't quite remember how he described him. The court usher was told to bring in the prisoner, and Mitya made his appearance. There was a hush through the court. One could have heard a pin drop. I don't know how it was with others, but Mitya made a most unfavourable impression on me. He looked so dandified in a brand-new frock coat. I heard afterwards that he had ordered it in Moscow expressly for the occasion from his own tailor, who had his measurements. He wore brand-new black kid gloves and exquisite linen. He walked in with his yard-long strides, looking stiffly straight in front of him, and sat down in his place with a most unperturbed air.

At the same moment the counsel for defence, the celebrated Fetyukovitch, entered, and a sort of subdued hum passed through the court. He was a tall, spare man, with long thin legs, with extremely long, thin, pale fingers, clean-shaven face, demurely brushed, rather short hair, and thin lips that were at times curved into something between a sneer and a smile. He looked about forty. His face would have been pleasant if it had not been for his eyes, which, in themselves small and inexpressive, were set remarkably close together, with only the thin, long nose as a dividing line. In fact, there was something strikingly birdlike about his face. He was in evening dress and white tie.

I remember the President's first questions to Mitya, about his name, his calling, and so on. Mitya answered sharply, and his voice was so unexpectedly loud that it made the President start and look at the prisoner with surprise. Then followed a list of persons who were to take part in the proceedings – that is, of the witnesses and experts. It was a long list. Four of the witnesses were not present – Miüsov, who had given evidence at the preliminary enquiry, but was now in Paris; Madame Hohlakov and Maximov, who were absent through illness; and Smerdyakov, through his sudden death, of which an official statement from the police was presented. The news of Smerdyakov's death produced a sudden stir and whisper in the court. Many of the audience, of course, had not heard of the sudden suicide. What struck people most was Mitya's sudden outburst. As soon as the statement of Smerdyakov's death was made, he cried out aloud from his place: 'He was a dog and died like a dog!'

I remember how his counsel rushed to him, and how the President addressed him, threatening to take stern measures, if such an irregularity were repeated. Mitya nodded and in a subdued voice repeated several times abruptly to his counsel, with no show of regret: 'I won't again, I won't. It escaped me. I won't do it again.'

And, of course, this brief episode did him no good with the jury or the public. His character was revealed, and it spoke for itself. It was under the influence of this incident that the opening statement was read. It was rather short, but circumstantial. It only stated the chief reason why he had been arrested, why he must be tried, and so on. Yet it made a great impression on me. The clerk read it loudly and distinctly. The whole tragedy was suddenly unfolded before us, concentrated, in bold relief, in a fatal and pitiless light. I remember how immediately after it had been read, the President asked Mitya in a loud, impressive voice: 'Prisoner, do you plead guilty?'

Mitya suddenly rose from his seat.

'I plead guilty to drunkenness and dissipation,' he exclaimed, again in a startling, almost frenzied, voice, 'to idleness and debauchery. I meant to become an honest man for good, just at the moment when I was struck down by fate. But I am not guilty of the death of that old man, my enemy and my father. No, no, I am not guilty of robbing him! I could not be. Dmitri Karamazov is a scoundrel, but not a thief.'

He sat down again, visibly trembling all over. The President again briefly, but impressively, admonished him to answer only what was asked, and not to indulge in irrelevant outbursts. Then he ordered the case to proceed. All the witnesses were led up to take the oath. Then I saw them all together. The brothers of the prisoner were, however, allowed to give evidence without taking the oath. After an exhortation from the priest and the President, the witnesses were led away and were made to sit as far as possible apart from one another. Then they began calling them up one by one. The witnesses for the prosecution were called first.

2

From the first moments of the trial one peculiar characteristic of the case became apparent to everyone, that is, the overwhelming strength of the prosecution as compared with the arguments the defence had to rely upon. I imagine that even the ladies, who were so impatiently longing for the acquittal of the interesting prisoner, were at the same time, without exception, convinced of his guilt. What's more, I believe they would have been mortified if his guilt had not been so firmly established, as that would have lessened the effect of the closing scene of the criminal's acquittal. That he would be acquitted all the ladies, strange to say, believed firmly up to the very last moment. The men were more interested in the contest between the prosecutor and the famous Fetyukovitch.

But Fetyukovitch remained an enigma to all up to the very end, up to his speech. Persons of experience suspected that he had some design, that he was working towards some object, but it was almost impossible to guess what it was. His confidence and self-reliance were unmistakable, however. Everyone noticed with pleasure, moreover, that he, after so short a stay, not more than three days, perhaps, among us, had so wonderfully succeeded in mastering the case and 'had studied it to a nicety'. People described with relish, afterwards, how cleverly he had 'taken down' all the witnesses for the prosecution, and as far as possible perplexed them and, what's more, had aspersed their reputations and so depreciated the value of their evidence.

So, for instance, when Grigory, Fyodor Pavlovitch's old servant, who had given the most damning piece of evidence about the open door, was examined, the counsel for the defence positively fastened upon him when his turn came to question him. It must be noted that Grigory entered the hall with a composed and almost stately air, not the least disconcerted by the majesty of the court or the vast audience listening to him. He gave evidence with as much confidence as though he had been talking with his Marfa, only perhaps more respectfully. It was impossible to make him contradict himself. The prosecutor questioned him first in detail about the family life of the Karamazovs. The family picture stood out in lurid colours. It was plain to ear and eye that the witness was guileless and impartial. In spite of his profound reverence for the memory of his deceased master, he yet bore witness that he had been unjust to Mitya and 'hadn't brought up his children as he should. He'd have been devoured by lice when he was little, if it hadn't been for me,' he added, describing Mitya's early childhood. 'It wasn't fair either of the father to wrong his son over his mother's property, which was by right his.'

In reply to the prosecutor's question as to what grounds he had for asserting that Fyodor Pavlovitch had wronged his son in their money relations, Grigory, to the surprise of everyone, had no proof at all to bring forward, but he still persisted that the arrangement with the son was 'unfair', and that he ought 'to have paid him several thousand roubles more'. I must note, by the way, that the prosecutor asked whether Fyodor Pavlovitch had really kept back part of Mitya's inheritance with marked persistence of all the witnesses who could be questioned on the point, not excepting Alyosha and Ivan, but he obtained no exact information from anyone; all alleged that it was so, but were unable to bring forward any tangible proof. Grigory's description of the scene at the dinner table, when Dmitri had burst in and beaten his father, threatening to come back to kill him, made a sinister impression on the court, especially as the old servant's composure in telling it, his parsimony of words and peculiar phraseology were as effective as eloquence. He observed that he was not angry with Mitya for having knocked him down and struck him on the face; he had forgiven him long ago, he said. Of the deceased Smerdyakov he observed, crossing himself, that he was a lad of ability, but stubborn and afflicted, and, worse still, an infidel, and that it was Fyodor Pavlovitch and his older son, Mitya, who had taught him to be so. But he defended Smerdyakov's honesty almost with warmth, and related how Smerdyakov had once found the master's money in the yard, and, instead of concealing it, had taken it to his master, who had rewarded him with a 'gold piece' for it, and trusted him implicitly from that time forward. He maintained obstinately that the door into the garden had been open. But he was asked so many questions that I can't recall them all.

At last the counsel for the defence began to cross-examine him, and the first question he asked was about the envelope in which Fyodor Pavlovitch was supposed to have put three thousand roubles for 'a certain person'. 'Have you ever seen it, you, who were for so many years in close attendance on your master?' Grigory answered that he had not seen it and had never heard of the money from anyone 'till everybody was talking about it.' This question about the envelope Fetyukovitch put to everyone who could conceivably have known of it, as persistently as the prosecutor asked his question about Dmitri's inheritance, and got the same answer from all, that no one had seen the envelope, though many had heard of it. From the beginning everyone noticed Fetyukovitch's persistence on this subject.

'Now, with your permission I'll ask you a question,' Fetyukovitch said, suddenly and unexpectedly. 'Of what was that balm, or rather, decoction, made, which, as we learn from the preliminary enquiry, you used on that evening to rub your lumbago, in the hope of curing it?'

Grigory looked blankly at the questioner, and after a brief silence muttered 'there was sage in it'.

'Nothing but sage? Don't you remember any other ingredient?'

'There was plantain in it too.'

'And pepper perhaps?' Fetyukovitch queried.

'Yes, there was pepper too.'

'Etcetera. And all dissolved in vodka?'

'In alcohol.'

There was a faint sound of laughter in the court.

'You see, in alcohol. After rubbing your back, I believe, you drank what was left in the bottle with a certain pious prayer, only known to your wife?'

'I did.'

'Did you drink much? Roughly speaking, a wine glass or two?'

'It might have been a tumblerful.'

'A tumblerful, even. Perhaps a tumber and a half?'

Grigory did not answer. He seemed to see what was meant.

'A glass and a half of neat alcohol – is not at all bad, don't you think? You might see the gates of heaven open, not only the door into the garden?'

Grigory remained silent. There was another laugh in the court. The President made a gesture.

'Do you know for a fact,' Fetyukovitch persisted, 'whether you were awake or not when you saw the open door?'

'I was on my legs.'

'That's not a proof that you were awake.' (There was again laughter in the court.) 'Could you have answered at that moment, if anyone had asked you a question – for instance, what year it is?'

'I don't know.'

'And what year is it, Anno Domini, do you know?'

Grigory stood with a perplexed face, looking straight at his tormentor. Strange to say, it appeared he really did not know what year it was.

'But perhaps you can tell how many fingers you have on your hands?'

'I am a servant,' Grigory said suddenly, in a loud and distinct voice. 'If my betters think fit to make fun of me, it is my duty to suffer it.'

Fetyukovitch was a little taken aback, and the President intervened, reminding him that he must ask more relevant questions. Fetyukovitch bowed with dignity and said that he had no more questions to ask of the witness. The public and the jury, of course, were left with a grain of doubt in their minds as to the evidence of a man who might, while undergoing a certain cure, have seen 'the gates of heaven', and who did not even know what year he was living in. But before Grigory left the box another episode occurred. The President, turning to the prisoner, asked him whether he had any comment to make on the evidence of the last witness.

'Except about the door, all he has said is true,' cried Mitya, in a loud voice. 'For combing the lice off me, I thank him; for forgiving my blows, I thank him. The old man has been honest all his life and as faithful to my father as seven hundred poodles.'

'Prisoner, be careful in your language,' the President admonished him.

'I am not a poodle,' Grigory muttered.

'All right, it's I am a poodle myself,' cried Mitya. 'If it's an insult, I take it to myself and I beg his pardon. I was a beast and cruel to him. I was cruel to Aesop too.'

'What Aesop?' the President asked sternly again.

'Oh, Pierrot . . . my father, Fyodor Pavlovitch.'

The President again and again warned Mitya impressively and very sternly to be more careful in his language.

'You are injuring yourself in the opinion of your judges.'

The counsel for the defence was equally clever in dealing with the evidence of Rakitin. I may remark that Rakitin was one of the leading witnesses and one to whom the prosecutor attached great significance. It appeared that he knew everything; his knowledge was amazing, he had been everywhere, seen everything, talked to everybody, knew every detail of the biography of Fyodor Pavlovitch and all the Karamazovs.

But Rakitin, in his youthful ardour, made a slight blunder, of which the counsel for the defence at once adroitly took advantage. Answering certain questions about Grushenka, he went so far as to speak somewhat contemptuously of Agrafena Alexandrovna as 'the kept mistress of Samsonov'. He would have given a good deal to take back his words afterwards.

'Allow me to ask,' began the counsel for the defence, with the most affable and even respectful smile. 'You stated just now that you were very intimately acquainted with Madame Svyetlov.' (It must be noted that Grushenka's surname was Svyetlov. I heard it for the first time that day, during the case.)

'I cannot answer for all my acquaintances . . . I am a young man . . . and who can be responsible for everyone he meets?' cried Rakitin, flushing deeply.

'I understand, I quite understand,' cried Fetyukovitch, as though he too were embarrassed and in haste to excuse himself. 'You, like any other, might well be interested in your acquaintance with a young and beautiful woman who would readily entertain the élite of the youth of the neighbourhood, but . . . I only wanted to know . . . it has come to my knowledge that Madame Svyetlov was particularly anxious a couple of months ago to make the acquaintance of the younger Karamazov, Alexey Fyodorovitch, and promised you twenty-five roubles, if you would bring him to her in his monastic dress. And that actually took place on the evening of the day on which the terrible crime, which is the subject of the present investigation, was committed. You brought Alexey Karamazov to Madame Svyetlov, and did you receive the twenty-five roubles from Madame Svyetlov as a reward, that's what I wanted to hear from you?'

'It was a joke . . . I don't see of what interest that can be to you . . . I took it for a joke . . . meaning to give it back later . . . '

'Then you did take . . . But you have not given it back yet . . . or have you?'

'That's of no consequence,' muttered Rakitin, 'I refuse to answer such questions . . . Of course I shall give it back.'

The President intervened, but Fetyukovitch declared he had no more questions to ask of the witness. Rakitin left the witness box with a slight stain on his character. The effect left by the lofty idealism of his speech was somewhat marred, and Fetyukovitch's expression, as he watched him walk away, seemed to suggest to the public 'this is a specimen of the lofty-minded persons who accuse the prisoner'.

Captain Snegiryov's evidence was a failure, too, but from quite a different reason. He appeared in ragged and dirty clothes, muddy boots, and in spite of the vigilance and expert observation of the police officers, he turned out to be hopelessly drunk. On being asked about Mitya's attack upon him, he refused to answer.

'God bless him. Iliusha told me not to. God will make it up to me yonder.'

'Who told you not to tell? Of whom are you talking?'

'Iliusha, my little son. "Father, Father, how he insulted you!" He said that about the stone. Now he is dying . . .'

The captain suddenly began to sob and fell down on his knees before the President. He was hurriedly led away amidst the laughter of the public. The effect prepared by the prosecutor did not come off at all.

Fetyukovitch continued to make the most of every opportunity, and amazed people more and more by his minute knowledge of the case. Thus, for example, Trifon Borissovitch made a great impression, of course, very prejudicial to Mitya. He calculated almost on his fingers that on his first visit to Mokroe, Mitya must have spent three thousand roubles, 'or very little less.

Just think what he squandered on those gypsy girls alone!' He recalled, in fact, every item of expense and added it all up. So the theory that only fifteen hundred had been spent and the rest had been put aside in a little bag seemed inconceivable.

'I saw three thousand as clear as a penny in his hands, I saw it with my own eyes; I should think I ought to know how to reckon money,' cried Trifon Borissovitch, doing his best to satisfy 'his betters'.

When Fetyukovitch came to cross-examine him, he scarcely tried to refute the evidence, but began asking him about an incident at the first carousal at Mokroe, a month before the arrest, when Timofey and another peasant called Akim had picked up on the floor in the passage a hundred roubles dropped by Mitya when he was drunk, given them to Trifon Borissovitch, and received a rouble each for doing so. 'Well,' asked the lawyer, 'did you give that hundred roubles back to Mr Karamazov?' Trifon Borissovitch shuffled in vain . . . He was obliged, after the peasants had been examined, to admit the finding of the hundred roubles, only adding that he had religiously returned it all to Dmitri Fyodorovitch 'in perfect honesty, and it's only because his honour was in liquor at the time, he wouldn't remember it'. But, as he had denied the incident of the hundred roubles till the peasants had been called to prove it, his evidence as to returning the money to Mitya was naturally regarded with great suspicion. So one of the most dangerous witnesses brought forward by the prosecution was again discredited.

The same thing happened with the Poles. They took up an attitude of pride and independence; they vociferated loudly that they had both been in the service of the Crown, and that 'Pan Mitya' had offered them three thousand 'to buy their honour', and that they had seen a large sum of money in his hands. Pan Mussyalovitch introduced a terrible number of Polish words into his sentences, and seeing that this only increased his consequence in the eyes of the President and the prosecutor, grew more and more pompous, and ended by talking in Polish altogether. But Fetyukovitch caught them, too, in his snares. Trifon Borissovitch, recalled, was forced, in spite of his evasions, to admit that Pan Vrublevsky had substituted another pack of cards for the one he had provided, and that Pan Mussyalovitch had cheated during the game. Kalganov confirmed this, and both the Poles left the witness box with damaged reputations, amidst laughter.

Then exactly the same thing happened with almost all the most dangerous witnesses. Fetyukovitch succeeded in casting a slur on all of them, dismissing them with a certain derision. The lawyers and experts were greatly impressed, but were somewhat at a loss to understand what good purpose could be served by these tactics, for all, I repeat, felt that the case for the prosecution could not be refuted, that it was indeed growing more and more tragically overwhelming. But from the confidence of the 'great magician' they saw that he was serene, and they waited, feeling that 'such a man' had not come from Petersburg for nothing, and that he was not a man to return unsuccessful.

3

The evidence of the medical experts, too, was of little use to the prisoner. And it appeared later that Fetyukovitch had not reckoned much upon it. The medical line of defence had only been taken up through the insistence of Katerina Ivanovna, who had sent specially for a celebrated doctor from Moscow. The case for the defence could, of course, lose nothing from such an opinion, and might, with luck, gain something from it. There was, however, an element of comedy about it, through the difference of opinion of the doctors. The medical experts were the famous doctor from Moscow, our doctor, Herzenstube, and the young doctor, Varvinsky. The two latter appeared also as witnesses for the prosecution.

Dr Herzenstube roundly declared that the abnormality of the prisoner's mental faculties was self-evident. Then giving his ground for this opinion, which I omit here, he added that the abnormality was not only evident in many of the prisoner's actions in the past, but was apparent even now at this very moment. When he was asked to explain how it was apparent now at this moment, the old doctor, with naïve directness, pointed out that the prisoner on entering the court had 'an extraordinary air, remarkable in the circumstances'; that he had 'marched in like a soldier, looking straight before him, though it would have been more natural for him to look to the left where, among the public, the ladies were sitting, seeing that he was a great admirer of the fair sex and must be thinking much of what the ladies are saying of him now', the old man concluded.

The Moscow doctor, being questioned in his turn, definitely and emphatically repeated that he considered the prisoner's mental condition abnormal in the highest degree. He talked at length and with erudition of 'aberration' and 'mania', and argued that, from all the facts collected, the prisoner had undoubtedly been in a condition of aberration for several days before his arrest, and, if the crime had been committed by him, it must, even if he were conscious of it, have been almost involuntary, as he had not the power to control the morbid impulse that possessed him.

But apart from temporary aberration, the doctor diagnosed mania, which promised, in his words, to lead to complete insanity in the future. (It must be noted that I report this in my own words, the doctor made use of very learned and professional language.) 'All his actions are in contravention of common sense and logic,' he continued. 'Not to refer to what I have not seen, that is, the crime itself and the whole catastrophe, the day before yesterday, while he was talking to me, he had an unaccountably fixed look in his eye. He laughed unexpectedly when there was nothing to laugh at. He showed continual and inexplicable irritability.' But the doctor detected mania, above all, in the fact that the prisoner could not even speak of the three thousand roubles, of which he considered himself to have been cheated, without extraordinary irritation, though he could speak comparatively lightly of other misfortunes and grievances. According to all accounts, he had even in the past, whenever the subject of the three thousand roubles was touched on, flown into a perfect frenzy, and yet he was reported to be an open-handed and not a grasping man.

'As to the opinion of my learned colleague,' the

Moscow doctor added ironically in conclusion, 'that the prisoner would, on entering the court, have naturally looked at the ladies and not straight before him, I will only say that, apart from the playfulness of this theory, it is radically unsound. For though I fully agree that the prisoner, on entering the court where his fate will be decided, would not naturally look straight before him in that fixed way, and that that may really be a sign of his abnormal mental condition, at the same time I maintain that he would naturally not look to the left at the ladies, but, on the contrary, to the right to find his legal adviser, on whose help all his hopes rest and on whose defence all his future depends.' The doctor expressed his opinion positively and emphatically.

But the unexpected pronouncement of Dr Varvinsky gave the last touch of comedy to the difference of opinion between the experts. In his opinion the prisoner was now, and had been all along, in a perfectly normal condition, and, although he certainly must have been in a nervous and exceedingly excited state before his arrest, this might have been due to several perfectly obvious causes, jealousy, anger, continual drunkenness, and so on. But this nervous condition would not involve the mental aberration of which mention had just been made. As to the question whether the prisoner should have looked to the left or to the right on entering the court, 'in his modest opinion', the prisoner would naturally look straight before him on entering the court, as he had in fact done, as that was where the judges, on whom his fate depended, were sitting. So that it was just by looking straight before him that he showed his perfectly normal state of mind at the present. The young doctor concluded his 'modest' testimony with some heat.

'Bravo, doctor!' cried Mitya, from his seat, 'just so!'

Mitya, of course, was checked, but the young doctor's opinion had a decisive influence on the judges and on the public, and, as appeared afterwards, everyone agreed with him. The chief sensation in Mitya's favour was created by the evidence of Katerina Ivanovna, which I will describe directly. Indeed, when the witnesses *à décharge*, that is, called by the defence, began giving evidence, fortune seemed all at once markedly more favourable to Mitya, and what was particularly striking, this was a surprise even to the counsel for the defence. But before Katerina Ivanovna was called, Alyosha was examined, and he recalled a fact which seemed to furnish positive evidence against one important point made by the prosecution.

4

It came quite as a surprise even to Alyosha himself. He was not required to take the oath, and I remember that both sides addressed him very gently and sympathetically. It was evident that his reputation for goodness had preceded him. Alyosha gave his evidence modestly and with restraint, but his warm sympathy for his unhappy brother was unmistakable. In answer to one question, he sketched his brother's character as that of a man violent-tempered perhaps and carried away by his passions, but at the same time honourable, proud and generous, capable of self-sacrifice, if necessary. He admitted, however, that, through his passion for Grushenka and his rivalry with his father, his brother had been of late in an intolerable position. But he repelled with indignation the suggestion that his brother might have committed a murder for the sake of gain, though he recognised that the three thousand roubles had become almost an obsession with Mitya.

'Did your brother tell you, anyway, that he intended to kill your father?' asked the prosecutor. 'You can refuse to answer if you think necessary,' he added.

'He did not tell me so directly,' answered Alyosha.

'How so? Did he tell you indirectly?'

'He spoke to me once of his hatred for our father and his fear that at an extreme moment . . . at a moment of fury, he might perhaps murder him.'

'And you believed him?'

'I am afraid to say that I did. But I never doubted that some higher feeling would always save him at the fatal moment, as it has indeed saved him, for it was not he killed my father,' Alyosha said firmly, in a loud voice that was heard throughout the court.

The prosecutor started like a warhorse at the sound of a trumpet. 'Let me assure you that I fully believe in the complete sincerity of your conviction and do not explain it by or identify it with your affection for your unhappy brother. Your peculiar view of the whole tragic episode is known to us already from the preliminary investigation. I won't attempt to conceal from you that it is highly individual and contradicts all the other evidence collected by the prosecution. And so I think it essential to press you to tell me what facts have led you to this conviction of your brother's innocence and of the guilt of another person against whom you gave evidence at the preliminary enquiry?'

'I only answered the questions asked me at the preliminary enquiry,' replied Alyosha, slowly and calmly. 'I made no accusation against Smerdyakov on my own initiative.'

'Yet you gave evidence against him?'

'I was led to do so by my brother Dmitri's words. I was told what took place at his arrest and how he had pointed to Smerdyakov before I was examined. I believe absolutely that my brother is innocent, and if he didn't commit the murder, then . . .'

'Then Smerdyakov? Why Smerdyakov? And why are you so completely persuaded of your brother's innocence?'

'I cannot help believing my brother. I know he wouldn't lie to me. I saw from his face he wasn't lying.'

'Only from his face? Is that all the proof you have?'

'I have no other proof.'

'And of Smerdyakov's guilt have you no proof whatever but your brother's word and the expression of his face?'

'No, I have no other proof.'

Fetyukovitch began his cross-examination. On his asking Alyosha when it was that the prisoner had told him of his hatred for his father and that he might kill him, and whether he had heard it, for instance, at their last meeting before the catastrophe, Alyosha started as he answered, as though only just recollecting and understanding something.

'I remember one circumstance now which I'd quite forgotten myself. It wasn't clear to me at the time, but now . . .'

And, obviously only now for the first time struck by an idea, he recounted eagerly how, at his last interview with Mitya that evening under the tree, on the road to the monastery, Mitya had struck himself on the breast, 'the upper part of the breast', and had repeated several times that he had a means of regaining his honour, that

that means was here, here on his breast. 'I thought, when he struck himself on the breast, he meant that it was in his heart,' Alyosha continued, 'that he might find in his heart strength to save himself from some awful disgrace which was awaiting him and which he did not dare confess even to me. I must confess I did think at the time that he was speaking of our father, and that the disgrace he was shuddering at was the thought of going to our father and doing some violence to him. Yet it was just then that he pointed to something on his breast, so that I remember the idea struck me at the time that the heart is not in that part of the breast, but lower down, and that he struck himself much too high, just below the neck, and kept pointing to that place. My idea seemed silly to me at the time, but he was perhaps pointing then to that little bag in which he had fifteen hundred roubles!'

'Just so,' Mitya cried from his place. 'That's right, Alyosha, it was the little bag I struck with my fist.'

Fetyukovitch flew to him in hot haste entreating him to keep quiet, and at the same instant pounced on Alyosha. Alyosha, carried away himself by his recollection, warmly expressed his theory that this disgrace was probably just that fifteen hundred roubles on him, which he might have returned to Katerina Ivanovna as half of what he owed her, but which he had yet determined not to repay her and to use for another purpose – namely, to enable him to elope with Grushenka, if she consented.

'It is so, it must be so,' exclaimed Alyosha, in sudden excitement. 'My brother cried several times that half of the disgrace, half of it (he said *half* several times) he could free himself from at once, but that he was so unhappy in his weakness of will that he wouldn't do it . . . that he knew beforehand he was incapable of doing it!'

Katerina Ivanovna was called to the witness box. As she entered something extraordinary happened in the court. The ladies clutched their lorgnettes and opera glasses. There was a stir among the men: some stood up to get a better view. Everybody alleged afterwards that Mitya had turned 'white as a sheet' on her entrance. All in black, she advanced modestly, almost timidly. It was impossible to tell from her face that she was agitated; but there was a resolute gleam in her dark and brooding eyes. I may remark that many people mentioned that she looked particularly handsome at that moment. She spoke softly but clearly, so that she was heard all over the court. She expressed herself with composure, or at least tried to appear composed. The President began his examination discreetly and very respectfully, as though afraid to touch on 'certain chords', and showing consideration for her great unhappiness. But in answer to one of the first questions Katerina Ivanovna replied firmly that she had been formerly betrothed to the prisoner 'until he left me of his own accord . . .' she added quietly. When they asked her about the three thousand she had entrusted to Mitya to post to her relations, she said firmly, 'I didn't give him the money simply to send it off. I felt at the time that he was in great need of money . . . I gave him the three thousand on the understanding that he should post it within the month if he cared to. There was no need for him to worry himself about that debt afterwards.'

I will not repeat all the questions asked her and all her answers in detail. I will only give the substance of her evidence.

'I was firmly convinced that he would send off that

sum as soon as he got money from his father,' she went on. 'I have never doubted his disinterestedness and his honesty . . . his scrupulous honesty . . . in money matters. I don't remember any threat uttered by him against his father. He certainly never uttered any such threat before me. If he had come to me at that time, I should have at once relieved his anxiety about that unlucky three thousand roubles, but he had given up coming to see me . . . and I myself was put in such a position . . . that I could not invite him . . . And I had no right, indeed, to be exacting as to that money,' she added suddenly, and there was a ring of resolution in her voice. 'I was once indebted to him for assistance in money for more than three thousand, and I took it, although I could not at that time foresee that I should ever be in a position to repay my debt.'

There was a note of defiance in her voice. It was then Fetyukovitch began his cross-examination.

'Did that take place not here, but at the beginning of your acquaintance?' Fetyukovitch suggested cautiously, feeling his way, instantly scenting something favourable. I must mention in parenthesis that, though Fetyukovitch had been brought from Petersburg partly at the instance of Katerina Ivanovna herself, he knew nothing about the episode of the five thousand roubles given her by Mitya, and of her 'bowing to the ground to him'. She concealed this from him and said nothing about it, and that was strange. It is more than likely that she herself did not know till the very last minute whether she would speak of that episode in the court, and waited for the inspiration of the moment.

Never shall I forget those moments. She began to tell her story. She told everything, the whole episode that Mitya had related to Alyosha, how she bowed to the ground, and her reasons for doing this. She told about her father and how she went to Mitya, and did not with one word, or by a single hint, suggest that Mitya had himself, through her sister, proposed they should 'send him Katerina Ivanovna' to fetch the money. She generously concealed that and was not ashamed to make it appear as though she had of her own impulse run to the young officer, relying on something . . . to beg him for the money. It was magnificent! I turned cold and trembled as I listened. The court was hushed, straining to catch each word. It was something unique. Even from such a self-willed and contemptuously proud girl as she was, such an extremely frank avowal, such sacrifice, such self-immolation, seemed incredible. And for what, for whom? To save the man who had deceived and insulted her and to help him, in however small a degree, by creating a strong impression in his favour. And, indeed, the figure of the young officer who, with a respectful bow to the innocent girl, handed her his last five thousand roubles – all he had in the world – suddenly appeared in a very sympathetic and attractive light.

The prosecutor did not venture upon even one question on the subject. Fetyukovitch felt that now the charge of theft, at least, was as good as disproved. 'The case' assumed quite a different aspect. There was a wave of sympathy for Mitya. As for him . . . I was told that once or twice, while Katerina Ivanovna was giving her evidence, he jumped up from his seat, sank back again, and hid his face in his hands. But when she had finished, he suddenly cried: 'Katya, why have you ruined me?' and his sobs were audible all over the court. But he instantly restrained himself, and cried again: 'Now I am condemned!'

Then he sat rigid in his place, with his teeth clenched and his arms folded across his chest. Katerina Ivanovna remained in the court and sat down in her place. She was pale and sat with her eyes cast down. Those who were sitting near her declared that for a long time she shivered all over as though in a fever. Grushenka was called.

She too was dressed entirely in black, with her magnificent black shawl on her shoulders. She walked to the witness box with her smooth, noiseless tread, with the slightly swaying gait common in women of full figure. She looked steadily at the President, turning her eyes neither to the right nor to the left. To my thinking she looked very handsome at that moment, and not at all pale, as the ladies alleged afterwards. They declared, too, that she had a concentrated and spiteful expression. I believe that she was simply irritated and painfully conscious of the contemptuous and inquisitive eyes of our scandal-loving public. She was proud and could not stand contempt. She was one of those people who flare up, angry and eager to retaliate, at the mere suggestion of contempt. There was an element of timidity, too, of course, and inward shame at her own timidity, so it was not strange that her tone kept changing. At one moment it was angry, contemptuous and rough, and at another there was a sincere note of self-condemnation. Sometimes she spoke as though she were taking a desperate plunge; as though she felt, 'I don't care what happens. I'll say it . . .' Apropos of her acquaintance with Fyodor Pavlovitch, she remarked curtly, 'That's all nonsense, and was it my fault that he would pester me?' But a minute later she added, 'It was all my fault. I was laughing at them both – at the old man and at him too –

and I brought both of them to this. It was all on account of me it happened.'

Samsonov's name came up somehow. 'That's nobody's business,' she snapped at once, with a sort of insolent defiance. 'He was my benefactor; he took me when I hadn't a shoe to my foot, when my family had turned me out.' The President reminded her, though very politely, that she must answer the questions directly, without going off into irrelevant details. Grushenka crimsoned and her eyes flashed.

The envelope with the notes in it she had not seen, but had only heard from 'that wicked wretch' that Fyodor Pavlovitch had an envelope with notes for three thousand in it. 'But that was all foolishness. I was only laughing. I wouldn't have gone to him for anything.'

'To whom are you referring as "that wicked wretch"?' enquired the prosecutor.

'The lackey, Smerdyakov, who murdered his master and hanged himself last night.'

She was, of course, at once asked what ground she had for such a definite accusation; but it appeared that she too had no grounds for it.

'Dmitri Fyodorovitch told me so himself; you can believe him. The woman who came between us has ruined him; she is the cause of it all, let me tell you,' Grushenka added. She seemed to be quivering with hatred, and there was a vindictive note in her voice.

She was again asked to whom she was referring.

'The young lady, Katerina Ivanovna there. She sent for me, offered me chocolate, tried to fascinate me. There's not much true shame about her, I can tell you that . . .'

At this point the President checked her sternly, begging her to moderate her language. But the jealous woman's heart was burning, and she did not care what she did.

'When the prisoner was arrested at Mokroe,' the prosecutor asked, 'everyone saw and heard you run out of the next room and cry out: "It's all my fault. We'll go to Siberia together!" So you already believed him to have murdered his father?'

'I don't remember what I felt at the time,' answered Grushenka. 'Everyone was crying out that he had killed his father, and I felt that it was my fault, that it was on my account he had murdered him. But when he said he wasn't guilty, I believed him at once, and I believe him now and always shall believe him. He is not the man to tell a lie.'

Fetyukovitch began his cross-examination. I remember that among other things he asked about Rakitin and the twenty-five roubles 'you paid him for bringing Alexey Fyodorovitch Karamazov to see you'.

'There was nothing strange about his taking the money,' sneered Grushenka, with angry contempt. 'He was always coming to me for money: he used to get thirty roubles a month at least out of me, chiefly for luxuries: he had enough to keep him without my help.'

'What led you to be so liberal to Mr Rakitin?' Fetyukovitch asked, in spite of an uneasy movement on the part of the President.

'Why, he is my cousin. His mother was my mother's sister. But he's always besought me not to tell anyone here of it, he is so dreadfully ashamed of me.'

This fact was a complete surprise to everyone; no one in the town nor in the monastery, nor even Mitya, knew of it. I was told later that Rakitin turned purple with shame where he sat. Grushenka had somehow heard before she came into the court that he had given evidence against Mitya, and so she was angry. The whole effect on the public of Rakitin's speech, of his noble sentiments, was now finally ruined. Fetyukovitch was satisfied: it was another godsend. Grushenka's cross-examination did not last long and, of course, there could be nothing particularly new in her evidence. She left a very disagreeable impression on the public; hundreds of contemptuous eyes were fixed upon her, as she finished giving her evidence and sat down again in the court, at a good distance from Katerina Ivanovna. Mitya was silent throughout her evidence. He sat as though turned to stone, with his eyes fixed on the ground.

Ivan was called to give evidence.

5

I may note that he had been called before Alyosha. But the usher of the court announced to the President that, owing to an attack of illness or some sort of fit, the witness could not appear at the moment, but was ready to give his evidence as soon as he recovered. But no one seemed to have heard it and it only came out later.

His entrance was at first almost unnoticed. The principal witnesses, especially the two rival ladies, had already been questioned. Curiosity was satisfied for the time; the public was feeling almost fatigued. Several more witnesses were still to be heard, who probably had little information to give after all that had been given. Time was passing. Ivan walked up with extraordinary deliberation, looking at no one, and with his head bowed, as though plunged in gloomy thought. He was irreproachably dressed, but his face made a painful impression, on me at least: there was an earthy look in it, a look like a dying man's. His eyes were lustreless; he raised them and looked slowly round the court. Alyosha jumped up from his seat and moaned 'Ah!' I remember that, but it was hardly noticed.

The President began by informing him that he was a witness not on oath, that he might answer or refuse to answer, but that, of course, he must bear witness according to his conscience, and so on and so on. Ivan listened and looked at him blankly, but his face gradually relaxed into a smile, and as soon as the President, looking at him in astonishment, finished, he laughed outright.

'Well, and what else?' he asked in a loud voice.

There was a hush in the court; there was a feeling of something strange. The President showed signs of uneasiness.

'You . . . are perhaps still unwell?' he began, looking everywhere for the usher.

'Don't trouble yourself, your excellency, I am well enough and can tell you something interesting,' Ivan answered with sudden calm and respect.

'You have some special communication to make?' the President went on, still mistrustfully.

Ivan looked down, waited a few seconds and, raising his head, answered, almost stammering: 'No . . . I haven't. I have nothing particular.'

They began questioning him. He answered, as it were reluctantly, with extreme brevity, with a sort of disgust which grew more and more marked, though he answered rationally. To many questions he answered that he did not know. He knew nothing of his father's money relations with Mitya. 'I wasn't interested in the subject,' he added. Threats to murder his father he had heard from the prisoner. Of the money in the envelope he had heard from Smerdyakov.

'The same thing over and over again,' he interrupted suddenly, with a look of weariness. 'I have nothing particular to tell the court.'

'I see you are unwell and understand your feelings,' the President began.

He turned to the prosecutor and the counsel for the defence to invite them to examine the witness, if necessary, when Ivan suddenly pleaded in an exhausted voice: 'Let me go, your excellency, I feel very ill.'

And with these words, without waiting for permission, he turned to walk out of the court. But after taking four steps he stood still, as though he had reached a decision, smiled slowly, and went back.

'I am like the peasant girl, your excellency . . . you know. How does it go? "I'll stand up if I like, and I won't if I don't." They were trying to put on her sarafan to take her to church to be married, and she said, "I'll stand up if I like, and I won't if I don't." . . . It's in some book about the peasantry.'

'What do you mean by that?' the President asked severely.

'Why, this,' Ivan suddenly pulled out a roll of notes. 'Here's the money . . . the notes that lay in that envelope' (he nodded towards the table on which lay the material evidence) 'for the sake of which our father was murdered. Where shall I put them? Mr Superintendent, take them.' The usher of the court took the whole roll and handed it to the President.

'How could this money have come into your possession if it is the same money?' the President asked in amazement.

'I got them from Smerdyakov, from the murderer, yesterday . . . I was with him just before he hanged himself. It was he, not my brother, killed our father. He murdered him and I incited him to do it . . . Who doesn't desire his father's death?'

'Are you in your right mind?' broke involuntarily from the President.

'I should think I am in my right mind . . . in the same nasty mind as all of you . . . as all these . . . ugly faces.' He turned suddenly to the audience. 'My father has been murdered and they pretend they are horrified,' he snarled, with furious contempt. 'They keep up the sham with one another. Liars! They all desire the death of their fathers. One reptile devours another . . . If there hadn't been a murder, they'd have been angry and gone home ill-humoured. It's a spectacle they want! "Bread and circuses". Though I am one to talk! Have you any water? Give me a drink for Christ's sake!' He suddenly clutched his head.

The usher at once approached him. Alyosha jumped up and cried, 'He is ill. Don't believe him: he has brain fever.' Katerina Ivanovna rose impulsively from her seat and, rigid with horror, gazed at Ivan. Mitya stood up and greedily looked at his brother and listened to him with a wild, strange smile.

'Don't disturb yourselves. I am not mad, I am only a murderer,' Ivan began again. 'You can't expect eloquence from a murderer,' he added suddenly for some reason and laughed a queer laugh.

The prosecutor bent over to the President in obvious dismay. The two other judges communicated in agitated whispers. Fetyukovitch pricked up his ears as he listened: the hall was hushed in expectation. The President seemed suddenly to recollect himself.

'Witness, your words are incomprehensible and impossible here. Calm yourself, if you can, and tell your story . . . if you really have something to tell. How can you confirm your statement . . . if indeed you are not delirious?'

'That's just it. I have no proof. That cur Smerdyakov won't send you proofs from the other world . . . in an envelope. You think of nothing but envelopes – one is enough. I've no witnesses . . . except one, perhaps,' he smiled thoughtfully.

'Who is your witness?'

'He has a tail, your excellency, and that would be irregular! The devil doesn't exist! Don't pay attention: he is a paltry, pitiful devil,' he added suddenly. He ceased laughing and spoke as it were confidentially. 'He is here somewhere, no doubt – under that table with the material evidence on it, perhaps. Come, release the monster . . . he's been singing a hymn. That's because his heart is light! It's like a drunken man in the street bawling how "Vanka went to Petersburg", and I would give a quadrillion quadrillions for two seconds of joy. You don't know me! Oh, how stupid all this business is! Come, take me instead of him! I didn't come for nothing . . . Why, why is everything so stupid? . . .'

And he began slowly, and as it were reflectively, looking round him again. But the court was all excitement by now. Alyosha rushed towards him, but the court usher had already seized Ivan by the arm.

'What are you about?' he cried, staring into the man's face, and suddenly seizing him by the shoulders, he flung him violently to the floor. But the police were on the spot and he was seized. He screamed furiously. And all the time he was being removed, he yelled and screamed something incoherent.

The whole court was thrown into confusion. Before everyone had completely regained composure and recovered from this scene, it was followed by another. Katerina Ivanovna had an attack of hysterics. She sobbed, shrieking loudly, but refused to leave the court, struggled, and besought them not to remove her. Suddenly she cried to the President: 'There is more evidence I must give at once . . . at once! Here is a document, a letter . . . take it, read it quickly, quickly! It's a letter from that monster . . . that man there, there!' she pointed to Mitya. 'It was he killed his father, you will see that directly. He wrote to me how he would kill his father! But the other one is ill, he is ill, he is delirious!' she kept crying out, beside herself.

The court usher took the document she held out to the President, and she, dropping into her chair, hiding her face in her hands, began convulsively and noiselessly sobbing, shaking all over, and stifling every sound for fear she would be ejected from the court. The document she had handed up was that letter Mitya had written at the Metropolis tavern, which Ivan had spoken of as a 'mathematical proof'. Alas! its mathematical conclusiveness was recognised, and had it not been for that letter, Mitya might have escaped his doom or, at least, that doom would have been less terrible. It was, I repeat, difficult to notice every detail. What followed is still confused in my mind. The President must, I suppose, have at once passed on the document to the judges, the jury, and the lawyers on both sides. I only remember how they began examining the witness. On being gently asked by the President whether she had recovered sufficiently, Katerina Ivanovna exclaimed impetuously: 'I received it the day before the crime was committed, but he wrote it the day before that, at the tavern – that is, two days before he committed the crime. Look, it is written on some sort of bill!' she cried breathlessly. 'He hated me at the time, because he had behaved contemptibly and was running after that creature . . . and because he owed me that three thousand . . . Oh! he was humiliated by that three thousand on account of his own meanness! This is how it happened about that three thousand. I beg you, I beseech you, to hear me. Three weeks before he murdered his father, he came to me one morning. I knew he was in need of money, and what he wanted it for. Yes, yes – to win that creature and carry her off. I knew then that he had been false to me and meant to abandon me, and it was I, I, who gave him that money, who offered it to him on the pretext of his sending it to my sister in Moscow. And as I gave it him, I looked him in the face and said that he could send it when he liked, "in a month's time would do". How, how could he have failed to understand that I was practically telling him to his face, "You want money to be false to me with your creature, so here's the money for you. I give it to you myself. Take it, if you have so little honour as to take it!" I wanted to prove what he was, and what happened? He took it, he took it, and squandered it with that creature in one night . . . But he knew, he knew that I knew all about it. I assure you he understood, too, that I gave him that money to test him, to see whether he was so lost to all sense of honour as to take it from me. I looked into his eyes and he looked into mine, and he understood it all and he took it – he carried off my money!'

'That's true, Katya,' Mitya roared suddenly, 'I looked into your eyes and I knew that you were dishonouring me, and yet I took your money. Despise me as a scoundrel, despise me, all of you! I've deserved it!'

'Prisoner,' cried the President, 'another word and I will order you to be removed.'

'That money was a torment to him,' Katya went on with impulsive haste. 'He wanted to repay it to me. He wanted to, that's true; but he needed money for that creature too. So he murdered his father, but he didn't repay me, and went off with her to that village where he was arrested. There, again, he squandered the money he had stolen after the murder of his father. And a day before the murder he wrote me this letter. He was drunk when he wrote it. But read it, read it attentively – more attentively, please – and you will see that he had described it all in his letter, all beforehand, how he would kill his father and where his money was kept. Look, please, don't overlook that, there's one phrase there, "I shall kill him as soon as Ivan has gone away." So he thought it all out beforehand how he would kill him,' Katerina Ivanovna pointed out to the court with venomous and malignant triumph. Oh! it was clear she had studied every line of that letter and detected every meaning underlining it. I remember that the letter was read aloud by the clerk, directly afterwards, I believe. It made an overwhelming impression. They asked Mitya whether he admitted having written the letter.

'It's mine, mine!' cried Mitya. 'I wouldn't have written it if I hadn't been drunk! . . . We've hated each other for many things, Katya, but I swear, I swear I loved you even while I hated you, and you didn't love me!'

He sank back on his seat, wringing his hands in despair. The prosecutor and counsel for the defence began cross-examining her, chiefly to ascertain what had induced her to conceal such a document and to give her evidence in quite a different tone and spirit just before.

'Yes, yes. I was telling lies just now. I was lying against my honour and my conscience, but I wanted to save him, for he has hated and despised me so!' Katya cried madly. 'Oh, he has despised me horribly, he has always despised me, and do you know, he has despised me from the very moment that I bowed down to him for that money. I saw that . . . Oh, he didn't understand, he had no idea why I ran to him, he can suspect nothing but baseness, he judged me by himself, he thought everyone was like himself!' Katya spat out furiously, in a perfect frenzy. 'And he only wanted to marry me because I'd inherited a fortune, because of that, because of that! I always suspected it was because of that! Oh, he is a brute! I tried to conquer him by my love – a love that knew no bounds. I even tried to forgive his faithlessness; but he understood nothing, nothing! How could he understand, indeed? He is a monster.'

The President and the prosecutor, of course, tried to calm her. I can't help thinking that they felt ashamed of taking advantage of her hysteria and of listening to such avowals. I remember hearing them say to her, 'We understand how hard it is for you; be sure we are able to feel for you,' and so on, and so on. And yet they dragged the evidence out of the raving, hysterical woman. She described at last with extraordinary lucidity, such as comes so often, though only for a moment, when the nerves are overwrought, how Ivan had been nearly driven out of his mind during the last two months trying to save 'the monster and murderer', his brother.

'He tortured himself,' she exclaimed, 'he was always trying to minimise his brother's guilt and confessing to me that he too had never loved his father, and perhaps desired his death himself. He tormented himself with his conscience! He told me everything, everything! He came every day and talked to me as his only friend. I have the honour to be his only friend!' she cried suddenly with a sort of defiance, and her eyes flashed. 'He had been twice to see Smerdyakov. One day he came to me and said, "If it was not my brother, but Smerdyakov committed the murder (for the legend was circulating everywhere that Smerdyakov had done it), perhaps I too am guilty, for Smerdyakov knew I didn't like my father and perhaps believed that I desired my father's death." Then I brought out that letter and showed it to him. He was entirely convinced that his brother had done it, and he was overwhelmed by it. The doctor from Moscow, at my request, examined him the day before yesterday and told me that he was on the eve of brain fever – and all on his account, on account of this monster! And last night he learned that Smerdyakov was dead! It was such a shock that it drove him out of his mind . . . and all through this monster, all for the sake of saving the monster!'

Oh, of course, such an outpouring, such an avowal is only possible once in a lifetime – at the hour of death, for instance, on the way to the scaffold! But it was in Katya's character, and it was such a moment in her life. It was the same impetuous Katya who had thrown herself on the mercy of a young profligate to save her father; the same Katya who had just before, in her pride and chastity, sacrificed herself and her maidenly modesty before all these people, telling of Mitya's generous conduct, in the hope of softening his fate a little. And now, again, she sacrificed herself; but this time it was for another, and perhaps only now – perhaps only at this moment – she felt and knew how dear that other was to her! She had sacrificed herself in terror for him; conceiving all of a sudden that he had ruined himself by his confession that it was he who had committed the murder, not his brother, she had sacrificed herself to save him, to save his good name, his reputation.

And yet one terrible doubt arose – was she lying in her description of her former relations with Mitya? – that was the question. No, she had not intentionally slandered him when she cried that Mitya despised her for her bowing down to him! She believed it herself. She had been firmly convinced, perhaps ever since that bow, that the simple-hearted Mitya, who even then adored her, was laughing at her and despising her. She had loved him with a hysterical, tortured love only from pride, from wounded pride, and that love was not like love, but more like revenge. Oh! perhaps that tortured love would have grown into real love, perhaps Katya longed for nothing more than that, but Mitya's faithlessness had wounded her to the core of her heart, and her heart could not forgive him. The moment of revenge had come upon her suddenly, and all that had been accumulating so long and so painfully in the offended woman's breast burst out all at once and unexpectedly. She betrayed

Mitya, but she betrayed herself, too. And no sooner had she given full expression to her feelings than the exaltation was over and she was overwhelmed with shame. Hysterics began again: she fell on the floor, sobbing and screaming. She was carried out. At that moment Grushenka, with a wail, rushed towards Mitya before they had time to prevent her.

'Mitya,' she wailed, 'your serpent has destroyed you! There, she has shown you what she is!' she shouted to the judges, shaking with anger. At a signal from the President they seized her and tried to remove her from the court. She wouldn't allow it. She fought and struggled to get back to Mitya. Mitya uttered a cry and struggled to get to her. He was overpowered.

I will not detail the evidence of the other witnesses, who only repeated and confirmed what had been said before, though all with their characteristic peculiarities. Everyone was excited, everyone was electrified by the late catastrophe, and all were awaiting the speeches for the prosecution and the defence with intense impatience. Fetyukovitch was obviously shaken by Katerina Ivanovna's evidence. But the prosecutor was triumphant. When all the evidence had been taken, the court was adjourned for almost an hour. I believe it was just eight o'clock when the President returned to his seat and our prosecutor, Ippolit Kirillovitch, began his speech.

6

Ippolit Kirillovitch began his speech, trembling with nervousness, with cold sweat on his forehead, feeling hot and cold all over by turns. He described this himself afterwards. He regarded this speech as his *chef d'oeuvre*, the *chef d'oeuvre* of his whole life, as his swan song. He died, it is true, nine months later of rapid consumption, so that he had the right, as it turned out, to compare himself to a swan singing his last song. He had put his whole heart and all the brain he had into that speech. And poor Ippolit Kirillovitch unexpectedly revealed that at least some feeling for the public welfare and 'the eternal question' lay concealed in him. Where his speech really excelled was in its sincerity. He genuinely believed in the prisoner's guilt; he was accusing him not as an official duty only, and in calling for vengeance he quivered with a genuine passion 'for the security of society'. Even the ladies in the audience, though they remained hostile to Ippolit Kirillovitch, admitted that he made an extraordinary impression on them. He began in a breaking voice, but it soon gained strength and filled the court to the end of his speech. But as soon as he had finished, he almost fainted.

'Gentlemen of the jury,' began the prosecutor, 'this case has made a stir throughout Russia. But what is there to wonder at, what is there so peculiarly horrifying in it for us? We are so accustomed to such crimes! That's what's so horrible, that such dark deeds have ceased to horrify us. What ought to horrify us is that we are so accustomed to it, and not this or that isolated crime. What are the causes of our indifference, our lukewarm attitude to such deeds, to such signs of the times, ominous of an unenviable future? Is it our cynicism, is it the premature exhaustion of intellect and imagination in a society that is sinking into decay, in spite of its youth? Is it that our moral principles are shattered to their foundations, or is it, perhaps, a complete lack of such principles among us? I cannot answer such questions; nevertheless they are disturbing, and every citizen not only must, but ought to be harassed by them . . . Look how our young people commit suicide, without asking themselves Hamlet's question what there is beyond. Look at our vice, at our profligates. Fyodor Pavlovitch, the luckless victim in the present case, was almost an innocent babe compared with many of them. And yet we all knew him, "he lived among us! . . ."

'What, after all, is this Karamazov family, which has gained such an unenviable notoriety throughout Russia?' he continued. 'Perhaps I am exaggerating, but it seems to me that certain fundamental features of the educated class of today are reflected in this family picture – only, of course, in miniature, "like the sun in a drop of water". Think of that unhappy, vicious, unbridled old man, who has met with such a melancholy end, the head of a family! A petty knave, a toady and buffoon, of fairly good, though undeveloped, intelligence, he was, above all, a money lender, who grew bolder with growing prosperity. His abject and servile characteristics disappeared, his malicious and sarcastic cynicism was all that remained. He had no feelings for his duties as a father. He left his little children to the servants, and was glad to be rid of them, forgot about them completely. He swindled his own son and spent his money, his maternal inheritance, on trying to get his mistress from him. No, I don't intend to leave the prisoner's defence altogether to my talented colleague from Petersburg. I will speak the truth myself, I can well understand what resentment against himself he built up in his son's heart.

'But to return to the eldest son,' Ippolit Kirillovitch went on. 'He is the prisoner before us. We have his life and his actions, too, before us; the fatal day has come and all has been brought to light. While his brothers seem to stand for "Europeanism" and "the principles of the people", he seems to represent Russia *as she is*. Oh, not all Russia, not all! God preserve us, if it were! Yet, here we have her, our mother Russia, the very scent and sound of her. Oh, he is spontaneous, he is a marvellous mingling of good and evil, he is a lover of culture and Schiller, yet he brawls in taverns and plucks out the beards of his boon companions. Oh, he too can be good and noble, but only when all goes well with him. What is more, he can be carried off his feet, positively carried off his feet by noble ideals, but only if they come of themselves, if they fall from heaven for him, if they need not be paid for. He dislikes paying for anything, but is very fond of receiving, and that's so with him in everything. Oh, give him every possible good in life (he couldn't be content with less), and put no obstacle in his way, and he will show that he too can be noble. He is not greedy, no, but he must have money, a great deal of money, and you will see how generously, with what scorn of filthy lucre, he will fling it all away in the reckless dissipation of one night. But if he has not money, he will show what he is ready to do to get it when he is in great need of it . . .

'By the way, gentlemen of the jury, we've just touched upon that three thousand roubles, and I will venture to anticipate things a little. Can you conceive that a man like that, on receiving that sum and in such a way, at the price of shame, such disgrace, such utter degradation, could have been capable that very day of setting apart half that sum, that very day, and sewing it up in a little bag, and would have had the firmness of character to carry it about with him for a whole month afterwards, in spite of every temptation and his extreme need of it! Neither in drunken debauchery in taverns, nor when he was galloping into the country, trying to get from God knows whom, the money so essential to him to remove the object of his affections from being tempted by his father, did he bring himself to touch that little bag. Why, if only to avoid abandoning his mistress to the rival of whom he was so jealous, he would have been certain to have opened that bag and to have stayed at home to keep watch over her, and to await the moment when she would say to him at last "I am yours," and to fly with her far from their fatal surroundings.

'But no, he did not touch his talisman, and what is the reason he gives for it? The chief reason, as I have just said, was that when she would say "I am yours, take me where you will," he might have the wherewithal to take her. But that first reason, in the prisoner's own words, was of little weight beside the second. While I have that money on me, he said, I am a scoundrel, not a thief, for I can always go to my insulted betrothed, and, laying down half the sum I have fraudulently appropriated, I can always say to her, "You see I've squandered half your money, and shown I am a weak and immoral man, and, if you like, a scoundrel" (I use the prisoner's own expressions), "but though I am a scoundrel, I am not a thief, for if I had been a thief, I wouldn't have brought you back this half of the money, but would have taken it as I did the other half!" A marvellous explanation! This frantic, but weak man, who could not resist the temptation of accepting the three thousand roubles at the price of such disgrace, this very man suddenly develops the most stoical firmness, and carries about a thousand roubles without daring to touch it. Does that fit in at all with the character we have analysed? No, and I venture to tell you how the real Dmitri Karamazov would have behaved in such circumstances, if he really had brought himself to put away the money.

'At the first temptation – for instance, to entertain the woman with whom he had already squandered half the money – he would have opened his little bag and have taken out some hundred roubles, for why should he have taken back precisely half the money, that is, fifteen hundred roubles; why not fourteen hundred? He could just as well have said then that he was not a thief, because he brought back fourteen hundred roubles. Then another time he would have opened it again and taken out another hundred, and then a third, and then a fourth, and before the end of the month he would have taken the last note but one, feeling that if he returned only a hundred it would answer the purpose, for a thief would have stolen it all. And then he would have looked at this last note, and have said to himself, "It's really not worth while to give back one hundred; let's spend that too!" That's how the real Dmitri Karamazov, as we know him, would have behaved. One cannot imagine anything more incongruous with the actual fact than this legend of the little bag. Nothing could be more inconceivable. But we shall return to that later.'

After touching upon what had come out in the proceedings concerning the financial relations of father and son, and arguing again and again that it was utterly impossible, from the facts known, to determine which was in the wrong, Ippolit Kirillovitch passed to the evidence of the medical experts in reference to Mitya's fixed idea about the three thousand owing him.

7

'The medical experts have striven to convince us that the prisoner is out of his mind and, in fact, a maniac. I maintain that he is in his right mind, and that if he had not been, he would have behaved more cleverly. As for his being a maniac, that I would agree with, but only in one point, that is, his fixed idea about the three thousand. Yet I think one might find a much simpler cause than his tendency to insanity. The object of the prisoner's continual and violent anger was not the sum itself; there was a special motive at the bottom of it. That motive is jealousy!'

Here Ippolit Kirillovitch described at length the prisoner's fatal passion for Grushenka.

'After a month of hopeless love and moral degradation, during which he betrayed his betrothed and appropriated money entrusted to his honour, the prisoner was driven almost to frenzy, almost to madness by continual jealousy – and of whom? His father! And the worst of it was that the crazy old man was alluring and enticing the object of his affection by means of that very three thousand roubles, which the son looked upon as his own property, part of his inheritance from his mother, out of which his father was cheating him. Yes, I admit it was hard to bear! It might well drive a man to madness. It was not the money, but the fact that this money was used with such revolting cynicism to ruin his happiness!'

Here the prosecutor described the meeting of the family at the monastery, the conversations with Alyosha, and the horrible scene of violence when the prisoner had rushed into his father's house just after dinner.

'I cannot positively assert,' the prosecutor continued, 'that the prisoner actually intended to murder his father, before that incident. Yet the idea had several times presented itself to him, and he had deliberated on it – for that we have facts, witnesses, and his own words. I confess, gentlemen of the jury,' he added, 'that till today I have been uncertain whether to attribute to the prisoner conscious premeditation.

'But I was only uncertain till today, till that fatal document was presented to the court just now. "Tomorrow I shall try and borrow the money from everyone," as he writes in his peculiar language, "and if they won't give it to me, there will be bloodshed." '

Here Ippolit Kirillovitch passed to a detailed description of all Mitya's efforts to borrow the money. He described his visit to Samsonov, his journey to Lyagavy. 'Harassed, jeered at, hungry, after selling his watch to pay for the journey (though he tells us he had fifeen hundred roubles on him – a likely story), tortured by jealousy at having left the object of his affections in the town, suspecting that she would go to Fyodor Pavlovitch in his absence, he returned at last to the town, and there he learns that Smerdyakov is in a fit, that the other servant is ill – the coast is clear and he knows the "signals" – what a temptation! Still he resists it; he goes off to a lady who has for some time been residing in the town, and who is highly esteemed among us, Madame Hohlakov.'

After describing the result of this conversation and the moment when the prisoner learned that Grushenka had not remained at Samsonov's, the sudden frenzy of the luckless man, worn out with jealousy and nervous exhaustion, at the thought that she had deceived him and was now with his father, Ippolit Kirillovitch concluded by dwelling upon the fatal influence of chance. 'Had the maid told him that her mistress was at Mokroe with a former lover, nothing would have happened. But she lost her head, she could only swear and protest her ignorance, and if the prisoner did not kill her on the spot, it was only because he flew in pursuit of his false mistress.

'But note, frantic as he was, he took with him a brass pestle. Why that? Why not some other weapon? But since he had been contemplating his plan and preparing himself for it for a whole month, he would snatch up anything like a weapon that caught his eye. He had realised for a month past that any object of the kind would serve as a weapon, so he instantly, without hesitation, recognised that it would serve his purpose. So it was by no means unconsciously, by no means involuntarily, that he snatched up that fatal pestle.' At this point Ippolit Kirillovitch broke off to discuss exhaustively the suspected connection of Smerdyakov with the murder. He did this very circumstantially, and everyone realised that, although he professed to despise that suspicion, he thought the subject of great importance.

8

To begin with, what was the source of this suspicion? (Ippolit Kirillovitch began.) 'The first person who cried out that Smerdyakov had committed the murder was the prisoner himself at the moment of his arrest, yet from that time to this he has not brought forward a single fact to confirm the charge, nor the faintest suggestion of a fact. The charge is confirmed by three persons only – the two brothers of the prisoner and Madame Svyetlov. The elder of these brothers expressed his suspicions only today, when he was undoubtedly suffering from brain fever. But we know that for the last two months he has completely shared our conviction of his brother's guilt and did not attempt to combat that idea. But of that later. The younger brother has admitted that he has not the slightest fact to support his notion of Smerdyakov's guilt, and has only been led to that conclusion from the prisoner's own words and the expression of his face. Yes, that astounding piece of evidence has been brought forward twice today by him. Madame Svyetlov was even more astounding. "What the prisoner tells you, you must believe; he is not a man to tell a lie." That is all the evidence against Smerdyakov produced by these three persons, who are all deeply concerned in the prisoner's fate. And yet the theory of Smerdyakov's guilt has been noised about, has been and is still maintained. Is it credible? Is it conceivable?'

Here Ippolit Kirillovitch thought it necessary to describe the personality of Smerdyakov, 'who had cut short his life in a fit of insanity'. He depicted him as a man of weak intellect, with a smattering of education, who had been thrown off his balance by philosophical ideas above his level and certain modern theories of duty, which he learned in practice from the reckless life of his master, who was also perhaps his father – Fyodor Pavlovitch; and, theoretically, from various strange philosophical conversations with his master's second son, Ivan Fyodorovitch, who readily indulged in this diversion, probably feeling dull or wishing to amuse himself at the valet's expense. But, if the epileptic fit from which he seemed to be suffering on the night of the murder was a simulated attack, then the question arises at once, what was his motive? What was he reckoning on? What was he aiming at? I say nothing about medicine: science, I am told, may go astray: the doctors were not able to discriminate between the counterfeit and the real. That may be so, but answer me one question: what motive had he for such a counterfeit? Could he, had he been plotting the murder, and did he desire to attract the attention of the household by having a fit just before?

'You see, gentlemen of the jury, on the night of the murder, there were five persons in Fyodor Pavlovitch's house and garden – Fyodor Pavlovitch himself (but he did not kill himself, that's evident); then his servant, Grigory, but he was almost killed himself; the third person was Grigory's wife, Marfa Ignatyevna, but it would be simply shameful to imagine her murdering her master. Two persons are left – the prisoner and Smerdyakov. But, if we are to believe the prisoner's statement that he is not the murderer, then Smerdyakov must have been, for there is no other alternative, no one else can be found. That is what accounts for the artful, astounding accusation against the unhappy idiot who committed suicide yesterday. Had a shadow of suspicion rested on anyone else, had there been any sixth person, I am persuaded that even the prisoner would have been ashamed to accuse Smerdyakov, and would have accused that sixth person, for to charge Smerdyakov with that murder is perfectly absurd.

'Gentlemen, let us lay aside psychology, let us lay aside medicine, let us even lay aside logic, let us turn only to the facts and see what the facts tell us. If Smerdyakov killed him, how did he do it? Alone or with the assistance of the prisoner? Let us consider the first alternative – that he did it alone. If he had killed him, it must have been for some reason, for some advantage to himself. But not having a shadow of the motive that the prisoner had for the murder – hatred, jealousy, and so on – Smerdyakov could only have murdered him for the sake of gain, in order to appropriate the three thousand roubles he had seen his master put in the envelope. And yet he tells another person – and a person most closely interested, that is, the prisoner – everything about the money and the signals, where the envelope lay, what was written on it, what it was tied up with, and, above all, told him of those signals by which he could enter the house. Did he do this simply to betray himself, or to invite to the same enterprise one who would be anxious to get that envelope for himself? "Yes," I shall be told, "but he betrayed it from fear." But how do you explain this? A man who could conceive such an audacious, savage act, and carry it out, tells facts which are known to no one else in the world, and which, if he held his tongue, no one would ever have guessed!

'No, however cowardly he might be, if he had

plotted such a crime, nothing would have induced him to tell anyone about the envelope and the signals, for that was as good as betraying himself beforehand. He would have invented something, he would have told some lie if he had been forced to give information, but he would have been silent about that. For, on the other hand, if he had said nothing about the money but had committed the murder and stolen the money, no one in the world could have charged him with murder for the sake of robbery, since no one but he had seen the money, no one but he knew of its existence in the house. Even if he had been accused of the murder, it could only have been thought that he had committed it from some other motive. But since no one had observed any such motive in him beforehand, and everyone saw, on the contrary, that his master was fond of him and honoured him with his confidence, he would, of course, have been the last to be suspected. People would have suspected first the man who had a motive, a man who had himself declared he had such motives, who had made no secret of it; they would, in fact, have suspected the son of the murdered man, Dmitri Fyodorovitch. Had Smerdyakov killed and robbed the old man, and the son been accused of it, that would, of course, have suited Smerdyakov. Yet are we to believe that, though plotting the murder, he told that son, Dmitri, about the money, the envelope, and the signals? Is that logical? Is that comprehensible?

'When the day of the murder planned by Smerdyakov came, we have him falling downstairs in a *feigned* fit – with what object? In the first place that Grigory, who had been intending to take his medicine, might put it off and remain on guard, seeing there was no one to look after the house, and, in the second place, I suppose, that his master seeing that there was no one to guard him, and in terror of a visit from his son, might redouble his vigilance and precaution. And, most of all, I suppose that he, Smerdyakov, disabled by the fit, might be carried from the kitchen, where he always slept, apart from all the rest, and where he could go in and out as he liked, to Grigory's room at the other end of the lodge, where he was always put, shut off by a screen three paces from their own bed. This was the immemorial custom established by his master and the kind-hearted Marfa Ignatyevna, whenever he had a fit. There, lying behind the screen, he would most likely, to keep up the sham, have begun groaning, and so keeping them awake all night (as Grigory and his wife testified). And all this, we are to believe, that he might more conveniently get up and murder his master!

'But I shall be told that he shammed illness on purpose that he might not be suspected and that he told the prisoner of the money and the signals to tempt him to commit the murder, and when he had murdered him and had gone away with the money, making a noise, most likely, and waking people, Smerdyakov got up, am I to believe, and went in – what for? To murder his master a second time and carry off the money that had already been stolen? Gentlemen, are you laughing? I am ashamed to put forward such suggestions, but, incredible as it seems, that's just what the prisoner alleges. When he had left the house, had knocked Grigory down and raised an alarm, he tells us Smerdyakov got up, went in and murdered his master and stole the money! I won't press the point that Smerdyakov could hardly have reckoned on this beforehand, and have foreseen that the furious and exasperated son would simply come to peep in respectfully, though he knew the signals, and beat a retreat, leaving Smerdyakov his booty. Gentlemen of the jury, I put this question to you in earnest; when was the moment when Smerdyakov could have committed his crime? Name that moment, or you can't accuse him.

'But, perhaps, the fit was a real one, the sick man suddenly recovered, heard someone shouting, and ran out. Well – what then? He looked about him and said, "Why not go and kill the master?" And how did he know what had happened, since he had been lying unconscious till that moment? But there's a limit to these flights of fancy. In a fit of melancholy arising from his disease and this catastrophe Smerdyakov hanged himself yesterday. He left a note written in his peculiar language, "I destroy myself of my own will and inclination so as to throw no blame on anyone." What would it have cost him to add: "I am the murderer, not Karamazov"? But that he did not add. Did his conscience lead him to suicide and not to avowing his guilt?

'Well, now: notes for three thousand roubles were brought into the court just now, and we are told that they are the same that lay in the envelope now on the table before us, and that the witness received them from Smerdyakov the day before. But I need not recall to you the painful scene we witnessed, though I will make one or two comments, selecting such trivial facts as might not be obvious at first sight to everyone, and so may be overlooked. In the first place, Smerdyakov must have given back the money and hanged himself yesterday from remorse. And only yesterday he confessed his guilt to Ivan Karamazov, as the latter informs us. If it were not so, indeed, why should Ivan Fyodorovitch have kept silence till now? And so, if he has confessed, then why, I ask again, did Smerdyakov not avow the whole truth in the last letter he left behind, knowing that the innocent prisoner had to face this terrible ordeal the next day?

'The money alone is no proof. A week ago, quite by chance, the fact came to the knowledge of myself and two other persons in this court that Ivan Fyodorovitch had sent two five-per-cent coupons of five thousand each – that is, ten thousand in all – to the chief town of the province to be cashed. I only mention this to point out that anyone may have money, and that it can't be proved that these notes lying here are the same ones that were in Fyodor Pavlovitch's envelope . . .

'Gentlemen of the jury, I have told you already why I consider this story not only an absurdity, but the most improbable invention that could have been brought forward in the circumstances. If one tried on a bet to invent the most unlikely story, one could hardly find anything more incredible. The worst of such stories is that the jubilant inventors of such stories can always be put to confusion and crushed by the very details in which real life is so rich and which these unhappy and involuntary storytellers neglect as insignificant trifles. Oh, they have no thought to spare for such details, their minds are concentrated on their grand invention as a whole and fancy anyone daring to pull them up for a trifle! But that's how they are caught. The prisoner was asked the question, "Where did you get the rag for your little bag and who made it for you?" "I made it myself." "And where did you get the linen?" The prisoner was positively offended, he thought it almost insulting to ask him such a trivial question, and would you believe it, his resentment was genuine! But they are all like that. "I tore it off my shirt." "Then we shall find that shirt among your linen tomorrow, with a piece torn off." And only imagine, gentlemen of the jury, if we really had found that torn shirt (and how could we have failed to find it in his chest of drawers or trunks?) that would have been a fact, a material fact in support of his statement! But he was incapable of that reflection. "I don't remember, it may not have been off my shirt, I sewed it up in one of my landlady's caps." "What sort of a cap?" "It was an old cotton rag of hers lying about." "And do you remember that clearly?" "No, I don't." And he was angry, very angry, and yet imagine not remembering it! At the most terrible moments of man's life, for instance when he is being led to execution, he remembers just such trifles. He will forget anything but some green roof that has flashed past him on the road, or a jackdaw on a cross – that he will remember. He concealed the making of that little bag from his household, he must have remembered his humiliating fear that someone might come in and find him needle in hand, how at the slightest sound he slipped behind the screen (there is a screen in his lodgings).

'But, gentlemen of the jury, why do I tell you all this, all these details, trifles?' cried Ippolit Kirillovitch suddenly. 'Just because the prisoner still persists in these absurdities to this moment. He has not explained anything since that fatal night two months ago, he has not added one actual illuminating fact to his former fantastic statements; all those are trivialities. "You must believe it on my honour." Oh, we are glad to believe it, we are eager to believe it, even if only on his word of honour! Are we jackals thirsting for human blood? Show us a single fact in the prisoner's favour and we shall rejoice; but let it be a substantial, real fact, and not a conclusion drawn from the prisoner's expression by his own brother, or that when he beat himself on the breast he must have meant to point to the little bag, in the darkness too. We shall rejoice at the new fact, we shall be the first to repudiate our charge, we shall hasten to repudiate it. But now justice cries out and we persist, we cannot repudiate anything.'

Ippolit Kirillovitch passed to his final peroration. He looked as though he were in a fever, he spoke of the blood that cried for vengeance, the blood of the father murdered by his son, with the base motive of robbery! He pointed to the tragic and glaring consistency of the facts.

'And whatever you may hear from the talented and celebrated counsel for the defence,' Ippolit Kirillovitch could not resist adding, 'whatever eloquent and touching appeals may be made to your sensibilities, remember that at this moment you are in a temple of justice. Remember that you are the champions of our justice, the champions of our holy Russia, of her principles, her family, everything that she holds sacred! Yes, you represent Russia here at this moment, and your verdict will be heard not in this hall only but will reëcho throughout the whole of Russia, and all Russia will hear you, as her champions and her judges, and she will be encouraged or disheartened by your verdict. Do not disappoint Russia and her expectations. Our fatal troika dashes on in its headlong flight perhaps to destruction and in all Russia for long past men have stretched out imploring hands and called a halt to its furious reckless course. And if other nations stand aside from that troika that may be, not from respect, as the poet would fain believe, but simply from horror. From horror, perhaps from disgust. And well it is that they stand aside, but maybe they will cease one day to do so and will form a strong wall to confront the hurrying apparition and will check the frenzied rush of our lawlessness, for the sake of their own safety, enlightenment and civilisation. Already we have heard voices of alarm from Europe, they already begin to resound. Do not tempt them! Do not heap up their growing hatred by a sentence justifying the murder of a father by his son!'

Though Ippolit Kirillovitch was genuinely moved, he wound up his speech with this rhetorical appeal – and the effect produced by him was extraordinary. When he had finished his speech, he went out hurriedly and, as I have mentioned before, almost fainted in the adjoining room. There was no applause in the court, but serious persons were pleased. The ladies were not so well satisfied, though even they were pleased with his eloquence, especially as they had no apprehensions as to the upshot of the trial and had full trust in Fetyukovitch. 'He will speak at last and of course carry all before him.'

Everyone looked at Mitya; he sat silent through the whole of the prosecutor's speech, clenching his teeth, with his hands clasped, and his head bowed. Only from time to time he raised his head and listened, especially when Grushenka was mentioned. When Ippolit Kirillovitch described how he had questioned and harassed him at Mokroe, Mitya raised his head and listened with intense curiosity. At one point he seemed about to jump up and cry out, but controlled himself and only shrugged his shoulders disdainfully.

People talked afterwards of the end of the speech, of the prosecutor's feat in examining the prisoner at Mokroe and jeered at Ippolit Kirillovitch. 'The man could not resist boasting of his cleverness,' they said.

The court was adjourned, but only for a short interval, a quarter of an hour or twenty minutes at most. There was a hum of conversation and exclamations in the audience. I remember some of them.

'A weighty speech,' a gentleman in one group observed gravely.

'He brought in too much psychology,' said another voice.

'But it was all true, the absolute truth!'

'Yes, he is first rate at it.'

'He summed it all up.'

'Yes, he summed us up too,' chimed in another voice. 'Do you remember, at the beginning of his speech, making out we were all like Fyodor Pavlovitch?'

'And at the end too. But that was all rubbish.'

'And obscure too.'

'He was a little too much carried away.'

'It's unjust, it's unjust.'

'No, it was smartly done, anyway. He's had long to wait, but he's had his say, ha-ha!'

'What will the counsel for the defence say?'

In another group I heard: 'He had no business to make a thrust at the Petersburg man like that; "appealing to your sensibilities" – do you remember?'

'Yes, that was tactless of him.'

'He was in too great a hurry.'

'He is a nervous man.'

'We laugh, but what must the prisoner be feeling?'

'Yes, what must it be like for Mitya?'

In a third group: 'Who is that lady, the fat one, with the lorgnette, sitting at the end?'

'She is a general's wife, divorced, I know her.'

'That's why she has the lorgnette.'

'She is not much good.'

'Well, she is a piquante little woman.'

'Two seats beyond her there is a little fair woman, she is prettier.'

'They caught him smartly at Mokroe, didn't they, eh?'

'Oh, it was smart enough. We've heard it before, how often he has told the story at people's houses!'

'And he couldn't resist doing it now. That's vanity.'

'He is a man with a grievance, he-he!'

'Yes, and quick to take offence. And there was too much rhetoric, such long sentences.'

'Yes, he tries to alarm us, he kept trying to alarm us. Do you remember about the troika? And then something about "They have Hamlets, but we have, so far, only Karamazovs!" That was cleverly said!'

'That was to propitiate the liberals. He is afraid of them.'

'Yes, and he is afraid of the lawyer too.'

'Yes, what will Fetyukovitch say?'

'Whatever he says, he won't fool our peasants.'

'Do you think so?'

A fourth group: 'What he said about the troika was good, that piece about the other nations.'

'And that was true what he said about other nations condemning us.'

'What do you mean?'

'Why, in the English Parliament a Member got up last week and speaking about the Nihilists asked the Ministry whether it was not high time to intervene, to educate this barbarous people. Ippolit was thinking of that, I know he was. He was talking about the speech in the English Parliament last week.'

'Those English wouldn't have an easy job.'

'Not an easy job? Why not?'

'Why, we'd shut up Kronstadt and not let them have any wheat. Where would they get it then?'

'In America. They get it from America now.'

'Nonsense!'

Just then the bell rang, all rushed to their places. Fetyukovitch mounted the tribune.

9

All was hushed as the first words of the famous orator rang out. The eyes of the audience were fastened upon him. He began very simply and directly, with an air of conviction, but not the slightest trace of conceit. He made no attempt at eloquence, at pathos, or emotional phrases. He was like a man speaking in a circle of intimate and sympathetic friends. His voice was a fine one, sonorous and sympathetic, and there was something genuine and simple in the very sound of it. But everyone realised at once that the speaker might suddenly rise to genuine pathos and 'pierce the heart with untold power'. His language was perhaps more informal than Ippolit Kirillovitch's, but he spoke without long phrases, and indeed, with more precision. One thing did not please the ladies: he kept bending forward, especially at the beginning of his speech, not exactly bowing, but as though he were about to dart at his listeners, bending his long spine in half, as though there were a spring in the middle that enabled him to bend at right angles.

At the beginning of his speech he spoke rather disconnectedly, without system, one may say, dealing with facts separately, though, at the end, these facts formed a whole. His speech might be divided into two parts, the first consisting of criticism in refutation of the charge, sometimes malicious and sarcastic. But in the second half he suddenly changed his tone, and even his manner, and at once rose to pathos. The audience seemed on the lookout for it, and quivered with enthusiasm.

He went straight to the point, and began by saying that although he practised in Petersburg, he had more than once visited provincial towns to defend prisoners, of whose innocence he had a conviction or at least a preconceived idea. 'That is what has happened to me in the present case,' he explained. 'From the very first accounts in the newspapers I was struck by something which strongly prepossessed me in the prisoner's favour. What interested me most was a fact which often occurs in legal practice, but rarely, I think, in such an extreme and peculiar form as in the present case. I ought to formulate that peculiarity only at the end of my speech, but I will do so at the very beginning, for it is my weakness to go to work directly, not keeping my effects in reserve and economising my material. That may be imprudent on my part, but at least it's sincere. What I have in my mind is this: there is an overwhelming chain of evidence against the prisoner, and at the same time not one fact that will stand criticism, if it is examined separately. As I followed the case more closely in the papers my idea was more and more confirmed, and I suddenly received from the prisoner's relatives a request to undertake his defence. I at once hurried here, and here I became completely convinced. It was to break down this terrible chain of facts, and to show that each piece of evidence taken separately was unproved and fantastic, that I undertook the case.'

So Fetyukovitch began.

'Gentlemen of the jury,' he suddenly protested, 'I am new to this district. I have no preconceived ideas. The prisoner, a man of turbulent and unbridled temper, has not insulted me. But he has insulted perhaps hundreds of persons in this town, and so prejudiced many people against him beforehand. Of course, I recognise that the moral sentiment of local society is justly excited against him. The prisoner is of turbulent and violent temper. Yet he was received in society here; he was even welcome in the family of my talented friend, the prosecutor.'

(At these words there were two or three laughs in the audience, quickly suppressed, but noticed by all. All of us knew that the prosecutor received Mitya against his will, solely because he had somehow interested his wife – a lady of the highest virtue and moral worth, but fanciful, capricious, and fond of opposing her husband, especially in trifles. Mitya's visits, however, had not been frequent.)

'Nevertheless I venture to suggest,' Fetyukovitch continued, 'that in spite of his independent mind and just character, my opponent may have formed a mistaken prejudice against my unfortunate client. Oh, that is so natural; the unfortunate man has only too well deserved such prejudices. Outraged morality, and still more outraged taste, is often relentless. We have, in the talented prosecutor's speech, heard a stern analysis of the prisoner's character and conduct, and his severe critical attitude to the case was evident. And, what's more, he went into psychological subtleties into which he could not have entered, if he had had less conscious and malicious prejudice against the prisoner. But there are things which are even worse, even more fatal in such cases, than the most malicious and consciously unfair attitude. It is worse if we are carried away by the artistic instinct, by the desire to create, so to speak, a romance, especially if God has endowed us with psychological insight. Before I started on my way here, I was warned in Petersburg, and was myself aware, that I would find a talented opponent whose psychological insight and subtlety had gained him peculiar renown in legal circles of recent years. But profound as psychology is, it's a two-edged knife that cuts both ways.' (Laughter among the public.) 'You will, of course, forgive me my comparison; I can't boast of eloquence. But I will take as an example any point in the prosecutor's speech.

'The prisoner, running away in the garden in the dark, climbed over the fence, was seized by the servant, and knocked him down with a brass pestle. Then he jumped back into the garden and spent five minutes over the man, trying to discover whether he had killed him or not. And the prosecutor refuses to believe the prisoner's statement that he ran to old Grigory out of pity. "No," he says, "such sensibility is impossible at such a moment, that's unnatural; he ran to find out whether the only witness of his crime was dead or alive, and so showed that he had committed the murder, since he would not have run back for any other reason."

'Here you have psychology; but let us take the same method and apply it to the case the other way round, and our result will be no less probable. If I am so bloodthirsty and cruelly calculating that when I kill a man I only run back to find out whether he is alive to witness against me, why should I spend five minutes looking after my victim at the risk of encountering other witnesses? Why soak my handkerchief, wiping the blood off his head so that it may be evidence against me later? If he were so cold-hearted and calculating, why not hit the servant on the head again and again with the same pestle so as to kill him outright and relieve himself of all anxiety about the witness?

'Again, though he ran to see whether the witness was alive, he left another witness on the path, that brass pestle which he had taken from the two women, and which they could always identify later as theirs, and prove that he had taken it from them. And it is not as though he had forgotten it on the path, dropped it through carelessness or haste, no, he had flung away his weapon, for it was found fifteen paces from where Grigory lay. Why did he do so? Just because he was grieved at having killed a man, an old servant; and he flung away the pestle with a curse, as a murderous weapon? That's how it must have been, what other reason could he have had for throwing it so far? And if he was capable of feeling grief and pity at having killed a man, it shows that he was innocent of his father's murder. Had he murdered him, he would never have aided another victim out of pity; then he would have felt differently; his thoughts would have been centred on self-preservation. He would have had none to spare for pity, that is beyond doubt. On the contrary, he would have broken the old man's skull instead of spending five minutes looking after him. There was room for pity and good-feeling just because his conscience had been clear till then. Here we have a different psychology. I have purposely resorted to this method, gentlemen of the jury, to show that you can prove anything by it. It all depends on who makes use of it. Psychology lures even most serious people into romancing, and quite unconsciously. I am speaking of the abuse of psychology, gentlemen.'

Sounds of approval and laughter, at the expense of the prosecutor, were again audible in the court. I will not repeat the speech in detail; I will only quote some passages from it, some leading points.

There was one point that struck everyone in Fetyukovitch's speech. He flatly denied the existence of the fatal three thousand roubles, and consequently the possibility of their having been stolen.

'Gentlemen of the jury,' he began. 'Consider, how have we heard of that sum, and who has seen the notes? The only person who saw them, and stated that they had been put in the envelope, was the servant, Smerdyakov. He had spoken of it to the prisoner and his brother, Ivan Fyodorovitch, before the catastrophe. Madame Svyetlov, too, had been told of it. But not one of these three persons had actually seen the notes, no one but Smerdyakov had seen them . . .

'The charge of robbery I repudiate with indignation. A man cannot be accused of robbery, if it's impossible to state accurately what he has stolen; that's an axiom. But did he murder him without robbery, did he murder him at all? Is that proved? Isn't that, too, fiction?'

10

'Allow me, gentlemen of the jury, to remind you that a man's life is at stake and that you must be careful. We have heard the prosecutor himself admit that until today he hesitated to accuse the prisoner of a full and conscious premeditation of the crime; he hesitated till he saw that fatal drunken letter which was produced in court today. "All was done as written." But, I repeat again, he was running to her, to seek her, solely to find out where she was. That's a fact that can't be disputed. Had she been at home, he would not have run away, but would have remained at her side, and so would not have done what he promised in the letter. He ran unexpectedly and accidentally, and by that time very likely he did not even remember his drunken letter. "He snatched up the pestle," they say, and you will remember how a whole edifice of psychology was built on that pestle – why he was bound to look at that pestle as a weapon, to snatch it up, and so on, and so on. A very commonplace idea occurs to me at this point: What if that pestle had not been in sight, had not been lying on the shelf from which it was snatched by the prisoner, but had been put away in a cupboard? It would not have caught the prisoner's eye, and he would have run away without a weapon, with empty hands, and then he would certainly not have killed anyone. How, then, can I look upon the pestle as a proof of premeditation?

'Now, thank God! we've come to the real point: "Since he was in the garden, he must have murdered him." In those few words: "since he *was*, then he *must*" lies the whole case for the prosecution. He was there, so he must have. And what if there is no *must* about it, even if he was there? Oh, I admit that the chain of evidence – the coincidences – are really suggestive. But examine all these facts separately, regardless of their connection. Why, for instance, does the prosecution refuse to admit the truth of the prisoner's statement that he ran away from his father's window? Remember the sarcasms in which the prosecutor indulged at the expense of the respectful and "pious" sentiments which suddenly came over the murderer. But what if there were something of the sort, a feeling of religious awe, if not a filial respect? "My mother must have been praying for me at that moment," were the prisoner's words at the preliminary enquiry, and so he ran away as soon as he convinced himself that Madame Svyetlov was not in his father's house. "But he could not convince himself by looking through the window," the prosecutor objects. But why couldn't he? Why? The window opened at the signals given by the prisoner. Some word might have been uttered by Fyodor Pavlovitch, some exclamation which showed the prisoner that she was not there. Why should we assume everything as we imagine it, as we make up our minds to imagine it? A thousand things may happen in reality which elude the subtlest imagination.

'But we shall be told at once, "There is his father's corpse! If he ran away without murdering him, who did murder him?" Here, I repeat, you have the whole logic of the prosecution. Who murdered him, if not the prisoner? There's no one to put in his place.

'Gentlemen of the jury, is that really so? Is it positively, actually true that there is no one else at all? We've heard the prosecutor count on his fingers all the persons who were in that house that night. They were five in number; three of them, I agree, could not have been responsible – the murdered man himself, old Grigory, and his wife. There are left then the prisoner and Smerdyakov, and the prosecutor dramatically exclaims that the prisoner pointed to Smerdyakov because he had no one else to fix on, that had there been a sixth person, even a phantom of a sixth person, he would have abandoned the charge against Smerdyakov at once in shame and have accused the other. But, gentlemen of the jury, why may I not draw the very opposite conclusion? There are two persons – the prisoner and Smerdyakov. Why can I not say that you accuse my client, simply because you have no one else to accuse? And you have no one else only because you have determined to exclude Smerdyakov from all suspicion . . .

'I made some enquiries: he resented his parentage, was ashamed of it, and would clench his teeth when he remembered that he was the son of "stinking Lizaveta". He was disrespectful to the servant Grigory and his wife, who had cared for him in his childhood. He cursed and jeered at Russia. He dreamed of going to France and becoming a Frenchman. He used often to say that he hadn't the means to do so. I fancy he loved no one but himself and had a strangely high opinion of himself. His conception of culture was limited to good clothes, clean shirt fronts and polished boots. Believing himself to be the illegitimate son of Fyodor Pavlovitch (there is evidence of this), he might well have resented his position, compared with that of his master's legitimate sons. They had everything, he nothing. They had all the rights, they had the inheritance, while he was only the cook. He told me himself that he had helped Fyodor Pavlovitch to put the notes in the envelope. The destination of that sum – a sum which would have made his career – must have been hateful to him.

'The talented prosecutor, with extraordinary subtlety, sketched for us all the arguments for and against the hypothesis of Smerdyakov's guilt, and asked us in particular what motive he had in feigning a fit. But he may not have been feigning at all, the fit may have happened quite naturally, but it may have passed off quite naturally, and the sick man may have recovered, not completely perhaps, but still regaining consciousness, as happens with epileptics.

'The prosecutor asks at what moment could Smerdyakov have committed the murder. But it is very easy to point out that moment. He might have waked up from deep sleep (for he was only asleep – an epileptic fit is always followed by a deep sleep) at that moment when the old Grigory shouted at the top of his voice "Parricide!" That shout in the dark and stillness may have waked Smerdyakov, whose sleep may have been less sound at the moment: he might indeed have awakened an hour earlier.

'Getting out of bed, he goes almost unconsciously and with no definite motive towards the sound to see what's the matter. His head is still clouded from his attack, his faculties are half asleep; but, once in the garden, he walks to the lighted windows and he hears terrible news from his master, who would be, of course, glad to see him. His mind sets to work at once. He hears all the details from his frightened master, and gradually in his disordered brain there shapes itself an idea – terrible, but seductive and irresistibly logical: to kill the old man, take the three thousand, and throw all the blame on to his young master. A terrible lust of money, of booty, might seize upon him as he realised his security from detection. Oh! these sudden and irresistible impulses come so often when there is a favourable opportunity, and especially with murderers who have had no idea of committing a murder beforehand. And Smerdyakov may have gone in and carried out his plan. With what weapon? Why, with any stone picked up in the garden. But what for, with what object? Why, the three thousand which means a career for him. Oh, I am not contradicting myself – the money may have existed. And perhaps Smerdyakov alone knew where to find it, where his master kept it.

'But why, why, asks the prosecutor, did not Smerdyakov confess in his last letter? Why did his conscience prompt him to one step and not to both? But, excuse me, conscience implies penitence, and the suicide may not have felt penitence, but only despair. Despair and penitence are two very different things. Despair may be vindictive and irreconcilable, and the suicide, laying his hands on himself, may well have felt redoubled hatred for those whom he had envied all his life.

'Gentlemen of the jury, beware of a miscarriage of justice! What is there unlikely in all I have put before you just now? Find the error in my reasoning; find the impossibility, the absurdity. And if there is but a shade of possibility, but a shade of probability in my propositions, do not condemn him. And is there only a shade? I swear by all that is sacred, I fully believe in the explanation of the murder I have just put forward. What troubles me and makes me indignant is that of all the mass of facts heaped up by the prosecution against the prisoner, there is not a single one certain and irrefutable. And yet the unhappy man is to be ruined by the accumulation of these facts. Yes, the accumulated effect is terrible: the blood, the blood dripping from his fingers, the bloodstained shirt, the dark night resounding with the shout "Parricide!" and the old man falling with a broken head. And then the mass of phrases, statements, gestures, shouts! Oh! this has so much influence, it can so bias the mind; but, gentlemen of the jury, can it bias your minds? Remember, you have been given absolute power to bind and to loose, but the greater the power, the more terrible its responsibility.

'I do not withdraw one iota of what I have said just now, but suppose for one moment I agreed with the prosecution that my luckless client had stained his hands with his father's blood. This is only a hypothesis, I repeat; I never for one instant doubt of his innocence. But, so be it, I assume that my client is guilty of parricide. Even so, hear what I have to say. I have it in my heart to say something more to you, for I feel that there must be a great conflict in your hearts and minds . . . Forgive my referring to your hearts and minds, gentlemen of the jury, but I want to be truthful and sincere to the end. Let us all be sincere!'

At this point the speech was interrupted by rather loud applause. The last words, indeed, were pronounced with a note of such sincerity that everyone felt that he really might have something to say, and that what he was about to say would be of the greatest consequence. But the President, hearing the applause, in a loud voice threatened to clear the court if such an incident were repeated. Every sound was hushed and Fetyukovitch began in a voice full of feeling quite unlike the tone he had used hitherto.

'Gentlemen of the jury, you remember that awful night of which so much has been said today, when the son climbed over the fence and stood face to face with the enemy and persecutor who had begotten him. I insist most emphatically it was not for money he ran to his father's house: the charge of robbery is an absurdity, as I proved before. And it was not to murder him he broke into the house, oh, no! If he had had that design he would, at least, have taken the precaution of arming himself beforehand. The brass pestle he caught up instinctively without knowing why he did it. Granted that he deceived his father by tapping at the window, granted that he made his way in – I've said already that I do not for a moment believe that legend, but let it be so, let us suppose it for a moment. Gentlemen, I swear to you by all that's holy, if it had not been his father, but an ordinary enemy, he would, after running through the rooms and satisfying himself that the woman was not there, have made off, posthaste, without doing any harm to his rival! He would have struck him, pushed him away perhaps, nothing more, for he had no thought and no time to spare for that. What he wanted to know was where she was. But his father, his father! The mere sight of the father who had hated him from his childhood, had been his enemy, his persecutor, and now his unnatural rival, was enough! A feeling of hatred came over him involuntarily, irresistibly, clouding his reason. It all surged up in one moment! It was an impulse of madness and insanity, but also an impulse of nature, irresistibly and unconsciously (like everything in nature) avenging the violation of its eternal laws.

'But the prisoner even then did not murder him – I maintain that, I cry that aloud! – no, he only brandished the pestle in a burst of indignant disgust, not meaning to kill him, not knowing that he would kill him. Had he not had this fatal pestle in his hands, he would have only knocked his father down perhaps, but would not have killed him. As he ran away, he did not know whether he had killed the old man. Such a murder is not a murder. Such a murder is not a parricide. No, the murder of such a father cannot be called parricide. Such a murder can only be reckoned parricide by prejudice.

'But I appeal to you again and again from the depths of my soul; did this murder actually take place? Gentlemen of the jury, if we convict and punish him, he will say to himself: "These people have done nothing for my upbringing, for my education, nothing to improve my lot, nothing to make me better, nothing to make me a man. These people have not given me to eat and to drink, have not visited me in prison and nakedness, and here they have sent me to penal servitude. I am quits, I owe them nothing now, and owe no one anything for ever. They are wicked and I will be wicked. They are cruel and I will be cruel." That is what he will say, gentlemen of the jury. And I swear, by finding him guilty you will only make it easier for him: you will ease his conscience, he will curse the blood he has shed and will not regret it. At the same time you will destroy in him the possibility of becoming a new man, for he will remain in his wickedness and blindness all his life.

'But do you want to punish him fearfully, terribly, with the most awful punishment that could be imagined, and at the same time to save him and regenerate his soul? If so, overwhelm him with your mercy! You will see, you will hear how he will tremble and be horror-struck. "How can I endure this mercy? How can I endure so much love? Am I worthy of it?" That's what he will exclaim.

'Oh, I know, I know that heart, that wild but grateful heart, gentlemen of the jury! It will bow before your mercy; it thirsts for a great and loving action, it will melt and mount upwards. There are souls which, in their limitation, blame the whole world. But subdue such a soul with mercy, show it love, and it will cure its past, for there are many good impulses in it. Such a heart will expand and see that God is merciful and that men are good and just. He will be horror-stricken; he will be crushed by remorse and the vast obligation laid upon him henceforth. And he will not say then, "I am quits," but will say, "I am guilty in the sight of all men and am more unworthy than all." With tears of penitence and poignant, tender anguish, he will exclaim: "Others are better than I, they wanted to save me, not to ruin me!" Oh, this act of mercy is so easy for you, for in the absence of anything like real evidence it will be too awful for you to pronounce: "Yes, he is guilty."

'Better acquit ten guilty men than punish one innocent man! Do you hear, do you hear that majestic voice from the past century of our glorious history? It is not for an insignificant person like me to remind you that the Russian court of justice does not exist for the punishment only, but also for the salvation of the criminal! Let other nations think of retribution and the letter of the law, we will cling to the spirit and the meaning – the salvation and the reformation of the lost. If this is true, if Russia and her justice are such, she may go forward with good cheer! Do not try to scare us with your frenzied troikas from which all the nations turn aside in disgust. Not a runaway troika, but the stately chariot of Russia will move calmly and majestically to its goal. In your hands is the fate of my client, in your hands is the fate of Russian justice. You will defend it, you will save it, you will prove that there are men who guard it, that it is in good hands!'

II

This was how Fetyukovitch concluded his speech, and the enthusiasm of the audience burst like a magnificent storm. It was out of the question to stop it: the women wept, many of the men wept too, even two important personages shed tears. The President submitted, and even postponed ringing his bell. The suppression of such enthusiasm would be the suppression of something sacred, as the ladies cried afterwards. The orator himself was genuinely touched.

And it was at this moment that Ippolit Kirillovitch got up to make certain objections. People looked at him with hatred. 'What? What's the meaning of it? He positively dares to make objections,' the ladies babbled. But if the whole world of ladies, including his wife, had protested, he could not have been stopped at that moment. He was pale, he was shaking with emotion, his first phrases were even unintelligible, he gasped for breath, could hardly speak clearly, lost the thread. But he soon recovered himself. Of this new speech of his I will quote only a few sentences.

'. . . I am reproached with having woven a romance. But what is this defence if not one romance on the top of another? All that was lacking was poetry. The weak-minded idiot, Smerdyakov, transformed into a Byronic hero, avenging society for his illegitimate birth – isn't this a romance in the Byronic style? And the son who breaks into his father's house and murders him without murdering him is not even a romance – this is a sphinx setting us a riddle that even a sphinx himself cannot solve. If he murdered him, he murdered him, and what's the meaning of his murdering him without having murdered him – who can make head or tail of this?

'Then we are admonished that our tribune is a tribune of true and sound ideas and from this tribune of "sound ideas" is heard a solemn declaration that to call the murder of a father "parricide" is nothing but a prejudice! But if parricide is a prejudice, and if every child is to ask his father why he is to love him, what will become of us? What will become of the foundations of society? What will become of the family? Parricide, it appears, is only a bogey of Moscow merchants' wives. The most precious, the most sacred guarantees for the destiny and future of Russian justice are presented to us in a perverted and frivolous form, simply to attain an object – to obtain the justification of something which cannot be justified. "Oh, overpower him with mercy," cries the counsel for the defence; but that's all the criminal wants, and tomorrow it will be seen how much he is overpowered. And is not the counsel for the defence too modest in asking only for the acquittal of the prisoner? Why not found a charity in the honour of the parricide to commemorate his exploit among future generations? Religion and the Gospel are corrected – that's all mysticism, we are told, and ours is the only true Christianity which has been subjected to the analysis of reason and common sense. And so they set up before us a false semblance of Christ! "What measure ye mete so it shall be meted unto you again," cries the counsel for the defence, and instantly deduces that Christ teaches us to measure as it is measured to us – and this from the tribune of truth and sound sense! We peep into the Gospel only on the eve of making speeches, in order to dazzle the audience by our acquaintance with what is, anyway, a rather original composition, which may be of use to produce a certain effect – all to serve the purpose! But what Christ commands us is something very different: He bids us beware of doing this, because the wicked world does this, but we ought to forgive and to turn the other cheek, and not to measure to our persecutors as they measure to us. This is what our God has taught us and not that to forbid children to murder their fathers is a prejudice. And it is not seemly for us from this tribune of truth and good sense, to correct the Gospel of our Lord, whom the counsel for the defence deigns to call only "the crucified lover of humanity", in opposition to all orthodox Russia, which calls to Him, "For Thou art our God!" '

At this the President intervened and checked the overzealous speaker, begging him not to exaggerate, not to overstep the bounds, and so on, as Presidents always do in such cases. The audience, too, was uneasy. People were restless: there were even exclamations of indignation. Fetyukovitch did not so much as reply; he only mounted the tribune to lay his hand on his heart and, in a reproachful voice, utter a few words full of dignity. He only touched again, lightly and ironically, on 'romancing' and 'psychology', and in an appropriate place quoted, 'Jupiter, you are angry, therefore you are wrong,' which provoked a burst of approving laughter in the audience, for Ippolit Kirillovitch was by no means like Jupiter. Then apropos of the accusation that he was teaching the young generation to murder their fathers, Fetyukovitch observed, with great dignity, that he would not even answer. As for the prosecutor's charge of uttering unorthodox opinions, Fetyukovitch hinted that it was a personal insinuation and that he had expected in this court to be secure from accusations 'damaging to my reputation as a citizen and a loyal subject'. But at these words the President pulled him up, too, and Fetyukovitch concluded his speech with a bow, amid a hum of approbation in the court. And Ippolit Kirillovitch was, in the opinion of our ladies, 'squashed for good'.

Then the prisoner was allowed to speak. Mitya stood up, but said very little. He was fearfully exhausted, physically and mentally. The look of strength and independence with which he had entered in the morning had almost disappeared. He seemed as though he had passed through an experience that day, which had taught him for the rest of his life something very important he had not understood till then. His voice was weak, he did not shout as before. In his words there was a new note of humility, defeat and submission.

'What am I to say, gentlemen of the jury? The hour of judgment has come for me, I feel the hand of God upon me! The end has come to an erring man! But, before God, I repeat to you, I am innocent of my father's blood! For the last time I repeat it, it wasn't I who killed him! I was erring, but I loved what is good. Every instant I strove to reform, but I lived like a wild beast. I thank the prosecutor, he told me many things about myself that I did not know; but it's not true that I killed my father, the prosecutor is mistaken. I thank my counsel, too. I wept while listening to him; but it's not true that I killed my father, and he needn't have surmised that. And don't believe the doctors. I am perfectly sane, only my heart is heavy. If you spare me, if you let me go, I will pray for you. I will be a better man. I give you my word before God I will! And if you will condemn me, I'll break my sword over my head myself and kiss the pieces. But spare me, do not rob me of my God! I know myself, I shall rebel! My heart is heavy, gentlemen . . . spare me!'

He almost fell back in his place: his voice broke: he could hardly articulate the last phrase. Then the judges proceeded to put the questions and began to ask both sides to formulate their conclusions. But I will not describe the details. At last the jury rose to retire for consultation. The President was very tired, and so his last charge to the jury was rather feeble. 'Be impartial, don't be influenced by the eloquence of the defence, but yet weigh the arguments. Remember that a great responsibility is laid upon you,' and so on and so on.

The jury withdrew and the court adjourned. People could get up, move about, exchange their accumulated impressions, refresh themselves at the buffet. It was very late, almost an hour past midnight, but nobody went away: the strain was so great that no one could think of repose. All waited with sinking hearts; though that is, perhaps, not quite correct, for the ladies were only in a state of hysterical impatience while their hearts remained untroubled. An acquittal, they thought, was inevitable. They all prepared themselves for a dramatic moment of general enthusiasm. I must own there were many among the men, too, who were convinced that an acquittal was inevitable. Some were pleased, others frowned, while some were simply dejected, not wanting the prisoner to be acquitted. Fetyukovitch himself was confident of his success. He was surrounded by people congratulating him and fawning upon him.

'There are,' he said to one group, as I was told afterwards, 'there are invisible threads that bind the counsel for the defence with the jury. One feels during one's speech if they are being formed. I was aware of them. They exist. Our cause is won. Set your mind at rest.'

'What will our peasants say now?' said one stout, angry-looking, pockmarked gentleman, a landowner of the neighbourhood, approaching a group of gentlemen engaged in conversation.

'But they are not all peasants. There are four government clerks among them.'

'Yes, there are clerks,' said a member of the district council, joining the group.

'And do you know that Nazaryev, the merchant with the medal, a juryman?'

'What of him?'

'He is a man with brains.'

'But he never speaks.'

'He is no great talker, but so much the better. There's no need for the Petersburg man to teach him: he could teach all Petersburg himself. He's the father of twelve children. Think of that!'

'Upon my word, you don't suppose they won't acquit him?' one of our young officials exclaimed in another group.

'They'll acquit him for certain,' said a resolute voice.

'It would be shameful, disgraceful, not to acquit him!' cried the official. 'Suppose he did murder his father – there are fathers and fathers! And, besides, he was in such a frenzy . . . He really may have done nothing but swing the pestle in the air, and so knocked the old man down. But it was a pity they dragged the valet in. That was simply an absurd theory! If I'd been in Fetyukovitch's place, I should simply have said straight out: "He murdered him; but he is not guilty, damn it all!" '

'That's what he did, only without saying, "Damn it all!" '

'No, Mihail Semyonovitch, he almost said that, too,' put in a third voice.

'Why, gentlemen, in Lent an actress was acquitted in our town who had cut the throat of her lover's lawful wife.'

'Oh, but she did not finish cutting it.'

'That makes no difference. She began cutting it.'

'What did you think of what he said about children? Splendid, wasn't it?'

'Splendid!'

'And about mysticism, too!'

'Oh, drop mysticism, do!' cried someone else; 'think of Ippolit and his fate from this day forth. His wife will scratch his eyes out tomorrow for Mitya's sake.'

'Is she here?'

'What an idea! If she'd been here, she'd have scratched them out in court. She is at home with a toothache. He, he, he!'

'He, he, he!'

In a third group: 'I dare say they will acquit our little Mitya, after all.'

'I wouldn't be surprised if he turns the Metropolis upside down tomorrow. He will be drinking for ten days!'

'Oh, the devil!'

'The devil's bound to have a hand in it. Where should he be if not here?'

'Well, gentlemen, I admit it was eloquent. But still it's not the thing to break your father's head with a pestle! Or what are we coming to?'

'The chariot! Do you remember the chariot?'

'Yes; he turned a troika into a chariot!'

'And tomorrow he will turn a chariot into a troika, just to suit his purpose.'

'What tricky fellows there are nowadays. Is there any justice to be had in Russia?'

But the bell rang. The jury deliberated for exactly an hour, neither more nor less. A profound silence reigned in the court as soon as the public had taken their seats. I remember how the jurymen walked into the court. At last! I won't repeat the questions in order, and, indeed, I have forgotten them. I remember only the answer to the President's first and chief question: 'Did the prisoner commit the murder for the sake of robbery and with premeditation?' (I don't remember the exact words.) There was a complete hush. The foreman of the jury, the youngest of the clerks, pronounced, in a clear, loud voice, amidst the deathlike stillness of the court: 'Yes, guilty!'

The same answer was given to every question: 'Yes, guilty!' and without the slightest extenuating comment. This no one had expected; almost everyone had reckoned upon a recommendation to mercy, at least. The deathlike silence in the court was not broken – all seemed petrified: those who desired his conviction as well as those who had been eager for his acquittal. But that was only for the first instant, and it was followed by a fearful hubbub. Many of the men in the audience were pleased. Some were rubbing their hands with no attempt to conceal their joy. Those who disagreed with the verdict seemed crushed, shrugged their shoulders, whispered, but still seemed unable to realise this. But how shall I describe the state the ladies were in? I thought they would create a riot. At first they could scarcely believe their ears. Then suddenly the whole court rang with exclamations: 'What's the meaning of it? What next?' They jumped up from their places. They seemed to fancy that the verdict might be at once reconsidered and reversed. At that instant Mitya suddenly stood up and cried in a heart-rending voice, stretching his hands out before him: 'I swear by God and the dreadful Day of Judgement I am not guilty of my father's blood! Katya, I forgive you! Brothers, friends, have pity on the other woman!'

He could not go on, and broke into a terrible sobbing wail that was heard all over the court in a strange, unnatural voice unlike his own. From the farthest corner at the back of the gallery came a piercing shriek – it was Grushenka. Mitya was taken away. The passing of the sentence was deferred till next day. The whole court was in an uproar, but I did not wait to hear. I only remember a few exclamations I heard on the steps as I went out.

'He'll have a twenty years' trip to the mines!'

'Not less.'

'Well, our peasants have stood firm.'

'And have done for our Mitya.'

Epilogue

I

Very early, at nine o'clock in the morning, five days after the trial, Alyosha went to Katerina Ivanovna's to talk over a matter of great importance to both of them and to give her a message. She sat and talked to him in the very room in which she had once received Grushenka. In the next room Ivan Fyodorovitch lay unconscious in a high fever. Katerina Ivanovna had immediately after the scene at the trial ordered the sick and unconscious man to be carried to her house, disregarding the inevitable gossip and general disapproval of the public. One of the two relatives who lived with her had departed to Moscow immediately after the scene at the court, the other remained. But if both had gone away, Katerina Ivanovna would have adhered to her resolution and would have gone on nursing the sick man and sitting by him day and night. Varvinsky and Herzenstube were attending him. The famous doctor had gone back to Moscow, refusing to give an opinion as to the probable outcome of the illness. Though the doctors encouraged Katerina Ivanovna and Alyosha, it was evident that they could not yet give them positive hopes of recovery.

Alyosha came to see his sick brother twice a day. But this time he had specially urgent business, and he foresaw how difficult it would be to approach the subject, yet he was in great haste. He had another appointment that could not be put off for that same morning, and there was need of haste.

They had been talking for a quarter of an hour. Katerina Ivanovna was pale and terribly fatigued, yet at the same time in a state of hysterical excitement. She had a presentiment of the reason why Alyosha had come to her.

'Don't worry about his decision,' she said, with confident emphasis to Alyosha. 'One way or another he is bound to come to it. He must escape. That unhappy man, that hero of honour and principle – not he, not Dmitri Fyodorovitch, but the man lying the other side of that door, who has sacrificed himself for his brother,' Katya added, with flashing eyes, 'told me the whole plan of escape long ago. You know he has already entered into negotiations . . . I've told you something already . . . You see, it will probably come off at the third stage of the journey from here, when the final group of prisoners is actually being taken to Siberia. Oh, it's a long way off yet. Ivan Fyodorovitch has already visited the superintendent of the third group. But we don't know yet who will be in charge of the party, and it's impossible to find that out so long beforehand. Tomorrow perhaps I will show you in detail the whole plan which Ivan Fyodorovitch left me on the eve of the trial in case of need . . . That was when – do you remember? – you found us quarrelling. He had just gone downstairs, but seeing you I made him come back; do you remember? Do you know what we were quarrelling about then?'

'No, I don't,' said Alyosha.

'Of course, he did not tell you. It was about that plan of escape. He had told me the main idea three days before, and we began quarrelling about it at once and quarrelled for three days. We quarrelled because when he told me that, if Mitya were convicted he would escape abroad with that creature, I felt furious at once – I can't tell you why, I don't know myself why . . . Oh, of course, I was furious then about that creature, and that she too should go abroad with Mitya!' Katerina Ivanovna exclaimed suddenly, her lips quivering with anger. 'As soon as Ivan Fyodorovitch saw that I was furious about that woman, he instantly imagined I was jealous of Mitya, and that I still loved Mitya. That is how our first quarrel began. I would not give an explanation, I could not ask forgiveness. I could not bear to think that such a man could suspect me of still loving that . . . and when I myself had told him long before that I did not love Mitya, that I loved no one but him! It was only resentment against that creature that made me angry with him. Three days later, on the evening you came, he brought me a sealed envelope, which I was to open at once, if anything happened to him. Oh, he foresaw his illness! He told me that the envelope contained the details of the escape, and that if he died or was taken dangerously ill, I was to save Mitya alone. Then he left me money, nearly ten thousand – those notes to which the prosecutor referred in his speech, having learned from someone that he had sent them to be changed. I was tremendously impressed to find that Ivan Fyodorovitch had not given up his idea of saving his brother, and was confiding this plan of escape to me, though he was still jealous of me and still convinced that I loved Mitya. Oh, that was a sacrifice! No, you cannot understand the greatness of such self-sacrifice, Alexey Fyodorovitch. I wanted to fall at his feet in reverence, but I thought at once that he would take it only for my joy at the thought of Mitya's being saved (and he certainly would have imagined that!), and I was so exasperated at the mere possibility of such an unjust thought on his part that I lost my temper again, and instead of kissing his feet, flew into a fury again! Oh, I am unhappy! It's my character, my awful, unhappy character! Oh, you will see, I shall end by driving him, too, to abandon me for another with whom he can get on better, like Mitya. But . . . no, I could not bear it, I would kill myself. And when you came in then, and when I called to you and told him to come back, I was so enraged by the look of contempt and hatred he turned on me that – do you remember? – I cried out to you that it was he, he alone who had persuaded me that his brother Mitya was a murderer! I said that malicious thing on purpose to wound him again. He had never, never persuaded me that his brother was a murderer. On the contrary, it was I who persuaded him! Oh, my vile temper was the cause of everything! I paved the way to that hideous scene at the trial. He wanted to show me that he was an honourable man, and that, even if I loved his brother, he would not ruin him for revenge or jealousy. So he came to the court . . . I am the cause of it all, I alone am to blame!'

Katya never had made such a confession to Alyosha before, and he felt that she was now at the stage of unbearable suffering when even the proudest heart painfully strangles its pride and falls vanquished by grief. Oh, Alyosha knew another terrible reason of her present misery, though she had carefully concealed it from him during the days since the trial; it would have been for some reason too painful to him if she had been brought so low as to speak to him now about that. She was suffering for her 'treachery' at the trial, and Alyosha felt that her conscience was impelling her to confess it to him, to him, Alyosha, with tears and cries and hysterical writhings on the floor. But he dreaded that moment and longed to spare her. It made the mission on which he had come even more difficult. He spoke of Mitya again.

'It's all right, it's all right, don't be anxious about him!' she began again, sharply and stubbornly. 'All that is only momentary, I know him, I know his heart only too well. You may be sure he will consent to escape. It's not as though it must happen immediately; he will have time to make up his mind to it. Ivan Fyodorovitch will be well by that time and will manage it all himself, so that I shall have nothing to do with it. Don't be anxious; he will consent to escape. He has agreed already: do you suppose he would give up that creature? And they won't let her go to him, so he is bound to escape. It's you he's most afraid of, he is afraid you won't approve of his escape on moral grounds. But you must generously *allow* it, if your sanction is so necessary,' Katya added viciously. She paused and smiled.

'He talks about some hymn,' she went on again, 'some cross he has to bear, some duty; I remember Ivan Fyodorovitch told me a great deal about it, and if you knew how he talked!' Katya cried suddenly, with feeling she could not repress, 'if you knew how he loved that wretched man at the moment he told me, and how he hated him, perhaps, at the same moment. And I heard his story and his tears with sneering disdain. Brute! Yes, I am a brute. I am responsible for his fever. But that man in prison is incapable of suffering,' Katya concluded irritably. 'Can such a man suffer? Men like him never suffer!'

There was a note of hatred and contempt in her words. And yet it was she who had betrayed him. 'Perhaps because she feels how she's wronged him she hates him at moments,' Alyosha thought to himself. He hoped that it was only 'at moments'. In Katya's last words he detected a challenging note, but he did not take it up.

'I sent for you this morning to make you promise to persuade him yourself. Or do you, too, consider that to escape would be dishonourable, cowardly, or something . . . unchristian, perhaps?' Katya added, even more defiantly.

'Oh, no. I'll tell him everything,' muttered Alyosha. 'He asks you to come and see him today,' he blurted out suddenly, looking her steadily in the face. She started, and drew back a little from him.

'Me? Can that be?' she faltered, turning pale.

'It can and ought to be!' Alyosha began emphatically, growing more animated. 'He needs you particularly just now. I would not have opened the subject and worried you, if it were not necessary. He is ill, he is beside himself, he keeps asking for you. It is not to be reconciled with you that he wants you, but only that you show yourself at his door. So much has happened to him since that day. He realises that he has injured you beyond all reckoning. He does not ask your forgiveness; "it's impossible to forgive me", he says himself, but only that you show yourself in his doorway.'

'It's so unexpected . . .' faltered Katya. 'Yet I had a presentiment all these days that you would come with that message. I knew he would ask me to come. It's impossible!'

'Let it be impossible, but do it. Only think, he realises for the first time how he has wounded you, the first time in his life; he had never grasped it before so fully. He said, "If she refuses to come, I shall be unhappy all my life." Do you hear? though he is condemned to penal servitude for twenty years, he is still planning to be happy – is not that pitiful? Think – you must visit him; though he is ruined, he is innocent,' broke like a challenge from Alyosha. 'His hands are clean, there is no blood on them! For the sake of his infinite sufferings in the future, visit him now. Go, greet him on his way into the darkness – stand at the door, that is all . . . You ought to do it, you ought to!' Alyosha concluded, laying immense stress on the word 'ought'.

'I ought to . . . but I cannot . . . ' Katya moaned. 'He will look at me . . . I can't.'

'Your eyes ought to meet. How will you live all your life, if you don't make up your mind to do it now?'

'Better suffer all my life.'

'You ought to go, you ought to go,' Alyosha repeated with merciless emphasis.

'But why today, why at once? . . . I can't leave our patient . . . '

'You can for a moment. It will only be a moment. If you don't come, he will be in delirium by tonight. I would not tell you a lie; have pity on him!'

'Have pity on *me*!' Katya said, with bitter reproach, and she burst into tears.

'Then you will come,' said Alyosha firmly, seeing her tears. 'I'll go and tell him you will come directly.'

'No, don't tell him so on any account,' cried Katya in alarm. 'I will come, but don't tell him beforehand, for perhaps I may go, but not go in . . . I don't know yet . . . '

Her voice failed her. She gasped for breath. Alyosha got up to go.

'And what if I meet anyone?' she said suddenly, in a low voice, turning white again.

'That's just why you must go now, to avoid meeting anyone. There will be no one there, I can tell you that for certain. We will expect you,' he concluded emphatically, and went out of the room.

2

He hurried to the hospital where Mitya was lying now. The day after his fate was determined, Mitya had fallen ill with a nervous fever, and was sent to the prison division of the town hospital. But at the request of several persons (Alyosha, Madame Hohlakov, Lise, etc.), Dr Varvinsky had put Mitya not with other prisoners, but in a separate little room, the one where Smerdyakov had lain. It is true that there was a sentinel at the other end of the corridor, and there was an iron grating over the window, so that Varvinsky could be at ease about the indulgence he had shown, which was not quite legal, indeed; but he was a kind-hearted and compassionate young man. He knew how hard it would be for a man like Mitya to pass at once so suddenly into the society of robbers and murderers, and that he must get used to it by degrees. The visits of relatives and friends were informally sanctioned by the doctor and overseer, and even by the police captain. But only Alyosha and Grushenka had visited Mitya. Rakitin had tried to force his way in twice, but Mitya persistently begged Varvinsky not to admit him.

Alyosha found him sitting on his bed in a hospital dressing gown, rather feverish, with a towel, soaked in vinegar and water, on his head. He looked at Alyosha as he came in with an enigmatic expression, but there was a shade of something like dread discernible in it.

He had become terribly preoccupied since the trial; sometimes he would be silent for half an hour together, and seemed to be pondering something heavily and painfully, oblivious of everything about him. If he roused himself from his brooding and began to talk, he always spoke with a kind of abruptness and never of what he really wanted to say. He looked sometimes with a face of suffering at his brother. He seemed to be more at ease with Grushenka than with Alyosha. It is true, he scarcely spoke to her at all, but as soon as she came in, his whole face lighted up with joy.

Alyosha sat down beside him on the bed in silence. This time Mitya was waiting for Alyosha in suspense, but he did not dare ask him a question. He felt it almost unthinkable that Katya would consent to come, and at the same time he felt that if she did not come, something inconceivable would happen. Alyosha understood his feelings.

'Trifon Borissovitch,' Mitya began nervously, 'has pulled his whole inn to pieces, I am told. He's taken up the flooring, pulled apart the planks, split up all the gallery, I am told. He is seeking treasure all the time – fifteen hundred roubles which the prosecutor said I'd hidden there. He began playing these tricks, they say, as soon as he got home. Serve him right, the swindler! The guard here told me yesterday; he comes from there.'

'Listen,' began Alyosha. 'She will come, but I don't know when. Perhaps today, perhaps in a few days, that I can't tell. But she will come, she will, that's certain.'

Mitya started, would have said something, but was silent. The news had a tremendous effect on him. It was evident that he would have liked terribly to know what had been said, but he was again afraid to ask.

Something cruel and contemptuous from Katya would have cut him like a knife at that moment.

'This was what she said among other things; that I must be sure to set your conscience at rest about escaping. If Ivan is not well by then, she will see to it all herself.'

'You've spoken of that already,' Mitya observed musingly.

'And you have repeated it to Grushenka,' observed Alyosha.

'Yes,' Mitya admitted. 'She won't come this morning.' He looked timidly at his brother. 'She won't come till the evening. When I told her yesterday that Katya was taking measures, she was silent, but she set her mouth. She only whispered, "Let her!" She understood that it was important. I did not dare to try her further. She understands now, I think, that Katya no longer cares for me, but loves Ivan.'

'Does she?' broke from Alyosha.

'Perhaps she does not. Only she is not coming this morning,' Mitya hastened to explain again; 'I asked her to do something for me. You know, Ivan is superior to all of us. He ought to live, not us. He will recover.'

'Would you believe it, though Katya is alarmed about him, she scarcely doubts of his recovery,' said Alyosha.

'That means that she is convinced he will die. It's because she is frightened she's so sure he will get well.'

'Ivan has a strong constitution, and I too believe there's every hope that he will get well,' Alyosha observed anxiously.

'Yes, he will get well. But she is convinced that he will die. She has a great deal of sorrow to bear . . . ' A silence followed. A grave anxiety was fretting Mitya.

'Alyosha, I love Grushenka terribly,' he said suddenly in a shaking voice, full of tears.

'They won't let her go out there to you,' Alyosha put in at once.

'And there is something else I wanted to tell you,' Mitya went on, with a sudden ring in his voice. 'If they beat me on the way out there, I won't submit to it. I shall kill someone, and shall be shot for it. And this will be going on for twenty years! They speak to me rudely as it is. I've been lying here all night, passing judgment on myself. I am not ready! I am not able to resign myself. I wanted to sing a "hymn"; but if a guard speaks to me, I have not the strength to bear it. For Grushenka I would bear anything . . . anything except blows . . . But she won't be allowed to come there.'

Alyosha smiled gently.

'Listen, brother, once for all,' he said. 'This is what I think about it. And you know that I would not tell you a lie. Listen: you are not ready, and such a cross is not for you. What's more, you don't need such a martyr's cross when you are not ready for it. If you had murdered our father, it would grieve me that you should reject your punishment. But you are innocent, and such a cross is too much for you. You wanted to make yourself another man by suffering. I say, only remember that other man always, all your life and wherever you go; and that will be enough for you. Your refusal of that great cross will only serve to make you feel all your life an even greater duty, and that constant feeling will do more to make you a new man, perhaps, than if you went to Siberia. For there you would not endure it and would repine, and perhaps at last would say: "I am quits." The lawyer was right about that. Such heavy burdens are not for all men. For some they are impossible. These are my thoughts about it, if you want them so much. If other men would have to answer for your escape, officers or soldiers, then I would not have "allowed" you,' smiled Alyosha. 'But they declare – the superintendent of that party told Ivan himself – that if it's well managed there will be no great enquiry, and that they can get off easily. Of course, bribing is dishonest even in such a case, but I can't undertake to judge about it, because if Ivan and Katya commissioned me to act for you, I know I would go and give bribes. I must tell you the truth. And so I can't judge of your own action. But let me assure you that I shall never condemn you. And it would be a strange thing if I could judge you in this. Now I think I've gone into everything.'

'But I do condemn myself!' cried Mitya. 'I shall escape, that was settled apart from you; could Mitya Karamazov do anything but run away? But I shall condemn myself, and I will pray for my sin for ever.

'Now listen to the rest; I'll open the other side of my heart to you. This is what I planned and decided. If I run away, even with money and a passport, and even to America, I should be cheered by the thought that I am not running away for pleasure, not for happiness, but to another exile as bad, perhaps, as Siberia. It is as bad, Alyosha, it is! I hate that America, damn it, already. Even though Grushenka will be with me. Just look at her; is she an American? She is Russian, Russian to the marrow of her bones; she will be homesick for the mother country, and I shall see every hour that she is suffering for my sake, that she has taken up that cross for me. And what harm has she done? And how shall I too put up with the rabble out there, though they may be better than I, every one of them. I hate that America already! And though they may be wonderful at machinery, every one of them, damn them, they are not of my soul. I love Russia, Alyosha, I love the Russian God, though I am a scoundrel myself. I shall suffocate there!' he exclaimed, his eyes suddenly flashing. His voice was trembling with tears. 'So this is what I've decided, Alyosha, listen,' he began again, mastering his emotion. 'As soon as I arrive there with Grushenka, we will set to work at once on the land, in solitude, somewhere very remote, where there are wild bears. There must be some remote parts even there. I am told there are still Redskins there, somewhere, on the edge of the horizon. So to the country of the *Last of the Mohicans*, and there we'll tackle the foreign grammar at once, Grushenka and I. Work and grammar – that's how we'll spend three years. And by that time we shall speak English like any Englishman. And as soon as we've learned it – goodbye to America! We'll run here to Russia as American citizens. Don't be uneasy – we would not come to this little town. We'd hide somewhere, a long way off, in the north or in the south. I shall be changed by that time, and she will, too, in America. The doctors shall make me some sort of wart on my face – that's what their technical talents are for! – or else I'll put out one eye, let my beard grow a yard, and I shall turn grey, fretting for Russia. I dare say they won't recognise us. And if they do, let them send us to Siberia – I don't care. It will show it's our fate. We'll work on the land here, too, somewhere in the wilds, and I'll masquerade as an American all my life. But we shall die on our own soil. That's my plan, and it will not be altered. Do you approve?'

'Yes,' said Alyosha, not wanting to contradict him. Mitya paused for a minute and said suddenly: 'And how they worked it up at the trial! Didn't they work it up!'

'If they had not, you would have been convicted just the same,' said Alyosha, with a sigh.

'Yes, people are sick of me here! God bless them, but it's hard,' Mitya moaned miserably. Again there was silence for a minute.

'Alyosha, put me out of my misery at once!' he exclaimed suddenly. 'Tell me, is she coming now, or not? Tell me? What did she say? How did she say it?'

'She said she would come, but I don't know whether she will come today. It's hard for her, you know,' Alyosha looked timidly at his brother.

'I should think it is hard for her! Alyosha, it will drive me out of my mind. Grushenka keeps looking at me. She understands. My God, calm my heart: what is it I want? I want Katya! Do I understand what I want? It's the headstrong, evil Karamazov spirit! No, I am not fit for suffering. I am a scoundrel, that's all one can say.'

'Here she is!' cried Alyosha.

At that instant Katya appeared in the doorway. For a moment she stood still, gazing at Mitya with a dazed expression. He leaped impulsively to his feet, and a scared look came into his face. He turned pale, but a timid, pleading smile appeared on his lips at once, and with an irresistible impulse he held out both hands to Katya. Seeing it, she flew impetuously to him. She seized him by the hands, and almost by force made him sit down on the bed. She sat down beside him, and still keeping his hands, pressed them violently. Several times they both strove to speak, but stopped short and again gazed speechless with a strange smile, their eyes fastened on one another. So passed two minutes.

'Have you forgiven me?' Mitya faltered at last, and at the same moment turning to Alyosha, his face working with joy, he cried, 'Do you hear what I am asking, do you hear?'

'That's what I loved you for, that you are generous at heart!' broke from Katya. 'My forgiveness is no good to you, nor yours to me; whether you forgive me or not, you will always be a sore place in my heart, and I in yours – so it must be . . . ' She stopped to take breath. 'What have I come for?' she began again with nervous haste: 'to embrace your feet, to press your hands like this, till it hurts – you remember how in Moscow I used to squeeze them – to tell you again that you are my god, my joy, to tell you that I love you madly,' she moaned in anguish, and suddenly pressed his hand greedily to her lips. Tears streamed from her eyes.

Alyosha stood speechless and confounded; he had never expected what he was seeing.

'Love is over, Mitya!' Katya began again, 'but the past is painfully dear to me. Know that will always be so. But now let what might have been come true for one minute,' she faltered, with a drawn smile, looking into his face joyfully again. 'You love another woman, and I love another man, and yet I shall love you for ever, and you will love me; do you know that? Do you hear? Love me, love me all your life!' she cried, with a quiver almost of menace, in her voice.

'I shall love you, and . . . do you know, Katya,' Mitya began, drawing a deep breath at each word, 'do you know, five days ago, that same evening, I loved you . . . When you fell down and were carried out . . . All my life! So it will be, so it will always be . . . '

So they murmured to one another frantic words, almost meaningless, perhaps not even true, but at that moment it was all true, and they both believed what they said implicitly.

'Katya,' cried Mitya suddenly, 'do you believe I murdered him? I know you don't believe it now, but then . . . when you gave evidence . . . Surely, surely you did not believe it!'

'I did not believe it even then. I've never believed it. I hated you, and for a moment I persuaded myself. While I was giving evidence I persuaded myself and believed it, but when I'd finished speaking I left off believing it at once. Don't doubt that! I have forgotten that I came here to punish myself,' she said, with a new expression in her voice, quite unlike the loving tones of a moment before.

'Woman, yours is a heavy burden,' broke, as it were, involuntarily from Mitya.

'Let me go,' she whispered. 'I'll come again. It's more than I can bear now.'

She was rising to her feet, but suddenly uttered a loud scream and staggered back. Grushenka walked quickly and noiselessly into the room. No one had expected her. Katya moved swiftly to the door, but when she reached Grushenka, she stopped suddenly, turned as white as chalk and moaned softly, almost in a whisper: 'Forgive me!'

Grushenka stared at her and, pausing for an instant, in a vindictive, venomous voice, answered: 'We are full of hatred, my girl, you and I! We are both full of hatred! As though we could forgive one another! Save him, and I'll worship you all my life.'

'You won't forgive her!' cried Mitya, with frantic reproach.

'Don't be anxious, I'll save him for you!' Katya whispered rapidly, and she ran out of the room.

'And you could refuse to forgive her when she begged your forgiveness herself?' Mitya exclaimed bitterly again.

'Mitya, don't dare to blame her; you have no right to!' Alyosha cried hotly.

'Her proud lips spoke, not her heart,' Grushenka brought out in a tone of disgust. 'If she saves you, I'll forgive her everything . . .'

She stopped speaking, as though suppressing something. She could not yet recover herself. She had come in, as appeared afterwards, accidentally, with no suspicion of what she would meet.

'Alyosha, run after her!' Mitya cried to his brother; 'tell her . . . I don't know . . . don't let her go away like this!'

'I'll come to you again at nightfall,' said Alyosha, and he ran after Katya. He overtook her outside the hospital grounds. She was walking fast, but as soon as Alyosha caught her up she said quickly: 'No, before that woman I can't punish myself! I asked her forgiveness because I wanted to punish myself to the bitter end. She would not forgive me . . . I like her for that!' she added, in an unnatural voice, and her eyes flashed with fierce resentment.

'My brother did not expect this in the least,' muttered Alyosha. 'He was sure she would not come . . .'

'No doubt. Let us leave that,' she snapped. 'Listen: I can't go with you to the funeral now. I've sent them flowers. I think they still have money. If necessary, tell them I'll never abandon them . . . Now leave me, leave me, please. You are late as it is – the bells are ringing for the service . . . Leave me, please!'

3

He really was late. They had waited for him and had already decided to bear the pretty flower-decked little coffin to the church without him. It was the coffin of poor little Iliusha. He had died two days after Mitya was sentenced. At the gate of the house, Alyosha was met by cries from the boys, Iliusha's schoolfellows. There were about twelve of them, they all had their school bags or satchels on their shoulders.

Alyosha went into the room. Iliusha lay with his hands folded and his eyes closed in a blue coffin with a white frill round it. His thin face was hardly changed at all, and strange to say there was no smell of decay from the corpse. The expression of his face was serious and, as it were, thoughtful. His hands, crossed over his breast, looked particularly beautiful, as though chiselled in marble. There were flowers in his hands and the coffin, inside and out, was decked with flowers, which had been sent early in the morning by Lise Hohlakov. But there were flowers too from Katerina Ivanovna, and when Alyosha opened the door, the captain had a bunch in his trembling hands and was strewing them again over his dear boy. He scarcely glanced at Alyosha when he came in, and he would not look at anyone, even at his crazy weeping wife, 'mamma', who kept trying to stand on her crippled legs to get a nearer look at her dead boy. Nina had been pushed in her chair by the boys close up to the coffin. She sat with her head pressed to it and she too was no doubt quietly weeping. Snegiryov's face looked eager, yet bewildered and exasperated. There was something crazy about his gestures and the words that broke from him. 'Old man, dear old man!' he exclaimed every minute, gazing at Iliusha. It was his habit to call Iliusha 'old man', as a term of affection, when he was alive.

At last came the funeral service itself and candles were distributed. The distracted father began fussing about again, but the touching and impressive funeral prayers moved and roused his soul. He seemed suddenly to shrink together and broke into rapid, short sobs, which he tried at first to smother, but at last he sobbed aloud. When they began taking leave of the dead and closing the coffin, he flung his arms about, as though he would not allow them to cover Iliusha, and began greedily and persistently kissing his dead boy on the lips. At last they succeeded in persuading him to come away from the coffin, but suddenly he impulsively stretched out his hand and snatched a few flowers from the coffin. He looked at them and a new idea seemed to dawn upon him, so that he apparently forgot his grief for a minute. Gradually he seemed to sink into brooding and did not resist when the coffin was lifted up and carried to the grave. It was an expensive one in the churchyard close to the church, Katerina Ivanovna had paid for it. After the customary rites the gravediggers lowered the coffin. Snegiryov with his flowers in his hands bent down so low over the open grave that the boys caught hold of his coat in alarm and pulled him back. He did not seem to understand fully what was happening. When they began filling up the grave, he suddenly pointed anxiously at the falling earth and began trying to say something, but no one could make out what he meant; he stopped suddenly, and ran homewards. It was not far off and they all arrived together. Snegiryov opened the door hurriedly and called to his wife.

'Mamma, poor crippled darling, Iliusha has sent you these flowers,' he cried, holding out to her a little bunch of flowers that had been frozen and broken while he was struggling in the snow. But at that instant he saw in the corner, by the little bed, Iliusha's little boots, which the landlady had put tidily side by side. Seeing the old, patched, rusty-looking, stiff boots he flung up his hands and rushed to them, fell on his knees, snatched up one boot and, pressing his lips to it, began kissing it greedily, crying, 'Iliusha, old man, dear old man, where are your little feet?'

'Where have you taken him away? Where have you taken him?' the lunatic cried in a heart-rending voice. Nina, too, broke into sobs. The boys ran out of the room. At last Alyosha too went out.

They all stood still by the big stone. Alyosha looked and the whole picture of what Snegiryov had described to him that day, how Iliusha, weeping and hugging his father, had cried, 'Father, Father, how he insulted you,' rose at once before his imagination. A sudden impulse seemed to come into his soul. With a serious and earnest expression he looked from one to another of the bright, pleasant faces of Iliusha's schoolfellows, and suddenly said to them: 'Boys, I should like to say one word to you, here at this place.'

The boys stood round him and at once bent attentive and expectant eyes upon him.

'Boys, whatever happens to us later in life, let us always remember how we buried the poor boy at whom you once threw stones, do you remember, by the bridge? He was a fine boy, a kind-hearted, brave boy, he felt for his father's honour and resented the cruel insult to him and stood up for him. There is nothing higher and stronger and more wholesome and good for life in the future than some good memory, especially a memory of childhood, of home. People talk to you a great deal about your education, but some good, sacred memory, preserved from childhood, is perhaps the best education. If a man carries many such memories with him into life, he is safe to the end of his days, and if only one good memory remains, in our hearts, even that may sometime be the means of saving us. Perhaps we may even grow wicked later on, may be unable to refrain from a bad action, may laugh at men's tears. But however bad we may become – which God forbid – yet, when we recall how we buried Iliusha, and how we have been talking like friends all together, at this stone, the cruellest and most mocking of us – if we do become so – will not dare to laugh inwardly at having been kind and good at this moment!'

The boys were excited and wanted to say something, but they restrained themselves, looking with intentness and emotion at the speaker.

'I say this in case we become bad,' Alyosha went on, 'but there's no reason why we should become bad, is there, boys? Let us be, first and above all, kind, then honest and then let us never forget each other! I say that again. I give you my word for my part that I'll never forget one of you. Every face looking at me now I shall remember even for thirty years.'

'We will remember, we will remember,' cried the boys.

'Ah, children, ah, dear friends, don't be afraid of life! How good life is when one does something good and just!'

'Yes, yes,' the boys repeated enthusiastically.

'Karamazov, we love you!' a voice cried impulsively.

'We love you, we love you!' they all caught it up. There were tears in the eyes of many of them.

'Well, now we will finish talking and go to his funeral dinner. Don't be put out at our eating pancakes – it's a very old custom and there's something nice in that!' laughed Alyosha. 'Well, let us go! And now we go hand in hand.'

'And always so, all our lives hand in hand! Hurrah for Karamazov!' And the boys took up the exclamation: 'Hurrah for Karamazov!'

Afterword

Within three months of completing *The Brothers Karamazov*, Dostoevsky was dead, and the novel stands now in many ways as a summation of his works and a concentration of the preoccupations of a lifetime. Many regard it as his greatest work, even as one of the greatest books ever written. Its sheer size and complexity – presented here in a slightly more manageable abridgment – gave Dostoevsky the space in which to pursue his themes, and – through the words and development of his characters – promote the ideologies that he has spent his life forging and sharpening.

Such literary space was a relative novelty to Dostoevsky, who had spent much of his life mired in debt. He wrote many of his books in serial form, with the demands of creditors hanging over him. However, while Dostoevsky wrote *The Brothers Karamazov* without this menace, the factor of debt remains an active force within the novel.

Dostoevsky may have found financial freedom by the time he began writing *The Brothers Karamazov*, but he was still haunted by the events of a lifetime. When he was a young man, away from home while studying at the St Petersburg Engineering Academy, his father was killed by the serfs on his family's estate. It was an event that was to leave its mark on almost all of Dostoevsky's writing: time and again in his books he explores murder and criminality, as well as the process of police work, an allegory perhaps for the internal investigation his characters go through. Moreover,

Dostoevsky's own father was apparently almost as amoral as the senior Karamazov, and the whole community was implicated in the murder, if not by action then by sympathy. And so, in *The Brothers Karamazov*, Dostoevsky outlines his belief in the collective responsibility for all transgression.

The pivotal role of the father in *The Brothers Karamazov* extends beyond simple biological paternity: it is present in the symbolic father-figure of Zosima, in the relationship of man to God the Father, and in Alexey's relationship to his protégé children. It would seem hardly surprising then that Sigmund Freud regarded *The Brothers Karamazov* as one of the three greatest works of fiction ever written (the others being *Oedipus Rex* and *Hamlet* – both dealing with the subject of parricide). The relationships within *The Brothers Karamazov* – filial, fraternal, sexual – as well as the motivations – conscious and unconscious – would indeed seem ripe for Freudian analysis, and Dostoevsky has attracted sustained interest from Freudian psychoanalytical critics. Taken on its own, such an approach tends to be too limiting (not least because of the inherent problems of the whole of the Freudian system), but that it not to say that Dostoevsky ignores those experiences of the human condition that Freud was later to study. For example, in *The Brothers Karamazov*, as in his other works, Dostoevsky uses the agency of dreams both to provide us with insight into the characters' psyches and as turning points in their psychological development: the change coming not from their conscious reasoning but from their subconscious dream states. Thus Dostoevsky can be seen not as a patient to be psychoanalysed, but more as the psychoanalyst, drawing out the mental fragments of his characters.

It is this ability, displayed since his debut work *Poor Folk*, to present the fully realized complexity of human psychology that is among the qualities that mark Dostoevsky as a great writer. He sees that people are a mass of conflicting urges, often leading to contradictory viewpoints and actions. Dmitri ('Mitya') is in many ways totemic of this sort of character in Dostoevsky's writing, with his fluctuation between the sinning sensualist and the man who loves God and desires salvation; between Sodom and Madonna. His quoting from Schiller, the German dramatist and lyric poet (1759-1805), is also telling: while Dmitri sees himself as something of an unrefined savage, one of the ideals Schiller embodies is a return to nature that accords with Dostoevsky's own beliefs of the sacred union between the soil of Russia and its peoples. Even Dmitri's name has echoes of 'Demeter,' the Greek goddess of the harvest. Moreover, Schiller was overwhelmingly concerned with the problems of the often mutually antagonistic freedom and responsibility, a theme in which Dostoevsky immerses his characters.

Dmitri is not alone in psychological conflict: Alexey ('Alyosha') is torn between the purity of monastic existence and the more practical Christianity required in worldly life; Grushenka's journey mirrors that of Dmitri's in reconciling her current capriciousness with an inherent faithfulness and acceptance of responsibility; and even the thoroughly rotten character of Fyodor is "sentimental" as well as "wicked." For one character, Ivan, the internal conflict becomes unbearable. While he professes a sincere love for mankind in general, he cannot generate genuine human love for individuals (hardly a unique character trait in many people publicly perceived as humanitarians).

Furthermore, while he appears at first a master of reason and rhetoric and entirely confident in his own opinions, beneath the surface lies the struggle between what his reason dictates should be the case, and the revulsion that his moral sense perceives in the ramifications of what his pursuit of pure rationality would lead to. He cannot believe in a God that is beyond the comprehension of human reason, and yet he perceives that without God there is no reason for virtue in the world and anything is permissible, a sentiment the servant Smerdyakov (whose name derives from the Russian word for a foul smell) takes literally in his murder of Fyodor. When Ivan realizes his ideological complicity in the death of his father, he is driven insane.

Madness is a recurrent theme in Dostoevsky's work, particularly in relation to the committing of crimes: the guilt of his characters is often manifested in physical symptoms (see, for example, Raskolnikov's episode of delirium and fever after his murder in *Crime and Punishment*.) While Dostoevsky perceived dualism everywhere, he also perceived connections that ran from the smallest of actions to the largest and most abstract of ideas: his is a world where characters have become deformed not only physically, but ideologically, mentally, and morally. It appears that Dostoevsky's own handicap – his epilepsy – started at the time of his father's death, which led Freud to theorize that this condition was caused by repressed childhood neuroses. That a retrospective medical diagnosis points to the biological cause of a temporal-lobe disorder does not, perhaps, diminish the added psychological importance this condition held for Dostoevsky himself.

As mentioned, despites its grand scope, *The Brothers*

Karamazov is a deeply personal book, in that the narrative dialectic it pursues is a reflection of the journey that Dostoevsky had taken in his life, and of the competing forces at work within him. In this sense, as well as being points on the ideological and moral compass of the novel, the characters reflect these elements of Dostoevsky: Ivan represented his rational mind and Alexey (also the name of Dostoevsky's child, who died in infancy) his spiritual side; Dmitri represented the admission of his own guilt and sin, and Father Zosima stood as the idealized vision of how he tried to live his life. Smerdyakov took on his epilepsy, and Karamazov senior got his name, Fyodor. Encompassed by the experiences of the individual characters is the central argument that Dostoevsky had been conducting with himself perhaps all his life, and certainly since his time in the Siberian prison. There, having only the Bible to read, he began to rebel against the socialist radicalism of his youth and turned toward a faith in the Orthodox Church and the Russian people. The picture he paints of Ivan is almost then of a younger self: a brilliant mind setting reason against faith, an opposition which *The Brothers Karamazov* – if it can be said to concern any one thing – is primarily about.

With Ivan's madness, Dmitri's voyage toward redemption, and Alexey's embodiment of the positive Christianity within the novel, it might seem obvious on which side of the argument the novel is. However, Ivan's poem of the Grand Inquisitor has intrigued those with an alternative perspective. Central to this opposition is the Inquisitor's charge against Jesus that only a few elect are able to accept God through faith alone. The rest of mankind needs the miracle, mystery and authority provided by the Church, which therefore, despite its love for mankind, becomes of the devil's party because it yields to the temptations that Jesus resisted. For example, the celebrated and controversial English novelist D. H. Lawrence (1885–1930) wrote that "We cannot doubt that the Inquisitor speaks Dostoevsky's own final opinion about Jesus. The opinion is, baldly, this: Jesus, you are inadequate. Men must correct you. And Jesus in the end gives the kiss of acquiescence to the Inquisitor, as Alexey does to Ivan." It is true that Dostoevsky often seems to be his own worst enemy, bringing his considerable intellect to bear on the side of the argument that he ultimately opposes, and it was a danger he was him-self aware of. Luckily, as if the novel in itself was not enough, we have many other writings and correspondence from Dostoevsky that establish his true view. Writing in his notebook after completing *The Brothers Karamazov*, Dostoevsky made it clear that the whole of the novel stands as an answer to the accusations of the Inquisitor. The apparent acquiescence in the two kisses (the one Jesus gives the Inquisitor, and the one given to Ivan by Alexey) in fact stands as perfect illustration of the opposition of reason and faith. Jesus and Alexey chose not to argue because they saw that rational argument on matters of belief is pointless: the latter cannot be reached by the former. The kiss is thus not a kiss of approval, but a kiss of forgiveness, of pardon, and one symbolic of the quiet power of faith.

The novel's attitude toward the occurrence of miracles is an interesting adjunct to this. Very early on, the book's narrator proffers the opinion that faith does not spring from miracles, but rather that only once a person has found faith will they be capable of accepting miracles. (While the narrator may express Dostoevsky's own opinion, the character of the narrator would seen to be a separate entity from that of the author: Dostoevsky shows sensitivity throughout his career of the difficulties inherent in defining a narrative voice.) Many had anticipated a miracle at the death of Father Zosima – whose teachings are central to the type of Christianity that Dostoevsky is promoting – but in fact the corpse quickly putrefies, which many take as a sign of spiritual and moral corruption. Even Alexey is thrown into doubt by this, but the reaffirmation of his faith come through his interaction with the living, specifically with children, who Dostoevsky believed represented the future hope for the salvation of mankind, and with Grushenka who through her repentance represents the idealized Russian woman. Thus Dostoevsky's God is lifted from the level of the cheap conjurer that he is so often portrayed to be by lesser novelists of a religious bent.

What is made more important than the outwardly miraculous is the acceptance of responsibility and suffering. While Ivan rejects the notion that suffering – particularly that of the innocent – is a price worth paying for salvation and truth, Dostoevsky wrote in his notebooks: "There is no happiness in comfort; happiness is bought with suffering." This is not a perspective unique to the author, but one that is integral to the Russian Orthodox faith. All Christianity is based upon accepting that Jesus suffered and died for humanity's salvation, but the Orthodox tradition is one that extends this to the notion of collective human suffering and responsibility. It is significant that the cross of the Russian Orthodox Church carries an extra crosspiece representing the two thieves who were crucified and suffered with Christ. The crosspiece is slanted, the raised end for the one who accepted his suffering and was granted a place in paradise, and the lower one for the thief who rejected Jesus and salvation. Thus the motif of the repentant criminal, which crops up again and again in Dostoevsky, has for him the most holy of precedents. Moreover, to be Orthodox was – and is – to be Russian, and to be Russian is to be Orthodox, and Dostoevsky is not immune to the faintly messianic view that it would be the Russian people who would prove the hope of salvation for all mankind. In the poem of the Grand Inquisitor, Dostoevsky stresses the separation of Orthodoxy from the Church of Rome by the almost satirical notion that the institution that succumbed to the temptations of the devil that Jesus resisted could really be the earthly voice of salvation. Even today there is hostility in the Russian Orthodox Church to any Roman Catholic proselytizing in its territory.

The mystical leanings of Father Zosima and Dostoevsky's vision of a transforming spiritual collectivism of the populace might have put him at odds with traditionalists even within the Russian Orthodox faith, and it would be a mistake to cast Dostoevsky as simply a reactionary fundamentalist. While he rejected the radicalism of his youth and that growing in the generation directly after his, neither was stasis an option. Nor does he reject reason outright – he was after all an immensely intelligent man – but believed that reason can only hope to gain any sort of purchase on Truth within the framework of faith.

All this is not to say that we have to accept that Dostoevsky is right in his beliefs and vision. For a start, he appears mistaken in the notion that the Russian people would never allow a godless system of authority: the rise of Marxist-Leninism put paid to that. One could, of course, argue that communism was as much as a religion as any other, and in a sense that is the distinction – between faith and organized religion – that the Inquisitor's poem reveals. The Inquisitor's plan of total obedience and lack of freedom for mankind in exchange for protection and peace of mind for all is in effect a template for totalitarianism, albeit of a benevolent variety. However, the years since Dostoevsky's death have proved far too often that totalitarian systems have a nasty habit of turning out to be anything but benevolent.

Dostoevsky's religious Orthodoxy has nonetheless remained somewhat problematic for his more progressive readers. The French Existentialist Albert Camus (1919–60) revered Dostoevsky as a prophet of the dilemmas that would confront twentieth-century man. However, Camus was uncomfortable with Dostoevsky's recourse to God. Existentialism requires an acceptance of the essential meaningless and absurdity of existence, and requires the individual to find the possibility of happiness without the hope of an afterlife. Whilst Dostoevsky paints a vivid portrait of the alienation central to the existentialist experience and conveys a strong sense of the absurd, Camus felt that Dostoevsky fell back on his Christian faith, unable to face the existentialist paradigm. For Camus, Ivan is remarkable not because he questioned the existence of God, but because, even if eternal life existed, he would not accept the bargain necessary to achieve it. With his assertion that if there is no immortality, everything is permitted, Camus marks Ivan out as the father of contemporary nihilism and poser of "the question that constitutes the real progress achieved by Dostoevsky in the history of rebellion: . . . can one live and stand one's ground in a state of rebellion?" The solution to continued rebellion against God is, of course, revolution – which Dostoevsky feared but which many men since have embraced.

All this, of course, only scratches the surface of *The Brothers Karamazov*. While Dostoevsky certainly exhibits a didacticism that authors of lesser narrative skill could not get away with, his characters are much more than simply allegorical figures in a grand philosophical set-piece. Indeed their very 'reality' is enforced by, from the very first paragraph, a narrative device of a true story being told. These fictional characters of a novelist seem as more real than the abstract examples of a philosopher, and the fact that in *The Brothers Karamazov* Dostoevsky perfects his skills as both stands as a testament to his lasting genius.

This abridgment is by W. Somerset Maugham (1874–1965). He initially trained as a doctor, before forging a career as a novelist and playwright. He traveled extensively and produced a large number of works, including *Of Human Bondage*, *The Moon and Sixpence*, and *The Razor's Edge.* He was also a master of the short story.

Further Reading

Bakhtin, Mikhail, *Problems of Dostoevsky's Poetics* (1929); tr. and ed. by Caryl Emerson, (Minnesota: University of Minneapolis Press, 1984)

Camus, Albert, *The Rebel* (many editions, including: New York, Vintage, 1992, and Penguin, 2001)

Frank, Joseph *Dostoevsky: The Mantle of the Prophet, 1871–1881* [Part 5 of a 5-volume biography] (New Jersey: Princeton University Press, 2003)

Pearce, Richard, *Dostoevsky: An Examination of the Major Novels* (New York: Cambridge University Press, 1971)

Biography

Fyodor Dostoevsky was born in Moscow in 1821. Between 1838 and 1843 he studied at the St Petersburg Engineering Academy. His first work of fiction was the epistolary novel *Poor Folk* (1846), which met with a generally favorable response. However, his immediately subsequent works were less enthusiastically received. In 1849 Dostoevsky was arrested as a member of the socialist Petrashevsky circle, and subjected to a mock execution. He suffered four years in a Siberian penal settlement and then another four years of enforced military service. He returned to writing in the late 1850s and traveled abroad in the 1860s. It was during the last twenty years of his life that he wrote the iconic works, such as *Notes from the Underground* (1864), *Crime and Punishment* (1866), *The Idiot* (1868) and *The Brothers Karamazov* (1880), which were to form the basis of his formidable reputation. He died in 1881.

years of his life that he wrote the iconic works, such as *Notes from the Underground* (1864), *Crime and Punishment* (1866), *The Idiot* (1868) and *The Brothers Karamazov* (1880), which were to form the basis of his formidable reputation. He died in 1881.

Library Collector's Library Collector's Library Collector's Library C
ary Collector's Library Collector's Library Collector's Library Collec
Library Collector's Library Collector's Library Collector's Library C
ary Collector's Library Collector's Library Collector's Library Collec
Library Collector's Library Collector's Library Collector's Library C
ary Collector's Library Collector's Library Collector's Library Collec
Library Collector's Library Collector's Library Collector's Library C
ary Collector's Library Collector's Library Collector's Library Collec
Library Collector's Library Collector's Library Collector's Library C
ary Collector's Library Collector's Library Collector's Library Collec
Library Collector's Library Collector's Library Collector's Library C
ary Collector's Library Collector's Library Collector's Library Collec
Library Collector's Library Collector's Library Collector's Library C
ary Collector's Library Collector's Library Collector's Library Collec
Library Collector's Library Collector's Library Collector's Library Co
ary Collector's Library Collector's Library Collector's Library Collec
Library Collector's Library Collector's Library Collector's Library Co
ary Collector's Library Collector's Library Collector's Library Collec
Library Collector's Library Collector's Library Collector's Library Co
ary Collector's Library Collector's Library Collector's Library Collec
Library Collector's Library Collector's Library Collector's Library Co
ary Collector's Library Collector's Library Collector's Library Collec